THE WATCHERS
AT THE WELL

THE WATCHERS
AT THE WELL

ECHOES OF THE
WELL OF SOULS
SHADOW OF THE
WELL OF SOULS
GODS OF THE
WELL OF SOULS

JACK L. CHALKER

GUILDAMERICA
B O O K S ®

Published by arrangement with:
Ballantine Books
201 East 50th Street
New York, NY 10022

ISBN 1-56865-123-6

PRINTED IN THE UNITED STATES OF AMERICA

CONTENTS

Echoes of the
Well of Souls

This one's for my family:
For my father and mother, Lloyd Allen Chalker and
Nancy Hopkins Chalker,
who lived to see their son "make it" but not
to see this book, but whose strength and support
continue with me;
For David Whitley Chalker,
the unknown Super Mario Brother
who wasn't even born when the last one appeared;
For Steven Lloyd Chalker,
whose birth was another delaying factor in getting
this one finished;
And for Eva, as always.

A FEW WORDS
FROM THE AUTHOR

DURING A TRIP TO the North Cascades up Lake Chelan in Washington State back in 1976, the Well World was born. This account has been published elsewhere (*Dance Band on the Titanic,* Del Rey, 1988) and won't be repeated here, but if you missed it, it gives as fully as I can explain it the creative processes which led, later that year, to the writing of *Midnight at the Well of Souls* (Del Rey, 1977 and ever after).

Midnight became my big hit, all the more so because it did it without any prior successes (my first novel, *A Jungle of Stars,* published the preceding year, sold okay but wasn't exactly a massive hit). Its fate was that it became, through means that no one can explain, a "campus cult classic" of the period—that is, a book everybody just *had* to read. Its sales, not only in the U.S. but in Britain, Germany, Denmark, and many other countries, have continued strong in the sixteen years since it was written, and it essentially made my career as a professional novelist.

It also brought me to a kind of personal fork in the road where I either jumped one way and risked everything or took the other and played my life safe. I was thirty-three years old and teaching history, and I had tenure at a time when history positions were few and far between. The safe road was to keep teaching until retirement and write, perhaps, a book every year or two when I had the time as a kind of profitable hobby. The other route was to go for broke and see if I could make it as a professional writer—even though it would mean giving up all that security, even tenure, at a time and age where I might not be able to get any of it back. I had the insight to realize that this was a once-in-a-lifetime opening and, ultimately, the ego to think I could make it.

To be practical, though, I'd need some real money, and fast. My publishers were paying me more than most beginning writers made, but it certainly wasn't enough to provide any security, and while I had ego and guts, I was practical enough and selfish enough not to want to starve in a garret someplace. Contrary to popular myth, starving in garrets has nothing to do with art; it has to do with your ability to recognize that after you do the art, it's a business. Shakespeare, Dickens, Twain, and Melville never starved in garrets, and I'd already gone through a sufficient number of life traumas that I didn't need to wallow in any more.

My publishers wouldn't pay enough to make me feel secure for other projects, but they would if I did a Well World sequel.

Now, understand, *Midnight* was never intended to be the start of a series. If it had been, I would have laid out things a lot differently. And I hadn't intended to write more, because what in the world do you do when you have already established that your hero is, at least in a science-fictional context, a god? The answer had to be to make him a peripheral character while featuring someone else, someone quite different. *Exiles at the Well of Souls* involved some of the same characters and time line but featured someone new and not godlike, the space pilot and high-tech thief Mavra Chang, and a mostly new supporting cast who went much farther afield geographically and otherwise.

I found I *liked* Mavra and the expanded Well, and on the manuscript page when I had ended *Midnight,* a fairly big book, I instead was introducing a new character into *Exiles.* Since the publisher had some length limitations (because of cost—buyer resistance to a much higher price for a gigantic volume meant they couldn't price it profitably), we split the book in two, with the second half published as *Quest for the Well of Souls.*

Doing a few independent novels as well during that period with totally different plots, settings, ideas, and objectives kept everything in at least creative perspective for me. Thus, when I finished *Quest,* I discovered I had enough unused notes to actually do another book. I had always wanted, for example, to go to the northern hemisphere of the Well World, and that was enough of a challenge (and had few of the layout problems compared to the south), so I wrote what my publisher titled *The Return of Nathan Brazil,* and then, in a big finish, I destroyed and re-created the entire universe, killed countless trillions of people, destroyed most civilizations, and had an upbeat ending in *Twilight at the Well of Souls.* It was a good ending, and I had no intention of ever writing another fictional word about the Well World.

Twilight was written in 1979 and published in 1980. The three novels in five volumes created a tight and, I thought, satisfactory epic. In spite of pleas from very large numbers of readers, I resolved that I was done, finished. I started work on *Four Lords of the Diamond.*

Now, I *did* have a couple of smart-ass lines I got used to giving at autographings, appearances, speeches, and SF conventions when I would inevitably be asked to do more Well World material, the most common of which was naming a dollar figure so impossibly high compared to what even the best in the field were getting paid at the time and saying that if somebody offered me *that* much, *and* if I had an idea I thought would not cheapen, and might possibly enhance, the existing books, I *might* consider it.

I have found that when you *are* actually offered *that much,* good ideas somehow pop out of the woodwork.

This book, and two more to follow, comprising the single work titled *The Watchers at the Well,* are the result. I have better titles than the ones we use, but the old experience with *The Return of Nathan Brazil* showed that some folks out there don't realize it's a Well World book unless it says Well of Souls in the title. While the story eventually caught up to the huge total of sales made by the other books in the series, it was a much slower starter. Don't blame me—blame yourselves.

And this brings up a last question. If you're too young or new to this literary form of ours or you're reading this because your wife/husband/brother/sister or whatever said you should, and you haven't read even *one,* let alone all five, of the previous books, what should you do?

The *correct* thing to do is to go and buy them. The friendly folks at Del Rey assure me that they will all be readily available at your nearest bookstore when this title comes out. They've never been out of print in any event, so if by chance they *aren't* there, either find a better, more aware bookstore or have them ordered.

But if you're not sure, or maybe cannot afford to invest twenty bucks, and want to just start reading this book, could you?

The answer is yes. This one, with the two that follow, has been constructed in such a way that while it contains two main characters from the earlier books and takes a few elements from them to move the plot along, everything here is explained and opened up as new. It will be quite a while before you actually get *on* the Well World, anyway, and by then the new characters who are partially the focus of this work will have to find out what you must know. Longtime readers will find it something of a refresher course, although I hope the information is what you need and not an encumbrance.

I enjoyed going back after such a long time, although I nearly went crazy trying to keep the Well World straight myself. The original books were done at a time when I was still using a (gasp!) *typewriter,* and so I didn't have my usual computer files to check and had to do it all the hard way. I have tried very hard to do justice to my own concept and my own convictions about my art, and I think I have. I haven't just dashed this off; indeed, this novel has taken the longest period I have ever used to write a book, and it's been among my most difficult to do as well. Over the period, too, I've thought that God or at least a great supernatural power was against me. Everything happened from my computer breaking down to having to undergo not one but two eye operations during this period. Well, the Powers lost. Here it is, and I wouldn't be offering it to you unless I thought it was as good as I could make it.

As I say, there are two more to come. Will I write others beyond that one? Well, I'm not going to say a flat "No," just as I didn't in 1980. And I'm not about to name another dollar figure, either. Maybe I will sometime, though—if this or its companion makes the *Times* bestseller lists . . .

Hey—naming a goal worked the *last* time, didn't it?

JACK L. CHALKER
Uniontown, Maryland
February 29, 1992

Prologue
NEAR AN UNNAMED NEUTRON STAR IN THE GALAXY M-22

IN THE NEARLY ONE billion years it had been in its lonely imprisonment, it had never lost its conviction that this universe required a god.

For eons beyond countless eons it had traveled through space in its crystalline cocoon, imprisoned until the end of time, or so those who'd fashioned the cage had boasted, yet what was time to it? And could any prison hold one such as it? Not entirely. They could hold the body, but the mind was beyond imprisonment.

The universe had been re-created, not once but many times, since it had been cast adrift by the only ones who could achieve such a feat, those of its own kind. It had been startled at the first re-creation, for it had been separated and walled off from the master control lest even in its eternal damnation it should somehow get inside once again. The Watchman had done it, the Watchman had reset all, but even the Watchman could not reset its own existence or alter its imprisonment, for it was of the First Matter.

Indeed, each time the system had been reset, its own power had increased; each re-creation required so much energy drawn from dimensions beyond the puny universe of its birth that for moments, for brief moments, there was no control at all, no chains, nothing to bind or hold, and its mind had been able to contact more and more of the control centers.

The jailers had not counted on that. They had not counted on a reset of their grand experiment in any way touching it, in any way influencing it; indeed, there had been much debate about whether to have a reset mechanism at all, and even those who argued in favor of it never dreamed it would actually be used, let alone more than once. Nothing was supposed to influence the prisoner in its eternal wanderings, but even gods can make mistakes; their mistakes, however, were of the sort that no one but another god could ever know of them.

But then, of course, freed of time, they nonetheless could never free themselves of its frame of reference; it was too ingrained in their genes and psyches. Unbound by instrumentalities, they had created their own boundaries in their less than limitless minds—minds indeed so limited that they could never accept the fact that absolute power was an end and not a means.

The last reset had done it. Intended to repair some sort of rip in the fabric of space-time itself, apparently wrought by *artificial* means, the reset had proved the need for a cosmic governor beyond doubt. The shift had been subtle, as they all had been subtle, yet the mathematics of its own prison were absolute, while that of the rest of the universe was not. At the crucial moment of the massive power drain, the one tiny fraction of a nanosecond when energy was not being equally applied as parts of the universe were selectively re-created, it was subject to the absolutes of physics without an interfering probability regulator.

It had been enough, *just* enough so that when the regulator kicked back in, it hadn't allowed for that most infinitesimal of lapses.

A neutron star grabbed at its prison, pulled it with ever-increasing speed, not enough to crash into the terribly dense surface but enough to create massive acceleration, to eventually propel it, like a missile in a sling, to speeds approaching that of light, bending time and space, catching it in the eddies and currents of space and punching it right through a tunnel, a hole in space-time created by the series of massive bodies here.

As usual, the prisoner did not know where or when it would emerge, but it also knew that for the first time the regulator didn't know either and would be slow to attempt adjustment. In that period it would be free of the regulator; in that period there might be a chance.

Then only the Watchman would stand between it and ultimate power. It was a being that even space and time could never fully contain, a being that had spent long eons planning its rule and reign. It would have to meet the Watchman eventually; it knew that and welcomed it, for the Watchman was in a way very much a prisoner as well, doomed to wander forever until needed yet always alone.

It looked forward to that meeting. In a billion years it had never been able to imagine who they'd gotten that was stupid enough to volunteer for the job and yet so slavishly loyal that, in all this time, it had never once taken advantage of the position.

A SMALL TOWN
IN GEORGIA

IT HAD BEEN A shock opening the door to the apartment and seeing just how much was missing.

Have I accumulated so little in my life as this? she wondered, oddly disturbed as much by the thought as by the emptiness.

Even most of the furniture had been his. He'd been nice, of course, offering to leave some of it, but she wanted everything of his, everything that might bring her back into contact with him, removed.

The effect was as if thieves had broken in and stolen anything that could be carried but had gotten scared off just before finishing the job. The drapes were hers, and the small stereo, the TV and its cheap stand, the six bookcases made of screw-it-together-yourself particleboard that sagged and groaned under the weight of her books, and the plants in the window. But only the big beanbag chair with the half dozen patches afforded a place to sit.

She went over to the sliding glass door that led to the tiny balcony and saw that the two cheap aluminum and plastic patio chairs and the little table she'd picked up at a garage sale were still there. So, too, were the worn chairs at the built-in kitchenette. He'd been sparing of the cutlery and glassware and had taken nothing save his abominable Cap'n Crunch cereal.

Feeling hollow and empty yet still distanced from the emotional shock, she put the small kettle on for tea and continued the inventory.

All her clothes were still there, of course, but even though they took up the vast majority of the closet space, there was an emptiness. The dresser and makeup table were just where they always were, but the room looked grotesque without the water bed, just the impression of where it had rested on the discolored and dirty carpet. She would have to tend to that right off the bat. She wondered if she could get a bed in four hours and doubted it; she'd have to either go to a motel tonight or sleep on the floor with just a pillow and sheets until it was delivered. There was no way in heaven that she could get as much as a twin mattress in the little Colt she was driving.

A sudden wave of insecurity washed over her, almost overwhelming her, and she dashed into the bathroom and then grabbed the sink as if to steady herself.

Funny how the bathroom had a calming effect. Maybe it was because, other than being minus his toiletries, it was intact. Then she looked at herself in the mirror, and some of the fear, the emptiness, returned.

She was thirty-six years old and, thanks to the two years she'd spent working at various odd jobs while waiting for an assistantship to open up so she could afford grad school, only seven years out of college. All that time she'd been a single-minded workaholic—push, push, push, drive, drive, drive. Two years teaching gut courses at junior college because even in an age when they were crying for scientists to teach, she'd discovered, there was a lot of resistance from the older male-dominated science faculties to hiring a young woman. All the research and academic excellence counted for little. Oh, they'd never come right out and said anything, but she knew the routine by now; at first she had been merely frustrated but was quickly clued in by her female colleagues at the junior college. *"They never take you serious unless you're well over forty because they think you're going to teach for a while and then quit and have babies"* and *"They still believe deep down that old saw about women not being as good as men in math and science."*

But they also, she had to admit, credited experience. Not that she hadn't tried that route, but the big openings for her were in the oil industry, and that meant both swallowing a lot of her principles and old ideals and also facing the probability of going off to Third World countries where women had no rights at all and trying to do a job there.

Finally she got *this* job, one she really loved, thanks to an old professor of hers who had become department head. As an instructor, teaching undergrads basic courses, it hadn't been the fun it should have been, but it allowed her to work as an assistant on the real research, even if it wasn't *her* grant and wouldn't merit more than a "thanks" in the articles that might be published out of it. Still, she'd done more work in the lab than the professors who *would* get the credit, trying to show them, prove to them that she was in their league and on their level.

And now she was thirty-six going on thirty-seven, not yet tenured, teaching elementary courses to humanities students who didn't give a damn but needed these few basic science courses so they could get B.S. instead of B.A. degrees. And she was alone in this mostly stripped apartment, going nowhere as usual and doing it alone.

Not that *he'd* dropped *her*. She had been the one to break it off, the one to give the ultimatum. It was always understood that they had an "open" relationship, that they were free to see others and not be tied down. They even laughed at the start about making sure they both had safe sex and got regular tests for any nasties that might be picked up. And she'd meant it at the time. The problem was she'd never fooled around with anybody else after he'd moved in, even though she'd had the chance. She simply didn't need anybody else. But he'd kept doing it and kept doing it and kept doing it until he'd done it with a regularity that finally showed that he was not about to slow down or become monogamous.

She felt guilty, even now, for being jealous. Worse, it wasn't based on morality but on her ego. She'd never expected to be so wounded, and it bothered her. *What do they have that I don't? What do they give him that I can't? Am I that bad in bed?*

Best not to dwell on it now. Best to pick up the pieces and go on to something else. She was good at that, she thought ruefully. It seemed like all her life she was picking up the pieces and going on to something else.

She slipped out of her clothes, removed her glasses, grabbed some towels, and went in to take a shower. The mirror on the shower wall reflected her back to herself with no illusions. She stepped very close to the glass so that she could see it clearly, her vision without the glasses being perfectly clear for only a foot or so in front of her, then stared at the reflection as if it were someone else, someone she hardly knew.

Her black hair was cut very short, in a boyish cut; it was easy to wash and easy to manage, and it had fewer gray hairs to pluck that way. Her face was a basic oval shape with brown eyes, thin lashes, a somewhat too large nose, and a mouth maybe a bit too wide, but not much. Not an unattractive face, neither cute nor beautiful, but with maturity creeping into its features, hardening them a bit—or was that her imagination?

Average. That's what she was: average. Not a bad figure but no bathing beauty type, either. Breasts a little too small, hips too wide. With the right clothes she could be very attractive, but this way, unadorned, her body would win no prizes, no envious gazes, no second looks. She looked like a million other women. *Generic, that's me,* she thought glumly. *I ought to have a little black bar code tattooed on my forehead.*

That was the trouble, really, in academia as well. There *were* women at the top of most scientific disciplines, including hers, none of whom would have any problems being wooed from one major chair to another, writing their own tickets their own way, but they were very few in number because the deck was still stacked. Those women were the geniuses, the intellects who could not be denied. As "attractive" was to "knockout," so 'smart" was to "brilliant." Intellectually, she knew that the vast majority of people, male or female, could not have attained a doctorate in a field like hers, but it just wasn't *quite* enough. Enough to finally teach at a great university, but only as "Instructor in the Physical Sciences"—not just Physics 101, which was bad enough, but, God help her, "Introduction to the Sciences for Humanities Students"—and a lowly assistant on research projects whose grants and control were held by middle-aged male professors.

The shower helped a little, but not much, since it left time for more brooding. Was it the fates that struck her where she was, or was it rather lapses in herself? Was she demanding too much of a guy and maybe too much of herself? With people starving around the world and the working poor standing with their families in soup kitchen lines, did she have any right to complain about a dead-end life if it was such a comfortable, yuppified dead end? Was she being just daddy's spoiled little girl, in a situation many would envy, depressed because she couldn't have it all?

A line from one of her undergraduate seminars came to her, fairly or not, and tried to give her some relief from those hard questions. The professor had been a leading feminist and sociologist, and she'd said, *"It's not tough enough being a woman in this day and age, we also have to be saddled with some kind of constant guilt trip, too."*

She was, she knew, at a crisis point in her own life, no matter how miserable other lives might be. She was at an age when biological clocks ticked loudly, at an age when ease of career change was fading fast with each passing page on the calendar, when any move that could be made had to be made or the status quo would become unbreakable. At some point in nearly everybody's life there came the time when one came to a cliff's edge and saw a monstrous gap between oneself and the other side, a side that was nearly impossible to make out. She was up for tenure and possible promotion next year, and she'd not heard anything to indicate she wouldn't get it, although one could never be sure. It was something she wanted, yet it also meant being here, on this side of the chasm, for the rest of her life.

Or she could break away and take real risks and, like most people who did so, fall into the chasm. But all the people who got what and where they wanted, the satisfied movers and shakers, had taken that same risk and made it to the other side. Not all of *those* people were happier than they'd been before, but many were. The trouble was, she was on the old side for making that leap. She was, after all, in this situation now because she craved stability, not earthquakes. Taking a risk in her personal life would mean saying yes to the first guy who proposed who wasn't a geek or a pervert. And professionally, to take a risk would mean first having someplace to jump to, and the offers weren't exactly pouring in, nor did risky opportunity just fall from the sky.

The vortex was never black; rather, it revealed the underside, the sinews, the crisscrossing lines of mathematical force that sustained and essentially stabilized the relevant parts of the universe. The Kraang examined those lines, noted the symmetry and precision, and, this time, noted the relay and junction points. Now, after all those millennia, the slight deviation the Kraang had been able to induce in the last reset had paid off; a line was being followed, not avoided as always before. The Watchman's line, the focal point for probability itself, the emergency signal and warning beacon for the physics of the governable portions of the cosmos . . .

The emergence, as always, was like suddenly being catapulted out of a great tunnel; there, ahead, a solar system, a governed construct in a pattern the Kraang understood well, although it had no knowledge of what sort of creatures might live there or their current stage of development. It did not matter. The Kraang was not supposed to be in this sort of proximity, and already the signal of an aberration would be flowing back to Control, but it was a very long way, and even at the sort of speed such messages could travel Underside, it would be several seconds before it reached Control, and then Control would react.

By now the Kraang knew how it would react.

Control was not self-aware, for if it were, it would be a living god of the universe with no limits and no governor. Automatic maintenance meant automatic response; the experiments were supposed to be controlled, not supervised.

The Kraang's great mind searched frantically for the now-invisible termination of the force line. Great Shia! Where was it? A world incredibly ancient, a world with an artificial yet living core . . .

For a moment the Kraang experienced panic. No such world existed in this system! The nine planets and dozens of assorted larger moons were all dead save the experiment itself! A billion years the lords of chance had made the Kraang wait for this moment! A billion years, and now to be faced with failure . . . ! It would be too much for even the Kraang to bear.

And then, suddenly, it found what it was looking for. A planet once but no more, pulled apart by the strains of gravity and catastrophe, broken into impossibly small fragments that still worked together, trapped into sufficient cohesion by Control's grasp of the energy of probability. Although in a million million pieces, the living heart still somehow functioned in what remained, two tiny steering moons and a vast additional ring . . .

Its mind reached out. Success! Connection! *I give a small part of myself to you!*

A sudden and violent bump, a wrenching jar—its container had been struck head on! An asteroid, small yet effective, had slammed into the container, altering its trajectory. It began to move quickly away, toward the still-distant inner gas giant. The Kraang relaxed and understood. Control was correcting. At this speed and trajectory the Kraang would rush headlong toward the giant world beyond, well away from the active matrix, and the giant's great gravity would slingshot the container around, accelerate it to tremendous speed, sufficient to generate a space-time ripple, to take it out of this system, perhaps out of this entire galaxy.

But it would take two years, as time was counted here, for it to reach the giant and the better part of a third to achieve the desired effect. Out here, in the real universe, Control was constrained by its own laws and the basic laws of physics. Corruption of the system had now occurred; the experiment was now invalidated. It would have no choice but to use whatever mechanism it created to call the Watchman, down there, somewhere, on the experiment itself, the blue and white world third from the sun . . .

"Lori, could you step into my office for a minute?"

It was symptomatic of the problems in her professional life and of her feelings of hitting brick walls. Whiz kid Roger Samms, Ph.D. at twenty-four, was always "Dr. Samms," but Lori Sutton, Ph.D., age thirty-six, was almost always "Lori" to Professor George Virdon Hicks, the department head and her boss. Hicks was basically a nice guy, but he belonged to a far older generation and was beyond even comprehending the problem.

She entered, somewhat puzzled. "Yes, sir?"

"Sit down, sit down!" He sighed and sank into his own chair. "I've got an interesting and fast-developing situation here that's causing us some problems and may be opening up some opportunities for you. Uh—pardon me for asking, but I'm given to understand that you're living alone here now, no particular personal ties or local family?"

She was puzzled and a little irritated at the speed of campus gossip. "That's true."

"And you did some of your doctoral research at the big observatories in Chile?"

She nodded. "Yes, under Don Mankowicz and Jorje Paz. It was the most fun I've had in science to date."

"Did you get over the mountains and into the Amazon basin at all?"

It was hard to see where this was going. "Yes, I took a kind of back-country trip into the rain forests with the Salazars—they finance their fight against the destruction of the rain forest and its cultures by taking folks like me on such trips. It was fascinating but a little rugged."

Hicks leaned forward a little and picked up a packet in a folder on his desk and shoved it toward her. She opened it up and saw it was full of faxes, some showing grainy photographs, others trajectory charts, star charts, and the like. She looked them over and read the covering letter from the MIT team down in Chile who'd sent them. And she was suddenly very interested.

"About nine days ago, during some routine calibration sweeps for the eighty-incher that's just been overhauled, they picked this up. We're not sure, but we think it's a known asteroid—at least, a small one discovered about a dozen years ago should have been in that vicinity at about that time. It should have cleared the orbit of the moon by a good two hundred thousand kilometers, but something, some collision or force unknown, seems to have jarred it just so. It's big—maybe as big as eight hundred meters—and it's just brushing by the moon right now."

She shrugged. "Fascinating, but we've had ones as big as or bigger than this come in between us and the moon."

"Yes, but they missed."

She felt a cold, eerie chill go through her, and she looked at the computer readouts again. "It's going to hit? This is—this could be Meteor Crater or Tunguska!"

He nodded. "Yes, on page three, there, you see that the current estimate based on angle, trajectory, and spectrum analysis of the composition estimates that possibly a third of it will survive to impact, possibly as a single unit. The explosion and crater are going to be enormous."

"And it's going to hit land? In South America?"

"We can't be completely certain, not for another ten to twelve hours, maybe not even then. There are a lot of questions as to the exact angle of entry, how much true mass it represents, whether it will fragment, and so on. They're now giving better than even odds that it'll impact off the Chilean or Ecuadorian coast in the Pacific, but if it's very heavy and hard inside and if the mass is great enough, it'll come down short, possibly in the Andes, more likely in the Brazilian rain forest short of there. Fortunes are being wagered in every observatory and physics department in the world, or will be. It'll hit the news shortly; there's much debate, I understand, on how early to release it, since we'll inevitably get special media coverage with experts talking about global warming and a new ice age from the dust and you name it and people living in both the wrong hemispheres panicking anyway. It'll be out regardless by the evening news tonight."

She nodded, fascinated but still puzzled. "So what has this to do with me?"

"There'll be scientists from all over and news organizations as well gearing up to go in, but the Brazilian government is very concerned about possible injuries or deaths and wants nobody in the area. They have troops already up there trying to get the few settlements evacuated in time, and that, plus the usual red tape, is putting the brakes on most efforts. The exception is Cable News, which has some contacts there and a good relationship with the Brazilian press and government. They've used us before for science pieces and are mounting a team to cover it. To the frustration of the others, they'll probably be the pool. They need somebody with them to tell them what the devil it is they're seeing, or not seeing, and they've called us."

She sat for a moment, not quite wanting to believe the implications of the conversation. Finally, worried that she *had* misunderstood, she asked, "Are you asking if I would go?"

He nodded. "Very short notice." He looked at his watch. 'You'd have to leave for home now. Pack in an hour or so. Your passport is current?"

"Yes, but—"

"Don't forget it. They've got the visas. They'll send a helicopter here for you and your stuff. You'll be on a private charter with their team leaving Hartsfield at seven tonight."

"But—but . . . Why me?"

He looked almost apologetic. "Grad assistants can cover your courses with no sweat, but Doctor Samms is in a rush to get his research organized for a presentation at the AAS next week, and both Kelly and I are, frankly, too old for this sort of thing, as much as I'd love to see that sucker come down—pardon the expression. Nobody else is qualified to observe the event and free enough to go who also wouldn't be stiff as a board and look like an ass on television. So it's either you or they call another university. And I'm afraid I have to call them back in less than ten minutes or they're going to do that anyway."

"I—I hardly know what to say. Yes, of *course* I'll go. I—oh, my God! I better get packing!" The fact that he was being fairly left-handed about it all, that she'd gotten the job only because she was the only one so unimportant that she could be easily spared, didn't bother her. This was the kind of luck she dreamed about, the one break upon which she might be able to stake out a scientific position that would be so unique that it would ensure her stature and prominence.

"We'll make sure you're covered," Hicks assured her. "Five o'clock this afternoon they'll land to pick you up at the medical center heliport. Don't forget your passport!"

She wanted to kiss the old boy, who now could call her "Lori" any time he wanted, but she was in too much of a hurry. Jeez—she'd have to get the suitcases out of the storage locker, haul them up. What to take? She had little clothing or equipment for this kind of trip. And makeup—this was television! And the laptop, of course, and . . . How the *hell* was she going to pack and make it in just three hours?

It was tough, but she managed, knowing she'd forgotten many vital things and hoping that she would have a chance to pick them up in Brazil before going into the wild. The mere hauling of the suitcases and the packing had her gasping for breath, and she began to wonder if she was up to the coming job. She began to feel both her age and the effects of letting the spa membership lapse about a year earlier. She also worried about how much of that clothing, particularly the jeans, would fit. In the months since she'd thrown Harry out, she'd found solace for her dark mood in large quantities of chocolate and other sugary things and generally letting herself go.

Well, the hell with it. If they were going to give her this kind of notice, they could damned well buy her appropriate jungle clothing.

She locked up and hauled the suitcases to the car, discovering for the first time that one wheel on the big suitcase was missing. She just wasn't *ready* for this, not with this kind of deadline—but she knew she needed it, needed it bad.

The helicopter was just about on time. It was, she saw, amused, the one Atlanta's pop radio station used for traffic reports and had that big logo on the side. She wondered how the commuters were going to get home tonight.

The pilot got out, bending slightly under the rotors, and put out his hand. "Hello! I'm Jim Syzmanski," he said in a shouted Georgia-accented voice. "You're Doctor Sutton?"

"Yes. I'm sorry for the bulk, but they didn't give me much notice on this."

He looked at the two suitcases. "No sweat. You ought to see what some of 'em take to a mere accident." He picked them up as if they weighed nothing and stored them in back of the seats. "Get in, and we'll get you goin'."

Although not new to helicopters, she'd never been in one of these small, light types with two seats and a bubble, and it was a little unnerving for a while. Still, the pilot knew his business; it was smooth and comfortable, and they were approaching the airport in a mere twenty minutes, about two hours less than it would have taken to drive and park.

"Sorry to rush you here so you could wait," the pilot told her, "but they need the chopper back over the highways, and this was the only slot I had to get you. Your bags will be okay here. Not many facilities in this area, but unless you want to hike a bunch to the terminal and back, I'd say just head for that waiting room over there. It's pretty basic, but it'll do. I'll radio in once I'm up and tell them that you're here and waiting. It shouldn't be long."

She thanked him, and he was off as soon as he got clearance, leaving her alone in the hangar area. There was a sleek-looking twin-engine Learjet just beyond the barrier with the news organization's corporate logo; she assumed that it was the plane they were going to use.

She turned and walked toward the indicated lounge area, which wasn't much more than a prefabricated unit sitting on the tarmac. A few official-looking people were around beyond the fence, but she suddenly felt nervous about being there without some kind of pass or badge. What if she got arrested for possible hijacking or something?

The lounge proved to have a few padded seats, one of those portable desks so common at airport check-ins, a single rest room, a soft drink machine, two candy machines, a dollar changer, and an empty coffee service. Suddenly conscious that she hadn't taken the time to eat anything since breakfast, she looked at the machines and sighed. The cuisine in this place wasn't exactly what she needed, but it would have to do. Hartsfield was such an enormous airport that getting to a point where she could even catch a shuttle to a terminal was beyond her current energy level, and she was afraid to leave. If they showed up and didn't find her here, they might just leave without her. One of Murphy's ancient laws—if you stay, they'll be late. If you go, they'll show up almost immediately. This wasn't exactly scheduled service, and any rules beyond that weren't very clear.

She fumbled through her bag. At least she had some ones and what felt like a ton of change at the bottom.

Nothing brought on depression faster or made time crawl more than having rushed like mad only to wind up stuck in an empty building, she reflected. The adrenaline rush was wearing off, replaced by a sense of weariness. If the pace had continued, it wouldn't have been so bad, but to be dropped suddenly into lonely silence was murder.

It also gave her time to worry. Had she packed everything that she needed? Was she dressed right for this? Thinking of utility, she'd pulled on some stretch pants, a Hubble telescope T-shirt because it was the only thing she could find that would mark her as perhaps a scientist, and some low-top sneakers. Her old hiking boots were packed, at least, but she doubted that she had a pair of jeans that still fit. Prescription sunglasses, check. But her spare pair of regular glasses were still in her desk in her office. Damn! *That's one,* she thought glumly. The pair she had on and the sunglasses would have to do.

She also hadn't stopped the mail or papers or arranged for her car to be picked up. It was too late to call anybody who could do much tonight; she'd have to call Hester, the department secretary, from Brazil tomorrow.

She went over to the window and looked out on the field. The sun was getting low, and the tinted windows reflected her image back through the view. *God! I look awful!* she thought, worried now about first impressions. She hadn't really realized how much she'd let herself go. She was becoming a real chubette, even in the face, and the very short haircut that had proved so convenient and would also be best for the tropics somehow looked very masculine against that face. *I look like a middle-aged bull dyke,* she thought unhappily. She was supposed to go on TV looking like *this*?

She was suddenly struck with a twinge of panic. What if the television people saw her and decided that there was no way somebody looking like her could go on? What if they told her at the last minute that they were getting somebody from the observatories in Chile? There had to be quite a scientific team assembling there for this event.

It was the deserted civil aviation terminal, she told herself. Rushing around from a standing start and then being dropped into this lonely silence. She wasn't very convincing, however. She was getting old and fat and unattractive at an accelerating rate, and it scared the living hell out of her.

She kept going to the windows and peering out at the Learjet, wondering if she shouldn't be outside, even in the dark. They might miss her, might not even know she was there.

Suddenly she heard voices approaching. The door opened, and two people walked in. The first was maybe the thinnest woman she'd ever seen short of Ethiopian famine pictures on TV; the woman almost redefined the term "tiny." Maybe five feet tall, weighing less than some people's birth weights, dressed in jeans and a matching denim jacket, she was perhaps in her mid-thirties, although it was hard to tell for sure, with a creamy brown complexion and one of those Afro-American hairstyles that looked like the hair was exploding around the head.

The other was a tall, lanky man in jeans and cowboy boots with disheveled sandy brown hair and a ruddy complexion who needed only a stalk of wheat in his hand to be the perfect picture of somebody who'd just stepped off the farm.

"So, anyway, I told George—" the thin woman was saying in one of those big, too-full voices small people seemed to have or develop, when she saw the stranger and paused. "Oh! Hi! You must be Doctor Sutton!"

"Uh—yes. I—I was beginning to think I was forgotten."

The tiny woman sank into a chair. "Sorry about that. When stories happen this fast it's always a mess, and this won't be the last of it. I'm Theresa Perez—'Terry' to all—and this is, believe it or not, Gustav Olafsson, always 'Gus.' I'm what they euphemistically call a 'producer,' which means I'm supposed to make sure everything's there that needs to be there and that the story gets done and gets back. It sounds important, but in the news biz it's a glorified executive secretary to the reporter. Gus is that peculiar breed of creature—we're not sure if they're human or not—known as the 'news photographer.' The kind of fanatic who'll insist on taping his own execution if it'll get a good picture."

" 'Lo," said the taciturn photographer.

"They tell us it'll be five or ten minutes and then we'll board, taxi out, and wait two hours to get out of this damned mess," Perez continued. "The traffic in this place is abominable. You know the saying, 'A wicked man died, and the devil came and took him straight to hell—after, of course, changing in Atlanta.' "

Lori smiled, although it was an old joke. "I know. Is that our plane out there?"

"Yeah. Don't let it fool you. The boss has a *real* fancy one just for his own use. The rest of them are corporate jets. We almost always fly commercial, but if we took Varig down, with all the changes and schedule problems, we'd never be sure of getting where we need to get in time. When you have a schedule problem, the Powers That Be unfreeze their rusted-shut purses and spring for a special. You have bags?"

"Two. They're still in the hangar over there—I hope."

"We'll get them."

"I hope I'm going to be able to pick up something before we go into the bush," Lori told her. "I'm not even sure my old stuff fits."

"I know what you mean. Well, we've got about seventy hours total, and it'll be tight, but we should have a little time in Manaus to get *something,* anyway. It's a decent city for being out there in the middle of nowhere, particularly since it became a main port of entry for airplanes. I was down a year or so ago when we did a rain forest depletion story. One of these times I'm going to be able to see something of these places we get sent. It's always hurry, hurry in this business, and after being ying-yanged around the world, when you get some time off, you want to spend it home in bed."

Lori nodded and smiled, but deep down she envied somebody with that kind of life.

"She never stops talking," Gus commented in a dry Minnesota accent that fit him well. "Ain't gonna get no sleep at all on this trip."

Perez looked up at him with a wry expression. "Gloomy Gus, always the soul of tact. No wonder you can't keep a job."

Lori looked puzzled, and Perez said, "Gus is a free-lance. Half the foreign photographers, sound men, and technicians are, even for the broadcast networks. Nobody can afford to keep on a staff so large that it can be all the places with all the personnel it needs to cover the world. I have a list of hundreds in different categories. This time Gus was the first one I called who was available."

"What she really means is that they don't want to pay top dollar to the best in the business during the long times when there's nothin' happening," Gus retorted.

"I gather you two have worked together before."

Perez nodded. "Twice. Once on the Mexican earthquake and again on one of those stock 'volcano blows its top' stories from Hawaii. Beats me why folks still have houses around that thing to begin with. Gus specializes in natural disasters. That's how he got tagged 'Gloomy' as much as his shining personality."

The door opened again, and a middle-aged man in a pilot's uniform came in. "We're ready when you are," he told Perez.

"Let's go, then," the producer responded, getting up, and they all filed out after the pilot.

"My bags!" Lori said suddenly.

"Need help?" the pilot asked her.

"No, not if they're still there, thanks. Just bring them out to the plane?"

He nodded, and she dashed into the hangar. Somebody had moved them to one side, but they were still there and apparently otherwise untouched. She picked them both up and walked toward the jet. The pilot—actually the copilot as it turned out—took them and stowed them in an external baggage compartment, along with Perez's overnight bag and Gus's small suitcase and huge mass of formidable-looking cases containing, she supposed, his camera, lenses, and the like.

The Lear *was* the way to fly, she decided almost instantly. It was like the first-class cabin of the finest airliner but no coach section behind. Just four extralarge and comfortable swivel airline seats with extended backrests and two pairs of standard seats against the aft bulkhead between which was access to the rest room. There was a small table in the center of the four swivel chairs that looked like a junior version of a corporate boardroom conference table. There were compartments overhead and other places to stow gear. There were also ashtrays, something she hadn't seen on many planes for a while. Not that she needed one, but clearly the regulations didn't apply if one owned the plane.

"Turn forward and you'll feel the seat lock into place," the copilot instructed them. "Everybody fasten your belts and keep your seats in the forward locked position until we have altitude. Once we're up, I'll come back and show you the rest. We've got a window coming up, though, and we don't want to miss it. You get bumped to the back of the line here, you may sit for hours."

They still sat for a little while, but finally the small jet taxied out to the starting position and in a very short time was rolling down the runway at what seemed breakneck speed, although it probably wasn't any faster than the 767 that had gone before them.

The flight was surprisingly smooth and comfortable once they were airborne; more so, she thought, than a bigger plane, although it had been much bumpier taxiing. She had been surprised to see the "Fasten Seat Belt" and "No Smoking" signs just like on a commercial jet. In a few minutes, the panorama of Atlanta at night was obscured by clouds and there was nothing to do but wait until those magic lights vanished, signaling freedom. Not that she wanted to get up right at the moment; the angle of climb was pretty steep and seemed to go on forever.

Finally they leveled off, and the seat belt lights went out. Almost immediately the copilot came back to the cabin. "Anybody hungry?" he asked.

"Starved," Lori responded.

"We get our meals from the same caterer as the big boys on flights like this. The executives have their own food specially prepared, but this is cuisine à la Dobbs House, I'm afraid. No better or worse than the usual airline fare. I'll stick them in the microwave, and we'll at least be full up until breakfast." The small kitchen was cleverly concealed and easy to manage. He put the dinners in, set the controls, then came back and pressed a large square button on one of the bulkheads. A section opened outward, cleverly revealing an impressive-looking bar.

"It's more or less serve yourself," the copilot told them. "Anything you might want is here. Hard stuff, soft stuff, beer, wine—good wine—as well as coffee, which I'll start when we reach altitude. Ice is in the hopper there, glasses in the bin. Trash goes in here, and dirty glasses go in this other bin over here."

A bell went off, and he went back to the small kitchen. "Let's see . . . we've got Delta fish, United Salisbury steak, and USAir lasagna. I'll just put them on the cold trays and set them on the table, and you can fight over which one you want."

"What about you and the pilot?" Lori asked him.

"Oh, we have to eat yet different meals, but that's later. Both of us ate before we came."

He showed them how to unlock the seats so they would swivel once more and also demonstrated that they were nearly full recliners with a nice footrest emerging when the backrest was lowered. Pillows and blankets were above.

Lori didn't care which meal she got and wound up with the Salisbury steak. She couldn't help noticing that Terry had the fish and a diet Pepsi. Only the congenitally thin acted like they were obese all the time.

"So—is this it?" she asked the two newspeople. "I mean—no reporter?"

Terry chuckled. "Oh, there'll be a reporter, all right. Himself." She lowered her voice as deep as she could. "John Maklovitch, CNN news," she intoned solemnly. "He'll meet up with us in Manaus. Flying in from God Only Knows, as usual. In fact, he should beat us there if his connections work out right. We'll use local free-lancers. I've already set up with my counterpart from TV Brasil. Right now they think it's fifty-fifty that the meteor will come down before dawn, so we're going to try and catch its act as it comes in, from the air. It would be neat if we could catch it hitting the earth, but they still can't predict exactly where within a couple of hundred miles last I heard, and it'll be traveling a lot faster than we can."

"Might be for the best we're not that close when it hits, if it hits land," Lori noted. "A big one like this could have the force of a decent-sized atomic bomb, in which case you'd get everything you might expect from a bomb, maybe including radiation—the great mystery explosion at Tunguska in Siberia in 1908 was radioactive, although that might not have been a meteor. The estimates I saw in the papers I read today indicate that this might be the largest one in modern times. The shock wave alone will be enormous, and the crater will be fantastic, like a volcanic caldera, very hot and possibly molten."

"Sounds like fun," Gus commented. "No chance this thing isn't a meteor, though, is there?"

"Huh? What do you mean? Little green men?"

"Well, I saw *War of the Worlds* on TBS last week. Good timing."

She laughed. "I seriously doubt it. The only danger, and it's very remote, is that this is going to be something like the Tunguska explosion I just talked about. Massive blast damage for hundreds of miles with no evidence of what caused it. Many people think it might have been antimatter."

"Auntie what?"

"Antimatter. Matter just like regular matter only with opposite electrical charge and polarity. When antimatter hits matter, they both blow up. Cancel out. Don't let that worry you, though. I never bought the antimatter Siberian explosion. Nobody ever explained to me why it didn't cancel out when it hit the atmosphere if it was. Others say it was a comet, although there's no sign of the meteorite fall that would accompany one. At least one major Russian physicist thinks it was a crashed alien spaceship, but I don't think we have to take that one seriously. Don't worry— it'll be plenty big enough if it's the size they predict even after losing the bulk of its mass in friction with the atmosphere. I *hope* it lands either in the jungle or in the sea. The track prediction I saw takes it over some fairly populous parts of Peru if it clears the Andes. There's no way they could evacuate all that region, not in three days."

"Don't get Gus hoping," Terry cautioned. "If it came down in downtown Lima, he'd be so ecstatic about the photo ops, he wouldn't even *think* of the misery. And no matter what he says, he'd *love* it to be an invasion from Mars. As I said, news photographers aren't quite human."

Gus looked sheepish. "Well, it ain't like this happens every day."

"In fact, it *does* happen every day," Lori told him. "Meteor strikes, that is. It's just that the particles hitting the Earth are usually small enough that they burn up before they reach the ground and just give pretty shooting stars for folks to look at. The ones that *do* reach the ground are often the size of peas or so, and most land in the ocean, in any case. It's just the size of this monster that makes it so unusual."

"Well, wherever it hits and no matter what damage it does, we'll be the first on the scene," Gus told her. 'That's our job."

"Actually, we're praying for Brazil," Terry added. "The other organizations will be forced to use our pool in that region. If it goes into Peru, well, there's a ton of broadcast teams in there now from dozens of countries and more arriving every day. We want to be first and exclusive. If we're not, we're not doing our job."

"If it *does* land up in the upper Amazon, at or near the Peruvian border, it'll be hell to get to on the ground," Lori pointed out. "No roads or airstrips up there, and what natives there are will be primitive and not very friendly. But I'm mostly worried about the idea of covering it from the air."

"Huh? Why?"

"While it's huge, it's not going to come down in one piece. As it comes through the atmosphere, it'll fragment. Some decent-sized chunks and a huge number of little ones will come off. Some will be large enough to fall on their own over a wide swath and cause enormous damage. Even so, on the ground you can take advantage of some cover, and the odds of being hit by a fragment in the open are still pretty low. In the atmosphere, though, it will be extremely turbulent, and if even a very tiny fragment hits the plane, it could be disaster. And when it hits, like I said, it'll be like an atomic bomb."

"It's what we get paid for, Doc," Gus commented, sounding singularly unconcerned. "Can't cover a war without gettin' in the line of fire once in a while."

"I'm afraid he's right," Terry agreed. "Listen, Doctor, if you feel it's ridiculous to risk your life being with us, we can rig up something on the ground for you to join in the comments, but we have to be where the action is, risk or not. In this business you have to develop a kind of insanity, sort of like being a permanent teenager, taking risks and never thinking about the consequences. If not, we might as well stay in Atlanta and just cover the aftermath. We're good at what we do, which is why so few of us get killed, but reporters *do* get hurt sometimes, even killed sometimes, in the pursuit of a story, and this is a major one. I thought that was understood. We'll have a ton of very famous scientists back in Atlanta and around the country feeding stuff to the anchors from their safe offices in the States. *You're* the one who'll be on site. You have to think about that, and now."

It was a sobering thought she hadn't considered up to that point. There was risk in this, not the career risks and romantic risks she'd thought about before—those suddenly seemed very minor—but *real* risk to life and limb. As the meteor came in over the coast of west Africa, it would begin to burn and shatter, and pieces would begin to break off. Most would fall in the Atlantic, but by the time it reached the Brazilian coast, it would be quite low and quite hot and coming in incredibly fast. Those pieces would be raining down over an area perhaps hundreds of miles wide. Parts of the country would look as if they had been bombed by an enemy air force. Fortunately, the region was in the main lightly populated, although there would be some towns that would suffer. But if it cleared the Andes, it would rain over populous portions of Peru like a carpet bomb attack. And there was nowhere that was totally unpopulated anymore except most of Antarctica.

This could be a major disaster, and she was being taken right into the middle of it, as dangerously close as possible to get the right pictures.

She could die.

My God! No wonder they passed the buck to me! That probably was unfair, she told herself, but she still wouldn't put it past them.

Of course, a lot of science was achieved at great risk. The geomorphologists who worked with exploding volcanoes took risks as a matter of routine; medicine and biology since well before the days of Madame Curie took risks as well. It could be a dangerous business, but it usually wasn't. The last astronomer to take a risk greater than pneumonia from spending a long, cold night at the telescope was probably Galileo before the ecclesiastical court in Rome.

Of course, it would be easier if she really *were* here doing science, but she wasn't. There were teams of top scientists all over the region doing that kind of work; with the level of prediction achieved by the computers on this event, it would probably be the most studied and viewed happening in contemporary science. She had no equipment, no labs waiting back home for her findings and samplings, no support at all. She was a mouthpiece, a witness for the cable TV audience.

Terry was getting a bunch of papers out of her briefcase. "Unless you want to bug out in Manaus, you'll have to sign these," the producer told her, shoving the papers over. "I have to fax signed copies back when I arrive and then Fedex the originals. It's mostly standard stuff."

She took the papers and started to look through them. The first was the personal release—she agreed that she had been told there was risk to this job and that she accepted the risk and wouldn't sue the company if something happened, in exchange for which they'd cover all medical expenses from on-the-assignment injuries. The second was the general waiver and promise to abide by the rules of the corporation and do what she was asked to do, etc., etc. The third covered her under the group lawsuit insurance policy in case she said something on the air that somebody else didn't like. The usual.

The fourth, however, was of more positive interest. It was basically a set of rules for an expense account for a foreign assignment, how to prepare one, what they would and would not cover, and the like. The list of what they covered was pretty damned extensive, but the rule apparently was to receipt everything and give it to Terry before a certain cutoff date. And finally, there was an agreement that she would work for up to seven days on this assignment as their exclusive agent and on-camera representative as a free-lance commentator, and licensed unlimited use of any and all footage and commentary given during that period for the onetime fee of—my heavens! That was hundreds of dollars *per day*!

"You look surprised," Terry noted.

"I—I never expected to be paid for this."

"You aren't plugging a book, you haven't got a forthcoming PBS series or whatever, so you're hired as a free-lancer. Just remember that your fee is based on doing satisfactory work and I'm the one who decides if you do."

Lori sighed. She knew at that point that even if she wasn't being paid a dime she'd have to see it through, grit her teeth and go through with the whole thing. Very dangerous or not, this was the chance of a lifetime, the potential turning point in her life she'd abandoned all hope of ever getting.

"I'm in," she told the producer.

AMAZONIA: ROCKFALL MINUS ONE

MANAUS LAY SO FAR into the Amazonian interior of Brazil that since its founding, its major connection to the rest of Brazil and the world as well had been just the Amazon River. Although now it was possible to reach the city by road, the river and the airplane were the primary twin connectors of the city to the rest of civilization.

Still, Manaus was a very large city, born during the boom in gold and other treasures of the Amazon discovered and developed in the nineteenth century. Great old houses and a magnificent if now rundown center city, with its old-world buildings defiant against the jungle, looking more like Lisbon at its finest, displayed Manaus's past, and with the development of the interior in full swing, it was something of a boomtown again. Its airport, always vital since the founding of the national airline decades before, was as grand and modern as any in the western world and was the main port of entry for foreign airliners, almost as if Brazil were intent on reminding all its visitors that there was more to the country than Rio and São Paulo. There were first-class hotels here once more, with all the amenities of modern civilization, and in its bustling streets one could buy almost anything.

With a corporate credit card, it wasn't hard for the two women to pick up what they needed, although it was a hardship to do so in the couple of hours allotted to the task. Terry had to be back at the hotel in a hurry; she'd been on the phone and fax in the hotel's business center almost since arriving, and she still had much to do. By the time they returned, messages had piled up, and before heading back down to the business center, Terry told Lori to order from room service and unpack and repack as needed.

A bellman came up a few minutes later with a folder full of papers, and Lori looked them over after being told they were from Terry. They turned out to be faxes of the latest computer summaries, including maps and tracking data. It was now felt that the angle and velocity would not take the approaching meteor over the Andes, which was a relief to Peru and Ecuador, of course, but the projections also indicated it would track a bit north of the original estimates.

She grabbed a map of Brazil and did a plot. If the projections held up, it would luckily hit in one of the remotest and least populated areas left in the country, but that would also present new dangers. If anything happened and the news crew went down in that region, they might never be found.

She decided to talk to the concierge. He was an old man with more Indian in him than anything else, and it took little imagination to imagine him in the midst of the jungle in some primitive tribe.

"*Sí, senhora.* The region, it is very, very wild. The natives there, they still live in the old ways and would not think too well of strangers. Strangers have cut, burned, destroyed much forest, many animals. Ruin the land and ways of the peoples. Those tribes, they will know of this. They will think anyone who come is come to steal their forest. Best you no go there."

"We'll try not to land if we can avoid it," she assured him. "What do you think the effect will be of the meteor hitting there?" She knew he'd heard all about it. Everybody had, and it was all anybody was talking about.

"They will think it a god, or a demon, or both. They will be very afraid."

She nodded. "Good. They will avoid the impact area, then. It might actually be safe to at least inspect the area afterward."

"What you say is true of the natives, senhora, but I still would not land there or even fly a small plane there."

"Oh? Why not?"

"Ah—how to put? There are certain people just over the border there who also do not like strangers."

He would say no more, but she got the idea. What a place to be heading for! One of the wildest jungles left in the western hemisphere, with snakes and dangerous insects, fierce natives who would see any stranger as a despoiler of their land, and not far away revolutionaries, drug lords, or worse seeing strangers as spies or narcs.

She went on down to the business center to see if any new information had come through. Terry was on two phones at once but looked up when she saw the scientist walk in.

"Hold on a minute," she said into both phones, then said to Lori, "Pick up that line over there—three, I think. You can get more than I can from him."

She wanted to ask who "him" was, but the producer was back on the phones again, so she went over, punched line three, and said, "Hello, this is Dr. Sutton."

"Ah! Somebody who speaks English, not telebabble!" responded a gruff voice at the other end, a voice with just a trace of a central European accent.

"And who am I speaking to?" she asked.

"Hendrik van Horne."

She knew him at once by reputation. Van Horne was something of a living legend among near-object astronomers. "Dr. van Horne! It's an honor. Where are you? Chile?"

"Yes. Things are going quite crazy here. We've had to get the army up to protect us."

"You're under attack?"

"From the world press, yes! It's insane! Those people—they think they own you! I am told you are going to try to track it down by air."

"If we can, more or less. I doubt if we can be there when it hits, but we should be first over it after it does, I would think."

"Ah! I envy you! No one in living memory has seen such a sight! Your account will be very important, Doctor, since you will be first on the scene. By the time that bureaucracy over there gets things set up, the trail will be days or weeks old. You must record everything—*everything*. Get a dictating recorder."

She hadn't thought of that. "I will. I think I can get one here in the hotel. But—I have no instruments. I'm with that same press, you know, and they're only interested in the story for the television."

"Yes, yes. They said they didn't have room for such things since they had to have all their own equipment," he responded with total disgust in his voice. "Nevertheless, the Institute for Advanced Science in Brazil is sending over a basic kit. Get it on board if you can and use it. Tell them it's a condition of their permission to go. Lie, cheat, steal. They deserve it, anyway. Do whatever you can."

"I will," she promised. "Do you have any hard data on the meteor, so I can know a bit more what to expect?"

"Not a lot. It is crazy. The spectrum changes almost as you watch. Whatever it is made of defies any sort of remote analysis. It drives our instruments crazy! That is why we cannot even estimate its true mass. Assuming it is very hard mineral, though, we estimate that the object when it hits will be at least a hundred or more meters across. A hundred-plus *meters*! Think of it! There will be no doubt when *this* one strikes. It will shake every seismograph in the world. The impact site should be at least the size of Meteor Crater in Arizona, perhaps larger and deeper. There will be a tremendous mass expended into the atmosphere by its impact, so be very cautious. It will also be quite some time cooling, which is just as well. We are all dying to know what its composition is that can give these insane readings."

"What do you mean by 'insane readings'?" she asked him, curious.

"I mean that from scan to scan, from moment to moment, the instruments start acting like there are shorts in the systems. They'll give you any result and any reading you want if you just wait. It is almost as if the object is, well, broadcasting interference along a tremendous range. Satellite photos, radar, and laser positioning seem to be the only reliable things we can use. We know what it looks like, more or less—and it's unexceptional in that regard—and its size, speed, trajectory, and so on, but as to its composition—forget it."

That *was* weird. "What's the estimated impact time?"

"If it acts like a conventional meteor and stays true, and if our best guess on mass is correct, and if it remains relatively intact, it is likely to impact at about four-forty tomorrow morning."

She nodded. Still in the darkness. If the sky was even partially clear, it should be one of the most spectacular sights in astronomy.

She thanked van Horne and hung up, then turned to Terry. "What's the weather supposed to be over that area in the early morning hours?"

"Hold on," Terry said into the single phone she was now using. "What?"

"The weather over the region we're going to. They say impact before dawn, about four-forty."

"Scattered clouds, no solid overcast at that hour."

"Good. Then we should be in for quite a show."

Lori was really getting into it now, the excitement of the event overtaking her fear. This, after all, was the kind of thing that had brought her into the sciences to begin with. Unlike some of the small number of other women in her field who'd studied with her, she hadn't gone into physics to prove any points. She had gone into it because, as a child, she'd stared up at the Milky Way on cloudless summer nights and imagined and wondered. She had glued herself to televisions during every space shot and had dreamed of becoming an astronaut. She had even applied for the program, but competition was very stiff, and so far NASA hadn't called.

NASA and the U.S. Air Force, of course, were tracking the meteor with satellite monitors and airborne laboratories with all the most advanced instruments, but they wouldn't be allowed in until well after the impact. Lori's news crew was going to be close, the first ones in, and they would, as van Horne reminded her, have the all-important first impressions. A grandstand seat for the cosmic event of the century.

Terry hung up the last of the phones. "That's it," she said flatly. "Let's get this show on the road."

"We're leaving *now*?"

"Take your smallest suitcase and just pack three days worth, including some tough clothes just in case we can get down near it." She looked at her watch. "My God! Three o'clock! Let's go! We've got to be in the air in an hour!"

They went back up to the room quickly. "What's the rush? It's still thirteen hours away," Lori pointed out.

"We're shifting our base for the evening to a private ranch closer to the fun. Took one *hell* of a lot of work to get permission from them, but they've got the only airstrip in the entire region."

"I didn't think *anybody* civilized lived up there."

"Well, 'civilized' is a matter of opinion. Francisco Campos isn't exactly a great humanitarian. More like a cross between the Mafia and the PLO."

Lori gave a low whistle. "How'd you ever get him to agree to help us?"

Terry grinned. "You'd be surprised at the contacts you have to develop in this business. Truth is, he's so afraid of the inevitable army of media and scientists and government officials, he's allowed us to be the initial pool while he treads water and tries to figure out how to handle what might be coming. It's one reason why we're exclusive in the area. He's been known to shoot down jet planes with surface-to-air missiles."

"And they let him just *stay* there?"

"He's inches over the border. He's worth more than the entire Peruvian treasury and has better arms and maybe a larger army than the government. The Peruvians also have enough trouble with their own revolutionaries, the Shining Path. Sort of a Latin American version of the Khmer Rouge. Compared to them, Campos is a model citizen."

In the lobby Lori met the man Terry always referred to as Himself for the first time. He looked tall and handsome and very much the network type; in his khaki outfit, tailored by Brooks Brothers, he looked as if he'd just stepped off a movie set.

"Hello, I'm John Maklovitch," he said in a deep, resonant voice that made Terry's parody seem right on target. "You must be Doctor Sutton."

"Yes. Pleased to meet you at last."

"Had a problem getting in," he explained to them. "I wound up having to get here from Monrovia via England, Miami, and Caracas." He turned to Terry. "Everything set with Campos?"

She nodded. "As much as can be."

"Let's get cracking, then. It's going to be one of those long, sleepless nights, I'm afraid."

Once up in the air, it was easy to see why the natives would hate strangers. What once had been a solid, nearly impenetrable jungle now had vast cleared areas, and other huge tracts were on fire, spilling smoke into the air like some gigantic forest fire. It was as if the jungle had leprosy, the healthy green skin peeling away, revealing huge ugly blotches that were growing steadily. It was hard to watch, and after a while she turned away.

Maklovitch was going over his game plan with Terry and working over some basic introductory script ideas. "The equipment already there?" he asked worriedly.

"They flew it in this morning before coming back for us," Terry told him. "We have a couple of local technicians from RTB in place and checking it out. When we get there, we'll do as many standups as they want us to, time permitting, but then we fly. We'll tape from the plane if we can and do live commentary—audio is firm and direct, and they can pick up the NASA pictures until they get our feeds. It's the best we could do with the equipment we had available. Plan is to take off about two and take a position on the track of the meteor about four hundred miles out —that'll be sufficient for us to link via Manaus. Then we follow it in. Plan is, if it comes down anywhere in our area, we'll find it, circle and shoot what we can, then get back to the ranch and raw feed whatever Gus has along with your standups. Then, if it's within a couple of hundred miles, we'll use one of Campos's helicopters to get in to the site. If it flattens as much of the jungle as they say it will, we might be able to land for a standup. If not, we'll be able to get some pretty spectacular close-in pictures."

"I hope this won't be like Matatowa," the reporter sighed. "Everything set up for it to blow, half a million bucks spent, and the damned earthquake hits three hundred miles south. I'd hate like hell to have this thing drop into the lap of ABC."

Their attitude was reassuring to the novice scientist. No talk of danger, no talk of risks, no reservations—just how to get the story. It may have been foolish to dismiss those thoughts, but it was also infectious. Maybe one *did* have to be crazy to do many of the things others took for granted; maybe those who took the risks were the ones who knew how to live, too.

"You're going to have to be on your best behavior and bite your tongue at this ranch, Doc," Terry said to her.

"Huh?"

"These are *extremely* dangerous guys," she explained. "Nobody knows how many people they've killed or what they're capable of, but no matter how macho or weird they are, go with the flow. I haven't dealt with these guys face to face before, but I've dealt with their type in Colombia. The Nazis must have been like these guys—smart, articulate, well educated mostly, often charming and cultured, but nutty as fruitcakes in the most psychopathic way. No comments, questions, or moral judgments. We're not here to do their story this time. Let's just do *our* job, okay?"

She nodded. "I'll try and just stay out of their way if I can. We won't exactly have a lot of time, anyway."

"We'll probably have one of them with us," Maklovitch noted. "I seriously doubt if they're going to like a lot of low-level photography of that region without some controls on their part. They'll have a man with us and another with the ground station just to make sure that nothing they don't want seen gets out. Don't worry too much about it, though; satellites can take better pictures of the region than Gus can."

"Like hell," the photographer growled. "Give me an altitude of just a few hundred feet and I'll tell you what's real and what's camouflage. Besides, we don't have a lot of satellite coverage in the southern hemisphere. They'll be on their toes with us. Bet on it."

"Yeah, well, don't you go trying to get away with shots you know are taboo," Maklovitch warned. "This thing's dangerous enough as it is. It wouldn't take much convincing if we were to wind up dead and burned from what they'll say is a tragic accident with the debris from this meteor. There're too many of these crackpots down here for us to cause trouble with Campos. Let the powers that be handle that. You just get the shots you're being paid for and not the kind in the back of the head."

The "Seat Belt" sign went on, and they heard the engines slowing; they were coming in on the Campos airstrip.

Darkness fell fast in the tropics, and it was difficult to see much. It was clear that the strip wasn't commercial caliber; it was bumpy as hell, and they could hear cinders hitting the wings and underside of the plane as they taxied in and slowed to a stop.

It was almost seven-thirty; seven and a half hours to go.

The door opened, and the heat and humidity streamed in. If anything, it seemed far worse than even Manaus, although climatologically there wasn't a lot of difference. A beat-up old station wagon, a full-sized American model not seen on U.S. roads in a decade, bounced up, and several men got out. They carried submachine guns and looked incredibly menacing.

One of the men shouted something to them in rapid Spanish, and Terry responded in kind. She turned to them and said, "Everybody's supposed to get into the wagon and go up to the main house. Air crew, too. They say they'll unload the rest of the gear and bring it along. I think they're supposed to search the plane—and the gear—although they don't say that."

"No problem," responded the voice of the pilot behind them. "They did this earlier today, although Joel and I just had to stand behind the wagon."

Terry said something sharply to the men in Spanish, then explained, "I just told them not to touch the communications equipment and relays. If they get out of whack, we might as well not be here."

The Americans all squeezed into the wagon, and the driver slid in, put his Uzi between his legs, and roared off. Lori was glad to see that she wasn't the only one suddenly holding on for dear life.

The ride was mercifully short, and soon they were in front of an imposing Spanish-style structure that seemed out of place in the middle of nowhere. Three men were waiting, two of whom had weapons and looked like bodyguards; the third was a tall, dignified man who seemed to have stepped out of the pages of some Latin novel. White-haired, including a thick but extremely well-groomed mustache, his skin almost blackened by the tropical sun, he nonetheless was more Spanish than South American and a far cry from the Brazilians they'd been with the past day. He was also the sort of man who clearly had not only been handsome when young but had remanied so into advancing age.

So help me, he's even wearing a white suit! Lori thought, somewhat amused in spite of her nervousness at being around so many guns.

John Maklovitch got out first, followed by the others. He approached the man in the white suit casually and nodded. *"Buenas noches,"* he said in a friendly and seemingly unconcerned tone.

"And good evening to you, my friend," responded the older man in a deep, rich baritone with only a trace of an accent. "I am Francisco Campos, at your service. I must apologize for all the guns and procedures, but this is a very dangerous area. To the west, we have some of the most ruthless revolutionaries on this continent; to the east, some of the most savage tribes remaining on Earth. We have a rigid set of precautions, and although some really are not appropriate for your visit, it is easier for my men to maintain their routine. The sort of men who are willing to live out here are not always the most intelligent, but they are good people."

"We understand perfectly," the newsman responded smoothly. "We were a bit concerned that they might disturb our transmitting equipment. It's delicate and needs to be calibrated as it was in Manaus this afternoon. If it's thrown out of whack, we will have disturbed you for nothing."

"They have been alerted by your technical staff here as to what to look for and what not to touch," Campos responded. "Please be assured that none of my men will harm your equipment in any way. Of *that* I can assure you. But come, you will be eaten alive by the insects out here. Come inside and relax. I can get you drinks and perhaps a light supper."

"Thank you. Your hospitality is most gracious. Uh—may I present my companions? The air crew you have seen, but this young lady is my producer, Theresa Perez, and this other lady is Doctor Lori Sutton, our science adviser for this story. The tall one here is Gus Olafsson, our cameraman."

"Delighted to meet you all," he responded, bowing slightly. "Perez?" he said quizzically. "You are from a Latin country?"

"Some say that," she responded. "Miami, actually."

"*Cubano?*"

"Partly. My father was—a *Marielito*. My mother was from Grenada. But I was born in Florida." She paused. "I apologize and mean no insult, but we have to get set up and in communication with Atlanta. We'll have to do one or two standups before we take off. They're already running nearly continuous coverage, and they'll be expecting us. Perhaps when we are done we can avail ourselves of your generous hospitality, but it *is* our job."

He paused, and for a moment they weren't sure if he was going to take this as an insult, but then he smiled and said, "Of course! I apologize for my stupidity! You see, we are very remote here, and schedules, time clocks, and such are as foreign as snow to us. *Mañana* is our watchword here, I fear. But there is but one meteor, *sí*? And it will not wait. I understand." He turned to one of the other men and barked some crisp orders in Spanish quite different in tone from the one he was using with them, then turned back to them.

"I have asked Juan, my son, to accompany you. With him along, you will find few barriers. His English is fairly good, so you should not need the lovely Señorita Perez to translate, and Juan is a very good helicopter pilot who can assist when you need it." He paused again and for the first time seemed slightly nervous. "This meteor—it is huge, yes?"

"Very large," Maklovitch acknowledged. "Maybe the biggest thing to hit the Earth in thousands of years."

"What will happen when it hits, if I may ask? Here, for example."

Lori decided it was time to take over. "Señor, I don't think we should mince words. Perhaps nothing, although the last track I saw takes it within 150-kilometers of here. There will be debris, some of it possibly as large as heavy rocks and some of it extremely hot. The explosion itself when it lands will be gigantic, like an exploding volcano or worse. How much of the effect you'll get here, whether fallout of rocks or blast damage, will depend on how close it hits. Make no mistake—if it does not clear the Andes, and we do not believe it will, it will hit within a 150-kilometer radius of this estate. Within fifty, you will suffer some strong damage. Within a hundred, some minor damage analogous to an earthquake about that far away. I would certainly take some precautions to secure things, tie them down, get breakables off shelves, that sort of thing, but I wouldn't panic. The odds are very good you won't be in the direct path—but you will know when it comes."

Campos seemed impressed by this. "I thank you. I will do what I can to 'batten the hatches,' as they say, then watch you and pray."

"They hooked up a relay to the house?" Maklovitch asked, impressed.

"No, no. I will watch you on my satellite television. On CNN."

The reporter seemed momentarily taken aback. "Good heavens!" he muttered, more to himself than to the others. "I wonder if the ratings people know about places like this?"

Just then a figure emerged from the house, summoned apparently by one of the bodyguards.

There was no question that Juan Campos was the son of Francisco, but there was a difference far greater between them. What was handsome and cultured on the older man seemed somehow raw and violent in the younger, almost as if the veneer of civilization had been stripped off with the years. His hair was long and black, his mustache was large and bushy, and the eyes were—well, *mean.* He wore green military fatigues that showed custom tailoring and combat boots, and the leather gun belt around his waist held a holster with a mean-looking automatic pistol sticking out of it.

Lori thought, but didn't dare say, that the younger man looked almost like the generic poster of a Latin American revolutionary.

Francisco introduced them around, and the younger man nodded to each in turn, giving each of the news team a penetrating stare, as if he were trying to memorize every detail he could see about them.

Finally he said, in a voice both deeper and more gruff than his father's as well as more heavily accented, "All right. We go."

Terry gave Lori a sudden look that was understood almost instantly; this wasn't their guide but their keeper, and no matter what kind of bastard he was, he was in charge.

They walked around the very large hacienda toward some large outbuildings in the rear, and almost instantly they could see where the crew had set up. A small area against a nondescript green-painted barn was being test lit by some very bright portable lights, and a generator rumbled to give the whole thing power. Gus was happy to see that they'd brought his gear around, and the crew, almost all Brazilians, had already unpacked some of it and set up for the spot.

Terry looked around in the darkness. "Too bad we couldn't get a better backdrop," she commented. "This could just as well be Macon County with that barn."

"No photographs of the ranch," Juan Campos growled. "Your plane or this barn only."

She shrugged. "Too bad. John will have to carry the remoteness with his personality."

The reporter chuckled, but then he turned to Juan Campos to get the other ground rules straight. "What do you want me to say about where we are?" he asked. "Just that we're on a remote airstrip well inside the jungle, or can I say more?"

"You may mention my father and his hospitality," the man in green responded. "In fact, we want you to do so. But do not mention me or what you have seen here."

"Fair enough. Uh—for the record, what does your father officially grow and export from here?"

"Bananas," Juan Campos responded flatly. Terry rolled her eyes, and Lori had a hard time not laughing in spite of the danger. It was all too, well, *comic book,* real as it might be.

"Doc, you and John stand over there against the barn," Terry instructed. "We want to play with the lighting, and Gus wants a camera test. We'll have to adjust to get rid of some of the shadows. John, I'm going to talk to base and see what they want and when."

They were already getting bitten by all sorts of small insects—a medical crew had met them at the airport in Manaus and had filled them with shots, but in spite of that and liberal doses of industrial-strength bug repellent on the plane, Lori was still not sure what was biting her or how hard it would be to look into a camera and not keep scratching and swatting. Thoughts of assassin bugs and malaria mosquitoes came to her unbidden. Once in the lights, though, the little bastards seemed to gang up in swarms. It was going to be a very tough few minutes with those lights on.

Almost as surreal was the little Brazilian man with the pancake and small kit of makeup who actually came in and touched both of them up while Gus took his own sweet time doing his tests and also rearranging the lighting. Finally the main lights went off, leaving them with enough electric light to see but still giving an almost eerie sense of darkness after that brightness.

"Can't do with available light and get a decent shot here," Gus told them, "but I think we can manage with just the one portable light there."

He seemed oblivious to the bugs. "Aren't you getting eaten alive, Gus?" Lori asked him. "How can you keep that steady?"

"Aw, shucks, this ain't no worse than a Minnesota lakes summer," he responded casually. "Up there the bugs got to get in all their eating in a real short time. You catch 'skeeters in little teeny bear traps."

"Yeah. Sure." She remembered an old boyfriend once saying that anybody who started something with the words "Aw, shucks" should be closely watched and never totally trusted. Gus wanted everybody to think of him as just a country hick from the Minnesota backwoods, but this was a man who made a living as a free-lance cameraman for foreign correspondents. She couldn't help but wonder what that country hick act concealed. Perhaps he was the type of person nobody could *ever* really know.

It was amusing to watch Maklovitch at work. He'd stand there with his scribbled notes, lights on, camera running, and go through the short-hand script several times, often stopping and looking disgusted and then starting all over again. Occasionally he'd examine himself in the tiny monitor and call for somebody to adjust his hair or put a little makeup here or there, and then he'd also go back and forth with someone on the microphone as if he were on the telephone. It was a moment before she realized that he *was* sort of on the telephone; he had an earpiece connected to the large apparatus beneath the satellite dish just beyond and was clearly in direct communication with Atlanta.

Suddenly he looked around. "Doctor Sutton!" he called.

"Yes?"

"Get over here! We want to introduce you and go over the initial spot."

She hurried over, suddenly as self-conscious of her appearance as Maklovitch was of his, but it was too late to do much about it.

Terry came up to her and handed her an earpiece similar to the reporter's. She stuck it in her ear. A small microphone was clipped to the front of her blouse.

"Hello? Doctor Sutton? You reading us?" a man's voice came to her.

She was suddenly panicked, unsure of how to reply. Maklovitch was an old hand at this sort of thing and said, "Just talk. That little mike you have on will pick you up. Just use a normal tone. It's pretty sensitive."

"Uh—yes, I hear you fine," she responded, feeling sudden panic and stage fright.

"All right. We'll be coming to your location after the next commercial spot."

"That can take twenty minutes," Maklovitch commented dryly. Then he said to her, "It's going to be easy. Just relax, I'll make some introductory remarks, introduce you, then ask you the same kind of questions we've asked all along. They might have a few extra questions as well, but don't expect anything complex or anything you might not be ready for. This isn't brain surgery, and the audience aren't physicists. Okay?"

She nodded nervously. Up until now this was the one thing she'd thought the least about; now, oddly, it was the thing that was making her the most nervous, and she tried desperately to calm down.

"All I want to do is not make a fool of myself," she told him honestly.

"Don't worry. You'll do fine. The one problem is the audio. You'll be hearing two channels at once sometimes—the director or supervising producer in Atlanta and the anchors. Just don't let it confuse you."

The next few minutes were something of a blur, but all thoughts of the discomfort, the lights, the bugs, and the heat and humidity faded. She remembered being asked, "Is there any danger that this asteroid is large enough to cause worldwide problems?" and answering reflexively.

"If you mean the sort of thing that wiped out the dinosaurs, a nuclear winter, no," she told them. "At least not from the figures I've seen so far. We *did* have a near miss with an asteroid that might have done us in a few years back, but this isn't in that league. Still, it is a very large object, relatively speaking, and there will be some very nasty aftereffects. We might well have some global cooling for a period of years, much as if a couple of very big volcanoes erupted at the same time, and, depending on the upper-level winds here, an even more dramatic effect on the South American and possibly African continents for some time. It will be impossible to say anything for sure until we see it hit."

"Then we don't have to find a survivalist with a fallout shelter," one of the distant anchors said jokingly.

"No. Although if you're living in the western Amazon basin and know somebody with one, it might not be a bad idea," she responded.

There was more of that sort of question and answer, but considering she wasn't even going on current data, there was, she reflected, nothing she could say that any nonscientist might not have said from somewhere in the States.

Still, when the light went down and somebody, probably Terry, said, "Okay, that's enough for now," Lori felt almost stunned, not quite remembering what had gone on. Almost everything—their questions, her replies, even her annoyances—seemed distant and unfocused, beyond remembering clearly. She was suddenly afraid that she'd just made an absolute fool of herself on national television.

Terry came up to her and asked, "Well, what do you think about the new data?"

"Huh? Oh—sorry. It's all something of a blur. New data?"

"Yeah. Impact point ninety kilometers west southwest of here in—" She looked at her watch. "—about three hours, give or take."

"They're that certain? There are so many variables . . ."

"NORAD's computers are pretty good these days, I hear, since they got into such hot water over muffing even the *continent* Skylab was gonna hit some years back. If this asteroid hadn't gone into unstable low Earth orbit, they might be guessing still, but it's deteriorating now right on schedule. They fed in the wobble and decay characteristics, and their computers came up with the predicted mass, and that was the missing element. They say they're ninety-plus percent sure. Didn't you hear *anything*?"

"I—I *heard* it, but it just didn't register. I guess I was just too nervous."

The producer grinned. "You did fine. Look, we'll keep getting data for the next hour or so, and if this prediction continues to hold, we'll do one more standup and then it's off to the plane. Take it easy, relax. Don Francisco's men brought out some sandwiches and drinks. Take the coffee, go easy on the beer, and don't touch that sangria—it's like a hundred and fifty proof."

She looked over at the small but elegant-looking spread. "I see Gus isn't taking your advice on the sangria," she noted.

"Aw! He's a cameraman. He has a reputation to uphold."

Lori was much too excited and nervous at that point to think about putting anything in her stomach, so she wandered over to where the technicians were monitoring the steady satellite feed and listened to the program.

It appeared that there would be no fewer than a dozen instrument-laden airplanes aloft at rockfall, after all, although Lori's group would be the on-site news pool. If nothing else, this would be the most covered impact in history, witnessed and monitored by more people around the world than any other. And even though they would have a ringside seat, the best view would be from the big tracking telescopes in Chile, which could lock on to the meteor while it was still coming in. She only prayed this wouldn't be another one of those overhyped duds astronomical science was famous for. If the thing *did* break up as it entered the atmosphere, or if the resistance was stronger and the angle less steep than projected, it might be nothing more than an anticlimactic meteor shower with very little reaching the ground. Still, this rock was so large that *something* would hit, and it would be bigger than a baseball, that was for sure.

If it did hit with real force, it would be very dangerous, but then they'd be in the perfect position to view the impact. The newspeople were concerned only with their pictures and an event opportunity which allowed them to build audience and sell diet plans and commemorative plates and such via commercials; *she* wanted to be in the neighborhood when a big one hit and see it just afterward. It was the chance of a lifetime.

Terry was preoccupied with her clipboard, which was constantly being updated to the point where it resembled the tracks of drunken worms more than a comprehensible schedule, listening to cues and the remote director's queries and commands from the tiny transceiver she wore like a hearing aid in her left ear. Oblivious to anything beyond the moment, she was startled to the point of near shock when somebody grabbed her rump and squeezed.

"How *dare* you!" she spit, whirling around, only to see the leering grin of Juan Campos. He was obviously high, possibly from drink—he smelled like it, anyway—but also, possibly, from something more. "You touch me again and I will grab your balls and twist them off!" she snapped in Spanish.

He just grinned and gave a low chuckle. "Spirit. I like a pretty girl with spunk."

"You are a pig!" she snapped. "Would you dishonor your father's hospitality in his own home?"

"My father is an old man," Juan Campos responded. "In his time he did as much and more, but now he remembers himself only as a gentleman. He sits here in his palace and acts the *patrón*, Don Francisco, the great benefactor of his people. It is I who now make it all possible, not him."

"Shall we tell him that? He is not far."

Campos stiffened. "You will not *approach* my father!"

"Then we will approach him together and ask him what he thinks of his son's behavior to his guest!" She started toward the house, and he suddenly reached out, grabbed her arm, and pulled her violently back. High or not, there was a homicidal, lunatic look in his eyes and manner, the kind of dark malevolence that would give anyone chills.

"All right, bitch! For now! But you will not always be in this place and so—*protected*. You forget where you are and how long a journey you have to get anywhere else!"

And with that, he faded back into the shadows.

Terry put on a good, tough front, and she *was* tough after all she'd been through in her job, but she was badly shaken by the encounter. It was a sudden mental free-fall back to Earth, a reminder of just how dangerous this place and these people were and how vulnerable she and her people were, too.

She hoped that one of those damned meteors would strike the bastard or perhaps wipe out this whole sordid place, but she knew that there would be no such luck. Her father's caution years ago, when she'd first gone out on her own, floated back to her. "Always remember that God reigns in heaven," he'd told her, "but Satan rules the Earth."

Perhaps, she thought sourly, she'd seen so much of the latter's evil, she just took it for granted.

John Maklovitch came over to her. "We've got one quick standup in five minutes, then we'd better get to the plane," he told her. "It's coming in." He was suddenly aware that she was hardly listening. "Something wrong?"

"The pig of a son just made a move on me and threatened me," she told him.

The newsman nodded. "I figured as much. Think you can handle him?"

"Alone? Sure. I've got a black belt, remember? But against him and some cronies with their big guns—well, I'm not so sure. Besides, what would the old man do if I broke his son's neck? We've got to get *out* of here, you know."

He thought a moment. "Maybe, but I'll report it in to the studio so they'll know to check up if something happens after the story. Nobody is dumb enough to do anything until we're breaking down. Tell you what . . . You remember the massacre in Chad? Why don't we just try the same gimmick? I'll have sound rig a trigger switch on the remote mike for me. Stick close to me, and if he pulls anything, at least he'll be broadcasting it back to the studio. You can imagine what the old man would be like if he heard *that* on his satellite TV!"

She gave him a weak smile. "Thanks, John. Let's get this show on the road!"

He hesitated a moment. "What about the doc? Think she'll get the same treatment?"

"I dunno. Maybe. She's kinda old and frumpy for Juan, but some of these other guys—you haven't seen many women around here." She sighed. "We'll *all* stick close."

The second spot went smoothly, and then everybody started to move fast. Gus and an assistant from the Brazilian network gathered their material and headed for the front of the big house; the sound man, also Brazilian, stuck with the newsman and the two women, his portable pack energized. Neither Maklovitch nor Terry said anything about Juan to Lori; no sense in alarming her unnecessarily and then possibly having to spill the backup plans where other ears could hear.

"We'll be on almost continuously from about five or ten minutes before anything shows up right through the strike and aftermath," the newsman warned the scientist. "Just comment on what you see and don't worry about what's going out. Just remember to watch your language."

"I'll try," she assured him. "I'm getting used to it now. I think once I'm away from this place, well, it'll be more relaxing."

"I know what you mean. We have to return and drop off the backup tape and the like for uplink, but we'll have to play it by ear from that point. If the main body hits anywhere within 150 or so miles of here, as it's supposed to, we'll probably have to use Don Francisco's helicopter to get in close. I, for one, want to see it close up after it hits if conditions permit and before the military and scientific teams get in and start blocking everything off. Still, if the thing looks like a nuclear blast, it might be too dangerous."

"It still depends on how much burns away and whether it fragments," Lori told him. "But if it's a good size, it's going to be a very nasty sight."

They took the station wagon back to the plane with guards and the technical crew riding in a truck behind. The pilot and copilot were there, looking a little uncomfortable and anxious to be off, but they helped the crew stow its gear.

"Wait a minute and let me and Hector here check the remote exterior cameras," Gus asked them. He and his Brazilian associate climbed aboard, and in a couple of minutes Gus stuck his head back out and said, "Come on in! Gonna be kinda crowded, though."

Terry walked up to the plane and went inside and saw immediately what Gus meant.

Sitting in the last row were Juan Campos and a big smelly bodyguard.

Campos grinned when he saw Terry. "Come in, come in! We are all one big happy family here, no?"

It was fifty-nine minutes to rockfall.

THE BEACH AT IPANEMA, BEFORE SUNRISE

IT WAS NEARLY DESERTED before dawn, this beach that was famous in song and story but would, before the morning was run, be crowded almost to bursting with bodies craving the sun and wind and waves. He liked the waves, the warm bodies wearing nothing or nearly so, the fun and general *life* of it all, and he came here often to watch, often entertained most by the reactions of puritanical American tourists seeing their first nude and topless bathers in what was basically an urban resort, but he liked this time, too, when he could still hear the waves, smell the salt air, and see that, indeed, there was sand on the beach.

The homeless, particularly the bands of pitiful, roving children, were also pretty much absent now, huddled away in corrugated cartons, abandoned buildings, and other hideaways, away from those who might prey even on them. Also absent for the moment were the hustlers, con men, pickpockets and petty thieves who roamed the area near the beach.

Not that he was alone, nor did he particularly want to be. Here and there, walking along the waves, barely visible in the beginnings of false dawn, were occasional couples and a determined jogger, and, up on the walk, a big man in a colorful shirt was either walking two enormous dogs on leashes or they were walking him. In the small cafés within sight of the beach there was already activity as they prepared for the morning onslaught of tourists and urban escapees, and as always in Brazil, the overpowering aroma of brewing coffee was beyond even the abilities of the morning breezes to completely dissipate.

This, in fact, was his favorite period of any year or season, when he was not working, and had nowhere to go, and could just walk around and enjoy the sights, sounds, smells, and, yes, people.

That would surprise those who'd known him over the long course of his life or even the few who currently knew him more than casually. He liked people; he genuinely liked them, else he'd never be here and certainly wouldn't be stuck in this rut. He just couldn't, wouldn't get *close* to individual people, not if he could help it. No matter how good or how wonderful or fascinating they were, they had a fatal flaw, all of them, that would eventually break his heart.

People grew old. People *died*.

That was why he particularly relished times like this. A few weeks in a town far from his normal haunts, an anonymous stranger to everybody he might meet. And they in turn were here temporarily from, usually, very mundane pursuits, here to have a good time and be convivial and then go home.

So long as he didn't stay very long or they remained an even shorter time, all was equal. The people he'd met, the experiences he'd had while on these faraway holidays, were golden; they were, in fact, what kept him going. No matter who he met, they were equals, and, at least in his mind, they would always stay that way, for he could be close and friendly or cold and distant as it suited him to be, and those people with whom he interacted would be forever young, forever alive, because he would never see or hear of them again.

He liked this age, too, or at least he liked things more from this age onward. Those who idealized the past, whether recent or ancient, should have had to live through and endure it. Then, perhaps, they would appreciate what they now had and just how far things had come.

It also continued to astonish him how much of history duplicated itself, sometimes in the smallest details. It would have astonished even great Caesar to know that he, or one nearly his twin, had crossed the Rubicon before, and what measure of futile toil had been done on a Great Wall for inner China long before the first brick was laid for that wall in this world; to know that Michelangelo could accomplish more than one David—and more than one Sistine Chapel; that Great Zimbabwe had stood before, almost but not quite on the same exact spot, and that Alexander had marched and Aristotle had thought not once but over again on more ancient ground. That Cyril, whom they would make a saint, would again and again commit the atrocity of burning the great library at Alexandria, and, once again, what remained of Greco-Roman writings would be preserved for Europe against Europe's best efforts by black Songhai at its library in great Timbuktu. Only the Hindus seemed to know, as they always did, that the cosmic wheel eternally came back again and again to the same place.

He understood why this was so, that the first natural development of

Earth had been recorded through him in a vast data base so distant that none here could comprehend such a gulf and that "reset" meant just that, not a random restart, lest the experiment be spoiled.

He knew more or less what he was and had his own dim memories of before, but even now he found it more and more difficult to recall specific details, to remember all that much. The human brain could manage only so much. It was not a factor with these mortals, who died before they approached a fraction of their capacity, but for such as him it was . . . spooled off.

Still, there *were* differences; there were always differences, but until now, through the countless centuries that preceded it, they were relatively minor ones. Even major changes tended to rectify themselves over time, allowing history to rejoin the original flow. Still, he hadn't remembered the collapse of the Soviet Union at any point in this age, nor the creeping fascism edging out idealistic if no less abhorrent communism. It was so hard to remember, but that change had jolted him as nothing else he could remember with its sense of wrongness. If such a major departure was somehow allowed, did that mean that the experiment was inevitably corrupted or that perhaps this time history was running true? Certainly it would delay space exploration and colonization, perhaps for a century or two. He recalled fleeting snippets of time spent in the Soviet Mars colony. It was so long ago, and the thought was so fragmented, he could not be certain if it was a true memory or not, but he felt that it was. It sure wouldn't be now. It would be interesting to see which *would* be the nation to get out to the stars. Or was there still some "rectification" to come?

It bothered him, not so much in principle—he didn't really care if things went differently or not, let alone who did what—but the mere fact that the difference existed at all. It seemed far too big to "rectify." Something just as bad or worse might well come out of it all, but it seemed far too huge a departure for correction, and, lost memories or not, he was certain that a change this major had never happened before.

Could it be some new glitch in the system? He hoped not. He *prayed* not. He wanted no more of that sort of thing, and anyway, if it was a glitch, the emergency program should call him and provide a means for him to come and fix things. That hadn't happened. And it wasn't as if, at this stage of technological development, he could just hop aboard an interstellar spacecraft and steer for one of the old portals. These people had barely made it to the moon the old-fashioned way, and when they had, they'd lost interest. He could never comprehend that; it seemed like social devolution. Oh, well . . .

His thoughts were suddenly broken by the sight of a couple standing on the walk above looking out at the sea. There seemed something decidedly odd about them, but he couldn't figure out what it was. Curiosity and the lack of anything better to do took him toward them. He saw that the woman was in a wheelchair—one of the elaborate, expensive, motorized kinds. There was something odd about the man, more than the fact that he was overdressed for the area and the occasion, something in the way he stood, in the carriage of his head, and in the sunglasses he was wearing.

It was enough to draw him closer to them. One did not often see a blind man and a wheelchair-bound woman out on these streets at *any* time, particularly on their own. Perhaps they were merely naive—thieves and muggers were not at all uncommon near the beach, and this couple was in no position to either defend themselves or give chase should they be threatened with violence. But he admired their courage and their obvious insistence that just because they were both handicapped did not mean that they were going to shut themselves away for the rest of their lives.

The woman sat oddly in the wheelchair, a position no one would naturally assume. A quadriplegic, most likely, with some limited control of at least one hand and arm sufficient to move the power joystick but not much else. She looked to be in her early to mid-forties, an attractive woman with short brown hair and lively eyes that seemed to pick up everything in a glance. She saw the stranger approaching and said something to her companion, who nodded.

The man had on a white business suit and a well-knotted dark tie and wore a broad-brimmed Panama hat. He was a handsome man, too, perhaps a shade older than the woman, with signs of gray in the black hair that emerged beneath the hat, and he was fairly tall, almost a head taller than the man who was now walking toward him. He also had a look about him one saw only in this country—a curious mixture of nationalities, part Amerind, part European, part black, that had merged over the past four centuries into a unique and distinct new race, the Atlantic Brazilian.

"Good morning, sir and madam," the small man greeted them in an oddly accented but still very good Brazilian Portuguese dialect. He could see them both tense, as if they both had also just realized their vulnerability. "Please rest easy. I was simply walking along and could not help noticing you here. This is not a terribly safe place, you know."

"I was born only two kilometers from here," the man responded in a deep, elegant baritone. "I have no more fear of this place or these people than would you."

"What is he saying, Tony?" the woman asked in English with a clipped

British Midlands accent. "I'm afraid I can't make out more than a word or two."

The stranger immediately switched to English. "I'm sorry, I hadn't realized that you both weren't locals." His accent was still odd, but the words were clear.

"Just small talk, my dear," the blind man assured her.

"I distinctly got the impression of a warning," she persisted.

"I was just saying that this is a dangerous area these days, what with so many homeless youth gangs, thieves, and the like around," the small man explained.

"And I told him I was very familiar with the area," her companion added.

"Well, I said much the same," the woman noted. "Your memories of this beach are about twenty years out of date."

"You do not live here, then?" the small man asked.

"No," responded the Brazilian, "we live in Salisbury, in England, actually. But I have been promising myself that I would return home someday no matter what, and after passing up previous opportunities, I decided that this was the time."

"You are staying with family, then?" The small man hesitated, feeling suddenly a bit embarrassed. "I'm sorry. My name is David Solomon— Captain David Solomon."

"Air force?"

"No. Merchant. My ship is the *Sumatra Shell* out of Bahrain. One of those huge supertankers filled with oil. I live aboard her for four months at a time, going back and forth from wherever there is crude oil to where they want me to unload it, seldom getting off for more than a few hours or a day at a time. When I'm rotated off, I like to come to places I either have never been or haven't been to in a very long time."

"I shouldn't think that someone with a name like yours would be too welcome in Bahrain," the man responded. "I, by the way, am Joao Antonio Guzman, and this is my wife, Anne Marie. I generally use 'Tony' as a first name because, frankly, the British do a terrible job on 'Joao.' They still pronounce Don Juan as Don Jew-an, you know."

"I can imagine," the captain replied. "And you're right. I'm Jewish, and that's neither popular nor even particularly legal in the Gulf, but nobody really minds so long as I stay out of Saudi Arabia. Besides, I am also Egyptian, which helps a great deal in such things. In fact, for practical reasons I'm listed on my documents as a Coptic Christian. Nobody ever cares or checks, and frankly, as religiously observant as I am, one faith is as good as another. In any event, I'm not there long when I'm there, and quite often I'm nowhere near Moslem territory. I've been running from Brunei to Sydney most recently, and neither of them gives a damn what religion I might be. Certainly my Dutch employers don't."

"And you're here on holiday, then?" Tony Guzman asked him. "First time?"

"First time in—a very long time. I've rented a small cottage at outrageous rates a few kilometers south but still near the beach. I just started walking and wound up here this morning. I like to watch the sun rise."

"As do we," Anne Marie told him. "It's such a huge, warm sun at this latitude. Tony, of course, can't see it come up except in his mind's eye, but he can feel it, and of course he has many more of these in his memories than I do, growing up here. We did this yesterday, too, taking a taxi from the hotel."

"Then you're not staying with family?"

"I have little family left here now. None close," the man told him. "The few that are left tend to be uncomfortable either with my condition or with the fact that I married an Englishwoman and am now a British citizen."

"And one that makes them *more* uncomfortable," Anne Marie put in.

"Well, I don't find either of you uncomfortable," he said with a casual honesty they instantly knew was real. "In fact, I find you very interesting people, and I salute you for not letting anything get in the way of your enjoyment."

"Do you have a wife? Children?" Anne Marie asked him.

He shook his head. "No, no one, I'm afraid. The kind of life I lead, the kind of job, just doesn't lend itself to marriage, and I'm unable to have children, so that point is moot."

She sighed. "That's one thing we have in common. I used to be able, it's true, but going through it would have killed me, they said."

"Your accident was early, then? Sorry—again, I don't mean to pry. If you'd rather not discuss it, we'll drop it."

"Oh, I don't mind a bit. I minded the *accident,* and I'd much rather be walking about and feel something below the armpits, but I certainly don't mind talking about it. I just wish it were more spectacular than it was, really, so I'd have a story to tell. An IRA bomb perhaps, or an aircraft accident, or perhaps a sport injury, but it was nothing so dramatic. Truth is, I don't even remember it. It was winter, I was sound asleep in the family car coming home from some Christmas visit to relatives, we hit a patch of ice, slid off, and rolled down an embankment. I was always a sound sleeper, so all I remember is tumbling and some very sharp pain in my neck and back, and that's it. I woke up unable to move anything below the neck. Years of therapy got me to this point, where I stuck. There're just no more connections to make."

"Mine was a bit more exotic," her husband added. "I was a pilot for Varig, and we had fuel and mechanical problems coming into Gatwick. We came in all right, but the nose wheel collapsed on landing, and we slid off the side of the runway and into a ground control radar hut. The base was concrete. All the passengers survived with only minor injuries, but we hit the small building head on. It shattered the windscreen, which is very hard to do, and crumpled in a part of the nose around the cockpit. My copilot had eleven broken bones and eventually lost his leg. I, on the other hand, had a piece of metal driven right into my skull. I have a *very* large metal plate in my head that makes it impossible for me to withstand airport security today—you should see their expressions when they use the hand scanner!—and although there is nothing wrong with the eyes themselves that we know of, there was internal bleeding and damage, and I've been unable to see since. I spent three years in British hospitals of one sort or another and remained there, partly because I had little to come home to and partly because, with the military government in power here and Brazil in such a bad shape economically, I could get much better care in the English system. Besides, I had to relearn even the basics of balance and get my confidence as a sightless man, and the therapy was quite good. I met Anne Marie while I was still in therapy."

"You shared hospitals?"

She laughed. "No, by that time I'd been this way for years. But I found I could sit and rot at home, watching the telly and being spoon-fed by doting relatives and nurses, or I could get out and do something. When an old friend of Father's who'd been working in the physical therapy wards voiced frustration that many people with relatively minor disabilities compared, say, to my own were so depressed and suicidal that they put themselves beyond help, I thought I might be able to do something. After all, if you've lost an arm, or legs, or even your eyes but you are confronted with someone with a more serious disability, like me, actually *doing* something, what sort of excuse do you have?"

The captain liked them more and more as he heard their stories.

"In truth, we are one person," Tony Guzman noted. "Most of me works all right, except my eyes, and Anne Marie's eyes work quite well. So she guides me and describes the world to me, and I do for her what she cannot do for herself. You would be surprised at how one could get used to almost anything."

"No," the captain responded, thoughtful. "No, I wouldn't. We all have crosses to bear. Some are just more obvious than others."

"But what of you?" Anne Marie said. "No wife . . . Do you have family of any sort?"

"No, not really. Well, there is one person, but I have no idea now where she is or what she is doing."

"A sister?"

"Not exactly. The relationship is rather—*complex*. Hard to describe. It's been so long, though, that I find it difficult now to even remember what she looked like. We had some sort of fight. I can't remember what it was about or even if I understood it then. She walked out, I thought for a little while, but she never returned, not even for her things. I never saw her again, even though I half tore that city apart looking."

"You speak of it as long ago, but you are not that old, surely," Tony noted.

He returned a grim smile the man could not see. "I am much older than I look." *Much* older. The city, after all, had been Nineveh at the time of its glories.

"I hesitate to say it, but from your account I would say that she met with foul play," Tony noted.

"Foul play possibly," he agreed, "although she's not dead. Once or twice I've run across someone who had known her, but never did I learn of it in time to track her. Like me, she is a survivor. If I had a clue as to where she might be, I'd still drop everything and go hunting for her, but, again like me, she could be anywhere in the world."

"You still think of her like that, even though you say you can hardly remember her looks?" Anne Marie asked, amazed. "Surely there must be someone else for you out there."

"I'm afraid not. We are bound in a way. Two of a kind. It's no use going into details, but trust me on that." He turned. "Ah! Here comes the sun!"

The three of them grew silent and let the great orb appear from the ocean depths, seeming huge enough to swallow the whole world. Finally Solomon said, "Have you two had breakfast yet? There is a café just a couple of blocks inland from here that is excellent. I would be honored if you would join me. My treat."

Tony said nothing but seemed to wait for his wife to speak. She mulled it over, then said, "Thank you, I believe we will. But then we must get back. I have to keep to something of a schedule, and I have some medications to take. But right now I feel all energy. We shall do some things this morning and go to sleep early."

"What? With all the nightlife here?"

She laughed. "Not tonight. Haven't you heard? They say there's some huge meteor that's going to come in tonight and crash in the western jungle. Some of these bloody locals are panicking and moving out for the night or staying in church or whatever, afraid that God is going to smite them or something. They say, though, that it might be visible here in the early morning hours. Between one and three A.M. Atlantic time. They say it might fragment and give us all a spectacular natural fireworks show. I shouldn't like to miss that, with the luck of being here when it comes."

"I had to pull every string I know just to get into our room," Tony told him. "There is not a vacant room anywhere in the area or farther inland, either. All the scientists and *touristas,* the sort of people who go on eclipse cruises, are all here for it, as are the newspeople from a hundred countries."

"I haven't paid much attention to the news," the captain admitted. "I *did* hear something about it when I noticed the shops selling lucky charms and meteor repellent in the last week or so. I thought it was far away and inland, though."

Anne Marie roared with laughter. "Meteor repellent! That's wonderful!"

"Don't laugh," the captain responded in a serious tone. "I will be willing to wager a good amount of money that nobody who uses it has ever been hit by a meteor."

They all laughed at his little joke, and then Tony said, "It is supposed to be visible from here—if it is clear. Of course, it is rarely clear here."

The captain thought a moment. "Look, I've got a minivan. If you're really keen to see it, we might manage the wheelchair and drive up into the inland mountains for a while, maybe above some of the coastal weather. That's if you feel up to it."

"Oh! That would be *delightful*!" Anne Marie exclaimed excitedly. "Sir, I will *ensure* that I am up to it. It is only one night, and we *are* on holiday, after all!"

Tony frowned and started to say something, then thought better of it, but it didn't escape the captain's notice. He had the distinct impression, though, that Tony was not all that thrilled by her being out on an expedition, however conservative. It made the captain wonder if there was something else important he didn't know but should.

They had an excellent breakfast, and Anne Marie couldn't stop talking about their good fortune in meeting the captain and how excited she was to be going somewhere where she was *sure* to see the big show.

After eating, Solomon accompanied them back to their hotel, one of the better ones in the area, as it turned out, with some handicapped-equipped rooms. Tony took his wife from the wheelchair with well-practiced motions and found the bathroom, acting as if he could see very well, indeed. He was certainly well adjusted to his blindness and had the room memorized.

He took some time with her in the bathroom. Finally they were done, and he brought her out and laid her on one of the beds.

"Thank you, Captain, for a *delightful* morning," she said, sounding suddenly very tired. "I can hardly wait until tonight!"

Tony pulled up the covers on the still unmade bed, then made his way back to the door. The captain went outside, and Guzman followed, keeping the door slightly ajar.

"Captain, I think there is something you should know," the blind man whispered, switching to Portuguese.

Solomon responded in kind. "I thought there was something."

"We are here, at grave expense, because it is the last chance we will have. She has been growing weaker and weaker, and eventually even the automatic organs like the heart and lungs will fail. It is only a matter of time. This is, most likely, our last holiday."

"I suspected as much. How long do they give her?"

"God knows. The doctors argued against this trip. I asked them how long she might last if she went into a hospital or was under constant home monitoring. They said a few weeks to no more than six months. Then I asked them how long it would be if she made the trip. They responded that it might be a few weeks to no more than six months but that it would certainly shorten her time. You have been with her this morning. I think you have seen why I fell in love with her. If she were to die today, here, it would be as she would want it, still out, still active, still doing new things. I think the doctors are wrong. I believe she would have died far sooner rotting at home. Certainly she would have died in misery instead of here, in my homeland, about which I have spoken all too much, watching the sun rise and smelling the smells and meeting the people. You see?"

He nodded. "But even you think this kind of silly trip tonight might be too much for her, is that it? Shall I make some excuse and call it off?"

"No! Not now. Had this been suggested only to me, I would have refused, but—well, you saw her. Perhaps it *will* kill her, but not before she sees the meteor. I just—wanted you to know."

The captain nodded. "I'll keep it an easy drive. And I suspect you might be underestimating the power of her will. She may die within the period the doctors say, but I think she'll pick her own time and place." He patted the blind man on the shoulder. "I'll see you at six."

There seemed to be only three kinds of people in metropolitan Rio that night: those who were terrified of the meteors, those who were profiteering from it, and those who were anxious to see what they could of the big show. Bars served meteor cocktails—which differed from bar to bar, but who cared?—and one main hotel advertised an Asteroid Ball in its roof-top club.

The captain found his new friends waiting for him, and once he was shown how the wheelchair collapsed, they managed to get everybody in the Volkswagen minivan. Getting out of town wasn't difficult, but though traffic normally thinned out going farther inland, the two-lane road through the mountains that formed the natural barrier between the city region and the dense jungle beyond was almost bumper to bumper.

"It looks like everybody else had the same idea we did," the captain noted sourly.

"Well, there are not many roads back here, and even those give out not far beyond the mountains," Tony noted. "I do know a few places that might be less traveled, but the road may not be paved."

"I'm willing, but I don't want too rough a road, not only for Anne Marie's sake but also because even though this is a good, solid Brazilian-made car, it doesn't have four-wheel drive," Solomon responded.

"These would be service and old military roads no longer in use. I do not know how rough they might be, but you should not need four-wheel drive for them. At any rate, we can take a look and you can make a decision from there."

The captain shrugged. "If your memory can get me to them, by all means," he said. He was a bit surprised. It had been Tony, after all, who had worried so much about Anne Marie's fragility that he hadn't been enthusiastic about the more civilized trip they had planned.

For a blind man who hadn't been in the area in twenty years, though, Tony was proving remarkably accurate.

"There should be a dirt road going up the side of the mountain on your right about two kilometers after that intersection," Tony told him. "It will have a sign marked DO NOT ENTER—MILITARY DISTRICT ROAD. Ignore it and go on up. It has not been used as more than a lover's rendezvous in more than a decade."

The captain was a bit suspicious at Tony's detailed recall. "How do you know all that?"

Tony smiled knowingly. "Well, I will tell you the secret. For a thousand cruzeiros the head porter was more than willing to suggest this and to write out the directions for Anne Marie. He has used the spot himself, you see. It is not likely, however, that there will be many up there to-night, or so he said, although he doubted we would be alone and suggested we use discretion with our lights."

"All right, I'll do what I can," the captain responded, chuckling. "Yep. There it is. Pretty imposing sign and the remains of a gate and gate-house." He pulled off, slowed to a crawl, then went into second gear for the climb. It was steep, and he would not have liked to have met someone traveling in the opposite direction, but it was manageable. The climb also seemed interminable, and he kept a wary eye on the temperature gauge, which was climbing precipitously, but just as he wondered what was going to happen when he boiled over before reaching the top, the road swung around and there was a pulloff. He took it and waited for the temperature to come down. "Hard to say how much farther the top is and how many switchbacks we might face," he explained. "I think we want to not only get up there but be able to get back down without having to coast." He looked at the dashboard clock. "It's a little after midnight. What time did they say the big show was?"

"Sometime after two," Anne Marie told him.

"We'll make it," he assured them. "Plenty of time. How are you holding up?"

"I'll be all right. I had hoped to nap partway, but I was too excited earlier, and at the moment this drive is a bit too unnerving and too steep for any such thing. I'm afraid to close my eyes."

"Don't blame me," Solomon responded. "I'm not the one that came up with this place. All I can say is that there better be a nice view of a clear sky up there or I'm gonna be mightily pissed off. Uh—pardon the language."

"Take no mind of me," Anne Marie responded. "I'm feeling a bit, well, you know, myself."

He started up again and, three switchbacks later, reached a level, debris-filled area that went back quite a ways. The headlights revealed it to be deserted.

The captain looked at the crumbling remains of buildings and gates and fences and frowned. "Did your porter tell you just what this place used to be for?" he asked.

"No," Tony admitted. "It would have to be either something very secretive or something very mundane, such as a storage area for road-grading equipment—there are many rock slides through here, or there were in my day."

The captain took the minivan on a very slow circuit and stopped when the headlights illuminated a large concrete pad. "A helipad. That's what that is," he told them. "Either this provided a quick getaway for VIPs or it was used to spirit people out of the city in secret. You could take somebody out from a rooftop in Rio, bring him here, then transfer him to just about anywhere. The buildings seem too small for a real jail but perfectly adequate for some quiet interrogation with no prying eyes around."

"Oh, dear," muttered Anne Marie.

Tony just nodded. "As military governments go, the one that ruled here for more than a decade wasn't all that horrible, but particularly in the early days, they went after communists, labor union people, vocal opponents of the regime . . . It wasn't as bad as Argentina or even Uruguay, but the military mind is rather consistent, and security is always the most zealous and secretive, particularly at the start of a military regime. It was because they were not totally fascist that the army is still held in some esteem here, and they were not overthrown—they finally admitted they hadn't the slightest idea how to run a large country and essentially quit. Still, there was probably much sadness here, and now it has become a lover's hideaway and a refuge for would-be stargazers. There is something very Brazilian in that."

"Well, we've got a fairly clear view from here except in the direction of the city," Solomon noted. "We still have a lot of light pollution but if there's anything to see in this area, we should see it."

"Try the radio," Tony suggested. "There is most certainly some coverage of it somewhere."

From the evidence of a slow turning of the dial, the "coverage" was mostly Brazilian music, the only obvious tie-in being a classical station playing *The Planets*. At the half hour, though, after the general world news headlines and local stories, the announcer said, "And finally, throughout the region, thousands of people are up in the hills or on rooftops or out at sea awaiting the arrival of what scientists say will be the most spectacular meteor display in centuries. If you are still up and listening to me, you should delay going to sleep another three-quarters of an hour and go outside and find a clear view to the northeast. Scientists tracking the meteor state that it should land somewhere in the remote upper Amazon basin, possibly near the Peruvian border, but it should be quite low over Rio when it arrives at approximately two-fifteen local time. Authorities state that the meteor will probably look much like a huge burning moon, but traveling very fast. Nothing is expected to strike Rio or anywhere within a thousand kilometers of the city, but as a precaution, police and fire teams are on the alert. Remain tuned to this station for updates."

"I'm not at all sure I like that last business," Anne Marie commented. "It sounds like they aren't bloody well sure of anything."

"Hundreds of meteors strike the Earth every single day," the captain reminded her. "Most are very small, and most fall into the ocean, but getting hit by one is not exactly the sort of thing sane people worry about. This one is unusual because it's so large, because it's going to strike land, and most of all because it was spotted early, so we know it's coming. But your odds of winning the Irish Sweepstakes three years in a row are far greater than the odds that even a splinter of this meteor will strike where you are. All that was, as he said, just precaution. You can never predict these things a hundred percent, and if it breaks up, pieces of it might fall in the region. Even then, it'll just make a more spectacular show for us to see—but it'll also mean even less damage to the world when the main body hits."

"Is that true?" Anne Marie asked. "Can the thing really do damage to the world? I realize I shouldn't like to be under it when it crashes, but—the world?"

"One of them killed the dinosaurs," Solomon said. "The whole climate of the planet was changed because so much dust and debris was kicked up high enough that it gave us twilight for several years. The plants died, the swamps dried up, things grew too cold, and the giant creatures couldn't eat or adapt to it."

"But that is just a theory, is it not?" Tony put in.

The captain was silent for a moment, staring off into space. "Yes, just a theory," he responded. "But the right one."

Anne Marie stared at the strange little man in the darkness and frowned. "Indeed? And how can you know that?"

Because it was a pain in the ass, even with the greatest computers in creation, to figure out just the exact spot to aim it where it would do exactly that, he thought to himself. Aloud, in a lighter tone, he said, "Well, I *told* you I was older than I looked."

They weren't sure whether to laugh or edge away from him at that, but since he had the car and the keys, a nervous laugh seemed the most prudent choice.

The captain got a blanket out of the car and spread it on the ground, then went back and got out a small hamper and a cooler. He then helped Tony get Anne Marie's wheelchair set up and her into it.

"Some light snacks, sinful sweets," the captain told them. "And some good wine, although in case you couldn't or wouldn't drink, some fruit punch as well."

The stars were out, not as many as would be visible farther out from the city but far more than could be seen in Rio itself. There was a quarter moon at this season, but it was a late moonrise and had not yet shown itself, nor would it until almost an hour after the meteor arrived. That much luck was with them.

The captain amazed them with his knowledge of the stars and constellations. There didn't seem to be a single one he couldn't name, or tell its distance from Earth and details about its composition.

"You know more than most astronomers could keep in their heads, I think," Tony noted, unable to see the stars but nonetheless fascinated by the tour. "This is from navigating a ship?"

"From navigating a *lot* of ships, and of different types," the captain responded.

"Do you think there is other life out there?" Anne Marie asked him. "Strange creatures, alien civilizations, all that sort of thing?"

"Oh, yes," he answered confidently. "A vast number. The hugeness of the cosmos is beyond anyone's comprehension. Some of them may already have spaceships and be in contact or even commerce with one another."

"You mean in this solar system?" Tony responded. "I would doubt it."

"No, no, there's nothing else in our solar system worth mentioning. I mean beyond. *Far* beyond. Thousands and millions of light-years, in this galaxy and many others."

"You are a romantic, Captain," Tony said skeptically. "What you say about other creatures and civilizations might well be true, but those same distances would prohibit contact. The speed of light alone says no."

"Well, that *is* something of a stopper," Solomon admitted, "but not as much as you'd think. Gravity bends space, light, even time itself, and it's but one of a great many forces at work. If a ship could be built to withstand those forces and make use of them, both space and time might be bent, reducing a journey of many centuries to a matter of days or weeks. They once said that heavier-than-air craft could never fly under their own power, and for many years it was believed that the sound barrier was so absolute, its vibrations would tear an airplane apart. *Nothing* is impossible—absolutely nothing. It just takes a lot of time, work, ingenuity, and guts to eventually figure a way to cheat."

Tony shook his head. "My education was as an engineer, and I know about solving such things, but I believe that practical interstellar flight is just outside the rules of God."

"Well said, sir! You sound like a medieval pope!"

"Oh, stop arguing, you two!" Anne Marie scolded. "I don't care if it's possible or not, since even if it is, none of us will live to see it, but it is fun to imagine. I wonder what sort of creatures there *are* out there."

Captain Solomon looked at the stars. "Oz, and Olympus, and Fairyland, and a hundred other lands not quite imagined here on Earth. If you like, play a game. Suppose you could wish yourself up there, become one of those other creatures—what sort of creature might you like to be?"

She laughed. "I'm not much good at imagining *creatures,* and most of the ones on the telly are pretty slimy."

"Well, there'll be slimy ones, of course. But, if you can't think of some creature out of whole cloth, pick one out of mythology or classical fantasy."

"*Umph!* It's so difficult to do! I suppose I should fall back on the obvious, as my therapists would say in the old days. Lying there, unable to move for so long, I used to dream of being a racehorse. Isn't *that* a silly thought, even if an obvious fantasy for me? Anne Marie, interplanetary racehorse!"

"Well, be a centaur, then, or is that 'centauress'?" the captain responded in a light mood. *I knew another centauress once, but I can't even remember her name . . .*

"What about you, Tony?" Anne Marie prompted. "What sort of creature would *you* be? How about an eagle? Flying about, and with remarkable eyesight as well."

"Possibly," Tony responded, sounding a bit irritated with the game but nonetheless going along for Anne Marie's sake since she was getting such a kick out of it. "But, and I am being fully honest here, if such a thing were possible, then I should like to be whatever you were." And he meant it, too. The captain could feel the love that was there and was almost consumed with envy for this unfortunate blind and crippled pair of mortals.

"How sweet, my darling," she said with a smile. "But what of you, Captain? We haven't heard your own choice."

"I'm afraid I have grave limits on that part of my imagination," he answered seriously. "I can think of myself only as Gilgamesh, or the Wandering Jew. Always the same, never changing, walking through the world but unable to fully become a part of it."

"I believe I'd like that," Tony said. "Never changing, never aging, and never beyond repair, as it were. Watching the ages come and go, empires rise and fall, and great events as they occur. Yes, I might find that quite enticing."

"No, you wouldn't," the captain came back a bit sharply. "Suppose you had to do it without Anne Marie? Without *anybody* to share it with? Watching everyone you knew or liked grow old and sick and then die, watching as many horrors as great things and being unable to do more than bear witness to them? Always alone, without even anyone to talk about it with or share experiences with on an equal basis? Is that a blessing or the worst of curses? You tell me."

"Without Anne Marie? Hmmm . . . I think I see what you mean. But I would insist on Anne Marie as well!"

"I'm not so certain of that myself," she put in. "I mean, after centuries together I'd expect even the most loving of people to get rather sick of one another."

Both men were startled by her comment, Tony because he could not conceive of such a thing and the captain for far different reasons.

Was that ultimately what it was? Did I need her so much that I failed to realize that I could be a pretty boring and predictable stick-in-the-mud that might eventually drive anybody nuts? Could it be as simple as that?

"You might grow sick of *me*?" Tony asked her, genuinely a little upset.

"Don't worry, darling, I'll give you a few thousand years or so," she answered playfully. She paused for a moment, sensing that her response had really bothered him. "Oh, come off it, Latin lover! It's just a silly game to pass the time!"

The captain turned and looked back toward the northeast. "Sorry I caused any problems. As Anne Marie said, it's just a ga— *Holy smoke!*"

Anne Marie suddenly looked up in the same direction and gasped. "Tony! *The whole sky is lighting up!* It's like the sun's about to rise!"

But it was thirteen minutes after two in the morning.

ROCKFALL: RIO

IN SPITE OF MANY predictions to the contrary, it was quite clear to astronomers that as the meteor dug into the atmosphere, it was coming apart. Not enough to keep a large mass from striking fairly close to where they had predicted but enough so that pieces, some fairly large, would shower down along the route inland. This had been feared but was not completely unexpected.

It began while still well over the Atlantic, a brilliant, shining fireball that turned darkness into eerie twilight while providing a surprisingly multicolored display in its wake for those watching openmouthed on ships at sea and from monitoring aircraft. This caused a lot of attention but little concern; the ocean was vast and swallowed whole the splinters that managed to make it all the way to the surface.

As the meteor approached the continent, however, it was lower in the sky and slowing slightly, although its speed was still so great that observers on the ground saw the fireball flash past in the space of but a few seconds.

To the captain and Anne Marie, sitting atop the hill not many kilometers from Rio, it was an eerie, awesome sight nonetheless. The meteor approached from over the horizon, illuminating the eastern sky like the coming of dawn, slowly obliterating the stars, and overwhelming even the glow of the city lights. When it suddenly appeared, much lower on the horizon than they had expected, it was a miniature sun, a massive fireball that seemed several times the size of a full moon. Even the captain had to admit that he'd never in his incredibly long life seen anything quite like it before.

It came with blinding speed almost directly over them, and at just about that moment the captain, who'd gotten to his feet without even realizing it as he gaped at the sight, suddenly reeled, cried out, and dropped to his knees.

The sensation was momentary but powerful: a sudden loss of orientation and a pervasive, cold, desolate emptiness that struck to the core of his soul, as if someone had just walked across his grave . . .

At the same moment there was a series of thunderous explosions that echoed all around them and a brief but violent wind that came out of nowhere and struck with surprising force.

"Wha—what's happening?" Tony cried. *"What's happening! Anne Marie!"*

"I'm all right!" she shouted to him, although already the wind and explosions seemed to be dying down, vanishing into pale echoes as if they had never been there. "Oh, good lord! There are streamers—sparkling things, hundreds—no, thousands of them, falling all over. Reds, yellows, greens, golds, pure white—incredible! Captain, can you—" For the first time she looked over and saw Solomon bent over double, looking agonized. *"Captain!* Are you all right?"

The captain gulped down several deep breaths. "Yes, yes! I'm all right. It was—strange. I've never felt anything like that before. Never. It's fading now. Did you feel it?"

"Only the wind."

He was getting some self-control back but was clearly still shaken. "That was just the fireball sucking up some of the air in its wake. It must have come almost directly over us. The explosions were sonic booms. It's still going *very* fast, unless it's already crashed by now." He looked out at the spectacular fireworks display still raining down all around them. "Some of those are *big*! I think I can see smoke in the direction of the city!"

There was a sudden, jarring explosion very close by, an explosion so near that the ground trembled and Anne Marie's wheelchair began to vibrate, almost tipping over. The captain again fell, this time from the tremors.

"What now? Earthquake?" Tony asked, frustrated that he could see nothing.

"I don't think so," the captain responded. "I think a big chunk came down pretty damned close to us." He picked himself up off the ground and wiped off some dirt. "Everybody okay?"

"Yes—I think so," Anne Marie responded. "Oh, my! This was quite the adventure, after all. I doubt if I will ever forget this. I'm *so* glad we came!"

The captain began looking around and immediately saw a reddish-orange glow from the direction of the road below—the road they'd used to get there.

"You two stay here and try to relax," he told them. "I'm going to walk over and see just what hit and where." He had visions of landslides that might possibly trap them atop the mountain, but he didn't want to alarm his companions until he knew just what the situation was.

He was also still somewhat shaken by that terrible paralyzing sensation he'd had as the meteor had passed overhead. Nothing, but nothing, had ever felt like that before.

It had felt like death.

Not the warm, dark cessation of life he'd imagined but cold, terribly lonely, empty, corrupt—the cold of decomposition and the grave.

He reached the point where the road started down, but he didn't have to walk far along it to discover what had hit and where. No *wonder* the earth had shaken! He couldn't imagine why it hadn't knocked them off the hilltop and toppled the car, for all the good the car was going to do now.

Below, near the point at which the dirt road met the main paved highway, was a large glowing object. There was a lot of steam and a hot, acrid smell as if the area had suddenly gone volcanic and melted rock and road. It was impossible to see much detail without going down quite a ways and it wasn't terribly clear how much of the dirt road remained intact, but he didn't dare leave his two companions to go down to check.

He started back toward them, reaching into his pocket and taking out a large cigar, which he stopped to light. He had refrained from smoking near Anne Marie, but this was the kind of situation that called for a good cigar. The hilltop was dark again, and all the debris made it a tricky walk, but he made it back to them without falling or twisting an ankle.

"We've got a real problem," he told them straight out. "Our friend that just passed over left us a present right at the base of the hill, and it's none too clear if we're going to be able to get down very easily."

"Oh, dear!" Anne Marie exclaimed. "What will we do, Captain?"

"There's a good-sized meteor chunk that came in and hit right down there. That was the earthquake we felt. It's still glowing hot—probably will be for days—and I'm not sure how much of that road is still there or whether there are any rock slides or other obstacles. The only thing we can do is try very carefully to make it down in the car. If it's impossible, then we'll have to go as far as we can, get out, and manage on our own. I'm pretty sure that if we can get down to the main road one way or another, people will be along fairly soon who might help. But the plain fact is, we have to get down there, since nobody knows we're up here and neither of you is exactly in condition to climb down the side of this hill even if we had ropes and such to do it with."

"I don't like it," Tony told him. "The whole road might be undermined, and there might well be rather narrow passages. Not only would that cause me obvious problems, but Anne Marie's chair would never make it."

"Couldn't we build a signal fire or something from all this junk?" Anne Marie asked. "I mean, there are sure to be all sorts of folks out here sooner or later, right? If it's big enough, possibly helicopters. You *did* say that this was once a helicopter landing pad, didn't you?"

Solomon nodded. "The trouble is, I think this is only one of a *lot* of fragment strikes, and it's pretty far out. I would expect people along the main road any time now, particularly others who came out here like us to get a better look, but in terms of the authorities and helicopters and the like—possibly sometime. The glow toward Rio has increased, I think, and I suspect that there are a number of fires and possibly worse."

"Check the radio," Tony suggested. "At least we'll know where we stand."

The captain nodded, went over to the minivan, and, after discovering he had to start the engine to power the radio, flicked it on.

There was mostly static.

"I think Jesus may have lost his power," the captain said a bit sarcastically. The great statue that sat on the mountain that directly overlooked Rio was the symbol of the city, but that same mountain and two others nearby were where the transmitting towers for radio, television, and other telecommunications were located. If power was out up there, it wouldn't matter what was going on below.

He slowly turned the dial, finally getting a low-powered broadcast heavy with static.

". . . out in two-thirds of the city, and there are numerous fires from sparks and cinders all over. Because we have managed to keep our power and remain on the air, we will keep broadcasting information as we know it. Civil authorities have asked that no one attempt to use the telephones and that they remain in their homes and remain calm. Fire brigades are out all over the city, and police are trying to free people trapped in buildings and cope with dozens of accidents as most of the traffic signals are out. A declaration of martial law is expected and may be in force now; we have no way of knowing from here . . ."

Solomon got out but left the radio on. "Sounds pretty bad. Martial law, fires, power outages, you name it. They didn't expect this. Not knowing anybody in particular is up here, I seriously doubt if anyone's going to be out this way for some time—maybe a day or two. Even if they knew we were here, I think we'd be a pretty damned low priority. We've got the remains of the little picnic I packed, but that's it, and there doesn't appear to be any water or other facilities up here. If you're too nervous to make the attempt down, my next inclination would be to go myself and see if I could find help—but, again, that might take a very long time, and I really wouldn't like leaving you two up here for an extended period."

"Ordinarily I would agree on getting down, but I am afraid that Anne Marie might get stuck halfway and then what do we do?" Tony asked.

"This is one of those 'there's no good solution' problems," the captain replied. "Anne Marie, you said you had medicine you had to take religiously, and you've been fairly weak as it is. How much of an extra supply of that medication did you bring?"

"Oh, my! Yes, I see what you mean," she said thoughtfully. "I'm afraid, dear, that he's right—we have no real choice in this."

Tony sighed. "I don't like it, but all right. Let us get packed up."

The captain helped, then, as they got settled in the van, he tried the radio again. One of the big stations at least had gotten back on the air, albeit with lower power than usual, and the details of what had happened in the city and beyond were soon clear.

Possibly hundreds of pieces from the meteor had come down, ranging from fingernail-size to a few as large as soccer balls. A number of homes and buildings had been hit; there was a crater in the center of the financial district about ten meters wide that had, among other things, severed the main electrical and phone cables to and from the city center; and many other fragments had been large enough and hot enough to touch off fires. A few, in poorer and rundown areas, had quickly become conflagrations. Although only two people were known to be dead and perhaps a dozen others had injuries serious enough to need hospitalization, the massive fires in the densely populated poor areas gave an unspoken but implicit promise of a much higher toll.

The swath cut by the shedding meteor was twenty to twenty-five kilometers wide, and reports of isolated rockfalls in other areas were still coming in. A large segment, larger than any that had struck the city, was seen to have fallen somewhere in the mountains beyond the city, but at the moment it wasn't known where it had fallen or if it had caused any major damage.

The main body had landed, perhaps only seconds later, in the remote upper Amazon basin, still within the country and inside of one of the new native reserve areas designed to protect the rain forest and the habitat of primitive tribes who lived there. Early reports said that there was massive damage at the main site, with the forest knocked down and ablaze, like the aftermath of an atomic bomb. The Archbishop of Rio had announced a special mass of thanks and salvation for tomorrow, noting that if the impact had come sooner, along the coast, there would have been massive loss of life.

The announcer then paused to gather more information, and the station began playing Jobim's *Quiet Night and Quiet Stars* . . .

The captain switched off the radio and drove slowly over to the road.

"Well, that big one in the mountain must have been the one that hit below," Tony noted.

The captain frowned. "Maybe. But I can't understand—if it was that big, and much smaller pieces caused so much damage, why we didn't have a minibomb effect here as well."

"That was quite a jolt when it hit," Anne Marie pointed out.

"Exactly. The jolt, yes, but something that hot, hitting with that kind of force, should have done far more if it's anywhere close, and I think it is. I'm beginning to have a very bad feeling about this."

"What do you expect? Martian invaders?" Tony joked.

"No. Nothing like that." He took a deep breath. "Well, here we go."

Solomon was surprised at how far they managed to get before fallen rocks and other debris stopped them. They were actually at the lower turnout of the last switchback before the main road and could see down the steep kilometer or more to the paved road below even though they couldn't reach it.

Anne Marie gasped at the sight on that main road. "What is it?" Tony pressed her.

"The meteor! Or at least the big piece of it! It's *huge*! It's stuck half in the road and half in the opposite hillside. It looks mostly buried in the hill and there's a lot of bubbling and hissing around the edges, but you can see a big part of it! It's *glowing*—a dull, almost golden yellow, and it looks like some huge gemstone, kind of like stained glass. Good heavens! I'd almost swear it *was* something artificial!"

The captain stared at it. *Just my imagination?* he wondered. *Or is that huge flat area facing outward the shape I'm afraid it is?*

He got out and surveyed the path, dully illuminated by the glow of the strange object. Surveying the scene, he went back to them and said, "I think I can angle the car so it'll give us light from the headlights the first part of the way down, after which, if that thing keeps glowing, we won't need any more light. It might be a tight fit, but I think we can get the wheelchair down, though we might have to lift it over at one or two places. Are you willing?"

"I think better down than back up at this point," Anne Marie replied.

It was not an easy task, but it was manageable. At one point dirt and rock had covered much of the road, making it difficult to get the wheelchair around without going off the side, but the captain managed, then, bracing her on the other side, got Tony around as well. Several times the blind man stumbled, but he was game all the way, and in about thirty minutes they made it down to the road.

The meteor had taken out much of the paved area, and between its own extrusion and the landslides the impact had caused, it would clearly be some time before any vehicle could get past. Still, there was more than enough room for them to manage, if no more slides occurred, and once on the other side, they would at least be well positioned when the first cars driven by the curious or investigators made it to the scene.

"I'm surprised there aren't a lot of people on both sides already here," Anne Marie said. "I know we were hardly the only ones to come up this route."

"We don't know how bad some of the slides are elsewhere, and perhaps other pieces fell as well, doing damage," Tony pointed out. "It might well be a while, but at least I believe we have more of a chance down here than up there. What do you think, Captain? What should we do now?"

Solomon was staring at the meteor. "Huh? Oh, sorry, I wasn't paying attention." He paused a moment, then said, "You two stay right here. I've got to get something off my mind one way or the other. I won't be but a moment."

With that, he walked down toward the still-glowing object. As he approached, the thing seemed to change somehow; the glassy surface took on a duller sheen, and then other forms seemed to appear just underneath.

Anne Marie gasped. "It looks like—something *alive*!" she said. "Like a network of arteries and veins or fluids going through pulsing tubes. I've seen this sort of thing under microscopes!"

"Your imagination is getting the best of you," her husband responded. "You've been through a lot tonight."

"No, no! I'm serious! I swear it! And it seems to be getting more and more detailed as the captain goes nearer to it. Captain!" she called out worriedly. "Don't go any closer! Watch out!"

The captain gestured confidently with his right hand. He walked around to the left, where the shoulder of the road still allowed passage, and as he did, a single gemlike "face" in the center seemed to darken on its own, becoming in a moment jet black, while the rest of the object remained unchanged.

"Son of a bitch! I *knew* it!" the captain grumbled. "A damned *hexagon*!"

He stood there staring at it and said, louder, "You coulda been a little more *subtle,* damn it!"

The object didn't respond. He knew it wouldn't. Although so advanced that it would be incomprehensible to Earth science, it was just a machine.

"I don't want to go through it all again!" he told it, knowing he was talking only to himself. "I didn't even want to do it the *last* time, and you forced me. What do you want me to do? Wipe out everything again? Just when they've gotten to the start of the fun part? Before I've even completely forgotten who and what I am? Screw up thousands of civilizations because one damned thing went refreshingly wrong in history? Well, I won't do it! Get *her* to do it! *She* knows how! I encoded her and linked her to the Well!"

He stopped for a moment, trying to calm down. Maybe it *had* gone for her as well. It would be ironic if she, too, were in Brazil, although what she'd be doing in the Amazon basin was beyond him. Still, he knew the machine wouldn't let him stay here while somebody else did the reset. He hadn't taken himself out of the core matrix. If somehow it allowed him to get around the embedded fragment without taking him in, swallowing him up, it wouldn't matter. It would send more of these, and more, until he would feel under constant bombardment. Either that or it would figure some other way. When one had the power to manipulate probability, one could be staved off for a while, but eventually one would get one's way. Besides, suppose he walked away and this gate stayed open? An invasion of people at this stage would not exactly be in anybody's best interest.

He sighed. Perhaps this time he could minimize the damage. Perhaps this time he could opt himself out. Still, it was pretty clear that he had no choice at this point, not until he was there, inside, at the controls. There simply weren't any options left open to him.

He had to go to the Well one more time.

But he also had certain other, more immediate responsibilities. He turned and walked back to the waiting couple.

"Don't ask me questions," he said to them, "but I know what this is. You remember that game we played up top? What would you like to become if you could?"

"Yes," Anne Marie responded nervously, suddenly not certain of the captain's sanity.

"Tony?"

"Yes, but what's the point of this?"

"That thing's a door. Now, you've *got* to trust me on this, and no, I'm not losing my mind. I once spent a lot of time and effort trying to avoid going through such a door before and failed. I'm not going to make *that* mistake again. The result is, I'm going to go through it. When I do, I think it will close behind me. If the two of you go with me, I can promise you that Anne Marie will walk again and that you, Tony, will see again. It's no heaven where that door leads. Remember, even Oz had wicked witches and the land of Jason was filled with dangerous people and more dangerous creatures. But it's not a bad place. It will heal you."

"You're raving mad," Tony responded, shaking his head.

"Look, I'm offering you a single chance. If there's no door there, then we go on by and we wait for help. If there *is* a door, you walk through it with me. Understand?"

"This is ridiculous!" Tony fumed. "I won't stand for any more of this! We'll wait right here!"

But Anne Marie, while more in tune with Tony's viewpoint than the captain's strange comments, nonetheless felt that something within the man was not lunacy but sincerity. "Just who *are* you that someone would send such a thing for you?" she asked him.

"I'm not going to tell you that, for your own protection and mine," he replied. "And if you decide to come with me, not a word that I knew anything about it to begin with. Not one word. We were just three people who went to see a meteor and found this curiosity and walked through. Understand?"

"I'm not going to listen to any more of this rot," Tony fumed.

The captain stared at him. "I understand how you feel and what it sounds like. But when I leave, you'll be stuck here alone, the two of you. I'm not certain *when* help will arrive. And the best way to reach the most likely source of help is around that thing over there. The door is that blackness that opened when I approached. You saw it, didn't you, Anne Marie? I can see that you did. It'll open again. What do you have to lose?"

She almost believed him. She *wanted* to believe him. "If—just granting your point for argument's sake—if what you say is true, would Tony and I still be together?"

He shrugged. "I can't promise that. I can only promise that he will see and you will walk and be strong again." He looked at Tony. "I remember our conversation. Is it worth it to take a chance, considering the alternative? We don't have much time. Sooner or later there will be hundreds, maybe thousands of people up here. Sightseers, rescuers, newspeople, scientists, road crews—you name it. I can't have them accidentally going through. I'm going now. You can go with me and what I have said will come to pass, or you can go on past and wait and hope that rescue comes quickly for Anne Marie's sake and enjoy your few weeks or months or whatever."

It was Tony's turn to sigh. "Captain, I will allow you to lead us past that thing. Beyond that I will not go."

"We love each other, Captain," Anne Marie said simply. "I'm not at all certain I would wish to live without Tony, healthy or not."

The captain gave them a humorless smile. "However, that option's not open to you, is it, Tony?"

"Haven't you understood, Captain?" the Brazilian asked him. "That is not the option you believe. We shall not wait for the inevitable, or survive each other."

The comment stunned Solomon. "Now there are two ways I envy you," he told him. "The kind of love you show is rare, and the ability to end your lives by your own decision is something I have always wished to be able to do."

"What? Do you believe you are a vampire or some such, too?" Tony asked derisively.

"No. But I told you all along that I am a lot older than I look. The same thing that sent *that* and knew just where and when to drop it insulates and protects me." *And controls me,* he thought to himself. *Walk this way in the early morning. Meet these two. Go up into the hills to a remote area . . .*

He sighed. "Well," the captain added, "we might as well get on with it. You have a great choice at this moment that I wish I had but do not. You can choose life or death for the both of you. Anne Marie in particular hasn't had that choice before, so it was an easy decision. Now your choice has a complication. Do you both *want* to die? Or are you merely reconciled to it? I'm giving you another choice." He paused a moment. "Let's go and get this over with."

He walked slowly forward, and Tony began pushing the wheelchair as Anne Marie gave short instructions that kept them going in the right direction. Still, beneath the automatic commands she was giving, she was also thinking, wondering if this strange little man was telling the truth and, in the impossible event that perhaps he was, whether the price was worth it.

She saw the activity just beneath the surface of the fragment speed up as they approached, and as they moved to the right, she saw the big facet, more than two meters high even though slightly buried in the ground at its bottom edge, open to an impossible, impenetrable darkness.

The captain stopped dead center of the opening. "Well, here is where we possibly part company," he told them. "I have enjoyed meeting you, and I am happy that at least some of the good that is within this race of humankind shines so brightly in you. It knows you're here. It won't close until you go on past. In any event, spending this evening with you has made it somehow easier for me." And with that, he walked straight into the blackness and vanished.

Anne Marie's heart leapt at the sight. The captain hadn't gone into the darkness or been enveloped by it, he had simply touched it and vanished.

"Captain?" Tony asked, frowning.

"He's gone, dear, just like he said," Anne Marie told him. "He went into it, and that was that. Strange. I think we've just had a close encounter, as they call it."

"Gone? What do you mean, 'gone'? Is there an opening in the thing? Did he crawl inside? What?"

"No, dear. He just walked into it and vanished. *Poof!* One moment he was there, the next he wasn't."

"An illusion of some kind. Or he was burned up or this thing has some sort of radiation. What he said just *can't* be true! It's not *possible!*"

"Perhaps. But it looked awfully quick and painless, you know, and there's no trace of him. I am feeling very, very exhausted, my darling, and I am in a great deal of pain. I am not at all certain I can stand it at this altitude until someone comes."

He swallowed hard, his emotions in turmoil. He wasn't *ready* for this! Not yet! It wasn't anything like what they'd planned! "What do you want me to do?" he asked in anguish. "Go into that thing? Now?"

"You don't have to if you don't want to. You know that."

"I go where you go!" he snapped. "But—"

"But what? It's quick, painless, no bodies, no traces, no one to grieve over and no mess left for others to deal with. They'll find the car, the porter will remember us, and we'll be listed as victims of the meteor. I *know* it's not what we wanted, but it is here, and there will not be a better time. I *know* I shall not survive to get even to hospital, and I do not want to die in hospital or be kept alive on machines. Do it for me. You may make your own decision afterward."

He neither moved nor spoke to her. The blackness on the face of the object remained unchanged.

"Come! Why do you fear the moment when it's at hand? We've discussed this over and over. Do it for me."

He was almost in tears, but he knew he had to give her the truth of his deepest fears.

"I—I am afraid that what the captain said might be true."

"Then we will be healed, isn't that right?"

"And separated in some strange, unknown place!"

"If I am healed, I will find you. Come. My pain grows with each moment, and no matter what he said, this thing could close at any moment. Go right and just walk ahead."

She suddenly pushed the joystick. The wheelchair lunged forward and lurched to the right, and both chair and occupant vanished into the darkness, leaving only silence.

"Anne Marie? *Anne Marie!*" His fear of losing her overcame all other thoughts. He turned right and walked straight ahead.

And without warning, he felt a sensation of falling.

Back on the paved mountain road above Rio, the dark hexagon winked out and the meteor began to undergo a dramatic transformation. The other facets, which had pulsed with an analog of a living circulatory system, began to fade; circulation failed, patches of decay began to appear, finally spreading over the surface of the object.

Its purpose accomplished, the Watchman and all others evidencing a desire to do so having passed through, the device had no other reason to exist, and very quickly it died.

By the time the first of the curious and investigators reached it, shortly after dawn, it resembled a huge, irregular lump of granite or gneiss laced with enormous veins of obsidian.

ROCKFALL: UPPER AMAZON

THERESA PEREZ WAS NOT amused. "What in hell are *you* doing here?" she asked Juan Campos acidly. "There is no room on this plane for you two. We have to work."

Campos grinned evilly at her. "So? We give you our hospitality and you would then deny me seeing this great sight? Even my father thought that we were owed this."

"What's the problem?" Maklovitch called, squeezing into the plane. He saw Campos and the bodyguard. "This wasn't part of the agreement," he noted with irritation. "We're on a tight schedule here and even tighter quarters."

"The agreement has been changed," Campos responded. "We are staying right here. If you choose not to take off, then sit. My father believes one of the family should be aboard."

Maklovitch thought fast. Right now the deadline outweighed all else, and in this plane Campos was as much at their mercy as they were at his. "All right—you come. *He* goes, and now!" the newsman added, pointing to the bodyguard.

"Ramón goes where I go."

The newsman thought a moment, then decided to call the bluff. "Very well. Terry, get on the horn and tell them that Don Campos has insisted on placing two armed men aboard. Because this exceeds our weight and room limits, we cannot go. Tell them the Campos file is to air rather than be sent to Don Campos. Understood?"

The gangster jumped. "Now, wait one minute. *What* file? You—bitch! You radio *nothing* without my permission!"

"Too late," she told him with a smile. "We're already live to the studio.

They're hearing every single word we say. Are you ordering me to switch us out, knowing that it means that here, on live audio, you are forcibly kidnapping us?"

This was getting a little too complicated too quickly for Juan Campos. *"What file?"*

"Your father knows," the newsman responded. "Why do you think we were offered his hospitality? I thought you told us that you really ran things around here." He paused a moment. "Now, since we're going nowhere, shall we all go see your father and explain the situation?"

Campos suddenly didn't know what to do. His first impulse was to take them all out and shoot them, but he was in fact acting on his own and he was not at all certain how his father would react when word of that came down. Nobody had said anything about a deal, but it explained much.

"All right. He goes, I stay."

"And you give him your pistol and stay in that seat as long as we're in the air," the newsman said firmly. He looked at his watch. "Better make up your mind right now or it won't make any difference. That meteor won't wait."

Campos threw up his hands in disgust, then handed a pistol over to the bodyguard and told him to get off and wait. The bodyguard, hesitant and not without some protest, complied.

None of them were fools enough to believe that Campos didn't still have various weapons on him, but at least it was one less. Now, with the bodyguard out, Lori climbed on, looking confused, and they took their seats.

The technicians had been working steadily since they'd arrived. Gus now had a console bolted in the center rear of the plane through which he could control several exterior cameras and see what each showed on small black-and-white monitors. The pictures were being recorded in a compartment beneath the cabin and also being sent by a computer-controlled *ku*-band satellite uplink mounted atop the aircraft that would relay them back to the U.S. studio if, of course, conditions were right and the aircraft was level. A similar microwave system was mounted on the plane's underside and might work for pickups in Manaus or at the makeshift hacienda uplink site. Provided that either system worked, directors far away in the States would pick the feed and also give Gus general direction.

"Probably none of it will work," Gus grumped, "which is why we're also taping, but it's worth a try."

Audio wasn't a problem, and Terry had on a headset that connected her by radio with the studio. Both Maklovitch and Sutton also had similar headsets, but those were on a different frequency and would be used mostly for contact and commentary to the live anchor desk.

They roared off into the night, climbing through a low cloud layer that bumped them around a bit and caused horrible noise on the audio. Then they broke free and had the clear sky above and all around them, with a tremendous view of the stars.

"I've got us on course and ready," the pilot reported. "We should be in position with, no thanks to the delays, about ten minutes to spare. For a region with cleared airspace, though, there's a fair amount of traffic on the radio. Not just the two science planes and the Brazilian Air Force tracker, but it seems there's a number of small civil aircraft up in violation of the clear airspace order. Two air force jets are trying to track them and force them down, but there's a *lot* of damned fools up."

"Yeah, and probably all three U.S. networks and a dozen others," Terry commented. "Wonder what would happen if they shot down an anchor or two."

It was very dark but very busy in the plane's cabin as everything was checked out one last time, and they even did a last-minute on-air audio report to the news desk. Everybody tried to forget about Campos, who at least was just sitting there uncharacteristically behaving himself. Still, the time dragged impossibly.

Lori felt keyed up but also suddenly very tired, almost drained. It was the waiting, she decided. She wanted things to start. They *all* wanted things to start.

"Contact! Visual contact by Science One!" the pilot reported excitedly. Science One was the combined Brazilian-Smithsonian research plane about 350 miles out in the Atlantic. "If what they're reporting is true," the pilot added, "then we're in for a dizzyingly fast lalapalooza! Buckle in tight! She's coming down dirty!"

"What does he mean by 'dirty'?" Juan Campos asked, breaking his long silence.

"Shedding," Lori told him. "Coming apart. Raining big, hot rocks."

The plane turned slowly and then reduced speed. Maklovitch was already on the air, and Lori knew now that she, too, was live.

"We should be seeing it any second now," the newsman said with a professional calmness his tense face belied. "It's coming right over Rio."

"There! Got it!" Gus cried. *"Oh, my God! What a whopper!"*

Things changed in an instant; the horizon suddenly turned from night into a creeping twilight, then, suddenly, it was there, coming straight for them for all they could tell.

"Madre dios!" Juan Campos breathed, and crossed himself.

Lori watched with a mixture of awe and fascination as the huge object sped toward them and then was suddenly past. It looked like some enormous flaming lump of charcoal, the size of a dozen full moons, blazing a yellow and white-hot tail.

"Wahoo!" Gus roared from his console, apparently very pleased with the pictures. It was only later that Lori realized that the man was so intent on his screens that he never actually saw the meteor.

The plane banked sharply and took a course perpendicular to the meteor's path so they could see it go down. The pilot's reactions were good, although suddenly the entire aircraft was rocked as if shaken by a giant hand, and unsecured items went flying. There was a roller coaster-like sensation of falling for what seemed an eternity, and then the pilot boosted power and pulled out of it.

"Did you get it? Did you get it?" Terry called repeatedly.

Now the plane headed back west, following a huge but ragged contrail left by the meteor. It took better than five minutes to reach the point where it dipped into the clouds, a distance the big rock had covered in seconds. There was no question, though, as to where to look. A giant mushroom-shaped plume was still rising from out of the clouds, and both plume and clouds seemed to be on fire.

They tensed again as the aircraft dipped below the clouds, and there were general gasps at the scene below. It looked like the whole forest was on fire, and the impact site, many miles away, resembled nothing less than an active volcanic caldera.

"It looks like an atom bomb," Lori commented, her throat dry and constricted. "Look at the blast area down there. The firestorm had to be incredibly hot to reach that distance in that wet, green growth."

Tremendous thunder and lightning were all around as well, making the scene look and sound like the end of the world.

"What is all that? Blast effect?" the anchor prompted her.

"No. It's very wet here, and the heat and blast cloud have created massive convection currents. The heat is rising, taking the humidity in the air with it, and it's condensing. Those are thunderstorms created by the impact. There's no telling how long it will rain on this area, but at least it will help extinguish the fires and keep the smoke from rising too high."

"I see a huge crater, but there's something glowing at the bottom," Maklovitch noted. "Is that the meteor itself?"

"Possibly, but unlikely," she answered. "It's probable that the whole thing disintegrated on impact, leaving only small fragments. More likely that is partly molten rock and mostly existing bedrock uncovered for the first time in a million years."

"I estimate that we are probably at least ten miles from the crater, yet it's clearly visible. It must be enormous. A mile, maybe two miles across. The fire and blast damage extend, oh, at least twenty or thirty miles all around, possibly more." The newsman suddenly remembered Juan Campos. "Señor Campos, does anyone live down there to your knowledge?"

Campos stared at the scene out of hell. "Not *now*," he responded in almost a whisper.

"No, no. I mean *before* it hit. I know there wasn't much in the way of evacuation because of the sparse population and the primitiveness of the people."

"Depends," the gunman managed. "Where are we now?"

Maklovitch saw what he meant. All of this region looked pretty much alike, even more so in the dark, and nothing much was left down there that might provide a landmark.

"I've got the position from Science Three," the pilot called back. "Call it, oh, a hundred, maybe a hundred and twenty kilometers south-south-east from the Campos airstrip."

The Peruvian nodded. "Then there *were* some Indians down there. Now?"

"Can we get in closer?" Gus asked the pilot. "I'd like to go straight over that crater if I could."

"I could try, but with these storms and downdrafts all over the place there's no predicting anything. You can feel her shaking now," the pilot replied. "I've been circling out some fifteen miles, and you feel what it's like. If I did it, it would have to be at a fairly fast speed."

"Well, the clouds and smoke are obscuring everything," the camera-man complained. "Either we get in there or we wrap, people. I'm for giving it a try."

Terry nodded, giving a quick satisfied glance at the terrified face of Juan Campos strapped in the back. *Welcome to the news business,* she thought acidly. "One pass, as low and slow as you dare," she told the pilot. "That's it. Gus will have to make do with what he can get."

Lori wasn't much more thrilled than Campos, as much as she wanted to see the sight closer up. With the tremendous turbulence, she found herself thinking less of the view than of headlines in the paper. LOCAL SCIENTIST AND NEWS CREW DIE COVERING ASTEROID.

"Hang on, everybody!" the pilot called, and circled first out, then back in toward the glow, climbing and increasing speed. The vapor, rising now mostly from the rainfall striking the still extremely hot object, obscured clear view, and the ride was the scariest any of them could remember. Then the turbulence subsided, and the fear and tension drained from all of them like water through a sieve, leaving them all more or less limp—except Gus, who was muttering that he hadn't really gotten a decent pass.

"One's enough, I think," Terry told him. "It's only going to get smokier for a while down there." She paused for a moment as someone far away asked her a question. "Gus? Can you replay that last pass, the straight-down shot, through a monitor here? They got it back at the studio, but they say there's something weird about it."

"Huh? Yeah, I guess, if you're finished shooting."

"We are for now. We're heading back to the ranch to uplink the tapes as backup. They want us, and particularly Doctor Sutton, to look at it and see if she can explain it. You, too, Gus, since it might be a trick of the light or something with the camera."

"Yeah, okay. Hold on. That's . . . lemmesee . . . three. Rewind. All right. Wait. There. Okay, it may have to run a little, but I think it's in the neighborhood. I'll switch it to the overhead monitor."

They all looked, and for a moment there was a jiggly freeze-frame of the crater and smoke cloud. Then they saw the picture flip, angle dizzyingly from one side to the other as the plane got into position, then zoom straight in. The picture was bouncy but clear enough. They saw the smoke flash past and, for a very brief moment, were looking straight down through billowing white smoke and rain.

"There! Did you all see it?" Terry asked them. "It looks like something dark, something black, straight down as we went over, with bright stuff all around it."

"Sorry, it was so fast," Lori responded apologetically.

The picture stopped, and Gus rewound the tape.

"Hold it!" Terry shouted. "No, up a little more. Frame advance. *There!* Hold it!"

The picture was still jumpy and distorted, but they could now all see just what the control room back in the States had noticed. Through the smoke, the red and yellow glow of the crater was visible, if not completely clear. Right in the center of the glowing mass was a black shape, distorted and indistinct but still some sort of regular form.

"I couldn't guess," Lori told them. "I'd need a much clearer photo than that to really say much of anything about it. It could be a different mineral, much harder than the surrounding rock, that has a higher melting point and maybe is already cooled down, or a fissure in whatever's left of the meteor, or a trick of the light."

"I don't know meteors, but *pictures* I know," Gus said firmly. "That's no trick of the light. Something's down there."

Maklovitch looked back at Campos. "Any way in there? To land, I mean."

"This plane? No, señor. Nothing, even if it would have survived that blast. And there are no roads in this region of any sort. On foot—days under the best of conditions."

"You have a helicopter at the ranch," the pilot called back. "I saw it on the field back there. What about that?"

Campos shook his head. "No, no, no. That is our private helicopter. Besides, if you could not even safely fly this plane through that smoke and the storms, flying a helicopter in there close would be suicide!"

"I flew choppers in hairier conditions than that in the Marine Corps," the pilot replied. "Thunderstorms, sandstorms, and under fire. It wouldn't be a big deal, I don't think, particularly if we're allowing another hour or two for things to calm down."

"No, no, *no!*" Juan Campos shouted. "It is out of the question!"

"It may be," Terry said, "but even as we speak, my boss is on the phone to your father, and it looks like we might just have a deal." She paused. "Of course, *you* don't have to come if you don't want to."

Even Lori thought the idea bordered on madness. "It's pretty dangerous," she noted, "and you'll get better pictures, as well as better conditions, after daylight."

"That's true," Terry agreed, "but we don't know how long after daylight the first choppers will be arriving from elsewhere, full of geologists and astronomers and military people and bureaucrats—"

"Not to mention NBC, ABC, CBS, CBC, the BBC, and maybe Fox, God help us," Maklovitch put in. "In this business being first is everything. That's why folks watch us and advertisers pay top dollar—we can do things like this the others can't. Nobody remembers the *second* newsman into Kuwait City."

"Forrest Sawyer, ABC," Terry responded instantly. "We were third!"

"Okay, nobody outside the business remembers. But we remember most that we were third. It's the name of the game. Not that we're trying to commit suicide. If Bob there wasn't sure he could get us in and out in one piece, I don't think we'd risk it ourselves. If you're really against it, you can stay behind, but if we can put this together, you'd be invaluable on the scene."

Lori thought a moment about remaining behind with all those ruthless men on the drug lord's ranch and wondered which was more dangerous. "I'll go," she told him, wondering if she was in fact being stupid.

"Good girl! Oops! Sorry, Doc. No offense," the newsman added.

"That's all right." *Mother always said I should be a good girl. I just want to know if I'm being a dumb broad by doing this.*

"You seem certain my father will say yes," Juan Campos noted.

"We plan for a yes. If it's no, we haven't lost anything," the newsman told him.

"Even if he agrees, the helicopter carries only six and not much cargo," the gunman pointed out. "With you, your pilot, your cameraman, the two señoritas, and a sound man, it will be full."

"He's got a point there," the pilot, Bob, agreed. "We're not gonna be able to truck in a suitcase unit or much of anything except a hand-held."

The newsman thought a moment. "All right, then, we'll try two trips. Terry, you can handle Gus's sound, right?"

"In a pinch, sure."

"All right. A suitcase, Terry, Gus, me, and the doc."

"What's a 'suitcase unit'?" Lori asked, puzzled.

"A portable uplink," Gus replied. "It's actually a kit in the form of three large suitcases. You can put it together with battery power and have it sending pictures and sound to a comsat in under an hour. The foreign correspondent's constant companion since it was invented."

They had the agreement by the time they landed, but, looking over the helicopter, they discovered that it wasn't as large as they'd hoped. When the suitcase unit was added, it left room for five, but only by a whisker.

Juan Campos wasted no time at all calling in from a dedicated phone at the aircraft parking area. When he returned, he did not look all that happy.

"My father, he says that I must go with the helicopter," he told them. "This time it is not my idea!"

"He's right," Maklovitch told them. "I just spoke to him myself on the same line. Mr. Campos is a little nervous about somebody taking up the chopper without one of his men along to see that we go only where we're supposed to go and shoot just what we're here to shoot, particularly since we'll probably be gone well into daylight and they *do* expect others from the Brazilian side there not long after that. There was no talking him out of it; either Campos here goes or it's no deal."

It didn't need to be spelled out. After daylight in particular, coming in on this side of the border would reveal some sights camouflaged from routine aerial or satellite surveillance. If they saw them, it wasn't any big deal, since they couldn't be sure of their exact location. But no pictures. No more blackmail possibilities or nice photos for experts and their computers to mull over.

"With the suitcases, that leaves only five seats, including the pilot," Terry noted, not at all pleased by this turn of events. Flying into a disaster area fraught with sudden dangers and possible horrors didn't faze her, it seemed, but the idea of being stuck out in the middle of nowhere with Juan Campos sure did. "Who stays?"

"Well, I want you and Gus out there setting up and getting what you can," Maklovitch told her. "They want me to do some more standups here and an initial wrap piece, so it looks like I come out with the second flight. They're not at all sure if we can uplink with the rain, so you'll need the extra setup time. I'll bring a sound man and Brazil network people with me on the second ride. We'll be in contact by radio." He edged closer to her and added in a low whisper, "Besides, he's got to come back with Bob to ensure he flies right."

Terry nodded. "Okay, then. Doc, you want to come with us now or wait for the second run? It's probably going to be pretty wet and rough out there, but if you want to come along, feel free. At least you'll be the first person with any scientific training at all to see the thing."

Lori didn't like it, but she knew she had to go. "I'm coming. Nobody in the history of known science has been able to get this close to an impact of this magnitude so soon. What about rain gear?"

"Señorita Doctor," Juan Campos said, "you could wear anything you wished and it would not help when the rain falls. Even with little wind, the rain is so strong and so powerful, it cannot be described but must be experienced. Best to seek shelter when it starts, dress light except for the mud boots, and have one or more dry changes of clothes packed away."

"Well, we don't have any rain slickers, anyway," Gus noted. "Got some wide hats that'll help and a couple of umbrellas, for all the good they'll do, but that's it."

"We'll manage," Lori said, not at all certain that it was true. "I've been drenched before."

Once up in the air, they didn't need a map to find where to go even in the darkness of the jungle. There were still fires burning all around, and the eerie yellow glow from the crater seemed almost like some great aircraft beacon.

"What's causing that pulsing?" Terry asked the scientist. "I mean, I don't know much about this, but that's not normal, is it?"

"Nobody quite knows what's 'normal' in a situation like this, but I can't explain it and wouldn't have expected it. It could be rapid heating and cooling, but it seems almost too regular for that. That's one of the things we might be able to find out if we can get close enough."

"Looks pretty promising," Bob told them. "There's still lightning and thunderstorms all around, but the area immediately around the crater looks like just smoke from the thing itself."

"The white smoke coming from it now is probably mostly steam," Lori told them. "Groundwater or runoff from the storm is going down the crater, hitting that very hot bottom, and instantly coming back up."

"Kind of like a geyser," Gus said, nodding.

"Something like that. Or a fumarole. That's a relative of the geyser that erupts constantly, spouting steam with a roar. It may be days, weeks, even longer before the crater is cool enough to allow people to descend, although the scientific teams probably have moon suits and could do it in a matter of a day or so. They go into still-active volcanic calderas in them."

"Too bad we don't have any of those suits in the budget," Gus commented. "I'd like to get a down-the-throat shot."

They were quite close now, close enough to see the strange yellow-gold shape at the bottom, even though that bottom was a quarter of a mile deep and still shrouded in steam.

"Funny," Terry said, looking at the unearthly scene. "I don't see that dark spot now. Maybe you were wrong, Gus. Maybe it was just a trick of the camera."

"Not like that," Gus maintained. "There's nothin' to cause that kind of thing." He frowned. "I tell you, Terry, if that thing opens up and some Martian machine pops out, I'm runnin'!"

"I'm more curious as to why the crater isn't deeper," Lori commented. "It's amazingly shallow for something that large coming in at that kind of speed."

"Looks plenty big enough to me," Gus replied.

"Sure, but the velocity at impact had to be close to Mach 3, maybe more. You crash anything going at close to three thousand kilometers per hour and you're going to get one *whale* of a deep hole. With an object twenty, maybe thirty meters across or more—it was very hard to tell—the crater should be many times deeper than it is. There are a lot of unexpected phenomena here. Enough, I'm afraid, to shake up several disciplines. They'll be *years* figuring this thing out! And that firestorm—it shouldn't have happened. An asteroid's just a huge piece of rock, and there's nothing in the jungle to ignite or explode that way. There must have been some sort of gas or explosive material that went up on impact. This is a *very* strange thing, indeed, we have here."

"Like that place in Siberia you were talking about?" Terry asked.

"As mysterious as that, only very different in the phenomena. At least this time we're on the scene." She sighed. "I wish I had some instruments here. At least I could take initial measurements. It might be nice to know if this area's now radioactive, for example."

"Radioactive!" Gus exclaimed nervously. "You mean we might be going into something like *that*?"

"It's possible. We don't really know *what's* orbiting out there in space." *Another cheery thought, that comes too late,* she mused to herself.

Terry looked down at what was rapidly resembling a moonscape. "Think any natives are down there? I heard all sorts of stories about some of these tribes."

"Impossible!" Juan Campos responded. "You see it. What could have lived through that impact, not to mention the firestorm?"

"I wouldn't be too sure of that," Bob noted. "I've seen bombardments so thick you couldn't believe a gnat could live through it, but when they went in afterward an amazing number of people were still alive and in fighting shape afterward. You never know. Still, I'd think that any of the primitives alive in these parts are still running. To them, this had to feel like the end of the world. It's possible to live through a bombardment, but those who have say it's the most terrifying thing imaginable, and they *knew* what was going on. Imagine how afraid these savages must be with no idea of what was going on."

"Yeah, well, I've seen that sort of thing, too," Gus admitted. "But I ain't so sure about the reaction. I wish we'd brought along a couple of those guns."

"You would never be able to use them, señor," Campos said matter-of-factly. "The Indians would not be seen until they wished to be seen. The darts in their blowguns are tipped with poisons and sharp enough to go through clothing, and they are accurate. These people also know what guns do and will guard against them. There *may* be a tribe or two that still are ignorant of the outside world, but I doubt it. They just do not like our world and ways, rejecting them in favor of the jungle and their own ancient life-style. But I think our pilot friend is right. This would have frightened them and awed them far too much for them to become curious. In a few days, or weeks, they might investigate, but not right off."

The pilot surveyed the area. He didn't need the helicopter spotlights to see the general area, not with the glow from the crater and the illumination of the newly risen moon, but the searchlight gave detail to the immediate ground surface. "I can't tell how hot it is, particularly with all the charred vegetation, but there's a clear spot over there about a kilometer from the crater that looks like good, solid rock. It's not raining now; you might just get lucky if it's cool enough."

"I don't see why it wouldn't be," Lori responded. "The immediate area was burned quickly in the firestorm."

The pilot set the helicopter down gently. Terry cautiously opened the door, looked down, grabbed a large flashlight, and then stepped out onto the surface. Fine dust and ash blew around from the backwash of the rotor blades, but she reached down and felt the soil and nodded. "Slightly warm, but no big deal," she shouted back into the cabin.

They all got out now except the pilot and Campos, who handed down the three large silver suitcases containing the portable dish unit to Gus. The three quickly moved away so that the helicopter could lift off. They all had their canteens, first-aid kits, and sufficient rations for the short time they would be there.

They watched the chopper rise, hover a moment as if reluctant to leave, then head out to the west toward the Campos compound. It was quickly swallowed up in the clouds and night. The blowing ash settled, and when they moved back in to retrieve the equipment, they were startled to see a form standing there.

"I decided to remain with you," said Juan Campos. "Even under these conditions, this is a dangerous place for two señoritas and one unarmed man."

All three of them had an uneasy feeling about the man, but there wasn't much they could do. *Forty minutes,* Terry thought frantically. *Maybe less, each way, with maybe twenty on the ground. Not even two hours. He has to know that.* But the animal lurking under that civilized veneer of his wasn't buried very deep, and it might not think that far ahead.

"I thought you had to guide the helicopter back and forth," Terry said aloud to him.

"Oh, he does not have any equipment in the helicopter. It is ours, after all. He will have no trouble finding his way back, either—he is a good pilot—and there is little for him to see until dawn. It is safe enough for now."

She sighed. "Well, then, help us lug this stuff over to a reasonably flat, stable area and help us set it up."

There was the sound of not so distant thunder. "Is all that water-proof?" Lori asked. "I think it might well get rained on, and us, too."

"Oh, it's pretty well sealed," Gus assured her. "Just keep the control box lid down tight and latched in a direct downpour. The big problem is stabilizing the dish, particularly in a heavy wind, along with the fact that *ku*-band signals are real bad in rain and heavy weather."

"We better think of some shelter for ourselves, too, just in case," Lori said. "This place looks pretty blasted, but over there the trees seem scorched but still standing."

"You can take the small flashlight and have a look-see," Gus told her, "but I wouldn't go too far 'round here. There's all sorts of mean, nasty critters live in these places, and it's pretty damn sure not all of 'em got blown to hell or had the sense to run."

"Thanks a lot," she came back sarcastically. What she *really* wanted to do was have a look at that crater, but until they were set up, there wasn't much she could do about that. She could see it, though, so tantalizingly close, with its eerie yellow glow and its strange, regular pulsing. It might be irresistible after a while.

From the jet, the whole region had looked more like the landing zone, but here, on the ground, it was much different. A surprising amount of the jungle was intact, although it showed the effects of blast and fire. Huge areas had been uprooted almost instantly, the giant trees lying there, all pointing away from the crater. Still, even here, the roots of some were so deep, and the underbrush was so thick below them, that large stands survived, and it appeared that the blast had affected barely another kilometer or two of the jungle beyond their camp. It indicated that the blast had been far less powerful than she'd originally thought and that the firestorm had occurred not on impact but *ahead* of it, not destroying the jungle but burning away the top instead.

She suddenly thought she saw something moving in the darkness and swung the flashlight toward it. The beam fell on an enormous, hairy multicolored spider standing atop one of the blasted trees. For a moment she couldn't tell if it was dead or alive, but then, suddenly, it *jumped* out of the beam and to her right.

She decided that she'd had enough exploring for the night and hurried back to the others.

"Find anything?" Gus asked as he finished the assembly of the main dish with a socket wrench.

"Jumping spiders," she told him nervously.

"Bird spider," Campos elaborated, helping Gus mount the dish into the suitcase console. "Very common here. They will attack if threatened but will try to run away if they can. So something *did* live through all this, then?"

Gus was a little more worried. "Sounds like we was talkin' sense up there. I bet there's more life still around here than anybody'd thought."

"Perhaps you are right, señor," Campos agreed. "In which case it will be a very good idea to stay away from the trees unless we must use them for shelter. The spiders and most insects are not big problems, but the snakes can be very dangerous, and if anything would survive all this it would be *la anaconda* and her kin."

The satellite dish was mounted into the main suitcase unit; Gus took out a small sledgehammer, pounded stakes into the rock and anchored the dish to them with a strong wire. He jiggled the thing a few times, then seemed satisfied.

"Next thing we do is see if we have juice from the battery pack, and then I'll try and align this sucker," he said.

One whole suitcase, it appeared, was a battery. "How long does that thing last?" Lori asked him.

"Oh, about an hour at full power, maybe more at a lower setting." He used a small electronic device to take a preliminary sighting, then switched on the unit and plugged in a tiny Watchman-style television that showed only snow. Checking the instrument often, he turned a few cranks on the dish mount, and suddenly a very snowy test pattern came in. It was somewhat distorted, weak, but it was there.

Terry plugged in a headset and threw a small switch. The television went black, but she paid no attention and instead said, "Hello, Atlanta. Hello, Atlanta. This is Terry at the crater. Do you receive us? Over." She toggled the switch down.

"Audio is fair," a tiny voice in her ear responded. "No video. Over."

Toggle. "We don't have a camera plugged in yet. Because of power limits and distance to the crater, we are unable to do live shots from the rim, but as soon as John gets here, we'll go out with the hand-held and then immediately feed tape. Over."

"Understood. There is a storm over the base at the moment delaying everything. Best guess is that it'll be about two hours until it clears and they can get to you. Advise you use the time for pickup shots if the weather is still clear there. If Sutton is up to it, try her in a standup. Feed what you get when you get it, but leave at least fifteen minutes. Over."

Two hours! "Uh—we might have a problem before that," she said low into the mike. "We have the nonteam member present and armed. Over."

"Can't do much about it. Handle it the best you can. We are advised of the situation from the pilot at base. Do whatever you have to. Suggest you shut down now until you are ready to feed. Over."

When you make deals with the devil, make sure it is you making the deal.

"All right. As you said, nothing much can be done about it. Out." She looked over at the cameraman. "Shut it and seal it, Gus," she told him. "They want us to do pickups at the crater if the weather holds."

The thunder rumbled across the ghostly landscape.

"That storm is toward the rancho," Campos noted. "I can tell. The storms do not last all that long, but they are fierce and they can be a problem. I think perhaps the helicopter will be late."

Damn it! Terry thought sourly. *At least he could have been a little less clever.* "It's raining there now," she admitted to him. "But they don't think it'll be a serious problem unless it comes this way."

There was a sudden, extremely bright bolt of stroboscopic lightning close by, and then a very loud explosion of thunder.

"I hate to say it," Gus yelled, "but I think we got that serious problem!"

Before anyone could reply, there was a sudden rush of wind and the heavens opened with a vengeance. It wasn't like any storm Lori had ever known; the rain was so heavy and dense, it was nearly impossible to see, and the roaring sound was deafening. Campos and the two women grabbed the flashlights and Gus snatched up the portacam unit, fortunately still in its case, and they headed for the shelter of the trees, spiders and snakes be damned. There was no hope of staying dry; as Lori ran toward the jungle, she was soaked through in an instant, and she could feel the intensity of the downpour as it pounded her through her clothing.

The trees were not the shelter they would have been only hours before, but there were places where the rain was deflected by higher foliage in spite of the fire damage. Surrounded by gushing waterfalls of runoff from the tree tops, the spot she found was fairly well protected.

She'd been afraid that she would slip and fall on the rock or trip over some wreckage of the destroyed forest, but somehow she'd managed to make it without mishap. Now, sheltered and catching her breath, she was aware of a series of sharp, thundering explosions that reverberated through the jungle. In a moment she realized that they were all coming from the same direction—the crater!

Either it was still extremely hot or some sort of reaction was taking place the nature of which she couldn't guess. She suddenly worried that it might somehow explode and take them all out, or shatter, or who knew what?

She wondered where the others were. Not far, surely, in spots just like this. There wasn't any sense in going looking for them in the incessant rain, and a few attempts proved the futility of trying to yell over the constant roar.

A crazy thought came to her of Gus's fears of a live rerun of *The War of the Worlds*. The repeated explosions from the crater certainly *did* sound very regular, like something, well, *venting*. Nerves, she told herself. Just nerves.

Terry, too, had found shelter, leaning against the tree and gasping for breath. She had fallen, and it felt like she'd bruised and skinned her knee. It hurt like hell.

God! This is one I'm gonna remember for an awfully long time, she told herself. *Like all the rest of my life. I been shot at, chased, slapped around, and treated like shit, but this may be the worst. And all for a damned hole in the ground! Maybe this is it. Maybe this is God telling me that it's time to pack it in, demand a studio job, or find something else. And those damned explosions! Bang! Bang! Bang! Like some kind of ghostly war.*

She had just decided that it couldn't be much worse when she felt something press against the side of her head. She started; powerful hands pushed her back, and there was a gun right in her face.

"Go ahead!" Campos yelled at her in Spanish with angry satisfaction. "Yell your head off, bitch! They could be five meters away and not hear you!"

He grabbed her, and she tried to kick him in the balls, but he side-stepped her attempt, which was weak because of the pain in her knee and her general state of near exhaustion. He twirled her around and pinned one of her arms behind her back, twisting it painfully as he drew her to him.

"Try anything more like that and I will break it! I will break your arms *and* your legs."

"My God, Campos! What do you want? You can't get away with this!" she yelled back defiantly.

"You know what I want, you whore!" he snapped. "And what if you do not turn up when the rain stops? They will suspect, but they will not *know.* Do you not remember where you are? Your friends come at our invitation and leave at our demand, and if they reject our story of your disappearance, they can do nothing. We are already on the wanted lists of a dozen countries. Your only hope is to do what I say and pretend you like it. If you convince *me,* then maybe, just maybe, I will let you live!"

He pushed her back against the tree and grabbed with his free hand for her rain-soaked khaki safari shirt, the other hand still holding the pistol, now pointed at her abdomen.

"Why? You're gonna kill me anyway. You *must*! And we both know it."

He grinned evilly. "Perhaps the rain will stop. Perhaps then they will hear us, no? You can never tell."

And, with that, he ripped the shirt, almost literally tearing it off her.

She closed her eyes and sank down, resigned now to her fate at the hands of this monster. She waited and waited, and nothing came.

Finally she opened her eyes and frowned, then her eyes grew wide in amazement.

Juan Campos had collapsed in a heap and was lying there facedown, more in the rain than out of it. The pistol had fallen from his hand, and she moved painfully to retrieve it, not comprehending what sudden miracle had saved her. Gus? But where was he? A falling branch? It didn't look like anything like that.

And then, only a few meters beyond, she saw shapes. She was so shaken that for a moment she imagined they were Gus's Martians or some other kind of creatures from the crater, and they *did* look like nothing on Earth. Their faces were tattooed with elaborate designs, with great earrings of wood or bone. Small, dark, and threatening in their own right, each figure held a small blowpipe in its hand, eyes wide but fearfully flinching with the sound of each small explosion.

She made a movement for the pistol, and the pipes went up. She stopped, backed away into the tree, and the pipes came down. Primitive, yes, like out of some *National Geographic* special, but they knew what guns could do.

Terry tried to think of how to say "friend" in every language that she knew, but only English and Spanish came to mind. She tried them, but only blank stares were returned.

And then, as dramatically as it had started, the rain stopped, as if someone had turned off a faucet.

Quickly, almost without sound, a trio of the primitives moved in toward Juan Campos's body, first turning him over, then going through his clothing with a thief's skill.

Inanely, Terry could only think, *If only I had a camera here! What a story this would make!*

With sudden amazement coming over her, she realized that the three stripping Campos were all girls—no, women, and, from the look of them, ones that had already lived rough lives. Their faces and bodies were decorated with well-worn designs, and they wore that primitive jewelry but not a stitch of clothing. Their black hair was long but obviously not without attention; it was shoulder-length on some, waist-length on others, and trimmed at the ends. Nor was it matted or tangled; much attention was clearly paid to keeping it groomed. Their awareness of how things connected on the clothing and of the gun and its purpose showed some knowledge, but everything about them said that they, if not ignorant of anything beyond the Stone Age, rejected all such things totally.

They *were,* however, thorough, and before two minutes had passed they had extracted from Campos's body an incredible assortment of weaponry, from two more small pistols to an assortment of knives and other instruments of violence. One of the women in the rear brought up a thick tray of woven straw, onto which all the weapons were carefully placed. By the time they were through, Campos was nude, his clothing put in a heap, and signs of various wounds and scars could be seen all over the man's body. Clearly his life hadn't always been one of idleness and ease.

Terry heard noises to her left and looked over to see several more of the women with a very frightened Dr. Lori Sutton in tow and others dragging another form which the newswoman recognized. "Oh, my God! *Gus!*"

She started to go to the cameraman, but for the first time, one of the women made a sound, saying sharply and menacingly, *"Azat!"*

Blowguns went up, and Terry got the message.

When Lori saw Terry's torn shirt and Campos on the ground nearby, she gasped, instantly putting two and two together. The scientist reached the newswoman and whispered, "Did he . . . ?"

"No. They stopped him. If they hadn't—"

"Azat! Azat!" came the menacing protest again. Gus by now was also stripped, and they gestured that the two women were to strip as well. Clearly they trusted nobody, not here.

Oh, God! The damned bugs are already eating me alive as it is! Lori thought, but she was too frightened not to comply.

"Guza! Guza!" the seeming leader said, pointing, indicating that they were to move toward the rest of the primitives, who still had their blowguns trained on the captives.

They're not going to give us back our clothes and equipment! Lori thought with sudden panic, but there wasn't much else to do, and she didn't want to argue, not right now.

They went back into the forest, and the tender feet of the two civilized women were soon feeling bruised and cut by the rough forest floor, compounded by insect bites that the natives seemed to just ignore.

They're taking us away, away from the base camp! Terry thought in panic. The rest of the news team would search, of course, but what chance did anyone have of finding them in the natives' jungle, even if it had just recently undergone massive alterations?

It seemed like a very long march, but hardly hours considering that dawn had not yet broken. Finally they reached what the two women first thought was a village but which, on closer inspection, appeared more to be a temporary camp rather than a permanent settlement.

Terry's curiosity competed with her fear, and she wondered if these women had been here when the meteor had hit. There were signs of debris about, a number of recently fallen trees and the remains of a crude stone fire pit that had apparently blown over. A camp fire burned in the wreckage, giving the whole area an eerie, flickering glow. On one side of the camp several women were lying on thick grass mats, and they had what looked like dried mud and leaves over parts of their bodies, some secured with vines. At least one showed signs of singed hair and had the natural bandages over part of her face and one eye.

Yes, they'd been here during impact. It was a wonder any of them had survived unscathed, let alone so many, and it was equally wondrous that any of them could still hear.

The two captive women were taken near the fire, although they hardly needed the extra heat, and with signs were ordered to sit. It was mostly mud there, thanks to the runoff from the rainstorm.

To their surprise, they saw the bodies of the two men being dragged into the camp, bound with vine ropes. *Then they aren't dead!* both thought almost at once, for why bind dead bodies? Some sort of paralyzing drug, then, rather than a lethal poison. Terry was happy that Gus wasn't a casualty, after all, but couldn't help wondering with a little bit of satisfaction what Campos would be like as the captive of a tribe of female savages.

Now what? they both wondered. Neither had any experience with anything like this, but it wasn't hard to think of movies, television shows, and books that told of the savage nature of the jungle people of the upper Amazon. And if they were taken far into the jungle before searchers could find them, what hope would there ever be of escape?

AMAZONIA

SHE WAS NOT OLD, she was ancient, although she no longer possessed the word to express it. The People believed that she was the daughter of a goddess and almost worshiped her, and after all this time she could no longer recall her own origin.

She sensed that in the distant past she'd been many things, but it was increasingly difficult to remember much of it. She *did* know somehow that the longer time passed and the more she remained in any one place, the more her memory faded, leaving only the present and immediate past. But the present and immediate past were such a long stretch of existence that she knew somehow that she was coming to a point where memories were falling into a deep and bottomless pit beyond recall. Some of the knowledge useful to the People remained, but it seemed now to come from nowhere, accepted as readily as magic, without question as to its origin but rather taken for granted as some divine gift. Vast periods of time passed when she never even thought of the Past, or that there had *been* a past, even in her dreams. She didn't mind; in fact, she felt better for it, slept more soundly for it. The present was enough. It was sufficient.

The language of the People was simple and pragmatic; they had all the words that were necessary for them and could express any concepts that were relevant to their simple but demanding lives, but there was no subtlety to it, no multiple meanings, no indirectness. There were also no words for lying, deceit, dishonesty, or most other sins, nor was there a word for property or any great concept of it.

Although there were spirits everywhere—not just in the sky but in the trees, the rocks, the water, the animals, even the wind—who were prayed to in the context of a view of the cosmos both simple and complete, they had no names, only attributes and powers. The names of the

People were also simple and generally descriptive: Little Flower, Big Nose, Soft Wind. They had named her Alama long ago, which meant "spirit mother."

She had used no other tongue for so long that she recalled no other. Like the rest of her forgotten past, she had no need of another.

Even time was different here, for the climate never changed, and the only temporal reference, beyond the passing of day and night, was the births, aging, and eventual deaths of the others. She had tried on occasion to figure out how long she had been with the People by generations, but she kept going back and back so far that all the faces and personalities blurred together in her mind. She did remember vaguely coming across an immense river in a very large canoe powered by the Spirit of the Wind, with huge, ugly men dressed in bright cloth and metal, with four-legged animals that they rode. She recalled that sometime afterward she had been beaten and whipped by some of those men and had fled into the jungle, but even that was a blur now, fading and soon to disappear with the rest of the past.

She had a hazy memory, almost a dream, of fleeing inland, encountering a tribe, and settling with them. She had felt safe, but something had happened—an accident—and she'd lost a hand. She could never remember which hand it was, anyway, since it wasn't important. It wasn't the loss that had caused the trouble with the tribe but, rather, the fact that the hand eventually had grown back. She had been cast out by the tribal leaders, men who had come to fear her, and she had pressed on, learning when to stay with a tribe and when to leave it, until she had found the People.

Legend said it had been a tribe where the men had grown lazy and no longer provided for the women and children or respected the gods and spirits. The women had learned how to hunt and forage and do all the things men did, after which the spirits had slain the men for their evil abandonment of their natural duties. Since that time they had allowed no man in the tribe. Now and then they would find men of other tribes in the forest and capture some of them, and, using the ancient potions made from the forest plants, the prisoners would be kept drugged and would mate with whoever of the tribe chose to do so. After a while the men would again be put to sleep and carried back to where they had been captured, to wake up wondering whether their experience had been real or some kind of dream. Male children born of these unions would be taken to some other mixed tribe and left. Only girl children were kept by the People. It was a part of the blood oath taken at adulthood, and there was a stark but well-understood price for not agreeing to do so: death to the mother, although not to the child, who was then taken to another tribe. It was a hard rule, but this was a hard life in a very hard land, and it had kept them free.

Was that one of *her* rules? Or had that been here before her? She couldn't remember. She wasn't even really certain if the People had predated her arrival or had come about as a mixture of circumstance and her own invention. Certainly she strictly enforced the rules: Use nothing not of nature, or of your own making, or the making of those you know. All things of others, even of other tribes, are unclean, to be buried when found and the handler purified afterward. Refuse nothing that another needs; have nothing that you would not willingly give away.

She worried about that sometimes, that perhaps she was not helping these women but was instead forcing them into a system to meet not their needs but hers. But wasn't that what a deity did? They did not seem to hate her for it, were not unhappy. If, perhaps, her perception of them as being happier than their counterparts in the more traditional tribes was colored by her own need to be right, they never seemed *less* content than the others. That would have to be enough. Provided that the tribe could continue to exist, that the forest would continue to exist, even her worries would not trouble her, for even now it was hard to imagine that she had not always been here.

She took no man herself, nor had she in such a long time, she could barely remember the experience. She felt no need for it anymore, and, more important, the survival of the tribe depended on procreation, particularly when they could keep only the girl children; she knew she was barren. There was only one man who was of her own kind, a man of godlike power that she *did* remember, but she could not remember even him with much clarity.

Still, while she'd banished all the worries of the past, she was concerned about the future. What made the People so attractive to her was their permanence, their unchanging yet challenging life, and their isolation. But it was getting a lot harder to maintain that isolation. The forest was being chewed up by monstrous machines, cleared, farmed, then abandoned because the land was neither loved nor understood by those new men and women who exploited her. The tribe had moved many times and more than once had barely escaped discovery, and it was getting harder and harder to find a place that would provide for the needs of the People in their jungle wilderness. Watching the cutting and burning of the forest had brought back old hatreds and fears; it was no less rape for being inflicted on the land rather than on a woman, and it was no less brutally violent.

That was why they were near the remote impact site, searching out a new place to call a home, a new refuge against the rapists of the land. It was a good region and held much promise, although there were others about—violent men, men with deadly weapons and a callous disregard for life, who were also planting and growing in the region. These men, at least, seemed to protect the forest to hide their activities from the rest of the world as much as she wanted to hide the People from those same eyes. That made them less of a problem to her and one she could accept. Their traps were elaborate and particularly nasty, but she could discover them easily, and they posed no real threat. And with the poisons and potions that were the legacy of tens of thousands of years of experience by the forest people, an uneasy truce was possible. The men understood that the People had no interest in what they were doing and wished only to be left alone. They also understood that in the forest their murderous guns and traps were little help should they decide to hunt down the forest tribes. After a few disastrous attempts, the men had abandoned any ideas of that.

This place would probably do, but locating a good site for a more permanent village would take some time. In the meantime, they would camp and move as one.

It had been quite late, and only the guards and the forest were awake. There had been good hunting, the Fire Keeper had a good flame, and everyone had a full belly and was content. The women had been sleeping off the large meal; even the Spirit Mother herself had been fast asleep, when it happened.

Suddenly she had awoken with a start, a horrible feeling sweeping over her like nothing she could dredge up from the most distant of remaining memories. It was an almost inexplicable form of dread, as if—*as if she were dead, sleeping forever with nature, and someone was digging at her grave* . . .

From above there came a crackling sound and a series of booms like thunder yet unlike any thunder she or the People knew. The night flared suddenly into day, and a great sun came almost upon them and vanished in a horrible explosion, beyond anything they could have imagined, powerful enough to shake the earth, collapse the lean-tos, throw the guards to the ground, and even topple some of the great trees.

Then, for a moment, there was a stillness almost as terrible as the crash, and suddenly, a searing wave of heat that burned and blackened whatever it touched swept over them. Women and children screamed both in terror and in pain, and there was fire, awful fire, all around.

Although in shock, she realized that somehow she'd received only a minor burn on one side and was otherwise all right. But others had been badly hurt and needed immediate attention. She got up on her feet and ran to the center of the camp, calling loudly, "Keep calm! Keep calm! We must help those who are hurt, and quickly!"

The sight of her and the sound of her commanding voice rallied those who were no more injured than she was, and the entire tribe went into immediate action.

Those who had been caught out in the open in the firestorm had suffered. Two were dead, struck full in the face by the heat, and another had been crushed to death by a falling tree. There were several broken limbs to be set, some seared hair that smelled and looked ugly but wasn't serious, and three or four serious burns.

"Susha! The healing herbs!" the Spirit Mother snapped, examining the badly burned side of Mahtra's face. There was a virtual pharmacy in the oils, balms, herbs, saps, and leaves of the great forest, and she had made certain that a kit of such things was always available. "Utra! Bhru! We will need water, both cold and very hot. Get urns! Bhru, fix the fire pit! The rest of you—if you are uninjured, help carry the hurt to the mats over there so they will be seen to quickly! Get any burning limbs out of the camp! Quickly! Time is all for the living! We will mourn and tend to the dead when we can!"

It was a frantic time, but in a way that was good, for the practical needs of their tribe, their family, drove out the terror that would have otherwise consumed them, and within an hour or two they were too weary to clearly remember their panic and fright. But though they were tired, they were not without curiosity. *Something* had blown up; something had exploded with enormous force very near to them. If it was something made by the Outside, what their tongue called "not forest," it might bring other Outsiders. If it was something run by the men of violence, that would be important to know, too. And if it was some kind of evil spirit come from the night sky to Earth, then that needed to be known most of all.

Alama, however, could not go. As she was the religious as well as temporal leader, her duty was to remain with the injured and to see that the ceremonies of the dead were performed, lest their spirits, deprived of a return to the bosom of the Earth Mother, be doomed to wander eternally without rest.

"Susha will remain and see to those who are burned," she ordered. "The guards must also remain, for none can travel until healed. Bhru, as Fire Keeper you will help me in the preparation of burial. The others, those who can, will go and see what has happened. Then you will come back and tell us what you see. Two groups, one under Bhama, the other under Utra, will go, one toward the great fire, the other below it here. Take care. The fire still burns at the tops of the trees, and there is much danger." She stopped, feeling a sudden drop in air pressure. "Rain comes. Rain will help with the fires and will make your journey better. Go now. Come back and tell us what you see, but do not be seen yourselves. Those too hurt for such a thing but able to help here, stay. There is much to do. All must be back before first light. Go!"

The long and exhausting night wore on. The graves were quickly and expertly dug, and the victims were wrapped in leaves, in spite of the driving rain. Most of the trees in and around the camp still stood, and Alama was proud of that. She always seemed to pick just the right spot when unforeseen danger lurked.

The rain continued intermittently. Finished with all but the ceremonies and the actual laying in the earth, Alama and Bhru came wearily back into the camp and stopped dead in their tracks. Two naked strangers, Outsider women, were being kept by the fire under guard, and two others, naked Outsider men, were lying unconscious on the side of the camp opposite the wounded tribeswomen. The women knew that the men were not dead, for why bring dead men into camp and defile it?

"Bhama! Utra!" Alama snapped angrily. "What is this?"

The two squad leaders, as weary as their chief, jumped to her call.

"They all hiding in the trees," Utra tried to explain. "One of the men, *that* one," she added, pointing to Juan Campos, "attack the dark woman. We put darts in him to stop him. Mother, we cannot just sit and watch such a thing! She sees us. It is not a time for deciding but just doing. If others come, she will say that she sees us and how many we are. Then they come try and find us. You say the wounded cannot travel, so we take them with us."

Alama sighed. She wished she'd been with them. Sometimes direct, pragmatic logic wasn't always the best course, particularly when dealing with Outsiders. "And the other two?"

"Mother, it rains hard then," Bhama told her. "We come up to the burning place from below. All at once we see this man there, under the trees. It was so sudden, we do not expect it. We are in the open to his eyes, and he sees us. Then he smiles. He reaches for something and holds it up to his face. We think it is some kind of weapon, and so we shoot him with darts. We still trying to decide what to do next, when the rain stops. Then this white woman comes toward us. She seems afraid of us when she sees us, but she does not try and run from us but runs to the man. We stop her. Then we hear our sisters nearby. We see that they have the others. We know there are no more. So we agree, all of us, to purify them. We bury their unclean things as the law commands. Then we bring them back with us for you to decide."

In a direct sense, what they had done was exactly right, if the facts were true. "How do you know that it is only these? That no others are here?"

"We see them come," Bhama assured her. "They come on a big, terrible bird that roars like thunder. They and their things get off, nobody else. Then the bird fly away."

This was not good, not good at all. There were certain to be others coming, and they would look for the missing foursome. Still, they couldn't just be released, not now. She looked up and sensed the wind through the charred and smoky atmosphere. It was raining again over there, and here soon as well. The sensible thing would be to destroy the camp, disguise the wounded, leave a few volunteer guards to watch over them, and move everyone away as far and fast as possible until they could find a place to hide. There would be a search, yes, but it would not be a major one, not in this jungle. But what then? The men couldn't be kept, nor could they be left bound and drugged forever. Even now they would slow everyone down. If these two women were their wives, they'd never give up searching, and the places where they could continue to hide out from the encroaching Outside were becoming more limited each day.

But if they killed the two men, what reaction would that bring in the women? They both already seemed too old to ever accept and adjust to the life of the People; there were potions, of course, drugs that would dull the mind and control it so that one could never disobey. Still, it was a distasteful business, and she didn't like it at all. In all these years she'd not faced a problem this complicated.

She looked at the two warriors. "And the thing that burns? What of it? Did any see it close?"

Utra nodded. "Yes, Mother. We see it. It is the heart of the Moon Goddess come to Earth. It is all black and burned around where it sits, and it is in a great hole that it makes for itself. It is bright and yellow, and it look like a great jewel the size of the full moon in the sky. And it beats, like the heart."

Alama frowned. A big jewel? Beating like a heart? That made no sense at all in any traditional lore, nor did anything from that buried past come to explain it, either. This was something totally new. Like the horrible feeling that had awakened her and still made her shiver when she thought about it.

Still, her past of fog and mist did not totally desert her. *Meteor,* it said, and she had an instant vision of a great rock in space coming down toward the Earth and striking with enormous force. But meteors didn't glow yellow and beat like hearts.

Now another concept came, like *meteor* without a true word but rather as an idea and picture: *Satellite*. In a world as primitive as this? Or had it been longer than she thought since she'd entered the forest? Far longer . . .

Bomb. The most worrying concept to come from that mental unknown and the most likely to be something that throbbed. How advanced might portions of Earth now be, anyway?

Spaceship. No, surely not that advanced. She was certain of that. But what if it wasn't a human spaceship? What if it was from something or someone *really* Outside?

"I must see it, and soon," she told them.

"But what of the ceremonies?" Bhru asked worriedly. "It is almost first light now."

Yes, that was the trouble. It was almost first light, and at some point, perhaps even now, certainly within hours, others would come to search for these missing four. Others would come to see what had fallen here, as the four captives probably had, for why else would they be here? There just wasn't enough time! And only a few hours earlier she had felt the luxury of timelessness.

There was no way around it, though. They *had* to break camp and play for time, no matter what. She gave the orders, and the two exhausted Outsider women watched as the camp became a frenzy of activity, turning a primitive campsite back into wild jungle.

"They're covering up to run!" Lori hissed. "And taking us with them!"

"Nothing we can do now," Terry whispered back. "At least Gus isn't dead. I wish they'd used more of that stuff on Campos, though."

"But we can't go like *this*!"

"I don't even want to go if I had on a safari suit, but we're gonna go, that's for sure. Either walking or carried like them."

They heard rather than saw the burial ceremony. It was done quietly, with the sound of chanting coming from somewhere out of sight, and it was Terry who guessed the meaning of the sound, not from any experience but from the sadness on the faces of their guards and the workers who paused, many with tears in their eyes.

But when the burial party returned, it was all business. It was no longer dark, but the mist from the ground still obscured even the tops of the trees. Alama was counting on that heavy mist not only to keep the investigators away a little bit longer but also to allow them to cross the open patches of jungle caused by the impact. A last, unpleasant touch was to be smeared, almost covered, with a thin paste made of herbs and clay that dried a sickly pea green. The whole tribe did it, and one of the tough warrior women supervised treating Terry and Lori.

Camouflage. Primitive but effective.

And just as primitive and effective was the simple pantomime the warrior woman did for their benefit, taking an ax with a stone blade that was polished razor sharp and showing how easy it was to cut things with it using a large leaf. She then pointed to their mouths and put a hand over each in an unmistakable warning message. Then she stuck out her own tongue and pretended to cut it out. It was amazing how easy it was to get some concepts across.

They trussed up Campos and Gus Olafsson with rope made of tough vines and slid logs through so that they could be carried on poles. Clearly, they were being kept drugged.

Although Lori was taller than any of the tribe and felt she could hardly lift herself, it took only two of the tribeswomen, one on each end of the pole, to carry each of the men with ease. All these women were muscular, many as well muscled as body builders. It was in its own way as intimidating as the blowguns and stone-tipped spears. And none of them was more intimidating than their leader, although she was perhaps the smallest of all the women there, certainly under five feet and thin and limber as an acrobat. It was her manner, her fire, her arrogance that commanded instant respect and obedience. She had the kind of personality and confident manner that a Napoleon probably had possessed.

There *was* something decidedly odd about her, though. She simply didn't look like any of the others. Rather, it was like a Chinese or Japanese woman amid a group of Mongols. She even had the almond "slanted" eyes that had vanished, if they were ever there, from the Amerind over the millennia.

The trek was arduous, though they would break for short periods every once in a while, mostly for their captives' benefit. Gourds were offered, one containing a fruit juice of some kind, another some sort of thick and nearly tasteless cold porridge with the consistency of library paste. Terry and Lori took it and managed to get some of it down, mainly because at this point anything seemed good. How the two trussed-up men were managing wasn't clear, but they at least were barely, if at all, aware of their circumstances, and as terribly uncomfortable as they were bound and carried, they at least hadn't had to walk.

Mercifully, they stopped for the day after what seemed like an eternity, deep within the thickest part of the jungle. Other than the occasional glimpses of the sun high above the nearly unbroken canopy indicating they were heading north, it was impossible to tell where they were. It was also incredible that so many of them—there must have been fifty or more, plus small children and supplies—could move through such dense jungle with confidence and leave no apparent trace.

Lori had not thought that she'd make it to the end of the journey, though when the day's march ended, she wasn't certain that it was such a good thing, after all. Too exhausted even to sleep, too uncomfortable even to relax, she could only think, and that was the last thing Lori Sutton wanted to do.

Just a few days before she'd been in a funk over her personal problems, which now seemed so trivial. The speed at which she had been plucked from obscurity and plunged into a dangerous but romantic adventure culminating in the professional event of a lifetime for an astronomer left her mind spinning. Now, naked, hot, exhausted, and in pain, she was trapped in the Stone Age, where virtually all her hard-won knowledge was totally useless.

She had to admit that she felt a little better that her captors were women. At least she would be spared the horrors that she imagined she'd be subjected to by a tribe of primitive men. Still, there were children here—all female, she'd noted—and that meant these women had to have mates somewhere. Had the meteor wiped out the men? Were they all away? It seemed unlikely, but it only made the puzzle deeper.

Terry looked only slightly better for the experience than did Lori, but Terry was younger and in better condition and was the kind of person who never gave up hope. She, at least, lay in a deep sleep on the forest floor, oblivious to the world.

They were probably the story now, Lori thought. Maybe the hunt for them would be massive, but it wouldn't last forever. Not in this jungle— and these primitive women knew the forest as no one else did; it was their entire world. Where was all this massive deforestation the environmentalists were always protesting about? She could use a little open clear-cut land right now.

Alama checked on her people, then saw that the white woman was still awake and made her way over to her. It would take a while for these soft Outsiders to build up their strength and become wise in the ways of the forest; until then they would be both captives and liabilities, a fact on Lori's mind as well as she eyed the leader nervously and wondered what was next.

The tiny but tough woman knelt, and black almond eyes looked deeply into the scientist's own. After a moment the leader pointed to herself and said, "Alama."

Lori realized that the woman was at least attempting to communicate. Alama was probably a name, possibly a title. It didn't matter. She pointed to herself and said, "Lori."

"Lo-ree," the small woman repeated, nodding.

Sutton pointed to her sleeping companion. "Terry," she said.

Alama looked over at the newswoman. "Teh-ree," she said.

Lori sighed. She was now convinced that this woman, so different in appearance and manner, could not have been a member of the tribe originally. She wished she knew some Portuguese or even Japanese, but her languages had been German and Russian. Not much practical help here. Terry's Spanish might do, but Terry was going to be out for some time.

Still, Alama seemed adept at this sort of communication and appeared to want to teach some basics of the tribe's language.

She pointed to her breasts and genitals. *"Seku."* She pointed at Lori. "Seku." Pointing to others of the tribe, she said, "Seku, seku, seku," and to the two bound and drugged men, *"Fatah. Fatah."* Then to the guard next to them, "Seku."

Seku. Woman. *Fatah.* Man.

Walk in place. *Kaas.* Run in place. *Koos.* The lesson proceeded slowly, with much repetition when a new word was added. Alama knew what she was doing.

At the end of perhaps an hour Lori thought she understood the bare basics. Of course, when any one of the others talked, it still sounded mostly like gibberish, but that was to be expected. Attempts to return the teaching by matching words in English were abruptly rejected. This was not a lesson for mutual benefit and understanding so much as for the benefit of the tribe. *The better to give orders, my dear,* Lori thought.

Finally, Alama said, "Lo-ree sleep," and it was understood. On the other hand, there was still no way to be as sophisticated as to convey "I want to sleep but I just can't." Alama, however, seemed to understand. She went away for a moment, then came back with a small gourd and taught another word. *Kao.* Drink.

Lori was still dehydrated, and she took it and drank. It was some sort of fruit juice again, with a slightly bitter aftertaste. Still, after a few minutes, the pain seemed to fade away and the inner turmoil quieted. She went over her new twenty- or thirty-word vocabulary in her mind, settled down, and was suddenly as deeply asleep as she had ever been.

The next few days were unpleasant but in some ways less traumatic. The men were allowed to come out of their stupor, although it seemed clear that repeated doses of the same drug on the blowgun darts kept them in partial paralysis. The guards were able to keep them quiet with a demonstration of what a Stone Age knife or ax might do to not only their tongues but their genitalia.

In the meantime the language lessons continued, sometimes with

Alama, sometimes with others doing the teaching to both women. No talking in any language but the tribe's was permitted. Absolutely none. Even an unthinking comment uttered in English or Spanish was punished with a quick lash delivered with a vinelike whip to the back or buttocks. It *hurt* and could cause welts or even draw blood. As bad as that was, it caused amused giggles among those nearby, particularly the children, which made it embarrassing as well. They were under constant watch during the day and were made to sleep apart with tribeswomen during the terrible pitch-dark nights. Alama had forbidden all use of fire, and under the thick jungle canopy not even the late, waning moon could be seen.

Eating without cooking was another thing, and it was several days and a bad case of gastric distress before their bodies, if not their minds, fully tolerated the raw—well, *creatures*—that were offered them and which the rest of the tribe ate with relish. Indeed, both had to be forced, more or less, to eat anything other than the fruit and greenery, which was only slightly more palatable.

A number of times they heard helicopters, often very nearby, and the sound of small planes, but neither seemed to come close enough. Once the sound of voices caused the entire tribe to hide in the underbrush, tensely waiting to attack, but the voices soon faded away. Clearly, though, there was a massive search going on, but these women were in their element, and soon the searchers moved on, finding nothing.

The two men continued to have the worst of it, and it worried both Lori and Terry. Not that either had much sympathy for Juan Campos, whose manner suggested that he knew he was going to die eventually and wanted just one chance to die fighting. Gus, however, was a different story. He just didn't deserve this, and his former irrepressible spirit had gone out of him, almost as if he'd retreated into a world of his own.

For the two American women it was a total immersion into a culture and life and language in which all their education and experience meant nothing. They lacked even basic knowledge. What was edible? What would harm them? What animals were a threat, and how did one deal with them? What water was fit to drink? What water contained things that might harm or even eat one?

Still, the tribe quickly put them to work doing what little chores they could manage, such as walking with large gourds filled with water balanced on their heads. First they got lessons, then help, then they were on their own. Either they got it right the first time or they kept at it—all day, if necessary—until the job was done. They did fetching, hauling, even bathing the wounded, removing small bugs and other creatures from skin or hair. All the while they were derisively called *dur* or *dua*—child, or even baby—because they were so helpless and ignorant. They were *in* the tribe but not *of* it; to become one of the People, one had to earn and desire the privilege.

True to her nature, Terry did not lose hope that one day she would be able to escape or be rescued, and she kept seeing the book she'd write and the movie it would make. These thoughts kept her going, but they were also mixed with pragmatism: Such a time might not come soon, and until then, she wanted to be a member of the tribe, not a slave. In that sense, she was adapting better than Lori.

The scientist was in turmoil over the situation. She was no longer waking up each day surprised that it hadn't been some awful dream; she wasn't even daydreaming much about her nice apartment, bathtubs, showers, and flush toilets, but she hated this place and this existence. She was becoming afraid again, not so much that she might die at any moment but rather fearful that she might actually live, and that she wasn't sure she could stand.

The worst part was that she realized that Alama's sophisticated immersion system was working as easily on her as it would on a woman from another primitive tribe. The only way to avoid that wicked little lash was to try to *think* in their tongue. Both Terry and Lori had learned enough to be able to do that, but it required constant observation and attention. Many of the women seemed to make a game out of trying to force them to make an accidental slip, which would earn another lash.

The language was more complex than it seemed. Terry had the basics down pat, but there were subtleties and nuances that were still a mystery to her. For one thing, they had no real concept of time except on a physical level: baby, child, child bearer, old. But "day" and "night" were all the clock or calendar they had or needed. The language itself was basically all in the present tense, as if they had no need of a past or future. The ideal of this culture was that every day be like the last and the next; change was evil.

Lori hated it. Hated it and knew that if this kept on and on, well, one day she'd just snap. And yet somehow she had to admit that there was some good as well. While there was individuality here, the tribe came first, and sharing and helping others were simply taken for granted. They had a genuine love for this hostile steam bath of a jungle and seemed to really respect it and all its inhabitants, even apologizing to the animals and plants they would kill and use. There were no signs of jealousy, greed, envy, or hate. Alama was still a curiosity. There was mystery, harsh experience, and much pain behind those enigmatic eyes. The tribe spoke of her not as a chief or leader but as some kind of deity; supposedly she had been here before any of them, never aging, never changing. But even with a deity living among them, there was trouble in the paradise of the People.

"Mother, the men cannot stay," Bhru pointed out one day. "There is much unhappiness in them. One just stares and barely eats. The other has our death in his eyes. Both are weak and grow sick. They cannot stay as they are. They cannot stay if they are free. They are no good to us."

Alama nodded. "I know. I think much on them. I try hard to say not to kill them. I pray but do not find a new trail for them." She sighed. "I wait for the scouts to come back. Then I will say of them what is done."

"As you will."

"The two women do well."

"We see the wisdom of your way. We do not give them rest to think. Their feet and hands grow hard. They grow strong. They speak no Outside, even when we trick them. The dark one thinks she plays a game with us, but the game is just to stay not People. White woman knows she is with us but does not like it."

"Yes, if things are as always, they will come around in the seasons. Things are not as always. The People need a safe home. The People need more babies. That may bring us close to Outsiders who hunt them. It *will* bring us close to tribes who speak with Outsiders. We cannot wait for them. They must know that they are of the People to death. They must not *want* to leave."

"But how would this be done?"

"I know a way. I know more of how Outsiders think. There is danger to it. They can go mad. They can think of killing selves. Like the men, I see no other trail. Can you make the mark of spirit potions?"

"Now that you say we can have fire, yes. What little I do not have, the forest has here."

"Good. Then make. Chsua has the thorn needles. I will speak to her and say what is to be done. Mix the sleep herbs in their drink so they will not wake. We will do this at dark."

Bhru now realized what the Mother had in mind. "But they cannot marry the forest, Mother! Not now! They need to be ready!"

"Do what I say and believe in my wisdom. I know it is not what is done, but this will make them ready. Just do and see."

Alama sighed, wondering again if what she was doing was right or wrong, doubts she could never express or share with the others. But they had to move and, depending on what the scouts reported, most likely back toward the thing that had burned the forest. What they'd already done, particularly to the men, would cause them to be hunted down if it were known. It *had* to be done. Anyone could be broken. Anyone. It was just a cruel procedure.

She knew that well, even if the specifics were lost in that mental fog. How many times had *she* been broken? she wondered. More than once, that was for sure.

Sleep was odd and restless, even in these strange circumstances. When Lori awoke just after first light with the mists still hanging halfway up the forest heights, it was with odd memories of lights and chanting, but the memory was too distant for her to be certain if it was reality or dream. It wasn't something to grab hold of; there were more immediate concerns. She felt, well, odd. Her skin tingled with a slight burning sensation all over, more an itch than pain, and her nose and ears actually ached.

She turned over, sat up, stretched, and reminded herself as she always did to think in the tribe's tongue. She put her hand to her sore nose and touched something hard that hurt enough to bring her fully awake.

Something clicked softly on either side of her head, and she put a hand to her ear and discovered that she now had earrings of the type common to the tribe, fashioned from bone and held together with the epoxylike resins they distilled from one of the plants. She looked down at herself and saw that she also now had on the bone bracelets and anklets also common to these people, and a necklace of fresh green carefully braided vines. But . . . her *skin!*

It was still somewhat dark, but she could see that her skin, probably her whole body, had been dyed a dull shade between olive and brown, and around her breasts, upper arms, and thighs somebody had drawn a series of bold, primitive designs in the flat colors used by the tribe to denote rank and position. Those areas were particularly uncomfortable, with a stinging sensation, and she felt similar areas on her face. They also had cut most of her hair off, leaving only a thin fuzz on top.

"Lo-rhee pretty now," commented Ghai, one of her keepers, sounding sincere. "Look like forest people. Is good, too, to keep hair short. Things live in hair."

Lori wet her fingers and tried rubbing on a small part of a design on her thigh. It remained as it was.

"Spirit marks not come off," Ghai told her, amused at the attempt.

Tattoos! They'd tattooed her! She was too upset at the realization to cry, although that might come later. *That bitch Alama!* She wanted to kill now but knew that she'd never get anywhere near the leader, and if she did, the leader would easily break her arm.

"Terry?"

"Same thing. You are wives of forest now. Do not worry. All pain goes away in one sleep, maybe two."

Pain was not what she felt so anguished about. She sank back down, fully understanding the logic Alama had used. There would still be some kind of hunt on for them, and people would probably be looking for them for years. Not even this sort of group would be fully undiscovered forever. But now, tattooed, dyed, with bones in ears and nose—the last a cruel overkill, since few of the tribe did it—they would be indistinguishable from the rest of the tribe. Even if they were found, would they want to be rescued like *this*? With these tattoos and such? And even if the doctors could get the cemented bone jewelry out, removing tattoos of this size would be a massive job. They'd be just medical challenges to the doctors and freaks to everyone else.

Damn it! It just wasn't *fair*!

She was happy that there weren't any mirrored surfaces around. She wasn't ready to see herself as they'd remade her, not yet, but she got some idea from seeing Terry. Of course, they had done nothing with her skin tone, since that wasn't necessary, but she was still barely recognizable: her hair shorn to virtually scalp level, large bone earrings with another through the inside nostrils from which a larger curved and polished bone hung almost like a ring, solid blue ovals tattooed from the eyes out past the brows, cheeks adorned with yellow finger-width lines to her ears, her lips framed in a pale white, and her body covered with very obvious and suggestive fertility signs. Terry was clearly to be a baby maker, while Lori, it appeared, was to assist the Fire Bringer and learn the potions and ways of healing.

The tribe, it seemed, had spared no art or effort in making the two appear so primitive that not even their parents would recognize them.

Terry was taking it harder even than Lori; the older woman at least had already given up hope, while it wasn't until now that Terry was forced to face the fact that this wasn't merely a reporter's hazard but a permanent condition.

Alama looked at them both, then gestured for Lori to come to her. As much as the American wanted to throttle the little woman, she obeyed.

The mysterious leader of the tribe, who came barely up to Lori's shoulders, looked her over approvingly.

"You are now of the People," Alama said after the examination. "Be one of us, take our way. There is no other trail for you. You join us, take the ceremonies. Lo-rhee die. You will take a new name. Think like us. Act like us. *Be* us. There is *us,* and there is *them.* All that is not us is them. You must be happy here with us. What do you say?"

Lori sighed. "I think I will be dead soon. Killed by the forest and this life. While I live, I see no other trail."

And then Alama took on a different aspect, almost soft and human, and she said quietly, "I did not wish this. We did not want any of you. The spirits of fate did this. You must know—*I had no choices.*"

It was so direct, so out of character, that it startled Lori for a moment. This small leader of this primitive tribe was actually *sorry* about all this! She realized suddenly that this had been an ordeal for them as well and that Alama, too, had been searching without success for a way out of the mess. Still, Lori could not forgive or forget. Not now. And because of that, she didn't know what to say.

At that moment there was a commotion on one side of the camp, and Alama looked over, then stood up anxiously to see a very tired warrior woman come through the excited crowd toward her.

Lori was suddenly forgotten as Alama first hugged the scout, then pressed her for information.

"All are well," the warrior told her. "Some of us stayed with the hurt. One hurt has died, Tagi, and was returned to the Earth properly; the others grow stronger."

Alama nodded. "My soul goes to her and all of us. What of the Outsiders and their hunt?"

"It is given up, we think. No more go out. There was much busy stuff around the great fire pit, but now there are only a few there. They have strange things with them. Outsiders in green with big weapons guard them."

"How many?"

"Of the ones that watch the great pit, it changes. As many as four hands are there, but mostly just one hand. Of the green ones with weapons, one hand and one. Two are on guard always. They watch the others, not the fire pit. But the fire pit is what they look at. A great bird like the one the first night comes two times a day, early and then late but in light. Sometimes men come and get off. Sometimes other men get on."

"And the thing in the fire pit? You see it?"

"It is hard to see it and not be seen. Yes, we see it, by climbing trees at night. It still lights and beats like a heart. It is like a big gemstone, but with sides of many parts of one shape. At the top, one of the shapes changes. It gets deep black. Then it is the same as the rest again."

Alama frowned. "This shape. Can you draw it here in the dirt?"

"Yes, Mother. It is like this all over, of what we can see." The scout took a stick and carefully drew a series of connected lines.

Alama gasped and stared at it as if it were the worst kind of magic for quite some time, and it made some of the others afraid to see it.

Lori, peering over, making use of her greater height, recognized it immediately but could not understand why it had had any effect on Alama. Still, the scientist in her was fascinated not only by the shape but by the idea that the entire meteor was made of interconnections of this shape.

She didn't think a sphere could be covered with hexagons.

Alama stayed by the fire most of the night, staring into it, deep in thought. The sight of the hexagon in the dirt had brought back memories so long buried that they seemed to be from someone else who had lived and died a long time ago. It was almost as if there were two of her inside her head: one Alama, the other someone she'd once been who was so totally different as to be some creature from another world.

But she *was* a creature from another world. She knew that now, although the details were far too distant, the concepts too vast to fully grasp.

This is what you've been waiting for, isn't it? Waiting all those years, until you could find a hexagon that would turn dark? And here it is, come to you, far sooner than you expected it.

There was a sudden realization that she had not made the decision to find the hexagon, that she had not gone to it. Rather, it had found her. It was no accident, certainly; it had been sent. It had been sent to pick her up.

Those men with the "strange stuff." Scientists certainly, trying to figure out what it was. She wondered what those very smart men thought of it. It must be confusing the hell out of them.

What kind of emergency would trigger it to find her? What could she do if she went? She had helped last time, certainly, but *he* had done most of the real work. He just didn't want to do it anymore. Could she do it without him? Did she want to? Was it sent for her because *he* had refused? Or would refuse? As murky as memories of that time were, she could remember nothing covering this kind of thing.

And if she did decide to go, she would have to have the help of the People with all those guards around, but she had no doubt that somehow a path would be opened for her. *She* could make it, but what about her People? How many might die so she could get through? That they would do it for her she had no doubts, but was it *right* to ask? And if she didn't go, *he* most certainly would. Somehow the system would make him go, and he would restart it all again, just as he always did.

She hated this world. It was filth and death and decay without end. She had been hiding from that, as much as she could hide, these past centuries, waiting, waiting, until one day she might again have the stars. When a woman could be a captain of a great ship and not a wife or lover or chattel slave.

She sighed. She would do what she could for the People, but like all others except *him,* they would die. Perhaps, just perhaps, she could at least try to solve her more direct moral dilemma at the same time.

In the morning she summoned both Lori and Terry to her. The language was inadequate for the task, but they had no other in common.

"The scouts say that there is a way out for all of you. All of us."

"Us?" Terry asked, more than hateful at what had been done to her.

"Yes. Us. Not a way to your village or mine but to another place. A place where you will no longer be of or look like the People. A place where you may be free. It is a—*different* kind of place. It is where I came from many, many lives ago."

"Where do you come from?" Lori asked, wondering where this was leading.

Alama pointed up. "From there. From *after* there. From the stars behind the stars."

Oh, great! Terry thought sourly. *First she's the Amazon Queen from Hell, now she thinks she's E.T.*

Lori, however, while not ready to accept it, was ready to at least not reject it. "You come from the stars?"

The small woman nodded. "I am here since the first tribes. I am in a trap. My way out is sent. You can come or stay and be of the People. You choose. I must go."

"The star that made the great fire pit that brought us here. That is a boat to the stars?" Lori, too, was having trouble fitting the language to these concepts.

"Not a boat. A door. A boat is not needed."

"And if we go there with you, they can take away these marks? These bones? This glue?"

Alama smiled. "The sacred word of Alama. You will not see those things again if you go." She paused. "One thing more. The men with you die. Left here, they die. They go with me if you help and live. You will have to carry them. Can you? Run and climb and carry heavy man?"

"I do not know. I can try."

"You can leave the hateful one to die!" Terry told her. "I will not carry him!"

"Both must go or not one of them. I cannot choose on your saying. If the one is evil, he will find the other place a way to change or die. It has a way of law, it seems. You need not choose now. First I must find a place for the People to live and prepare them for my going. And it will be hard to get to the door. Many men, many big weapons so that no more go away like you. For now I give you leave. Go to the tree in back of me. There in quiet voice you may speak your own tongue on this. There and no other place or time but I choose."

It was another unexpected gesture, but if she really believed what she was saying, then it hardly mattered to them anymore. They were anxious to take advantage of it, no matter what.

"Is she crazy or what?" Terry whispered in the first English she'd tried in she didn't know how long.

"I don't think she is," Lori replied. "I know it sounds mad, but it's no crazier than this. Look, I heard the other women talking. They were preparing to ritually kill Campos and Gus. Like you, I don't care about Campos, but I can see her point. But if it's Gus and Campos or nothing, I say take them both."

"You really think you can just walk into this meteor and come out on some other world?"

"Probably not. If we aren't machine-gunned by the armed guards, we'll wind up splat on top of that thing as targets or we'll be burned to death. But there *was* something really weird about that meteor. You remember it. And Alama—she knows too much about too many things to be only an aboriginal priestess. Besides, have you looked at a reflection of yourself? You look like something out of *National Geographic*. So do I. I know I couldn't go back like this, and I probably won't make it a year out here. Or, worse, maybe I will. Can you imagine living the rest of your life with these people? At this point I am willing to accept even space creatures. The bottom line is, if it really doesn't matter anymore if I live or die, what have I got to lose?"

Terry shook her head in wonder at the situation. "I don't know. I sure don't want to live as one of the tribe forever, but I couldn't go back looking like *this*. Some of the women said that the tattoos use some kind of stuff that penetrates deeply, that they've seen the color on *skulls*. So much for plastic surgery. But the truth is, I've been doing a lot of soul-searching lately, and bad as it is, I'd rather live like this than die. I dunno—I've interviewed too many saucer nuts in my time to accept a story like that."

Lori understood, in a way. "Still, how many leaders of Stone Age tribes could spin a story like that? These people don't know anything outside the rain forest. *Something* was sure screwy about the way that meteor came in, the way it hit, the way it just sat there, the pulsing—even the dark shape on top that winked in and out. If I were normal, I would be on your side, but I'm not normal, I'm a Ph.D. turned into a Stone Age jungle girl. She may be crazy, but I'm desperate. Besides, think of poor Gus. If we try and Alama's crazy, at least Gus will get out and get attention. If we don't go along, they're going to kill him."

"You really think you can carry him all the way to that meteor?"

"Ordinarily, no. But I've *got* to."

Terry stared at the strange little woman by the fire. "I wonder how she's going to do it."

METEOR SITE A,
UPPER AMAZON BASIN

IT WAS IRONIC THAT the two women adapted quicker and better to the life of the People after being offered a way out. Terry in particular took some delight in looking after the two men, particularly Campos, who had no idea who she was. Bound and drugged most of the time, allowed only a little exercise under watchful blowguns, neither was in great shape, but they at least seemed to have stabilized a bit.

Terry and Lori took the ceremonies of full initiation into the tribe, which involved a rather complex set of rituals culminating in drinking the blood of all the members of the tribe, which had been mixed with some juice in a gourd. This didn't free them from work, but it gave them equal status with the others. Both spent long periods learning the ways of the People; Alama encouraged them and seemed quite pleased by their actions.

They finally picked a village site, well hidden and deep in the densest region of the jungle but located within two or three days walk of several more traditional tribal villages, so that they could at least get the one thing from men that nature could not provide. Making the huts, building the specialized structures of sticks and straw, coping with the driving rains—it was a real education.

Terry went along on a scouting expedition to one of the villages and saw that the tribe had at least some remote contact with the outside world. The bronze cross and small empty hut showed that missionaries had been there.

It said something about how easily she was adapting to the life that Terry never once considered that such contact provided a means of escape. Instead, she was quite pleased with how confidently she now moved through the forest and how well she had adapted to the hard life and way of survival of the People.

It was almost as if, Lori thought, Terry had burned all her mental bridges and was acting out some sort of fantasy. Lori, too, had acclimated well. She had certainly learned a lot of skills and had grown strong and self-reliant in her own way.

All of which pleased Alama no end. If she could get those two through, she thought, they would probably be the best prepared individuals ever to be dumped on that world.

Now, though, she would have to face the first barrier to be overcome.

She had told the tribe that the thing from the sky had come for her, to take her home. They hadn't questioned it, but they were not at all happy about it. They had the law and well-trained leaders, but now they would have to see if they could survive on their own. Oddly, she felt worse about putting them in danger to get to the meteor than about leaving. After all the millennia, she was tired of the dying; she wanted, *needed* a challenge. This time, more than ever, she felt that she was ready for it.

Only the one small stand of trees remained for any sort of cover; the darkness would have to suffice the rest of the way, although the meteor still glowed brightly like some great floodlight in the ground, waiting for her.

The quartzlike hexagonal facets were incredibly regular, but the thing was not round. It might have been round once, but the part that had plowed into the ground here was irregular, jagged and misshapen, as if parts of it had been consumed and other parts had been broken off as it had made its way in. The crater should have been a couple of kilometers deep; instead, it was fairly shallow, only ten meters deep.

Looking at it from the treetops, Alama felt its energy and its life, felt its pull. Somehow she was certain that it *knew* she was there. And not quite on top but angled a little back was the spot that now and again turned into the deepest black, beckoning her.

She wished it were that easy. She wished that she'd been quicker recognizing it when it had struck, that she'd simply gone to it and seen it for herself before any of the scientists or military had gotten there. It would have been so much simpler.

The guards were Brazilian soldiers in camouflage fatigues, nasty-looking automatic rifles slung over their shoulders. They were a tough-looking bunch, but they looked extremely bored. Weeks, months—who could say how long it had been since the thing had hit?—of no activity and little else to do were taking their toll. Only two stood perfunctory guard, one at the camp and the other farther up at the equipment tent next to the crater, the other four playing cards and smoking cigars outside their big tent.

There seemed to be only two scientists currently in the camp, although the crater was ringed with instruments and, clearly, some effort had been made to take large samples. Probes ran from a portable generator right onto and into the meteor itself; long cables carried power to instruments guarded against rain and anchored against sudden wind.

It had become routine.

There were signs all around that a near army had been there at one time, that many other tents and structures had once been set up here, and that a huge area had been cleared for such a group. Now just these few remained.

Lori in particular was somewhat shaken by the small size of the camp. How long had they been in the jungle? It had seemed weeks, no more, and the events of that frantic and terrifying night were still fresh in her mind, but mere weeks would not have reduced the world's interest so much. The search after their mysterious disappearance would have slowed them down, and scientists the world over with visions of Nobel prizes would have been clamoring to be here—that the camp was so small and the scientific inquiry so routine meant it must have been a year . . . or longer.

It *couldn't* be that long. Gus and Campos could not have survived their miserable half-drugged imprisonment that long. Then again, how long had it taken to build these tough, callused feet that no longer felt the jungle floor, these hard hands that did much heavy work, or the muscles she had developed? It all seemed to make no sense.

What did make sense was the two days they spent observing every move of the camp. The military helicopter came in the morning and often deposited a few people, probably scientists and research assistants, who checked the data, read out information from the instruments into their portable computers, and did a lot of routine maintenance work. They remained all day and were picked up by the helicopter again before nightfall, leaving only the guards and the two permanent party members there: an old white-haired man in khaki shirt and shorts and a young bearded man who wore boots and jeans and a kind of cowboy hat but usually went shirtless.

Terry climbed effortlessly up one of the trees and stared at the pulsing, glowing meteor during the night. She watched as the black hexagon came on and saw, or thought she saw, some kind of shimmering just above it. Then, startled, she saw a small black shape crawling on the meteor near the hole. A lizard of some kind, she realized. It reached the black area, seemed to pause for a moment, then stepped into it. For a brief second it seemed frozen, suspended in dark space, and then it winked out.

The equipment around the edge of the crater became more active, clicking and whining, then subsided. The scientists had measured the effect and the fate of the hapless reptile.

She came down the tree and stood there, chewing absentmindedly on a finger while in thought, then sought out Lori.

"I am going to the men to see if they are able to help themselves," Lori said. "I can carry one if I have to, but if they walk, is much help."

"Bimi," Terry said hesitantly, using Lori's tribal name, "I cannot go with you."

"You can! You have to! This life is not for you. Death comes young with the People. You belong Outside!"

"Outside I cannot go," Terry reminded her. "And I just watch a lizard go into the black hole, and it cooked in fire! Alama takes you all to death now, not life. Life can still be long."

"I, too, watch things go in the hole. It is not like cooking. She says it is a door."

"It is death! You stay here with me! For Alama, the men, it is quick and with no hurt. But not you!"

"Something says to trust Alama. I do. I must. Best take the risk than live as the People to death."

"You *are* of the People! You think, speak first as one of the tribe. Have to think to speak other tongues. You are strong, tough. You know the magic of the potions. We can live happy here."

"No. I cannot. I do not think you can, but we are not the same. Alama says the door will be no more when we go. If you do not come now, you cannot come." She shifted mental gears, suddenly aware that Terry had a point on how they were thinking, and began whispering in English.

"Terry, I'm a scientist, not a witch or medicine woman. That is a great mystery. I've watched it as you have. I don't know just what it is, but I am convinced that it is a machine, not a monster. I recognized some of the monitoring devices. *They* know it's a machine, too. They're trying to figure out what it is. They probably lost somebody to that door in the early stages, which is why they're so low-key here. It's too heavy to move, and I think they're still too scared it'll blow up. And a lot of that equipment is military stuff. Not Brazilian but American. I think they've evacuated the area as much as they could and are waiting until they figure out what to do next."

"Suppose she's right. Suppose it's what she says. What's it like in there or wherever you come out? You think they'll be *people*, like Alama? Suppose it's a probe or something? Poke and study and dissect you for science. *She* couldn't tell you if she wanted to. Our one common tongue can't handle it."

"I'll take the chance. I may not like her much, but I think I trust her. And is this life any better? No doctors, no vaccines, constant dawn-to-dusk hunting and gathering to eat? You're an educated woman of the modern world."

"I dunno. I spent ten years since college batting my head against the wall, getting shot at and beaten up and worse, no real home, no personal life to speak of, working sixty-, seventy-, eighty-hour weeks sometimes just to prove I was better than any of them. And what am I? After all that I'm still a line producer, no on-air anything, doing the same job they're giving to twenty-two-year-old bimbos fresh out of school. And when I had my one shot, a year ago, a real producer's job in Washington with ABC, I put them off because they begged me to cover the fighting in Zaire. So I got stuck in this jerkwater hotel up the Congo. These soldiers came along; they shot most everybody and raped me and left me for dead. I came out anyway, but the ABC job's gone and the rumor is that I lost my nerve! Lost my nerve! And now *this* happens. But, it's a funny thing. I'm good at this. I have a family here. All women, and nobody but nobody questions my nerve! This *is* another planet, and I am already living on it."

"But your family! Your friends!"

"My parents split when I was ten. My father sits in Miami, laundering drug money and dreaming of the old Cuba. My mother spends her alimony sitting in a beach house on Dominica and stuffing white powder up her nose. I don't have a family—I have a series of Catholic boarding schools. And I don't have friends. I thought I did, but they all started whispering about my 'nerve' the first chance they got. I've had years of one-night stands and little else. Nobody is gonna miss me, even now."

Lori was shocked. "I—I never knew . . ."

"Well, we never had the time to get to know each other well. Go if you must—I pray that it is as wonderful as you dream. I don't know if I can live like this forever or not, but I realized a long time ago that if anybody was to get away without all of us getting killed, I would have to stay. I accept that."

"What? No! I want you to come!"

"You know Alama's plan. The four of us disappeared here—who knows how long ago now, but they still have guns up there. It will be necessary to have someone who can speak with them."

"But you don't know Portuguese!"

"No, but it is close enough to Spanish."

"But *you* can't go up there! You know how they're supposed to be diverted!"

"It is not the same. If it is to work, I must go with them."

"You have spoken to Alama about this?"

"Yes. She made some of the same arguments, sort of, but she said it was up to me. She knew, though, that the plan had a much better chance with me staying behind than going with you."

"You can still change your mind."

"Perhaps. Maybe I'm crazy. Maybe I will always regret this. But the fact is, I have little choice. I really believe I might wind up thinking this was the best choice for me. Time will tell."

Lori could only hug her and say, "I hope for your sake that it is."

Terry shrugged. "Besides, I can always come out someday. Be the tattooed lady, the sole survivor who lived as a Stone Age savage. The *Enquirer* alone would pay me enough, with book and TV movie rights, for me to live out my old age."

Lori sighed. "Then I better *really* see Gus."

Gus was still drugged, as was Campos, but he was conscious. After a long period of apparent catatonia, he was able to be coaxed out on occasion, although he did not recognize what had happened to him and still seemed only vaguely aware of his surroundings. He was thin and weathered; his bindings had scarred his wrists and ankles, and he looked almost like a living skeleton. It was pretty clear that he'd need a lot of help, but he was so wasted away and Lori was in such good shape now that she found she could carry him with little trouble.

"Gus, hang on," she said to him. "One more day and we'll get you out of here."

He smiled sleepily like a little child. "Big story?"

"The biggest."

"Lots of pictures?"

"As many as you can take."

He seemed happy at that. She squeezed his hand and went over to Juan Campos. Compared to Gus, Campos was in great shape. He was one very tough cookie, and he had eventually made the best of a mostly intolerable situation. After two early attempts at escape, when he'd shown enough strength to break the tough natural rope bonds and shake off the effects of a very mind-dulling drug, he'd accepted his punishment and the improbability of getting away and tried to make the most of it. He had begun to play up to his captors and to show unmistakable invitations and intent, and he'd been taken up on it by many, and one, possibly two, had conceived with him.

He'd still remained drugged and mostly bound and always well guarded, but he had managed by this to gain extra food and drink and, while weak for lack of any regular exercise, might well be able to make it on his own.

He had figured out who Lori and Terry were and found their transformations into native jungle girls highly amusing.

"All right, Campos. Listen up. The tribe wants to dispose of you, but the chief has other plans. Tomorrow your legs will be freed, and we'll try and give you a little time to exercise them. You're going for a walk, and you'll wear a gag and have rope binding your arms. You do *exactly* what you're told and you might get out of this alive. Understand? You make one funny move and you'll be full of darts with enough curare to kill you in midstep. Understand?"

He nodded sleepily.

"Do one thing right and you're home free. Be stupid and you're dead. And be aware that nobody here really cares which."

There was nothing else to do now but get some sleep and wait for the next day. It was not easy to do. *Please, God! Let Terry and I* both *be making the right decision tomorrow!*

Professor Umberto Alcazar-Diaz, visiting professor of astrogeology at the University of São Paulo, director general of Site A, and, not incidentally, also a research fellow at the National Aeronautics and Space Administration in Houston, had just taken off his glasses and settled back for a nap. He had been working almost nonstop on the lab findings dropped off by the morning helicopter, and his eyes were killing him.

Suddenly he heard a commotion among the guards outside. He was curious but too tired to see to it. "Carlos. You want to see what that's all about?"

"*Sí*, Professor," the young man replied, getting up from his bunk and putting aside the routine security report he'd been writing up in English so that his bosses at the Agency could quickly read it back in Washington. He opened the frame door on the elaborate tent with a casual air and felt something sting him in the neck. He fell back inside, out cold.

The professor couldn't see much without his glasses, but he knew that the young man had fallen, and he jumped up and went to his aid. Seeing that he was unconscious, Umberto Alcazar-Diaz opened the door to call to the guards, but he felt a sting in his neck before he could call out, and that was the last he remembered. The door came shut again.

Outside, the guards were oblivious to the happenings in the tent some twenty meters from any of them, but the armed soldier on duty in the camp was staring at something in the evening sun and had his rifle to the ready, while the other off-duty guards stopped what they were doing and tensed, guns not far away.

"*¡No tire! ¡Somos amigos simpáticos!*" a young woman's voice called from not far away. It wasn't Portuguese and was oddly structured, but one of the men at the card table made it out.

"Antonio! Hold up!" he called in Portuguese. "It's some woman speaking Spanish!"

"Woman? Women?" the duty guard called back in amazement. "Can you understand them?"

"Let me see." The Spanish-speaking sergeant looked out and saw a number of native women standing nervously in a clearing just in front of one of the few immediate stands of trees that had survived the blast. They were all naked and painted up, but that wasn't all that unusual, although he'd never seen markings quite like those before.

"*¿Habla español?*" the same woman asked. She seemed to be the leader.

"*Sí. ¿Quién es?*" the sergeant called back, not too nervous but puzzled.

"*Soy llamado Teysi.*"

"*¿Dónde viene de?*"

"*Somos de la aldea.*"

"She says her name is Teysi and that they come from the village. That must be the one about three kilometers southeast that refused to evacuate."

"What are they doing out here so late in the day and all by themselves?" the duty guard asked, not suspicious but just as curious. "I have been out here so long that even *they* look good to me."

"You never know about these natives, but the ones in the village are friendly so long as you don't ask them to leave." He turned back to the small group of women—six, no *seven* of them! "*¿Porqué vienen ustedes niñas aquí?*" he asked them.

The answer came in halting, not very good Spanish, but the message was clear.

"*Nuestros hombres son enfermos o muertos,*" Teysi explained. "*Nos mantienen lejos de hombres. Ninguno de nosotros ha tenido un hombre en mucho tiempo. Nos mantienen lejos de hombres. Somos muy solo y triste. Vemos que hombres guapos son aquí. Vamos fuera verle. ¿Le gustaríamos vernosotros?*"

The sergeant grinned. "I wonder . . . She says that they are the widows of men who are dead or something like that. That they are being kept locked away and haven't had men in a long time and that they are very lonely. They heard that some handsome men were here and snuck out to see us. I think they want to come up and see us close."

"Some of these tribes are sneaky," another guard warned.

"You ever heard of any of the tribes using women as bait? It would be dishonorable to the men. No, they are too simple and too primitive to be other than what they say. What do you think? Should we invite them up?"

"Why not?" one guard asked. "If they do not smell too bad, maybe we can have some fun. I do not think we will have to search them for concealed weapons!"

They all laughed at that.

"Yes, but what about the professor and his shadow?" another asked.

They glanced at the tent, whose door was shut.

"If they want some, let them get their own," the sergeant joked. "Maybe they will just sleep through it, eh? If they object, I will handle them."

With that, he gestured the women to approach the camp.

"Soy el único aquí que hablo español," explained the leader, a dark girl with a ring of bone in her nose. She might be hell to kiss long and hard, but she had quite a body, and her other assets were . . . outstanding.

The sergeant responded that he was the only one who spoke Spanish among his crew, too.

The lead girl gave a soft laugh. *"Queremos tocar y palpamos, no hablamos."*

"I think she says they want more touch and feel than talk, boys! Her Spanish is terrible, but what the hell! I think we will finally break the monotony of this wretched post!"

A couple of the women pointed to the guards and made comments.

"Le dicen son hombres muy bonitos," the dark one said as she reached them.

"She says they think we look *pretty,* boys!" the sergeant laughed. "If it wasn't coming from them and out here, I think I'd be insulted!"

Terry had been nervous before they had revealed themselves. Using the halting, stilted, not quite correct Spanish had been easier; it wasn't as if the soldier's Spanish was much better.

She found that she actually was turned on, too, perhaps as much by the danger as by the desire. Somehow it was poetic that here, on almost the very spot where they had been taken captive who knew how long ago, she had returned as one of her captors to break, in the most dramatic of ways, all ties to her past.

That left the guard near the equipment.

It would have been easier to have just taken him out, but they weren't at all certain they could do it without the others seeing or perhaps calling to him. He had seen and heard most of what was going on down at the camp and had come almost halfway back to see the scene he'd liked to have been a part of.

Each of the women had one of the men, but that left two women, and they came toward the remaining guard with innocent smiles, strutting to be sure he understood them. It wasn't very long before he was totally distracted and effectively out of direct sight of the crater itself.

Alama nodded. Lori again picked up poor Gus, who seemed light as a feather, and Alama pushed Campos forward. "Down *there*?" he said with amazement, but he knew how many of these women were around and knew that Lori's threat wasn't an idle one. He might escape even now if he felt he could, but he wasn't going to do anything until he was pretty damned sure he'd live through it.

The crater wall was thick with fine dust and shiny fragments—it wasn't as easy as it had seemed to get to the meteor. The ground was littered with micalike hexagonal fragments, like tiny odd geometric forms from some bizarre workshop, many of which were fairly sharp, making walking difficult. Lori almost lost Gus once, and Campos actually slipped and fell.

"Up there! Fast!" Lori ordered.

"What? On the *meteor*? We will get burned!"

"There's nothing to burn you. Do as I say. You're almost free."

Alama had already scrambled up, showing the way, and was now standing on a jagged outcrop very near where the so-called doorway to the stars was. She was keeping an eye on Campos, and she had a poison-tipped spear poised in case he tried to flee. She felt a moral obligation to take him along, but she understood what slime he was.

There was a sound of happy commotion coming from just beyond her line of sight, and she smiled to herself and thought, *Do good, my children. Get many fine babies. Farewell.*

But *was* it farewell? Where the hell was the doorway? Damn it, it had been *expecting* her! *Beckoning* her! Why didn't it show up?

Campos passed her and at that moment gave her something of a shove. It was hard to tell if he'd slipped or if it was deliberate, but it knocked Alama down, sending the spear clattering down to the bottom of the crater.

He turned, looked at Lori, struggling up with Gus, smiled, and said "*Adiós, muchachas!* I will return, and your tribe will serve me forever!" He turned his back, took a step . . .

And vanished as if a three-dimensional television image had been abruptly turned off.

"Alama! Are you all right?"

The small woman struggled back to balance. "I am good enough. Where is he?"

"He winked out!"

"Ah. It knows when to come, as always." She gave Lori a hand, and together they hauled Gus the last little bit. Alama pulled him a little, then said, "You will have to take him in with you. When I go, it goes."

Lori nodded, saw the blackness, but hesitated, looking back toward the camp.

"I know what you think. If she do that, she will make it. Now hurry! Go!"

Lori picked up Gus once more, half dragging him, and backed into the black area. As soon as Gus's feet cleared the black boundary, there was total darkness all around her and a sensation of falling.

Alama sighed and for the first time noticed the cameras. She hadn't ever seen their like, but she knew what they were. It didn't matter. Not anymore.

She stood there for a moment in all her Amazonian glory, bowed to each, then jumped into the blackness and winked out.

Terry lay on the blanket next to the sergeant and tried to catch her breath. A whole range of strange emotions and thoughts whirled in her head, and she needed time to regain control.

Suddenly, as it always seemed to do in this country, it began to rain hard, ending the trysts with a start and sending people scrambling.

Her sergeant rolled off the blanket and made for the nearby tent without even thinking of her for the moment, assuming she would follow. She, however, was used to the rain now, even this driving rain, and she got up and looked toward the crater.

The meteor was still glowing and pulsing. Maybe faster now; there was something different about it, but it was still active.

Curiosity and a certain sense of emptiness and loss overcame her, and she made for it. The crater guard ran past her, half-dressed and cursing in Portuguese, without ever being aware of her.

She reached the low point between the two sets of covered equipment and stared for a moment. *They must have made it*, she thought. *There's no sign, and we sure gave them enough time.*

But the thing hadn't died down; the black "hole" was still there, but it looked odd. It looked, in fact, like something was keeping it open when it wanted to close.

Sweet Jesus! she thought, staring at it. *Do I have the nerve, after all?*

The rain pounded all around, and she had a tense feeling that some dramatic event was imminent.

"The hell with it. I never could pass up a great story," she said aloud to herself, and ran into the crater, ignoring the dust that was turning to mud and the piles of glassine hexagonal minerals. With a surefootedness she could never have imagined before this, she made her way up the side of the meteor and to the edge of the hole, certain that it would close just as she reached it. As she neared it, she slipped, bruised a knee, then managed to get up and, with supreme effort, drag herself on top of the blackness. It felt solid as a rock, and for a moment she felt the oddest mixture of relief and disappointment.

The world winked out, and there was only blackness and a sensation of falling fast through space.

Back at the meteor site the ground started to shake, and there were cries of "Earthquake!" from the camp.

Almost too fast to see, the meteor became duller, its surface fading to a dull rock sheen; cracks appeared, and fissures opened up along its fracture points.

The glow died; the pulsing stopped, and it grew suddenly very dark at the camp.

When the scientist and the intelligence agent came around two hours later, there were no native women, no real sign of what had happened to them or why, and six very confused soldiers who had already vowed to tell no one of the night's activities.

Alama was falling in the blackness, and then suddenly she stopped, not on a cold, hard surface, as she had expected, but suspended somehow in the gate's usual emptiness, a state she could never comprehend.

And then a voice came to her. A voice speaking an ancient tongue, but the tongue of her birth, and speaking it directly into her mind.

"*Mavra! Mavra! Oh, you* must *hear me and understand! Mavra!*"

A vast scene unfolded from her memories, a scene of a huge artificial moon filled with great equipment of impossible complexity, a moon that had a name, personality, and a soul. A name so dear to her that it was wrenched back even after all this time by the "sound" of that voice in her mind.

"*Obie?*"

"*Mavra! Please! You must listen! I can't keep this gateway open long!*"

"*Obie—you're dead. You're many thousands of years dead and gone.*"

"*No! We're not dead. And yet not alive. We're shifted over, like ghosts, unable to do much but still very much here!*"

"*What? Who's 'we'?*"

"*All of us. The trillions and trillions of us of all the races that ever were except the first. All the beings from the past universe, from* our *universe, and all the beings from the universes before. We're stored, stored in the records of the Well, so we can be reused if needed. Only I am strong enough to retain some independent action, because I can manipulate, too, in a way. I've been waiting, waiting a long time until you intersected the Well matrix again and I could reach you!*"

"Obie! You're inside the Well?"

"I am part of it! We are all part of it now! We provide the templates for the re-created universe as needed. It is a horrible existence. Not even a half of living. Those—Markovians—or whatever they're called never cared about what they were doing to all those lives if a reset was needed. I don't think they ever thought that there would be *a reset. But, like the Watcher, we are mere—insurance."*

This was too much all at once. *"Obie, I—"*

"Keep quiet for once and let me talk! I can't hold this gate open very much longer, and I don't think I can contact you again until you're here, inside the control computer, where we're all stored."

"Obie—you want me to come to you? Is that it? What would I do? I don't know how anything works. I just pushed the buttons Nathan told me to push! You'd need him to help you."

Nathan! That was his name! That was the other one like her!

"No! No! Not Nathan! That is what we fear most! He will come again and he will reset, and we will have more company and be pushed farther back in the memory banks, leaving even less of what little remains of us and cutting us off completely!"

"He wouldn't do that if he knew!"

"He not only would, he will. He doesn't know it, but he will. He has no choice, Mavra! He is the Watcher! He is programmed to do it each and every time."

"Programmed? Obie—it has been a long time. I remember very little of the old days. It is coming back, but it is still hazy."

"It means that he has no choice. He was designed by the Markovians to do just one thing."

"You speak of him as if he were a machine!"

"Mavra, he is *a machine! And he doesn't even know it! Only a machine could bear these long, long lives, re-creation after re-creation. He is the only self-aware construct of the ancient ones, and he is rigidly compelled to act in only one way when he is needed. You were not on Earth before, and you had no formal educa-tion. You do not know history. All the monsters of history, all the mass killers, the armies, the hatreds, the diseases, the things that represent all evil in the universe are re-created time after time as well, very much as they were, to do their evil over and over again to the same people over and over again. He has the power to change it. He has the power to make things better, to alleviate suffering and misery and death, to create a wonderful universe for all the Last Races, but what does he do? He makes it all the same. He uses the templates. He does it over and over just the same. He doesn't even change himself. Oh, no, that would corrupt their dam-nable experiment! The ultimate evil, unintended though it was. They were so sure they were gods. They were so certain that they could not make mistakes. The reset mechanism, the Watcher, were there to ward off* natural *deviations. They allowed for randomness and chaos to possibly require that the experiment be restarted, but*

they were certain that they were right! If it goes wrong, the Watcher puts it back exactly *as it was. He doesn't want to. He fought it the last time. But he still did it. And he will do it again. He will reset the experiment, kill trillions on over fifteen hundred worlds, and the evil will start anew. He* has *to, even if he doesn't understand why. He cannot refuse, even if he learns the truth himself and believes it. It is built in that he will do it.*"

Nathan a—what was the word?—a *robot*? She could hardly believe it, yet it explained much. It was the first time he really made any sense at all.

"*He—he is already there?*"

"*Yes, but he will fight it. He will fight it until he is forced to act. Mavra—you must use that time! You must get here before him! You must act as if he were your enemy, although he is ours. You must do it for* our *sake and the sake of anybody you ever cared about back on Earth.*"

"*But—Obie? I told you—I wouldn't know what to do!*"

"*The last time he made a mistake. He thinks, he feels, he cares. Outside of his one mission, he is basically good. He recoiled at the reset and had you do it. He remade you into a being like himself. The Well will let you in if you come. And once inside, we can speak together without these limits! I can tell you what to do, Mavra! Together we can break this vicious cycle and create a better, more stable universe based on good. But you must get here first!*"

There was sudden silence, and she called out mentally, "*Obie?*"

"*I can't hold it anymore, Mavra. Come! Get here ahead of him! Let me live again and we'll have a universe that is glorious! I know how. You can do it. Come!*"

"*Obie! Wait!*"

But there was no answer; the falling sensation resumed.

Only her quick reflexes kept her from falling right on top of Gus. She rolled and got immediately to her feet and looked around at their surroundings with mixed emotions. After the unexpected "conversation" in transit, she had much to think about, and it wasn't of a sort she wanted to deal with, at least right now. On the other hand, the familiarity of the great chamber after such a very long time was beyond satisfaction; she felt suddenly *alive* again.

Lori watched in amazement as the woman she knew as Alama got to her feet, raised her arms and turned slowly around in a circle, as if drinking in the cold and bizarre view, then gave a surprisingly deep yet joyful laugh that echoed through the chamber. Lori could not, however, understand the words the tiny woman called out in that same tone of joy and amusement, said in an odd, melodic tongue like none she'd ever heard before.

"Hello, you big, beautiful Well World, you! *Mavra's back!*"

"Alama," Lori called out, interrupting the scene in the only common language the two now shared, that of the People, "when you do not come, I do not know what to do next."

She was more than a little relieved to find that contrary to Terry's fears, she was still very much alive and none the worse for wear, but she had felt very alone and exposed there, with Gus so weak and out of it.

The small woman stopped, frowned, then, abruptly all business, turned toward Lori. "Where is the other man?"

"Campos? He knows not where he is. He is very angry. He said he will find a way out of this trap. He walks in that direction." She pointed.

"He is still tied?"

"His hands."

The small woman smiled. "He will be easy to find. Do not worry."

"Alama, Gus is bad off. We must find help for him."

She nodded and knelt to examine the man, who was conscious but still clearly in something of a fog. Then she looked back up at Lori. "Take him up there. I will follow. Do not worry. He will be all right." She paused a moment, then added, "*Not* Alama. No more Alama. I am Mavra. Mavra Chang."

"Mavra Chang," Lori repeated. It sounded odd and not quite right, but the family name was most interesting. Chang. So she *was* a true Oriental! Chinese probably, with a name like Chang. But that didn't solve the mystery. If she was Chinese, then she wasn't a native of wherever *this* was. "The stars beyond the stars." The idea of some hidden, ancient group of Chinese from another planet seemed ludicrous.

That is, if this place *was* another planet. It was true that the trip had been a bizarre one, but it hadn't seemed long, and while this vast chamber was like nothing she'd ever seen before, it certainly didn't have the feel of some extraterrestrial locale.

It *was* a huge place, though. She wasn't certain if she could see the end of it in either direction. The shiny, slightly concave coppery surface of the floor reflected bright, indirect light from an unseen source, giving an illusion of great distance. On two sides of the floor was a low barrier wall topped by a dark rail, and here and there, there were openings in it so that one could get up onto whatever was beyond. With a tired sigh, she hoisted Gus and made her way carefully over to the nearest opening, and, going through, she deposited him again on the floor.

This area was quite different in many respects. The "floor" was brown and felt like padded plastic; it gave slightly to her weight, and she felt a slight stickiness on her bare feet. The barrier wall was a dark brown inside and seemed to mesh seamlessly with the floor surface. It was surprisingly wide; several people could walk abreast on it and not touch the main wall or barrier wall. It, too, seemed to go on forever.

What was almost as unnerving as the size of the place was the deathly silence, so that every sound they made seemed magnified. Suddenly they heard a terrified scream far ahead of them and then the sound of a panicked running. Lori tensed, but Alama—Mavra—seemed to find it amusing.

In another minute they could see the frantic form of Juan Campos racing toward them, and as he drew close, his expression looked as if he had just gazed upon the most gruesome of ghosts.

He would have run right past them, or so it seemed, except that Mavra stuck out a leg and tripped him.

"Campos! What did you see?" Lori pressed, nervous. This was not a man who scared easily.

"A monster! Horrible! Help me up! We can't stay here! It is right behind me!"

She looked up at Mavra, who she knew couldn't possibly have understood what the terrified man had said yet who didn't ask about it, either.

Up ahead, from the direction Campos had come, there was the sudden whine of machinery, and she felt a vibration through the floor.

Campos heard and felt it, too, and he whimpered, then turned, wide-eyed in fear, toward the sound of the noise.

Lori gasped and felt the same panic rise in her that had already mastered Juan Campos; only Mavra's cool assurance and bemused expression kept her where she was.

Seemingly floating toward them was a huge apparition, a monstrous reptilian form perhaps three or four meters high, with a mean-looking head much like a tyrannosaurus Lori had seen in museum dinosaur exhibits. The head, however, was perched on an even wider body, with a burnt-orange underbelly fully exposed, all supported by two monstrous legs that vanished below the barrier wall. It seemed to have a tail as great as its body, and gigantic bony plates extended from just below the neck down to, and perhaps onto, the tail.

Its primary coloring was a passionate purple, broken with crimson spots so thick and regular, they seemed almost like polka dots.

The creature filled perhaps eighty percent of the width of the walkway, and it was coming straight for them, riding on a section that was moving.

Mavra turned to them and said, "Tell them do not move. Just wait and all will be safe."

Lori swallowed hard but said, "Come on, Campos! Be the macho man you always wanted to be! She says don't move and nobody will get hurt."

It was clear that Campos wanted to get up and run, but he was stopped both by the fact that his bound wrists made it hard to get back on his feet and by the sheer bravado of the two women. There was just no way Juan Campos could run away from anything in fear if two women stayed.

"Very well, but if I am to die, let me die with my hands free."

It seemed like a fair request. Lori allowed herself to take one eye off the still-approaching Leviathan and gesture to the bonds for approval. Mavra nodded, and Lori untied him.

He sat up, rubbing his wrists. "What sort of lunatic place is this, and how did we get here?" he asked, both eyes still on the approaching monster.

"I only promised you'd be free," Lori reminded him. "I didn't say where."

The creature was now very close, and it reached over and down with one of its fully formed hands at the end of long, spindly arms and struck the side of the barrier wall. The belt it was on stopped moving, leaving it about ten feet from them.

Lori gaped at the thing in wonder and saw now that it wore some kind of sash around its neck and upper torso with a complex symbol embossed on it by a method suggesting some advanced technology. Around its neck and over the sash hung a thick gold chain like some kind of giant necklace, and at the end of it hung what appeared to be a ruby-colored gemstone, hexagonal in shape.

The creature looked *them* over as well, and its head shook a bit from side to side and its eyes widened. The gem on the necklace seemed to light up and emitted a very soft whine, followed by a voice that Lori heard in English, Campos in Spanish, and Mavra in her ancient native tongue. It was a high-pitched, slightly nervous voice that didn't at all match the monstrous visage before them.

"Oh, my! Goodness gracious!" said the voice. "Savages!"

SOUTH ZONE

IN AN INSTANT THAT silly, high-pitched voice with a trace of a lisp in it, the riotous colors, and the comment and tone made Lori think more of the Reluctant Dragon than of a terrible monster.

"I don't know what this place is coming to," the creature went on, speaking aloud mostly to itself. "Gentlemen, soldiers, and savages, all Type 41 Glathrielians, of all things, plus dumb animals, outright junk—what's next? This used to be such a *peaceful* posting!"

"Who are you?" Mavra Chang asked him in a normal, civil tone. Interestingly to Lori and Campos, the device on the necklace—obviously some sort of advanced translating computer—picked up her strange tongue and echoed it to them.

"I am Auchen Glough, Ambassador from Kwynn and the unfortunate current Duty Officer at South Zone. I assume you all fell in from this terrible planet called Dirt just like the others?"

"Close enough," Mavra responded. "There have been others?"

"Oh, my, yes! Not on my watch, I admit, but we've all seen the pictures and gotten the reports. First there was a party of three, then, a day or so later, two more, and now, after an *interminable* period when it's rained junk in here, the four of you. How many more?"

"No more, I shouldn't think," Mavra told him.

"Most unusual, most odd," muttered the ambassador. 'We have had new arrivals here, but never, *never* from a planetbound group. Well, I suppose we should get this over with. If everyone will stand, I will take us back to the office for indoctrination and briefing."

"He can't stand," Lori said of Gus. "He's very weak and ill. He needs attention."

"Hmmm. Well, carry him over the junction points, and that will be enough for now. He's not likely to die in an hour or two, is he?"

"No. At least I don't *think* so. But if he doesn't get some kind of attention, he's going to die fairly soon."

"Then we'd best get on with it. Come."

Juan Campos felt some of his confidence coming back. "I am not following that *thing* until I find out where I am and what the hell this is all
about!" he stated.

"If you follow me, I will tell you," the ambassador responded. "If you
don't, you will get very hungry and very thirsty out here. We are headed
for the only exit."

For now, at least, that seemed good enough.

With Gus in her arms, Lori stepped past the wall opening. Mavra was
already there, and Campos followed last, wary but more worried about
remaining alone than about going with what he still thought of as a
potentially vicious monster.

The ambassador turned around, showing that the spiny plates did
indeed extend down the tail and that the tail itself terminated in a very
nasty-looking bony spike. He struck the side twice, and the moving walkway started, carrying them back down the chamber toward the unknown.

They were barely out of sight when Terry materialized on the concave
floor.

She was a little confused and disoriented, having gone from a very
unusual encounter with the Brazilian sergeant to a rain-soaked climb
and then a fall through darkness, but she felt glad to be alive and looked
around, amazed at the size and strangeness of the place.

I don't know where this is, but it sure isn't Brazil, she thought, gaping. *Sweet
Jesus! I thought the People were weird enough, but this is getting weirder by the
minute!*

She got up, unarmed and naked as the day she was born with nothing
that wasn't glued in or tattooed on, and looked around. She was wondering what to do next when she heard sounds of what might have been
voices coming from very far away to her left. It wasn't much, and the
sounds seemed to be diminishing with each passing moment, but, naked
and unarmed or not, there wasn't much choice but to head off in that
direction. She eyed the openings and the low barrier wall and scrambled
up to the top of the nearest one.

She looked around, but the sounds were gone now, and there was an
unnerving quiet and stillness about this massive place. There seemed
nothing to do but head in the direction she'd thought the sounds had
come from and hope for the best. She was certainly exposed as hell here.

She stared off into the distance and sighed. It was going to be a *long*
walk.

* * *

No seats in the South Zone conference room seemed to be designed for humans, but there was plenty of floor space.

The Kwynn ambassador went to the front and pushed a concealed panel in the wall, and a small lectern and operating console rose from the floor until it was at the considerable height most useful to him.

"I realize that you all are very confused right now as to where you are and all the rest," he began hesitantly, trying to find the right words for what he considered the most primitive-looking bunch he'd ever known to come through. "I will try to make it as simple as I can. You are no longer on the planet on which you were born and raised. Somehow, by accident or design, you entered a device which transported you here. Never mind how—you could not possibly understand it even if you were the most advanced of races."

You don't understand it at all yourself, you old fraud, Mavra thought, but kept silent.

"Seeing you, I believe it," Juan Campos responded. "But my only question is, How do I get back?"

"Um, well, you don't. It's strictly a one-way system now, although it once went in both directions. That was ages ago, beyond any living memories and all but the most basic of our records. I'm afraid you are here to stay."

"That is impossible! If one can get somewhere, one can get back!"

"Well, you are welcome to try, but I wouldn't suggest poking blindly even around here. You would be taken as a Glathrielian and could wind up being in a deadly situation. Glathriel doesn't really have any representation here except the Ambreza, and I doubt if you'd fare too well with them, either."

"What will you do with us?" Lori asked nervously.

"If you will kindly just allow me to continue, I think I can answer all your questions!" the ambassador snapped irritably. "It is difficult enough trying to simplify this when you don't have the background to understand it. Uh, you *do* know what planets are, don't you?"

"We are not as we appear," Mavra told him. "I think everyone will understand what you say. Do not simplify anything. If there's something we don't understand, we'll ask questions afterward."

"Oh, very well. You might understand what this place is a little better if you have some basic background, though. The universe as we know it is around twenty-four billion years old, give or take a few billion. On the vast number of worlds in the vast number of galaxies that it contains, life of all sorts evolved. It stands to reason that someone had to evolve up to a high standard first. There are many terms for them, but the one we use these days is simply the First Race. They were nothing like anything you know or even I know, and we have little direct information about them. What we *do* know is that they came up just like every other race does in the natural system and reached a level well beyond where any races are today. At least a billion or maybe more years ago they reached the top. They were everywhere, they'd explored everything that could be explored, and they were so advanced, they didn't need spaceships or much of anything to move from point to point. You arrived by one of their methods of travel. We call them hex gates, for obvious reasons. They did an awful lot of things based on sixes, and the hexagon was their sort of 'pet shape,' as it were. Finally they reached the point where they were like gods, permanently linked to their machines and able to have or do or experience almost anything they wanted just by, well, thinking of it."

Lori tried to imagine what they must have been like and failed. A race so advanced that they were magic. Whatever they wished, they could have. "Where are they now?" she asked. "Here?"

"No. And yes. And maybe. That is the impossible question, and it has a lot of answers, not all of them verifiable. You—all of us—would think that such an existence would be the ultimate one, and it probably was for quite a while. They banished fear and want and desire and even death. They probably had a lot of fun, maybe for millions of years, but after a while something we might not imagine happened."

"They started losing it?" Campos guessed.

"No. They grew bored. Horribly, horribly bored. Have any of you ever played any gambling game? Any game of chance at all?"

They all nodded. "Of course," Campos responded.

"What would happen if you discovered one day that you couldn't lose. That you could *never* lose?"

"I would settle a lot of old scores and wind up owning the world!" Campos replied.

But Lori said, "I think I see what you mean. It would get boring. It wouldn't be any fun anymore. If you can't lose, then winning is meaningless."

"Yes, precisely so. And that's what happened to them. Life lost all its meaning. There was nothing more to learn, nothing more to do that they hadn't all done a thousand times, no surprises, no reason for existence anymore."

"You mean they *killed* themselves out of boredom?" Lori was appalled.

"The ancient records imply that this is indeed what started happening; others went a bit mad, imagining a higher state beyond where they were and believing that they had a way to get there—which also, of course, meant death if they were wrong. It was the first crisis they faced in so long it was beyond their memory, so they got together and tried to figure out why being omnipotent was so empty. They couldn't believe that a permanent state of ultimate happiness was impossible, since their whole racial effort had been directed for so long at attaining just that, so they came up with the only other answer they could. They figured that they were somehow flawed. That they had evolved *incorrectly.* And since their experiments showed that they would wind up the same way if they started from scratch, they decided that their whole race had evolved wrongly, that it was impossible to reach that state as the First Race. It sounds crazy, I know, and perhaps it is, but that's the way they thought. Which of us could understand their thinking? And thus came about their Great Project."

"I do not think that I would get so bored," Campos commented. "Such power!"

"Perhaps. But we are not they. As I was saying, the Great Project. Even now I don't think we can even understand it. It is very unclear. It seems, however, that a giant experiment and computer—you know what a computer is? Good!—was built the size of a reasonable planet. On it, 1,560 laboratories, in fact, were built, each containing a unique ecosystem. They took beings from worlds where life had evolved, and they in many cases altered or speeded up the evolution of those races. In some cases, what had once been animals became a thinking and dominant race. In other cases, they made things up from whole cloth, often taking variations of ideas done by others. The idea was to create and test as large and varied a selection of potential master races starting from different worlds and backgrounds, to try and design the one system that would in fact produce the heaven they dreamed of. The laboratory areas, tightly controlled to make them simulate the theoretical planets and systems they'd invented, were divided into two segments. Since about half of all life that had evolved in the universe, including apparently them, was based on carbon, half the world was given over to carbon-based life-forms. The other half, just to be sure, was given over to *non*-carbon-based forms, like silicon, even pure energy, and for forms with alternative atmospheres like ammonia and methane. A great barrier was placed between the two halves so that they could not interact with one another, and the non-carbon-based half had extra barriers guarding against one environment polluting another. The southern half was the carbon-based half. You are carbon-based, as am I, so we are in the south."

Lori was fascinated. "You mean *this* is the laboratory? And the experiment is still going on?"

"Well, this is the laboratory world, yes, but we *think* the experiment is long over with. In fact, it is somewhat humbling to realize that someone else got first crack. The *last* ones to have at it were the bottom of the barrel—still godlike creatures, nonetheless. We here now are, sad to say, among the last created. We call our current state the Last Races, for obvious reasons."

"Fifteen hundred and sixty different races?" Lori said as much as asked. "All here? Now? How big *is* this place, anyway?"

"Not huge, but big enough. Unfortunately, the translator has limits, one of which is measurement systems. From what I have learned from watching the recordings of prior entries here, I gather we are somewhat close to the same size as your home world."

"Huh? On a world the size of Earth, you've got 1,560 little worlds? It sounds like a collection of small domes."

"No, no, it's not like that. You will see."

"You were talking about those god creatures," Juan Campos put in. "You never said why they did this thing or what happened to them." He didn't like the idea of a whole race of godlike beings looking over his shoulder.

"Oh, yes. Well, it is unclear what happened, but it *is* clear that for the experiments to prove that their systems had possibilities, they used themselves."

"What?" This was getting too much for Lori to handle. "You mean they became the races they invented?"

"So it would seem. All but the control group. That one worked on the 'next phase' of evolution some thought must exist. They were also supposed to be the guardians to ensure that those who became part of the experiment might be able to back out. After a while, though, it didn't happen. The control group vanished—nobody knows where or how or why. Some say they found their higher state. Others say they killed themselves attempting it. It is unknown what happened, but one thing was sure: When they left, no pure members of the First Race remained. The First Race had been consumed by retaking on mortality in the course of its experiment. The new races that had proved themselves were moved out to worlds to begin a natural evolution. Only the last series of experiments were left, and because there was no control, they were never shut down even when they were used as the templates for worlds like the one you came from. Nobody left here knew how to get off of this world or how to get to, much less operate, the computer and machinery, so we have been here ever since, maintained by the master computer as we were, free only within the limits of its programming. You are here because all the First Race hex gates all over the universe were left switched on, all with this place as their terminus; there was no one to turn them off."

"I see," Lori said, nodding. But she *didn't* see, not totally. How did that explain this Alama, this Mavra Chang?

"Two ancient terms have come down from those past ages," the ambassador told them. "The word that appears to refer to this laboratory world seems to translate out, for no discernible reason, as 'well.' Thus we refer to this as the Well World. The operating computer that maintains it and us, and possibly a lot more, has the ancient name of the Well of Souls. Very poetic, actually."

"You said that most of them left the way we came in," Juan Campos noted, thinking of what he and his family might do with access to all this. "Then there *is* a way to get out."

"Oh, certainly. You simply have to get into the master computer and give it the proper instructions. That's obvious. The trouble is, the last race to leave locked the master computer and took the keys with them, as it were. It is likely that the gate you used—a meteor, I believe—was one of the gates used when your world was being prepared and designed for full habitation. A work-gang gate, as it were, parked somewhere after it was no longer needed. Some cosmic catastrophe jolted it out of its orbit, and it came down and snared you and the others. This happens. Some races, as I have said, who are already spacefaring sorts have accidentally bumped into them, mostly on ancient, deserted worlds once inhabited by the First Race. The gates are locally controlled, and it appears that because the races involved are the recognized designs of the First Race, it can't tell *you* apart from *them*. So it brings you here. And here you will remain for reasons I have already stated."

"You said that we were—what did you call it?—Glath something?" Lori said, thinking.

"Glathriel. Yes. You are different in minor details but basically the same race and clearly of their origin. It is understandable that, stuck here over vast periods of time, differences would fade as evolution produced single uniform races, and that is pretty much the rule in all of the hexes."

"Hexes?" Campos prompted.

"Yes. All of the experimental areas, the 'nations' of the Well World now, are hexagonal in shape except at the equator and at the poles. The ones abutting both are of more a wing shape but still manage six sides. The equator, as I said, is an impenetrable barrier. None of us could survive for long in most of the North, and few of those races could survive here. There are a couple of exceptions, but not many. We do some limited trade and contacts through this zone—there is a local hex gate that goes between them—but very little. We haven't much in common. Each hex also has its own local gate, but it will carry you only to here and then will return you back to your 'native' hex when you leave."

"Where is 'here' exactly in all this?" Lori asked him.

"South Zone. The south polar region. The 'cap,' as it were. You cannot enter this zone except by the local hex gates or the way you arrived. You can leave only through the local gates. This area was once the social control center, transport hub, you name it, of the Great Project. Now it is used essentially as embassies for the various hexes. Not every hex has an ambassador or representative here—some do not socialize much with other races—though about half do, mostly the high-tech hexes and some of the semis."

"Huh?"

"I told you each hex was an artificially created environment in which various conditions were duplicated or enforced to simulate real worlds. Resource- and food-rich worlds would eventually evolve technological civilizations. Those hexes are fully controlled by natural law, and many, like my own, are extremely developed. Others might have a very livable ecosystem but lack the sort of resources that would allow the easy development of a high-tech civilization. In those, some natural laws are, for lack of a better term, deactivated. Those are the semitech hexes, in which things like steam power are allowed, but not more advanced systems. In yet others, those with few resources or particularly harsh environments, survival itself was the primary aim and the races had to be tested on that basis. It was also thought, or so it is surmised, that these hexes might be an attempt to see if a race could attain perfection in a natural state and to explore the idea that machines and high technology might well be the corrupting influence. In these hexes only direct mechanical energy works. Muscle power, water power, and the like, but always in a preindustrial stage. Do not take them lightly. Some of them have developed amazing powers that seem almost like magic to the rest of us, although most are stagnant to a large degree."

"The other creatures—they are like you?" Campos asked.

"Oh, my, no! Only the Kwynn are like the Kwynn. Our land is on the equator west of the Sea of Storms. And yes, there are vast ocean areas and water-breathing races who live here under the same rules. There are 1,560 different races. There are some similarities among these, even some outright mixture of racial traits. A Dillian might be considered a mixture of a draft animal from Glathriel and the dominant Glathrielian race, for example. There are also somewhat similar combinations of my own kind, from cold-blooded to warm, short to tall, and all sorts of mixtures. A few are, well, unique."

"You brought up this Glathriel again," Lori noted. "Why don't they have an embassy here?"

"Glathriel was, as you might expect, a high-tech hex," the Kwynn replied. "It reached a very high level very fast, partly because, it is said, they were so violent and warlike. In ancient times a king arose who decided to expand beyond his hex and conquer other hexes, either enslaving or exterminating the natives to increase his own race. A peaceful nontech agrarian hex that had an abundant supply of food and an extremely fertile land was to be the first target, since Glathriel had become too developed to support its own population and did not have sufficient trade to buy what it needed. This other race, the Ambreza, got wind of the plot and somehow created a kind of gas, harmless to Ambreza, that would interact with the atmosphere in Glathriel and become quickly pervasive. It appears to have altered brain chemistry or some such. In quite a short period of time, before they could even realize what was happening, it reduced the entire Glathrielian population to moron level, barely more than animals. The Ambreza then moved into Glathriel and enjoyed the benefits of high technology, then they rounded up the Glathrielians, perhaps a million of them, and forced them into Ambreza, where they are used as draft animals, tilling the fields under Ambreza plantation supervisors. Of course, the only account we have is the Ambreza one, so we don't know if the Glathrielians were really that mean or simply outsmarted themselves by forgetting that nontech is not a synonym for 'stupid,' 'ignorant,' or 'defenseless.' "

"How horrible! And you said 'are used.' You mean they were genetically altered? They remain—moronic?"

"No, not at all. But they remain a rather primitive bunch, I fear. Apparently, over the generations they achieved a tolerance for the gas, which is actually a derivative of a natural marsh product. The Ambreza retained a fairly good-sized chunk of the place for their plantations bordering on the new Ambreza, and the rest was left to the remaining Glathrielians, who regained their senses over time but never more than a fraction of their previous numbers. Indeed, their population has been stable at about fifteen or twenty thousand for as long as we have valid records. The rest of the hex that the Ambreza didn't need was allowed to grow wild. Today they live in tribal groups as simple hunter-gatherers and remain very primitive. The Ambreza say that a wild plant they always considered a nuisance proved a mild drug to Glathrielians, who use it quite a lot. It has sapped their ambition as well as their fierceness and is at the center of their primitive homegrown religion. A few of the tribes are willing to work on the Ambreza plantations as farm labor, getting good-quality fruits and vegetables for their effort. Most consider the Ambreza devils, although they don't really know why. They have totally lost their past."

Lori could just imagine the Glathrielians. All the Amazonians might feel right at home there. "But isn't there some sense of guilt that these people should be so limited because of crimes by an ancestral group that nobody remembers except in the winner's legends?" she asked.

"One might say that," the ambassador conceded, "but the vast gulf of time also argues for leaving them just that way. We are, after all, the *leftovers* from the Grand Experiment, no matter what we think of ourselves now; we are not the experiment itself. They are not that much different, and no worse off, than many other races and hexes. Indeed, we have only the Ambreza legends and the fact that when Ambrezans come here, they must leave to Glathriel, not their own hex, to show that there is any truth to it, anyway. After all this time, no one is much worried about it."

"Ain't nobody gonna expose me to a gas that turns me into no animal!" Juan Campos declared. "I won't let it happen!"

"Nobody said it would," the ambassador pointed out.

"But you said we were Glath—those people! The place used to be ours and is now in the hands of these guys who steal our minds with drugs! I mean, it took the people *generations* to get used to it. We're not used to it. We breathe that stuff, and we're just big hairless apes!"

"No. It *is* true that there is a slight danger, but if you *were* going to Glathriel, you'd emerge not there but in Ambreza. Besides, whoever said you were going to Glathriel? The odds are something like 779 to 1 against it."

Even Lori was suddenly confused. "But you said that's where we'd go!"

"Uh, yes, if you were *Glathrielians*. But that is not how it works. After all, our ancestors also used this mechanism to *become* our ancestors, you see. The computer here keeps things in a careful balance. If a hex becomes overpopulated, then no babies are born until the population levels out. If a hex is underpopulated, it can't *avoid* having more children. You are not yet in the census. When you go through the hex gate for the first time, you will be detected by the master computer as a newcomer not in its data base. It will then look at that data base and see where one extra person might fit without disturbing any balances. No one actually comes through a gate as he is. You are broken down and converted into energy, and the blueprint for 'you' is sent along with the energy packet. You are then reconstructed at the other end according to that blueprint. When you go through the first time, the computer will decide where you best fit in its system, and it will alter the blueprint. Just as the First Race were converted into their creations, so will you be. Your packet will be reconstructed with a new blueprint. Your mind, your memories, won't change, but your physical, racial form will. You will become a new creature of a race new to you."

"What!" both Lori and Campos exclaimed at much the same time.

"Yes. And certain—adjustments will be made so that you can survive. For one thing, you will begin at or just beyond the age of adulthood. That varies, of course, but you will be younger certainly. The primary thinking and memory areas of the brain will be retained, so you will still be pretty much the person you are, but the more animal levels of the brain and its functions will be those of the new race, not the one you have now. Thus, you will be able to handle the body comfortably and will not be repulsed by the sight of others. It is an adjustment mechanism, although, to be sure, making the sentient *mental* adjustment to fully *accept* what you are and that you will be that way forever is easier for some than for others. The rest you will learn from the natives. They will want to know about you as much as you will want and need to learn from them."

Campos was appalled. "You mean I could walk through that thing and come out looking like *you*?"

"I am a diplomat, so I will ignore the insult. Yes, you could. Race, sex, all that will be computer-selected based on the needs of the Well World. There have always been theories that the individual does unconsciously influence the selection to some degree, but it is not clear how or why. Don't be upset. You have a whole new life, starting with coming of age. A whole new start."

"Well, I don't want it!" Juan Campos proclaimed. "I want my old life back—as *me*!"

"You have no choice, as I say. You will either walk through or, to be blunt, you will be thrown through. I assure you that the personnel here in South Zone and even the automated systems here will use force if need be."

Campos let it go, but he was clearly not at all pleased.

"The others who came before—they have already all gone through?" It was Mavra's first question in the session.

"Yes, all, and quite some time ago."

"Who were they? Can you say?"

"Not exactly. Let me punch up the records. Hmmmm. First was a very civilized fellow named David Solomon—pardon the pronunciation. He came nicely dressed, along with two companions, both older, I believe— it is not easy for me to tell much about your race—who were both crippled in some way. The male, who said he was named Joao Antonio

Guzman, could not see, as I remember, and the woman, Anne Marie Guzman, presumably a relation, had a terrible disease and could not even move much on her own. Then, a few days later, two males came through. One was definitely an older man in a uniform who said he was Colonel Jorge Lunderman of something called the Brazilian Air Force, whatever that is, and the other was a much younger man in a different uniform named Captain Julian Beard of somebody else's air force."

"I wonder where *they* came from?" Lori mused. "I wonder if they were part of the first investigative team there and got caught?"

"You would not think it would be two officers," Campos commented. "I mean, always send the privates in first is the old rule."

"Perhaps. But if they were part of the science team, it might make sense," Lori said.

"And now the four of you. And I hope that is it for now," the ambassador added.

"Almost certainly," Mavra told him. "Umm . . . just out of curiosity, is there *any* account in any of the legends of any of the races here of a surviving member of the First Race? Of somebody who could work the big computer?"

"Odd you should ask. Yes. The name is part of so many similar legends and sagas here that it is believed that he must have once been real, although whether of the First Race is not known. Come to think of it, he is always said to be a Glathrielian! Indeed, there are so many stories and legends about him that it is not totally certain if he is a real character, a composite, or a part of our extensive mythology. That is hotly debated. But there are ancient battle sites and legends in many hexes, including some that are very alien to Glathriel and very far from it, that have their own stories."

"Uh huh. And his name?"

"It varies, but there is one that is most common. It is, and pardon the translator limitations, um, let's see—yes, that's it. Brazil. Nathan Brazil."

Nathan Brazil. Mavra remembered him now. She remembered a *lot* about Nathan Brazil.

"Is there any consistency to what he looked like?"

"I'm afraid not, and any records of him that might have contained such information are apparently lost. Besides, what sort of consistency might you expect from all those races, most of whom could not tell one of you from the other?"

"Point taken. Any other specific names and people in those legends?"

"Many. I am not too proficient in such things myself; the Kwynn were apparently not involved in that, and our sagas are different."

"No Glathrielian woman hero?"

"I do not recall one, although there may be. Why?"

"Just wondering." Mavra in fact felt some vague disappointment at the news that she wasn't even a footnote. Somehow it was a little insulting, all things considered.

Still, what was irritating to her ego might actually be an asset. It would be a lot harder to move around here if one were a world-class legend who could open the Well. Others would get ideas.

Still, she vowed that *this* time they would not forget her!

"I believe," said the ambassador calmly, "that it is time to process you through. This has been a *very* busy day."

"Two favors, if I might," Mavra responded quickly. "First, are pictures of the earlier arrivals available so that we may see if there is anyone we know in them? And second, may I use your translating device to speak to the others here briefly? We have no practical common tongue, I'm afraid."

Lori, astounded at the modern bearing and sophistication in Mavra's conversation, couldn't suppress a smile. In the tongue of the People she said, "I know you cannot explain this in the tongue."

Unexpectedly, the translator issued only an echo of exactly what she had spoken, untranslated, although it clearly caught the conversation. Even the ambassador was surprised. "I've never seen one of these do *that* before," he commented worriedly.

Mavra, too, was surprised and responded, "It knows not the magic of the People."

Again, the words were echoed unchanged.

Mavra gestured toward the ambassador. "Remember," she told Lori. "It might be very good to have a tongue that cannot be known here." Lori nodded, thinking much the same thing.

The ambassador sighed. "Well, stop doing that! It's annoying! Let's see . . . What was it you wanted? Oh, yes. Pictures of the arrivals. Of course, they do not look like this *now*."

He punched some buttons on the console, and a wall screen showed three people in the very same conference room they were using. A twist of a dial focused entirely on one and blew it up to full screen. It showed a very handsome man of clear Latin American ancestry, his hair in the process of going gray, dressed in casual but clearly expensive clothes.

"That's all right. Just one at a time, thank you," Mavra said.

Another twist, and the picture showed a woman, very frail although by no means old, with short hair in a prim bun and thick horn-rimmed glasses. She was in a wheelchair.

Another twist, and a third man came into view, dressed more casually than the other but still quite well. He was a small man, not merely short but thin and wiry, with a large nose and deep-set eyes that seemed almost black and neatly trimmed black hair. He was clean-shaven, but Mavra recognized him in an instant and a clear memory of his face, his voice, his personality filled in inside her mind. There was no question, no doubt about it.

Nathan Brazil had returned to the Well World before her.

"You say it has been a fairly long time since they came through," she noted. "Has he returned to South Zone at all since arriving?"

"I couldn't say. Those records would not be here, if any records of such a visit were actually kept at all. He'd be dealing with his hex ambassador in any event."

"But does it say what they became? The man and the woman in particular?"

"Well, that would be appended here for informational purposes *if* the race has an embassy here and *if* the ambassador bothered to register them. Let me check. Ah, yes. Two of them, anyway. The first man went to Zumerbald, the woman to Dillia, and the third—well, there's no record on him, although that means little, as I said."

I know where he went, she thought, *and I know just what he looks like.*

The picture changed, and two other men came up on the screen, neither familiar.

"This is the colonel and the captain?"

"Yes, if you prefer." A close-up of the older man, the colonel, showed a gruff middle-aged man with gray hair and dark complexion but with distinctly Germanic rather than Brazilian features—not uncommon in Brazil, although Mavra would not know that. The close-up of the other showed a much younger and quite handsome man with thick brown hair and a medium complexion which suggested he hadn't been in the tropics very long. His uniform was khaki-colored and had nothing on it but a name tag and captain's bars on the shoulders.

"The older man went to Nanzistu," the ambassador told her, "and the younger went to—odd, it's not there, but I could have sworn somebody or other said he went to Erdom. Well, they don't keep a permanent ambassador here, and they're a tribal people, so perhaps they didn't do much updating. But that's the lot."

"He looks familiar somehow," Lori said, looking at the handsome man. "I wonder if I met him somewhere. I wouldn't forget a face and body like *that.* It's an American uniform."

"Well, perhaps you will remember; it might be useful," Mavra replied, then turned to the ambassador. "And one other favor," she reminded him.

"Eh? What?"

"Your translator. I would like to speak directly to my companions for a moment. A few minutes, no more."

"Well, you can do that now, can't you?"

"It would be easier if I didn't have to shout. May I just borrow it for a moment and place it right here? Where are we going to go?"

"Oh, very well." He lifted it from around his neck, and she went and took it from him. "Be careful with it, though!"

She took it over and knelt beside Gus. "Gus, can you hear me?"

"Um . . . Huh? Yeah. Been listenin' to this bullshit. Still hung over from them drugs, though. I'd swear that guy over there was a giant pink talking dinosaur."

"You're not hung over, and he's more or less exactly that," Lori assured him. "Look, Gus, you heard it. Whether you believe it or not, they're going to force us through, and who knows where or even *what* we'll be if he's telling the truth?"

"Believe it, Gus," Mavra said firmly. "But that's not the point right now. The point is what happens *after*. I'm going to tell you all right now that I will not change. I am already registered here. I'm going to Ambreza, the old Glathriel, and so did that small fellow up there. You heard my questions about the legends?"

Lori frowned. "Yes, but I don't see—"

"You don't have to. That man is Nathan Brazil. The one in the legends. The man who can work the computer that runs not only this place but *every* place. Sooner or later that is going to get out. Sooner if I have anything to do with it. And although I doubt he's even started yet, sooner or later he's going to head north, to the equator, and go inside. When he does, he is going to become like one of the ancient people that built this place. He'll go down into the guts of this world, check it out, then he'll do a reset."

"A *what*?" Juan Campos and Lori almost said together.

"A reset. It won't affect this world, but it will affect Earth. Drastically. Time, space, everything will be changed. They had few rules, those ancient people. In the end he'll bring Earth and the other inhabited planets back up to speed, to where, in our case, true humans develop. But everybody now alive on Earth, and everybody who's lived up to that point, will be destroyed first. It will all start out from scratch. I—I *think* that they'll all be stored here in the memory banks of the Well World. But all of it, everything and everyone you ever knew, will be gone."

Lori shook her head in wonder. "I'm still having trouble with *this* place. I can't really handle *that*."

"Yes, how do you know this to be true?" Juan Campos added.

"I was there the last time he did it. I—helped. It was necessary, I swear. It was do that or the entire universe would die forever, even this place. But when we started it back up, nothing was made better. Everything developed exactly as it had before. All the suffering, the misery, the evil. I don't know if this crisis is as serious as that one. I don't think it is. Lori, you trusted me enough to come this far, and I wasn't lying, was I? Trust me on this one, too. I want to stop him this time. I want to see if it's necessary to destroy the universe and reset it when a few minor repairs and adjustments will suffice. Maybe this time I can save everybody and make things a little better. I can do that, but only if I beat him inside, to the master control."

"What are you?" Lori asked her. "One of those creatures like him?"

"No. I was born on a distant planet so long ago, it doesn't matter. I was a product of the *last* creation, or re-creation, maybe. There is a certain bond between us, and I helped him then. He repaid the kindness by making me more like himself, registering me with the master control and making me virtually immortal. That is why a gate was sent for each of us. Never mind—time is short, I'm afraid, and they like this to go very fast once you're briefed. The plain fact is, I have to beat him there."

"He's got one hell of a head start," Juan Campos noted.

"Not necessarily. You don't know him like I do. He will do anything to put it off, but he finally will be forced to do it. The Well will see to that. Right now he's probably enjoying himself, finding out what's new and what's old here, and trying to think of a thousand reasons why he should not go. At some point he will also try to at least make contact with his companions. That is in his nature, and I know in any event that he has a special fondness for Dillians. It is a very long and very dangerous journey from Glathriel, not far north of Zone, to the equator."

"But you said he couldn't be killed!" Lori pointed out.

"He can't, and neither can I, but almost everything else bad *can* happen to us. This is unlike anyplace else. It is like crossing dozens of little alien worlds, each a few hundred kilometers across. Many are friendly, but others are hostile to all outsiders, and even the weather and climate change. Some of the places, and races, have great power and can be downright ugly. It is almost a cosmic joke that we both start far away in Glathriel. Almost as if, perhaps unconsciously, he *wanted* it to be as hard as possible. And whichever of us gets there first will have great power— and great discretion. I don't know if I can beat him there, but if I waste little time and get to it, I might. *He* won't go alone, and if any of the natives here pick up on who he is, they will try and insure that they are there, too. I cannot beat him alone. That is why we are having this conference. I need your help. I won't do much selling. Come to save your family, friends, and world. Come to gain what rewards I can shower on you if I win. Come for the most unique adventure of your lives. But I need friends and allies."

"But what can we do?" Lori asked her. "We don't even know where or, if I can believe it, *what* we'll be!"

"No, you don't. But any hex gate—and there is one in each hex—will bring you back here. Leave a message telling me where you are. I will find you. Do *not* try and find me. I will have to avoid Brazil, and you will not be prepared for such a journey. But I need to know where and what you are. If you cannot do it yourself, send word. I will find you. I have already had the worst done to me on this world, and I am better suited for it. Understand?"

"Yes, I think so," Lori answered, and Juan Campos nodded thoughtfully. *If she can work this thing, then she has access to all that power . . .*

"Gus?"

"Yeah, sure. Do they have cameras here? And news?"

"Some hexes do, of various kinds. Some do not. Depends on where you are. It even depends on where you are whether any sort of camera will work. As to news, that, too, varies. You will find something, Gus. The Well is random but not *completely* random. The important thing is that you will be hale, hearty, healthy, and ready to go no matter *what* you are, and soon."

"You can count on me," Juan Campos told her, and Lori looked over at him and frowned.

"I'll come," she said, "if only to make sure you don't get to like this slime ball before you get to know him."

Campos looked pained.

"I don't believe a word of this, so why the hell not?" Gus told her.

Mavra smiled. "Good. You get that word to me, and I will get to you. Do it as soon as you can. I cannot wait in Ambreza for long, and I certainly will not want to return here again once I have set out. I will give you—let's see—a month. Four weeks. That will give you enough time and will allow me to find out what I need to know and secure what I will require for the journey. Four weeks."

There was a sudden loud series of grunts and roars from across the room. The translator said faintly, "That's enough! Let's go!"

"Good luck to you all," Mavra told them, and hugged Lori. Then she picked the translator up and returned it to the Kwynn.

"I thought you were saying good-bye, not giving speeches," he harrumphed. "All right, everyone! Outside that door and to your right!"

Lori bent down to pick up Gus, but he said, "I might make it. Help me to my feet."

She did, worried about his long captivity in bonds and his weak condition, and sure enough, he collapsed. She reached down and picked him up gently.

"Damn! This is *embarrassing*!" Gus muttered.

They followed the ambassador down another long series of corridors, past rooms with strange-shaped entrances that contained a variety of horrific or mythical creatures and even worse smells and noises. Mavra could see Campos looking for a way out. Finally they reached the end of a dead-end corridor, and in front of them was a black hexagon as dark and nonreflective as the one atop the meteor.

"I still don't see how this is possible," Lori muttered aloud.

"Matter to energy conversion," the ambassador replied. "And energy to matter. Quite simple in principle, although of course none of us know how to do it. Who is first?"

"Ah, hell," Gus said with some disgust. "Does she have to carry me into that thing?"

"While there's nothing specific against it, it's not traditional to send two through at once," the Kwynn replied. "However, it is not exactly a transit point. You could literally be *thrown* in and it would not matter. You would still feel as if you'd fallen asleep, so they tell me, and then awaken on the ground wherever you are assigned."

"Well, if somebody'll stand me up and give me a little push, I'll go," Gus told them.

Mavra went over and helped Lori, and together they got the man, taller than Lori by almost a head and taller than Mavra by head *and* shoulders, on his wobbly feet. Then, together, they gave him a push forward, and he managed a step into the blackness, pitched forward, and was gone.

Lori stood there looking nervously at the gate. "I really don't know," she sighed. "I never much liked the sight of myself in a mirror, but there's a lot worse things to be than me. Now's a hell of a time to find that out, though, isn't it?" She took a deep breath. "Well, here goes nothing." And with that, she leapt into the blackness.

Mavra looked at Campos, who bowed slightly and made a gesture that could only mean either "ladies first" or "after you." She shrugged, smiled at him, and jumped in.

"Now you, sir," the ambassador told him. "Go ahead."

"I think I want to consider this a little more carefully," Juan Campos replied. "Like a day or two. Maybe next year?"

The ambassador sighed and turned as if to lead the way back, and his huge tail came around, struck Campos a hard blow, and flung him into the blackness.

"Thank goodness for *that!*" sighed the ambassador, and began the walk back to his offices.

It had taken Terry some time to catch up with the others. She made several false turns, and though she had barely avoided some terrifying creatures, the place had been pretty deserted. She'd finally found them just as they were being led away by a pink dragon.

Hearing nothing of the briefing and knowing nothing of where they were, she made the instant assumption that her companions had been captured by the creature. She followed at a distance, hoping at least to see where they would be taken. Maybe, just maybe, she could get them out.

They went through a winding maze of corridors with so many twists and turns that she was not sure if she could find her way back. *One problem at a time,* she told herself.

She found that the last corridor ended in another of those black hexes. It figured, somehow. They were being sent someplace else. There was nothing to do but follow, she thought, but at least she had not been captured, and that might still come in handy.

From the corridor's far corner she watched them disappear into the hex, too far away to distinguish what they were saying. She suppressed a giggle when she saw Campos being knocked in, though. When Campos, too, had gone, she backed off, found an empty room, and hid there until the pink dragon returned back up another corridor.

She wasn't sure what was going on, where she was, or what lay on the other side of that black hex, but if Gus and Lori and Alama were there, then she had to follow before she got caught as well. It was sure better than staying here with those creepy monsters.

Allowing a good fifteen or twenty minutes to pass, hoping that whoever or whatever waiting on the other side of the black hex would be gone, she got up and made her way down the dead-end corridor where her companions had disappeared.

She was tempted to sleep first—she felt unimaginably tired as well as hungry and thirsty—but she knew she couldn't let the trail grow too cold, and while sleep might be possible, she couldn't chance discovery by any of the weird creatures she had glimpsed earlier.

Summoning up her last bit of willpower, she stepped into the blackness.

AMBREZA

SHE SENSED THE WRONGNESS long before she came to full consciousness, a sense that something was missing or had been taken away. And yet she knew who she was. All the "pictures" were there in her mind: her mother, her father, friends and acquaintances, going to school, working, all that.

But she couldn't *articulate* those mental snapshots or put labels on them. It was as if she had words, even in her mind, only for the things that could be expressed in the language of the People. No, not even that. It was even more primitive, more basic.

Even that thought had no words to it but was rather an assemblage of mental pictures and feelings. She was aware that her thought process was far different from what it had been before, as if all the rules for gathering, organizing, and interpreting information had been suddenly and radically changed. It was as bizarre and alien a way to think as anything she might have imagined, and it seemed slower and harder to assemble thoughts or ideas and, once assembled, impossible to express them. All of her old languages had gone from her mind; they just weren't there anymore. Not even the People's. She could call up a memory or scene in her mind and remember the gist of what was said, but could not recall saying it.

There *was* a language there, but it was a strange one, composed of a series of images and concepts that seemed to form as if by magic in her mind, conveying real messages, real thoughts and decisions, but with no words.

To even be able to think such complex concepts using such a method was amazing to her, but to be unable to express even the slightest sense of them was frustrating and likely to become more frustrating as time went on. And it was *hard* to think; she had to concentrate.

What was happening to her?

She sat up, opened her eyes, and looked down at herself and was shocked at what she saw—or, more accurately, what she *didn't* see.

Her body, in fact, looked perfectly normal, but the cemented bones in both her nose and her ears were gone. It felt odd not to have them there after so long, but also it was something of a relief. The tattoos, too, were gone, and her body didn't look all that different to her than it had before the People had done their stuff. Well, that wasn't *exactly* true. Her skin seemed, well, smoother and younger, and the scars were gone—even the appendix scar—and she seemed, well, maybe a little chubby, like she'd been when she was in her early teens. And she had long hair again, the same stringy jet black hair she'd always had, but it was down well below her shoulders, almost to her ass, and it seemed to have a slick, slightly wet feel to it although no residue came off on her hands. She knew that hair didn't grow *that* fast; either she'd been unconscious a long time or something beyond her understanding had happened to her.

In fact, in spite of those differences, she felt *great*. She couldn't remember when she'd felt this good, in top condition, no aches or pains or *anything*. She felt like a kid again, although her fair-sized but firm breasts and the rest of her body assured her that she wasn't. If her mind were just working right, if she just had her language skills back, if it just weren't so hard to think complicated thoughts, she would have felt vast relief.

She sprang to her feet and looked warily around. The weight and swing of the hair felt very odd; she'd never had it this long before. Still, it was the least of her problems, and for some reason it felt *right* for the hair to be there.

She was in a stand of trees, but it was no jungle or rain forest; rather, it was almost parklike. The trees were not *quite* familiar but were far less strange than the ones of the Amazon. She felt thirsty and a little hungry, which was natural, but she also suddenly felt a sense of danger and tension, of being too exposed. All her brooding, her attempts to think complex thoughts and sort things out, suddenly vanished, replaced by something else, something that required no thought, no deliberation, but seemed in retrospect almost instinctual.

Almost before she knew it, she was climbing up a very tall tree that rationality would have said could not have been climbed. It was tall and had a long regular trunk with few opportunities for handholds or footholds, yet she went up it as if it were a stairway. Before she knew it, she was perched on a heavy limb seven or more meters above the ground below. The uncertain perch, the sheer drop, the smoothness of the trunk going back down did not bother her at all. Her sense of balance was absolutely perfect, and she didn't think the situation odd at all.

The upper parts of the tree bore a bananalike fruit; she walked over to a nearby bunch, picked one of them off, and began eating it, skin, stem, and all, all without conscious thought. The fruit had a banana's consistency but was green and brown on the outside and a bright orange color inside. It was moist and sweet and went down so well, she picked another. Somehow she just *knew* which ones were ripe and which ones to leave alone.

She did, however, shrug off the immediate feeling of contentment a full belly gave her, because the sense of tension and danger still remained. Before she could relax, something impelled her to assess her location and the lay of the land. She climbed farther up, to where she could see out in all directions with little effort.

The immediate area was a sort of park with well-manicured trees and grassy areas filled with both sun and shade. The land beyond seemed to be gently rolling, with a number of rivers or streams and a road that came from off the horizon, made its way lazily around various stands of tilled and grooved farmland and across small bridges of stone or wood, and continued off to her right through more of the same sort of country. There was something odd about where the road vanished from sight; just before the horizon there was a sort of shimmering, like heat distortion but extending along the horizon as far as she could see. But the shimmering was too steady and regular for it to be caused by rising heat —it seemed substantial, almost solid, and an image of a giant window came into her mind.

To her left a side road seemed to wander up to a huge, elaborate building with many more outbuildings beyond. The mind-picture that most matched was of a farm, but that was mostly because of the surrounding fields and the layout of the buildings; neither the house nor the outbuildings looked like anything she'd seen before. It was a picturesque, almost idyllic scene nonetheless, and she knew it; why, then, did she have such a strong emotional reaction to it, bordering not on fear but on repulsion? Had she been in the jungle so long that what once would have seemed a pleasant, peaceful, even charming scene now looked and felt so wrong? By contrast, that shimmering skyline in the opposite direction felt equally *right*; it had an emotional attraction she could feel, as if it were a magnet softly pulling at her.

Recent events had been so strange and had moved so fast of late that she felt frightened and confused by almost everything. She tried to put her thoughts in order and found that she couldn't. Putting the memory pictures together in some sort of context was hard. Worse, her experiences with the People felt more real, more understandable to her than anything she had experienced before. When she tried to recall her past life, all she got was confusion and conflicting feelings. It was all there, but it just wasn't much use. And if she couldn't think clearly and figure out what was happening to her, what was she going to do?

She went back down the tree partway until she found a thick branch that forked into two only slightly thinner ones. With a little shifting, she discovered it made a pretty solid and secure seat, shielded from the ground by branches. She was so *tired*; perhaps sleep would help. It never even occurred to her that even her second incarnation among the People would never have considered this sort of perch either safe or secure. She was too tired to mentally fight herself right now. It was best to clear the mind, relax, and sleep it off. Perhaps it would let her think more clearly.

Settling back, eyes closed, as relaxed as she could be, she felt a concept come to her by a process that was completely unfamiliar. It was hard not to have the words to use. It went against her entire cultural upbringing. Even the People were as linguistically sophisticated as they needed to be. This was completely different.

Words can obscure as well as clarify. With this way, there was never an error in understanding, if what she was trying to comprehend was understandable at all.

Was that it? Was there something she was missing here?

Was it better not to think, too? She was here, hunger quelled and safe, because of unthinking action.

No. That would make me nothing more than an animal.

Then what?

Just as you speak when you need *to speak, think when you* need *to think. Know when to speak and when not to. Know when to think and when not to.*

But didn't she always need to think?

Learn to let go. Do not fight impulses, let it go. It is when nothing comes that thinking is required. Learn to trust yourself.

Her impulse just then was to go to sleep. She did not fight it.

It was almost dark when she awoke, but rather than feeling nervous about the setting sun, she felt less afraid, more confident. It was already becoming easier for her to not impose her own old mind-set on this weird situation and to embrace this new and different inner way of thought. It was as if thoughts and decisions were debated and assembled far away in her mind, out of consciousness, then the entire set of possibilities was almost magically laid before her as a series of picture objects.

This place was not where she was supposed to be or she wouldn't feel its wrongness. The direction toward the odd farm buildings felt even more wrong; so it was toward that shimmering wall that she must go, for only that way felt right. There was also a feeling of undefined danger in this area, so the quicker she got out of it, the better.

First she surveyed the area once again. There was an odd noise from the direction of the farm, and what she saw in the rapidly waning light made her gasp and brought on an intense feeling of danger and irrational distaste that was like nothing she had ever experienced.

Two creatures were in some sort of vehicle that was making a whining noise. It seemed to sway from side to side as it turned into the small road up to the farm. The vehicle was basically an open cabin mounted to a thick oval slab, but while it bounced along, it seemed to be hovering an elbow's length above the road, with nothing touching the road itself. It was the sight of the two creatures that caused her overpowering sense of dislike.

They looked like two giant beavers, each the size of a man; one was dressed in some sort of waistcoat, and the other wore a flowered bib and a silly-looking hat with a big flower sticking out of it.

The hovercar pulled up finally in front of the house and settled to the ground, its whine now cut off. The driver with the waistcoat got out, stretched, and walked around to open the door for its companion with the hat.

Standing and walking, they looked less like beavers than like something entirely new. It was just the rodentlike head and prominent buckteeth that gave the initial impression. They were covered with thick brown hair, they walked upright on thick bowed legs extending from wide hips, and they were like nothing human.

She wanted to meet them even less than she had wanted to meet that purple polka-dotted dragon. Just as curious was her nearly instant reaction to the vehicle, the bright clothing the creatures wore, even the buildings. Somehow all of them were *wrong*. This was far more than the aversion the People had to things they did not make themselves; it was more general, as if anything artificial or manufactured by *anyone* was wrong. She did not even wish she had some sort of weapon; that would be wrong as well.

It was time to eat and run.

It was getting easier all the time to process information and think in this new way, which didn't *seem* like thinking at all but was in fact as complex a method of reasoning as the one she'd been raised on. The trick *wasn't* not to think, after all; it was not to fight doing things in your head in a whole new way.

She came down the tree almost as easily as she'd gone up it, jumping the last couple of meters and landing expertly on her feet. For someone who had no idea where she was, her sense of direction seemed absolute. She headed toward the edge of the trees, paused to take stock of all her wide-open senses, and, perceiving nothing nearby, darted out into the open and across the road to the rows of thick bushes beyond. The bushes bore some large pear-shaped, cream-colored fruits, but she never gave them a second glance. Something, more of that new inner knowledge, told her that none of the strange-looking fruits were ripe and ready to eat yet.

She began to make her way through the groves at a steady pace, pausing only now and again to check the smells, sounds, and other bits of information that the gentle breeze might bring. Darkness was falling quickly now, yet she proceeded on, drawn by some inner road map of the region. She had no idea where she was or where she was going, but somehow she knew how to get there.

Finally she came to a shallow stream that burbled over a bed of rocks. She paused, crouched, and took some water in her cupped hands and sniffed it. It smelled right, so she drank deeply, discovering a fierce but previously suppressed thirst. After she drank, she relaxed for the first time since leaving her tree, and, seeing very little around in the darkness, she looked up—and gasped.

There were countless stars up there, in some places so thick that they seemed to be a single burning mass, and parts of the sky were bathed in clouds of gold and magenta and deep royal purple, all seemingly frozen in midswirl. There were more stars than she'd ever seen before, and features out of deep space astronomical photographs right there, sitting in the night sky.

She did not have to gaze but an instant upon the incredible beauty of that vast fairyland starfield to know that there was nowhere on Earth from which it might be seen. The sight and that knowledge fell upon her instantly, generating a sense of awe, excitement, and some fear.

Alama had not lied. This was another world, far, far away from the one she had known.

And still there was that inner urge to press on, to proceed as quickly as possible to wherever it was that was calling her. Tearing her eyes away from the spectral scene, she waded across the creek and went on through the brush on the other side.

Even pushing her pace as much as she dared, it took hours to reach that shimmering boundary glimpsed much earlier from the top of the tree. It wasn't easy to see even in the bright starlight, but she could sense it, almost feel it. And yet it *could* be seen, for on this side of the barrier things had a brighter, more orderly look, while beyond it things seemed much darker. She had no sense of it as something dangerous or even unusual, but it *was* unique in her experience, and she could not be absolutely certain that it was safe.

She approached it cautiously, then stood right up to it, finally putting out a hand to touch it. It radiated warmth and a sense of thicker air, and after hesitating a moment, she thrust her right hand into it.

It passed through with no resistance, but the feeling on the other side was quite different. Hot and wet were the two impressions that came to mind, and the sense of something striking and tickling her caused her to withdraw the hand. It seemed all right, and when she touched it, the hand was wet; what she'd felt were raindrops.

Her new self did not react, but her old self caught the immediate sense of incongruity. She looked up—and, to the very boundary itself, the starfield shone in a cloudless sky. Rain? From where?

Taking in a deep breath, she walked straight through the barrier—feeling a change in environment but no resistance—and into a pitch-dark land of steady, gentle warm rain. The temperature was considerably warmer than it had been on the other side, almost steamy and very reminiscent of the Amazon jungle. The rain, however, was more subdued, which was actually a welcome change from what she'd been used to.

She turned and stuck her head back through the "barrier." Although it hadn't seemed cold to her, the shock of suddenly going, wet-faced, from a steam bath to a spring night made it feel almost frigid. It was fascinating, as if the whole world were one huge house and each "room" in the place had its own weather and climate.

She withdrew her head. It felt somehow better to be over here, even with the extreme darkness and the rain. She wasn't certain if this was because of her newfound instincts or because this region was more like the northwest Amazon, but it felt more like, well, *home.*

She walked away from the boundary slowly and carefully, almost tripping on wild, junglelike vegetation, until the soft glow coming through from the other side of the barrier was no longer visible. Suppressing as much as possible her feelings of disorientation and fear, she tried to empty her mind, relax, and let that new set of senses take over.

And slowly, strangely, she began to see her surroundings in a way she'd never seen anything before.

Ancient trees rose all around her; she saw them as a throbbing, pulsing reddish color, the leaves almost black in the inky darkness. Variations of the same red color also appeared in the bushes, other plants, even mosses, everything alive that was organic, all glowing with the energy of life.

Other spots glowed yellow and purple and orange. Smaller things mostly, but brighter, often moving either in or on the vegetation or occasionally on the ground or even in the air. The yellows were some form of reptile, perhaps many forms; the purples were small warm-blooded creatures; and the oranges were flitting insects of the night.

The ground seemed mostly to remain black close by, but not too far off it seemed to shimmer as if something transparent and yet also reflective were on top of it, distorting the colors or auras that she saw clearly above it.

Water, she realized. Mostly standing water, except for the effect of the raindrops. The vegetation was dense, but it was no jungle, and there were openings among the trees that were not overgrown. Neither was it any sort of farm or orchard as on the other side; it was random, natural . . . *as it should be.* It was, she realized, some sort of vast swamp.

Curious, she closed her eyes for a moment and found that the scene was still there. She moved a little, cautiously, keeping to the "black" areas, and saw that the scene moved with her, changing point of view as if all this were the same as the vision her eyes brought.

But she was not seeing with her eyes; rather, she was somehow seeing the essence of life in the wild and its reflections in her mind.

She began to walk slowly but confidently, using the black areas as her guide. Some points were quite small, but overall they seemed to almost form a network of paths through the wilderness, paths taking her through great beauty in a direction that seemed to draw her.

Navigating by this new second sight also became easier the longer she did it. While it hardly gave full circular vision, it was far superior in some ways to normal sight because it covered a wider area. Several times she was aware of large creatures she took to be snakes of some kind lurking high in the trees; when they watched her, they burned exceptionally bright, and she avoided them. The water was mostly just the reflective sort, but occasionally it, too, would have brightly glowing forms in it. Most of these had pale greenish tinges—fish, perhaps? That was what came to mind. Here and there would be large orange masses, sometimes in the water, sometimes out, and these, too, she quietly avoided while always looking for an unoccupied nearby tree just in case those orange shapes became a bit too interested in her. Once or twice one seemed to do just that, but none of them ever really approached her with any speed, and she never felt in real danger from them.

It was also getting easier to isolate sounds and smells and associate colors with them. As the night wore on and her journey continued, these supplemental senses and her discriminatory abilities concerning them increased greatly, the data fed and either filed or rejected automatically as it rushed in.

Crocodiles to the left, thirty feet, floating lazily . . . Two big snakes above and to the right, neither hungry . . . Colony of strange birds roosting in the tree to the left . . .

At a junction of "paths" she stopped suddenly, catching an odd scent from the ground. She realized suddenly that it was fecal matter of the sort whose smell would have repulsed her even days earlier. Now it was just information. It wasn't all that fresh, but the odor put a picture in her mind that excited her.

People!

Was it just a random dropping, or did it also have another purpose? A territory marker, perhaps, like animals used? Or an indicator of a trail to follow? But if the latter, which direction did it mark to go? Surely, if it *was* some sort of message as well as a simple call of nature, it meant to go up the path it was on. Having no other road signs to guide her, she went up that path.

There were more at other junctions, each having a different scent. That meant that these *were* trail markers, laid out by intelligence, not mere territorial boundaries that would involve the same few people—or so she hoped. Such a system, however primitive or however revolting it might have seemed to "civilized" people, made a lot of sense. Only those who *could* sense and figure them out would understand their meaning.

Was this something new, a function of this strange place, or were things like her new mind-sight and such finely honed senses of smell and hearing something all people had once possessed but had somehow lost? The latter seemed more likely; she, after all, was using them, and that meant that they were a natural part of her, perhaps sealed off in that unused part of the brain. Were those untapped parts of the human brain really unused excess capacity, or were they vestigial remains of senses civilization had made unnecessary?

What other powers might these people possess, these people who were clearly up ahead, clearly at the place where she felt driven to go?

There was only one good way to find out.

The Ambrezan came out on the porch and said, "We have just had a report from the capital that a second party has come through the Well."

Nathan Brazil took his feet down from the porch railing, slowed his idle rocking in the chair, and took the cigar out of his mouth. "All Glathrielians?" he asked.

"It seems so. Two males and two females in a single party, and then a third female later, who, it is said, evaded the alarms and security measures and went through without detection."

Brazil stopped rocking and stood up. "That's probably the one. No word from anywhere else that a Glathrielian female like myself came through here unaltered?"

"None, although it's a big place. If she didn't want to be found, it is entirely possible that she's made some sort of deal. Not everyone might advertise as blatantly as you, you know."

Nathan Brazil grinned. "You're just trying to get rid of me. I make you uncomfortable."

"No, not at all—"

"Oh, come on, Hsada! A civilized, talking, technologically sophisticated Glathrielian must awaken ancestral nightmares."

The Ambrezan stared at the little man with its big brown eyes outlined by a slight frown. "I never know when you are joking."

Brazil chuckled. "Don't worry about it. As soon as I can link up with her, I'm out of here. Promise. I have friends that are a very long way from here that I promised I'd see, and I already feel guilty I haven't done it yet."

The truth was, he didn't really *want* to see either Tony or Anne Marie, even though he wouldn't mind a trip up that way. He really didn't want the burden of getting the two of them together as they were now. Deep down, he was hoping that each, being now healthy and hearty, and both, to his relief, in rather comfortable hexes, would use these months to settle in and build new lives and new attachments. It wasn't as if he'd forced either or both into coming, after all, or as if they wouldn't be dead by now if they hadn't chosen to come through, but if ever a match of love and devotion had been made in heaven before, he hadn't seen it in all his long life. He *could,* of course, fix them up if he went up to the Well, but he didn't really want to do that just yet. He felt no sense of urgency, and he wanted to stay here a while and enjoy the difference.

The Ambreza had not initially been all that thrilled at his appearance, and he knew it—they hadn't reacted much differently the last time or two, either. But they were civilized in the extreme, suckers for a good story, and, well, he'd been *useful* to them, working for a few months helping them redesign rather than merely repair and upgrade their failing irrigation system, saving them a lot of investment and foreign involvement. Now he had clothes specially made to his design, some local money, and chits for a decent supply of the prime Ambrezan export, tobacco, with which to make his way anywhere he wanted to go. He lacked only Mavra, and he very much wanted to find her, see her, have things *explained* to him. It would be like old times, and *this* time he'd teach her the full operational details of the Well—as soon as he got there and could remember them again—so he might not ever have to carry this burden again.

He knew that last was selfish, but damn it, it was hard to be all that sentimental toward somebody he could hardly remember and last saw maybe twenty-five hundred years ago.

Maybe now it was time for a reunion.

He walked into the house and back to the communications room. The Ambreza had quite a sophisticated setup, able to call just about anywhere they had people in what was now Ambreza, the high-tech hex that very long ago had been the common ancestral home of the Terran races.

The furniture in an Ambrezan house was *not* made for his anatomy, but he could make do. He sat at the console and dialed in the communications ministry in the capital city of Khor.

"Oh, Solomon—yes. The group that came through. We had the ambassador run a systems check for placements, but it was inconclusive. However, we are certain that the last one, the female who didn't clear entry, came to Glathriel. We registered a surge in section—um—B-14. Yes. Agricultural district up north not far from the border with Glathriel, which is where you'd expect a deposit, matching *exactly* the time of Zone entry. It's always easier to track an individual than a group, although this is hardly an everyday thing. In fact, counting you, I can remember no other but this one even in the records."

"All right. But she made no contact with the locals?"

"Not that we can determine. A search of the area using the local manager's dogs indicated that she went south into Glathriel. Beyond that we can't say, since it's too much of a mess in that district to do decent tracking, and frankly, it's far too much trouble for something that is your business, not ours. As long as she's gone to Glathriel, she's not our problem."

He frowned. "Gone to Glathriel . . . Well, I suppose that if she didn't want a lot of immediate attention, she might head for the coast strip there. I don't suppose that there's any word from them."

The technician was not terribly patient with this imposition. "Look, Glathriel is a nontech hex. No communication works except the direct kind, and no vehicles work except animal power. The people along there are mostly a religious sect that's antiprogress, and we and they don't talk much to one another except when they come south twice a year to sell their crops. It might be weeks, even *months* before we hear any news from them. I admit that a talking, civilized, and sophisticated Glathrielian might cause quite a stir, even some sort of religious crisis among them, but it's still not something we'd hear anytime soon."

Brazil scratched his chin and thought about it. "I don't know. If she's heading toward them, it'll almost certainly be ones near the border. I suspect we'd hear pretty fast for those very same reasons." He sighed.

"Okay, that's all you can do now. I'll take it from here. Thank you very much."

"Very well. Out," the comm tech responded curtly, and switched off.

Nathan Brazil sat there a moment trying to decide what to do. Finally he got up and went over to a far wall where a map of Ambreza and part of Glathriel was tacked to a cork board.

B-14 . . . There it was. Not that far from the Ambrezan strip in Glathriel. A country road was marked as heading through the district toward that point, so that was the logical place to start. It looked to be maybe three, four hours drive if he could bum one or a day on horseback if he couldn't. It was certainly worth getting off his duff and going after her. He had no doubt that it was Mavra Chang; it was inconceivable to him that any of the new entries would wind up Glathrielians. He'd pretty much seen to that long ago.

He turned and saw Hsada standing there looking sternly at him from the doorway.

"No, you cannot borrow the car," the Ambrezan told him flatly. "You will be going into Glathriel, and I would have to send somebody down there and lose a day getting it back. However, delivery trucks go through town all the time, and some may have stops at or near there. I *will* get someone to drive you in, and from there you can make your own arrangements."

Brazil grinned and shrugged. "Good enough. What can I say?"

"Say good-bye," responded Hsada. "And don't forget to settle your rent through today before you leave."

It turned out that settling the rent was more of a problem than finding a ride to near the border. Hsada was a very hard bargainer and was more creative in finding extra charges to spring on him than anybody since that lowland Scotswoman at a bed and breakfast about a hundred years ago. Extra sheet charge, indeed.

There were only five cities plus the capital worth the name in Ambreza, and maybe forty small towns spread all over, but the two basic occupations of those in the country were raising crops for export and truck farming. Over the centuries truck farming had become quite sophisticated, with regular routes and a whole guild of middlemen doing the shipping to and from the markets on a daily basis. Tobacco was grown best in the southeast; the southwest was better suited to longer-growing but high-demand produce like subtropical fruits due not to location but to a strong warm current off the Gulf of Zinjin that came in very close to shore and created a more or less subtropical pocket. This, of course, had been allowed by those who had created the hex; weather and climate were not of the natural sort on *this* world, but when they saw that the water hex of Flotish had such currents designed in, they simply made use of them.

By that evening he was within a few kilometers of the plantation nearest the designated spot, and he stayed over with some very surprised and curious farm supervisors that night so he'd have the full next day for the quest. While the field bosses were somewhat taken aback at a glib Glathrielian wearing clothes and speaking like them, they were suckers for a good set of stories and even worse suckers at cards and dice.

The next morning he saw the first Glathrielians he'd seen since—well, a *very* long time ago. He had forgotten their rather exotic "look," a unique yet homogenized blend of just about every racial type on Earth. Being of a near uniformly brown skin, with a variety of Oriental features yet with brown, black, and reddish hair was only the beginning of it. One could look at anyone and see suggestions of somebody one thought was familiar, yet the entire amalgam was something totally unique.

This time, though, they also seemed decidedly, well, *odd.* There was no other way to explain it. True, their tropical hex didn't really require clothing, but these people wore *nothing.* Not amulets or paint or markings of any kind, nor earrings, nose rings, bracelets, anklets—nothing at all, men or women. They also seemed to let their hair and, on the men, facial hair as well simply *grow.* He couldn't understand why some of them didn't trip over all that hair or strangle on it. Some of the shorter women seemed to have to wrap it around themselves to keep it from dragging on the ground, and he had never seen men with hair that long. Hair that, oddly, didn't seem to tangle or get matted. Had *he* done that? He didn't remember doing it, but if he'd altered them significantly, the computer would have filled in the logical items which he'd left out but which might be required for some reason.

Other things also bothered him. Their remarkable silence for one thing. Watching them, it seemed at times as if there was some kind of communication going on, judging from the gestures, the playful actions, the coordination they exhibited, but aside from some grunts and occasional laughter they said nothing.

He wondered if they were at all aware that they now worked the fields that their distant ancestors had once owned. He watched as they seemed to have some kind of silent prayer vigil before starting to work, then they went to it, picking fruit and stacking it in neat piles every few bushes.

"They have an almost unnatural ability to figure out just which fruit is ready to be picked," one of the Ambrezan supervisors commented to him.

"But they don't fill baskets or containers," Brazil noted. "They just pile it all neatly."

"They won't touch them. No Glathrielian will touch *anything* manufactured, even a box. They even make several trips carrying their 'pay,' which is a small percentage of the crop, back to their home in Glathriel in their arms."

"What about that home? Don't they have some sort of village or whatever with shelter?"

"No, they don't. Not as we understand it, anyway. They *do* have tribal lands that they consider their home, but the few structures are very crude and very basic and formed entirely from gathered dead wood and dropped leaves. They don't build as such. The few crude structures tend to be shelters for the babies and for bad weather. Mostly they sleep either out in the open or in hollow trees, some caves, and shelters formed from fallen logs and the like. They don't even build or keep fires, although if a thunderstorm comes along and sets something off, they might use it until it goes out. They don't kill unless something is trying to kill them and there is no other choice—and whatever *that* unfortunate animal is, they then eat it raw that same day."

"They seem to eat okay from what I can see," Brazil noted. "The women seem to range from chubby to fat, and the men are built like bricks."

"They eat a complex variety of things, some of which we, and perhaps you, would find disgusting, but it seems the perfect balance for them. They make great workers, though. No complaints, virtually no mistakes, and they won't touch, let alone eat, anything they haven't picked themselves. They're always good-humored in a childlike sort of way, and they're so placid, they don't even swat flies that land on them."

"How'd you ever get them to work for you?"

"It's been this way since long before my time or my grandfather's time, too," the Ambrezan supervisor replied. "Only a few tribes will do it, but they've been doing it forever on the border plantations and, I think, along the Zinjin Coast strip. The vast majority live way in the interior, which is mostly swamp and jungle with some volcanic areas. We used to try and survey them once upon a time, I'm told, but they can vanish like magic, and it just wasn't worth the time and trouble. The fact is, we know very little about them beyond these border tribes."

"I know about that," Brazil told him. "They asked me to do a report on them if I went in, figuring that since I'm related in a way to them, I might be taken as one of them if I went in."

"Well, that figures. You gonna go?"

"Looks like it. I'm after another like myself. A female. Very small and very thin—even smaller and thinner than me. You haven't seen or heard much about somebody like that, have you?"

"Heard they was looking for somebody like that down the road apiece, but haven't seen or heard a thing myself, no. Of course, I can't tell any of you apart much, frankly, but I think I'd have noticed a female smaller and thinner than you, that's for sure." He sighed. "Well, if you're gonna find her, you got maybe two weeks."

"Huh? Why's that?"

"Oh, they haven't got any families as such. You can see the same kid with a different parent most any day. It's all communal. That's 'cause, I think, they have one short period of a couple of days when all the women get fertile all at once and all the men can think of nothing else and they go at it, breaking only for sleep, for up to four days. Then they don't do it anymore until the next month. Lots of animals like that, but I know of only a few races here that still have that old mechanism. They say we did back in prehistoric times or whatever, but not since."

The idea shook him. *Just what did I do to you, people?*

It was coming back to him now in bits and pieces. When he'd come through that time off the spaceship, he'd discovered that the Ambreza had literally reduced the Glathrielians to animallike status. When he'd done his work in the Well, he'd fixed that so there'd be a slow but steady generational rise back to normality through providing immunity to the Ambreza gas—but in a nontech hex, which, he'd guessed, wouldn't threaten the Ambreza.

He'd been wrong. The next time through, he'd caught wind that the Glathrielians had gotten to a point where they knew the legends and stories about how they'd been kicked out of their ancestral home and brought low and were getting *very* curious about Ambrezan technology and doing a lot of work on natural chemicals themselves. The Ambreza leadership had been getting nervous even then; the seeds of potential genocide were being sown even then as the Ambreza's imaginations started coming up with potential attacks far worse than the Glathrielians could have managed on their own.

So while he and Mavra had reset and checked out the system, he'd made other changes to ensure that this would all die down. He'd removed the translation abilities from the Glathrielians so that they could only communicate among themselves, and he'd put a blocker in there so that no other language but theirs could get through. If they couldn't reconnoiter and spy on their hated enemy, they wouldn't be much of a threat. And he'd made what he thought then were some minor physiological changes to ensure that they adapted nearly perfectly to their present hex and would not be as comfortable in the one that was now Ambreza or lust for it so much.

But *this*—these people, this totally primitive way—was not what he'd had in mind at all. He'd sought only to protect them from slaughter, not to reduce them to pre-Stone Age levels. What had the computer imposed logically on them that flowed from his premises? Just how badly had he goofed?

What have I done? he wondered again, watching them. This was all he needed, he thought sourly. A hyperdose of pure guilt right now. I'm not going to keep ying-yanging these people around forever for some sin of ancestors even I can't remember, he vowed. If I made a mistake, this time I'll correct it, but, beyond that, from this point on, as much as I like the Ambreza, I'm not going to keep these people down again. If any new adjustments need to be done, by damn, I'll do 'em on the Ambreza for a change!

He stared at them as they worked, trying to figure them out, and over a period of time he got a sense that he wasn't seeing the whole picture, but he couldn't put his finger on what was disturbing him that he hadn't already quantified.

And then he had it.

There were no lame, no crippled, not so much as a limper among them. Well, they might leave all of those home. But no, it was more than that. In the kind of rough environment and natural way they lived, their creamy brown skins should have the signs of all sorts of incidental injuries, scars, and whatnot. There were none. Every one of their hides looked as smooth and untouched as a baby's bottom. Not a scar or a scab among them, and some of them weren't young.

And that was impossible. It was something that just might not occur to the Ambreza, thankfully, but it was damned impossible. Something that they hid from everyone except themselves was definitely not kosher about the Glathrielians. Now he *had* to go in. Mavra was still the object, but he very much wanted to know just what the hell was going on there.

His strange appearance, so like them and yet so different both in features and in the fact that he was clothed and having a conversation with Ambrezans, naturally drew curious looks from the Glathrielians. No, it was worse than that. They looked puzzled as all hell.

Finally, one young woman came over to him a bit shyly but with definite purpose, a big smile of friendliness on her face. He smiled back at her, and she put out her hands, and after a moment of trying to figure out what she wanted, he put out his and they clasped hands.

Suddenly he felt a strange, slightly dizzy sensation, and at the same time she gasped, let go forcefully, and backed away from him, a look of near terror in her eyes. As he followed her with his gaze, she broke and ran not toward the other tribespeople but away, at top speed, in the direction of the border.

Now what the hell? was all he could manage.

The others were now also staring at him rather warily but just keeping their distance and working the grove. He decided to press on down the road and pick up the trail.

The old Ambrezan couple who owned the plantation square in the middle of section B-14 hadn't seen or heard much of anything, and they'd been very surprised when they'd gotten the call from the government, but they'd let the dogs out and had them sniff around, and sure enough, they had picked up some odd kind of trail in a grove of trees and followed it all the way to the border. It was quite puzzling to them; there were so many Glathrielian scents around that it would have to be something outside the dogs' normal experience to have them take off like that.

Nathan Brazil nodded but did not explain. If it were Mavra, and it certainly looked like there was no other possibility, she would smell of many alien things but little or nothing of the Well World.

"You ain't gonna track her with no dogs in there, no, sir," the old Ambrezan told him. "They get in Glathriel a ways, and they go nuts. Can't pick up anything—take you around in circles, they will. Horses and mules might work in some parts, but if you're goin' in here, you're goin' right into the Great Swamp. Runs for half the hex, it does. Lots of water, killer snakes, vicious swamp lizards, and a lot worse."

He shrugged. "The Glathrielians seem to do all right in there."

"Well, maybe. Maybe it's just 'cause they have enough young to keep pace, too. Ever think of that? You don't see no old ones, that's for sure, and as peaceful as they are, they might just figure the thing's got a right to eat 'em. Or maybe they smell as bad to the animals there as they do to us—no offense, son. But you take a riding or pack animal in there, all you'll do is give them vicious brutes a real feast and waste a good animal."

"I'll walk," he told them. "Been a while since I carried a full pack, but it won't be the first time. *She* walked in there with nothing at all, and it's only been two days or so. I might be able to pick up something. I was a pretty fair tracker once."

"Well, if she ain't got eaten, you might have a chance," the old gent admitted. "But I still wouldn't like to go in there far. That place like that other world they say you come from? Might make a difference."

"No, not much. Parts of it are like that, but not the parts I like. Actually, my home's more like, well, *here*."

And it *was,* too, he realized with a start. Maybe that was why he liked Ambreza and the Ambrezans so much. Given the same hex and a jump start, they'd either managed to develop a *very* Terranlike society and culture or, more likely, had co-opted parts of it, copied from those they had overthrown. Designed and bred for the hex they now found loathsome, the ones who'd been forced to take *their* place had come up very differently indeed, while the Ambrezan culture was, after all these thousands of years, virtually unchanged. Static. And they *liked* it that way.

The Ambreza of their original hex had been creative, aggressive, clever enough to meet a threat when they were woefully mismatched. Moving here, they'd done almost certainly a far better job of managing the hex, but they'd grown soft, stagnant, and complacent, devoid of the daring and creativity that their remote ancestors had had in abundance. They just weren't really in their element here, and they'd spent thousands upon thousands of generations treading water, never changing or adapting beyond what they had to do. Even he felt that comfortable sense of time standing still here, and in ways easy to take, with their horses and cows and hunting dogs and country manners.

What had the Glathrielians become in the Ambrezan hex? A tropical swamp and jungle was also an invitation to stagnancy for Terrans, and on a much more primitive scale. Even when the magic of technology was allowed to work, the regions of Earth covered by such unlivable areas had tended to keep the inhabitants in the Stone Age. He'd seen it in the Congo, the Philippines, the Amazon interior again and again, just as they'd remained rather primitive in the arctic regions, too busy surviving to go any further until technology came to them or, in more cases than not, was forced upon them.

And yet, even there they'd done the best they could with what they'd had. They'd become farmers where it was possible; fishers near seas, lakes, and oceans; hunters and managers of game, with social organizations of varying degrees as geography allowed. From the spear and blowgun to the igloo to vast irrigation channels, they'd adapted and innovated their way to some sort of culture.

Glathriel looked all the more an enigma because of it. Even the last time Terran types had managed all this, until they'd become a threat to others and he'd set them back a bit. Had they lost once too often? Had they given up as a people?

Or had they adapted and innovated in ways none on Earth had ever done?

What had the girl seen by holding his hands, and how had she seen it?

Had he perhaps set up the evolutionary mechanism and now forgotten that he had done so or, even more disturbing, done it without realizing it?

He allowed the old man to take him all the way, down to the stake in the ground just before the hex boundary where they'd stopped the dogs.

Bidding the old Ambrezan farewell with thanks, he adjusted the backpack and walked into the new Glathriel.

It was, he thought, a nearly unimaginable feeling to enter a hex populated by people who looked very much like him and somehow feel that he was going into territory more alien than some of the strangest hexes on the Well World.

GLATHRIEL

TERRY PEREZ HAD BEEN walking through the dense, wet jungle for several hours. She didn't have much of a time sense anymore, but the night and the strangeness of the place gave her no clues as to even immediate time. She *did* realize that she should have been exhausted by now, but she wasn't. Perhaps it was expectation or the creepiness of the surroundings that gave her the extra energy, but she knew she couldn't stop until she'd reached wherever it was that was calling her.

Certainly the signs were fresher now; she was on a main trail headed straight for a relatively large gathering of people, and that alone would satisfy her. She didn't know what they would look like or be like, but fears of alien monsters were far from her thoughts due mostly to this place. It was too much like the Amazon, right down to its animal inhabitants, to feel alien, and without that eerie, overfilled sky it might just have been a different part of the same forest she'd been living in for months.

In fact, she realized, without that bizarre kidnapping and the time with the People, she would have been totally unprepared and unequipped to deal with this and would have been back on the ground where she had "landed" in a sheer panic right now.

As it was, in the darkness of the swamp, she neared her goal.

They had not come to help her, but they appeared to be sitting there waiting for her to arrive. Two men, appearing eerily alien to her second sight, stood there in purple outline, looking like some skewed infrared or UV picture; both women had fuzzy, ball-shaped violet colorations below their breasts that neither the men nor she shared. Nor did she have the one thing that set them apart not only from herself but from the glow of animals as well.

They all had shimmering soft, pale white auras outlining themselves. For the first time she really felt nervous and more than a little awkward. The shapes *seemed* human, at least from what she could see in the dark, but just who and what were they?

She stopped, and there was the inevitable uneasy pause as each side waited for the other to make a move. She watched as, after a little bit, they clasped hands and saw in some surprise that the pale white auras broke and seemed to merge into a single glow. Finally, they seemed to make a silent decision, and the man on her far right raised his left hand and beckoned to her in an unmistakable gesture. After a moment's hesitation she came forward, butterflies in her stomach, until she stood right in front of the man, close enough to note that he had bad breath and sorely needed a bath.

He reached out and took her hand in his, and the white aura coming from the group broke and then ran slowly up her arm and around her. When it had completely enveloped her, she felt a sudden shock to her system, and then she felt their collective minds rushing to hers, engulfing her as the aura had engulfed her body. There were no words because words were not necessary. In that instant they were a part of her and she was a part of them; they *were* her and she *was* they, individually and collectively. In that instant she was male and female, Terran and Glathrielian. All that she was, all that she had ever been, they knew because they were she; all that they knew, all that they had ever been, she was, because she was all of them.

No introductions or explanations were required; the exchange of information, data, backgrounds, and points of view was instantaneous and total. How long it went on she did not know, but it wasn't long, for it was still dark when they separated and she was again alone. Alone but not the same.

Not quite a Glathrielian, although she knew exactly what it meant and felt like and was as comfortable here as any native. But because of that knowledge she was no longer quite a Terran, either. After she had shared minds, what was the use of names or most of the human foibles that had caused humanity to war and conquer and hate and become so prejudiced? If evil was rooted in a lack of communication and understanding, these people were without it, although they were far too knowledgeable about their world for it to be considered a new Eden. They had eaten of the Tree of Knowledge of Good and Evil, and they knew the difference. It just wasn't the difference most others thought it was.

The point was that she could never hide anything from any of them, or they from her. The idea would have disturbed her before she had touched their minds, but it could not now.

She understood perfectly what was going on and exactly what her role in it would be. She was content with that.

The region hadn't always been a swamp.

Sometime, in the times hidden by mists forever, it had been a far different sort of place. Not that its climate hadn't always been hot and muggy, but once these were actually agricultural districts in which the Ambreza raised rice and other grains, controlling the influx of water with a grand complex of locks, channels, dams, and movable dikes so intricate and so ingeniously perfect that under most circumstances they operated themselves with almost clockwork precision, leaving the designers only to do maintenance and harvest the crops. The Ambreza were equally comfortable on land or water then and pushed the art of the purely mechanical almost to its limits.

Now, after countless thousands of years of pure neglect, one could not see a sign of that once-great race of builders and innovators. What might yet be preserved was far down, under layers of rock-hard sediment, volcanic ash, plant spores, and the decomposed remains of innumerable animals and insects.

It was a dismal place now, overrun with dirty water and fallen, moss-covered logs, hidden under a blanket of high trees reaching for the light under skies more gray than clear, leaving the areas below in a twilight of swirling mist that hovered below the branches like a living thing.

It was hard to believe that such a place could ever be tamed, yet the Ambreza had done it, and they were not alone; back on Earth the Kingdom of the Congo had conquered just such a hot, steamy junglelike swamp ten times this size and had built a thriving civilization until slavery, disease, and finally a harsh colonial hand had reduced the population to a point where the control of the land could not be maintained and it had fallen rapidly back to this sort of state. In ancient Cambodia they had tamed such a place so thoroughly that they'd built great temples to their gods in the midst of it, not knowing that they were actually building those temples to their own genius.

The last time Nathan Brazil had been anywhere near Glathriel, the inhabitants had been slowly embarking on just such a taming project, and they were the distant ancestors of the people who lived in this gunk now. What had happened to them? Certainly, this time he'd found nothing in the Ambrezan records or stories to indicate that the former natives had done anything. Nor had it been a quick change, even after his last intervention. All the evidence was that it had been slow, a turning inward, a rejection of what might be, a withdrawal into themselves that spread like some plague from border to border.

What had it been? What had changed them not only mentally and philosophically but *physically,* as was clear, reverting them to some animal base for reproduction, supplanting even the concept of family in their culture? What now clearly healed them so quickly, a necessity in such a harsh environment for survival, yet made them so passive that they would not even build permanent shelters for themselves or make much of anything with their own hands? What, in fact, had happened to their language, which, as was typical of Terran-evolved tongues, had been quite rich and colorful? He hadn't taken *that* from them, just their ability to understand *other* tongues. Yet the Ambrezans were adamant that they barely had a language at all—a few dozen sounds, many imitative of native animals here, with very basic meaning, and rarely used even then?

Yet they held hands and silently prayed. To whom or what?

He refused to believe it. Something inside him told him that the impression was false. Terrans adapted. They were among the best adapters in the universe. Why, just starting from the plains of Africa and the Fertile Crescent they'd settled the Arctic and the jungles and vast deserts and every kind of climate and unlivable place in between.

As he trudged into the wet jungle, Brazil kept at the puzzle this place represented. Had they adapted *too* well? No, no, that was unheard of, ridiculous. But the last time at the Well he *had* done some design tinkering to make this hex their own, to become as if this, not the other place, were what they were originally designed to survive in.

That was what the Well World was, wasn't it? A gigantic set of laboratories, each with a race designed for the place or a place for the race, set together and wound up and allowed to run their course to see just how viable race and setting really were?

She had held his hands . . .

Wait a minute! He'd put them here last time to adapt, and they'd done just what the damned Well World was supposed to let them do.

They held hands in a circle and prayed . . .

They'd adapted.

They'd become something different, gone off in a whole new direction. Whether it was a good direction for people, or bad, or stagnant wasn't the point. But that was in fact what had happened; he was sure of it.

The human race had trotted off and become something else.

Now the job was to find out what the hell that "something else" was.

That, of course, and find the ever-elusive and apparently deliberately evasive Mavra Chang.

It wasn't easy to find traces of her, but it could be done. The twin keys were in the eternally wet ground between the marshes that formed a set of complex trails. Some of those trails retained the impression of footprints for very long periods, and one set of prints, appearing infrequently but often enough, was a bit different from the rest. The way this one person walked was different; the prints of the others showed that they walked in a more confident manner, emphasizing the forward area of the foot, while hers showed the full foot coming down with a slight emphasis on the heel.

Clearly, she wasn't at all unfamiliar with this sort of climate and terrain, but that, too, fit. Assuming that the meteor had finally struck where they'd said it would, it would have come down somewhere deep in the Amazon. What Mavra was doing there was a total mystery, but that was the way the master computer worked when it had to, and he knew that it had come for her as well as himself. The method had been a bit crude yet effective, but the meteor had come in only one way, and it had fragmented over Rio and then struck deep inside.

He wondered if she was doing smuggling or drugs or something or if she'd gone native. It didn't matter. In fact, it explained why she had headed down here almost immediately if, as now seemed clear, she wanted to avoid quick discovery and, maybe, him. She *had* to know that he was here.

Or did she? He'd been pretty far gone when he'd fallen into a hex gate on some far-off world so many lifetimes back. Hell, he'd been through it more than once, and even now he couldn't remember her face. Until quite recently he hadn't even remembered her name or anything about what she looked like.

Could it be that she no longer remembered who or what she was and had headed here because it was familiar?

If so, she was going to be in for a rude shock if what he now suspected had happened here actually had. This hex was really going to hell in a handbasket, that was for sure. His previous experiences here had been along the coast and once on the extreme southern savannas between the volcanic ranges, but *this* was a mess. The water had come in to great depths in some places but was shallow in most, and creatures either had managed to come in here or had evolved from more benign forms to some unpleasant types.

The big reptiles that floated in the water and sat along the banks, for example, were very close to alligators or crocodiles, but not quite. They had a leaner, smoother, more primitive look to them, and they seemed less like crocs than some dinosaur relative.

In fact, the whole area reminded him of the Age of the Reptiles before humans had developed. The trees, the giant ferns, the mean-looking fish all seemed from some ancient era. The insects looked pretty modern, the only difference being that some of them were pretty damned big. Mammals were around, but most were small, and it seemed like the smaller ones had tempers worse than the protocrocs while the bigger ones were constantly nervous.

There *did* seem to be several varieties of small monkeys, or maybe protomonkeys would be a better description, gathered in packs and hanging out in the trees, and there were other small tree dwellers that seemed squirrellike. There were birds of all shapes and sizes, many with very effective natural camouflage and others that would stand out against anything. Some of the creatures weren't birds or mammals or anything else, exactly. One of these looked like a medium-sized fish that had rows and rows of teeth and occasionally leapt from the water and *flew* on multiple wings.

Great. And unless I get lucky, I get to sleep with these critters tonight, Brazil thought glumly. He wasn't worried about being killed—*that* was never a worry—but being attacked was always a possibility, and he didn't like the thought of being savagely chewed up. It took up to two years to grow a new hand or arm or leg, even longer for scars to vanish, and he was not immune to pain.

The idea that this place might be home to thousands, maybe tens of thousands of people wearing nothing at all and living and sleeping in the open was difficult to accept. It was pretty easy to see why the Ambreza never saw any old Glathrielians.

He made good time in spite of his reservations about the wildlife and the thick mud that formed the only safe path. He realized that the paths seemed to follow a roughly logical plan and wondered if they had somehow been built up or maintained based on those ancient Ambrezan canal systems, but it seemed unlikely. They'd be many meters down by now.

It bothered him that he saw no signs of humanity other than the prints. All those Glathrielians who came and worked the plantations on the other side of the border had to come from *somewhere,* and that "somewhere" couldn't be all *that* far inside. He should see some signs of where they came from and where they went by now, he thought, but there was nothing.

He'd had a later start than he wanted, too, and he didn't relish bedding down in the pitch darkness in this region. Still, what else could he do?

As he moved in, though, he began to hear various sounds in the bush around him that were unlike the sounds of the creatures he'd been seeing and avoiding all afternoon. Once or twice he was certain he caught a brief glimpse of some man-sized shapes off in the foliage, but when he turned, they seemed to vanish. He wasn't really worried about the natives; hell, he *wanted* to find, or be found by, the natives. Rather, he was worried about far larger predators that might be around somewhere that had so far escaped his notice.

As the day wore on toward its end, though, he became more and more certain that he was being watched. There were too many such odd near encounters, and they were increasing—and, frankly, becoming more obvious. Through the swamp noises he occasionally heard what he was certain was a cough or perhaps a grunt. The third time he heard it, he knew that he was in the midst of a number of them and that they wanted him to know it.

What's the matter, boys? Afraid I'll touch you?

The worst concern he had was darkness at this point; there was simply no telling what they were waiting for, but darkness in their element would certainly make whatever it was much easier. He was deceptively dangerous for a little man in hand-to-hand combat, but even the biggest muscle man he'd ever seen wasn't a match for a horde of attackers unless those attackers were total incompetents, and he just didn't feel that these people were as dull or stupid as they wanted to appear to be to others. There was, after all, quite a good motive for cultivating just the sort of reputation they now had with the somewhat paranoid Ambreza. He couldn't have imagined that the furry race would have ever allowed Glathrielians free reign in the hex with no monitoring.

He had, however, deliberately placed himself in his current predicament, and he was getting pretty damned tired of it. He stopped at a fairly wide clearing that had some decent grass to hold it, removed his pack, then sat on it and looked around at the apparently silent wilderness.

"All right," he called out to them. "I don't know if you can understand me or not, but you sure as hell know you're being talked to. Now, I am tired and I am pissed off as all hell right now, and my purely mechanical watch here says that it's about a half hour to sundown. Now, I'm gonna wait here maybe five or ten minutes, and if you want to come out and talk, or fight, or whatever, that's fine. After that I'm gonna make camp, I'm gonna make a fire, I'm gonna eat something and have an Ambrezan beer with it and maybe then some coffee. If you want any, you're welcome. If you just want to watch, then piss on you!" He took out a cigar, bit off the end, then lit it with a safety match. More things worked in a nontech hex than most people thought.

He waited until the cigar was almost half-smoked. During that time he had the distinct impression that more and more natives were showing up and sitting out there staring at him. For a starkly lonely campsite in the middle of a jungle swamp, he had the oddest feeling that he was sitting alone on the field at Rio's largest soccer stadium and that the stands were full. Or was he, rather, sitting alone in the center of the Roman Colosseum with the crowd waiting until the lions were ready?

Well, he wouldn't wait for them. He was as tired and hungry as he'd said he was, and he was going to be set up before dark.

Before too long he had his tent set up and his supplies organized and he'd started a fire. In a nontech hex it was impossible to manufacture a good compressed-gas system, but as long as the mechanism was totally mechanical, nothing stopped anyone from bringing premanufactured canisters in and having a clean fire. He knew how rough he might have to live if he started heading north to the equator, as he would have to do sooner or later. He was not about to sacrifice any comforts at this point if he could avoid it.

He had pre-prepared his own food and had it vacuum-sealed. The Ambreza and he didn't really agree on what constituted a hearty, tasty meal, so these were his own creations, and he managed to use three containers to make a fairly decent simmering stew. The Glathrielians were allegedly all vegetarians or worse, but he had enough faith in his recipes that it would have to smell awfully good to humans no matter whether they'd actually eat the stuff or not. The beer was in small plastic containers that held in a cold gas that surrounded the inner bottles. The cap was released with a simple pull, and this, too, worked in a nontech hex. It was a most satisfying meal considering the conditions.

By the time he'd finished, it was dark. Darkness fell rapidly over the Well World almost anywhere, since its axial tilt was virtually nil, and by the time he'd put on the coffee, his fire was the only light. It was enough —for now. When he was done, he'd bring out his lantern and light it, filled as it was with an ingenious combination of small cylinders that fed a small amount of oil to a pan and allowed for a decent all-night light. They might come at him, but they wouldn't come in total darkness.

He poured the coffee and settled back comfortably, considering relighting the remaining half of his cigar, when he suddenly frowned and looked around by the glow of the fire.

She stood there, just at the edge of the fire, staring right at him. She looked to be maybe fourteen or fifteen years old, fully developed but very young, and she was stark naked and unblemished in any way.

He sat up and stared back at her big brown eyes and saw in them a great deal of intelligence and awareness. There was also something odd about her. She looked like a Glathrielian should look, and yet she didn't. That all-race exotic cast all the ones he'd seen exhibited wasn't there; this girl looked more like somebody on the beach at Ipanema. Her features were more classical—sort of an Afro-European mix found in the

Caribbean or parts of Latin America—with none of the Asian about her, and she was a lighter, smoother brown.

"Hello," he said pleasantly. "Want some coffee? I have some paper cups here if you do."

She frowned, and he really got the feeling that she was honestly trying to make out his words but to no avail. That in itself was odd. It was as if she *expected* to be able to understand him and was puzzled that she could not.

He gestured for her to come closer and have a seat, and without any hesitancy she did just that, sitting cross-legged on the ground to his left but between him and the fire.

"Excuse me for not offering my hand, but as bad luck as I have with women, I don't want you to suddenly start screaming and running away in terror or something." He got up and went to the fire instead, and holding an empty cup, poured some coffee into it and took it over to her and set it down near her. She watched him all the time like a hawk, but there was no fear in her. She didn't touch the cup or look at it again, though, and he remembered that they rejected all such things.

She seemed to be thinking about something for a moment, then she leaned over, got on her knees, and cleared a place in the wet soil, making it free of grass. With her finger, she did something in the dirt, then backed away and resumed her seat.

Curious, he walked over and crouched down to look at what she'd scratched there. At first he couldn't make it out. Some kind of drawing. A box, another box inside of it, and a kind of V mark under it. Shaking his head, he got up, walked around, and looked at it from another angle.

My God, if I didn't know better, I'd swear it was a drawing of a television set, he thought, wondering. He suddenly had an awful thought.

Crouching down again, he wiped out her drawing as best he could and traced a different, more irregular design.

She came over, looked at it, then nodded and put a finger at a point on the left and a bit up from the center of the picture.

It was a crude map of Brazil.

He turned and looked at her, then put his right hand up in the air, made a fist, and brought it down with a whistling sound to a *boom!* in the dirt.

She smiled and nodded, then repeated his pantomime and sound effects, this time taking her own fist into the crude map just where she'd made the dot.

His jaw dropped just a bit. *Maybe that* was *a television! If so, she's not just some native girl with bad luck, either.* He decided to get more ambitious and do a little signing. He'd been pretty good at signing once. It was the only thing that had saved his ass during the sack of Rome.

He traced a circle in the air, then slowly outlined a hex shape, then, with his hand, portrayed his arm going from the circle through the hex to here. She watched and nodded, smiling.

He shrugged to, he hoped, indicate total puzzlement as to how she'd wound up here. It wasn't supposed to work this way. Nobody was supposed to become a Glathrielian unless the race was in danger of dying out, and at least it hardly looked like *that.*

She waved a finger in the air, had it go to ground, had two fingers walk out, then made as if she were operating a very old-time camera, then mouthing into something she was holding. *A helicopter! She'd been part of a TV crew covering the impact!* That *had* to be it and would easily explain her appearance.

It still didn't answer why she was *here,* why she wasn't one of the other 779 races of the South, but it told him basically who she was and how she'd gotten here.

He had an awful thought. He pointed to her foot and then to the drawing area. With his own foot he mocked putting it down on the drawing. She didn't get it right away but eventually figured out what he wanted, although maybe not why, and stepped on the place, making a half footprint.

It was, of course, a standing rather than walking print, but he'd been following enough of a certain set of prints for his experienced tracker's eyes to relate the two.

He hadn't been following Mavra, after all. He'd been following *this* girl! And that meant that *she,* not Mavra, was the source of the pulse— and the source of the track the hounds had followed.

Well, some of the mystery was at least explained, why she'd gone pretty much straight into Glathriel and why she hadn't contacted the Ambreza. In one sense he was relieved, although he felt frustrated by still not finding who he was really looking for.

Now all he had to do was try to figure out why this girl was here. Not only shouldn't she have become a Glathrielian, she hadn't—not totally. The Well had done some of its work but had left her original form pretty much intact. Oh, he suspected she was a good deal older than she looked now—that was a fairly simple procedure for the Well program—and any diseases or infirmities or other problems, right down to fillings in her teeth, would have been repaired, but it had left her genetic code mostly untouched. It shouldn't have done that. As far as he knew, it *couldn't* have done that.

But it had.

It had also done its adaptation work internally in a way he'd never intended. She couldn't understand him because the program now specified that Type 41's could understand no language but their own. She couldn't speak even in *that* language because, as far as he could see, they didn't have a spoken language as such. She would have been given any attributes and abilities necessary to survive and integrate with the locals here, even ones developed independently, since that, too, was part of the program, but at the cost of being able to verbalize, and perhaps even use, what her education and training had prepared her to do. Hell, if she'd been some sort of TV personality, then she had to be going *nuts* with these limits!

"I didn't mean to do it," he told her sincerely, although he knew she couldn't understand and wouldn't have understood the comment even if she *had* comprehended the words. "I honestly didn't. It's not supposed to work this way." Maybe, just maybe, the Well was broken, after all.

And, he thought, if she was a reporter, why not take the coffee? He knew few of them who could resist coffee, and it would have immediately established her as someone more than Glathrielian if she'd taken it. Hell, it'd only been what? Two, three days tops. She couldn't have totally assimilated into their culture in that short a time, could she? Had, somehow, the Well imposed the culture upon her as well?

It wasn't designed to do that, either. Some stuff one had to learn.

More interesting was what he *wasn't* able to communicate to her. Some simple things, like "others" versus "alone," as in "Did you come with others or alone?" he could not seem to put over. She, too, tried a few times to communicate, but her attempts seemed random and confused. It wasn't an entirely new phenomenon to him; some of the other races of the Well World, most in the North but even a few in the South, simply did not fully follow the logical thought patterns that he and most of the southern races adhered to in one degree or another. A nonverbal society *might* develop along the same logic paths, and certainly in the case of the same race with the same brain structure, but even on Earth there were societies that saw things too differently to ever fully understand one another. This was a step further. In some ways it was like the card games at which he excelled. At one time, eons ago, he'd learned the basics of those games and played them so often that now he rarely thought about how or what to play and when; a part of his brain that he couldn't even consciously touch, let alone access deliberately, processed all the information according to experience, and he simply played automatically—and won. Writers, painters, other creators had the same experience; they didn't know where the words or visions had come from—they just were there and came from some unapproachable recess of the mind that they neither understood nor consciously used but that nonetheless they simply took for granted and used.

None of them could ever explain the process. "God-given talent" was an oft-quoted phrase for it, but talent came from somewhere, and it was called up from a mystery region of consciousness in a manner they could neither comprehend nor control.

Could a whole race operate *entirely* on that sort of processing? Could an entire culture somehow evolve that required no front-brained verbalizations? How could it work? Where was the shared experience, the teaching, the communication that would give such a people the tools with which to work? And to what end? To some animallike equilibrium in which survival was enough?

It was a real puzzle, and he didn't know the answer. There was only one place where he could get those answers, he knew, and that place was a long and hard journey from here.

He could help this girl there, too. Get her out of the trap she'd fallen into.

It never occurred to him to take her along, though. If she was so bound by the Glathrielian way, she'd never survive the trip, and she'd be more in the way than useful, anyway. Still, he wanted to try to tell her, to get through to her, that he *could* help her—and would.

That, however, proved impossible to get over.

After a while fatigue and frustration overcame him, and he managed to get her to understand that he had to sleep. She nodded but continued to sit as he went into the tent, zipped it shut, and, after a much longer time than he thought it would take, managed to get to sleep.

In the morning she was still there.

He wasn't actually fooled into thinking that she'd sat there all night, but she and the others he hadn't seen might think he was. Certainly there had been a lot of traffic through his camp during the night, all without disturbing him. The signs were quite clear that nothing short of a mob scene had occurred, yet none of his equipment had been touched, not even the now-cold cup of coffee still sitting there in the grass.

Well, regardless of the games they might think they were playing, he'd wasted a couple of days coming here, and he'd probably waste another two or more getting back to anyplace useful. At least now it was time to move on, time to actually *do* something other than sit. He'd appreciated the rest, but he was out of place both here and in Ambreza, and he now had a better reason to enter the Well than he'd had before.

After he had packed his gear, she got up, beckoned him, and started off back toward Ambreza with a surefootedness and confidence he certainly didn't feel. He did not argue, however—what good would that have done, anyway? And hell, maybe she knew a shortcut.

The paths she took were shorter, although it was still better than seven hours walking, not counting the breaks, until he once again saw the border. She stood there, letting him pass through, and then passed through herself. Now *she* was following *him*, but she seemed determined to stick with him.

He stopped, turned, looked her in the eye, and shook his head "no," but she had no reaction to that, although she must have understood it and continued to follow him.

Well, as much as he'd have *liked* to take her along, it was impossible. What would she eat? How could she withstand the climatic extremes of the journey in the nude? What would happen when he got on a truck or some other automatic device her people wouldn't touch?

Still, she followed him right up to the farm buildings and waited while he knocked.

The old Ambrezan male was there, apparently doing accounts. He stared out at the girl in the front yard and gave a typical Ambrezan *"Chi chi chi!"* which was basically an expression of thoughtfulness. "So she's the one you went in to get?"

"No, she's another. Somebody totally different."

"Yeah, I figured if you come back, it'd be empty-handed. I no sooner got back to the house than the wife called for me to go after you. Seems another female much like you showed up in the capital just about that time."

Brazil was delighted at the news. "Did they give a name?"

"Dunno. Got the note here someplace."

"Well, more important, is she still there?"

"Maybe, but I got the impression she was there to go to Zone. The gate's right in the city center, you know. Wanted to find out about her friends, I think they said. *Chi chi chi!* Now where in—ah! Here!"

"You'll have to read it for me," Brazil told him. "I'm all right with the translator at languages, but reading is something else again."

"Oh. All right. Let's see . . . 'Female Type 41 arrested near the city border at ten-fourteen this morning for being illegally out of a Glathrielian-allowed district. Proved to be alien of same origin as you. Received clothing, passage to Zone tomorrow for locating rest of her party.'"

"Hmmm . . . Wonder if she's still in Zone or the city? She'd have to come back there through the gate, anyway. May I use your communicator and call in and see?"

"Sure. No problem. What about the female there?"

"She'll wait." He went inside and placed a call to the comm center.

"Yes, her name was registered as a Mavra Chang," the comm tech informed him. "Went down to Zone yesterday, returned in the evening. Got provisions and left this morning. The law prevents any Type 41 from being in the city for more than two days, anyway."

"That's the one. How did she leave? And where did they take her?"

"She left by air shuttle. She was going south to the border with Erdom. I assume one of her party is down there someplace or she's going to try and make a boat connection of some sort. At any rate, she said she would probably not be back unless she needed to use a Zone gate as an escape route."

"Damn!" Brazil swore. "No chance I could get an airdrop to the same spot?"

"Maybe in a couple of days or so. Not right now. We don't run those for the convenience of aliens, you know."

The Ambreza had a small air fleet, operating, as it had to, totally within the hex, that basically consisted of a few dozen helicopterlike vehicles which were used for emergencies and for big shots to move around. How she'd talked herself into a ride down there was a mystery, but that she'd been able to do so sounded like the old Mavra.

"Was she informed that I was here and looking for her?"

There was an embarrassed silence for a moment, then the comm tech answered, "Yes, she was informed."

"And?"

"She said that she'd have to move fast or you might catch up to her."

He sighed. "All right. Thank you," and signed off.

The old Ambrezan chuckled. "Ain't it always the damnedest thing, son?"

"Huh? What do you mean?"

"Well, you come up here lookin' for her, and she's down there and she don't even want to see you. On the other hand, you pick up *another* one you didn't know, didn't want, and can't seem to get rid of!"

He nodded and sighed again. "Sure is. Well, thanks for your help. Any way to get some transportation out of this region?"

"Might be able to help. Dunno what your girl out there's gonna do, though. They don't like machines, you know. They don't like much of *anything* 'cept maybe each other. Where you goin'? South to Erdom? That's pretty mean country even if you know it. All desert 'cept right along the coast."

"No, I don't think so. In fact, while I'll probably get in touch with the embassy just to see where *she* might be going, it's not worth chasing her at this point, particularly if she has some reason for avoiding me. I think

I'm best off heading east from here. Catch a ship and get on my way. I, too, have some people I promised to look up far from here."

"Well, it's up to you, son. I'll see what I can do about a call in to the foreign ministry, and then we'll see about gettin' you a ride east. From this distance it might do you best to go overland by horse rather than go through all that convoluted bunch of roads that'll take you three hundred kilometers to go fifty."

He gave a small smile. "And I suppose you might have a horse for sale."

"Could be. Ain't got no saddles that'd fit you, though."

"I can make do with a blanket and a bridle," he assured the Ambrezan. "Let's go see what you have."

They went out and walked back beyond the outbuildings to a large open pasture between the headquarters and the parklike glade where Terry had entered the Well World. Quite a number of good-looking horses were there, and he looked them over.

He picked a strong-looking brown gelding after surveying the herd. "How much?"

"Oh, I reckon a hundred and fifty'll do it."

"A hundred and fifty! I'll *walk* before I'll pay a hundred and fifty for a gelding to get me fifty kilometers!"

"No, no, son. I ain't tryin' to cheat you. That's for the *two* of them."

Nathan Brazil looked around and saw the girl, now mounted atop a horse without blanket, bridle, or anything else but looking very much at home there. She smiled at him.

He felt like a cross between a sucker and merely a damned fool, but he paid anyway. Hell, otherwise he wouldn't have put it past her to just steal the damned horse or, worse, try to run along after him. At least he could get most of the money back at the port when he sold the two horses.

ERDOM

AT FIRST THERE HAD been the dizzying sensation of falling nearly identical to that first hex gate that had brought them all to this strange new world, but then the sensation had abruptly ceased and she had fallen into the deepest sleep she had ever known.

Doctor Lori Ann Sutton awoke feeling groggy, hung over, and a little sick to the stomach, lying on what felt like a bed of warm sand.

She opened her eyes and looked around and saw that it *was* a bed of warm sand. At least it was sand, and there was an awful lot of it under a mean hot sun that was still low on the horizon. Or was it going down? Who could tell?

She sat up, scratched where the sand had pressed against her side, and immediately felt a terrible sense of wrongness. The whole scene—sand, sky, sun—had all the colors she expected, but there seemed to be even more. She could actually *see* the heat, and there were darker areas as well.

I'm seeing into the infrared spectrum! she thought wonderingly. And maybe beyond. Maybe, just maybe, in *both* directions. The *entire* spectrum?

Suddenly she remembered everything. The gate, the lecture by the polka-dotted dragon, Alama's—no, *Mavra*'s words—and something about becoming some different creature.

She looked down at herself and saw that she was a very different creature, indeed. Her arms were long but very thin and ended in a huge pair of hands that were not human. They had only three fingers, long and thick, and an opposable thumb almost as long as the index finger and thicker than any of the others. The nails were huge and thick as well and seemed to run from halfway past the knuckle to beyond the tip. Put together in a relaxed way, they formed almost, well, a kind of supple, softer *hoof,* the palms fairly hard and thick and a pale brownish color.

Her feet were the same, only the hoof was cloven and seemed oddly shaped on the bottom, something like a horse's hoof crossed with the foot of a camel.

She was covered in a thick, hidelike skin that was itself almost covered by very short, thick, pastel beige hair that flared out at the ankles and wrists. But that wasn't the worst of it or the biggest shock.

Between her legs, emerging from a mass of thick, medium-brown pubic hair, was the *biggest* set of male genitalia she had ever seen, very dark brown in color and with a leatherlike texture.

She touched it and gave a slight gasp and then just stared down at it for quite some time.

My God! I'm a man! she thought, getting a queasy feeling in her stomach echoed by a strange but not altogether pleasant sensation in the genitals.

It was an oddball fantasy come to life, one she had played with in the past, mostly out of the frustration of having to compete at the top levels of her profession with men and wanting the same power and position they took for granted. But it was only a fantasy, not a serious wish. The reality of the change shook her.

And after all that time with the all-female tribe of the People, she felt an odd sense of aversion. *I'm going to miss my breasts!* she thought, trying to get a handle on things.

Finally she managed to overcome the tremendous shock to consider the next question. She was male. But a male *what*? What was beige and hairy and had big hooves and arms apparently evolved from a set of more equinelike forelegs?

The body was *very* slender and surprisingly supple. The body was a nearly perfect blend of equine and human, strange, yet somehow she thought of the term "erotic" to cover it. *Hah! If only Jeff could see me now, with* this *body and* this *big a sausage!* Of course, he wouldn't exactly be turned on by the idea, but it would be awfully nice to use these hard hands to slug him.

God! I'm a guy for all of three minutes and already I'm thinking like one! she admonished herself.

The fact was, mentally, where it counted, she was still the same person. Nothing had been changed that she could tell, no knowledge or memories lost, no feelings all that different. But it was as if her mind were now in another's body, someone whose differences went beyond just gender —*way* beyond.

While there seemed very little sensation in the rather large feet, the palms proved to have a lot of nerve sensors, and she could get a surprisingly good "feel," as good as or better than her old hands. *I'll never touch-type again, though,* she thought inanely. Not with two fewer fingers, even though the size of the hands and the length of the fingers gave her, if anything, more control.

She still thought of herself as a "she," and she knew that she probably would have to make a major mental adjustment on that score. Nobody in this new place would know that she'd been a woman most of her life; they'd see her in this man's body instead.

She felt her face. It *seemed* human enough—mouth, even with what seemed to be thicker lips and maybe a longer, slightly thicker tongue, but her jaw moved side to side as well as up and down, and the teeth indicated that whatever these people were, they were omnivores, not herbivores as she would have expected. The canines, in fact, seemed a bit larger and sharper than they used to be—and no caps, no missing back tooth!

She had always been farsighted, which was the reason she had been able to survive among the People without her glasses, but vision now seemed perfect, with every little hair easy to pick out even very close up. She couldn't remember when she'd seen this clearly at all distances.

Nose . . . Well, human, sort of, but there was something odd *inside* the nostrils, controlled by voluntary muscles. She flexed them and suddenly found her breathing cut off. She relaxed them again very quickly. Protection against blowing sand, perhaps? The eyes felt a little funny, too. She concentrated and found that she had double eyelids that could be independently controlled if she concentrated or would operate as one if she didn't. The outer lids were essentially what she thought of as "normal"; the inner ones, however, were transparent. They distorted her vision and in fact seemed to filter color so that the world became a study in contrasting grays, but she could see through them.

The ears were definitely *not* "normal." They went more back than up and were protected by large pointed lobes, more like a horse's ears or some similar animal's. They could, she discovered, be somewhat rotated, raised, or lowered, even independently of one another. There was a shock of bushy hair atop the head, but it didn't seem to grow long down the back. With some trepidation she pulled one and looked at it. It appeared nearly snow white in color and very long and thick.

Lori had a sudden thought and reached around to her behind. There appeared to be a bit of excess hair at the base of the spine but not the tail she almost expected to find. In a way it was kind of disappointing. She'd always wondered what it would feel like to have a tail.

She looked around, trying to figure out how to get up. Equinelike or not, this wasn't the body of a four-footed animal, no matter what its ancestors might have been like. It wasn't as easy as getting up in a human body, it seemed, but she figured it out with a little experimentation. She turned over and used the hands as forefeet and then pushed off, letting her back muscles lift her upright. The true feet were clearly designed for sand; she found no problems with footing at all.

She looked around, wondering where the hell she might go. In doing so, she saw her shadow, and it made an amazing vision to her eyes even though, with the sun not so high, it was distorted and lengthened. Curiously, though, it was only by seeing that shadow that she noticed the horn.

Her hand went up to the top of her head and found it easily, almost centered up there. A twisting, rock-hard spiral going up, not quite straight, to a very wicked point. Although it was hard and almost half a meter long, she had no sensation of it being there at all, not even weight or balance on the head.

A male bipedal unicorn? she wondered to herself. *Why would any evolving race keep a horn like that?*

For now she could only guess. A weapon perhaps, considering the thinness and fragility of the arms? Or . . . She had an awful thought it might be used in some way involving mating no matter how conventional it seemed.

All right, Lori, you know the basics about what they've stuck you with; now what?

Again she scanned the horizon, and this time a curious effect happened. When she concentrated on any far point, it was as if her vision suddenly became telescopic. She could bring her view of the horizon closer, *much* closer, seeing detail at very great distances indeed. Although there was about a half second's disorientation when she switched her focus to something more close up, the effect was the neatest thing about this body she'd discovered.

But what good was it to be able to zero in on the distant horizon if there was nothing but sand to be seen?

"Get to a zone gate and tell me where and what you are," Mavra had said, but how could she do that when there seemed nowhere to go to get *anywhere?*

Lori continued the horizon pan, stopping and magnifying, trying to see *anything*. What good was all this if she was going to be stuck, alone and without food or water, in this desert?

She suddenly stopped and zeroed in on a tiny black speck far, far away. She would never even have noticed it without this perfect vision, and she would certainly have never been able to tell that it was more than a dune shadow without the remarkable telescopic abilities. Even with them it was barely discernible, but it seemed to be a dark area of some kind protruding from the desert floor. Rocks? It didn't seem likely.

Trees! An oasis!

The sun was definitely climbing, and the day was heating up fast. Now was the time to make for any possible haven, and second-guessing was a luxury that she could not afford.

She started off toward the black dot and began to improve on her walking and balancing abilities with almost every step. She did not walk with those feet; she sort of trotted or even galloped, kicking up sand but making very good speed. She also learned rather quickly and a bit painfully that when moving fast, she had to lean a bit forward and keep the hips wide, otherwise that *thing* down there flapping away would get crunched between the upper calves.

It was getting progressively hotter, and she could actually *see* the heat both as it came down upon her and as it was first trapped and then radiated back by her body. She wondered just how hot to the touch she was right now.

She began to have trouble seeing. The heat radiation was coloring everything and distorting her sight. It suddenly occurred to her that there was more than one use for those inner lids, and she closed them. Virtually all colors snapped out and the world became a mass of infinite grays, yet the black dots that hadn't seemed to grow any closer no matter what speed she was making now began to resolve themselves a bit more clearly and did in fact seem to be getting ever so slightly larger.

It *was* an oasis! That might not mean people, but those were clearly trees of some kind, and trees needed water.

Or at least she *hoped* that trees here needed water.

She would have expected to become winded after a while and have to rest, particularly in the growing heat, but she found that running across the sands like this gave her a real rush; her chest apparently contained mostly lung, and it went in and out with each giant breath she took. But the rhythm of the breathing and the running was very easy to slip into, and even though it seemed like she'd been running for hours across many, many kilometers, she didn't feel the least bit tired or winded.

She was definitely hungry and thirsty, though, which only gave her more impetus to reach her goal as quickly as physically possible.

Soon the oasis loomed before her, filling much of her vision, and it was enough of a dark mass that she lifted the inner lids to get the full detail.

The trees weren't like any she'd ever seen before, but they had a tropical look, with thin and supple trunks rising to layers of oversized palm- or fernlike leaves.

She ran right through the first row and found the area larger than she had expected and the ground inside harder with much exposed white-veined gray rock that produced a "clopping" sound when her feet hit it. She slowed but found that she needed to go up to a tree and put a hand out to fully stop herself without falling over.

It was almost a letdown to stop running, but her chest continued to heave and she continued to gulp in air at the same rhythm until her breathing slowed to a more normal rate.

She looked around, and her ears automatically rotated about a hundred degrees on either side, checking for sounds. There wasn't much except the rustling of some leaves in the highest part of the trees, apparently in reaction to a slight breeze that didn't reach the ground.

Her nose, though, brought an overpowering aroma that she recognized immediately, even though she'd never smelled it before—*water!*

Finding it was as simple as following her nose.

She didn't hesitate a moment worrying that it might not be good water. It wasn't any new inner sense that told her anything about it but rather an all-consuming thirst that made it clear that the question was moot. She simply had to have water.

The water was in fact from a spring that bubbled out of the rocks and created an attractive, shaded pool about a dozen meters across. She headed for it, got on all fours, then dropped down and just stuck her face in it and began to suck and lap it in. Her natural nose plugs closed the instant her face hit the water, and she hardly noticed.

It was an eerie sensation, though, because she just drank and drank. She had never drunk this much of anything in her whole life, and long after a human her size would have been satisfied she continued to take it in. She could *feel* it, cooling down her whole body in stages, coiling around inside her like a living thing, and finally concentrating in her back. There was no telling how much she drank before, unable to take another gulp, she came up out of the water and settled back, lying there on her side. For several minutes she felt bloated but cool, and then, slowly, her body temperature seemed to come back to normal and that bloated feeling subsided.

She wondered where all the water had gone. She didn't *feel* like she'd grown some sort of camel's hump, nor did rolling on her back for a moment reveal one, but clearly this body had areas to store a lot of excess liquid. After a while she forced herself to get up, even though she actually felt sleepy. For one thing, the pool was not totally calm but it did reflect decently and she wanted to get a more complete image of herself. And then it would be prudent to look around. Although Lori the American college teacher wouldn't have resisted, Bimi of the People knew that it wouldn't do to just zonk out without checking the lay of the land.

The image of herself in the gently rippling water was both strange and familiar. She'd always had something of a long neck, and she still did; the face, although the same beige or light tan color, contained enough of the old Lori Sutton to be recognizable, although it had a harder, larger, rougher cast. It was, she realized, what her face would have looked like had she been born a man. She'd always had that boyish look to her face, and now it seemed to have firmed up and looked not nearly as bad to her as it had all those times in the mirror.

The lips *were* thicker by quite a bit and were a dark brown, the nose was a bit larger, the eyes were dark black blobs against a medium brown field, the ears were very equine and larger than she'd thought, and the eyebrows were thick and snow white and rose on either side of the eyes at a slight angle, giving her a slightly exotic look. The big shock of white hair was actually kind of cute. The horn, the same color brown as the skin fur, looked, well, different from what she had imagined. *That's one hell of a phallic symbol,* she thought. *Jeez! As weird as this body is, it sure would have turned me on!*

She tore herself reluctantly away from the self-examination and got up and looked around the rest of the oasis. It was, thankfully, deserted. Not that she wanted to hide out forever, but she wasn't sure she was ready for others of this kind yet, particularly not as a man.

This was clearly a popular stop. In the sandy soil were traces of great numbers of people—beings like herself, anyway—having moved through here, and probably not long ago, since clearly the winds came through this place and erased many signs as if they'd never been. There was also signs of some sort of civilized behavior as well—holes which clearly were some kind of tent pole supports, a central fire pit with more support holes that might indicate anything from a rotisserie to grates being placed there, and a veritable waste pile of damaged and broken crockery, much of it of fired clay and some of it inlaid with elaborate designs.

The designs were very interesting, since among the more abstract parts were some scenes of what might have been life in this place. The style was almost reminiscent of ancient Egyptian, all in profile and two very flat dimensions yet finely featured. She couldn't be sure if these were domestic or religious scenes, but a lot could be learned from them.

For one thing, they went in for decoration more than clothes, and *that* was instructive—not that clothes made a lot of sense out here with this kind of body. Either these beings came in a rainbow of colors or dyed fur in different colors and patterns was popular. So was decorating the horns, some of which were depicted as impossibly long. There was also a fair amount of jewelry on the males and what appeared to be serapelike capes with intricate designs worn over the head but extending down only chest-high and, on some but not all, a kind of highly decorated but very brief codpiece. Males didn't seem to grow facial hair, but the big clump of hair on top tapered down the back until it vanished completely about three-quarters of the way down in a manelike appearance.

The females were quite different. First, they were all depicted as at least a head shorter than any of the males, although that might be just the male artist's perspective. They had very soft feminine faces and no horn at all, but they had a huge amount of hair that trailed down their backs. They also had tails, much like horses' tails, that were almost mirror images of their hair and seemed to be deliberately styled to be that way and kept up with some kind of stays. They were not brown-furred but rather a soft, pale yellow, and their body hair and tails were a variety of browns, reds, even blonds, as well as black. How much was artificial and how much was "natural" color couldn't be determined.

They also had two pairs of breasts, one atop the other. It was a very strange sight, but with the erotic equine curves of the body it didn't look wrong, either. That got Lori to examining her own chest, where, after some effort even with the short hair, she did indeed locate four small nipples.

Did they have *that* many kids that they needed all that excess capacity? Or did they have a lot of kids and only a few made it past weaning? No, probably not. They didn't seem big enough to carry more than one or two routinely, any more than human women did. The breasts, which seemed almost "humanlike," had some of the short pale yellow fur about two-thirds of the way to the nipples but were otherwise all a very light brown.

Some of the decorations simply depicted scenes from some kind of tribal life: guards flanking a particularly decorated male who wore a lot of gold and a bright serape adorned with a sash, females preparing food in fire pits. The males carried spears, and some seemed to be wearing swords—there was one scene of two males dueling, possibly in sport, the swords thin and rapierlike, with hilts somewhat reminiscent of their horns. There were also scenes that were blatantly erotic, often two or more females with one male, and the sexual attributes depicted made her own rather large endowment seem downright trivial.

Still, aside from the alienness of the people depicted, the scenes for the most part looked right out of some ancient Near Eastern Earth culture. A tribal, nomadic people, but with a sense of art and, from the odd-looking bands around some of the broken pottery, with a form of writing as well.

She was about to abandon her look through the remnants when a large fragment caught her eye and she reached down, picked it up, and frowned. It gave her a sudden chill to look at the scene, the first one she really didn't like at all.

Their tents, crockery, ornamental stuff, all their goods moved on what seemed to be sledlike devices made to slide through the sand. Several had been depicted open or parked in other scenes, but this scene was of some in motion. She wondered why she hadn't seen any depictions of domesticated animals, and this was why.

The females were lined up on a series of wooden bars passed through a forward support, and teams of six to ten of them, depending on the size of the desert sled, were clearly pulling them while the males ran with their spears to either side.

The females were the draft animals.

In fact, suddenly flashing back through the other scenes, she realized that whenever work was depicted, it was the females who were doing it. The males might fence or look magnificent or whatever, but never were they shown actually *doing* anything, except in the erotic ones, of course, when they were doing what men always liked to do.

She felt outraged by the sight as all her old principles came to the fore, and yet she found herself thinking, *Thank God I'm not a woman here!*

She was ashamed of the thought, yet damn it, the idea of being one of the bosses rather than one of the servants was something of a turn-on. She hated herself for feeling *that,* too, and tried to get some self-control back. She didn't know what it was to be as oppressed as these women obviously were, but she knew what it was like to be a woman in a man's world, and she hoped she wouldn't descend to that level even if she had to adjust to this society.

She tossed the shard back in the pile, and it landed with a crash and cracked again.

This was too much to handle, coming all at once, she thought. It made the kidnapping and subsequent life among the People seem almost ordinary by comparison. Still, Alam—Mavra—had been right. Without that first experience, she wasn't sure if she could have handled this one at all.

She looked around, but there was clearly nothing to eat here. There *did* seem to be some kind of round, green fruit way up atop the trees, but even if it were edible and ripe enough to eat, this body was good for a lot of things, but tree climbing wasn't one of them. Filled with water, though, she was in no immediate danger of anything more than a growling stomach. She would pick a spot in the shade with some promise of concealment just in case and get the badly needed rest. *Then* she could think of what to do next.

* * *

It was a weird dream, mixing living scenes from the discarded pottery and the race that lived here with scenes of the Amazon and of the university, and at one point she was saying to her department head, *"Now that I'm a man, Dr. Avery, you can't deny me the Holburn Chair and the professorship that goes with it."*

The smell of odd spices and perfumes and the tinkling of bells brought her back to consciousness, but it wasn't until the sudden thought that she was no longer alone that she stiffened, rolled over, and tensely peered out from the rocks and bushes toward the pool.

It wasn't a big caravan like those depicted on the shards but, rather, a small party, no more than eight or nine people from the look of it, and one of those sleighlike wagons. Most, maybe all, were females, except for one big fellow reclining on a cushion. He looked, well, old—not really old but well into middle age from the cast and lines in his face and the wear and tear on his skin. He wore a somewhat faded and threadbare serape of faded red that had an even more faded yellow design too shopworn to matter and one of those codpieces that might at one time have been silvery but now just looked a dirty gray. His horn, either shorter than hers or worn down over time, was wrapped in a kind of turbanlike affair that made it appear that he was wearing a cream-colored pointed hat. Everything about him, from his overall look and manner to the faded remnants of once colorfully decorated skin, looked a bit old and a bit seedy.

So did the sleigh. Clearly it had seen a lot of use in its time and hadn't been cared for very well of late, but, like its owner, it was serviceable.

Watching the females, seeing them in person for the first time, was an odd experience. All were considerably smaller than either the old man or Lori, and the double pair of breasts on them all seemed quite a bit larger than in the pictures. The hair and the tails were nicely done up so that they were pretty well mirror images of one another, and the effect was quite nice indeed to look at. They all seemed to have a naturally feminine, sexy manner to them, and they would talk or whisper to one another, ears turning and twitching, and occasionally giggle like school-girls. Most wore some sort of jewelry—bracelets, necklaces—but little else, although the one at the fire pit had on a thick serape much longer than the male's, apparently not a garment but rather protection against heat. There was also something odd about their hands, but she couldn't make out what it might be.

She wondered just what the hell she should do now. Here was contact, and on a scale she might handle, but damn it, it was *scary* to be in this situation. Finally realizing that there was nothing else to do, Lori hauled herself onto the top of the rock, assuming a sitting position, and coughed politely.

The effect on the females was startling. They froze like deer in the meadow might have frozen at the first sense of danger. The male moved pretty quickly, though, whirling, grabbing a sword, and actually getting to his feet in a single series of motions.

"Who be you?" the old man called out menacingly in a low voice.

"Please, good sir, put down your sword," Lori responded, startled at how very, very deep her voice sounded to her ears but also relieved that language, at least, wasn't going to be a problem. "I sit here with nothing, not even clothes, let alone a weapon."

"Where'd ye come from?" the old man asked suspiciously, sword still in hand.

"I was already here," Lori explained. "I—I woke up in the sands near here as I am now."

"*Yesss . . . ?* And who dumped ye there, and why?"

"I—I don't know if this is going to sound crazy to you or not, but I was a different sort of—creature—from another world. I came through what I was told is a hex gate to a place called Zone, and then they forced me through another gate, and I woke up as you see me."

The old man sniffed, frowned, then put his sword away. "Not *another* one!" he said in disbelief. "Not in my lifetime, or my father's, or *his* father's lifetime has anyone come through there and been dumped here. Now suddenly yer fallin' from the skies!"

Lori's heart skipped a beat. "*Another* one, you say? You mean I'm not the first?"

"Not if yer what you says you are, anyways. Other was a girl, over in the Hajeb, a couple months ago maybe. Least, that's what I heard."

She shook her head. "That means nothing to me. I'm afraid I don't even know where I am, or what I am, for that matter." She was disappointed at the time frame. It meant that whoever the girl was, she was from one of the other parties—most likely the woman in the wheelchair, since that was the only female she recalled among the pictures shown to them back in Zone.

The old man chuckled. "Well, sonny, this land be Erdom, in the bottom of the World, and we all be Erdomites first. I be Posiphar of the Makob, a traveling merchant by trade. I buy and sell things, services, whatever be needed between the families and tribes of the Hjolai. I be on me route from oasis to oasis right now, headin' next fer the camp of Lord Aswab."

"The names mean nothing to me yet. I'm sorry," she told him. Guessing that the man's odd manner of speech was either a regional dialect or just the mark of a less than educated man, she made no attempt to duplicate it. "Uh, I'd like to come down, but I'm not really dressed fit for mixed company, I'm afraid."

Posiphar chuckled again. "Don't worry none 'bout the girls. Ye ain't got nothin' they ain't seen many times afore, I promise ye. Come, come, let me get a look at ye!"

She got down slowly and carefully. Although the body seemed easier to use, more familiar now, she wasn't about to take any chances with it. She then walked over to him, trying to be as natural as possible.

"Heh! Ye walk like some girl," the old man commented. "Well, ain't no nevermind of mine. Yer a big fella, though, I got to say."

Until now she really hadn't had anything for comparison, but it was clear that things were pretty much of a human-sized scale, and now, standing in front of the merchant, she found that as he was a head taller than the tallest woman in his party, she was almost that much bigger and taller than he was. Although she'd been by no means short, it was a novel experience to be the biggest and tallest of a group, and she found she liked the sensation.

"Well, son," the merchant said at last, "maybe ye and me can make a deal here. Ye needs a bit of educatin' on Erdom, I think."

"Not to mention food, clothes, and money," she added.

"Yeah, well, that goes without sayin', I suppose. As ye might have figured, I ain't exactly drippin' with gold and silver and precious gems, but I makes do, I does. Been some banditry about of late—ain't like the old times, I tell ye. I ain't no slouch in a fight, but I be gettin' on and slowed down in spite of meself, and with nobody coverin' me back, I ain't been feelin' too safe of late. Don't suppose ye be any good with a sword?"

She looked at the sword he'd put down by his side. It wasn't like a broadsword; in fact, it was more like a saber than anything else. She wasn't *great* with a sword, but she'd *almost* made the fencing team her undergraduate senior year. "I can use one of those if I had to," she told him. "I might be off balance with it, though. I'm still getting used to this body. But I'm even better with a spear," she added.

"Hmph! What were ye before? Some kinda hard-shelled twelve-armed insect or somethin'?"

She laughed. "No, nothing like that. In some ways not an *extremely* different sort than this, but far enough. More—apelike. You know what an ape is?"

"Sure I do! Seen some over in the port cities now and again. See most anything in this world at them docks. Where'd you think I seen them insect things?"

She was startled. "You mean there actually *are* creatures like that here? Man-sized insects that—think?"

"Sure. You got a whole *lot* t' learn, sonny. Um, what *is* yer name, anyways? One of them impossible-to-say words?"

"Uh, well, it's Lori. It *was*, anyway."

"That's a good enough nonsense word to serve," Posiphar responded. "Here ye be linked with yer family and tribal place name. Since ye ain't got no family or no tribe here, a place name'll do. It'll drive everybody else nuts tryin' to figure out how ye got it, too. How's Lori of Alkhaz sound as a name?"

"Uh, all right, I guess, but who, what, or where is Alkhaz?"

"Why, *this* is Alkhaz, of course! Just a transit oasis, not nobody's in particular. That's 'cause the water's decent here only part of the year. The rest of the time it's either too muddy or too alkaline for most folks' tastes. There's always another that opens up, so it's no big thing."

"I'll accept it, then," she told him. "And Erdom? Is all of it like this? Desert?"

"Well, a whole lot of it is, anyways. All except right on the coast. A few nice little cities there get some rain and have some hills with trees that keep the rain there to use. Got a decent-sized seacoast, but we're right smack up against that Zone wall, so the only place where everything piles up is in the southeast, where Erdom and the wall come together. Sand and stuff gets built up by the sea breezes there, and they get a decent amount of weather. Rest of the place, well, the rains just sink into the sands and get swallowed up, and these here underground rivers are the only water."

"And so it's just the coast and the rest is like this?"

"Well, there's some towns around inside, where you got really good springs, of course. Otherwise you couldn't do the Pilgrimage of the Seven Springs. Got some deep mines over in Jwoba. Them's gold mines. And Awokabi has the diamonds and so on. Don't like 'em much, though. Dirty, smelly, sad little towns where most folks work for nothin' but food and water and the lords live fat. I like the Hjolai better. Folks be friendly if ye don't overstay yer welcome, and they knows ye won't cheat 'em much, and there still be some honor."

She looked out at the desert. "How many people live out here, though? What do they live on?"

"Oh, the whole be divided into Holdings, we calls 'em, each with a pretty fair-sized oasis able to support some number of herd animals and even some farmin' of a limited type. Each is a hereditary family Holding headed by a lord, and the folks there pretty much work fer him. He in return gives 'em protection and security. It ain't a bad system. Hell, half the year the lord's movin' 'round his Holding from oasis to oasis, listenin' t' gripes, fixin' problems. They still think things go both ways out here. The people work for the lord, and the lord tries to help the people with their problems and make life better for 'em. Most do all right. You gets a bad one now and again, o' course—stands to reason—but he don't last long. Most of 'em, even the best, get knocked off sooner or later by one of their relatives anyways, and if you got the people cheerin' for it, well, that lord lasts all the shorter, see?"

Lori nodded, but she wasn't all that thrilled by the system. It sounded like something out of Arabia and a past age of Earth—monarchical tribal families, inheritance by assassination, feudalism. She wasn't all that sure how much she was going to like this.

"But you're not working for a lord," she noted. "Or are you?"

"*Haw!* Not likely! There be some of us around, kind of like a brotherhood. See, them lords need us, 'cause they don't get along with one another nohow, and we be the only ones can walk and talk between with nobody figurin' we like one side better'n the other. So if one wants t' send a message to the other, they use traders like me. If their breedin' stock's thin and needs freshening, they won't sell to nobody they won't even talk to, so they sell to me for a promise that I'll bring 'em back what they need. I takes the stock, trades it to another, then bring the trade back, and that settles that. Of course there's a fee, but we haggles fer it. I been around so long 'cause I always gives 'em a good deal. 'Course, you don't live as well or as rich as if you try'n jerks 'em around a bit, but ye keeps yer balls that way. Them lords got a real mean streak if they catch you!"

"I'll bet," Lori said glumly, having no trouble imagining Erdomite desert justice. "Uh, you mentioned some deal between us?"

"Sure. Kwaza! Bring me the serpent chest!" he called, and one of the women stopped what she was doing, went over to the sleigh, and started rummaging around. She finally found the chest and brought it over to them.

When she did, Lori could see what had been mystifying her about the females' hands. They were more hooflike, the three fingers fused together and bending as one, with just enough indentation for flexibility, while the opposing thumb was even wider and broader than the males' thumbs. The effect reminded her more of claws, but they were too soft and supple for that description to be accurate. It must be more like doing everything wearing mittens, she thought.

When the woman had gone back to her work, Lori asked in a low tone, "Are all females' hands like that? No independent fingers?"

"Huh? Oh, sure. That's 'cause, when they're well along carryin' a baby, they got to pretty much walk on all fours and use their arms like the forelegs of an animal unless they be leanin' on somethin'. Otherwise they couldn't get around at all for them last two months or so. If the fingers could spread like a man's, you'd never be able t' do it. It'd tear yer fingers right off after a while. Don't believe me, try it sometimes."

"Hmph! Seems too bad, though. It sure limits what they can do."

"Not as much as ye think," Posiphar replied. "There's an old sayin', of course, that if women had fingers they'd be dangerous, but actually they got a little over us. You'n me, we get a bad break in the leg, don't heal, and we're crippled and in pain fer life, hobblin' around and no good to nobody. They lose a leg, they can still get around, do most of what they could before. No, the Creator put a lot of thought into us. I seen some races down at the port, they got these big boobs or udders, and fer what? To feed the young for a few months after havin' kids. And how many kids do most women have, anyways? So they carry them things for life and use 'em hardly a'tall. Erdomite women, now, when they ain't suck-lin', they stores water in them. Ye, me, full of water here, couldn't last more'n eight days without a drink. Women—up to three weeks, and it's available not only to them from the inside but to anybody else what needs it from the outside. Now, *that's* useful!"

She didn't bother to bring up the fact that there were other, purely pleasurable uses for breasts, but she conceded him his point. Each gender had its strengths and weaknesses for this harsh society and environ-ment, but it was pretty clear that the men were, in every sense of the word, on top here.

The chest, with an exotic winged serpentlike creature carved into it, proved to have various articles of male adornment. Only one of the dozens of codpieces was big enough to fit, and it was a plain, worn black color, but somehow, although it was decidedly uncomfortable and not at all useful for concealment or protection, it made her feel dressed for polite company. She passed on anything else, though, figuring, as it turned out correctly, that anything she might choose to use would be charged to her account. While she had no objection to providing the old trader with some extra protection, she also had no intention of getting so into debt to him that he'd virtually own her.

The food was very spicy and very good, and Lori realized with a start that it had been a *very* long time since she'd eaten, let alone had a de-cently cooked meal. The meat seemed similar to lamb but was too salty to tell more, and it was cooked in a large woklike pan together with some kind of very long ricelike grain and a number of green and red vegeta-bles at least one of which was some kind of hot pepper. Out here the drink was water, period.

With more conversation both that night and the next day setting out across the desert, she learned much more about this strange place and its dominant race.

Women were definitely at the very low end of the scale here, as she'd surmised, bound there by religion, tradition, and some definitely chauvinistic attitudes among the males. Because they were smaller and therefore had smaller brains, Posiphar told her, women were not as intelligent as men and had shorter attention spans, so any education and position was reserved for the males. It was considered a logical as well as practical division, not the least of reasons for this being that females outnumbered males roughly three to one, not only in live births but because they tended to live longer. Because of this, too, polygamy was the norm, although many men had only one wife and some of the richer males had whole harems. The rule was that one could have as many wives as one could support. There was also a law that said if one could no longer support them, one had to find new husbands for them that could.

She was relieved to learn that one of her fears, at least, was unfounded. They did not buy and sell women, or anybody else, either, although the women, without any practical rights at all, were pretty much at the mercy of the exclusively male-dominated system. "Love matches" were simply beyond their comprehension; one married for political reasons, for social reasons, for a dowry, or sometimes because one liked their features and thought that the combination would produce superior children.

Infant mortality was horrendous in the cities and working towns but surprisingly low in the desert and oasis communities. Communicable diseases were rare; the way heat was handled and exchanged in the bodies produced regular temperatures for short periods almost every day that killed ninety-five percent of any viruses or bacteria that might lurk inside. In the cities and working towns it was often the living conditions and other environmental factors that killed the young.

There was almost no chance at social mobility for either men or women, though. Maybe one step up or down, but no more than that. Certain physical features and colorations were unique to certain classes and made it difficult to pass as another in any event. Although it would be a while before she could recognize those differences, Posiphar told her that her body marked her as pretty well in the middle of the scale, suitable for a soldier or merchant or craftsman, but she had no characteristics of the nobility at all.

Erdom itself was, like all hexes, six-sided, but because it abutted the South Zone wall, an impenetrable barrier, its six sides formed a wing shape with a long flat along the ocean to the east rather than a hexagon.

Initially, a newcomer would simply "appear" almost anywhere in a given hex, but once there, the gates were the only way to and from Zone. The gate for Erdom was located near the wall in the far southeast corner, outside the large port city-state of Aqomb, where sat the Sultan of Erdom. The Sultan, in fact, had little practical authority outside his city but was the titular ruler of the entire hex, and, as such, Aqomb was considered the temporal and spiritual capital of Erdom.

Law in Erdom was entirely religious law, not only out of conviction but also out of necessity—the religion and its laws were the only true unifying elements in the primitive "nation" and served as a guarantee of uniformity of social rules and taboos across the hex. A priesthood of monks, all voluntarily castrated and living a totally religious and mostly cloistered life, ran the temples and spent most of the time praying to a series of cosmic gods that looked like some kind of giant six-armed octopuses out of a nightmare. The damper was put on social mobility and even male-female treatment by a strong belief in reincarnation, in which all Erdomites spent endless cycles of death and rebirth in attempts to raise themselves up to the level of their gods. Each soul was born as a lower-class female first, and only a perfect life would result in rebirth as a lower-class male. From that point a soul went up or down the social scale depending on how its life went, first female and then male until it reached the top of male nobility, after which came divination as a monk and, finally, godhood.

The fact that the vast majority of the population were lower-class females was taken as a sign that not too many made it. It was also a rationalization for the whole sociopolitical structure and the treatment of both males and females within each level of the system. It also meant that complainers, chronic troublemakers, and potential enemies could be executed with a clear conscience, since they'd be reborn anyway.

In fact, maiming was considered a far greater punishment, since it meant suffering with the result of transgression instead of having a new chance at a full life. About the only thing one so maimed could become would be a bandit if physically able or a crippled beggar if not. Only males faced maiming; females who ran afoul of religious law were always beheaded.

It was not, however, a strict society overall if one just played the game. Punishment came from rocking the boat; so long as one paid lip service to the system and behaved, it was actually pretty relaxed. It was also pretty dull, which was why the men indulged in a lot of macho posturing, dangerous sports, and even duels.

Lori did wonder about the women. They all looked strong and did much of the drudge work yet were seemingly always cheerful; the talk around the wells and camp site sounded pretty dumb and vapid, and there was never the slightest sign she could find of disobedience or rebellion. Almost without exception, they really *did* seem as dumb as a box of rocks.

As the days passed, Lori no longer felt any physical strangeness either with her own body or in seeing other Erdomites. In fact, being a member of this race was now so natural for her that even in her dreams of Earth and her previous existence all the people looked like Erdomites. Still, there were problems.

As an astronomer she'd been thrilled and awed by the night sky; the Well World seemed to be in the middle of a globular cluster. But there was nothing familiar to her up there, and even the names meant little. And of course there was the additional restriction of being in a highly limited nontech hex where science was on a rather low level, ignorance even among the educated was fairly high, and much of what she always had taken for granted—great telescopes, computers, and all the rest—simply wouldn't work. Worse, one good solid look at the written language of Erdom showed that it was pictographic, like Chinese, and not the sort of thing learned easily or quickly. Even though she still could read and write in her Earth languages, they were of little use here except to make memos to herself. In this element she was stripped of her profession and lifelong passion, denied a chance at it again or anything like it, and essentially illiterate—just like much of the population. Education was in the hands of a few teaching monks, and even if she could get into that highest caste, which she could not, the price would be much too high for her even now.

The other problem, though, was her sense of identity. She felt like an Erdomite, true, but she still felt like a woman trapped in a man's body. Although she was tempted to try out the opposite sexual role, the females just didn't really appeal to her. The men of her age, on the other hand, seemed powerful, strong, and very, very erotic.

And it was tearing her up.

She liked being around them, liked playing around with them, too. Either her fencing was improving dramatically or most of them weren't very good at it, because she rarely lost and then usually by not fully concentrating on the mock duel. In fact, by betting on such competitions, she'd actually accumulated some cash—gold and silver coins that were accepted hexwide—and bought her own used sword, hilt, and belt as well as a decent bow and a quiver of bronze-tipped arrows. While she wasn't a real champion at the latter, she was getting very good at hitting what she aimed at.

The trouble was, she was enjoying being around the young men and sporting with them for all the wrong reasons, and she dared not let on what the real reasons were.

Being on the road with the merchant helped, though. It was tough to form too many attachments when she was three or four days in one place, another few days journeying across the desert, then another three or four days in a new town or camp. She had given up all thought of contacting Mavra by this point; it was far too late, even though such an expedition away from this place would be much to her liking and Mavra could probably use somebody Lori's size.

Another thing was rubbing her wrong, too, although it was even harder to control. She was finding day by day that she was treating the females—both Posiphar's two wives and four daughters and those she came in casual contact with—in the same callous manner as the other males. She was much too easily buying into that part of the system, one that went against her whole life and all her beliefs. She felt guilty as hell every time she did it—but always after she did it, and she didn't stop because of it. It called her entire personal belief system into question. Deep down, had she really craved the absolute sexual equality she'd always thought she wanted, or had she instead subconsciously *really* just wanted a reversal of the system? If the latter, then she really hadn't had any ideals, just rationalizations.

Things changed a little when they pulled into a small oasis town in the south. They really didn't have any business to do there, but it was on the way from Point A to Point B and was a convenient stopover.

She wandered over to the ubiquitous social club all such places had, where the young men hung out between jobs and the transients could relax. It was much like an English pub in atmosphere, although Erdomite desert tribes considered alcohol and most stimulants and depressants stronger than coffee or tea to be evil and did not serve them.

The name always started the questions.

"Lori of Alkhaz. Odd name. Who are the Alkhaz, and where? Never heard of them."

She'd explain that she was not a native and had come through the Well, and that would elicit what was now becoming a somewhat boring and repetitive set of explanations that nonetheless made the newcomer the center of attention for a while. This time, however, there was a difference.

"You ought to go over and see Aswam the Master Tentmaker, then," one of the men commented.

"Oh? I have no need for a tent."

"No, no. He's the latest recipient of what's rapidly being called 'The

Girl from All the Hells.' She's an emigrant from another world, just like you."

"Really? Yes, I very much want to speak with her! Where is this tentmaker's place?"

"I'll show you. I'm not certain that anybody can do much with her, though. She's too smart, too aggressive, hates everybody and everything, and they keep her locked up like a prisoner since she won't behave and nobody's been able to break her. We think she's mad. Would you believe that she claims she was once a *man*? She's been passed around from family to family for some time, and by the time poor Aswam took a crack at her, there was nobody left to pass her on to when he gave up."

"My God! I'm surprised she wasn't executed!"

"I think that's what she wants, but it would be immoral to punish someone who is mad for behaving like they are mad, you see."

She did see and quickly had the dwelling of the master tentmaker in sight. She wasn't sure who or what she expected, but male or female, crazy or sane, it was somebody she could *talk* to. The fact that the other emigrant claimed to have been a man explained a lot of the behavior. She wouldn't have much liked being a female in *this* society, but to have been a man and dropped female into it would be particularly awful.

Although most of the buildings in these permanent settlements were made of dried mud, Aswam, of course, lived in what looked like a tent city. He proved to be a prosperous middle-aged man with many wives and more kids than could be easily counted.

"*Ack!*" he exclaimed, looking disgusted. "*That* one! She is a demon!"

"Perhaps, but if she's from the same place I'm from, as I think she might be, maybe I can do something with her."

He led Lori to a small mud hut in back of the tents, not much bigger than the outhouse it sat next to. Unlike most buildings in Erdom, though, this one was not open or covered only with a blanket but had an actual lockable door of wood.

"I used to store money and records in here," the tentmaker grumbled. "Now I am saddled with this dead loss!"

"Why did you take her, then?"

"Ha! The dowry offered was fantastic, or so I thought. More than any pretty girl is worth. But I tell you, she is so much trouble that I now realize that I was taken!"

"Why do you keep her locked up? Is she dangerous?"

"Only to herself. She keeps trying to run off into the Hjolai."

"You have the keys?"

"Yes, here. Go ahead in."

"What is her name?"

"She calls herself 'Julian' or some such foreign name."

She felt some relief that at least it wasn't poor Gus. He'd had enough done to him up to now. She had to admit to herself that she was also somewhat disappointed that it wasn't Juan Campos. Being a female in Erdom was just what that bastard deserved.

"All right. You can leave us. I'll be responsible."

Lori turned the key in the lock, opened the door, and went inside the small hut. It was quite dark, with only slits at the top for letting in light, and quite barren. The floor was covered with a local strawlike grass, and on it a female lay on her side, looking up at the newcomer.

There was only one way to try to break the ice. She tried English first. "My name is Lori, and I'm from Earth."

The effect on the girl was dramatic. She pushed herself to a seated position and looked up at the newcomer. "You're from *Earth*?" she responded in the same language and with an American accent. The almost whispery alto voice, however, seemed out of place. "This isn't just some new trick, is it?"

"No, it's no trick."

"Well, where I come from, a guy named Lori would be a little suspect."

"That's because the same thing happened to me that happened to you, only in reverse. It's terrible and ironic, I know, but I was a woman just like you were a man."

She stared at Lori for a moment, frowning in the gloom, then shook her head sadly. "Crazy. They said when we got here that this Well was some kind of logical computer. So where's the logic of making me *this* and you *that*?"

"Yes, I know. I was also an assistant professor of astronomy, which does me precious little good in this place."

"You *were*? I was a shuttle astronaut. A mission specialist. A fancy engineer, really, not a pilot. I'm Julian Beard."

"Then *you're* one of the two men who came through ahead of us! I *knew* you looked familiar when they showed us your picture. Your 'before' picture, that is. I did some work in Houston a few years back, and you were one of the instructors. Lori Ann Sutton."

The name didn't register, but she didn't expect it to. Many such scientists and other types had come through there, and she had only stayed a week. Still, Julian said, "Well, that's a kick in the head and ass. This thing is *really* screwed up. Dropped us in the wrong bodies in a backward land where even if you were allowed to use what you know, what you know doesn't work. Would you believe *nothing* but mechanical energy functions here? Or at least in any controllable way."

"I know. But, while I understand your problems being female in *this* society, how'd you get stuck in *this* fix?"

Julian shook her head in disgust. "You just don't *know*. First you wake up looking like an alternative evolution from a prehistoric horse, then you find you're not only a girl but you've got four breasts and a big tail and hands like pincers. Then you wander into one of these Bedouinlike camps and you're treated like a fresh piece of meat. They didn't *care* about me. They weren't even *interested* in me except as new flesh. Just trying to talk civilly to them gets you a rap in the mouth or worse. Then they decide you're either high-spirited or too smart or both, and they start trying to break you, body and soul. They were just, well, *unspeakable*, barbaric, and while they didn't break me, they pretty much took my soul. I didn't even want to live anymore."

Lori sighed. "I think I can imagine. I'm not so sure I wouldn't have just killed myself."

"That's just the problem! You *can't*. Not really. I tried to figure this out, and even though I'm no biologist, I have a theory. I think, well, in humans, most all males have some female in them. I mean, it's half the chromosomes, right? And every female has some male hormones to one degree or another. Here the male chromosome seems to have all the male hormones. Either that or male hormones have no effect on females. All the male I am, all the maleness I ever had, is in my head, but the female hormones really take control of behavior. I can't explain it. I can't even tell you what it does to you exactly. It's not like I suddenly woke up a human female. That would be a whole different thing, one you could certainly understand. This is Erdomese, and it's like a hundred times anything in humans, I'm sure. You know the feeling of walking alone on a dark night in a place you don't know well? The kind of nervousness or outright fear that's there? *Everything* becomes like that. *Everywhere*. In sunlight as well as darkness. The insecurity is monstrous, overwhelming. You just can't handle it no matter how hard you try. Like a permanent, unshakable paranoia. You want to be in a group with others, others you *know*. The urge for security dominates you and overrides anything else. Anything odd happens, you freeze solid or you have an irresistible impulse to run and hide. You only feel safe when you're with a big group of women you know or there's a related man around—husband, big brother, father, whatever. For that matter, ever see a wife or daughter talk back or argue with a husband or father here? Most of them just— *can't*. They hate it, but they have to take it."

Lori nodded, having seen all this behavior in the females. "Maybe it's vestigial. Not just a sexual division of responsibilities but a true herd mentality. I think this race evolved, or was made to evolve, from some more primitive herd animals. The whole society seems to rise from those primitive roots. The males were the hunters and guardians of the herd. The horn was a natural weapon. I think that's why males here love this kind of swordplay. And that's why you kept trying to run off into the desert. It fit the pattern and would still be almost certain suicide."

"Yes, that's it. It was my only way out. That and the fact that I was maybe the only woman in this stinking place who could muster up the guts to say 'no' and have enough self-control to mean it. But I couldn't really fight it. All I could do was piss and moan and make the men's lives a little miserable. It would be nothing back home—I wouldn't have had anything to do with a woman who didn't have that kind of spunk—but here it's something the guys just can't handle. So they swapped me off, family to family, and it started all over again. Finally this tentmaker took me to one of their weird priests. I think they're smart and well educated, because he knew what an engineer was and what computers are and a lot more. We talked for quite a while about who I was and where I was from and what my problem was, and I thought maybe things would improve, but they didn't. They got worse."

"He led you on and then pounced, huh?"

"Pretty much. In the end their job is to keep everything just the way it is. Just *knowing* about the outside world isn't the same as *approving* of it. It was his idea to lock me up like this. He said it might take a long time, but I was very young—this body's about fourteen or so—and that eventually, with no stimuli, the biology—he actually called it 'programming'—would take over completely. He's right, too. Since I've been in here my dreams have gotten more and more mixed up and more and more erotic. My memories are becoming more and more confused, and I have trouble remembering what I was like—before. Even the math tables I used to stay sane when they were trying to break me more crudely fail me. Not that I've forgotten them, I just can't keep my mind on them. I also kept trying to always think in English, or sometimes German, but I just can't *concentrate* anymore, and the more my thoughts were Erdomese, the more Erdomese I became. I—I've lost so much already, I don't know how much of me is really left. Here, see? I'm starting to cry, and I just can't stop it. And I don't even feel embarrassed about doing it anymore."

"Sometimes a good cry is something we all need. Holding it in is what eats you up."

"Yeah?" she responded, sniffling and wiping away tears. "So if you're so miserable here, how many times have *you* cried since you got here?"

Lori didn't answer, but the truth was, not at all. For a man to cry here was to show weakness and lose honor and the respect of both males and females. No matter how much she'd wanted to, she'd held it in as a matter of course. It was another little shock to the system. *Maybe I've become more of a male than I think . . .*

"I don't know," Lori told her. "I still can't figure out my own self in this. I mean, no offense, but there's still some of me that's the human woman I was for most of my life. It won't go away. I liked men, and I still do. I assume you were pretty much of a straight arrow like me back home, but *your* orientation seems to be changing to fit what you've become."

"I—I think we fight it because it's the last real core of what we were," she suggested, still wiping away tears. "So long as we hold on to that, we're still something of our old selves. I mean, what defines us—how we grew up, how we related to other people—more than our sex? You let go, you throw that out, and you're not *you* anymore. You're somebody else, somebody with another person's memories. I think you can cling to it until you die—and there's certainly got to be gays in most all the cultures here, since we see it in animals, too. With men here, though, it's easier. You have a little of both male and female in you, so it's easier to control the physical aspects of the change. I don't so it was a lot harder to cling to, but I did, until I was put in here for so long. I could either fight that battle or stay sane fighting the others. I let it go. For *you,* it's the defining thing. For *me,* it was in the way, I think. You have more choices, but in the end you're going to have to decide who and what you want to be, 'cause you're going to be an Erdomite man for the rest of your life, just like I'm going to be an Erdomite woman."

"I think there's a lot more of Julian Beard in you than you think," Lori told her. "Otherwise you'd have given up and given in long ago." She decided she liked Julian—liked her a lot. It was the first time she felt she was really attracted to a female here.

"Maybe. When a female gets close to a male she trusts, she gets these *feelings,* these *urges* that are hard to control. I'm feeling them right now, in here, with you. Right now my mind, the one thing I've been able to somehow keep, is able to suppress them, but every day I'm here it gets harder and harder to fight, to keep control. I'm slipping more and more."

"Tell me something. The women here—are they really as dumb as they seem to be?"

That brought a smile to Julian's still-tearful face. "No, some are quite smart, but they've learned to hide it well. Being smart in this culture just means trouble if you're a woman. They're pretty ignorant, though, and they don't know any other system. Sometimes I think of those women in the countries back on Earth that went western and then returned to fundamentalism. They might resent the restrictions, but somehow they're comforted by the absolutism of the rules and religion. And like I said, security is everything."

"I just—I dunno—I just had a hunch that might be it," Lori replied. "It really offended me that they might all be frightened little bimbos. But I forgot to ask the one question I wanted to know more than anything. How did you ever get here in the *first* place?"

"Stupidity," Julian Beard replied. "That meteor that came down in the jungle—I was on assignment from NASA to take a look at it. Good publicity, too. Then that news team disappeared and the army took over, and it was *weeks* before anything serious could be done."

"Yes, I was one of the team."

"I thought so. I figured what happened to us happened to you. Anyway, this tough old Brazilian Air Force colonel who was in charge out there was more a politician than a military man. He finally called off the search and bent to pressures to let in researchers, at least a few at a time. Well, the whole world came down on us, or so it seemed, and they wanted pictures and all that for the publicity, and since a number of people had climbed all over that meteor before, we figured it wasn't any big deal. The colonel and I were asked to pose on top of it for the media; he talked me into it, and you can guess what happened."

"The hex gate opened, and you both wound up in Zone talking to a polka-dotted dragon."

"Actually, it was a mean-looking five-foot-tall talking butterfly. You?"

"Too long a story to tell here and now. The first thing we have to do is decide what to do about you."

"Huh?"

"Look, it may be backward, but we're here and we're stuck. That Zone had elaborate computers and all sorts of technology, and I happen to know that a third of the countries here—they call them hexes, after their shape—support high technology, some way in advance of Earth's. I'm going crazy here, and you want to kill yourself before you lose it all. There's a seacoast and ports here, believe it or not, and ships that go all sorts of places. We're both wrong-bodied opposites with a lot of the same background. I'd like to find a place where I could really study that astronomer's dream of a sky up there. You'd like to get someplace where you could still be an individual and not a harem girl. There's *got* to be such a place here somewhere."

Julian sighed. "You'd have to marry me to take me anywhere here," she pointed out. "And I have to tell you, I think I'd rather rot in here than have a name-only marriage. Earlier, maybe, but not at the stage I'm at now. I'm a woman now, an Erdomite woman, and I'd go bananas if I wound up a mere housemaid or a nun."

"Yeah, well, we're the original odd couple all right, but you've just given me the first decent conversation I've had since I got here." She was fighting with herself inside and trying to get the right words out. "I like you, Julian. I like you a lot. If you can accept your fate, I guess, with your help, I can accept mine. Like you, I'm here and I'm stuck this way. I think I might just be able to be a man, maybe the man I always said I wanted to see, with you. Okay. Deal?"

"You'd be responsible for me. And I don't know, like I said—I don't know how much of me is left and how much I can keep over time. This having a two-way conversation in English has really helped, but it's a real *fight*. It's like, well, half of me is an old air force jock clinging desperately to his old identity through real contact with a colleague and half of me lusts after your body and would become your slave if you'd just let her attend your needs. No, it's worse. There's not even close to fifty percent of Julian Beard left. I don't know, it sounds crazy, but this contact, this conversation, this *hope* is actually making the Erdomite part harder to control."

"Just take it easy," Lori said soothingly. "I'll go make the arrangements." And Posiphar would have to be told that his security was about to leave him.

Julian was already thinking ahead. "We'll need money for this . . ."

Lori grinned. "I get the idea that our tentmaker friend out there will pay me *handsomely* to take you off his hands."

And *he* was just the one to get the best deal!

ARMOWAK,
AMBREZA-FLOTISH BORDER

NATHAN BRAZIL HAD TO admit to himself that the Well World was probably the one place in all creation where a good-looking human woman could play Lady Godiva and not fear anything more than if she was over-dressed.

He really wasn't quite certain just what to do with the girl. Clearly she wanted to come along, but she wasn't an asset on a long trip as she was. It was as if she'd been reborn as a water creature who couldn't really communicate or travel any distance over land.

Still, he wasn't sure how to ditch her, either. She certainly had a mind of her own.

She also had something of an appetite. Any time they stopped during their journey, she'd find something edible around and down it. Like nearly all the Glathrielians he'd seen, she was chubby but not fat and apparently in excellent condition. He wondered if she wouldn't start putting on weight if she kept eating like that, but it was a moot point. Things she could eat that were so readily available would be few and far between in many of the hexes he'd have to travel, including Flotish itself, considering that the hex was part of the Gulf of Zinjin and was in fact salt water to near ocean depths.

He was nonetheless still fascinated by her and loath to cast her out. She should not have become a Glathrielian. And since she had, she shouldn't have retained what was obviously her natural coloration and features. The Well had changed her in many ways, including taking who knew how many years off her age, but the one thing it clearly had not done was change her genetic code.

He wished he could just know her name. He wasn't sure Glathrielians even used names anymore, but *she* had one, and no amount of blocking or rewiring of some brain functions would keep her from knowing it. The problem was in finding some way for her to tell it to him.

It was not a problem he could solve on the back of a horse, though, not with her on *another* horse.

That, too, was a wonder. He'd gotten the impression that the Glathrielians wouldn't even *use* a live animal, yet she'd picked her horse, gotten on, and now rode quite comfortably. Another mystery. When they were making speed, she'd go forward and hang on somehow up against the horse's neck, but she never kicked it to start, never seemed to guide it at all. The horse, though, did just what it was supposed to do every time. Sometimes he thought that the two moved so naturally and effortlessly together that it was as if somehow she and the horse were one.

Terry herself had no more answers beyond her old name, which indeed she did remember, although it was sometimes confusing because of the otherwise nonverbal processes now operating in her mind. Sometimes it seemed like it was Terry; other times, Teysi. She knew that there had been a lot more to the name than either of those once, but those were the defining words she retained.

As for the horse, she was discovering talents she didn't know she had as she went along. She had gone out back, had realized he was going to ride, and had simply touched a number of horses until one of the animals "clicked" with her in a way she could not explain. When one had and she had mounted it, all she'd had to do was relax and put everything out of her mind except that horse. As Brazil had imagined without believing, she'd become one with it, so that the two bodies, while in physical contact with one another, actually did become as one, operating as easily as one operated one's arms, legs, and head. Whenever she dismounted and contact was broken, it was as if she'd lost something of herself. The size and power of the animal were exhilarating. Still, she hadn't the vaguest idea how she did it.

At a stop to get something to eat and drink and give the horses time to do the same, he decided to try another experiment. If that first Glathrielian girl had reacted to him as if he had the plague, how would *this* one react?

He walked over to her, and she watched him come and stand right in front of her. He smiled, and she returned the smile. They were both almost exactly the same height, his computer-designed leather boots raising him just a bit, but only to match the added height of her thick black hair. Then, casually, he reached out and took her hands in his.

The initial contact was a shock, and the tumble of information that came through was incredibly confusing to her. There was a kindness in him that she found true, almost noble, and still the element of a little boy inside somewhere, either deep down or up front in the bravado that masked his deeper self.

There was also a sadness there, an incredible, deep, painful emptiness that was almost too much to bear. She grieved for anyone who could have that much sorrow within him, yet she admired him, too, for the strength to be able to carry it. It masked, even overwhelmed, the tremendous contradictions she could sense but not grab hold of inside of him.

And yet, deep down, there was something else, something hidden very deep, yet something he was aware of. It was so concealed, so cleverly masked with layer upon layer of pure humanity that it could not be directly seen, only glimpsed ever so briefly, like something seen only in the extreme corner of the eye. That was the heart of the confusion about him. There seemed to be two of him, two totally different creatures so alien to one another that the other would not come in, would not focus. Yet the man she *could* see, the man of sorrows, was not a mask, not a facade, but one and the same with what was hidden. It made no sense at all.

They had warned her, warned her that something lurked there that she did not want to see and should not and that only the man should be considered. She backed away from it, sensing somehow that what lay hidden was no more dangerous than the man and no less, being one and the same, but that it was somehow beyond her comprehension or ability to cope.

He liked her. That made her feel very good indeed, because she liked him and she wasn't certain how she was coming across. He wasn't a particularly handsome man, but he had a tough appearance, and his well-worn face echoed his inner strength and long experience. Even in her past life, she knew that if they'd met, she would have been attracted to him. The fact that she now could see so much of him yet not reach the central mystery of him fascinated her and made him all the more interesting. Sensing that he would never take advantage of her, she felt that at some point she might well be tempted to take advantage of him.

There was little or no sensation or information going in Brazil's direction, but he did somehow sense both her trust and her attraction to him, whether by some sixth sense or perhaps just from long experience. He did not consider it unusual, since, after all, if *he* were stuck in *her* current situation and found just one other human being who knew who and what she was or had been and where she'd come from, he'd probably react the same way. He had no sense that she had learned so much about him, but he had noticed an odd, almost electrical tingling when he'd touched her that was as mysterious as the rest of her. If he didn't know better, he told himself, he'd swear that she was somehow generating a weak force field of some kind from within herself.

There was still a lot of the old Terry in her, and she found herself getting turned on by the experience. That, right now, would never do, so she gave him a quick kiss and a big smile and broke the contact.

Well, at least she didn't run away screaming, he thought, *although, truth be told, that* was *the general idea.* Whatever the first girl had seen, this one either hadn't seen it or wasn't upset about it.

The fact was, he had mixed emotions about the result. On the one hand, to have gotten rid of her would have been in both their best interests; on the other, he had to admit that he liked her spunk and liked having somebody around who, however silent, didn't look or smell like a giant beaver.

Still, how could he take her along? Once she was on that ship and out to sea, there wouldn't be any way out for her.

It was almost nightfall by the time they intersected the main road, but by that time the city lights were in view ahead. Coming over the last rise, Armowak was spread before them, and beyond lay the great blackness of the sea.

For Terry, the scene was both pretty and scary. Old reflexes, old inner tensions from her past life resurfaced at the sight of a modern city, and for the first time it really hit home that she was about to be plunged back into modern civilization as a naked savage. Still, there was a certain confidence in that thought, and the kinds of things she'd been raised to fear in such places now had no hold on her. If she had nothing, it could not be stolen, and she doubted that giant beavers and most of whatever else lived in this world had much interest in her body.

Although traffic wasn't heavy, there were a number of the small personal cars going to and from the city at pretty good speeds, and their Ambrezan drivers seemed oblivious to anything on either side of them. A number of larger vehicles, including tandems and triples, passed as well, showing the importance of the port. She and Brazil kept to the side, well away from the road, and barely drew a glance from any passersby.

Armowak was Ambreza's western gateway to the rest of the world. Into it came the imports from other hexes that allowed a measure of variety in Ambrezan markets, products of perhaps hundreds of races. From it went the principal export, tobacco, both processed and "raw," as well as manufactured items for various trading partners from the computer-controlled and robot-driven factories of the interior. It was a busy, bustling place, a major seaport where great ships called constantly and where many of the races of the Well World mixed in a rare amalgam of shapes, forms, and languages. Here, too, one could buy almost anything with enough money, and here, too, one could lose everything if not careful.

The suburban areas were fairly quiet but well lit; the streets were mostly narrow, except the main highway, and made for pedestrian traffic only, since there was an extensive system of underground moving walkways and transit vehicles to move people quickly around the city. The layout and design of the city were exotic to Terry's eyes and definitely had an alien cast, yet were basically familiar and logical.

The old city area was along the docks. The port itself ran for a couple of miles, or so it seemed, with large piers, massive warehouses, brick and cobblestone streets, and broad silver-gray strips that proved to be much the same as the railroad tracks used by futuristic vehicles moving freight and supplies to and from the port area.

The services area of the port ran from the opposite side of the main north-south docks for about three blocks before a row of older, seedier-looking office buildings drew a line of demarcation between the actual port and the rest of the city.

There were a few larger ships in, although most of what was there seemed to be coastal steamers, tuglike boats, and even a few of what looked like fishing trawlers. What was fascinating was the odd juxtaposition of technologies between the ships and the shore services: the latter were very modern with magnetic trains and robotic longshoremen, and the ships often had smokestacks and, on the larger ones, two or even three tall sailing masts as well. It was as if ships of the American Civil War era were tying up and being serviced at some twenty-first-century port.

Nathan Brazil was familiar with the design and the reasons behind it. He was impressed to see that some of the ships weren't wood anymore but were metal-plated or, in a few cases, seemed to be made out of wholly artificial new plasticlike substances. Their odd nature, though, remained out of necessity; literally just a few meters outside the harbor entrance, visible by day but hidden in the night and city lights, was another hex boundary. Beyond it, where these ships had to sail, a different technology level was imposed. Flotish was a semitech hex; there steam or sail power could be used but nothing electrical worked. Batteries would not hold charges, generators and alternators might truly give off energy, but it could not be controlled and dissipated just about as fast as it was made. Even powerful broadcast signals from a high-tech hex like Ambreza would fade quickly once they passed that boundary, no matter how strong the source. Running an internal combustion engine large enough to be useful would result in the most beautiful and rapid burning up of an engine anybody had ever seen.

Beyond were a few hexes that restricted all technology except direct mechanical devices. There great steam boilers would virtually explode, making it impossible to power any device, ships included. To travel those distances one had to use the most ancient of methods, the wind in the sail.

That also meant that each ship had to carry a highly trained crew expert in both steam and sail and willing to live for long periods aboard ship. Such crews were highly paid and highly prized, and they acted like it. Ship's law was the only law they respected, and the companies tended to pay for or gloss over any excesses in port. They also tended to be from a great many races, and here, at this port, Terry began to get a sampling of just what other sorts of creatures this world contained.

Two large scorpionlike creatures moved down a side street to her left, startling her. They looked huge, mean, and menacing. Elsewhere were several man-sized bipeds wearing clothes that looked like they were out of some Renaissance movie epic, but they more resembled Sylvester the Cat, with their expressive, almost comical feline faces and fur and large fluffy tails. And there was a creature that looked half woman and half vulture, with a pretty face and mean killer's eyes that seemed to glow in the dark. Like the Ambreza, most embodied some aspects of creatures she knew or at least knew about, but the association with familiar Earth creatures was merely a way of cataloging them so that her mind could deal with what she was seeing. The reference points were far from exact, but they were the only way she could cope with the many alien beings she encountered.

Some, however, were beyond easy mental cataloging. Creatures with mottled, leathery dark green skin that went along at a fast clip on what seemed to be hundreds of spindly legs and whose entire bodies seemed to open into rows of sharp, pointy teeth; wrinkled, slow-moving dark gray masses that could only be thought of as hippos without apparent bones; squidlike monstrosities whose tails seemed topped with giant sunflowers. There were so many, and they were so bizarre both individually and collectively that she could only look at one and then another and hope nobody noticed her staring.

But this was no freak show or chamber of horrors; these were *people,* people of ancient races, races as established as her own, from their own hex-shaped countries. She had to always remember that.

Brazil pulled up in front of a lighted office and dismounted, tying his horse loosely to what he knew was a fireplug. Terry wasn't sure what to do. Her impulse was to remain outside, but she had no idea what this place was or how long Brazil might be. After a moment she got down and followed him into the office.

Almost immediately she felt a sense of claustrophobia, of being hemmed in, of the walls and ceiling maybe closing in on her. She repressed it as best she could and managed to stay with him, but she didn't like the feeling.

The creature behind a counter was a large, irregular lump maybe only a bit taller than their own height that seemed to be an animated mass of tiny red and green feathers from behind which, much farther down than would be expected, two huge, round yellow eyes looked back at them.

"Yes?" the creature asked Brazil pleasantly, barely giving Terry a glance.

"Are there any ships in now outbound to Agon or Clopta or anywhere else semitech or above in the northwest?" Brazil asked it.

"Nothing direct," the creature replied. "The *Setting Sun* down at Pier 69 may be your best bet. It stops at Kalibu, Hakazit, Tuirith, and Krysmilar. You might be able to change, particularly at Hakazit, since there's a lot of cross-channel stuff out of there."

"Nothing else coming in that might be more direct?"

"Sorry. Not until sometime next month, and that won't give you any time advantage. The only other possibility for Agon is something like the *Northern Winds* leaving in two days for Parmiter, but your chances of a westbound connection from there are slim to none, and you'd have to walk overland."

"Yeah, well, that would be a solution if Agon were my final destination, but it's not. I'll have enough overland without starting that early. When does *Setting Sun* sail?"

"Let me see . . ." The huge eyes dropped down to look at something below the counter. "They're still finishing off-loading, and they have a lot to get on. They're scheduled for high tide . . . the day after tomorrow. About nine in the morning local time."

"That sounds reasonable. I need to book passage on that sailing to Hakazit if it's available, with a cabin if possible."

"Yes, sir. For two?"

He turned and looked at Terry, who was showing her discomfort and staring around the office with a queasy look. Still, she was here.

"Yes," he sighed. "Might as well. What's the weather supposed to be en route?"

"Possible storms in west Ronbonz, otherwise choppy but not uncomfortable. The winds, however, are unpredictable in this crossing, particularly in storms."

"I'll still take it. You have anything on the basics of Hakazit or a general hex guide? I want to see if it's feasible to book the horses on as well."

"Animals are not guaranteed in shipment," the strange clerk warned him. "There is a bookshop on Vremzy Street, two blocks in and one left. It's closed by now, but it will be open all day tomorrow. You can get what you need there. Outfitters and suppliers are along that street as well. We can probably add two animals with no problem if you come back here by nine or ten tomorrow night with your prepaid ticket. In the meantime they can be quartered at the livestock area, Warehouse 29 just along this street. Now, I'll need to know your native hex so that sufficient edible provisions can be laid on for you and the cabin prepared properly."

Nathan Brazil grinned. "Glathrielian."

Those huge eyes seemed to double in size. "You are joking, of course."

"No, I'm not. We came through the Well from offworld, and that's what we are. It won't be hard even if your guide doesn't list us. I'll give you a half dozen or more races we're compatible with."

"Very well. So *you're* what Glathrielians look like."

"You work here and you've never seen any?"

"I'm actually the purser on the *Honza Queen*. When we're in port, we take the late shifts in the company offices. There isn't much here to interest me, anyway."

The fare was not cheap, but it was reasonable, and Brazil felt certain he could more than afford this leg. There would be other times when things would be a lot harder.

Besides, it might be interesting to see how hard the ship's crew and other passengers might gamble.

Finally, Brazil asked, "Is there any outdoor area nearby where we might be able to camp? I suspect that any hotels in this area won't be set up for us, and I have my own food." There usually were such places around ports, particularly because most of them naturally provided only for the races that were the most common visitors. The Gulf of Zinjin was an arm of the Well World's greatest ocean, and there were far too many possible visitors to economically provide for them all, and particularly not Glathrielians.

"Far northern end, past the last pier," the clerk informed him. "Rather nice, although a bit chilly some nights for hairless types. A number of small merchants have local stalls up there from dawn to dusk, too, if you can tolerate the local food."

"Some of it. Well, it sounds fine to me. Any permits required?"

"Not at the port one. All others, you'd need to report to the police first."

The clerk made a series of entries with two huge, clawed hands that extended from under the feathers, and the computer spit out very neat-looking ticket books. Brazil thanked him, put the tickets away, and went back outside, with Terry following. Just walking back out in the air seemed to lift an enormous burden from her, but she still felt a little shaken and a little sick from the experience. Being enclosed was going to be very, very rough on her indeed, she knew.

Brazil decided to take the horses with them rather than pay to have them quartered at the warehouse. The odds of their being in the way at the park were more than outweighed by the possibilities of selling them to the locals there if transporting them proved to be a problem, and it might. Hakazit and Agon were also high-tech hexes, and any layover in the former would just leave him with even more ravenous mouths to feed, not to mention the problem of horse droppings, which many places, and particularly high-tech places, tended to frown on.

The park wasn't much, just a large area that apparently had been part of a much earlier port and settlement, long abandoned. They'd planted some trees, as much to keep erosion down as for shelter, and it fronted right on the Gulf, with a small jetty leading out to guide lights warning off any incoming ships.

If anyone else was using the park right now, he couldn't see them, although with some clouds and only a few electric streetlights he might well have missed them. Still, there was a nice ocean smell coming in on the breeze and the quiet sound of waves lapping at the old pylons.

He picked a spot just inside the trees and set up the small tent and the camping outfit as he had in Glathriel. Thanks to the brevity of his trip, he still had a five-day supply of food and gas canisters, and there was a very nice if somewhat elaborate fountain in the middle of the park that, thankfully, had fresh water.

Terry used her new night sense to survey the area and found virtually nothing edible in and around the park. She knew she could wander farther afield, but this was a large and strange city and was unlikely to have any real groves close by. Here one didn't pick one's food, one bought it.

Thus, when Brazil opened up his food supplies and gestured an offer to share, she had no choice but to accept, although she made it clear with hand signals that it was not to be cooked. Something of an amateur gourmet who fancied herself a very good cook, she now found the thought of cooked food thoroughly repulsive.

Brazil did not compromise his own preferences for hers but did find a perverse fascination in watching her eat. Knowing that she must have been a civilized, modern woman, he was fascinated to see her take an open container of preserved fruit, for example, and just scoop it out with her fingers. He was even more surprised when she took and ate the beef he had, both ground and in small filets, also raw. He remembered then the Ambrezan foreman telling him that Glathrielians would eat meat, but only if it was already dead.

Terry, too, was surprised both at her appetite and at the fact that the meat tasted exceptionally good right out of the container. Until now she'd always liked her meat cooked through, and with sauces and all the trimmings if available. While he packed up and saw to the horses, she went to the fountain and then to relieve herself, and when she got back, he was getting ready to turn in. It had been a long, tiring day, and both keenly felt it.

A *very* chilly sea breeze was developing, and he was concerned for her. He offered her a spot in his tent, limited as it was, or his sleeping bag, but she declined both with a smile. Then she gave him a little hug and a kiss and went off.

Again he'd noticed that odd, almost static electricity feeling when they'd touched, but now he noticed another thing as well.

She'd been warm to the touch, with no sign at all of the chill he felt on his face and hands. As warm as summertime.

Terry didn't notice this because she really didn't feel it. The field around her that she could see, generated somehow by her own body, acted as insulator and even life support system in some odd way. She felt warm and comfortable, and she picked a tree almost over Brazil's tent and scampered up it, then found a comfortable notch and settled in for the night.

Terry awoke the next morning feeling nauseous, and for a moment she was afraid it was the food. Something inside her, though, told her that it wasn't, that it would pass, and she trusted her instincts as usual and they proved correct. She still felt a little queasy when Brazil finally got up and found her there waiting for him, but she didn't let on that anything was wrong, and after getting something to eat, the feeling gradually vanished.

Brazil bought breakfast from the promised local merchants, who set up small booths along the waterfront area of the park selling home-grown produce and other things. He discovered that Terry would eat bread, the first cooked item he had seen her accept, but not eggs. In point of fact, she ate two whole home-baked loaves of bread and two large melons, and Brazil began to wonder if he could literally afford to take her with that kind of appetite.

He walked back into the port district; he'd already made a decision that the horses would be far too much of a burden until they were needed to be worth the cost and had opened some discussions with a stall merchant who kept a couple of horses at his place outside the city.

Terry followed him through the now-bustling area, and her head began to reel with the number of races and weird sounds and smells that made the whole place come alive. She had already figured, though, that he was leaving by ship, and she no longer felt compelled to enter the buildings he entered.

So many sounds, so many races . . . how did they *understand* each other? She found the whole thing bewildering. The Glathrielians whose lives she'd shared had not prepared her for this.

Occasionally one or another of the creatures would say something to her, but she was always able to convey by some gesture or expression that she did not understand them. Still, she did feel the irony of being naked and exposed in a strange city and yearned for a dark alleyway. Once a particularly smelly and repulsive-looking reptilian creature had actually *touched* her, and she'd reacted instantly with a nearly panicky mental push that said "Go away!" And the creature had frozen, looked puzzled for a moment, then seemed to lose all interest in her and actually had gone away!

Could she really *do* that, or was it a coincidence? One of these times she'd find out.

Brazil emerged from the bookshop with something of what he needed. He had been surprised to find, in the first few weeks after landing in Ambreza, that he was able to figure out the written language almost as if it were something he'd forgotten rather than something he'd never known. It was a *little* cumbersome and not all of it read just right, but what he needed to read he had little problem figuring out.

The map was the most important thing. When he had the time, he intended to annotate it in Latin, the "stock" Earth language he'd found the most useful over the long haul, so he wouldn't have to keep looking up and remembering this term or that and figuring out things word by word and sentence by sentence. There was a sort of common written language here, one used for interhex trade and commerce—the ticket was in it—but he found *it* less familiar and less useful than Ambrezan.

Of course, he knew what had happened. He was remembering ancient Ambrezan, which had evolved greatly over the millennia since his last time here, and the common language he'd known had been entirely replaced, perhaps many times.

He then stopped at the ministry of commerce offices to call in to the capital, report *something* on his slight observations on Glathrielians— mostly to omit any of the oddities and report a very primitive life-style of no threat or consequence to the Ambrezans—and get what information he could on Mavra's group.

There was *some* information, but it was incomplete and not guaranteed. Of the two men and two women who came in, one was reported in Erdom, as he'd surmised, another was in Zebede, which did surprise him, a third was in Dahir, and a fourth, clearly Mavra, had shown up in Glathriel, as he already knew.

"But who's this other Glathrielian female I have with me?" he asked them. "If she didn't come in with me, and she didn't, since I know where mine are, and she didn't come in with *them,* she must have come in either alone or with another group."

"The only group we have other than yours and the larger party is two males about three weeks after you arrived. One of those is a Leeming, and the other—that's odd—also an Erdomite."

"Well, then, who *is* this girl?"

"You're sure she's not a native putting you on?"

He sighed. "Natives do not look like her. I know you might not be able to tell them apart, but I sure can. And natives don't draw maps of televisions and cameras and North America on Earth."

"Well, we have no reports of anybody coming through except those we told you about. Sorry. They are quite upset with this at Zone Security, you know. There's an investigation to find out just how this happened. Right now the only plausible theory is that she came in just after one of your groups, probably the larger one, and somehow snuck by security and went directly through the gate without being noticed. How that's possible nobody can say."

Nathan Brazil sighed and muttered, "Television reporters," in a disgusted tone. "All right, thank you. I'll be off now, and it's unlikely although not impossible that I'll be back. I thank you for all your help."

"Not a big problem," the comm tech told him. "However, I was told to inform you if you were heard from again that if you *do* return, you must proceed immediately to Glathriel and remain there. If you are picked up here again, you will be immediately transported there. You must make somebody nervous."

Damned paranoids, he thought, but he acknowledged the transmission and switched out.

The truth was, he'd like to do that at some point. Move into Glathriel and live there, "go native," as it were, if he could stand it, and uncover the real mysteries of the place. Now, however, wasn't the time.

Still, after seeing what was wrong with the Well, he seriously considered remaining this time, at least for a while. He wasn't really sure why he hadn't done so before, although, of course, the *last* time had been pretty dicey and leaving had been the only practical choice.

Hell, he could change his looks in there, even his race and sex, if he wanted to. He couldn't figure out why he'd never done it. Too much the uncomfortable god, he decided. Maybe this time would be different. Or maybe he should just try the current Glathrielian matrix and see just what the hell was going on inside those people. That was if this girl made it up there with him and couldn't tell him what he needed to know after removing her speech and language block.

They headed back up to the park with a detour past the ship they were going to take. It was a *big* one, larger than any he'd remembered from his still admittedly spotty recollections. Three-masted, made of superior fitted wood covered with some kind of synthetic laminate that protected and sealed it, two stacks, three decks above the main deck. Yeah, it looked like it could take an ocean, all right, and keep everybody comfortable and dry while doing it. It even had all sorts of smaller, exotic-looking masts atop the wheelhouse, indicating that if the hex allowed, it could use almost any technology known to Well World science.

It flew the Suffok flag, which meant it was a long way from home. He wished it were *going* home; it would make things very easy indeed, since that hex was virtually on the equator, but he suspected that it rarely went up that far. Considering that such a ship could not lie idle for long, he suspected that its profits, more than its hull, went to its home port in any given year.

Terry stared at the ship with a mixture of awe, wonder, puzzlement, and a little fear. The puzzlement was of course because she had no idea how the Well World worked or that there were nontech, semitech, and high-tech hexes, and thus its combination of features from every type of ship she'd ever known, and some she'd never thought of, seemed bizarre. Fear because even in normal times she'd never been that great on ships, and she really didn't know if her claustrophobia could stand it long on that thing. She knew, though, that something that big and that grand didn't make small voyages.

They continued walking back up the street to the park. By now it was late in the day and the merchants were mostly packing up, but Brazil was able to spot the one he'd spoken to about the horses, and now he figured he'd close whatever deal he could get. He'd paid a lot; now the Ambrezan, sensing Brazil was in something of a time squeeze, offered only half.

They haggled and argued and finally settled on a hundred plus as much of the unsold produce as Brazil and Terry could carry back to their nearby campsite. Brazil made out a bill of sale on some glorified butcher paper and signed and dated it, and the merchant took it and nodded.

Brazil had to admit to himself that he took far more of the produce than he could possibly consume, but he felt a little gypped by the guy and wanted to cost him as much as possible. Terry, however, once she got the idea, did even better.

Both of them ate until they were stuffed, understanding that little of it would keep, but after he watched Terry put away so much of it, he wondered if there were going to be leftovers, after all.

Finally, they cleaned up as best they could and found themselves again virtually alone in the park after dark. The sky had cleared, and the glow from the massive stellar display was almost like a full moon on Earth. It was one sight that neither he nor Terry ever tired of; those who were born under it and took it for granted rarely even looked up.

Terry felt oddly nervous about the coming day. For one thing, she had no idea if she'd have to sneak or bully her way onto that big ship to stay with him or whether he'd added her to the fare. For another, cut off from Earth, from her friends, and from Glathriel, she felt particularly lonely and insecure, and Brazil was the only one around she had to lean on.

He'd considered turning in early to insure having enough time to get the gear packed and board the ship, but he felt too wide awake, and there was that wonderful sky and the water. He finally decided that he'd take a walk and appreciate the scene. Acutely aware of her insecurity, Terry went with him, taking his hand as they walked along the ancient seawall where once great ships had called in some distant age. After a while they sat together on the seawall and looked out at the sky, the inner harbor lights, and the darkness beyond. To Terry, this moment was wonderful; she wanted it to continue.

She closed her eyes and allowed the night sense to come in, the scene took on a far different look. It wasn't dark anymore; instead, it was rippling, and within it she saw thousands of pale green shapes, many tiny, some very large, and, here and there, large shapes of an indigo color she'd never seen before. What were they? Some monsters of the deep, like whales, swimming yet breathing air? Or did intelligent races live even in the water here? Were they more creatures of some kind, creatures who had some sort of different civilization out there in the sea?

The concept, combined with the sky, made her feel even tinier and more lost and insecure, and her fear that Brazil might leave her grew. How could she follow him through *that*?

Without even realizing that she was doing it, she squeezed his hand and sent, *Love me! Don't ever leave me!* The white aura, particularly strong after all she had eaten, rushed from her and to him, and a bright white series of impulses traveled from her up his arm and into his head and seemed to explode there, then fade, although not entirely.

They hadn't invented a number high enough to count the women

Nathan Brazil had known in his life, and he'd spent millennia trying to never form an attachment or any real feeling for any short-lifer because of the inevitable heartbreak. It was always a battle, though, particularly because of his own intense loneliness. Somehow, though, right there, right then, with this mystery woman he could neither talk to nor understand, he lost the battle and the will to fight it at all. Suddenly, without even thinking, he drew her to him, and he kissed her, and suddenly the pent-up emotions held back for so many countless years overwhelmed him.

She had been both surprised and pleased when he'd embraced her and started to kiss her in a way far more than friendly, since that was just what she wanted and needed then, but with the kiss came a sudden massive surge of deep, blinding white from *him* into *her*. The closest she might have come to describing the feeling rushing inward, had she been capable of analyzing it or even cared to, was that it seemed as if her whole brain had been fried in a massive wave of pleasure and desire.

By the time they'd finished, under that magnificent sky, on the grass, near the ancient seawall, and were just lying there side by side, holding hands and looking up, she was incapable of even wondering if what she'd tried had backfired. She only knew that she'd never felt like this before, not *ever*, and that she could never bear to lose him or live without him. She was, even in the Glathrielian energy sense, linked to him now for life.

Brazil, too old, too wise, too strong, was unaware of the cause of what had happened but was nonetheless affected by it. *I swore when Mavra left that I would never allow myself to do this again,* he thought. *But I guess I made myself a little too human, after all. So, here I am, feeling totally illogical, in love with somebody whose name I don't know, whose background I don't know, and who I can't even talk to. Maybe after all this time I really have gone nuts.*

But he didn't want to reject it, even though he knew deep down he could purge it if he truly worked at it. He'd felt the same intensity of feeling from her, and for now maybe that was enough. He felt the odd linkage, as if something tangible actually connected the two of them like some umbilical cord, but he dismissed it as just too many years of holding in his emotions.

Finally, he got up and pulled her to her feet, and they walked back toward the camp, still in an emotional high.

The fact that a feeling of impending danger cut through the high was all the more dramatic. They both sensed it at the same time and moved over away from the campsite toward the darkest area of trees. They separated, but the link established between them did not weaken or falter. It was as if they could read each other's emotions, though not thoughts, and immediately accept and act on them. There was something out there, something not friendly, and it was waiting for them.

She separated from him and immediately tried her night sense. What had been invisible before now came in very, very clear. There were two creatures; one, larger than the other, holding some sort of instrument, was hiding behind a tree just down the path to the fountain, with a clear view of the tent; the other was in the trees, silent, still, waiting for them.

At the same moment Terry saw them with the night sight, Nathan Brazil suddenly knew exactly where both of the lurkers were. He didn't wait to wonder how he knew; he sensed that the girl was going for the one in the trees, so his target was the bastard down the trail.

Great! he thought sourly. *What the hell am I going to do? Hit him with my guidebook?* Anything he could possibly use as a weapon was back in the camp. Or was it?

He suddenly realized that he was carrying his clothes, not wearing them, and he fumbled in the pants pockets to see what he had. The map and book, safety matches, and . . . one of the spare little gas canisters he used for the camp stove. He couldn't remember putting it there and wondered if it was full or empty. There was no time to check; he'd have to trust to those little twists of fate that always got him out of nasty situations and hope this wasn't one of those times when he was going to wake up in a hospital.

Dropping everything but the canister, which lit much like a common cigar lighter, he silently made his way around through the trees, giving the ambusher a wide berth. Thanking fate that these two hadn't discovered them up by the seawall, he began to close in on his quarry from the fountain side.

He could see the lurker now. Humanoid, maybe a meter and a half tall, covered with brown fur or feathers, and, most important of all, holding a mean-looking rifle of no local manufacture with what must have been a sniper's scope on it. With the experience of countless lifetimes, Brazil approached the creature in absolute silence, slowly, slowly closing in, ready to pounce if the sniper suddenly noticed him.

Now he was practically standing next to the sniper, at the same tree. Carefully, silently, he turned the little gas jet on and prayed that the flint and wheel wouldn't screw him up.

The sniper suddenly straightened up a bit in puzzlement, then sniffed the air. Brazil lit the canister and shoved it at him. A huge sheet of flame roared out and caught the fur, and the creature roared in pain and turned, giving Brazil a look at one of the meanest-looking faces he'd ever seen.

As the creature straightened up, Brazil dropped the canister and leapt at it, grabbing the rifle and then dropping, rolling, and coming back up with it pointed back at the assassin in one fluid motion.

The creature banged its back against the tree and put out the fire but then glared down the barrel of his own rifle. There was no doubt from the way Brazil held it that the man knew just how to use it.

Over near the camp another creature had waited in the trees to pounce on whoever might have come to the tent. It clung, silent and still, to the side of the tree without any obvious means of support.

Terry had moved around to the other side after separating from Brazil and had gone up a tree well distant from her own quarry. She moved with silent precision, using the night sense to see the links whereby she could get from one tree to the other and finally to the one next to the tent. The thing glowed brightly in her night sense, a sickly red like dried blood against the glowing tan of the tree. The outline was clear and now familiar to her: one of those scorpionlike creatures, its long, curved tail poised and practically screaming instant death to her.

She was right above it now, and for the first time she wasn't sure what to do. She *sensed* that Nathan was about to pounce on the other one; whatever it was had to be done fast. If only she had a better angle . . . Nothing she could do would work unless she actually *touched* the loathsome thing!

At that moment Brazil moved, and from up the path there was a scream that she knew was not his. The creature was suddenly alert, then turned toward the direction of the sounds. At that moment, fidgeting, the deadly tail was pointed straight down, the curve right below her. Timing, of course, was everything, but there was no chance for anything else but direct force and a prayer that it would work.

She jumped feet first and struck the tail at its midcurve. The tail went forward and punctured the thick exoskeleton of the creature, who roared even as they both fell from the tree and onto the tent below.

She landed right next to the thing and gave a panicked cry as the poison-tipped tail flailed up and down in random directions. She rolled away just in time for it to miss her, but it was a near thing. She was entangled in the collapsed tent with the creature when it again struck within a hair's breadth of her arm. She reached out reflexively and shoved it, at the same time sending her own fear and panic.

The creature managed to right itself but seemingly forgot about her. It *leapt* a good ten feet, landing on its feet, and began running on all six of its legs away toward the port, emitting an eerie, piercing sirenlike scream as it did so.

She had no idea where it went, and she didn't care. She knew it was gone, and she felt that Nathan was all right as well.

Brazil was torn between his captive and his clear perception of her fright and panic. He turned slightly, distracted by the feelings he was receiving from her, and the would-be sniper took it as an opening, running into the man and knocking him down, sending the rifle into the grass. The creature didn't look for it or go at Brazil, though; instead, it ran at top speed away into the darkness.

Brazil got up quickly and looked around, but the assassin was gone. *"Damn!"* he swore aloud. "Damn! Damn! Damn!" He looked around for the rifle, certain that the creature hadn't retrieved it, and found it in about thirty seconds. The girl no longer worried him; he knew without even checking that she was safe and that the other assailant, too, had fled.

Instead, he walked back down to what remained of the camp, looking at the rifle, noting only now what had caused him to know that an ambush awaited.

The two embedded electric streetlights along the fountain path were out. Either put out or shot out, most likely.

He found Terry shaken but unharmed. She might have a bruise or two, and she had a couple of scratches where she'd fallen into the tent, but it didn't appear to be anything serious.

He smiled, winked at her, and kissed her, then turned his attention to the rifle. It was a damned good one, too. Expensive. But the previous owner was no pro; a pro would never have taken up that exposed position or allowed anyone to get that close. Similarly, the Ecundo, for that was what the scorpionlike creature had been, had acted less like an assassin than like some ship's crewman hard up for some spare cash and recruited on the spot for an "easy" job. Again, no matter what her own abilities, she shouldn't have been able to get close enough to nail him without his hearing, and he certainly should have nailed her with that stinger when they fell. These were amateurs. Amateurs hired by somebody with money and sources of illegal weapons.

They'd just survived a crude attempt by amateurs at a paid "hit."

"Now what the hell . . . ?" he mused, staring at the rifle. Who would want him dead badly enough to hire toughs to do it? Who would be dumb enough to think they could kill him? Yet if they didn't know who he really was and what that meant, why bother? The Ambreza? Hardly. They could have snared him a lot easier a thousand times and with far less mess. He'd been only in Ambreza and briefly in Glathriel, and certainly the latter was out as a suspect. The only one who knew both who he was and where he might be would be Mavra Chang.

But this wasn't her style. Remote-control hits by amateurs? And she of all people would know that he couldn't be taken out any more than *she* could. But who else could it be?

Damn it, Mavra was as much if not more of an enigma to him than the girl was. If it *was* Mavra, what might be the motive? To slow him up, perhaps, now that he was on the move? A real possibility. But the worst possibility was one he didn't want to think about.

That somebody here, somewhere, knew who and what he was and was bent on stopping him at all cost, a third player whose very race and motives were unknown.

He looked at the ruins of the camp and sighed. Then he went over to find his clothes and get dressed again. *She* might not mind, but it was damned chilly for him.

There wouldn't be much sleep tonight, after all, even with all that had happened. Tomorrow morning the ship would sail, and they would be on it. Plenty of time to sleep then. Or, at least, if there was another attacker aboard, they couldn't run away like these two and he might get answers to some questions.

It was the story of his life, he decided. Every nice turn was met with an unexpected plunge into something nasty.

ERDOM

LORI HAD BEEN WITH Posiphar long enough to understand the bargaining game, and it was a good thing, too, since the tentmaker wasn't offering a very good deal on getting Julian off his hands in spite of his professed disgust with her.

"Since the treatment has begun as the Holy One directed, she is coming along very well," Aswam argued. "In a few more months, with the herbs the monk gave us to add to her food and drink, she will have forgotten all this foolishness and become a good girl and bear many fine children."

Lori did find this particular scale of bargaining distasteful, though; it seemed too much like haggling over a sale price, and in this case the commodity was a woman reduced to the status of a brood mare. Still, the addition of drugs—"herbs"—to Julian's food explained a lot as well about her mood swings and collapse of will.

"And you are arguing that I should repay *you* for your losses to date, when you are telling me that she is as she is now only because of *herbs*? And other than your loss of use of the storage shed, how much has she cost you so far above what dowry you were paid for her? How much for those herbs and all the special attention?"

"My investment is considerable now. That is why I will not give her away!"

"Ah! But you said it would still be months, perhaps many months, before it ran its course and you had the girl you wanted. *Perhaps* it will be months. *Perhaps* it will be longer. And can you ever be certain that what you see is real, is not an act? Will you ever be able to trust her fully? Or will your wives and daughters always be preoccupied watching her, so that they can never concentrate on their duties? It seems to me that you are boasting of doubling your costs in a fifty-fifty chance that she might work out. Right now, thanks to the dowry, your losses are small, but now that dowry is gone and all the costs are on you. Is yet one more wife worth that much to you?"

They argued back and forth, and for a little while Lori was afraid that Aswam might well not budge too much beyond a "Take her and go," blaming Lori for Julian's newfound resolve.

Lori had fought so hard just to get the tentmaker to this point that he feared pressing the matter might lose everything. Still, there was just some feeling inside, some gut instinct, that the old man really *didn't* want Julian anymore. Lori wondered if he had the right to bargain beyond this point, considering that it was Julian's future, not his, that was at stake, but something inside made it impossible to stop. He did, however, decide to bring down the hammer.

Lori got up from the cushion and looked down at the still-reclining tentmaker. "I cannot accept the dishonor of a wife with no dowry," he said flatly. "If she is not worthy of it and I am not worthy of the respect, then there is nothing more to say." He turned, feeling uneasy and queasy as hell about what he was doing, and started for the exit from the great tent.

He actually thought the old bastard was going to let him go, but just as he reached the curtained doorway and made to push back the drape and leave, Aswam called, "Now, wait a minute! Perhaps *something* can be ar- ranged, young hothead."

Lori smiled and felt immense relief, then set his face in a very serious posture before turning and coming back to the old man. From this point the haggling would be over how much the tentmaker would pay, not the other way around.

The final price was not nearly as much as Lori had hoped for as a stake, but he just didn't have the heart or stomach to press it anymore. He kept thinking that if Julian had known what he'd done, she'd have killed him. In fact, if the old Lori Ann Sutton had seen this, she would have organized protests.

Once agreed, a marriage contract of sorts was drawn up, and then Lori had to go and see the village Holy One.

The monks of the hierarchy of the church looked and sounded quite odd. All males, castrated while still children, they tended to be small and wizened, with weak sopranolike voices, without hair or horn. Only the eyes showed that there was a lot more going on in the head than their appearance indicated.

"I must confess that I am not wholly in favor of this union," the monk told him. "The role of females in this society is quite tightly prescribed, and no matter why the gods have chosen to put that person in that body, it was their holy will that it be so, just as it was for you. You were a step beyond her in your spiritual development, hence you were reborn male, and she was a step behind. In a sense, both of you were given a great gift. Few may be spiritually reevaluated while still alive. You were promoted, Julian was demoted one step, as it were. The proof of the rightness of it is how well you have adapted under a mental and cultural burden the rest of us do not have to share. That is why Julian is having so many problems with it; it is always more difficult to go down than up. I know the argument for the randomness of the Well process, but we reject it. There is a reason for all that happens. Randomness is an illusion. I fear that the joining of the two of you might well undermine that process."

Lori remembered Julian's warning that this monk was both devious and dangerous. Maybe they all were. Playing god and meddler on some level was the only thing they had.

"Are you telling me then, Holy One, that you will not allow it?"

"I am of two minds on it. On the one hand, there must be a reason why, out of 780 racial possibilities for each of you, both of you were reborn Erdomese and have come together in this way. On the other hand, since Julian will tend to cling to her old self more in your constant company, by allowing it I might jeopardize her immortal soul." He sighed and thought a moment. "There is a possible compromise position here."

"Yes?"

"First, what are your plans afterward?"

"Um, well, I am weary of being a needless guard for an old trader. I need more of a challenge. I had thought to travel to Aqomb and find tutors to teach me the full written language of Erdom. Once I am reasonably proficient, I hope to gain a position in the civil service there."

The monk nodded, pleased with the answer. "Very well. Here is what I will do, then. I will marry the two of you, but on the official papers I will place conditions. First, you must swear to me on your honor that you will continue with the herbal additives until they are gone. This is not just a religious requirement; to discontinue them now might well cause her to become very ill and cause permanent mental and emotional problems. Do not believe that I say this just to make you do it. I swear upon the Holy of Holies that what I tell you is true."

She didn't like it, but there was nothing she could do about it for now. "All right, I swear it. But I must know what they are."

"They are simply aids. In layman's terms, they help her mind and body become one and her behavior to be consistent with Erdomese culture."

"And in nonlayman's terms? I was once a scientist."

The monk gave a thin smile. "In technical parlance, they are natural psychochemical blockers and facilitators of attaining desired hormonal balances. One, for example, is a hybrid of two herbs used for countless generations as aphrodisiacs. Over a period of time the body begins to treat the blockers and newly set hormonal levels as normal and produces them naturally as needed. Once that happens, the drugs have no further effect and can be discontinued. In midtreatment, however, the body's balances are quite disturbed and discontinuance can produce what anyone might call insanity. The pharmacology is quite complex, actually. To go into more detail would involve going through the *Pharmacopoeia,* and you cannot at the moment read it."

She was startled by this sudden rather sophisticated science and immediately saw what Julian meant when she said that this guy was no fool.

"I accept what you say. The problem I have is, what is it doing to her mind?"

"You won't notice any changes from the way she is now so long as you continue them. The bottom line is that she won't want to kill herself, and she will be accepting of her role."

"Okay, that's one condition. You said several."

"Yes. When you reach Aqomb, you must check in and present the papers to the Holy Office there. They will monitor your compliance and her progress."

"Very well."

"Next, you will speak only Erdomese to one another, even in private. Language is the primary definer of a culture. You must believe that the Holy Office can determine if you uphold this or not in their examination of you both."

She wasn't sure how they could tell, but right now she would agree to anything just to get it done and over with.

"And finally, as soon as practical after the marriage but certainly before you retire for the night, you *must* consummate the marriage and present her for examination by me the next day. *Then,* and only then, will I give you the papers. Failure in any one of these may result in the marriage being annulled, and if it is, you will not see her again and may yourself face criminal penalties. Once you are married, you are morally and legally responsible for her and you *will* be held accountable. Remember, too," he added, possibly guessing at her ultimate intentions, "that even if you leave our land, you have had your living rebirth. There will be no more change in race, sex, or anything else until you die and are again reborn. There is no running from it. There are no colonies here. You both will be Erdomese and nothing else."

Well, the monk had sure laid it on the line. "All right, I agree." Lori said. "I swear it to you here and now." He hoped he could fulfill the duties he was agreeing to. As a male and an Erdomese, he was still a virgin.

"Very well. I assume you can write in *some* language?"

"Several. Just not Erdomese—yet."

"All right, then, I will dictate the contract, and you will write it in the language of your choosing. One copy for you in your language, certified as a true copy by me, and the other in Erdomese for official use. Those, and the marriage contract, will suffice. When do you leave?"

"Well, Posiphar has indicated that he might well go to Aqomb himself for a while and take a rest. If he does, we'll go with him. The hope is to leave just before dawn the day after tomorrow so that we can hit a small oasis at midday."

"Very well. Then you will marry tomorrow. I will then be there before you leave the next morning to make my examinations and, if satisfactory, hand you the papers."

The interview was over. "Thank you, Holy One. I will try to be worthy of your trust," he said, rising, bowing slightly, and leaving the prayer sanctuary.

He headed for Julian, who was still locked up by decree until the marriage, to tell her the good and the not so good parts of the news.

"I speak in Erdomese," he said right off, "because one of the conditions was that we speak nothing else to one another, and I do not wish to have anything go wrong."

"It will be so," she agreed.

"The reason why you have changed so much in here is that they have been giving you herbs to facilitate the process," he told her. "They are strong, and the Holy One knows his business. I am commanded to keep you on them until they are gone. He said that to stop them now would cause you to go mad. He also said that they would not change you more than you are now, that it is just to ensure that you remain this way. He also said that an examination by others could tell. Does this bother you?"

"No," she responded. "It—gives me relief. Now I understand why I have been this way. It helps me. And if it frees me from this place, I will take anything they wish. I know they can probably tell. That is one thing they are experts at here. Getting what they want."

"Then we do it tomorrow."

"Tomorrow!" Julian was excited. "But—I will need more than *this*! I can't get married looking and smelling like *this*!"

Lori grinned. "You look just fine to me, but I'll speak to Aswam. Most likely his wives and daughters can help you. He'll probably try and rob me blind for the service, but until tomorrow he's stuck with you."

Julian laughed, the first laugh she'd had since she'd gotten here. "And I will be a good little girl until he has no hold on me. I promise."

"Um, one more thing. They require that we consummate as soon as possible after marriage."

"Well, I am ready for that. I would not have it any other way, as I told you before, even though it is another way they hope to hold us here."

"Huh? Why is that?"

"They hope I will get pregnant, which will restrict us, and that I will have children, which will limit us more. With nations so small and so different, it is unlikely that the others would welcome families as settlers. It does not worry me. One day I might like to have children, but it is not how you do it here that counts. Even births are regulated from on high, so that the nations do not get too many people to support. That is what they told us when we came in here."

Reminded of that, Lori felt a little more relieved. She didn't think they had a population problem here at the moment, and she'd seen some babies in her travels, but not a lot of them. The fact that at least by observation it appeared that twins were the norm made the chances even lower.

"That's supposing that we can do it right to begin with," she joked.

Julian gave a soft laugh. "That should not be a problem. *You* know what a woman wants; *I* know what a man wants. When you consider that, we should be the most perfect couple in all history!"

After Lori left to make the arrangements, Julian had to chuckle at the sudden realization that she was still of two minds. As a human male she'd been divorced with no children; now, as an Erdomese female, she was to be married and could have her own children, and something in her really craved the kind of family life Julian Beard had rarely experienced. Lori might find what he was looking for elsewhere, but she would never again fly a plane, let alone a spacecraft, never again do meaningful research—not with *this* body and *these* hands—and, curiously, she didn't really mind. She'd railed against that knowledge most of all in the beginning, but it no longer seemed to matter now. Oh, she was glad that she'd done those things and had those memories, but at the age of forty Julian Beard, from a broken home and with no wife or family, had accomplished as much or more on his own than his boyhood dreams had ever imagined. She hadn't realized until now how empty some of the triumphs had been without anyone to share them with.

She wondered if in fact the Well had screwed up or whether, somehow, becoming Julian Beard's complete opposite—sexually, technologically, and in every other way—wasn't what was exactly right for her at the moment. Now she was supporting Lori's show, and it felt comfortable to be in that role and stop fighting. Lori might never understand it, but that, too, was all right.

Husbands never understood their wives, did they?

Julian in fact looked stunning for the tiny wedding, with long golden earrings—a series of squares linked together with chain, hanging down from punctures in the lowest part of the equine ears—a matching necklace, a pinkish glow applied judiciously to her face and upper body, hooves and "fingers" shined to almost a reflective polish, and her hair and tail done up in the traditional style, rising from golden tubes out across her back and up from the rear and then slinkily down to almost the ankles. Aswam's women had done her up just right, and she had just the body for it.

Lori was stunned by the look. In the dark shed he hadn't even noticed that Julian's hair was a sultry light reddish-brown, and the combination now put the other women around to shame.

Somehow, too, he'd expected Julian to be taller. It was true that Lori was very large for an Erdomese male, and he'd gotten used to being higher than everybody else by a few inches, but Julian looked positively *tiny* beside him, with only that huge mane of hair bringing her up to near his shoulders. She also looked so *young*, although certainly amply developed.

The wedding was brief and simple, held in a small demonstrator tent on Aswan's property, with only the tentmaker and his women and Posiphar and his women in attendance. In some ways the oaths taken before the witnesses and priest were everything Lori had hated back on Earth; Julian had to promise to honor, respect, and "obey absolutely" her husband, while Lori was required to swear only that he accepted all responsibilities, morally and legally, for his wife's welfare. More interestingly, the word "love" was nowhere to be found. That, at least, Lori thought, was not dishonest; he wasn't in love with Julian, but he did find her incredibly attractive on all levels, and love might come later. Neither, however, really knew the other yet—which was in some ways also consistent with Erdomese tradition.

Then there were fruit drinks and exotic pastries and some of the exotic-sounding Erdomese music from two of his daughters who had some talent in that direction, and that was it. By the heat of midday they were in a guest tent not too far away, the floor of which was covered with the large, varicolored pillows that were the most common furnishings in the nation.

Julian sighed. "Well, now I am Lori-Julian, or Madam Lori. Husband's name goes first here, but even if you take a dozen more wives I'll still be the only Madam Lori."

"I know," Lori replied, stretching out on the pillows and sighing. "Sorry, I didn't get much sleep last night."

"You are lucky. I got none at all. I never thought I would ever get married again. And I *surely* never thought I would be somebody's *wife*."

Lori frowned and looked up at her. "You were married?"

"A disaster. I will tell you about it if you want. We were divorced years ago, and after she remarried, I never saw or heard from her again. You were never married?"

"No. I lived with a string of men off and on, the last one for five years. We had just broken up for good when I got the offer to cover the meteor strike." He smiled sadly. "Want to know the ultimate irony? I forced the issue. I was closing in on forty, and my biological clock was in screaming mode. The idea of children frightened him to death for some reason. I pressed, he left. Just moved out without a word." The smile turned to a nasty grin. "How I'd like to see him *now*!"

Julian chuckled. "Yes, it might be fun to see Holly now, too. I've got twice her cleavage in *both* ways. Useful, too. They actually *are* 'jugs,' you might say, holding water until near the time of birth, when Mother Nature throws a switch inside. You think *you* have problems. Erdomese gestation is almost a year long, and the little buggers have hooves." She lay down beside him. "We can get some rest now and do what we must later," she suggested, "but can you at least satisfy one bit of curiosity I've had since I woke up here?"

"Huh? What?"

"Will you take that thing off? I've got to know if it really is that big or if those things are falsies."

Lori shifted around, removed the codpiece, and put it to one side, then rolled back. He'd never seen *anybody's* eyes get that big.

"Oh, *my*! Oh *my, oh my* . . ."

It proved a lot easier, and a lot better, than either of them had thought it would be.

The land changed considerably as they neared the coast, becoming harder and more like the deserts of the American southwest or the steppes of Kazakhstan than like the Saharalike interior. Water here could be found coming from fissures in the rocks or occasionally in streams around which sprang dramatic vegetation. Because of this, they would often run into wandering herds of *amat, twon,* or *zalj,* the Erdom equivalent of the bison, the cow, and the antelope, respectively, and, here and there, signs of *mahdag,* the elephantine and vicious yaklike creatures of the steppes. Overhead, the fierce pterodactyllike *maguid* would swoop down in aerial packs; while preferring carrion, maguid were perfectly willing to do their own killing if they were really hungry.

Posiphar had exchanged the sand skis for wooden wheels, and it occasionally took all of them to get it up some of the grades and all of them to keep it from going down some grades ahead of them. Mostly, the daughters pulled it, the others walking beside.

"This place could be beautiful if you knew the rules and what was dangerous and what was not," Julian noted. "Unfortunately, I do not know those rules, and it seems pretty scary to me."

"I've seen little here that scares me," Lori assured her. "Nothing I couldn't take with a spear or arrow, anyway. Mahdag is a different story, but I don't *want* to try one of those."

"There be them who hunt them," Posiphar remarked. "And them who be offerings of mahdag to the maguid who have tried to hunt them, too. Luckily, they be few and far between, and the ground be shaken long afore they come."

"Have you ever seen one?" Lori asked him.

"Yes, several times in this district, always from a distance and going the correct way, which is not the same way the mahdag be going. The cursed beasts be a head or more taller than even y'self and weigh a couple of tons or more."

Lori shook his head in wonder. "What do they *eat*? It would seem that it would take a lot to satisfy just one of them."

"Oh, there be a lot more vegetation around on some of these plateaus and mesas than ye'd think," the old trader told him. "I be not sure anyone has ever had the opportunity to study livin' ones and survive, but I be certain that they be vegetarians and kill entirely for pleasure."

The church taught that the mahdag had once been people, evil ones beyond redemption, doomed to wander in the wastes until the end of the world.

The trip had been an uneventful one as usual, and Lori and Julian had pretty well stuck to the bargain. She was even mixing the herbs herself according to the instructions passed on to them. They also practiced some social rules that Lori at least had never even noticed before, although he'd been around Posiphar's wives and daughters since arriving in Erdom. He *should* have noticed, though, and he felt bad about his lapse, since most were really designed to keep women in their "place."

For instance, a wife or daughter could address a husband or father easily, and also any other woman, but conversing directly with any other man, unless specifically invited to do so by husband or father, was forbidden. Since Julian considered Posiphar's family a set of ignorant little airheads, she talked mostly to Lori, but *never* interrupting a conversation Lori was having with Posiphar. This grated a bit on Julian's nerves, but she held it in and practiced it anyway. She was well aware that she was still on some kind of probation and that it all could be yanked away, and that was her biggest terror.

Still, when they got to the start of the last mesa, they found themselves in an actual forest, which seemed strange and alien to them after so long in the desert, and when they emerged from it at the other end, the whole of the Sultanate of Aqomb was spread out below them in the late afternoon light, and even Julian had to gasp.

The town itself sat on a broad coastal plain, its towers and spirals and vast honeycomb of streets looking like something out of the *Arabian Nights*. The green of trees and grass, in parks within the city walls as well as outside and up the coast as far as the eye could see, made it seem literally a different world. But what was even more startling was the view beyond, not only just to the east of the city but also to the south of it, and it wasn't the vast expanse of the West Arm of the Sea of Turigen, either, although that seemed amazing enough. It was the shimmering curtain that seemed to follow the coast all the way through which most of the water was glimpsed, a curtain that seemed to rise up to heaven itself.

"That's right," Posiphar cackled, "Ye never seen a hex boundary afore. That there be the border with Hadron. All the nations be bordered like that, all over the world. It can be kinda odd sometimes, not like now. I hear tell of some where it be havin' ice fallin' from the skies and as cold as the lower hells on one side, and on the other side it be sunny and warm as the Hjolai at midday."

"And that to the right—it looks like the same sort of thing, only solid. You sure can't see through it."

The wall there did indeed look thick and translucent; it reflected the sun to some extent but was a mottled gray-black going from behind to ahead of them as far as could be seen.

"That be the Zone Boundary," Posiphar told him. "Inside there is where ye came in, somewheres. Damn thing's so huge, you can put dozens of nations in it at least. Even where they be havin' great weapons, they can't blast through it, chip it, even scratch it. The only way in or out of it is by the Great Zone Gate, which be hidden by that tall building down there built up against the wall. I hear tell it be a mighty strange thing. Ye walk through any of them, and it's like a tunnel and there you are in the Zone. But no matter if ye walk in your own, or someplace far away, even on the other side of the world, when ye leave the Zone, ye walk out right there. If ye travel as I know ye intends, remember that.

Any gate will take you to Zone, and any gate out of Zone will take ye right there. Be a whale of a shortcut home."

Both he and Julian stared at that wall. Inside there was where they'd awakened after dropping through, somehow, to Zone from Brazil. Inside there they'd received their briefings and gone through the gate the first time and wound up here.

"Can anybody just use it?" he asked.

"Well, yes 'n' no. Accordin' to treaties, anybody's *supposed* t' be allowed to walk through any gate, but not everybody likes everybody else and not everybody signs treaties, and some who does sign treaties don't always *remember* what's in 'em, if you gets my meanin'. Still, mostly you can, but you only can if ye turn 'round and come right back to home. Zone itself's for official types only. Kinda handy for some emergency-type trade, though. If ye needs somethin' quick, ye can always have a fellow someplace far off push it into Zone by *his* gate, then ye pick it up there and push it back and it's here."

"You mean *things* as well as people are transported? That's not like the ones we went through."

"Oh, it be handy, but limited. Mostly things like medicines and stuff and fancy stuff for the rich come through. Most all else goes in or out by ship and overland by all sorts of ways. It don't allow no animals or bugs or stuff through, so it's safe, but them critters *can* get into Zone, so they spray and inspect and all that in there, and they really don't allow much use of the thing for that kind of trade, you see. Most bugs and stuff don't like it outside their home, and most races can't catch other races' diseases, but there's always a few what can. And most *anything* can live inside the Zone."

"Have you ever been outside of Erdom?" he asked the trader.

"Me? A few times, yes. Not far, though, and not on any of them floating contraptions. Been up north where they grow tobacco. Be a big trade item here, only for the very rich. Gave it up, though, after a while. Them Ambrezans be mighty strange folks, and I don't much like them contraptions floatin' you in air and all that. Also it be wet and smelly, with water just hangin' in the air. They be also makin' smart remarks about our ways and looks and how I treats me wives and all that. The longer you're away, too, the better home seems. This place was *made* fer us."

Lori couldn't imagine himself having that problem, but he might. Who could tell what sorts of places those other hexes were? "Is there anywhere where we can see a map of the world? Find out about some of the other hexes and races and the like?"

"Oh, there's plenty books 'n' maps and stuff, but if ye can't read Erdomese, it don't matter, does it? Down by the port there ye can get stuff in a ton of crazy languages as well as the one they use for translators so we can talk to one another, even them what don't have mouths. But ye can't read that, neither, so what's the use? Best go down to the port and pump some of them funny critters that runs the boats."

Julian's head came up and looked at Lori, who had the same sudden thought. "You mean those translators work—even in Erdom?"

"Yep, they do. Got several kinds. Some folks wear 'em, some get 'em stuck inside 'em—don't recommend *that* be done in Erdom! I hear tell they be hexes where they can look right inside you and see what's there and do all sorts of miracle things. The rich and nobles go there when they needs stuff. 'Course, you and me, we can't afford it and don't have the contacts." He looked at the sun. "We better be gettin' on down there if we want to be on the flat afore dark. It be all downhill from here and windy. The woods don't stop here where ye think; they just go down, too."

The sun *did* set before they were all the way down; the road was good, but they were descending maybe two kilometers or more in a fairly steep grade, and the compensation was a serpentine roadway that switched back and forth on itself for what seemed like forever.

Still, even though it was some distance yet to the city, the flat made it easy going and the city was certainly not something anybody could miss. It was big and bright and seemed lit up like a million Christmas trees.

Julian's past military experience spotted a puzzle. "I wonder why they have city walls if they light the place up like that."

Even Posiphar didn't know the answer to that when Lori passed along the question to him. "Guess if anybody be attackin', they'd put them lights out," he guessed.

This was one city that did not close at night. Oh, the shops and bazaars were closed, but there seemed to be clubs and nightlife and eateries and music and gaiety all over the place, all illuminated by brilliant oil lamps, some, with stained glass, casting fairyland glows that ranged the spectrum.

Posiphar directed them to a small hotel. "Farewell, lad. It's been a very interestin' time we be with you, and the gods go with you. With my brood we be stayin' with some old friends in their place near the docks. Ye mind yer money, now. Ye ain't got much, and it goes quick."

Lori felt like he was losing his oldest friend, which in a way was true, but they parted on a handshake rather than the embrace he almost gave the old fellow. Men did not *do* that, not in Erdom.

Julian looked at the hotel. "Well, my husband, it looks a little seedy, but cheap at least."

Lori grinned. "You mind your manners and tongue here or we'll both be in trouble."

"Yes, *sir*, my Lord and Master," Julian responded mockingly, but she shut up.

The place *was* a little seedy, but it wasn't all that cheap. While he liked the city, its sights, sounds, and smells, Lori had to wonder how long he could afford to stay around this place before he had to find a job of some kind. At this rate, not long, and there was much to learn and probably a lot of money to raise before they could ship out of here.

The next morning he got directions from the desk clerk to the Holy Office. Best to get that out of the way as soon as possible, they'd both agreed, although it was not something they looked forward to. Posiphar had confirmed that the church was a master of drugs and potions, and it was here, in the unique climate and conditions of the south coast, that they grew and bred their stuff. He'd figured as much. If a monk in a jerkwater town like the one they were married in knew that much, imagine what the ones *here* knew and could do!

The monk read over the marriage contract and the annotations and paperwork from the desert monk. Then they were separated, somewhat to Julian's panic, and taken to different rooms that looked very much like Erdomese-designed versions of doctors' examining rooms, and that was what they proved essentially to be. The monk who examined Lori seemed a bit younger and in a little better shape than the others he'd seen, but the doctor knew his stuff and gave a pretty reasonable physical. At the end the monk left for a couple of minutes, then returned with three small cups filled with different colored liquids.

"Recline on the examining couch and take the orange liquid and then relax," Lori was instructed. "I will return in a few more minutes. Your wife is fine, and I'm sort of going between the two of you."

Lori noted that the doctor didn't leave until the liquid was clearly swallowed. It tasted like burned orange.

After a while things got very pleasantly hazy, although he was never completely out. He just lay there, kind of floating, and he didn't feel any anxiety when the monk-doctor returned and checked his eyes and reflexes.

After that came a whole series of questions, and he answered every one, although the moment he answered, he found he couldn't remember the question or the answer. Feeling good, he was agreeable when told to down the green liquid, and after a very short time, he was out cold, at least as far as he was concerned, and he never did know about the third cup.

He woke up later feeling absolutely *great*, supercharged with energy.

He also felt different somehow as well, but he couldn't quite put his finger on what it was at the start. Let's see . . . He knew who he was, and where he was, and why he was here . . . Something about a woman . . . His wife? No, that wasn't it. Oh, yeah. *He'd* been a woman, from a different world, and he'd carried part of her inside him since he got here. Now she was gone. Not the memory, although that seemed both alien and irrelevant to him. All those feelings, all those emotions, all those conflicts seemed to have vanished now. He felt no conflict; he was all man, and he liked it that way. He liked being Erdomese, too. He couldn't imagine being anything but what he was, even though the back of his mind assured him he had been. He was glad to be rid of that wimpish element.

Next door Julian awoke also feeling simply *wonderful*. She, too, had a feeling that something was gone, but, as with Lori, it didn't matter. *Nothing* mattered. All she could remember was that she'd been sick some way, and they'd made her well, and now she was First Wife to the most handsome, virile, *wonderful* man and that was that.

The monks studied them from hidden recesses in the walls and nodded to one another. Lori would take the prescription down to the pharmacy and get more of the second and third drugs. The second they would both take, and they would effectively rehypnotize each other. The third, which only Lori would take, would cause overwhelming hormonal changes that would wash the last traces of Lori Ann Sutton from his conscious actions and inner thoughts.

They would make good citizens.

The monks' plans might have worked well except for their own introduction of a factor that they never thought of as a threat.

A note on official government stationery had been left at the Holy Office for Lori, and it was given to him dutifully as the pair left.

Lori was quite puzzled at it and even more puzzled that anyone would think he might be able to read it, but he found that he could. It was written in, of all things, classical Greek.

> This is a just-in-case note. I have word from Zone that you were made into an Erdomese male. While it is difficult for me to imagine you other than as you were, it is a very good thing you were made male if it had to be Erdom, as you know.
>
> I had intended to come to you, but in your own port where this is being written and where I have been trying to locate you, there has been a serious attempt on my life. I cannot imagine any motive for this except from Nathan Brazil, and, since he knows I cannot be killed, I can only guess that he has learned of my intentions and is attempting

to slow me down, possibly lay me up for weeks or months in a nontech hex hospital, or at the very least kidnap me and imprison me somewhere in the interior. This means that the race is on, and time is not on my side. I need your help. The fate of countless thousands of worlds is at stake, as well as, quite possibly, this one. My best bet is to head for the Zone Gate if I can get to it safely, which will return me to Ambreza just to the north. If I cannot get into Zone, I'll have to take a ship, but few have ever been able to prevent me from going where I want to get into.

I have left messages everywhere I dare that I feel are reasonably secure. If you made it here and are reading this, I plead with you in the spirit of comradeship we once had not long ago to join me. I must get out of here today before more attempts are made—one might succeed. It is unlikely that they would know you by sight or current name, so you should be safe. I have left money on account with you at the Gryssod Shipping Line on Baszabhi Street at the port. Money right now is the least of my problems. Use the account to purchase tickets on the first ship north to the port of Sukar in Itus. Register at the Transient Main hotel. Someone will contact you there and get you in touch with me or provide the means to get to me.

I will not minimize the task. It is long, arduous, and dangerous. The prize, however, is that if we win and beat him to the Well, you can name any treasure, any reward, anything you like. There is literally no limit. I hope to see you very soon.

It was signed "Alama—Mavra Chang." The date was only four days old.

He gestured for Julian to follow and went out, trying to figure out what to do next. She followed meekly, without questions. Certainly this put a different light on things. He liked the fact that she was pleading with him to help her. He remembered her as small and weak compared to a big man like him. She needed a warrior, and that was at the moment the only thing he was qualified to do.

And the reward certainly beat working for a living.

Instead of going back to the hotel, he went to the port and, after a few inquiries, found the shipping agency. The clerk, who looked something like a Julian-sized bowling ball on stilts with two huge oval eyes, was disconcerting, being the first non-Erdomese he'd seen since the dragon back in Zone. It also had the most irritating high-pitched voice he'd ever heard.

"Is there a ship leaving any time soon for Sukar, in Itus?" he asked.

"There usually is, sir," the thing replied. "Drat these old-fashioned written schedules. It takes time to find anything. Itus, Itus . . . Yes, here it is. There is a ship leaving this evening, in fact."

"And how long would it take to get there?"

"Well, it is *quite* a long trip, sir, and the only ones likely to put in here are coastal steamers."

"Never mind that! How long?"

"With stops, five days, more or less."

Five days. "And how long is it from—" *What was the name of that place? Think!* "—from Ambrosia or something like that to Itus?"

"You mean Ambreza, sir?"

"It sounds right. North of here?"

"Immediately north, so just minus one day, sir."

One day. So if Mavra got back to Ambreza and set out for Itus from there, it meant that she was five days ahead of him. Five, plus the five days for Lori to get there by boat, was ten—maybe less if Mavra had to travel from the hex gate in Ambreza to the port and get transit. Clearly, overland wasn't an option from the way the letter was phrased.

The offered reward, however exaggerated, sure seemed better than working for years.

He looked at Julian. This wasn't a job for a *girl*, but she *was* his wife, and he was responsible, and he'd need somebody along to attend to him. The hell with it.

"Book two on that ship. There should be an account in my name left here to cover the tickets. Lori of Alkhaz and First Wife." Damn! That name sounded dumb to him now. He'd have to change it sometime, but not until he'd linked up with Chang.

There was in fact a pouch left for him, which included not only sufficient money for passage but some international coins for expenses and another copy of a similar letter in Greek that contained no new information.

He went back to the hotel, pausing only to stop at a chemist's shop and get a prescription from the monks filled. It never entered his head why he was doing it or that he shouldn't.

"Pack what we have," he told Julian curtly. "We're going on a trip."

She looked puzzled but neither objected nor asked questions about it.

The monks' plot would work for a while. But there was only a four-day supply in the vials, and when he felt the urge to get more, both he and Julian would be hundreds of kilometers away from the nearest chemist who could fill it and heading farther away from Erdom.

SOUTH ZONE

STANDING BEHIND HER DESK, Ursoma would have looked to any Terran like a pretty woman with very long blond hair, an exotic cast to her face, and a skin tone that one might not have placed exactly. Only the ears, which were pointed and set oddly on both sides of her face, would have seemed out of sorts.

When she moved from behind the desk, however, the differences were more apparent. She had no navel, but at about where the navel should have been, the skin became darker and light wheat-colored hair began—from this point on down, and back through all four hoofed feet to her tail, she was very much a horse. The fact that the seemingly unbalanced front and rear halves managed to work so well together was even more amazing.

There was a buzzing sound, and she turned and looked toward her office door. "Come in!"

A large creature walked in, in some ways the reverse of Ursoma. His body, while chunky, was quite humanoid, but upon his thick neck sat a face that most resembled a great bull's head set in a permanently pissed-off expression. Because of the differences in them, she was almost as tall as he was.

"You left a message that you wanted to see me?"

She walked over to him slowly, all four hooves clattering on the smooth floor. When she reached him, her face grew suddenly very angry and she slapped him hard.

Although she didn't look it, female Dillians were very strong, and the bull-headed creature reeled from the blow, then snorted and roared, "How *dare* you do that to me?"

"Because you are a pigheaded asshole, and I'm in charge by mutual consent of this operation. I can have you *executed* for what you pulled! Your punishment would be far worse than slapping if I reported you!"

"What do you mean?" the creature grumbled, but calmed down.

"I mean these reports! Brazil and that mute girl. Mavra Chang down in Erdom. I know you hired those killers. It wasn't hard to trace a turd-brain like you!"

"So they failed. They won't next time. I am tired of all this stupidity, this sneaking around and spying. Direct action is the answer! Just eliminate the threat!"

She sighed. "I think I *will* have you executed! That's *Nathan Brazil,* you idiot! You *can't* kill him! No matter what you do, the Well won't let you! And since we have no reason to disbelieve her, the same goes for this Chang woman. All you can do is scare them underground, put them on their guard, and if you kill any of their friends or associates, you'll have them so pissed off at us that when one or the other gets into the Well, they'll take a revenge more terrible than the legends! Didn't that ever *occur* to you? Didn't you *listen* at the briefings, when we played the tape of her talking to her compatriots before they went through? Didn't you hear the proof that it was Brazil coming through, unchanged but with a translator module implant so he could speak to the Ambreza as soon as he awoke? And the same for Chang? Our computers state that there is almost a dead certainty that at least one and possibly both are of the First Race, locked in Glathrielian bodies for some reason of their own but heading for the Well."

"It was boring and stupid. When you started on that immortal crap, I fell asleep. I'm an atheist. I do not believe in immortal godlike beings. I think we were being had with that briefing shit. Either that or the female is crazy. If it wasn't one or the other, she makes a pretty dumb goddess using a translator and never once thinking that it might be recorded or monitored."

"Well, wake up now and look at the evidence! Did it ever occur to you that after all those centuries Chang just might be a wee bit *rusty*? Oh, I don't know why I *don't* put you permanently to sleep. One more, just *one* slight deviation from plans, one *teensy,* infinitesimal attempt to *think* or *act* on your own and you will forfeit your lands, your possessions, all wives, everything you have, and then you will *beg* to be executed after we are through with you! Our chances of pulling this off are slim enough now. Once they get into the Well, who can limit their power? Who can override them? Not any of *us*! And *you*—you get them running scared and threaten any possibilities of a deal we might have!"

"All right, all right. So what do you want me to do?"

"Call off your assassins. At once. Then start attending briefings, and this time stay awake and *listen*! Brazil and the girl are now headed west across the Gulf of Zinjin. If they connect at the narrows, he will be almost two-thirds of the way there, while Chang is still getting organized in Itus. We must slow Brazil and direct Chang so that the two are likely to end up near the equator in the same general region at the same time. *That* is going to be tricky enough, but we can't depend on fate to do it for us. This is going to take a lot of coordination. And we must *all* work as a team. All of us! If we don't, then armies will mobilize once either or both get near their goals, and we shall be fighting each other over them! Understand?"

He nodded but said nothing.

"There is a briefing over the secured channels in one hour. Be on and be awake!" she snapped, then whirled and trotted back to her desk.

GLATHRIEL,
AT MIDNIGHT

IN THE DARKNESS, UNDER cloudy skies with a drizzly rain falling, with the air seeming heavy and solid and the mists moving like wraiths through the tops of the trees, there was a Gathering.

By the hundreds they came, male and female, young, old, and in between, to sit in the open on that wet, swampy ground, eyes closed, and to touch one another in such a way that both arms were linked to or clasped by different people. The Gathering itself was brief and silent. Thoughts, as most of the other races of the Well World had them, were not transferred, yet information was. The combined analytical data was sifted, sorted, and examined; all possibilities that might be foreseen were equally and clearly laid out in an instant, and a collective decision arose as if spontaneously out of the combined input of the Gathering.

It was over in just a few minutes, but had they been Ambrezan, or Erdomese, or Dillians, or even Terrans, they might have run on for hours and never even seen all the data or all the ways it might be used, let alone make decisions. But if the Gathering were translated to a linear form and distilled, it might have been something like this:

"The stepchild of the group does well.

"That which we imparted to her blends well with that which had come before. She has now ensured that she will enter the Well of Souls with the man of the First Race.

"It is surprising that the Power works even on one of his strength.

"The First Race was great enough to know, even at their height, that they were flawed beyond redemption. That is why the Great Experiment was decreed. But as the Watchman, he is less than he was, although all that he was is still within him. Consider the shock to the Monitors when he instinctively reacted to the Power! Yet,

in taking on the form of a Colonial Race, living as one with them, he shares their defects and weaknesses as well as their own strengths. Otherwise he would have recognized us and sensed us.

"And so he proceeds to do for us the one thing that we could never do for ourselves. Our opportunity comes early. We must seize upon it and hope that it has not come too early for us, as it did for them.

"So far, things go well. It is good that the girl was not given to know that she and the First One are proceeding toward the end of the universe as they know it."

VERGUTZ

THE COASTLINE WAS NOW out of sight behind them, and the mighty stacks of the great ship belched out plumes of white smoke as the ship accelerated to full speed.

Terry sat on the afterdeck next to Nathan Brazil, oblivious to the stiff wind and chill in the ocean air, looking not back but forward.

Brazil himself stared into the rolling waters, put his arm around Terry, and thought only of good possibilities. Since no one could possibly know which route he would take and no passengers or crew had signed on to the ship after he purchased their tickets, he was reasonably certain that whoever had hired those bumbling assassins was left behind. It would be next to impossible to set up anything serious at his destination before they arrived, unless somehow they already knew that destination and had allies there. Unlikely, but he could cope. If it *was* Mavra, she'd be more likely to go hell-bent north herself than worry anymore about him. She had started from the same place and at roughly the same time, so they had equal distances to travel. He would also have liked to have checked up on Tony and Anne Marie, but they, too, could wait. If there was any place a potential foe would figure he'd show up and be laying for him, it would be around either one of them.

At any rate, once he was on the northern land mass, they'd be damned difficult to track and he'd have many options open.

Once the entire Well World had marshaled to prevent him from getting up there. This was *much* easier. And once inside, he'd find out about this Glathrielian business, and maybe, once he normalized the girl here a bit more, they might stick around a while, take the grand tour of this place. Perhaps, if she still loved him then, he'd add her to the master Well matrix. Then, perhaps, he could also find out what the hell was the bug up Mavra's ass for the last three thousand years.

The hell with it. He was on a great ship going across a beautiful ocean, an attractive and loving if mysterious companion at his side, and things didn't look nearly as rough as the last couple of times.

Hell, after all he'd been through before, he was *owed* one easy one . . .

SOMEWHERE IN THE
CONSTELLATION ORION

IF PATIENCE WAS A virtue, the Kraang's infinite virtue was now within sight of the ultimate prize.

So far, so good, thought the Kraang.

Shadow of the
Well of Souls

For Fritz Leiber,
who enjoyed the original Well saga
but left us before this one was done, and
likewise for my old friend Reg Bretnor,
also gone too soon, my writing opposite of sorts,
who packed more laughs into fewer words than
any science-fiction author in history.
The worst thing about growing old
is the increasing number of missing,
and missed, friends.

SOMEWHERE
BETWEEN GALACTIC CLUSTERS

THE KRAANG HAD GOOD reason to be complacent. After so long, so *very* long, its plans were coming to a head, and with each passing day its link to and power within the Well Net grew. It could already send within the field and could receive and track and monitor as well. While none of the principals in the drama it had concocted were directly addressable— unless they were in a full Well field such as traveling through and be- tween hex gates and Zones—and the Watchers were outside its direct monitoring abilities, the others whom it had identified as they were pro- cessed by the system were far easier to track.

When the Kraang's ship itself was not in the slingshot gateways, it was now possible to see through the eyes and hear through the ears of the others who had been processed, and that was more than sufficient to monitor the Watchers' track, while both Watchers and their monitors were unaware even of its very existence. And although unable to send to them under normal circumstances, it could do more than merely re- ceive; it *knew* them. It knew their innermost thoughts, their loves, hates, fears, and nightmares. It knew that little band better than they knew themselves. That not only allowed the Kraang to filter out subjective impressions from the raw data, it also provided such deep individual knowledge of them that when more *was* possible, when they finally opened the gate that would bring it to them, they would be as soft clay, as easily remolded inside as they had been outside to serve the Kraang's purposes.

It had been nothing less than the remaking of the cosmos that had allowed the Kraang's liberation, although close to a billion years had passed until chance had ultimately given it access to the net once again, access the Ancient Ones believed had been denied it for eternity. The rest of the system had provided just a moment, mere nanoseconds, when the program that had bound it for billions of years could not control its destiny. That tiny moment had been sufficient for the Kraang to alter the system, however slightly, without detection by the net or the Watchman, so that when the program was reimposed, it was flawed. Afterward it had been a mere matter of waiting, suspended of activity, until eventually chance would place the Kraang and its prison within distance of possible direct contact with a Well Gate. The Well computer became aware of the flaw only when that contact came, and then it was too late: the Kraang had access to the net. And the Kraang could be disengaged from the net only by the Watchman, since the Well was powerless in and of itself to do harm to one of its creators. Only another Maker could do that.

So the Kraang had done what it had to do. The world upon which the Watchman lived was still primitive; there was no space travel of consequence, no way to create a situation by which the Watchman could be drawn to a gate. The gate, then, had to come to the Watchman by the crude but effective method of sending Well Gates down to the planet of the Watchman as meteors.

But there had been two Watchers instead of one at this juncture, the second created by the original Watchman when the cosmos was reset. Multiple gates were required because the two were separated. And so the gates had fallen, remaining open until the Watchers were collected, operating in their normal manner until the Well could safely close them. During that period it was almost inevitable that others, natives of the planet, would fall through, and it was amazing how few had actually done so.

Few, but enough.

The newspeople—Theresa Perez, the producer; Gus Olafsson, the cameraman; and Dr. Lori Ann Sutton, the university astronomer tapped as the expert for the newspeople—had been captured by a primitive Amazonian tribe deep in the jungles of Brazil. A tribe whose mysterious leader was the female Watcher, who had taken them through with her to the Well World, along with the Peruvian gangster and drug lord Juan Campos. And, before them, the two of the always-inevitable investigators of the meteor, Colonel Jorge Lunderman, Brazilian Air Force regional commander, and Julian Beard, U.S. Air Force scientist-astronaut. *Those* two had been taken while posing for photos atop the "meteor," perhaps as an object lesson for all others to stay away.

The other, the original Watchman, had also been in Brazil, but on the civilized coast, taking a sort of holiday in the nation that shared his name. Only two natives had been taken in with him, both at his invitation: the blind former airline pilot Joao Antonio Guzman and his dying British wife, Anne Marie.

Eight natives who were processed by the Well, each becoming *something else,* another creature, another race, yet with their memories and essential selves, their souls as it might be colorfully put, intact, for good or evil. The Kraang had no influence over what they had become, but it ever after had been along for the ride.

During the processing, a link could be and was established.

Even communication with the Watchers was possible during that period, but it was dangerous to go too far. Surface thoughts and surface memories triggered by the experience had been available even though the Watchers themselves remained essentially out of the Kraang's control. One thought, however, one memory, one weakness, particularly on the part of the newer Watcher, was sufficient. Had *been* sufficient.

Now the game was commencing. Now one of them certainly would open the way. Now one of them, at least, would be the unwitting agent freeing the Kraang and summoning it home. Home to the Well.

Home to become God.

HAKAZIT

ALTHOUGH IN MANY WAYS the Well World felt familiar, even comfortable to him, in other ways, Nathan Brazil reflected, he always had a sense of wrongness when on it.

It wasn't the bizarre variety of creatures and cultures, the things that made new entrants so uneasy; rather, it was the common things. *Some* things might be expected to change when crossing a national boundary, but not the climate, and absolutely not the gravity, yet one could cross from the tropics to snow in a few footsteps or have gravitational fluctuation of up to twenty percent in the same distance if one were near one of those borders. And of course it should be cold at the poles and grow warmer toward the equator, even more so than on Earth, as the Well World had no appreciable axial tilt and thus no natural seasons. The days, and nights, a bit longer than back on Earth, were nonetheless always pretty close to equal.

But Glathriel, near the south polar region, was tropical; Hakazit, a thousand kilometers or so west of Glathriel yet only a bit north, was raw and cold, the winds off the Ocean of Shadows brisk and biting, carrying small droplets of ice and snow and swirling them around, not in the sense of a storm but rather as persistent irritants, felt but not really seen.

He pulled his fur-lined jacket tightly about him, hoping to ward off some of the wintry chill, his breath causing huge puffs of steam as it came from his warm interior and struck the frigid air with every exhalation. He looked over at the girl standing atop the rocky cliff looking out at the pounding surf. Although as Earth-human, in some ways *more* Earth-human, than he was, she was wearing not a stitch of clothing, and Brazil marveled again at her total insulation.

He would have liked to know how they had pulled it off. Some sort of internally generated energy field, certainly, a true cosmic aura fueled from within by some autonomic source he couldn't imagine. Certainly she didn't do it consciously; it was simply too perfect for that. But even if he granted the unlikely and heretofore unsuspected power to Type 41 humans to do this sort of thing, he couldn't imagine why it would evolve in a primitive and totally tropical hex where only "wet" and "dry" had much meaning. Nor did it account for the selectivity. She was standing there in temperatures well below freezing on rock that itself was cold enough to freeze any water it had, but the cold didn't affect her. She was warm to the touch even on the surface of her skin, and the icy droplets that were turning his own hair into a miniature ice field were hitting her as well, as warm and liquid as a summer drizzle. Yet her long black hair blew free in the wind, a wind that made the chill factor almost Arctic on bare skin but that, in that incredibly small fraction of a millimeter before it struck any part of her, was suddenly turned as warm as a tropical breeze.

Clearly the talent had not been evolved for situations like this; it merely served this function as well. What was it, then? What was this mysterious inner-produced energy field's primary function?

Clearly it required a lot of energy. The photo he'd received here of her in the Zone Gate corridor, taken off the monitor recording, had shown her very lean and somewhat muscular; now she was, well, *fat*. Not obese —nobody who could move like she did could be considered that—but the thighs were very large, the ass ample, the breasts enlarged to substantial proportions and resting on an ample tummy. She ate a lot, yet it never seemed to slow her down, and he'd never seen her pant for breath once, even while running. That surplus wasn't there for the usual reasons; most of the Glathrielians he had seen were at the least chubby. It was there as fuel for whatever additional engine they had within themselves.

She was more than merely another of the Well World's many mysteries, though. The Well World left no one unchanged who entered through its Zone Gate save Mavra and himself, yet she was clearly not of Glathriel, the only Earth-human hex here. Her west African heritage showed clearly in her skin and lips, yet her naturally straight, lush, long black hair and general facial features betrayed an equally obvious Hispanic ancestry. She had been made by no Well computer; she had been born and had grown up like this. Whatever changes had been made, they had been inside, in the adaptation stage, in which the brain was slightly reprogrammed to accept a new situation.

But the Well World wouldn't have programmed in an evolutionary change made after the last reset. It would use the basic template.

Conclusion: She had not been changed inside by the Well at all, but by some other force, and that force could only be the Glathrielians themselves.

And *that* disturbed him most of all, because the last time Glathriel's template had been examined and revised, he had done it himself, and while he might well have expected some sort of tropical tribal primitive society or some other variation of it, he'd given them nothing with which to develop the society, if it could be called that, and the powers that they now possessed. A society that used no tools, built no structures, altered its environment not a whit, had no apparent spoken language or even the concept or need for one, consuming only what it found day by day, and not even using fire. Yet somehow they presented the sensation of a tightly knit and intelligent tribal society.

He had no idea who this girl was, or what she had been, or where other than Earth she'd come from. She'd almost snuck into Zone on her own and crept past the officious and preoccupied duty personnel there. The recordings of her from South Zone, discovered too late, showed a picture of a primitive savage, painted and dressed in little but bones, but she didn't look like any Amazonian Indian he'd ever heard of. The group she had followed in, Mavra's group, had entered similarly primitive-looking, yet had proved to be from a modern and articulate educated society. He'd like to know that story one of these days; it was probably a hell of a saga.

Was she from one of the primitive tribes of the Amazon, a native who had been caught in the hex gate, perhaps after seeing the others go through? Some orphan, perhaps, or a captive raised by them, which would explain her different look? She was tough and had guts; she'd taken on an Ecundo whose body was armored and whose tail meant death without a second thought—and with her bare hands. Yet even as she rejected all the fruits of technology as a Glathrielian would, she'd not been surprised or even curious about them. She seemed to know exactly what was dangerous to touch and what was safe, and she seemed to understand the setup of a developed society even if she did not join in on any of its activities.

Despite this, and for no logical reason he could determine, he found her attractive in ways he couldn't really explain. He hadn't remembered feeling this way about anybody, possibly ever, certainly not in countless thousands of years. It was oddly sexual, stirring in him feelings he'd believed dead so long that they'd ceased to be more than abstractions to him. He had of course felt closeness, friendship, even a sort of love for individuals over time, as much as he'd tried to repress such feelings, knowing the brief time they had compared to him, but not on this level. It was also clear that she sensed this and, in what ways she could, reciprocated. She was anything but naive and unsophisticated in the art of making love, and while nobody had longer experience than he in that sort of thing, she made him feel things, physical things, to a degree he knew he'd never reached before. It was as if she were some powerful and addictive drug, one that, once taken, he could never again be without. It was the first new experience he'd had since . . . since . . . since before he'd re-created the universe.

Of course, he suspected that it wasn't entirely natural. Glathriel's revenge, he thought with a trace of genuine irony. Take *us* out of our nice, comfortable high-tech little worldlet and stick us in a nontech swamp designed for a race of giant beavers, will you? Well, it took us a million years, but we finally figured out a way to get back at you! Then, through *her*, it is *we* who will control *you*!

He considered that a distinct possibility, although he wasn't certain how sophisticated the Glathrielians were along those lines. It did not, however, overly concern him. For one thing, she was at least partly Earth-human, no matter how changed she might be, and he'd had a very long time to learn to read beyond the surface of Earth people, to detect even slightly corrupt attitudes or motives as well as pure ones. He'd never sensed any deception in her. If it *was* something Glathrielian women did to snare men, it worked both ways, of that he was positive. If she was the only girl in his world—pretty well true at the moment, come to think of it—then he was her only boy. He was absolutely convinced that she would not, *could* not act against him. Whatever unsuspected potential lurked in the Type 41 brain, the link that bound the two of them together was empathic in nature, and that was the most revealing sense of all. Even telepaths learned how to cheat each other just to survive; an empath seldom could, since the very power dealt in emotions which no one could ever fully control.

Within their own subjective limits, he felt what she felt, and she felt what he felt. That was what made physical intimacy so intense, but it also left him convinced that she could not knowingly play false with him.

"Knowingly," of course, was an important distinction, but even if there was something sinister at work and he was deluding himself, he knew in the end that it didn't matter. Once inside the Well, he was invulnerable to anything the universe could throw at him, even betrayal. And once inside, he would be able to find out what the hell was going on.

In the meantime something deep within his own psyche, his own deep chasm of loneliness, despair, and alienation from others, assuaged over long years only with tiny morsels of hope and self-delusion, had been, however temporarily, partially filled, and for the moment that was enough.

Still, it was *too* damned cold for him, even if not for her, and the kind of warmth she could give him was not the sort he now required. He went over to her and put his hand on her shoulder. She turned and smiled at him, and he made an exaggerated shiver and gestured back toward the town. She nodded and looked sympathetic; clearly she was also no stranger to a cold environment, even if she couldn't feel it herself.

All seaport towns had a certain basic similarity to them. Although the towns themselves and their urban layouts tended to vary in wild and bizarre ways, reflecting the very different races that lived in them, there was always a section by the docks generally known as the International Quarter, even though it was a far smaller piece of the town than that. Where ocean ships crewed by a polyglot of races made ports of call like spaceships docking in new tiny worlds, a level of comfort, convenience, and service was necessary to cater to alien needs. Some were far better than others at this, of course, but Hakazit was a high-tech hex with a huge automated port, and its facilities were first-rate. The Hakazitians were a bit harder to take, if only because they resembled, to Brazil's mind at least, human-sized mosquitoes with a proboscis that looked like a giant version of one of those Happy New Year whistles that unrolled when blown. But the Hakazitians' "nose," when extended, proved to be not one but six sticky tendrils capable not only of feeding but also of doing almost any task hands could do and a few they could not. Their huge hivelike structures dominated the landscape as far back as anyone could see.

The girl—she'd never taken to or responded to any name he'd tried, so she'd just become the girl—never liked being inside a structure. Glathrielians, it seemed, were a bit claustrophobic even in fairly large rooms. It was a measure of how attached they'd become that she was willing to enter most buildings, even sleep where he did, although she was always clearly uncomfortable and still preferred floors to beds, at least for sleeping. She almost seemed to get a charge, though, out of walking unconcerned and unafraid stark naked down bustling streets and in crowded hotel lobbies, something unthinkable on Earth. But since the only other one of her species was her companion and lover, it gave her a rush of liberation that was as unique to her as his feelings for her were to him.

Vagt Damstrl, which meant "the Hotel Grand" in Hakazit, or so they said, was an imposing structure that dominated the skyline in a way only the huge port cranes could match, and its management prided itself on being able to provide both accommodations and necessaries for any race of the Well World that might be a guest. As usual, considering the state of Glathriel and its people, it had nothing *precisely* the way he'd want it, but many races liked carpeting on the floors and many others liked soft beds and many bathed in pools or tublike creations, so that they were able to assemble a spacious room for him that not only was to his standards but went beyond them. Nor was food a problem; a fair number of races who traveled for various reasons ate things close to or even the same as Type 41's, and a short scan by a clever little device he'd never seen before resulted in room service deliveries of meals, even some sort of meat and fish, that were tasty and had no unusual side effects. Even silverware was provided to his specifications.

The girl ate no meat, nor would she use tableware. Still, she could and did pack away an enormous amount of fruits, grains, nuts, and starchy vegetables, all raw, all completely consumed, including rinds, skins, and seeds. She also ate whole sticks of whatever butter they provided and large squares of what appeared to be lard. It was fascinating to see the lengths she would go to to avoid using tools or utensils, though. Milk— he wasn't sure what kind and didn't want to know, but it had a distinct buttery taste and a kind of goatlike aroma—was fine, but not in a glass. Put it in a large bowl, and she would not touch the bowl but would put her face into it and drink or, if it was ample enough, cup it in her hands. But just about everything she could eat she *did* eat.

The aversion to using tools or mechanical devices wasn't absolute, but it was as absolute as she could make it. She would not take the elevator; she walked up and down the stairs or often ran. Neither would she open a door or even indicate that she wanted it open; she would simply stand there until it was opened for her. Somehow, though, she always knew the right floor to stop at and wait for him.

Even dicier was when she had to go to the toilet. Although the one in the room wasn't built for Earth humans, it was close enough to be useful, but she would not sit on it or even touch it. She squatted, and that was that. But she had no aversion to the large oval-shaped sunken tub that filled and drained automatically. She had no problems adapting the tub to her bodily needs, which was okay, but it kept him from enjoying it. She, however, immersed herself in it with no compunctions. Overall, until he arranged with the management for an alternative shower, she smelled better than he did.

That night, feeling finally warm and comfortable, Nathan Brazil sat in the room and looked over some maps. The shortest route to the Well was over the Strait of Sagath to Agon, just three hexes away via the water route, then north through Lilblod, through Mixtim or Clopta, and across Quilst to the Avenue. It wasn't an area he knew from the past, being well off his normal track, but it was direct and didn't require too much travel in nontech hexes. Indeed, if he went via Clopta, Betared, up to Lieveru, and approached the Avenue from the west in Ellerbanta, although it would be a bit farther, he could limit the nontech part to Lilblod alone. That didn't ensure friendly receptions, of course, but high- and semitech hexes had means of transportation other than muscle power, and that meant speed. By getting on the ship the girl had shown that she would ride in such things even if she didn't like it, adjusting as best she could, as she was doing just being inside the hotel and the room.

The other alternative was to head northeast, but in addition to being longer, that route had the almost equal problem of being partly in areas well known to him. He wasn't at all certain he wanted to put himself under the authority of the Yaxa, whose high-tech devices might well contain some vestigial residue of suspicion or identification of one Nathan Brazil even after so very long a time. He didn't trust them much in any event.

Getting to Agon, however, was proving to be harder than he'd been led to believe. No matter what shipping company or booking agent he tried, nothing was going there. Coming *from* there, yes, but even when he found two ships on the schedule, he was informed that one had developed hull problems and would be in drydock for months and that the other was skipping the port because of scheduling problems and lack of business there. It almost seemed as if nothing was crossing the relatively short strait. Somehow some new natural law had been passed, or so evidence suggested, that ships traveled only east and west. It was almost making him paranoid.

If it wasn't so ridiculous, he thought, *I'd swear I was the victim of some massive conspiracy to keep me here.*

Well, he had to decide on something, however unsatisfactory, fairly quickly. At the rates charged by the Grand, they'd be on the street in two more weeks. In a way he envied the girl—that wouldn't bother her a bit, and he knew it. While she was mortal and he was not, the inseparable gulf between them that even empathic linkage couldn't get around, *he* felt the cold and hunger and was subject to many of the infirmities that she was somehow shielded against. He had no intention of being frozen stiff in some cliffside hideaway until somebody found him and thawed him out in years to come.

It was while coming out from yet another fruitless encounter with a shipping agent that he met the colonel.

"Of all the sights I have seen in this beautiful but accursed world, that has to be the most amazing," said a voice behind him, a voice that sounded both eerie and menacing, the kind of voice that would give the same impression if it just said "Good morning." It was Sydney Greenstreet, but on steroids and in a mild echo chamber.

Brazil and the girl both stopped dead at the sound and turned. Brazil felt her sudden reaction to the speaker and understood it. She never reacted to the outward appearance of anybody; he wasn't even sure she considered it relevant. But the inside, the important part of an individual, *that* she got immediately and with unerring accuracy. Not that he needed the loan of her talent for this case. The voice kind of *oozed* with a silky sliminess that would put anyone on guard. The fact that the figure who spoke matched the impression only reinforced the sense of menace.

"I beg your pardon," Brazil responded politely. "Were you speaking to me?"

The creature they faced was less a form than a mass; it seemed almost made of liquid, an unsettling, pulsating thing that had no clearly defined shape, its "skin," or outer membrane, a glistening obsidianlike shiny brown that reflected and distorted all the light that struck it. He couldn't imagine how it spoke aloud at all.

"Pardon," it said, revealing a nearly invisible slitlike mouth in the midst of the mass. "I had not even the slightest suspicion that there might be Earthlike humans on this planet, although God knows there is certainly every other nightmare creature."

Brazil frowned. "You know Earth?"

"Of course. I was born there and once looked much as you." The mass changed, writhed, and took on an increasingly humanoid shape, until, standing before them, it became what looked for all the world like a life-sized animated carving in obsidian or jade of an Earth-human man, middle-aged but ramrod straight. There was even a suggestion of a bushy mustache and the semblance of, yes, some sort of uniform. "Colonel Jorge Lunderman, late of the Air Force of the Republic of Brazil, rather abruptly retired but at your service."

"So *you're* one of the two officers that they told me about! I wondered who you were and how you wound up coming through. Oh—sorry. Captain Solomon is my name. David Solomon."

"Captain? In the service of what nation?"

"None, really. Merchant marine. Countless ships under the usual flags of convenience."

"You were in port, then, in Rio?"

"No, just on holiday there. I hadn't been in Brazil in—a *very* long time."

"I was commandant of the Northwestern Defense Sector—the area mostly of jungle and isolated settlements between Manaus and the western and northern national borders. A very large meteor struck, harmlessly, in the middle of the jungle, but a mostly American television news crew who went in to investigate and report on it vanished completely. There was quite a search using every resource at our command, but it was as if they had vanished into nothingness."

Brazil nodded. "I understand. Somehow they must all have fallen through to here."

"Well, some Peruvian revolutionaries had camps just along the border, and they were in alliance with some very powerful drug barons, one of whom had guaranteed the newspeople's safety. We had fears that the crew had been disposed of for some reason, but we found only cooperation from the Peruvians. It seems one of Don Campos's sons was among the group that vanished. We searched for weeks before giving up. Nothing. But this meteor, it was so strange that they were flying in scientists from all over to test and check and measure it. There seemed no harm there, though. They'd poked it and probed it and tried to drill into it, and nothing much had changed. The Americans sent a liaison, a NASA astronaut who was a geologist, to help coordinate. The two of us stupidly agreed to pose atop the meteor for the news media. It seemed harmless enough. The next thing we knew, we were here."

Brazil listened carefully to the account, musing over the implications he couldn't fully discuss with the colonel or anybody else. Why had a huge chunk of meteor with a fully operative Well Gate fallen so far inland? Hell, that was a thousand miles from Rio, where he was, and the Well computer hadn't had any trouble almost hitting him on the head with one. Had Mavra been in Brazil as well? Maneuvered there by the subtle shifts of probability the Well was capable of when it concerned a Watcher? That still didn't make sense. One didn't go to the upper Amazon for a casual trip, but he couldn't see her either in the drug trade or playing local revolutionary. Not unless she was leading the rebels, anyway. Or . . .

Just why *had* he decided to take his holiday in Brazil? Maybe it was *he* who'd been manipulated. The savage looks of the other party, the accounts of how primitive they and the girl had seemed . . . Mavra living with a tribe of Stone Age Indians deep in the jungle? That *had* to be the answer. How and why would have to remain a mystery, at least for now, but it explained a lot. But the colonel and the astronaut had come through *weeks*, maybe longer, before Mavra's group.

Maybe the colonel's initial search and, afterward, the colonel's and the astronaut's apparent on-camera disintegration would have made it hard as hell to reach the Gate. That *had* to be it. But then, who *did* come through with Mavra when she finally managed it? Others of her tribe? And if that was the case, where was that news crew?

"Captain? Are you all right?" the colonel asked.

"Oh, yes, sorry. I was just trying to fit events together. What brings you to Hakazit now, Colonel?"

"Why, I thought that would be obvious. You do. Both of you, in fact. I mean, it is still something of a shock to me to find myself here in this form and situation, but I accepted what had happened out of necessity. But I had not seen or heard of a race here that was like the one into which I was born, and suddenly there is news that at least two and perhaps more of what I still think of as 'humans' were around and apparently unchanged. I had to find out who you were and what you were doing and, of course, how the both of you manage to remain as you were. I *assume* she is as she looked before and is not some native human stock unknown to me. Your pardon, but the only surprise greater than seeing someone like you here is seeing her, standing there, stark naked, on a cold and windswept coast, apparently feeling no discomfort."

"You're right; both of us are from Earth. I suspect she came through the same gate you did. I came through in the hills behind Rio with two others I haven't located as yet. She's a mystery girl—arrived naked, painted up, bone jewelry and the like, and snuck right past everybody and entered the Well World without being noticed until too late. I have no idea why the computer they say controls things here decided to keep us both as we were, but I can hazard a guess as to why she's more changed in other ways, including the ones that are obvious, than I am. There *is* a human hex here, but the people don't quite look like any race or nationality we know and they're primitive, mysterious, and very un-Earthlike in their ways. They took a different path somehow. Seems that long ago their ancestors plotted to take over an adjoining nontech hex, Ambreza, and forgot that lack of machines doesn't equal lack of intelligence. The Ambrezians bred some kind of gas-producing plant that grew like weeds in the human hex and basically knocked their brains all to hell. Then they switched hexes, so now the humans are nontech and apparently have been ever since. It changed them. There was some sort of mutation. Had they remained high-tech, they'd have been fairly familiar, I think, but being nontech, they went to the ultimate nontech system. Because the computer still has them in their original hex, however, that's where both the girl and I came in. I stayed and made myself useful to the Ambrezians—they look like giant beavers—while she fled to the human hex and fell in with them. It was *they*, I'm sure, that made her this way, not the computer."

"Does she not speak?"

"I don't think she speaks or understands a word anybody says. Sometimes I'm not even sure she thinks the way most of us think. The Ambreza said that they did have a small number of sounds that were consistent, but not enough to be considered a language. I'm not so sure it's more than the equivalent of the sound codes used by many animal species. You know—warning the tribe of danger, warning enemies off, sounds that relate to fear, and things like that. A scream, a warning cry, a sigh, a purringlike hum—that's about the range of it. If they communicate more complex information, and I'm convinced that they do, it's by means other than what we think of as language. I hope she *was* one of the Stone Age Amazonians. I'd hate to think of the frustration I would have, let alone anyone from a more civilized and technological culture, under those limitations imposed on her."

"She is definitely not a native," the colonel noted. "However, she looks like many people in my old native land for all that. It is not unheard of for such tribes to find or adopt lost children of outsiders and raise them as their own. I pray that it is so, for then she is probably better off and will live longer by coming here. It would be terrible if, say, she was one of the missing television crew. I mean, I may look, even *be* very different, but inside, in my mind, I am still Jorge Lunderman. But like *that,* not even as you say *thinking* as we were raised to think, how much of either of us would be truly left after a period living that way? I am the same man that I was, living a different life in a very different place and as, frankly, something very different than what I was. Still, there is continuity, is there not? The mind and soul are my own. I would much prefer that to retaining my body and losing my mind, my memories, my very way of thinking. I would not be me anymore. I would be someone entirely different, but perhaps with just that lurking suspicion somewhere telling me that I was once someone else. Terrible, sir! Terrible!"

Brazil glanced at the girl, who was still looking at the creature with some disdain on her face but with no hint that she'd comprehended, or even *tried* to comprehend, any of the discussion.

"Well, she seems neither tortured nor unhappy," the captain noted, "so I will continue to just accept her as she is."

The colonel shifted a bit, the human statue distorting a bit eerily. "You must tell me what you are doing and why she is with you instead of remaining back there!" he said enthusiastically. "And about all the rest of what you know as well. It seems like *ages* since I was able to speak to anyone with a common frame of reference to my past! But sir, I apologize! While the cold is of some little discomfort to me and apparently none to her, you must be *freezing*! Forgive my manners. Have you a hotel?"

"Yes, I'm at the Grand. You?"

"I am currently living out of my cabin aboard the ship I used to get here. It will be in port here for three days, so there is little reason to consider my course of action beyond that until then. My cabin is, of course, at your service, but I'm afraid it would be neither spacious nor comfortable to one not of my new kind. Shall we go to your hotel, then?"

"Might as well," Brazil sighed. "It doesn't look as if I'm *ever* going to get out of here."

They began walking, or, rather, Brazil began walking, as did the girl, a bit behind, while the colonel sort of oozed along next to him.

"That *is* a good question to begin with as we walk," the colonel noted. "Why *are* you in this inhospitable and out-of-the-way place?"

"Well, if you must know, I'm in a far worse position than either you or the girl there. I can't set up anything permanent in Glathriel—the human hex—unless I want to take on her ways and life-style. The Ambreza could be strung along just so much, but they're still paranoid about humans, particularly the kind who can talk and know technology like me, and they've basically barred me from returning. I'm the man without a country. I am not, however, without a good deal of experience and skills that even the Ambreza found useful, which is how I have any cash at all. By the time you can command the kind of ships I did, you became something of an expert in almost everything practical and useful. Way up north around the equator there are two high-tech hexes separated by a narrow strait, neither of which has ever seen or heard of the likes of Glathriel, and both are highly dependent on shipping and import-export trade at this stage. They've both been looking for qualified ship's officers and as usual aren't particular about the race or nationality involved. They also serve as flags of convenience for hundreds of coastal hexes, particularly the nontech and semitech ones that have to get ships and crews from high-tech places. It's my best shot at a life here."

"Yes, I understand," the colonel said. "But you have been frustrated?"

"I can't get a ship north for love or money. It's driving me crazy—not to mention quickly broke before I've started."

The colonel thought a moment. "Tell me, Captain, do you think you could handle the sort of ship they must use here?"

The Well World *did* require rather bizarre ships, since there were water hexes as well as land ones and those water hexes had the same technological limitations as their dry counterparts. Thus, a large ship had to be able to move entirely by sail through nontech waters, switch to basic steam fed by manual labor or ingenious cog-driven mechanisms for the semitech, but could use an efficient fusion plant for the high-tech regions.

"I began in sail, if that's what you mean," Brazil told him. "And I've got—*had*—a master's license for steam as well. My latest ships were big diesels, but the power source of a modern plant isn't relevant if the power's fed to the engines in the amount the bridge demands. I'm a little out of shape to climb rigging myself, but I could handle most anything else."

"Then why do you not sail there yourself?"

"For the same reason you, as an air force colonel, didn't have your own personal supersonic transport. That would take an incredible amount of money, and I'm afraid I'm still a wee bit short."

The colonel chuckled, a very eerie sound. "Yes, I see. But there are much smaller craft making the runs. Private and government yachts, ferries that are built in one place and must be sailed to where they are needed, smaller fishing boats or their equivalents, that sort of thing. Like many other high-tech coastal hexes, Hakazit has a very competitive ship-building industry, you know, and they often have only skeleton crews to take those ships to their customers, as most experienced crew live on and have a share in their own ships. Forget shipping agencies, sir! Try the shipwrights! Why, I managed to finagle passage here because they needed someone familiar with government-type contracts to check on an overdue naval vessel my nation has on order. Permit me to ask around when I go down there tomorrow morning. Perhaps I can find something for you. One-way, of course, and probably not precisely to where you wish to go, but sufficient, I would expect."

"I have no papers for this world," Brazil reminded him, "so I never even thought of that route. But, if you can find somebody who'll take me north, I'll be glad to sign on."

"Done, sir!"

"You sound very confident," Brazil noted dryly.

"Why, sir, I am first and foremost a Brazilian! In my country you learn very quickly how to deal with mosquitoes, however large they are!"

In point of fact, Theresa "Terry" Perez *did* remember who she had been and where she had come from, but that only accentuated the change within her. What was different was that it no longer mattered to her, nor even did it disturb any part of her in the slightest that it no longer mattered to her. Nothing that mattered to virtually all the others in the hotel and in the city really mattered to her, except for a few basics. That was at the root of this new, nonlinear way of thinking that the Glathrielian group will be imposed upon her, and not unwillingly on her part although she hadn't known at the time what it would mean and the old Terry might well have fled instead.

In point of fact, the Glathrielians had not imposed a great deal; rather, they had in effect rewired her brain so that it processed information in a way more alien to Earth standards than most of the cultures of the wildly varying races of the Well World. It created a new Terry, one who automatically saw the world in a new and very different way.

The Glathrielian imperative was essentially quite simple: At all times, consider only all the things that are relevant to you, and miss not a one of those. Anything irrelevant or unnecessary was a distraction; distraction was the way to destruction, so anything unimportant must be literally factored out of the mind and not even allowed to register. It would take years of self-training to master it completely, but Terry, helped by the experience and self-training of the Glathrielian elders, had achieved an amazingly high level of mastery in so short a time.

If she could filter out all distractions, all things not directly relevant to her existence and what was of true importance to her, and automatically observe only what she needed, the amount of information that simply *came* to her was enormous, far beyond the sort of knowledge others might possess. Thoughts, actions, and processes that did not require decisions should be automated so that they, too, ceased to exist as a factor. The energy field that her brain could generate and her body could use for so many things was one such process she had already relegated to that status. Although she didn't know or care exactly what it was doing, or how, it protected her from the elements that might cause distraction—extremes of heat and cold, for example, or even adjusting gravitation or filtering out any impurities from an atmosphere so that if the chemicals needed to breathe were present in any mixture, it would extract only those and allow them into her lungs.

Of course, it was also useful both as a defense and as an offense, if needed, and those functions, too, were automated.

Without even realizing she had done so, she had reordered much of her digestive system and metabolism for maximum efficiency and maximum reserves of power. *What* she ate, so long as it was not poisonous to her system and was not of flesh, was irrelevant to her, and even much that might have made her ill or killed her was now separated out and isolated and passed through without harm. The body maintained its own vitamin, mineral, fat, and sugar requirements as best it could with whatever was at hand; it basically controlled what and how much she ate. She didn't even think of it.

All the knowledge of her past and the person she'd been was not gone, but it had been reordered and placed in an out-of-the-way, protected area of the brain. The sight of an object or an assemblage of objects brought forth an instant reaction based on that knowledge but only what was needed to deal with it. Thus, the sight of electrical cables or sockets might evoke a warning of danger rather than a definition or a picture of what they were. By simply obeying those impulses automatically, she did not have to deal with them, either. The standard senses—sight, smell, sound, taste, and touch—were processed on a wholly subconscious level, almost as if she had a second parallel mind with access to all the same data whose sole function was to evaluate each and every "frame" of information, sixty or more per second, calculate if an action was necessary, and send the irresistible order to her consciousness.

This alone gave her enormous abilities of which she was as yet not completely aware that when used would not be thought about or reflected upon but merely accepted.

She was totally unaware that she was in a city, let alone a strange city on another planet peopled almost entirely by creatures alien to her. Yet her senses and her past knowledge of cities allowed her to cross busy streets at peak hours safely and, quite literally, without thinking about it. That was knowledge the Glathrielians themselves would have lacked, and they would have been easy targets for the first speeding truck. That was why she was unique even for Glathriel. She could survive in wildly unfamiliar places because her previous knowledge base gave her sufficient information for her to do so.

She felt uncomfortable inside because walls and barriers blocked not only the irrelevant but the important as well. Enclosures distracted and had to be dealt with. Still, the knowledge base informed her that the object: mate was subject to environmental weaknesses that no longer plagued her, and it was unthinkable that she would keep him in discomfort when it was possible to do otherwise. The concept of separating from him any more than necessary was simply not allowable. She and he were linked in biophysical and biochemical ways that neither understood but that she realized and accepted. That she had in fact induced the linkage to ensure that he took her with him she no longer even remembered; it was irrelevant. *Is* mattered; *was* did not matter and was thus dismissed from the mind unless *was* was absolutely required for a current action.

And all of *is* was composed of objects. *Mate* is. *Interactor with Mate* is. At that moment those two objects were the only things in her mind. All else was filtered out as irrelevant. She understood nothing that was said; indeed, those very sounds were filtered out as irrelevant. But she *felt* what Mate felt; every little nuance of feeling was input, to a level he could not have comprehended. These were assimilated and appended to the Mate object's *is,* which in turn formed a complete and constantly changing whole object picture in her mind.

The Glathrielian way saw life as a series of assembled objects leading to clearly pictured objectives, the latter simplified to the most basic form.

Situation: hunger. Objective: find, consume sufficient food. Her one larger objective since turning Glathrielian had been to accompany now-mate. Having achieved that objective, she'd had no need for another. She understood, however, that Mate had his own objective. Because she lacked any data that the objective affected her in any way she would consider important and lacked any overall further objective of her own, Mate's objective was in control and she would support him as he required. Just what Mate's objective was she neither knew nor cared, nor would she care until and unless it affected what she considered important.

Her conscious mind saw no irrelevant external details; it saw other life as a seemingly infinite variety of colors and color mixes and patterns. She saw what was *inside* rather than what was *outside* in this circumstance.

Mate's *is* was warmth, comfort, interaction with Other; interaction produced in him a range of sensations, none of which were unpleasurable and which included some hope and optimism, which meant that Mate was interacting with Other in pursuit of Mate's objective. The Other, however, was radiating a very different *is* that Mate seemed oblivious to. *Deceit, dishonesty, coldness, cruelty—danger!* These impressions all came to her as they could only when her mind was freed of distractions. She could not interact with the Other, but she could with Mate, both empathically and physically. She knew that Mate was getting the information in the same manner as she was sending it, but while he did not reject it, and it seemed only to reinforce his own instinct about the Other; neither did Mate act upon it as she would have.

If she still could think in the old ways, she would have thought to herself, *He knows the colonel is a lying, two-faced bastard with ulterior motives, but for now he's stringing the creature along.*

She was uneasy about this only because she lacked any knowledge of what the creature was and how it might be dealt with. With the creatures she'd taken on in the past, she'd been able to absorb sufficient data from Mate to formulate a course of action; in this case, however, Mate didn't seem to know anything about the damned creature, either, meaning that the only course open if the thing turned dangerous was to run like hell.

For his part, Nathan Brazil was getting a little irritated by the waves of warning coming from the girl. He fervently wished there was some way to tell her, *"I know, the guy's a slimy, dangerous son of a bitch, but I need to know what he's up to."* Still, she seemed to actually be making an important point. If this creature were to try anything now, he hadn't the slightest idea how to hurt it or just what it could do to him. He was suddenly so astonished that she had actually managed relevant and intelligent communication with him that he almost fumbled acting on it. Repressing his excitement, at least for the moment, he got control and asked, "By the way, Colonel, I don't want to sound insulting, but just what the devil *are* you, anyway? Your race and nationality, I mean. You're a new species to me."

That wasn't quite true, but it must have been eons ago when he'd last encountered such a creature as this, and he just didn't have anything to go on.

"The nation is called Leeming, sir," the colonel told him. "At least, that is the way the translators spit it out, and that's acceptable. And our kind are called Leems, not Leemingites or whatever, which is very close to the actual sound."

The name, pronounced a bit differently but still close enough, did indeed ring a distant bell. They had no skeletal structure, and the brain case was a rock-hard ball that could move to any part of the fluid body. The outer membrane was thick enough to stop most projectiles, and yet they could control their skin and fluid interior almost down to the cellular level. What they needed, they could quickly create the internal musculature to make. Arm, hand, tentacles, functional eyes, functional mouths and voice mechanisms, ears, even the semblance of a former Brazilian Air Force colonel. They could maintain simple shapes or appendages almost forever but were unable to sustain complex forms for very long, especially when under stress. The Leem were asexual, but two were required to reproduce, each consuming a massive quantity of food and growing to almost one and a half times its normal size, then splitting off that new half, which then joined with a half from the other to produce a whole new being. They ate by secreting an acidic poison that could dissolve virtually any organic life to a puddle of warm goo, which was then absorbed directly through the skin.

Now where the hell did all that *come from?* Brazil wondered. From the Well data bank was the obvious answer, but it still startled him. The Well had never been so generous or so obvious or so detailed with him before.

The data flowed into Terry from him and were added to her own internal knowledge base. This in turn changed the conscious picture of the Other dramatically, and it startled her. Mate had not known; then, suddenly, there had been a tiny burst of energy and a data stream had come from no specific point into his mind and then secondarily from his mind to hers.

She felt his surprise and initial puzzlement at it, then his comfort of recognition and his surprised pleasure rather than continued bafflement. It was something unexpected, new data that could not now be correlated.

Like her, Mate had a knowledge base that gave important data, but unlike her, the source was *external*. And while he knew the source, he had not expected the data to be given. There was something very important about that fact beyond its obvious comforting factors and its convenience to Mate, but as yet she could relate it to no objective of hers. But if it was not important to his objective beyond the obvious, and not relevant to hers, but was relevant and important beyond a doubt, then to whose objective did it relate? The priorities were clear: SELF < FAMILY < TRIBE. Mate + external knowledge base = great power. Family + external knowledge base = great power^2. Tribe + external knowledge base = ?
∞?

Such speculation was fruitless and irrelevant to her now and was immediately wiped from her conscious mind as if it had never been considered. What remained was the relevant part: that she had a tribal objective that overruled all other actions, and that was for she and Mate to reach Mate's objective. Until that was attained, reaching Mate's objective was the sole motivator of all subsequent actions. And any actions on her part to further that objective were justified.

Without exception.

CIBON,
OFF THE ITUS COAST

IT HAD NOT BEEN a pleasant voyage for the former Julian Beard, although at the time she didn't realize how unusual the experience was.

The monks of Erdom, pledged to maintain a stable society, had been faced with a pair of Erdomites, one male, one female, from another world, another culture, another race, now in Erdomite bodies but with their old minds and memories. Lori Sutton, once a human female and an astronomy professor as well, was now an Erdomite male through the oddities and occasional sick humor of the Well, two meters tall, strong, fast, an equine humanoid with a horn on his head and a pair of legs that could propel him at up to twenty miles an hour in deep sand. Julian Beard, once a handsome human man, an engineer and a shuttle astronaut, was now a pastel yellow Erdomite female, small, with little upper body strength, with a mane of hair and a matching tail, coping with not one but two pairs of breasts, and with hands that were little more than mittenlike split soft hooves. Both were trapped in a Well World nation where only mechanical energy was allowed, a medieval desert society where females had neither status nor rights, and where education and knowledge were tightly held and controlled by a pervasive church run by Erdomese eunuchs. To the monks, these two were the very definition of a pair who just would not culturally fit.

The original plan had been simple: to use one of the monks' great herbal potions to essentially hypnotize them into being good Erdomites, with a posthypnotic command that each should take the drug every night and then reinforce the hypnotic commands on the other. Only the monks' failure to command them to forget their pasts and past knowledge and a fortuitous plea for help from Mavra Chang had taken them out of the monks' clutches before the conditioning could be completed.

Julian had found herself totally submissive, without any sort of aggression or defenses, in a mental state where her whole reason for living was to please her husband and anticipate his wishes. Lori had become the strutting, cavalier male, accepting Julian and *all* Erdomese females as incapable of more than pleasing men, doing household work, and having babies. He associated with other males and treated his wife as some kind of chattel slave without regard for her feelings.

Three days out of Erdom on the voyage north to Itus, they had taken the last of the drug without remembering it. The fourth day out, they went to take it and there was none left; they both went through the commanded ritual anyway, but without the potion they were aware of it and could understand what had been done to them. The effect was even worse because the old dosages had not worn off. When they said them, the statements sounded somewhat reasonable. It was only well after, when they awoke the next morning, that the full significance of it hit them.

The first realization was that they had been badly had by the monks of Erdom. The second was more than a little guilt and shame at having fallen for it.

That morning, in the cabin, they did not speak to one another for quite some time. Finally it was Julian, uncharacteristically, who broke the silence.

"I think for sanity's sake we should speak to each other in private *only* in English from now on. I think we both need the mental equivalent of a cold shower, and that's it. Not to mention the vocabulary."

"That's fine with me," Lori replied softly, not looking directly at Julian. "It seems to me that we're in enough trouble with those monks that it hardly makes a difference if we break our other promises now."

"Were you a feminist back in your previous life?" Julian asked. It seemed an odd question for the situation.

"Of a sort, yes. The word had come into some disrepute because it was co-opted by radicals with a different agenda from most women, but on the basic issues I was. Something of an activist, in fact." *Although,* Lori admitted, *I compromised my ideals more than once to get or keep a position.*

"Well, now you're going to find out the truth of one thing they told you and one other thing they didn't. First, men *do* control and set the rules in society—at least in the two I know, Earth's and Erdom's. Maybe a lot of other places. That's true. And now you're a man and have to know the second thing."

"Huh? What are you talking about?"

"The men who rule? You're not one of them. You're stuck with those stupid rules the same as every woman, and you can't change them much, either."

"Thanks a lot. After the way I treated you the last four days . . ."

"Think of it as an education, or the start of one," Julian sighed. "We were trapped. Both of us. But we couldn't escape because it was built into the society. If we hadn't agreed on the temple visit, I would have been stuck with that tentmaker and gotten the treatment later, when the local monk got the drugs he needed. If you agreed but then didn't show up, they'd have sent people looking for us, and in that society it's pretty hard to hide for very long. And *then* we'd have been *kept* in the temple, but instead of just being drugged and hypnotized, we'd have been the subjects for their chemical inquisition. We'd have come out of there with our brains scrubbed so clean that not a trace of Julian Beard or Lori Sutton would have remained."

Lori shook his head in wonder and sighed. "I wonder what would have happened if they hadn't passed me that letter. Or if they'd told me to simply forget I was ever anything but an Erdomite and *then* handed me a letter I couldn't read."

"I suspect that this friend of yours paid a handsome bribe to ensure that we'd get the letter. As to the other, remember, they'd never had two people like us before. They couldn't think of everything that quickly. But we'd have continued to drug and hypnotize each other, and over weeks, months, a year, we'd have had reinforcing visits to the temple so they could correct any problems. Eventually we'd be so steeped in our roles and behavior and so indoctrinated into the religion and culture, nothing else would have been needed. I shouldn't wonder that my next prescription might have included some mind-dulling chemicals, slowing down my mental processes until I couldn't keep two thoughts in my head at once or have much long-term memory. I'd just be another of those stupid bubbleheads."

"You think they're smart enough to have stuff like that?"

"I think it's about time we stop thinking of them as ignorant and stupid just because they live in a feudal, primitive society. They are a very old culture. Ancient by Earth standards. I think they know an awful lot about everything that is possible to use in a nontechnical society and even more about keeping things the way they are and under complete control."

"But—we're Erdomese! You said it yourself a week ago. We're Erdomese whether we like it or not. Sooner or later—"

She nodded. "Sooner or later we'll be back there and even more suspect because we've traveled abroad. I hope by then we'll have figured out some way to beat them."

"If we survive this, and if this woman's telling the truth or anything close to it, we might have a crack. The promised reward is 'anything we want.' Maybe even out of here, if we wanted it. I take it that you're not so enamored of being female after the last few days."

"Not treated like *that,* I'm not! I don't mind being the junior partner along for the ride, but I treated my *dog* better than I got treated by you! And the dog didn't have to work, either."

"I—I know. You think I'm *proud* of that?"

Julian grinned. "I think it's a lot tougher holding to principle when you're on the top of the heap instead of on the bottom. But for your information, it's not the gender I'm upset with, it's the bottom position and its permanence. Being a culturally correct Erdomese female is the pits, I'll tell you. If I were forced to go back to *that,* I'd *cheerfully* take their stupid pills. Like *this* I can manage, I think, although there's still some residual effect from that stuff. Alone in the cabin with just you, I find I can fight it, but out there, among others, particularly other Erdomese on the ship, I'm not so sure I won't have a relapse."

"Until we're well away from Erdomese it might not be so bad to keep to the fiction, anyway," Lori noted. "I wouldn't be at all surprised if some of these businessmen traders here didn't also report back to the temple on just about everything they see and hear. I doubt if they could do anything this far from home, but we are citizens of Erdom, and we can't hide that fact. They do all their diplomacy in the polar Zone, but it's as if they have a voice in every one of these hex-shaped countries. We left pretty suddenly. If they decided to trump up some charges against us, we could easily wind up being arrested and sent back through one of those gates right back to Erdom, with the monks waiting for us at the other end. I think it's best not to relax too much until we have some protection from others who know this place better than we do."

It was a sobering thought. "Thanks. Just what I needed—more reasons to jump at shadows. Actually, the residue of these past few days is different from what you think I meant. I mean, I *know* how to play the sniveling little bimbo if I have to. I hate it, but it's kind of a survival skill. No, it's not that—it's the fear."

"Huh? Fear of what?"

"Of anything. You see, up until we got the treatment, I was playacting. To a certain extent the lifetime and instincts of good old Julian Beard were still there. Spending these days as a 'pure' Erdomese woman, though, I didn't have those old senses to call upon. For the first time I faced the added burden of being a female in a male-dominated society that places women somewhere just above the herd animals or even below them. Without you around as a protector, I was absolutely *defenseless*. I had to take all the feelies from those merchants, all the guff, and all of a sudden every single one of them looked like a threat. My body was entirely at their mercy, and I needed, *required* you to stand in their way. I didn't want to be out of your sight, and if you went off, I got back to this cabin in a hurry and locked myself in, scared to death all the way here. Until now I hadn't understood why I felt the need to be locked up to be safe. I put it down to the drugs or the body or the changes in me. *This* brought it home. The old me, the *male* me, would have explored this ship from stem to stern and never had a second thought. Now, suddenly, I was in the midst of strangers, and I didn't know friend from foe. I was scared to leave and scared to stay."

Lori felt a sudden sympathy for Julian. "I think I know what you mean," he responded. "It explains a lot about how *I'm* reacting to all this, too. I've had a cavalier, adventurous attitude since becoming male and a kind of charge-straight-ahead-and-damn-the-consequences feeling. Until now I was only aware that some sort of burden had been lifted off me but not what it was. It was just that the sort of feeling I had growing up female back home was gone. When I was seventeen, I was raped by my prom date. At the time I felt disgusted, but I never said anything because there was always this feeling somewhere deep down that I'd encouraged him somehow, *let* him do it—I don't know. I *do* know I changed after that. Cut my hair real short, started to be a slob, got fat and stayed that way, just about never used makeup—made myself unattractive in general. I stopped dating for a long time, until after I'd gotten my Ph.D., really, hung out in women's studies centers and even socialized with a lesbian group, although I never really wanted to go to bed with them. I *did* go to bed with men—a lot of them—but they were always men I picked out, and they were mostly nerds who were desperate for any female interest. They were going to love me for *me,* no frills or compromises, or to hell with them. Don't get me wrong—I knew I was reacting—but I had a justification for everything. And, surrounded by lots of women I knew and trusted, or by men of my choosing, I managed to keep the fear down. I guess that's why I took to the all-women tribe so easily. No men to threaten, and women who were not only self-sufficient but actually dangerous."

"And now we both realize that, just like in physics, nothing is really lost, it's just transferred," Julian said with a sigh. "Now I've got the burden and yours is gone. About the only thing I can cling to as a real advantage is that this body sure delivers *dynamite* sex."

"I guessed as much, considering your responses. And that's the downside of my change. I can turn on like a light switch, but everything's concentrated in just one spot. It explains a lot about my previous lovers. I feel a lot less guilt now."

They had a laugh at that and then went on to more immediate worries.

"What do you know about this Chang woman, anyway?" Julian asked.

"Not a lot. As far as I was concerned, she was the leader and demigoddess of a tribe of primitive rain forest Amazons—literally. Tough, mean, and ruthless; that was her reputation among the tribe. Then, suddenly, all *this* comes about and suddenly she's claiming to be some immortal from this world. I would have sworn she'd have barely recognized anything beyond Stone Age technology as anything but magic and that she had no experience beyond the jungles, yet here she is, suddenly a different sort of person, comfortable with technology well in advance of our own and writing notes to me in ancient Greek!"

"Yeah, how'd she know you knew Greek?"

"I don't even know how she'd know I knew German, let alone Greek. Our only common language was that of a Stone Age tribe. I don't count it because I can't speak it, and I was surprised that I could read the note at all. She made it pretty basic, though, and it all came back to me. She certainly knows no English, and if she did, it would probably sound more like Shakespeare's or even Chaucer's. She'd been in that jungle an awfully long time. It was almost like she was hiding out from the world."

"From that other fellow with the appropriate name, perhaps. Brazil."

"Maybe. But I get the feeling it's not that simple. She's not just a small woman, she's *tiny*. Under five feet, skinny, wiry, but moves like a cat. She also has a confident, brassy voice and manner, but I wonder if that's just a mask for what we were talking about."

"Huh?"

"The fear factor."

"But—she's immortal, or she says she is. And according to you, the tribe at least believed that any injuries to her, no matter how severe, would heal without scars and that she could even regrow limbs."

"Yes, she's beyond some of our most common fears—if it's all true, anyway. But she still can be badly hurt, and she feels the same pain. I wonder if she also feels the same kind of psychological pain. She's strong for her size but no match for an average man. Suppose she is immortal and started life on Earth thousands of years ago? The way the Erdomese look at women and women's rights is about standard for most cultures in human history until fairly recently. I wonder . . . After a few thousand years of being a victim with no end in sight, *I* might run off to a rain forest and surround myself with cast-off and runaway tribal women, too.

I sort of ran away socially for years from just one incident. And this Brazil person—I *assume* they started out together and they got separated centuries or longer ago. I wonder if that's not part of the problem."

"What? That she lost her protection?"

"That she needed his protection in the first place. Her ego is pretty damned strong. There would be only so much protection she could stand before cracking."

"You think he was abusing her or something?"

"No, I don't think so. Even in Zone she described him as basically a good person. She would have cast him as the epitome of evil if he'd done anything to her. No, I think it's more basic than that. Thousands of years in a series of what must have seemed *very* primitive societies to her, always with that fear factor . . . Suppose he simply never noticed? Suppose he, the immortal *male,* just couldn't comprehend it?"

It was something to think about but not something that could be proved one way or the other, not until they actually met this mysterious Brazil—if, indeed, they ever did. This and their mental hangover and associated guilt produced a minute or two of silence.

Finally Julian spoke. "I really don't understand a lot of this at all. If what we're being told is correct, much of what I learned about creation, evolution, the birth and death of the universe—it's all wrong. Yet everything, all the laws of science, seem to be more or less holding in spite of all that, and it doesn't make any sense. We've gone from a solid foundation down through the rabbit hole to Wonderland."

"Not exactly," Lori responded. "We don't know enough to draw any conclusions about the universe at large. There were a lot of theorists in physics who postulated bizarre theories that were at least mathematically possible. White holes, parallel universes, and much more. Even in the Einsteinian sense we casually accepted gravity bending time itself. This doesn't show that what we knew was wrong, only that we knew far less than we thought we did. You know the old saw—I believe it was Arthur C. Clarke—that says that a civilization separated by countless years of development from our own would discover and know so much more that its technology would seem like magic to us. I think that's what's bugging you—all that work, all that knowledge, and we're as ignorant of this sort of stuff as the most primitive tribes of Earth are ignorant of our science."

"It's that," Julian admitted, "but it's more than that, too. We're not talking here about centuries ahead, or even thousands of years, but *millions* of years—maybe even more than that. All that time, and look at what they've come up with! Stagnant fundamentalism, ignorance, sexism, racism, violence—all the things *we* were trying to beat. All that knowledge, all that experience—and look at it! It's not the science that they know, it's what they *don't* have, or don't use!"

Lori sighed. "I know. Still, I keep telling myself that this *isn't* the future, it's an experimental slide. This is an artificial place, maintained by a computer. The civilizations here aren't futuristic, they're by definition stagnant, limited, leftovers after the experiment's done, left over and forgotten. Their populations are fixed, their capabilities are fixed, they can't grow, they can't progress, and they can't leave. Long ago— *very* long ago—they adapted to the situation. Some of them went mad, I suspect; some developed religious justifications for all that they had. Others went savage; still others just settled into a static condition where there's no future beyond the individual's. A few may have wound up like the People in the Amazon or some of the tribes of Papua New Guinea, where they repudiated all that had been learned, rejected all progress in the same way that we were told that the makers of this world rejected and turned their back on near godhood, equating progress with evil. In many ways this is less a romantic world than a tragic one."

"Maybe," Julian said thoughtfully. "But that brings up a nasty little thought for the immediate future. This Mavra Chang is from another age, another time, no matter what her name and appearance. I think we can take that much for granted."

"She sure knows her way around. And if she's been here before, and the only way out is through this Well, this control room, then we can assume she has even more knowledge."

"But knowledge isn't wisdom," Julian pointed out. "That's exactly what we were talking about. If she's been here before, she's very, very old. Maybe 'ancient' isn't even a good enough term for her. Never changing, never able to have a decent relationship with other human beings—they age and die in what for her would be a very short time— she's pretty much an individual example of what these hexes have gone through."

"Huh? What do you mean?"

"Well, if these hexes, trapped as they are, turned into the kind of things we're seeing, what must the effect be on an individual isolated from all around her? Maybe there's another explanation for why she might have shut herself off from the world, from all progress, in a never-ending primitive tribal group in the middle of nowhere for all those centuries. She *created* her own hex, a stagnant, never-changing one, just to cope. That doesn't make her sound very sane, either, does it?"

Lori didn't like the logic of that. "And if *she's* insane, in some sense, anyway, then what does that make this much more ancient Nathan Brazil? Thanks a lot. What you're saying is that we're on our way to help an ancient, probably insane demigoddess do battle with an even older and probably madder demigod. Now, *that* is a way to cheer me up!"

Julian shrugged. "At least it makes the whole problem of Erdom and the monks seem rather trivial, doesn't it?"

Itus was, if anything, as hot as Erdom but additionally was as humid as Erdom was dry. The air seemed a solid thing, a thick woolen blanket that enveloped one and made one slow, groggy, and exhausted from fighting against it. The gravitation, too, seemed greater; they felt heavy, leaden, and it took effort just to walk. Julian, particularly with the added dead weight of the four breasts, found it next to impossible to walk without support on just her thin equine legs and dropped to walking on all fours, something that didn't seem at all unnatural. Lori almost envied her after walking a couple of blocks. Julian did not seem as pleased, but the alternative was next to impossible. And frankly, even standing on all fours, bringing her height down to about a meter plus, she was still on a reasonable level for the natives of this place.

The Ituns were insectoids, large, low, caterpillarlike creatures with dozens of spindly legs emerging from thick hairy coats and faces that seemed to be two huge, bulging oval eyes and a nasty-looking mouth flanked by intimidating, curved tusks. They seemed to be able to bend and then lock themselves into just about any position they required and, supported by the hind rows of legs, use their many forelegs as individual hands, fingers, or tentacles. Far worse for the newcomers than the eternally nasty faces and fixed vicious expressions, though, was the sight of all that thick hair in the constant heat and humidity. It made them feel even hotter just watching.

The Itun behind the front desk of the transients' hotel seemed a bit larger and older and perhaps a bit more shopworn than the average denizen of the hex but was accustomed to dealing with alien types on a daily basis. Unable to form the kind of sounds that Common Speech required, it relied on one of the benefits of a high-tech hex: a small transmitter attached to the top of its head right above and between the eyes.

"Lori of Alkhaz," he told the desk clerk. "Party of two Erdomese. I was told that we would be expected."

Lower feet were already tapping something into an Itun terminal. The head cocked and looked down and read something on a screen.

"Yes," the clerk responded in a toneless electronic-sounding voice. "An Erdomese suite was prepaid for you. Do you have much baggage?"

"Very little," Lori responded. All that they owned was in one small pack.

"Very well," the clerk said, and pushed a small plastic card over to him.

"Um—are there any messages for me?"

"No, nothing. It would have shown on the console."

That was disappointing. "Uh, then—how do I find the room?"

"Follow the key, of course," replied the clerk, and turned to take care of someone else.

Lori picked up the plastic card, which seemed a plain ivory white in color, turned it over, and shrugged. There was nothing imprinted on it at all, not even an arrow or a magnetic stripe.

He was about to ask how the thing worked when he noticed that a tiny spot was pulsing a brighter white along one of the edges of the card. As he turned to face the lobby, holding the card out, the spot moved. He turned the card in his hand, but the spot moved to always keep the same relative position.

"Come on, Julian. I think I have this thing figured out," he said, and moved toward the rear corridor in the direction of the blinking light.

"Moo!" Julian snorted. "I feel like a damned *cow* like this!"

You are *a cow*, Lori thought, but checked himself before he said it. Damn it! It was *tough* not to reflexively say something that sounded patronizing or offensive! And the truth was, Erdomese, for all their resemblance to equine forms, really were biologically closer to the bovine family with perhaps a bit of camel. Even their sexual temperament was more bovine, with the male overly dominant, competitive, territorial, and violent, the female by nature passive. Even the native language was divided and reinforced the differing natures; there were strict masculine and feminine forms of every part of speech, without exception. They were in a sense speaking two complementary but different languages in which every word form had two variants. In this dual track of Erdomese, the male spoke Erdomo, which was what *he* thought in, and the female Erdoma, which was what Julian naturally used.

It was why they tried so hard to converse in English; to even *think* in Erdomese was to impose and reinforce the expected roles of attitude and behavior. It was, however, tough to get around without constant effort because the Well acclimation process imposed the native language as the primary one, since language defined a culture and the system was designed to ease the transition, not to fight it. Both of them lapsed into it more often than not; they thought in it, even dreamed in it, and it gave a heavy accent to and put a cast upon even their translations into their former native tongue.

Living in a high-tech cosmopolitan hex, however, the Ituns were well aware of the burdens their comfortable home placed on most other races and did what they could. Corridors back into the hotel were wide moving walkways, and there were very large elevators at regular intervals. The key, however, kept telling them to go straight back, until they were at the back of the building itself. It then indicated a turn to the right, and they walked slowly down a long, wide corridor until the key suddenly stopped blinking and became a bright white in front of an extratall, extrawide door. Lori saw the slot and inserted the key, and the door slid open.

"Air-conditioning!" Julian gasped in English, there being no term for it in Erdomese, but she quickly lapsed into the normal tongue, too tired to think straight. "I beg you please to shut the door, my husband, so that its coolness might not flee." She plopped down on the cushions, still wearing the pack, obviously exhausted.

Lori knew how she felt. Both had their tongues hanging out, panting, their forms, so suited to the desert need for retaining moisture, unable to sweat in the humidity.

It probably wasn't all that cool in the room; they were accustomed to greater heat than even Itus provided. But the air conditioner also dehumidified, and that created a level of comfort that was unbelievable.

"I am never going to leave this room again. Ever," Julian gasped. "I am going to live and die here."

He unhooked and pulled off the small pack on her back and tossed it into a corner, then slipped off the leather codpiece he wore that felt like it was cutting him in two and tossed that over with the pack. The thing was more for propriety than for protection, and he wondered if he really needed it so long as he wasn't going to pay a call on the Erdomese consul. While a number of races wore bright and ornate clothing, many others wore little or none, even some of the most developed, unless it was needed as protection against the elements. Here—well, he probably would, since there were enough Erdomese passing through Itus on various business that he might well be noticed. If and when they got farther away, though, so that he and Julian were more curiosities than familiar forms, he might just chuck it until needed.

Clothes had been a mania with him once, as an Earth female; now, as an Erdomese male, they seemed totally uninteresting except for utilitarian value.

He looked over at Julian and saw that she was asleep. She looked so tiny and nearly helpless without him, he thought. And so damned sexy . . . A whole rush of stereotypical Erdomese male attitudes, thoughts, and feelings came into his mind. The lingering aftereffects of the monks' treatments, he wondered, without really fighting them, or was it the onrush of male hormones shaping him into somebody he didn't know, somebody he should think of with disgust? Damn it, there was something new in his nature, something that made it a virtual turn-on that she was here and dependent on him. In a sense, that terrible feeling was beginning to define him. She was at least as smart as he was, perhaps smarter. Oddly, he valued that, too, so much that it was a real fear that she might *not* need him at some point, that she was essential to him while he'd been more an escape route for her. Away from that suffocating culture and away from any who might even know it, she might well eventually find him superfluous. The thought raised his insecurity to almost the fear level.

And the old conflicts surfaced as well. Damn it, he *liked* having someone dependent on *him* for a change, even though it made him feel guilty as hell.

What was at the heart of the conflict, though, was that he could continue to suppress or fight that kind of feeling, but now, as things were, did he *need* it so badly that he might not put up the fight?

Considering how mild her own reaction had been when the drug supply was exhausted and they became aware of the conditioning, he couldn't convince himself deep down that despite her protestations, she hadn't liked it in that role, too. No, *no*! That was a damned rationalization, no better than "Well, dressing like that, she asked for it."

Had she liked it? No, of course not, he told himself. Had *he* liked it, even to the far lesser degree that he'd experienced it growing up an Earth female? But the argument somehow failed to totally convince the dual nature within him.

Maybe it was simpler but more insidious than that. In the end it hadn't been a matter of liking it or not liking it. It had simply been easier, more comfortable not to be in a constant battle against one's own language and culture, particularly when every personal moral victory was no more than that. That culture, that society, wasn't about to change, ever. And neither were they from who and what they were now.

He felt confused and depressed, as if his whole life's attitudes had somehow now been proved bogus, a self-delusional sham. People on the bottom of systems always said they wanted equality, but did they, really? Or did they, deep down, yearn more to have the situation reversed? Did the oppressed really believe the ideals they espoused, or was that just rhetoric? Did they in fact *really* want to instead become the oppressors?

It was his most disturbing fear, a fear that it might well go deep down in the "human" psyche as the sort of flaw people did not want to admit, even to themselves. But how many times had sincere reformers run for office against entrenched corrupt politicians and won, only to slowly turn into exactly what they'd run against? How many idealistic Third

World revolutionaries had overthrown the horrors of dictatorship and been at best no better and often something worse? What kind of revolution had the feminist movement been when it had been limited to rich western nations, while the women who made up ninety percent of the rest of the world's female population remained mired in the muck?

"The first thing the freed slaves from America did after founding Liberia was to build plantations and enslave the African native population . . ." He remembered that from a history lecture long ago.

He wondered if that was why Terry and the news crew had been so cynical. They'd covered the Third World—Terry's parents had been from the Third World—and they had more perspective than the closed, ivory-tower lives of the American and west European crusaders. Maybe that was why so much of the press in general was so cynical.

How much easier it would have been for her if the Well hadn't played its cruel joke on the two of them. If Julian had emerged as the male and Lori as the female, both could have retained far more of their core beliefs. Neither was really comfortable staring their alternate selves in the face, both playing the other's role.

And there was still Mavra Chang, an enigma from a previous *universe,* for God's sake, who'd chosen for her own reasons to live as the leader of a band of Stone Age women deep in the Amazon jungles. Instead of trying to dominate men or help create a new equal society, she'd rejected men and all that they'd built.

And that brought up another point. It was only because of Chang's call that they were in Itus, but what the hell did he owe Mavra Chang? It was Mavra Chang whose abduction of the whole crew had destroyed his life and led inevitably to Erdom and what he was now. Indirectly, even Julian was here because of her, since without her jungle adventures he'd have been nowhere near that damned meteor.

True, Julian Beard and Lori Anne Sutton had both been at low points in their "real" lives when all this had happened, but he doubted that either of them had wanted *this.* But the question remained: Now that they were here, what did they owe that mysterious crazy woman?

Well, of course, it was a job of sorts, something definite to do, and it got the both of them out of Erdom and might allow them to see some of this strange world. Although if there were many more of these "hexes" as miserable as Itus, he wasn't sure his curiosity and enthusiasm could stand it. But that was exactly what it was and would remain. A job. A job that could be quit. A job in which he would feel no outstanding loyalties or long-standing obligations to the employer.

Most of all, maybe it would be a chance to sort out, removed from cultural and church pressures, who and what they now were and what options there might be for the future.

Fine words, but the dual nature persisted. The intellectual half wanted to make this a totally new start, to prove that things didn't have to be the way they were back home no matter who was on top. But the other half, that dark, primal part of the psyche, wanted to bury Lori Anne Sutton, her ivory-tower ideals, and her guilt trips and become the new Erdomese man that the monks wanted. Even her logical side couldn't work out a point to fighting it, considering how much everything was stacked against change. Without even a hope of change, how could clinging to the old ideals result in anything more than a life of frustration and misery?

"Some men do run the world," Julian had said. *"The bad news is that you are not one of them."*

Damn it all! It was a hell of a lot harder to fight this nature when a person was the one on top!

He finally did begin to nod off when suddenly there was a series of steady beeps from a small room between the main one and the bath. He went in, anxious mostly to silence it lest Julian awaken, and discovered that while the small room was of a very odd look and design, it had all the earmarks of a telephone booth. There was a red bar that was beeping on the far wall, and above it a small speaker that could be detached if need be, and above it a small screen. Thinking fast, he did what seemed logical and pushed the bar.

The screen popped on, and he was looking at the face of Mavra Chang.

"Wait a minute," he said, hoping he didn't have to pick up or push anything to be heard. "I'm going to close the door."

He peered out, but Julian seemed to have just shifted position and gone back to sleep. He pulled the sliding door closed and turned again to the screen.

"Holy shit!" Mavra Chang said, shaking her head. "Is that really *you*, Lori?"

Chang's whole appearance had changed. She seemed younger, her skin smoother, her hair expertly cut very short, wearing some kind of black pullover outfit. Cleaned up and made over, she looked very Chinese indeed. Only her big, dark eyes were the same, those ancient, weary, yet penetrating eyes.

"Yes, it's me. You knew how I wound up, surely. You were there."

"Yeah, I know, but it takes *seeing* for it to sink in, I think. I don't know what my mental picture of you was really, but it wasn't *that*. Don't get me wrong, but it's just not the Lori I knew."

"I—I'm not," he admitted. "I'm just not sure exactly who I am now, that's all."

"Yeah, well, it's a shame you had to undergo all this before we could talk normally, but we'll need brawn as well as brains on this trip, so it might just work out. I gather everything went okay. God knows the bribes I had to spread around—with accompanying curses and threats of curses—to make sure you got at least one of my messages. I decided to take a gamble on Greek; my Greek's rusty as all hell, but it seemed a better bet than Latin or Portuguese."

"You picked one of the few I could handle," he assured her. "Who would have guessed that we had something of a common language all along? We could have spoken back in the Amazon, at least by writing in the dirt."

"No, no. I was pretty far gone back there; it took the shock of coming through the Well Gate to bring some useful things back to me. I'd been in that jungle, by my best guess, maybe three hundred years or even longer. I think I was right on the edge of losing all memory of anything but the jungle. But that's a long story for another time. Things are different now, and in many ways I'm as different a person as you are from the life back then."

Different, yes, but not in the same ways at all, he thought.

He noticed that her words, although they sounded like they were coming in her voice with normal intonation and expression, weren't really matching what her lips were forming. He had seen this on the ship as well. In fact, it had been very strange to walk into a room filled with a number of races, and understand some plainly while others made just weird-sounding noises or spouted gibberish. "You have a translator now," he said a bit enviously.

"Yeah, well, the one I had originally gave out long ago, and they're only useful here, anyway. It was one of the first things I had done once I had the method and the means. It's very quick, and there's no more pain than the prick of a sharp needle. The trouble is, they're not available at just any shop and they're incredibly expensive. I've got quickly dwindling fortunes here and a very long way to go. And I assume that you have your wife with you— Jeez! That sounds funny to say!—and that she was some kind of soldier or pilot or something who came through ahead of us."

"Yes. *She,* in fact, was once a *he.* An American, like me and the news crew, only sent down by the government to help with the investigation of the meteor. He was in fact a space shuttle pilot. An astrogeologist, I think. Got sucked in long before we entered while posing for a picture on top of the thing."

"Huh! Think of that! And you thought *you* had a shock! Believe me, it's not at all unheard of for the Well to switch sexes when it switches forms, but it's very rare to have two from so small a sample wind up the same race, let alone *both* switching sexes. In fact, I know of only one other case, and at least I think I understand why that one happened."

"I was thinking of that myself. She was so despondent in that culture that she was on the verge of suicide when I found her. Our marriage, I think, was the only thing that saved her life. It seems like amazing luck."

"Yeah, well, there's luck and then there's the Well. I can tell you about luck. The Well doesn't have any means of reversing its first random decision once you're processed and incorporated into this strange big family, but it monitors everything that goes on. I can't help but wonder if it somehow sensed your Julian was in danger of death by its actions and used you to correct that when it had the chance. Now, though, you're both on your own. Don't count on the Well to save you anymore, either of you."

"Well, it might explain what happened, but I haven't counted on the Well to save either of us from anything, anyway. In fact, *you* saved us from becoming good little loyal feudal types." Quickly, he told her what had happened in the temple.

"Wow! Nick of time, sounds like! Well, look, as comfortable as this high-tech hex might be, I don't want to be here or any other spot too long. I'm already sure I'm being watched, bugged, and monitored, and I'm not even sure by who."

"You won't get any argument from us," he assured her. "This added gravity and tremendous humidity are doing me in slowly, and Julian is having even worse trouble with it."

"Oh, yeah. I've been here awhile and I've gotten somewhat used to the slightly higher G, and the climate's no worse than the Amazon, but I keep forgetting that you're a different species of creature now, designed more for a desert climate and sandy soil. You guys must be *miserable*! Well, at least in a high-tech hex you don't have to walk unless you want to. It might not be the soul of comfort, designed as they are for giant caterpillars, but there is a kind of train going to almost any point we need in this hex. But it's a long, nasty way to where we're going, and I've seen worse than this place. Look, I'll tell you what. I'll figure out how to float the two translators somehow, but I want to get the implant done fast, and then we're out of here. Could we do it this afternoon?"

"I suppose I could. Julian's asleep. But look," he found himself saying, almost without thinking, "if it's too much of an expense, then we could do without the translators. Besides, in Julian's case, an Erdomese female with a translator would in the best case be exiled from any contact with foreigners once we returned. It might do her more harm than good."

Mavra considered that. "Hmmm . . . I forgot about that damned culture down there. Woulda made me puke if I hadn't seen and been forced to live in so many similar cultures back on Earth. In China some families actually drowned girl babies because they had no value or status! And they were still having enough babies to one day overrun the planet!" She sighed. "Well, it would be a savings I could use, and she will be able to understand anybody else with one. Still, I'd like more than one of us to have one. Okay, I'm going to give you a name and address. The front desk will be able to tell you how to get there. It's not far. Just be warned—that loud crackling and buzzing you hear all over when you go out will sound like a huge mob of people all talking at once when you come back. You'll understand it, but don't expect to make full sense out of it. The Ituns don't exactly have the same frame of reference as we do."

Lori got the address and repeated it back several times until Mavra was satisfied. Fortunately, the city was on a grid system, and the streets were basically numbers and Itun alphabetical characters so that he could use an Erdomese equivalent and the concierge's translator would understand.

"Okay, then. Get it done, come back, have dinner—make sure you order room service; you won't even want to *see* Ituns eat—and get as much rest as you can. We'll finish up what we need to do today as well and meet you tomorrow at the hotel. Since I'm being so thoroughly and obviously shadowed, there's not much point to cloak and dagger stuff—yet."

"We?"

"Yes, there will be more of us."

"You mean you found Gus?" He hesitated a moment. "Not—*Campos*! Please, not *him*!"

"No, neither one, really. Your Gus wound up a Dahir, or so I'm told, and that's a fair distance from here, although we might be able to contact him somehow along the way. I didn't really know him, remember. We kept him and the other guy kind of out of it."

"Yeah, well, Campos is a psycho. Rapist, drug dealer, gangster—you name it. The lowest common denominator of all the worst things in humans. Now, *there's* somebody who should have been an Erdomese female! *That* would have been justice! Gus was a nice guy, very gentle, a photographer in fact."

"Well, I got no word on Campos, but I know the type. I doubt if he's anywhere near Erdom or even Itus, but the Well's been known to have a sense of humor about some people. I don't pretend to understand it, but I was led to believe that the Well actually takes your personality, both conscious and subconscious, your dreams and ambition, even your fantasies and your fears, into consideration, but on a kind of loopy basis I doubt if anybody but another giant machine could fully understand."

"Then—the colonel Julian spoke of, perhaps?"

"Nope. Don't know where or what he is, either. No, you don't know them. They came in with Nathan in about the same way that you wound up coming through with me. I needed a source of information on him, and we hit it off. It's a kind of sweet story, as unique, I suspect, in the very long history of the Well World as your own story and Julian's, and as oddly perverse as well. You'll have to see and hear the story for yourself. Let's leave it until tomorrow, when we'll all have to discuss our options. Besides, it's getting past midday, and I want your translator in today."

He sighed. "All right, then, until tomorrow."

The connection was broken.

Lori went out as silently as possible and saw that Julian was still asleep. He got his codpiece and put it on, then went silently to the door, feeling a pang of guilt at sneaking out for this without her. Why had he done that? Denied her a translator? The devices were unlikely to process Earth languages, so she'd have to speak Erdomese to be understood by them, and as with Mavra just now, the speech she'd hear from the translator would be in Erdomese to her as well. Erdomese didn't possess a lot of technical terms, the feminine form even less so. Anyone who didn't have a translator—rare and expensive, Mavra said, so uncommon—or speak Erdomese—highly unlikely, particularly as they went farther from Erdom—would be unable to communicate with her or she with them except through someone like him. And even then some very basic technical terms wouldn't translate at all—they'd be gibberish. She'd had to use English just to say "air-conditioning."

Outside the door he felt like a heel. As he was on the moving walkway, though, he began to rationalize. Mavra *had* been groping for him to give her an excuse not to spend the extra funds and had readily accepted his explanation. And he wasn't kidding, either. Back in Erdom, where they would surely eventually wind up, for a female to even *speak* in the male "voice" was considered a sin, and in Erdom sin equaled crime. Suppose, when she spoke to a male back there, the translator changed things to the male form of the language? Even if that didn't happen, he had every intention of living in the capital and not out in the middle of nowhere when this was all over with, and she was too smart to consistently fake ignorance of a foreign tongue if it said something interesting or relevant.

Lori knew he was groping for good reasons to get rid of the guilt, but by the time he had gotten his directions and left the hotel, he had decided that what was done was now done, and besides, if he was really wrong about this, he'd make sure she got a translator at some point along the way. By the time he reached the Interspecies Clinic near the docks, he had almost fully accepted that version.

The procedure to implant the translator really wasn't all that much. The medical personnel at the clinic, supervised by Ituns but of several races from hexes along the main coastal route here, put him through an imager, ran a three-dimensional scan of him through their medical computer, and determined exactly where and how to insert the translator—a tiny little gem that apparently was grown or cultured by one of the undersea races. They showed him how to activate it, then they put him under a light anesthetic with a simple and painless injection, and the totally computerized surgery began. In less than twenty minutes he was coming out of it with a headache from the anesthesia and a sore spot on the back of his neck.

An Itun and another creature entered and did a visual examination. The creature looked like nothing imaginable but was as close to a living version of an Earth child's toy—a long-necked little bird that hung on the side of a glass and dipped its bill into the water, then sprang back up, only to repeat the motion until the water ran out. Lori had the distinct feeling that the birdlike thing with the incredibly long, thin, straight neck could see right inside and through him, but he couldn't explain that feeling.

"How are you feeling?" asked the Itun, and Lori started to put his hand up to his neck and then hesitated.

"Uh—all right to touch the area?"

"Oh, yes. It is completely sealed. The soreness is internal bruising, but it will pass very quickly. You should feel nothing by tomorrow."

"And—it's in?"

"Oh, yes. I wear no speaker to allow someone to hear me in their native language, you will notice. You are hearing me directly in Erdomese, although I speak only Itun, a tongue you are as physically incapable of uttering as I am yours, and I am hearing you quite clearly in Itun at the same time that my colleague here is hearing you in what passes for a voice in Wukl."

"You be not born as form utilized," the strange, comic birdlike Wukl put in, the voice sounding like nothing Lori had ever heard or imagined. It was a kind of chilling sound, yet without any emotion or inflection whatsoever, and it seemed only partly said aloud and partly formed inside his own brain. It *was*, of course, male-voice Erdomese, but apparently the way the creature thought wasn't exactly compatible with the Erdomese language. There were limits on these things.

Still, he was amazed and impressed almost beyond words. "Incredible! Uh—no, I wasn't born Erdomese, if that's what you mean. I entered through the Well. But how do you know?"

"Conflict is," the Wukl attempted to explain. "Clear to sense. Know not base not knowable. If unpleased could mediate self."

"Don't try and follow it too closely," the Itun warned. "You will just turn your thoughts to boiling. We, too, think differently than you do, but I have had much training in dealing with others. The Wukl—well, they see things so differently from most races that we know it is difficult for them to understand others, but they are very skilled surgeons and they have good souls and desire to help. Their help, however, can be as convoluted and as unwanted as the initial problem. If given its own way, what would result would be what we might euphemistically call a surgical compromise that would be at best unique and not at all an improvement, as the injured and shipwrecked of a number of races have discovered when washed up on their shores. Nor should you take it too literally. The Wukl see everyone of us as horribly flawed, you see. We're not Wukls."

The headache was passing, leaving only the slight stinging. "Yes, I see."

"No want Wukl betterment?" the Wukl asked.

"Um, no, not at this time, thank you. But—as of now I'll be able to understand all the other races, whether they themselves have translators or not? And they will understand me?"

"Within limits, yes," the Itun responded. "You will find those limits can be daunting indeed, as the Wukl here demonstrates in one area, and there are some races simply too different in their thought patterns to allow any meaningful communication. But for the most part you will find that it will take more practice editing out the sounds than understanding what you wish. It will take a little getting used to, but for a traveler to foreign hexes it is the one thing to not be without."

"Can I go now? I think I'm all right," Lori told them.

"Yes, the Wukl is a superb diagnostician within limits, and if it hasn't noted a problem by this point in the procedure, then there is none. We have received payment in advance from your benefactor by messenger, so you are free to go as soon as you feel able."

He *was* still a little groggy, and the humidity and heavy gravity made him not totally steady, but he decided he should get back to the hotel.

He soon experienced the strangeness of hearing those alien speakers all about him, and the initial disorientation, since while the *words* were understandable, the meaning was in most cases more obscure than the Wukl. His respect for the Ituns like the doctor and the hotel people went up enormously; Ituns definitely did *not* think along the lines of humans or Erdomese.

Julian was awake and apparently had been for some time. Although Erdomese did not take baths on the whole—a complete immersion for any length of time would remove naturally protective oils and could lead to an ugly and sometimes painfully itchy skin condition akin to mange—spraying their faces and upper torsos with a showerlike wand could have a cooling and freshening effect. Clearly she'd spent some time in the bath area and had made some use of cosmetics and oils both from their meager case and from what the hotel provided. To him, at least, she looked refreshed and smelled quite sweet.

"Hello, my husband," she said in Erdomese. "You have been gone a long time. I was beginning to worry for your safety."

"Chang called and made arrangements for me to get a translator put inside my head. It was no worse than going to a dentist, but it was not pleasant. You were still asleep, and I decided you needed rest more than news at the time, and almost the last words you spoke were that you didn't want to leave this room again!"

She accepted it. "This thing in your head—it means you can speak to and understand all not-Erdomese speech?"

He nodded. "Pretty much. It was a simple task, but it is very expensive. I am sorry that Chang did not have the money for both of us to have one. Perhaps someday."

Julian had no reason to doubt him, but she was disappointed. "Yes, perhaps someday," she repeated, knowing how unlikely that "someday" might be. It did, however, increase her sense of isolation.

"This Madam Chang speaks not English?"

"No. I don't think so. She mentioned Greek, Latin, and Portuguese but not English. But it won't matter in that case. Since *she* has one of these things in her head, too, you will be able to understand her and she will be able to understand you—in Erdomese."

She sighed. "In Erdoma, you mean. Oh, well, it is better than silence." She paused a moment, then asked, "Is there no other news?"

"Oh, yes. She's coming by tomorrow, with others—I'm not sure how many. People from Earth who came in with the other fellow, her counterpart. I don't know what race. She wants to leave pretty quickly—don't worry! She says we're going to *ride* out of here. Hopefully all the way out, and quickly."

He thought that would make her happy, but she just let it go by. She seemed off, depressed, and he went over and stood behind her and massaged her back and neck. She *did* react as always to that, and she seemed to relax a little.

"We should eat and rest," she said at last. "After tonight we may not be able to do it when we need to."

He nodded. "I'll order something from the hotel. I'm starving, anyway; I didn't eat because of the surgery."

Nor did I, because you forgot, Julian thought, but said nothing. She couldn't quite explain her feelings even to herself, but she was generally irritated by him today, leaving without a word or a message, more like the drugged and hypnotized Lori than the one from before or even the one of this morning. She'd deliberately kept using Erdoma, which made her sound like some sort of Arabian Nights wimp by its very nature, maybe to test him and see if he'd switch to English. He hadn't. When that was coupled with sneaking out for so long, the apparent start of a new pattern depressed her. Well, maybe it wasn't a trend. Maybe he was just too tired to realize the way he was acting, she hoped. Maybe it was just this extra gravity that made her feel like a hippopotamus. Maybe she was just getting her period, and *that* was a wonderful thought to look forward to when they were starting off on a hard trip.

Most of all, she needed somebody else to talk to.

Mavra Chang arrived early the next morning, as promised. The door buzzed irritatingly, telling them that someone was there, and Julian, still feeling heavy and bloated but somewhat better than the day before, went to the door and pushed the opener so that it slid back. She'd hardly remembered that there would be more than one, but she had been curious almost since hearing Lori's story to see this mysterious, ancient immortal human female.

She was not prepared for someone so incredibly tiny. Julian, although petite compared to Lori, was nonetheless pretty much the same five foot ten she'd been as a human male; if Mavra Chang was over five feet tall, it was because of her high-heeled black leather boots, and it would be amazing if the woman weighed a hundred pounds. She had a nearly perfect waist but almost no breasts at all, and big almond-shaped eyes looked up at Julian from a classically pretty Han Chinese face.

The ancient, imposing immortal of Julian's mental image shattered in front of somebody who looked thirteen years old.

Chang's tiny form was set off even more by the two figures behind her. Both stood almost as tall as Lori and stared at Julian through big green eyes with the longest lashes Julian had ever seen. From the waist up, where it curved inward in the expected way, they seemed quite human-

looking except for the pointed equine ears that emerged from a thick
gusher of strawberry blond hair. They were, in fact, stunningly beautiful
young women of perhaps sixteen or so—from the waist up.

From the waist down they were most like palomino ponies.

They were female centaurs—centauresses, Julian thought, amazed.

And they were absolutely identical twins down to the smallest detail.

Mavra Chang smiled. "Hello. You must be Julian," she said pleasantly
in a deep female voice that nonetheless sounded hard-edged and tough
in spite of its speaking Erdoma. "I'm Mavra Chang. And the girls—well,
you two think *you* have problems! Don't worry, though. You won't have
any trouble telling *this* pair apart. Meet Tony and Anne Marie, the only
other case of two entries to the same species. You see, before they went
through, they were a married couple . . ."

HAKAZIT

FOR A COUPLE OF days now Nathan Brazil had had the oddest feeling based on long experience that he was being followed. He'd learned to trust those instincts, but over the countless years he'd also become nearly infallible in eventually tripping up any shadow that might try it, particularly over an extended period of time. This time he'd failed, even though more than once he'd become *certain* that he'd nailed the bugger. He'd walked down to the docks, gone down a very long deserted pier to the end, then used a little secret he'd discovered for ducking down below the pier and making his way back along a safety catwalk below. He'd *known* that the shadow had followed him onto the pier; he also knew that he could not possibly have been seen going below the pier and coming back, even with the girl inevitably in tow, and he'd heard the creak of timbers and the sound of a few heavy footsteps above, going out toward the end of the pier, yet, when he'd emerged and staked out the pier from the only exit, nobody had come.

The girl was another thing. She was absolutely uncanny at spotting any potential threats or irritants, and they'd been together long enough that he could read her reactions when somebody was around who was taking an inordinate interest in them. Several times she'd had brief flashes of this wariness when he'd sensed the tail, yet after a moment, she would frown as if puzzled, then seemingly dismiss it. She could sense the colonel coming three blocks away, but she barely reacted, and then only for this brief check, when he felt a shadow so close that he could almost smell its bad breath.

He had tried without success to convince himself that it was nerves. Certainly he was antsy and frustrated as hell at being stuck in this desolate place for so long, and his money was virtually gone while his prospects for earning any more were negligible unless he moved quickly. In this one sense he envied the girl; she appeared to need absolutely nothing except his companionship.

Still, he knew that someone was around, lurking, always near. At this stage in his life such feelings and instincts were almost never wrong. But what could it want?

He was as certain of the shadow's reality as he was that there was only one, and the same one, too. Like at the pier whenever he'd temporarily shaken the tail, he'd heard it, and it wasn't a tiny creature like the pixieish Lata, who could fly and hide in any number of small places, or any of the other obvious possibilities. The thing was *big*, bigger than he was, and certainly heavier by far.

In his hotel, away from close prying eyes, he'd gone through his reference books on the Well World. The standardized written trading language had definitely changed a lot, but the basics were still there and there wasn't a language with a fundamental multicultural linguistic base that he hadn't been able to master in the amount of time he'd wasted here. Not that his reading ability was perfect, but at least he was at the point where it was mostly nouns that stymied him, and those one could look up in a dictionary.

Fifteen hundred sixty separate species of sentient beings . . . That was a lot, but one could eliminate a couple of hundred off the bat: those who were not mobile, unable to function in the south, or too insular to leave their hexes, etc. That still left more than half, though.

Which could it be? And why?

The books, which were of course simplified and intended for businesspeople, diplomats, even tourists, were of little help in his attempts to solve the mystery, but they did give him a different sort of shock.

How they had *changed*! How much almost *all* of them had changed. Some socially and culturally—although few as radically as the Glathrielians—and physically as well. Up until now, the only familiar species he'd encountered were the Ambreza, who, while becoming even more xenophobic as the reasons for it had faded into half-remembered legend, weren't all *that* much different from what they had been the last time.

Dillians, though . . . He'd always loved the centaurs. The last time they'd been basically the stuff of ancient Greek legend, large and gruff and looking very much like ordinary Earth-human types welded to sturdy working-horse bodies.

If the two photos in the book could be believed, though, they looked quite a bit different now. Sleeker, smaller, almost streamlined. Of course, Dillia wasn't about to pose anything but its best-looking for an international publication, but the changes were too radical in the male and female shown to just be a matter of centaur public relations. They just, well, no longer looked like the hybrids they'd always seemed, but perfectly and logically designed as a whole. If those two were typical, he almost felt as if he were half a Dillian rather than a Dillian being half man, half horse.

And if they'd been the only ones, he still might have passed it off as a slick photograph, but they weren't. Quite a number of old familiar races looked at least as different. None were unrecognizable; none had undergone *that* radical a transformation. But the Uliks looked more streamlined, a bit less of the serpent, and the lower pair of arms seemed to be quite different, almost as if they were changing into clawlike feet. The Yaxa body had become fuller, a bit more humanoid, the head and chest enlarged as well . . . It went on and on. Nothing so glaring as to shout at a person, but noticeable in picture after picture.

Something was definitely going on here, something totally unexpected.

There was no shot of a Gedemondan, of course. He hadn't expected one, and for one to have been there would have been as radical a change in their culture as had happened in Glathriel. The book indicated that one could now climb their mountains if it were just for sport or passage and that Dillians had an actual trail network through there all the way to Palim and the Sea of Storms and through Alestol to the Sea of Turigen, giving them access to much of the Well World in spite of their less than hospitable neighbors. But, the book also warned, do not expect to see a Gedemondan at any point, and those who damaged their land or strayed off the prescribed trails or took anything with them had a tendency to suffer mental torments of one sort or another or, in cases of gross transgression, to simply disappear.

Well, it was nice to know that at least the Gedemondans hadn't changed much.

He wondered idly if the shadow might be a Gedemondan. It was certainly large and heavy enough. The Gedemondans could also play tricks with one's mind and had other strange powers and abilities, but overall, he doubted it. Their religion, their culture, the focus of their entire race required isolation. Sending one out into the world would be as radical a change for them as, well, the Glathrielians.

Maybe it *was* a Gedemondan, after all. It fit, and he hadn't really found much evidence of more mobile cultures who could perform the kind of vanishing act this one could. Several could blend in, chameleon-like, with their surroundings, but that wouldn't explain the speed and variety of places this tail had been or the wide-open spaces where he'd *felt* the thing nearby and yet could see nothing out of the ordinary.

Well, there was no way to get around the tail, particularly when he was stuck here. This invisible follower had also scotched his idea to just take a hike west, maybe to Jorgasnovara, a nontech hex that might well be a place to shake anyone. What difference would it make, though, if the shadow just followed at a discreet distance and remained invisible?

Better to get out by sea if possible. Such creatures as this had to eat and sleep; either they'd miss the boat or they would become more obvious, and more manageable, out in the middle of the ocean. He was pretty sure that a Gedemondan would have a tough time if forced to swim, although, damn it, the big bastards could probably walk on water by now.

He slammed the book shut. Damn it, he just couldn't stay around here! He didn't want to live in a damned tent out in this perennially lousy weather, and that was what would happen within another week. It was time to move, to do *something,* no matter whether it made a major difference or not. The colonel had been delaying and hemming and hawing about sailing opportunities but had yet to come up with anything concrete. Tomorrow he'd give the old bastard an ultimatum. Come up with something *now* or it was farewell. Damn it, if Jorgasnovara was any sort of option, he'd take it. If not, he'd use the Zone Gate and go back into Ambreza and get the hell out of there somehow via Glathriel to the Sea of Turigen. He could certainly work that out with the Ambrezan Zone ambassador, and *that* would shake up any tails and meddlers! If nothing else, this damned shadow would have to follow him through the Gate, where he'd be perfectly satisfied to sit and wait awhile for it, or give it up.

At least it would be doing *something. God knows where Mavra is by this time,* he thought sourly. *Probably doing better than I am, anyway.*

The shadow was there in the hotel lobby. He could *feel* it, even though, as usual, he could put neither face nor form to it. It was another reason why he felt he had to bolt. He'd shaken it once and was certain he could do it again. The watcher depended too much on its invisibility or whatever it was using; it hadn't been subtle in any other way, and that would be its undoing.

The colonel was his usual oozy self, and that didn't apply *just* to his external appearance, Brazil thought. In this case at least, the Well's oddball sense of humor—some sort of reflection, probably, of an early puckish programmer—had simply made the outside match what was already there inside.

"I can't wait any longer, Colonel," he told the Leeming. "I believe that this is farewell for us. I will be leaving very soon."

The colonel was visibly upset, as shown by his sudden involuntary imitation of a gelatin mold. "But—but just give me a few more days, Captain! The ship is almost completed. These things take *time,* you know, and one cannot *will* a complex ship into seaworthiness!"

"It doesn't matter. Either I'm on a ship within the next day or I'm out of here," Brazil said flatly. "And since, as you say, you can't materialize a working ship going anywhere near where I want to go, I'll be making other arrangements."

"Indeed? What other arrangements, if I might be so bold? I mean, there is considerable ocean between this continent and anywhere else."

"I have other possibilities. They're just more work, that's all. I've been getting too soft and lazy here, and too broke. No, Colonel, it won't do. I'm gone."

The colonel, still quivering, was also thinking furiously. "Well, give me until tomorrow morning at least. One more night. That is not asking too much, I think. If I do not come up with anything useful, you can still leave."

Brazil frowned. "And what makes you think you can come up with something in so short a time when you haven't been able to come up with anything for weeks?" he asked suspiciously.

"Oh, well, ah, we have been waiting for the ship to be completed to go where you wished to go, have we not? And if you leave on your own, you will have to make a very circuitous route, is that not so? While it is true that I might not be able to get you near your destination, I can certainly get you on the same *continent.* Let me look at what ships are in. What I find might not be very comfortable, but at least it will get you somewhere closer. Agreed?"

A half smile crept over Nathan Brazil's face. "I believe I understand things perfectly now, Colonel. In fact, I feel somewhat chagrined that it took me this long. Tell you what—you go and see what you can come up with and then contact me back here. If I'm still here, we'll talk some more. If you find that I've checked out, forget me. That is the best I can do."

"I—I think you are being very unreasonable, but I will try and find something with all speed, I promise you. Wait for my call. Until tonight at least."

"We will see, Colonel. We will see."

He watched the creature slither off and knew that he didn't have much of a window of opportunity. Within minutes the colonel would be calling in, reporting to whoever had sent him here, telling them to find him some kind of passage in a hurry, but something slow and sure to wind up going in the wrong direction. Others would be dispatched to put a close watch on him in case he did try to leave.

Of course, there was also the shadow, but somehow he didn't think that whatever it was worked for the same people who obviously employed the colonel. He wasn't sure why he felt that way, but as usual, he knew to trust his instincts.

The girl seemed surprised when he went back toward the room, but she followed. He'd gotten into the habit of using the stairs with her most of the time, not because it was easier for her but because he'd felt he was getting soft and needed the exercise. Well, he'd get his exercise now, that was for sure.

The shadow rarely followed them to the room either because it had trouble with the stairs or because it didn't feel it needed to cover him from that point.

He'd been settling his bill on a day-to-day basis, so he didn't need to clear anything with the desk. If they wanted to complain that he hadn't formally checked out and owed another day, well, let them find him to collect.

It was easy to pack, particularly now. He wanted to travel light and had almost everything he needed in a backpack. He already wore the warm clothing required, and while he might get a little gamy after a while from the lack of too many changes of clothes, he'd coped with that and worse before.

The thermal windows were not designed to open, not only to insulate the room but also to contain any climatic adjustments that inhabitants from other hexes might require, but he'd long ago figured out how they were fastened on and how they were removed for servicing and replacement. It took him about twenty minutes to undo the window he'd picked long ago and to scoop out the puttylike sealant. The window was stubborn, and while working it he almost caused it to fall outward and crash down below, but he managed at the last minute to catch it and carefully manipulate it into the room. Another bill they'd have to send him.

The girl watched, both puzzled and fascinated, as the cold, damp wind blew into the room. She watched, too, as he took out a thin rope of some very strong synthetic material, looped it and buckled one end to a grate just inside the window, then let the rest drop almost five stories to the extended lobby roof below. Satisfied that he had a good solid hold, he put on the backpack and his hat, hoping he wouldn't lose it in the wind, and went over to the open window. He looked down a bit nervously, then nodded to himself and turned back to her. There was no way around this, and he felt he knew her well enough that she'd figure a way to follow. Her refusal to use things was more a belief pattern than anything imposed, and as with most religious tenets, followers could and did compromise when they had to.

"Well, you either come out this way or you stay here," he told her. "I am going, and I am not coming back. At least I *hope* I'm not."

She stared at him, not comprehending the words, but she got the idea as he climbed up onto the sill and grabbed on to the rope. She knew that he was leaving, sneaking away so that he wouldn't be seen or followed, and it was no contest in her mind between using the rope and remaining until somebody opened the door. She ran to the window as he was making his way down the side of the building and looked down. When he was clearly close enough to the roof level to jump, she reached out, grasped the rope, and began to descend.

Brazil watched her come down, admiring her seeming effortlessness at the pretty daunting descent. When she reached his side, he took the rope and twirled and twisted one end; the other came free and fell at their feet. He quickly coiled it back up and went to the left side of the roof area.

They had been clever in making certain he had a front-facing room, although he doubted that they had expected anything like this. The roof ran the length of the building's front but had only a small turn on either side tapering quickly down to nothing. It was constructed of some metallic-looking synthetic, smooth as glass and unlikely to take anything driven into it with any power he could muster. The drop itself was five, maybe closer to six meters—makable, but he preferred not to unless it was forced on him since it would be onto a stone-hard surface. Nor was there anything he felt was secure enough to attach the rope to. He wished he had plungers or a basic chemistry kit, either of which would allow him to create some kind of suction cup, but while such things were readily available, their purpose would be easily divined by anyone watching him, and he *knew* they were watching him. Maybe more than one group.

He took a deep breath. Well, there was nothing for it but to jump and risk a break or sprain. He'd jumped worse and made it. He was just getting up the nerve when he felt her hand on his shoulder. He turned, puzzled, and she pointed to the rope. Curious, and relieved at least for the moment from thinking about the jump, he handed it to her. She took it and twisted a fair amount of it around her waist, then handed the rest back. He understood immediately what she was offering to do, but he was unsure about the wisdom of it. She wasn't, after all, any taller than he was, and while she undoubtedly weighed more, it still would be quite a load with no handholds. Still, he could hardly argue with her, and if she managed to hold long enough for him to get halfway, he could easily drop the rest of the distance. He assumed that she would then jump; she was extremely athletic for one of her hefty build.

It was starting to rain, one of the icy rains that passed for a warm front in beautiful Hakazit, but in this case he didn't mind since it had pretty well cleared the streets of general traffic. Not that there weren't various denizens of the hex and people of various stripes from the hotel bustling about, but they were hurried and busy. Still, it would have to be fast.

"Okay," he told her with a sigh. "Here goes." With that he dropped the rope over the side, took it, and climbed quickly down hand over hand. It wasn't until he dropped the last little bit to the sidewalk that he realized that the rope had been rock steady.

She did not wait to uncoil the rope but jumped the instant he was down, hitting on her bare feet, flexing the knees, then standing up straight. For all it had seemed, it might have been a one-meter jump. She slipped the rope off and handed it to him. He did not wait to coil it but took off for the rear of the building, the girl quickly following behind.

Walking the long distance out would have been absurd; both Brazil and the girl stuck out like lighthouses in this hex. The watchers would have the transport terminals covered, of course, and even if they didn't, they could trace them easily. That was why Brazil had decided not to leave in those ways but rather in his own.

As the rain came harder, mixed now with ice and creating a frigid slush, he made his way by the alleys and service lanes down toward the docks.

He didn't care if the Hakazit workers saw them; they were doing nothing illegal or improper using the back ways, and so they would be nothing more than idle curiosities in a boring routine. He was in his element once they reached the docks, where he'd even managed to give the slip to the mysterious shadow.

The lousy weather, even for Hakazit, was something of a blessing to him. He brushed wet snow from his beard and walked along an alley about a block from the docks, heading west toward the commercial fleet and the shipbuilding area.

Just beyond was Pulcinell, a water hex whose dominant race, he gathered, was a bottom-living species that somewhat resembled lobsters with tentacles and that tended vast undersea farms and built vast, strange cities out of coral, sand, and shell. The higher, lighter layers were inhabited by various kinds of the usual sort of sea life, including a kind of jet-propelled swimming clam called a *zur* that was considered a delicacy by many land races and by a species of water-dwelling mammals called *kata*, who, in carefully rationed numbers, were used for fur, leather, and meat. A delicacy and quite limited in the allowable catch, the creature was a high-profit item. The Pulcinell had been known to somehow punch large holes in the bottoms of poachers' boats. A nontech hex, they had some needs that required trading, and they wanted their share of the carefully managed harvest.

A *kata* boat was a bit too large for him to manage alone, but a small *zur* troller was generally a two-person craft and could, with its single mast, be handled by one man. It would be no picnic to cross an ocean in it, even at a narrow point, but he'd sailed halfway around the world alone in something not much better, and if he could move down the coast or use some of the small islands to get water and provisions, it might not be a dangerous trip.

Still, he fervently wished that he could somehow communicate with the girl and teach her how to set a sail and otherwise handle a boat. It would make life a lot simpler.

There were a *lot* of the small craft in. Small wonder, considering that the weather visible just beyond the hex barrier didn't look all that much better than the weather here. He didn't care. There were no conditions he could imagine that he hadn't already faced at one time or another in almost any type of craft.

Of course, he'd sunk quite a few times, too, but he preferred not to think about that.

And there they were, down the small street through the dock buildings, bobbing in the water between two long warehouses, "parked" in diagonal slots on both sides of three long piers.

Although the design of the small boats differed markedly, as would be expected considering the number of races that built and sailed them, there were certain basic similarities to all of them, and none looked so bizarre as to be unmanageable. The physics of floating objects didn't change all that much, either. At least, if it *did*, then more was wrong here than he suspected.

The trick was to steal the one owned or operated by a race that ate what he could eat and would be likely to have palatable supplies aboard.

He walked down the alley, crossed the main street, and walked out onto the center pier, where a large number of the boats were tied, the girl following. He was not worried about being spotted; for one thing, the sleet was turning to steady, fine snow and starting to lie on the street, piers, and boats, and the dock area was nearly deserted.

Experience had also taught him that one of the best ways to be barely noticed was to go where one wanted and act like one belonged there. With so many different races in at this ocean port, it was unlikely anybody would even figure out his species—or care.

A number of the small boats could be rejected out of hand. For one thing, about twenty percent of them had people aboard, and that disqualified them. He had no stomach for a fight if it could be avoided, particularly not against creatures that might have nasty natural defenses or firearms, and he was never big enough to win even a fair fight with his own kind.

Of the rest, about half could be dismissed as being too alien either to run efficiently or to have a chance of containing useful supplies. A winch was a winch, it was true, and a wheel was a wheel, but the designs were very different if one was using tentacles or suckers or something other than hands.

He was getting cold, wet, and somewhat snow-covered himself by the time he found what he was looking for. It was an attractive little sloop, sleekly built and designed to take heavy weather at a good clip under sail. The creatures who had sailed it here definitely had hands, and the design was in many ways quite conventional for Earth circa, perhaps, the early 1800s. There was no sign of a stack, so either it was built from the ground up as a no-frills sailing craft or it came from a nontech hex and did much of its business in similar places. That suited him, since the passage between Hakazit and Agon was either nontech or semitech and the useful high-tech navigational aids would be of no use anyway in those waters. He would in fact have little problem staying out of high-tech hexes entirely if he made a direct crossing and then proceeded along the coast.

Something inside him just told him that whatever these people were, they ate what he could eat. More of his "intuition," he supposed, drawn from the Well's own catalog.

Looking around and seeing no one obvious, he climbed down onto the trim little craft, and the girl followed, eyes darting around, ears alert for any signs of danger.

There were no tides to speak of on the Well World, but there were many currents, and ports in general were designed to take advantage of them. The diagonal boat slips were the first step; each was basically a small canallike lock which filled when the ship was docked and raised it a few meters above the surrounding sea. If he triggered the lock mechanism, it would open, and, casting off at the precise moment, the ship would float out into the harbor on the outflowing water. Then he could turn, raise a single sail by that winch over there, and make his way out and into Pulcinell. The wind wasn't entirely favorable in the storm, and it would mean moving quickly, but he thought it was possible.

Not for the first time did he wish he could at least tell the girl how to do something. It would be very useful if she could take the wheel, trigger the sail winch, or even push the damned lock button. He sighed. Well, he was on his own, and that was that. He checked the mechanical winch on the small sail he would need, figured out the safety and the release, and decided it would work. Then he walked over to the outside wheel aft of the mast and removed the blocks and wheel lock, testing it to ensure that it was free.

Gesturing for her to stay aboard, he then climbed back on the dock, found a small metal pole with a rectangular box on it, opened it at the hinge, and found two large buttons there, one depressed. He pushed the other one, cursed as it rang a *very* loud bell that seemed to echo over the entire harbor area, then ran back and jumped onto the deck from the pier, slipping and falling in the snow as he did so. The lock was opening pretty fast—a lot faster than he'd figured—and he let go of the bowline and rushed back, let go of the stern line, and almost slipped again as the small sailing vessel lurched free and then began to move with more speed than he wanted backward into the channel. He climbed up and grabbed the wheel, feeling out of breath, then worried that the damned lock wouldn't be completely out of the way by the time he passed the wall. It almost wasn't; he felt a bump, and the ship lurched and groaned, but it continued out into the channel.

There were several yells, curses, and threats from behind him as the bell and the launch had made it clear to some of those still aboard other boats that this one was leaving in the storm and probably not with its owners, but he didn't care. He spun the wheel for all it was worth, turning the little craft so its bow faced the inner marker buoys, then locked it with the latch and ran forward to trigger the sail. He barely noticed that the girl was watching him, fascinated, and it was probably a good thing. He would have been furious had he seen her just sitting there on a hatch cover when he was so frantic.

The winch jammed when he pushed the release; he cursed, then started hitting it and banging on it for all it was worth. The damned thing was frozen! He looked up and saw that the ship was turning slightly on its own and was beginning to drift sideways out of the docking area and back toward the other boats, many of which now had very nasty-looking creatures on them just waiting for him to drift near.

The girl sensed the danger and saw what he was trying to do. She got up, came over to him, and put her hand on the stuck lever. There was a sudden electrical crackle, and steam actually rose from the winch mechanism. The lever moved back, releasing the sail.

He was far too busy and too worried even now to consider what he'd seen. Two ropes came down from either side of the sail, and they had to be grabbed and tied to the pulley mechanism on either side of the boat. He grabbed one and tied it off as she watched, then the girl went over and caught the other and handed it to him when he reached her. It was a big help; he wouldn't have expected most people to know how to tie into the remote mechanism.

By this point they had drifted very close to the pier. At least a half dozen angry shapes were atop the various lock gates just waiting for him, and he wasn't at all sure he could get out of there in time to keep from bumping into one of the gates and giving whatever was there an open invitation to board.

He ran forward again, expertly engaging the intricate system of levers, pulleys, and gears that allowed a single pilot to handle the steering and sail adjustments, and brought the craft under some control. Momentum, however, wasn't that great, and he felt a mild bump as the ship's side struck the closest lock door. Something screamed and cursed at him, and a large black shape jumped aboard and fell to the deck.

By this time he had things under control and was working the ship back out into the docking area and toward the inner markers. That, however, had allowed the unwanted newcomer to regain its footing, and it now stood there, almost in front of and just below him, glowering menacingly.

It was two meters tall and covered in thick black fur, and its huge eyes glowed yellow; when it opened its mouth, it showed more teeth than a shark, all very large and very pointy. Although something of a shapeless mass with no clear waist, it had huge, thick fur-covered arms ending in clawed hands. On its feet was the only clothing it apparently wore or needed—an outlandish pair of what could only be galoshes, size twenty, extra wide. It did, however, have one other thing that was even more intimidating. In its right hand it held what looked very much like some kind of humongous pistol.

"Turn this ship around!" it thundered menacingly. "This is a Chandur ship, and you're no Chandur, thief!"

"And neither are you!" he shouted back, thinking fast and still steering for the markers. "I know very well whose ship this is! I was hired to repossess it for failing to make payments for much of this past season!"

"Repo—! That's *worse* than a damned thief!" the creature roared. "I *ate* the last repo agent who tried it on *my* ship! We watermen stick together!" It looked around and saw that they were still headed out. "I said turn this boat around! *Now!*"

"If you ate the last repo agent, then I've got nothing to lose, do I?" he responded, trying to sound as cool as possible. "If I'm going to die, I guess I might as well take you with me. That barge over there looks solid enough to crack us up and put us under."

The creature raised the pistol. "Get away from that wheel or I'll blast you where you stand! Move away, I say! Down here! I'll take her in!

Don't think I won't shoot, either. It'll blow your wheel, but I can use the other one in the wheel shack amidships!"

Nathan Brazil sighed and stepped back from the wheel and over to the right as directed. *Well, I* almost *got away with it,* he thought glumly.

Suddenly a dark shape moved from the center deck behind the creature forward to where it could sense something moving. It whirled and immediately faced the girl.

It towered over her, and the mouth opened, revealing the very nasty teeth, but she did not seem intimidated. Instead, she looked up at the thing and right into its huge oval eyes.

"You! You get over with your friend—" it began in the same deep, threatening tone it had used on him, but suddenly it stopped. The big eyes seemed to squint, and the huge mouth took on a look of undeniable surprise and confusion. "You—you get—I—uh . . ." it tried, then stopped, seemingly frozen to the spot, unable to move.

Brazil didn't wait to find out what was going on. With the gun no longer aimed at him, he went back to the wheel and began adjusting the course. Still, one eye was on where they were heading and the other was on the drama unfolding just below.

Slowly, jerkily, as if fighting something that was making the creature move against its will as if it were some sort of giant marionette, the right arm was coming up to the face, the gun still firmly in its hand, and when it was at mouth level, the wrist trembled and began to turn the barrel inward, toward that mouth.

"*No!*" Brazil yelled at her, trying to project as much emotion as he could that she should not go through with what she was obviously doing. What he particularly didn't like was what he was getting back from her.

Nothing.

A cold, empty nothing, devoid of pity, hesitation, question.

Devoid of humanity.

She felt his revulsion, though, and hesitated, as if waiting for instructions.

They weren't very far from the barges. The water was icy cold, but with that kind of insulation the creature shouldn't have any trouble making it to them before he froze to death. Frantic to try to communicate with her and upset by this terrible, almost machinelike coldness he felt inside her, he tried mental pictures of the thing jumping overboard and said aloud, "*Splash! Swish!*"

For a moment nothing happened, then she seemed to get the idea. The big creature turned, walked stiffly to the side of the boat, bent over the rail, then dropped into the water, still holding the gun.

He spun the wheel back toward the center channel and then shouted, "Let go of it! *Let. Go. Of. It!*"

She again seemed to get the message, and from perhaps ten meters behind he heard the creature break to the surface and roar with fury. When the curses and threats came, Brazil relaxed. The big thing would be okay.

The girl seemed to be back to normal now. The feelings he got were the basic ones, of satisfaction at dealing with a threat, of a job properly done. That deep, abiding coldness he'd felt was now once again hidden, but he would not forget it.

That would-be hero was too much like himself, a fellow sailor doing what honor required him to do. He would kill such a man in a fair fight if he had the chance and no other choice, but always out of necessity, never coldly and never without profound regret.

She either didn't understand that or had discounted it. It was almost as if she'd observed the situation, done a cold, mathematical calculation, and taken the easiest route. No regrets, no second thoughts, no recrimination, nothing. The fact that she had a kind of mental power that could do this at all was scary enough, but to do it so damned coldly was . . . scary.

He had never been this frightened of something. Not in a very, very long time. If she could do that to the sailor, then she could do that to him and might well do so. He tried very hard to suppress the fear, but it was there, niggling, and that was the worst of it: he knew she could feel it inside him as surely as if it were inside her. The only thing that gave him some comfort was that she had acted only for his protection, and she had listened to him when he had insisted that the sailor should live.

The truth was, he could sense in her no danger to himself, but that wasn't what scared him so much.

What if they can all do this? What kind of game is the population of Glathriel playing, and with how much of this world?

He was out into the full channel now and approaching the hex barrier, and he turned to a more practical concern. At least the weather had prevented the other sailors from pursuing them; now *he* had to prove he was enough of a sailor to get through it himself. The snowstorm wasn't a big deal, but the dark, swirling clouds in Pulcinell right ahead didn't promise anything better.

He passed through the barrier, feeling the very slight tingle that was all anybody felt when going through one of the energy walls, and he was suddenly in tropical heat and a roaring wind. For several minutes he was again frantically working for control of the boat in ankle-deep snow on the deck while sweating from the heavy clothing he wore.

He estimated the winds at gale force, no worse, but it meant trimming sail to the minimum, heading upwind, and battling the sea with a wheel that had a mind of its own. He only hoped that the girl didn't suffer from seasickness; this was going to be one rough time.

No rest for the weary, he thought glumly, but if he could hold out, it would be very much to his advantage. He didn't care how far he went or if he went very far at all; if the storm grew no worse and if he maintained his current heading, it would put a lot of water between him and any pursuers. He fully expected to use this wind once it slackened off enough to trust.

For now, though, it was a matter of keeping the damned boat afloat. He watched wave after wave crash into the bow and engulf it and then felt that bizarre sensation only those who had sailed into a large storm knew, that of the deck shifting suddenly both horizontally and vertically at once as the bow came up and broke free to await another wave.

There was a lashing post, and he considered tying himself to the wheel station, but he'd sailed worse-handling craft than this in even rougher weather over thousands of years and countless endless seas. Once he got his sea legs and the rhythm of the ship, he would feel fairly comfortable with it. Still, it would be nice to sit down, strapped to a fixed chair rather than having to stand through the storm for who knew how long. Still, he dared to lock the wheel long enough to slip off the heavy coat he was wearing and noted for the first time that he'd lost his hat somewhere along the way.

Finding himself pretty well soaked anyway, he slipped off his shirt and was just deciding if he could go any farther when the small boat gave a sudden, violent lurch to one side, throwing him to the deck.

"What the—?" he asked himself, getting up and looking around. It was still pretty rough, but it wasn't *that* rough. *Must have hit a reef or something,* he decided, shaking his head and turning back to the wheel.

He suddenly froze, a cold chill going through him to the bone even though it was as hot as ever. He looked around for the girl but found her sitting just behind the mainmast, cross-legged, looking forward at the huge swells exactly as she'd been when he'd locked the wheel. And, yet, and yet . . .

Wet and crumpled, his hat now sat atop the topmost spoke of the ship's wheel.

ITUS

"I UNDERSTAND THAT WE have something in common," one of the twin centauresses said to Julian in heavily accented English as they entered the hotel room.

"Yes?" was all Julian could manage, still startled both by the unexpectedly diminutive appearance of Mavra Chang and by the startling if imposing twins who seemed to have stepped out of *Fantasia.*

"You were a human male, were you not? And so was I. Not so Anne Marie, who was my wife."

"I'm afraid Tony is having a very difficult time with this," Anne Marie put in, her voice absolutely identical to the other's but with a definitely softer and gentler, almost "sweet" tone, while Tony's seemed much firmer, almost aristocratic. There were clearly two different personalities inside those mirror-image heads, not to mention the fact that Anne Marie's accent was very British.

"I will survive the shock," Tony commented, as if reassuring herself as well as Anne Marie. Tony was in fact looking at the very feminine, pastel-colored, and four-breasted Julian and already seeing how much worse things might have been.

Mavra walked over to Lori and stood looking at him. While she had always projected the feeling of someone much larger, in fact she now barely came up to the middle of his chest, heeled boots and all. She gave a low whistle. "Man! The Well outdid itself on this batch! The two guys become girls, one of the girls becomes a guy, and the other girl becomes the exact identical twin of her husband. Boy! Talk about screwing around with people's psyches!"

Lori was as stunned by the twin centauresses as Julian had been. "I thought you said two entries to the same species was just about unheard of," he said to Mavra. He left unsaid that he was startled to be "hearing" the centauresses in Erdomese in spite of the fact that since Julian could understand them, they were most likely speaking English. Was that, he worried, a price of the translator? That it translated even languages one *knew*? He wondered for a moment why he hadn't noticed this with Julian, then realized that they had uncharacteristically spoken only Erdomese to one another since his return the previous afternoon.

Mavra nodded at Lori's comment about same-species conversions being uncommon. "They are. Sex changes—no, they happen all the time. The reason generally is to maintain the balance in the hex, since you can't add territory. Dillians—that's what this pair is—tend to mate only a couple of times a year and have long gestation periods. I know the race well myself. The result is that they often have periods when there are fewer births than normal, so they're a natural to add to during one of those times, and newcomers are almost always females there because with that long gestation, they're not necessarily going to increase the population before the Well can balance things out. It would also be most common to be female if you got put in Erdom, as Julian was, since they have a lot more females than males. Lori, I think you were the exception for reasons we discussed. On the other hand, if *you* had come through first, you'd undoubtedly have been female, and Julian wouldn't even have wound up Erdomese. Hard to say. For my selfish purposes, anyway, I'm glad it worked out the way it did. Happy to have you both aboard."

The twins, as it were, were stunning creatures on both the "human" and nonhuman halves. Both stood about 215 centimeters tall, with thick, billowing strawberry blond hair that cascaded from their heads and went down the back like a mane, out of which stuck two very equine ears that seemed to be able to pivot independently of one another, and big green eyes set in an exotically beautiful face that contained elements of classical European but had other influences from many races. The complexion was a golden brown, although it was difficult to determine if it was tanned or naturally that way. The breasts were rather large and seemed designed more to hang down when the torso leaned forward, suggesting that centaur young nursed standing on all fours; otherwise, the figure was close to perfect, going down to a very small waist at the point where the humanoid torso merged into the equine half just about where a horse's neck would begin, so that the entire humanoid torso seemed to be slightly forward of the main body.

The lower half was not quite horse, either, but rather an equine extension of the torso, clearly having a single, supple backbone that ran from the humanoid shoulders all the way to the tail. The ponylike body tapered in just forward of the rear thighs and was covered with short golden hair, ending in a large, bushy tail of the same strawberry blond as the hair on their heads. They were for all that almost supernaturally supple; the backbone had to be able to flex effortlessly in almost any direction. They could bend the humanlike torso down so that they were able to actually touch the ground without bending at the knees, turning it almost backward, while swiveling the rear hips around to reach their own tails. It was in form a masterpiece of beauty and functional design.

They were the sexiest-looking creatures Julian had ever seen or imagined, all the more so because, while bipedal, she shared some of the equine look herself. She found herself thinking, *Now,* that's *the way it should be done!*

Lori had much the same reaction and was somewhat amazed and embarrassed to discover that he was becoming turned on just looking at them. He decided he'd better sit down.

The room, which had seemed large, was pretty cramped with the two centaurs inside, but they made do as best they could. "We ordered some coffees and teas," Julian told them. "It was all we could think of since we did not know the nature or needs of your companions."

"Tea is fine with me," Mavra told her. "Tony, being a native Brazilian, will probably complain about the coffee, but he won't drink much else. Anne Marie, being British, is self-explanatory."

"I feel like I should help you, dear," Anne Marie said apologetically, "but I'm afraid I haven't gotten used to all this excess baggage on my rear end in rooms like this yet. Both of us have already made some *frightful* messes knocking over things."

"No, no. You are our guests," Julian told her, and went into the corridor to the bath and prepared the drinks, then brought them back out. The sight of the two centauresses standing there holding cups and saucers was almost funny.

Anne Marie looked at Julian as if studying a sculpture. "You know, I always fantasized about becoming what I am now, but I do believe that had I known of or imagined your form, I should have preferred it. You are so pretty and combine much of the best of both human and animal form."

"I think you got the best of it," Julian told her. "The status of females in Erdomese society is that of objects. It would be unthinkable for one or two females to travel alone even there, let alone to other lands."

"Oh, yes, I'm afraid Mavra has told us about that. What a *shame* for you, poor dear! At least you are fortunate to be married to someone from your own culture. I will say that Dillian society is quite comfortable and relaxed. Oh, the men like to show off their strength and do a lot of man things like drinking heavily and boasting and competing in all sorts of games and silly contests, but women are equal on the councils and in education. The people are all quite civil, so there's not the fear and pressure there is back home. I can—and did—walk the trails alone at night with no more worry than that of tripping over a log. There's quite a lot of stock taken in family. Not much privacy, but you can't have *everything*, after all. It's quite pleasant, really. More than I hoped for and much less than I feared."

Julian looked over at Tony, who seemed in general a bit less happy about the situation, but she decided it was a matter for later, more discreet discussion.

"I'll get right to the point," Mavra told them, her sharp, penetrating voice more than compensating for her tiny size. "We've got passage on a cross-country train this afternoon that will take us directly to the Ogadon border. Ogadon's a water hex, so that means taking another ship." She unfurled a map on the cushions, and they all looked at it.

"There are some places here I'd rather not revisit if I can avoid it," she continued. "Makiem is definitely one of them; dealing with an absolute monarchy of giant toads with little love for their own kind, let alone others, is not something I want to do. Parmiter is a whole nation of professional thieves and scoundrels, I'm told. I have a fondness for Awbri, but it's not much for trade and few ships stop there, and since they're fliers, there are no roads or even trails to speak of. Agon is the most likely jumping-off spot and about as far as I think I can afford. Trouble is, once we're ashore, we're in totally foreign territory for me. I'm much more familiar with the regions north and particularly east of here."

"Then why not go north through that one, there?" Lori asked her, pointing to Wygon and wishing she could read the scratches that served for writing on Mavra's map. "Or even hop a ship east? There are lots of those."

"Well, several reasons," Mavra told them. "For one thing, while the Wygon are good folks, we'd be heading up to this point here, the Yaxa-Harbigor border. I don't know how the Yaxa are now, but I doubt if they're any nicer or dumber than they were, and they were not people easily tangled with. That route is also mostly overland; we've got no flying races in our group and will be walking or riding blind. In fact, this is the first time I ever had this big a party with me and only two races represented! As for water, it damn near broke me getting Anne Marie and Tony here from Dillia, which is *not* an easy hex to get out of, not to mention the bribes I had to spread around Aqomb to reach the two of you. If all I could get us back to was Zhonzhorp, we'd be as far from any possible goal as we are now and dead broke. I think I can get us a deal to

Agon. Not fancy, maybe, but it's only four days' sail. We'll also need supplies before we take off into unknown country. You can't assume anything about climate, edible food, or much else when you go overland, and in a lot of places you can't use money even if you have it. I'm not going to go over our exact route now; I'll wait until we're well away from here and in a place where I'm not certain I'm being recorded and examined. Any questions I *can* answer right now?"

"Yeah, one," Lori said, staring at the map. "What do you need *us* for, anyway?" Mavra had said more words in one gulp since entering the room than she'd spoken altogether in all that time in the Amazon. Her whole manner was as domineering and pushy as ever, but now it was accompanied by nonstop talking, as if she were making up for all those years of near silence.

"Basically, because it's between difficult and impossible to get any distance here by traveling only overland," Mavra responded. "You really have no idea yet. And also because somebody—either hired by Nathan or on their own or a combination of both—definitely doesn't want me to get up there, or at least not to get there first. If Nathan gets in before I do, the first thing he'll do is take me out of the Well master system. That'll mean I'll be processed just as you were, forced to go through a Well Gate and come out as something else. I'll also become just another mortal. I know that's my problem, but it means you guys will be stuck far from even your new homes with nothing to show for it. If, on the other hand, *I* get in first, I can pretty well call my own tune, and yours as well. You can't believe what power I can have inside there, and more important, if what I think is true really *is* true, I may well be able to take some of that power out with me. You can get whatever you want—the race and sex of your choice, riches, power, or, if it turns out that what I suspect is true, you can come with me and travel the whole damned universe."

"That sounds exciting," Anne Marie said with typical understatement. "But is it really as dangerous as you make it out to be?"

"There are things worse than death here," Mavra Chang warned. "Once I was captured and transformed halfway into a donkey. Human torso, donkey legs, ears, and tail. No hands, just legs and unable to raise my head. Then, getting away like that, I fell into the land of the Wukl, who decided to 'perfect' my design. I spent many long years as a fat piglike creature, always looking down at the ground. And that wasn't the *only* experience I had. No, you never know what's going to get you here, and with every evidence that somebody somewhere *is* trying to get me, there's more safety in numbers. Besides, I like the company."

*   *   *

There were passenger trains across Itus, but the kind of passengers they were designed to carry were built quite differently from the party of travelers. The result was that they had the choice of riding in the Itun equivalent of a boxcar—which looked as if it would easily heat up enough to fry eggs no matter how many hatches were open—or the same equivalent of a flatcar, with some thin but strong metal fencing, a meter or so high, placed around the edges. They chose the latter.

After watching the increasingly boring countryside go by, Lori decided to try to nap; Anne Marie—at least Julian *thought* it was Anne Marie—went over and spoke to Mavra, and that left Tony down on the other side of the flatcar staring off into space. Hesitantly, Julian made her way over to where the centauress who had said that they had much in common but had otherwise said little was standing. Julian wasn't really sure how to approach either of them or even if she should, but it was worth a try. Still, she stood there, waiting to be noticed.

For a few moments the centauress continued to stare vacantly to the side, but then she said in that same accented English, "I think you are even more unhappy than I, are you not?"

"I—I'm not sure. You are—Tony? Is that right?"

"Yes. And you are—Julian? Is that right?"

"Julian Beard. Or so I was. Lori-Julian now. I can understand how it can be tough on you, winding up the identical twin of your wife, but I still envy you. I would trade places in a moment, except I couldn't do that to *anybody*."

"Yours is one of those medieval cultures where women are chattel, I gather."

"Pretty much, yes. Sort of like some of those Middle Eastern societies back on Earth, only worse. This culture is built into the genes. The fight, the aggression just sort of drains out of you. Not all at once, but little by little. I was a hell-raising bitch like they'd never seen when I first woke up there, but over time it began to dribble away. The body chemistry, brain chemistry, whatever, just takes over. It's not that you like it—even the ones born this way mostly don't like it—but you just can't help yourself. I was able to keep a little of my old self, enough for my self-respect, so long as Lori was remembering his own former self and giving me some room, but lately he's been acting, well, as badly as I think *I* used to act when I was a teenager. I was a handsome guy—triple-letter athlete, honor student, you name it. The girls used to fall all over themselves trying to get my attention, and I was so macho and so full of myself, I pretty well treated them like toys. I admit it. Even after I got married, I cheated. Hotshot air force officer, poster boy, often away from my family."

"You were married?"

"Divorced."

Tony paused. "I see. But this Lori, she was on the other end of such behavior, was she not? Growing up, I mean. And now the tables are turned. Are you Catholic?"

"No. Not much of anything, really, although my parents were Methodists."

"I was just curious. I have many differences from you and your life, but in one way I find a certain sameness. I feel as if I am in purgatory, that I was not that bad a man, but the angels have found the one way to show me my sins and crumple my pride. Perhaps that is what this is. *Purgatorio*. Not as Dante imagined it but the same in the essentials. For Anne Marie it is different, because she never even had much chance to sin. For her this is a wondrous fantasy, and she is amused but not overly upset by my own state. One would think it would be more difficult to deal with having four legs and the bottom half of a horse than with changing to a woman, but I am a Latin and I was raised in a culture where this is simply unthinkable. I believe that if it were not for my love of and duty to Anne Marie, I would have killed myself." He hesitated. "No, that is not true. The nuns did too good a job on me for me to take my life. But I would have left alone and wandered this world until I died, a hermit to my own kind. This now I cannot do, so I must learn to deal with it. In a Latin culture, *macho* means more than merely what you Americans would call being a 'male chauvinist pig.' In fact, it should not even mean that at all. It is a code of behavior, a set of duties and responsibilities for men, a way of thinking and approaching life. Not that there are not millions of womanizers, but I was brought up too well to be one of those. I *respected* women and loved them, but as a man. Even though we could never have sex, I was never unfaithful to Anne Marie."

"You could never have *sex*?"

"She was badly crippled when we met. I was a pilot for Varig, and I was blinded in an accident. At one stroke my passion and livelihood were taken from me forever. It was while recovering in an English hospital that I met Anne Marie. She was so much more battered and broken than I, yet she was not there as a patient but as a giver of care and love. Other than her mind and soul, which shone through anything, even my darkness, the only other thing that worked perfectly on her was her eyes. So, together we became one person. She provided my eyes and my soul, and I provided the body and strength she never had. It was a love beyond anything you might imagine, and sex had virtually nothing to do with it."

Julian was absolutely amazed at hearing this. "I think that's an amazing story! My God! And you came through together and wound up the same species and still together, too."

"I fully admit to never quite believing the whole story until we went through that gateway in the fallen rock," Tony admitted. "Even then I did not believe that we were truly in another place, on another world. I was not sure that we had not died, except that I was still blind and my knee hurt from falling on that hard floor. Anne Marie almost *did* die; her wheelchair did not arrive with us, and the shock of being flung onto the floor was almost too much for her. Captain Solomon, as we knew him, led me as I carried her to the place where they gave us comfort and what is, I suppose, the standard briefing. Still I did not quite believe. I thought that it must be some sort of dream or trick, or a hallucination, that we had begun our suicide pact or perhaps that I had gone mad. *Still* I clung to her, afraid to let go, and they decided we should go through without delay because of her failing state. I thought she was at least unconscious, but just before we leapt, she whispered, 'Centaurs. There are *centaurs* here, Tony. I saw one! Hold me tight and leap and think of me and centaurs!' And I was so desperate that it was all I *did* think of, down to my core. At that moment, and only at that moment, I found myself believing it, believing all of it, and the thing that I was horribly afraid of was that we would be separated, that we would be separated forever by distance and perhaps by species itself. That we would become monstrous to one another. With all of that in my head, I went forward . . . And I awoke in a forest glade as you see me now."

The first thing, the very first thing he did, was open his eyes and see. See normally, see perfectly, see as well as he had when he had taken his first pilot's examination. There were colors and shapes and textures that had been but somewhat blurred and idealized memories.

He could see!

And then he had seen her, stirring, trying to get up, and he'd known instantly who she was although he'd never seen her picture or allowed anyone to describe her. He'd known her hair was blond and her eyes were green, and that had been enough.

He'd thought, wonderingly, that she made the most beautiful centauress in all creation.

He also felt the weight and the difficulty in breathing and orientation and hauled himself up to standing at almost the same moment that she did. Standing on all fours, facing her, looking at her, knowing that his prayers had been answered. They were together and of the same kind!

And then she had stared at him, first in awe, then in wonder, and said, "Tony?

That can't be you, *dear, can it?" And she had continued to stare, an expression that was half shock and half bemusement on her pretty face.*

"Then—it is true!" he'd responded, his voice sounding very strange to his ears. "Then we are still together! And whole!" He did not care what form they were, human, centaur, crocodile, or swamp rat, only that they were no longer blind or infirm but healthy and still together. Still, he sensed that something was wrong. "What is it, Anne Marie?"

"I'm afraid that we're a bit more together than either of us thought," she'd responded hesitantly. "I wish we had a mirror, but, well, look at as much of your new self as you can and be prepared for a bit of a shock."

"It was the one thing that I, that *neither* of us, had ever thought about, even *considered*," Tony continued. "It is still very hard for me. Not for Anne Marie, I don't believe. Not really. As before, she sees more inside a person than the surface. But for me, and the culture in which I was raised, it is much, much harder. I think it gives the old term 'soul mates' a whole new meaning, does it not?"

Julian could think of a lot worse fates, but needing sympathy, she decided not to deny it to another. Still, she really thought he was lacking a lot of perspective. "It could have been much worse. Both of you as females of *my* race, for example. Or the ultimate fear you mentioned— that you would be of two species monstrous to one another. I of all people understand your shock, but I would trade with you in a moment."

"Oh, I do not doubt that!" Tony responded. "And I sympathize. Still, hormones can only account for so much of anyone's behavior, true? Otherwise, why do both of you have minds and wills? Both you and Lori must learn to control your new selves. The real problem is that you see yourself in your husband because you grew up a man, and you see yourself as the equivalent of how you perceived those young girls who threw themselves at you in your youth. Neither of us grew up female. Neither of us has the grounding of experience in the differences that brings, so we do not know how to cope. You yield because you do not know how to defend as *she* would. I fight when I should yield because my subjective universe was far more rigidly divided sexually than yours by my culture and upbringing. You are in despair because you cannot be *her*, and you cannot be your old self, and you do not have the experience or tools to be someone new. I—I can accept this. I was, after all, prepared to die with her, and I find some old prejudices crumbling now, the most basic of which is that it really does not feel that much different to be a woman. The problem is not with the body but with the mind, with needing a whole new frame of reference—not just accepting it and living with it myself but accepting the way others now perceive me and react and interact with me."

"You mean the way men treat you."

"No, I mean the way all others treat me. The way men look at me even when they are being nice, the very words and approach they take when speaking to me, the way certain conversations are closed to me now. And it is not just the men. The women react differently as well. As I am certain you know, a conversation strictly among women is quite different from one between men or between men and women."

"You can say that again," Julian agreed.

"So it is a matter of learning the rules, as it were. But I can no longer be Tony, the old Tony. Not like this. Not even to her. And I do not know how to be anything else, particularly with her. And *that* is something that I understand and she, not having been male, cannot yet grasp. I can be her—sister, her best friend, but I can no longer be her husband."

"Maybe. Maybe you're right. We've all got a lot to learn." She decided that this was enough mutual wallowing for now. What Tony had said was true, but it was damned hard to feel sorry for the centauress when *she* would sell her soul to be either one of them. "On the other hand, this Mavra Chang is something else, isn't she? She reminds me of a couple of women astronauts I trained with. Tough, knowledgeable, able to handle almost anything or anyone no matter what her size and sex, but still undeniably feminine."

"She is indeed someone quite unusual," Tony agreed. "I can only hope that toughness rubs off on the rest of us."

"Um, I'm curious," Julian said cautiously. "Is this what Anne Marie says she looked like? I mean, are you now a clone of her?"

"Clone is a good term," Tony replied. "We *are* clones of a sort—they were so amazed at us that they sent us off to a hospital and took samples, which, I believe, were sent out to one of the high-tech lands. I believe the interest was in the fact that we even had the same fingerprints. Even identical twins do not quite have that. We are genetically absolutely identical. Only the personalities and experiences are different, and that makes quite a difference indeed."

That was fascinating but not the answer to the question. "No, I mean, do you look like she used to? I know you said you didn't want to have her described, I assume so you could hold a mental picture, but surely she's said something now."

"Oh, I see. No, we do not look like she used to. In fact, I can see something of my mother and one of my own sisters in us. I think that somehow, we were designed out of the genetic patterns of her mother and my maternal chromosome. Or so it was theorized. We are a combination of the pattern and look of the best of both of us. As for the horse part, well, I have never seen a horse built quite like this, with such style and grace, as it were, looking at her and thus myself from my old male vantage point, but I am certain that wherever it comes from, it is not in either of our ancestries."

Julian chuckled, then suddenly realized that it was the first time she had laughed at all on the Well World. Tony had at least a sense of humor about things, and that was what would certainly pull her through to some solution to her own inner conflict. The Erdomese could use something to laugh about, but there had been little to do up to now.

Anne Marie came over to them. "Oh, I'd hoped you two would get along!" she gushed. "Tony has been too much in a shell since all this, haven't you, dear? I, on the other hand, have been quite excited by it all. I've done more and seen more in the past few months than I had ever *dreamed* to do in a lifetime! I find everything here so *frightfully* fascinating!"

Julian wondered if that sense of adventure would last if they got into a really bad situation. She couldn't imagine that Anne Marie could kill a fly willfully and with malice aforethought.

The train ran silently along on a magnetic track, levitating just above the surface. There was no engineer, no crew; the entire process was automated, and each car could be switched in and out at will or become part of a new train at almost every junction. They'd gone through a large number of such junctions, when everything slowed to a crawl and pieces of train were diverted, some were added, some were taken away on spurs or alternate tracks, and a new train was put together. It was a marvel of efficiency and served the hex well.

Now they slowed for one more switching yard and in a matter of minutes watched the long train divide into five separate sections and go off in all directions. There was a slight bump as their own car was joined to other sections old and new, and then everything speeded up once more.

It was a few minutes after this that Mavra Chang had the odd feeling that something wasn't right. At first she couldn't put her finger on it, and she began to inventory her surroundings to see what it was that was setting off warnings in the danger-sensing area of her brain. The car was the same; the other cars were innocuous enough, and the surroundings looked little different from what they had looked like before. What was the problem?

She was almost ready to dismiss her feeling as being too jumpy when suddenly she had it. The sun!

They had been going generally due west. Now, suddenly, the sun was not behind them as it should have been in late afternoon with the Well World's west–east rotation, but on their left. They were still going west, but it was now south-southwest. Clearly the car was no longer heading for the port at all. Something, or someone, had ordered them diverted.

"Everybody! Listen up!" she shouted. "Lori, wake up! We've got trouble!"

Lori stirred and shook his head to clear it. "Huh? What?"

"They've switched us south onto another line," she told them as they gathered around the tiny woman.

" 'They'?" Lori asked. "Who's 'they'?"

"If I knew *that* for sure, I could deal with them!" Mavra snapped. "Never mind that now. Somebody with influence who definitely doesn't want me to get up to the Well first, that's for sure. Anybody here a good judge of land speed? About what speed do you think this car is making now?"

It was Julian who spoke up. "At its maximum, no more than two hundred kilometers an hour," she stated with a certainty that surprised them. "At average, about one hundred forty."

"That's a fair enough estimate," Mavra responded, impressed. "You were never in astronaut training."

"That's *right*! I'd forgotten you were a spacer! Okay, and according to this cheap watch I bought months ago, we've been going for three and a half hours. That would mean we're about two-thirds of the way, or were when we were switched. At the angle we're now traveling, if it stays fairly constant, we'll still reach the coast, but way, way south of where we want to be. There's only one decent harbor on the west coast, or so I'm told; the coastal waters are otherwise too shallow. Mostly small towns along there dependent on rail. I'd say that they're aiming to bring us in down there at one of the small towns on the southwest border, maybe the southernmost one, at or after dusk."

"But *why*? That's the question," Lori said, frowning.

"That's easy enough. We miss our ship, we've got a long, slow walk up, since we can't trust the trains anymore, and we're in the kind of area where we always will stick out like sore thumbs."

"But we can't *walk*, not in this humidity and gravity!" Julian protested. "At least *I* can't!"

"This is not as much of a problem for us," Tony pointed out. "If need be, I could carry you and Mavra, too, and I am certain that Anne Marie could carry Lori."

"Of course," the other centauress replied. "It is a *bit* more difficult for us, and we have to go slower because of the burden on these thin legs, but you would hardly add to the burden."

Mavra shook her head. "Uh uh. We might do that for a short distance but not a long one. Not only do I want out of here, I want to get lost. At least to whoever's behind this. And the *last* thing I want to do is make a grand march under these conditions to a place where somehow I know they won't have a ship for us."

"But what is the alternative?" Tony asked her.

"If we keep going this way, we'll come in to the southwesternmost yard in a small town almost at the Gekir border. Gekir's a nontech hex and I've never been there, but my experience has been that if you want to get lost, get into a nontech hex. No mass transportation, but no mass communications, either. Nontechs are also the most dangerous for a lot of reasons, but while I don't remember much about them, what was said indicates that the Gekir are not a mean or hostile people, and there's some trade between there and Itus. As to what kind of creatures they are, I haven't a clue, even though we might or might not have seen them among the races back in the capital. If we're lucky, there might be some kind of sailing vessels that call along the coast. It's worth a try."

"But if whoever is chasing you is influential enough to divert our railcar, they will have people watching out for us at the town, won't they?" Julian asked worriedly.

"Yes, so we'll have to get off before that point and avoid the town. It shouldn't be too hard to do. They're bound to have a decoupling yard just before the town to route the various cars to loading areas. When the train slows, we get off, fast. It'll still be moving, so watch yourselves, but it should be moving at a crawl, at least up to the switch. Tony, I assume you and Anne Marie could jump off."

"I don't think that would be a problem, but we'll have to time it right," Tony replied. "I don't think either of us should risk a broken ankle at this point, and the heavier gravity is a major threat. Wait a moment! Anne Marie, come give me a hand here."

The two centauresses went over to the left side and studied the short staked fence. "They look just placed in," Anne Marie said, and with both hands tried to pry one up. She tried as hard as she could, but it wouldn't budge. "No go, I'm afraid, dear."

Tony got close beside her. "Both of us together, then."

They tried, but it was as if the panel were welded on.

Julian came over and looked at the panel as well, bending down to see what might be holding it in. "I think it's more magnets," she said at last. "This train runs on the basis of magnetic polarity. There are two strong electromagnets underneath, one the track and the other on the undercarriage. When power is applied, they repel, we float essentially friction-free, and by moving one set, speed can be quickly achieved or slowed, even stopped on a dime. But the stakes, I bet, are matched to the polarity of the undercarriage. When it's powered, they're pulled tight." She thought a moment. "I wonder if there are any dead spots."

"Dead spots?" one of them asked.

"Yes. Have you ever ridden on a subway—underground, metro, or whatever—or an electric-powered train? There's often points where the track is either not powered because of some repair or connector or the power source changes. The lights might flicker or even go off, but it's brief and the train's forward momentum keeps it rolling until it gets to the next powered section. I thought I felt a slight loosening at one point while I was leaning on it here, and there were the vibrations rattling the stakes briefly, but then it was tight again. If there's another, then in that brief moment this panel should be able to be pulled. *If* it's really held by the electromagnets, that is."

"There is only one way to find out," Tony said. "I will just stand here and pull on it and see."

Although it was a rather simple explanation of the principle, Lori found himself momentarily taken aback by Julian's sophisticated knowledge, even though he knew her background. He hadn't been used to her being very assertive of late, and it gave him oddly mixed feelings he neither liked nor wanted to deal with. Julian had come up almost effortlessly with the solution to a problem of the sort that only seemed obvious when it was explained. The rattling had happened every few minutes off and on since they'd boarded, yet only Julian had put it together. Although he was quite proud of her, the two warring halves of his nature could not have been more divided on interpretation. The Lori Sutton part was cheering; the Lori of Alkhaz part was furious that she'd just given it to them all rather than tell him in private so that he could bring it up to the group.

Several minutes passed, and a bored Tony, feeling circulation going in her arms, was just about to give it up when suddenly the panel came up and she staggered back a bit, barely keeping balance. It didn't come all the way out but was now held only by two flat pins, no longer flush with the flatcar floor.

"If need be, I could probably kick it down at this point," Tony commented, "but I think that Lori might do better pushing up from beneath. Just be sure you don't fall off the train when it comes up!"

Lori looked at it dubiously. "Yeah, right," he said, but lay down, got his body in as close as he could with his legs well beyond the almost free panel, and pushed against the very solid-feeling section.

When the moment came, tense as he was, the panel almost did take him with it; it flew up and away, and he suddenly felt himself going forward into the opening. Only Anne Marie's strong hands grabbing his legs and bringing him back in saved him, and, being hauled back on his stomach, he was suddenly *very* thankful he'd kept wearing the hardened codpiece.

"Wow! Can she *bend*!" Julian gasped. "She didn't even have to *kneel*!" But she rushed to Lori.

Mavra nodded and said to herself, "Things aren't quite as static as they seem on the Well World. Dillian evolution has sure done a neat job on them!"

Julian bent down next to Lori, concerned. "Are you all right, my husband?" she asked in Erdomese.

He nodded. "Just bumped around a bit. I will be all right in a minute or two." He turned on his side and looked back and up at the centauress who'd grabbed him. "Thanks a lot, Tony."

"Think nothing of it, dear," responded Anne Marie, not taking any offense at all at being confused with her twin.

Mavra came over and inspected the opening. "Okay. That means Lori, Julian, and I can sit on the edge and then jump off rather than having to contend with a meter-high hurdle, and you two have a straight jump."

"How much longer will it be, do you think?" Julian asked her.

Mavra looked at her watch and then at the sun. "Maybe fifteen minutes. Okay, you've all seen these switching points; you know what they look like. Get as far away to the south—the direction that you'll jump—as you can as fast as you can and stay out of sight of anybody in the yard area. Assemble behind the first building that gives us cover and wait until we're all there. Understood? They may not be expecting us to jump, but they're sure to have somebody at the station to keep a tail on us, and it'll most likely be an Itun hired for the job. From this point we avoid Ituns until we're across the border."

They waited as the shadows grew and the light began to fade around them. Darkness came quickly to the Well World, and within a few more minutes it would be pitch black. That actually bothered the two Erdomese the least, since they could simply lift their natural eye filters and see the full spectrum. Mavra and the two Dillians, however, had no more night vision than ordinary Earth humans, a thought that occurred to Julian.

"We should jump off last," she said to Lori, "because we can see."

He shook his head. "No, I think we go first for that very reason. We can find *them* a lot easier than they can find *us*, and I think it would be better to be on the ground just in case one of them has a problem with the jump."

"All right, then. You go and I'll follow. Night is almost completely upon us, and there are many lights not far ahead. I can already feel us slowing just a bit."

Lori turned to Mavra, who had noticed the lights as well, and she nodded. "Any time you feel right after we're slow enough. Just don't take it too fast. We'll get out."

The Erdomese moved to the opening in the flatcar stakes. Lori sat, legs out over the side of the car, uncomfortable sitting on his behind because of the tail and tailbone. It was not a normal position for Erdomese, and he decided to jump as soon as he felt it was safe.

"Remember the heavier gravity," Julian warned him. "You will hit very hard, my husband."

"You take care, too."

The train was definitely slowing now, going perhaps thirty kilometers per hour, and it continued to slow. Lori's tailbone was hurting badly enough that when it was down to about twenty, he took a deep breath and launched himself into the night. He hit as hard as Julian had warned, pitched forward, and found himself rolling down a small embankment into a fetid, muddy drainage ditch. Covered with stinking mud, he almost panicked, got control, and clawed himself out of it and up onto dryer land. He lay there, breathing hard, for a minute or so, then picked himself up. He not only stank, he was sore, and his left ankle and right wrist stung when he moved them. For a moment he was afraid that he'd broken something, but he quickly realized that they were probably only sprains and not that serious. By force of will he made his way in the darkness just below the tracks toward the lighted area about half a kilometer farther on.

Julian came to meet him, walking on all fours. "Are you all right?" she asked, concerned, then twitched her nose. "You sure don't *smell* all right!"

"Rolled all the way down into the drainage canal. Didn't pay enough attention to the slope. I've got some twists, but I can handle it. You?"

"A little bruised but not bad. It was slower, and I had a more level area. About the only problem I'll have is getting grass stains out of my fur."

He managed a chuckle at that. "The others?"

"Mavra was right behind me. She just jumped out, rolled once, and landed on her feet almost beside me! Like an acrobat or something. She told me to find you and she was going to check on the Blondie Twins."

"Let's join up," he told her, gesturing forward.

"You are limping! Come! Put your hand on my shoulder, and I will help you," she invited, standing erect.

"I—I can make it on my own," Lori insisted, then grimaced and almost fell forward. She caught him and helped brace him, and this took just enough weight off that he was able to manage it.

"I thought you couldn't even move, let alone stand in this place," he noted.

"I grow strong when I am needed," she responded, quoting a female Erdomese proverb.

Both Dillians had jumped without a hitch and now waited with Mavra for Lori and Julian to join them in a dark area behind the first automated switching tower. Mavra, seeing them in the very dim glow of the tower lights, motioned for the much larger centaurs to remain where they were and ran toward the two Erdomese. "What happened?" she asked. "Are you hurt bad?"

"I'm not sure," Lori answered honestly. "I *thought* the ankle was just twisted a little, but now I'm not so sure. It doesn't feel broken, but I think it's a hell of a sprain."

"Well, a very ancient man who knows the Well World far better than I do once said to never travel without a Dillian if you can manage it. We can repack all the stuff on one of them and put you on the other. Don't argue! Whoever's watching us has probably already discovered that we're not there. The sooner we get away from here, the better!"

When they reached the Dillians, one of them was already repacking the saddlebags on the other. Then the one who carried all the equipment helped Lori onto the other's back.

"Ride forward," the centauress suggested. "That should take the pressure off your tail as well. And watch that horn on your head! I don't want to get stabbed if I have to make a sudden stop!" Left unsaid was the rather noticeable stink of swamp and mud permeating his hair.

He felt awkward and helpless and, even worse, stupid. It was almost like a horse riding a horse. He was just never designed to ride on the back of a soft animal, but there was little choice at the moment.

Mavra turned to Julian and said, "Well, you're leading the way because you can see and we can't. Can you handle it? I know how hard this high G is on you."

"I'll be all right," she assured the woman in black. "You said south, right? How far do you wish to go tonight?"

"Well, we're going to be moving a lot slower and more cautiously than I planned, but we ought to go on until at least one of us has to stop. It shouldn't be more than a dozen kilometers or so to the border if we head due south. That's a haul on foot in the dark under these conditions, but we haven't done much more than rest on our duffs all day. Can you make it?"

"Yes." No equivocation, no hesitancy. Mavra liked that.

"I think you're gonna do just fine, Julian. You sure you know which way's south? We had a bend just before we came in."

"I know. It is something in the Erdomese brain. Once we have a fix on the sun at any point, we always know direction, even when the sun is gone." She looked around, thinking. "The first thing is to find a road or trail of some kind going in our direction and parallel it. I do not think we should risk Tony or Anne Marie tripping over jungle vines or fallen logs. Just keep close and I will get you through."

"You sound like you've done this sort of thing before."

"Air force survival training. This is no worse than the jungles of Panama or Honduras."

"That's *right*! Lori said you were once captain of a spaceship."

"No, captain was my rank in the air force. A military service. I was a mission specialist on the space shuttle, not a pilot or commander, although I had a jet pilot's license."

"Too much of this is new to me," Mavra admitted, her translated voice coming to Julian's ears as an odd but understandable mixture of Erdomese and English, depending on the terms used. "I was in the jungle, cut off, for so long that it wasn't until a few years ago that I even realized that Earth had progressed to power tools, let alone flying machines and spacecraft, and by that time I saw them only as evil magic. Until I spoke with Tony and Anne Marie here, I had no idea Brazil wasn't still a Portuguese colony, let alone that your own country even existed. It was all very ironic. All I was doing was holding out in the wilderness until technology advanced to where I could get off that planet, and I managed to fall into a trap where I rejected all technology. Even now I'm sweating like a stuck pig. I still haven't gotten used to clothing, and these boots feel bizarre."

"What's stopping you from taking them off? The nearest Earth-human type is probably a thousand miles from here, if even that close."

"Practicality, mostly. Certainly not modesty. I was *born* without that word having much meaning. Back in the Amazon, that was *my* jungle. I loved it and still do, but I knew everything about it. Everything. This isn't my jungle. I don't know the effects of anything I step on here, and any protection is better than none when you've only got bare skin in an unknown land." She dropped her voice low. "Hell, I remember when female Dillians wore bras, and they weren't nearly as hung as those two."

Julian also lowered her voice to a high whisper. "Is it just me, or is it really difficult to tell which is which unless they speak? I mean, I've had the eeriest feeling that the same one I spoke to who was Tony, definitely Tony, was later talking like Anne Marie."

"I know what you mean," Mavra whispered back. "Actually, I'm sort of relieved that somebody else feels it, too. Maybe it's just how absolutely identical they look, but it's spooked me more times in the past few weeks than I can tell you."

"That is what I mean. Is there something else about them I do not know but should?"

"Could be, but if so, I don't know it, either. If it *is* more than mental confusion on our part, I'm absolutely positive that they aren't aware of it themselves. I just don't know. Every time I say that absolutely nothing can surprise me anymore, something does. How the two of them were processed is unprecedented; you and Lori make a different but equally unprecedented case. I don't know *what's* going on here, but until I get to the Well, I can't find out for sure myself. Even the Well World seems odd. I always thought of it as static, too tightly managed to change radically, but there are many differences. Differences you wouldn't notice from one time here, but it's *different*. Some of the cultures are changed, a few radically so. There are differences in alliances, attitudes, you name it. Even the races are different. Not a lot in some cases, a great deal in one or two that I've seen, but there are changes from radical to subtle in all the ones I knew. It may be a normal thing, as with all worlds, but this is not a normal world, nor was it ever intended to be. I can't help wondering if it feels the same way to Nathan, wherever he is."

That brought up a point Julian was even more interested in. "This Nathan. Tell me about him."

"He is—well, he cannot be described. Oh, I can tell you what he looks like, more or less, and from what Tony and Anne Marie have told me he's changed very little. You'd like him. Most people do. There's a kindness and gentleness in him that come through, and he's the loneliest creature in all the cosmos."

"You were not just—associates. Or even teacher and pupil."

"No."

"You still speak of him with affection, yet this kind, wise, gentle man you describe is out to get you and maybe worse."

Mavra sighed. "I think so. At least the evidence points that way, and it almost *feels* like his handiwork. You can be seduced by him in many ways, and at the time he means it, but deep down, where the soul resides, he's also something else. Something almost—monstrous. It's hidden most of the time, I think even from himself, but it's always there, and in the end it's always in control. You won't see it much when he's human, but inside the Well it's much clearer. It is nothing less than the collective will of the ancient creatures that built this place and remade the universe as they pleased. *He* doesn't even like it. Last time he fought like hell against it and wound up almost forced to do its will, kicking and screaming all the way. It is there, and I find it most significant that this time he didn't even try to fight it. He's surrendered to it, I think, and that alone makes him the most dangerous creature since the universe was born."

"And yet—he gave *you* immortality and the key to this Well, this God-computer," Julian noted.

"Yes. I've come up with many theories as to why, some more flattering to my ego than others, but it wasn't until I came here once again that I found out the truth. He is two creatures—the kind, gentle, but tough and resourceful man I knew and described and this—*thing*. He's been the man so long, it is more his true self than that hidden within him, but he knows he's in a trap, an eternal trap. By taking me in there, by making *me* reset things last time, he dodged his own conflict while still doing what he was compelled to do. Now I think it was more than that. I don't have this thing inside me. I was born to this form and grew up as you see me. I think his human half wants to be stopped. In the end, I think that was the idea all along. The next time, *this* time, I'd be there, too. Something inside him wants me to beat him and seize control. To stop his compulsive pattern. Maybe it's because he became too much like us; maybe it's simple logic. The stress of last time and its responsibilities brought it home to him that there was a flaw in the plans of those who created this place. They wanted a new, even greater race of true gods to evolve, but even they couldn't foresee all the things that could happen in so vast a universe over so much time. So they left him as their guardian, to keep it on track, but they blew it. They didn't just set it going, they made it a controlled experiment instead, all the variables taken into account."

Julian saw where she was going, or thought she did, as much as this whole place made any sense. "You are saying that they overcontrolled. That by insisting on things developing as they designed, they gave it no opportunity to develop differently."

"Well, they sure weren't as godlike as they thought they were, that was for sure," Mavra agreed. "They couldn't conceive that being a race of true gods *would* become boring as hell after some great length of time. Their whole racial history was motivated by a belief that true and absolute perfection was possible. They could not face the fact that it wasn't, and so they built this world, and the races that were successful here were sent out into the universe to see if *they* could attain that perfection. If anything loused up the experiment beyond repair, though, they had a mechanism for resetting things to start so absolute that everything would develop *exactly* the same, except that whatever caused the collapse would be factored out. Even you were probably there in the past creation, the one that I, many relative centuries in the future, wiped out and re-created. The same nations, the same races, the same *people*, being born, living, progressing, dying, over and over."

"My God! You mean I've done *this* before? Or someone exactly like me?"

"No. I have no doubt there was a Julian Beard who lived your life and did all the same things—up to the point where you were sent to investigate the meteor. And a Lori who remained the first female full professor of astronomy at wherever she taught, and a Tony and Anne Marie who probably died in a suicide pact, and the others as well. Your coming here changed that for you and for the others. I believe Nathan has at one point or another changed a number of individuals' lives. It is difficult to say this, but most individual lives, if removed or altered, won't change the fabric very much so long as the number of them is kept very small. It is said that the Well Gates react to people's wills and that no one who *would* mess up the master plan is ever transported here. I don't know. But I *do* know it can't continue. Reset after reset, the same people, the same races, the same lives over and over . . . In the end, if *that* keeps happening, then *nobody* really matters. Nobody at all. And if I fail this time, that's what is going to *keep* going on again and again. A continuous wheel, a perpetual replaying of the same damned recording over and over until the universe dies. That's what this is all about. That's why you're all here."

"Sweet Jesus!" Julian gasped, thinking of the implications of what she was saying.

"What are you two girls whispering about?" Lori called to them.

Mavra Chang gave a crooked smile. "Us *women* are talking *woman talk*," she replied aloud.

It was a long way yet in the dark to the border.

PULCINELL

THE SIGHT OF NATHAN Brazil's broad-brimmed hat, soggy and crumpled though it was, atop the top spoke of the ship's wheel made everything else, from the escape to the weather to the girl's extraordinary powers, seem distant and pale. More, his empathic link with the girl told him that not only had she not done it, she was unaware of anyone else around to do it, either.

Either I'm losing my mind or there's somebody else here, he told himself.

The girl, riding out the storm just behind the mainmast, instantly sensed his feelings of danger and confusion and turned to look back at him, all her vast array of senses and powers deployed against a threat.

There was nothing. No threat at all. She frowned. No threat, but there was something else, something *different* here. Something that had not been there before, not until that odd lurch the ship had taken. Whatever it was, it was no enemy, but why couldn't she see it or find it? There was only something vague, and that something, like a fuzzy, friendly ghost-like presence, was back there with Nathan Brazil.

Brazil had no choice but to retake the wheel, removing the hat first and throwing it forward. The wind caught it, but it was too soggy to blow away; it skidded across the deck and stuck against the side. He unlocked the wheel and began to try to think of ways to use this wind rather than fight it. It was no use, though. Somebody—or *something*—had put that hat on the wheel. Something that was there with him now. Something that even the girl could only dimly perceive.

"What are you? Who are you?" he yelled against the howling gale. "Stop playing children's games and show yourself! Where the hell are you?"

"Right here at your side, Captain Brazil," responded a low, deep resonant voice that nonetheless was not formed by humanlike lips.

Nathan Brazil almost jumped out of his skin. He whirled around, letting go of the wheel.

"Right here," said the voice, and when it spoke, he could suddenly see it, if only vaguely.

It *was* big, big enough to tower the better part of a meter over him, and broad and strong of body. It had a head much like a snake's or a giant lizard's, long and flattened with two big, yellow catlike eyes that popped up from its surface, and a large, thick serpentine body that was balanced on two thick legs that ended in clawed, webbed feet but started too far down the torso to be a main support for the rest of it. It balanced now on those two feet and on the remainder of that body, which ended in a broad, almost shovellike tail. Extruding from either side of the torso, a bit below where the shoulders ought to have been, were two very thin, frail-looking arms terminating in four clawed, long webbed fingers and an opposable thumb. Like the legs, they extended out from the torso, more like a reptile than a mammal. The whole thing was covered in silvery scales that seemed to give off a rainbow of colors as the swirling clouds varied the available light and which were probably spectacular in direct sunlight.

"Don't you think you'd better tend to the wheel first?" the creature asked him in a calm, pleasant voice. "I just had the very *devil* of a swim just to catch up with you. I'd rather not go back in the water again for a while."

"Uh, yeah, sure," Brazil commented, turning back to the wheel and, with some difficulty, wrestling it back under control. It was a miracle that the lone sail, even deployed as little as it was, hadn't been torn to shreds. Whoever had built this boat had *really* known how to build.

"Uh, if you don't mind," Brazil said, trying not to look around or away but keep his eyes on steering, "just who the hell are you and why did you go to all the trouble of swimming after us in the first place? And why couldn't we see you?"

"Survival trait, they tell me. The arms, as you might have noticed, are very limber, but they ain't real big or real muscular, and the legs, while strong, don't let you move real fast. That would've made us sittin' ducks in our own land, let alone from outside threats. Dahir's a nontech hex, you know."

"So you're a Dahir!" *Another one I don't quite remember looking like this, let alone with this trick,* he thought. "A *very* long way from home, aren't you? And a damned good swimmer for an inland race."

"It was another thing that just come naturally, sort of. Dahir's inland, true, but it's real swampy. Lowlands, wetter than the Everglades. The routine's to swim along pretty much like a snake and stand up to feed or do whatever else you feel like doin'. Of course, we walk around the houses and lodges and the like, but for any kind of travel, well, it's kinda like takin' the car even though the grocery store's only two blocks away. You know you *should* walk, but it's so much easier to ride. Even though this is ocean, to tell you the truth I never even *thought* about not bein' able to swim in it. I gotta admit, though, I almost lost it when it got so rough all of a sudden. I'd actually missed you and was gettin' dragged away to the side and then forward a little when one of them waves just picked me up and dropped me *kerplang* on the deck."

"So *that's* what shook the ship! You're another one of the people who came in through the gate from Earth, I gather. You're a long way from the Everglades and corner grocers here."

"Yeah, but I didn't have a lot of choice in the matter, neither. I was dropped, drugged, dragged around a jungle for I don't know *how* long, then carried through to here and more or less thrown in. I really don't remember a lot of it, except that I knew I was dyin'."

"You're from Mavra's group, then."

"I guess. I know who she is, but only by hearin' about it. I understand she was the leader of that group of nutty Amazons who grabbed us. As I said, I was drugged and sick most of the time, and it's all a daze. Not nearly as much of a shock as wakin' up like *this,* I gotta say, but the in between's a little fuzzy. For the record, I'm Gus Olafsson. Everybody just calls me Gus, even in Dahir."

"A Swede?"

"Minnesota. United States. To tell the truth, though, the area's kind of Scandinavia west, with the Swedes there, the Norwegians, and even the Finns up in the Iron Mountain district. You know the place?"

"No, sorry. I've actually spent very little time in the States, and I don't know much about the interior at all. I heard much of it was flat, dull, and cold."

"Well, not all of it, but that describes where I come from pretty well. Pretty area, though, up around the lake district. It was a nice place to grow up but not a great place to make a livin' in if you didn't want to do the same old things. I didn't. Instead, I picked a way to see the world, all right. More than one, as it's turned out. In fact, the things you can do as a Dahir woulda been real handy for my profession, except, of course, when somebody would have to see me, which would cause a right good monster movie–style panic, I'd say. Shame, though. It'd be a real advantage not to be seen in most cases. I coulda done great investigative work right in plain sight."

"You were some sort of reporter?"

"News photographer. Television, actually. Started at small stations, worked my way up until I got some really good footage, then went free-lance, gettin' work from the networks and local stations. Finally impressed folks enough, I guess, that I got an offer from the news network, and I've been doin' that, well, until them Amazons more or less killed me and I wound up here like this."

"You're the one who's been following us for the last week or so, then."

"Yeah, pretty much. You only gave me the slip once, out on the dock that one time. Pretty slick, but I figured it out. I also figured when I heard you talkin' to that bastard blob of Jell-O that you wouldn't've been so straight with him if you hadn'ta finally figured you'd been had and was already fixin' to light out. I got to admit you picked a lousy day in particular to do it, but I just had this feelin' you would."

"Yeah, but how'd you track us from the hotel? We climbed down a sheer wall on a rope."

"Hey! I was a news photographer, right? I mean, the only way to get the picture nobody else gets is to think like the guy you're shadowin'. The rubes and the lazy ones, they'd stake out the lobby just like the colonel's boys and wait for you to come through, figuring you would try and shake 'em. Me, I decided you was smarter than that, even if you did take a long time to catch on to the colonel's game, and then it was just figurin' how I would do it if I was you."

"I was able to at least sense your presence most of the time," he noted. "How come I didn't sense you back there?"

"Because a good stakeout depends on not bein' made, right? I mean, if you hadn't given me the slip back on that dock last week, I would never have guessed you'd figured I was there at all, but since you did, I thought you or maybe Terry might be feelin' me, and I hung back. I mean, you made tracks all through the snow, right? The only thing was, hangin' back and not knowin' how they launched these things, I couldn't get close enough to jump on the boat. When you had your problems, I wasn't in the right spot, so I couldn't jump on like that other fella, but I figured I was close enough to swim out to you. Almost caught up when you got over near the barges, but then that guy came overboard almost into my face, and by the time I got my bearin's back, you was headin' through the hex boundary. I hadta swim like the very devil to get even close after that."

Brazil frowned. "But, if you're not part of the colonel's crowd, then what are you doing here in the first place?"

"Lookin' for you, and Terry. She and I go back a long way. I was the only cameraman she worked with if she could manage it."

"Terry?"

"Her," responded Gus, and a small finger pointed out at the girl on deck.

Brazil was suddenly excited. "You *know* her? Know who she is?"

"Sure. Theresa Perez. Hotshot producer for the news channel. It was her I was workin' for when we come down to Brazil for the meteor coverage. Had an exclusive, too. Pretty good pictures, if I do say so myself. Hope they got 'em okay."

Theresa Perez. *Terry* . . . At last, at least, she had a name and a past.

"But—she can't see you, either? Even now?"

"I guess she could. She should if I was talkin' to her or tried to make her, I guess. It ain't somethin' I can turn on and off, you know. I don't even know how it's done. All I know is that we're like just about invisible to anybody except another Dahir. Works on every race I ever saw or met. Kinda handy, really, when you're off on your own with nothin' like I was. Just walk on any handy ship. They don't even notice you. Need some food? Just take it. Gets to be kinda fun after a while. The Dahir, they got somethin' of a religion about how not to abuse the power, but I didn't stay for the lectures. Hell, I wasn't a good Lutheran; why should I be a good and loyal follower of a religion I wasn't even born to?"

Nathan Brazil laughed at that. "You'll do fine around here, Gus. That's just the attitude to survive."

"Yeah, well, maybe. I dunno. It ain't foolproof. I found that out a couple of times. You can't fool a camera, or an electric eye, or any number of security devices. Recorders record your sounds even if the folks around don't notice them when they're made. I almost got picked up more than once back there in Hakazit, and I knew they'd just send me back home by the Zone Express, and with the kind of stuff I was charged with, that damned system woulda throwed the book at me. I guess I'm kinda on the lam myself now."

"Well, I won't turn you in, and I'm going to try as hard as I can to keep away from any more high-tech hexes for a while myself. The way you talk, though, everybody everywhere already knows who I am."

"Well, not everybody *believes* it, or at least all the stories and legends, but it's kinda the talk of government and official types, anyway. That's how I heard about it. They had me in the capital, in what you might call a school on how to be a good Dahir and love it. They was also tryin' to pump me for what I knew about the others, which wasn't all that much. I doubt if most folks in the country, most places, have heard of you, but the big shots all have. They're kinda in a whole set of arguments with each other, too. Some don't believe you're the guy in their legends; some believe you are, and it scares hell out of 'em. Some of the believers want to nab you; others want to just make sure you don't *do* whatever they're scared of you doin' without first makin' deals with them. Those who don't believe you're anybody special want to knock you off just to show the true believers they're right, and so on. No matter how you look at it, though, Cap, you're as made as me and twice as wanted."

Nathan Brazil sighed. "So that's the way it is. I'd kind of hoped nobody would spot me and I could be kindly Captain Solomon. So even the colonel knew all the time."

"Oh, he knew, all right. Kept givin' them regular reports on you. I stood there and listened to him give 'em. For now he was just gettin' orders to stall, stall, stall, so I guess they still ain't made up their minds. The guy was a perfect toady, I bet, back home, and he might have changed race, form, and loyalties, but he's right at home doin' just the same here. Uh—just out of curiosity, *are* you the guy they're scared of?"

Brazil shrugged. "I suppose it wouldn't hurt to admit what most of the leadership already half believes. Yeah, I'm the same guy. And yes, they have some reason to be scared of me, too. More reason now than before, if they get me too pissed off."

"They say you're some kind of like, well, god or something. That you're really one of them guys who built this nutty place."

"Well, that's a bit exaggerated. Right now I've only got one important power they don't, pretty much like your one big power. The Well—the master computer that keeps things running here—won't let them or anything else kill me."

"Huh! I'll trade you!"

"Don't tempt me! But still, it's not as big a deal when you think of it. I can be hurt, hurt bad. If it's *really* bad, I can take a very long time to heal. I can be kept prisoner, drugged, you name it. In other words, they might not be able to kill me but they can sure *stop* me, and if everybody and their sister knows about me, then I've got real trouble. I had this kind of situation once before, but then I had a number of friends and allies. Now—I don't know. And Mavra Chang's just like me, Gus. She's heading where I'm heading, too. If she gets there before I do, all bets are off, including on me. She doesn't really know how complicated this business is, but she can get me out of the loop, anyway. She could even . . ." He paused a moment, as if the very concept were hitting him for the first time. "She could even *kill* me."

"Yeah? Would she do that?"

"She might. I don't know, Gus. I haven't seen her in . . . well, a *very* long time. We're strangers, really, at this point. And you say she was leading a band of Amazons in the Brazilian jungle?"

"Yep. The Stone Age type, too. Naked and painted and little poison darts and all that. I wouldn't worry as much about her as you are, though."

"No? Why not?"

"Well, they like got the same idea about her as about you. She's not in their legends and stuff, but the ones that believe the stories about you also believe she's another one like you. They're doin' the exact same thing to her. You can bet on it."

That made him feel a little better, but not much. "So they have us both running on treadmills, pushing hard and hardly moving."

"You're movin' now," Gus pointed out.

"Yeah, I guess. But sooner or later I have to land this thing. Hell, maybe sooner than later. I haven't exactly had a chance to check below and see if we have any usable provisions. If not, we're all gonna get very hungry and very thirsty very fast."

"Well, that's a point. Is there anything I can do?"

Brazil thought a moment. "Yeah. I don't want to try you at the wheel in this weather, not unless you have some experience with these kind of ships."

"Canoes are my speed. Canoes and speedboats."

"I thought so. But you know what we need and you know what you need. You could look below and give me an inventory."

"No problem."

"Gus? Also look for charts. I know you probably can't read the stuff here, but you know what I mean by nautical charts. They have to have them somewhere. We're going to have to get our bearings when we get out of this blow and then decide where we have to go."

"Will do. I'll be back as soon as I can."

"Uh—Gus?"

"Yeah, Cap?"

"One more thing. You never answered my question as to why you didn't contact me before."

"Well, I started to, but then I saw Terry, and I didn't know what to do. I mean, you didn't know her before, Cap. She was bright and educated, spoke a half dozen languages, damned brave and good at her job, and real pretty, too. But more important, she was a talker, a real extrovert. I wasn't so sure I'd seen her lookin' anything like she did before, considerin' what happened to me and the colonel and all, but I didn't figure she'd be any more changed, you know, *inside,* than I was. Then I see her, and she don't notice me—it's not invisibility, Cap, it's just that folks don't *notice* me unless I wanta get noticed. And then she's stark naked, which is weird under most conditions but particularly weird in a climate like that one, she don't say a word, and she's got this weird blankness about her, even in her eyes. I mean, it didn't take no Einstein to know that somethin' far worse than what happened to me happened to her. Thing was, Cap, I didn't know how or why it happened, see? I mean, for all I knew, particularly with what they was sayin' about you, I mean, *you* coulda done it to her. I couldn't do nothin', see, until I was sure which side I wanted to be on."

Brazil didn't immediately look around, dealing as he was with keeping the ship righted, but finally he said, "Okay, fair enough. Let me know what you find!"

There was no response, and he looked around and saw nothing at all. For a moment he wasn't sure he'd seen the creature at all, but then he spotted the open hatch to the main cabin below and realized that the Dahir hadn't waited but had gone on down after their last words. Gone on down, and he hadn't seen him!

In a way, though, it was reassuring. The girl—Terry—hadn't seen him, either. Hadn't in fact seen him *yet*. There were limits on her as there were on him, after all.

He wondered just what the trick was about something that big being so invisible to others. Gus said it didn't work with cameras, so that meant it wasn't some kind of blending in, no chameleonlike attribute that somehow masked even so large a creature against a background. Sounds, too, seemed to be masked somewhat, maybe totally. He'd heard the creak of the timbers in that warehouse, and that had brought a sensation of footsteps, but had he really heard them? He certainly hadn't seen a damned thing when Gus hadn't wanted to be seen.

He also wasn't sure what Dahirs ate, but he certainly had sympathy for any of their menu items.

His thoughts drifted back to the girl. It was impossible to even imagine her as a worldly, vibrant mistress of technology and show business, a producer of highly visible news who'd probably been in a hundred danger spots all on her own and managed to survive and even thrive on that kind of thing. He had no reason to feel that Gus was putting him on; both he and the girl had, after all, been completely at the Dahir's mercy over the long haul, and Gus's own explanation of his actions rang true. But squaring the Terry that Gus had known, worked with, perhaps even loved, considering his devotion to finding her, with the eerie wordless mystic with the icy heart and strange and terrible powers who was back sitting behind the mast was next to impossible.

How much of that old Terry was still somewhere inside her? Had her essence simply walled off, or had she been reprogrammed beyond any hope of recall? Or was Terry the newswoman somehow still all there and along for the ride? Was her old personality erased or suppressed? Were her old memories gone or modified or merely filed under "old business" somewhere?

There *was* a real human being in there somewhere, he was sure of that. The girl who'd made love to him and fought alongside him and who had sent him signals on all those others with whom he'd come into contact was certainly no monster, and even if she had rejected or hadn't been able to use the sophistication of Ambreza or Hakazit, she'd understood it and coped with it. A savage would have been awed, amazed, confused by high-tech life; a savage would have had to be protected from being run over at the first busy street. She was neither ignorant nor stupid. What she did and what she would not do were conscious decisions to accept or reject, not the products of either upbringing or lack of understanding.

She manipulated that sailor as coldly as if he were a puppet . . . And with a coldness he'd never felt inside her before, not really. It was almost as if . . . as if she were two creatures, both Terry the human and *something else*. That something else, the coldness, had the power and made the rules, but in exchange it protected her against everything from the elements to sailors with guns, and so long as she followed its rules, then *it* was the passenger, emerging only as needed. Its control over her was not absolute; she, Terry, had overruled it and opted for his plea for mercy for the man over the other's computerlike direct and deadly course.

Not parasitism, then, but symbiosis of some sort. Terry had not been infected; rather, she had made a bargain and now had to live with the consequences.

If what he'd been told was true, if her news crew had been kidnapped out in the middle of the jungle by some Stone Age tribe of women, then the way Gus said he was treated made one kind of sense. But how did they treat the women they also took? From the pictures and data he'd gotten from Zone, they *all* looked like they'd walked in out of some cave in the distant past.

As with most primitive tribes who captured people, the prisoners were given a choice: join, assimilate, or die. All things considered, he'd have signed up if they'd have let him under those circumstances.

So they had been lost, taken captive, forced to live a Stone Age existence in a hostile jungle they didn't quite know and thus had become dependent on the tribe for survival—and then they had been translated here.

Terry hadn't come with the initial group, and that was a story only she could know. But she'd come before the gate had closed, alone, sneaking in past the monitors, seeing bizarre places and even more bizarre creatures. She'd followed to the Zone Gate and gone through, probably trying to catch her friends, and had wound up in Ambreza stark naked, defenseless, and scared to death. Why she went to Glathriel was another unknowable, but it was not hard to figure. Maybe she just saw some recognizable humans working for the Ambreza and followed them. It would be the natural, cautious choice of a survivor in a horrendous situation ignorant of where she was or what the hell was going on. So she'd gone in, made contact . . . and then what?

A bargain. Under the circumstances and considering what she'd just been through, who wouldn't take such a bargain? As in the jungle, what was the alternative?

It explained everything—and nothing. A bargain with whom? Or, more properly, *what*? There weren't any creatures like that on the Well World. At least no creatures designed and created here. The Well protected them from external influences, anything that would be a contaminant. It *couldn't* be an external force; even if it somehow got by the Well, such a thing would have caused the system to summon him long before it got this firmly established. Whatever it was, whatever had happened to the Glathrielians that had made them what they were, was homegrown, of *that* he was certain.

"There's what looks and smells like several kegs of beer, some fresh water, and those charts you wanted," Gus's voice suddenly said next to him.

Brazil jumped and lost the wheel again for a second. Wrestling it back, he yelled, "Now cut that out! You do that one time too often and we *are* going to capsize!"

"Hey, sorry! I *told* you I couldn't exactly turn it on or off."

"Well, make some noise, then! Yell at me as you're coming up! *Something!* At least when we're not in dangerous territory."

"Hey, I'll try, but it's always turned on. I practically have to shout in your face for you to consciously notice me."

And that, of course, was it. Somehow, something inside the Dahir broadcast something that could be received on some mental level by just about every other organic race. Something that made other beings simply not notice them. That was why he'd almost always been able to tell that somebody was there, following him. He *could* see Gus, would even give way for him, maybe with a "Beg your pardon." So could the girl; so could everybody else.

But some signal in the mind said, "Pay no attention to him. Don't notice him at all. He's not interesting or important."

Gus, he decided, for all his worldly experience and ambitions, was a bit too much the product of his roots to see the real possibilities here.

Why, with a little technical help, Brazil thought, the Dahir could become the greatest bank robber in history.

Still, for all the problems a being he never noticed until it yelled for his attention presented to his nerves and his long-standing paranoia, he was glad to have the big creature along. In one being Gus gave his team physical strength, unparalleled scouting, and spying potential, and most of all, Gus gave him somebody to talk to.

"How long can you keep this up?" Gus asked him worriedly, watching the small man fighting the wheel and seemingly doing three things at once all the time.

"Oh, a good while. I've had a lot of rest these past several weeks, and I've seen worse than this. If I can get us around the storm to where we can use it, you might spell me. Until then you'll probably have to find me something to serve as a chamber pot before long. Until then, could you get me a tankard or mug or whatever they use of that beer?"

"Sure. You want some of the bread, too? It's hard as nails, but it looks edible. At least, I'd have eaten it if I were hungry enough and still my old self."

"Yeah, thanks. You didn't mention the bread. That will help. But make sure those charts don't blow off anywhere! We're gonna need them bad as soon as I can get a look at them."

"I'll be sure. I'll leave them below until you want them. Beats me, though, how they'll do you much good here. I mean, how the hell do you know where you are now? We could be going in circles for all we know."

"No, I'm a better sailor than that. You're right, though, in the sense that we'll need to see the sun or stars to get a bearing and figure out exactly where we are. You see that little dome atop the wheel housing?"

"Uh, yeah, now that you mention it."

"Well, that's the equivalent of a compass here. That bubble is always at true north in this hemisphere. That's how I know we're not going in circles. We *have* been going farther west than I'd planned, but I couldn't guess at our speed or how far we've come, but against this wind it hasn't been all that much. That's why I'm trying to get the western edge of the storm. If I can catch it and keep steering forward with the wind at our back, we can hoist some real sail and make good time. Now, how about that beer and bread or whatever it is? And if you can, find me something to sit on!"

The wind was brisk but behind them, and under nearly full sail they were making excellent time in a north-northwesterly direction. Although he was more than a little hesitant, Gus took the wheel after some basic coaching by Brazil and found that it wasn't that hard, provided that little changed in the weather conditions and the seas remained fairly steady. Gus still didn't really want to do it, but he knew that Brazil had been at the wheel and fighting the storm for the better part of a day and into the night; he had to be totally exhausted.

Still, the little man hadn't gone down for a rest yet. He had taken the opportunity to inspect the ship from bow to stern and to inventory the supplies below, but he insisted on remaining near the wheel in case Gus should run into problems and need him in a hurry. Protesting that he was literally "too tired to sleep," he now used an oil lamp and sat there going over the charts and navigational books about the region.

Although they were out of the rain, the sky was still completely overcast, and in the darkness the stars could give him no guidance. He knew the bearing they were now on and had a fair estimate of their speed, but the hours of battling the storm itself gave him no clue as to just where on the charts he'd started from. He particularly worried that they might have gone far enough west to cross the Mowry border, though he thought he would have felt the passage through the hex boundary. While that wasn't in itself a problem, Mowry was a high-tech hex with all the sophisticated technology for locating almost anything on, above, or below its surface, and it was dotted with thousands of small volcanic islands, some of which were submerged and could easily wreck a ship.

Dlubine suited him far more. While he probably couldn't outrun a sleek steamer without a wind at least this good if not better, both mass communications and navigation were far more basic. Before he could be caught, they would have to know that it was he and immediately engage the chase.

Dlubine, too, had a number of islands, both volcanic and coral, but they would be more handy than a threat, or so he hoped. He wasn't at all sure what the Dlubine looked like, but the chart showed small harbors on some of the islands, indicating that they did a direct trade with surface ships. He was willing to take the risk.

If Gus could continue to bury his moral qualms, there should be little problem picking up what they needed on one of those. He hoped the natives were at least initially friendly, but that was a secondary concern. First, of course, he had to find them.

Finally, in spite of everything, he drifted off into a deep, deep sleep.

When he awoke groggily, feeling as if someone had beaten the hell out of him and he'd just recovered consciousness, he grew suddenly aware that the wind was down and there was direct sunlight hitting his skin. He opened his eyes, and for a moment sheer panic went through him as he saw no one at the wheel.

"Gus!" he called.

"Oh, you're awake," the gravel-voiced Dahir responded, and in the blink of an eye the huge, colorful snakelike form was there, less steering the ship than kind of leaning lazily on the wheel. "I was thinking of waking you up, considering I haven't had much rest myself."

Nathan Brazil nodded and got painfully to his feet. "God! I need an intravenous coffee transfusion," he groaned.

"Sorry. Fresh out. Never touch the stuff myself. You're stuck with water or beer for breakfast. I used to have a 'Beer—Breakfast of Champions' shirt once. Wouldn't fit now, though, I suppose, and I don't have much of a taste for beer anymore, either."

"Well, let me get some water on my face and see if I can wake up," the captain moaned. "Then, if you can hold on for another couple of minutes, I want to take some sightings of the sun and get a rough position." He went over to the small jug that was just where he'd left it in the night and splashed some of the water on his face and neck. It felt warm, but it was better than nothing. "How long was I out?"

"Can't say, not having a watch, but the sun's been up quite a while."

Nathan Brazil looked up and took a sight reading. "Um, yeah. *Way* up. Sun's not quite over the yardarm, though, so I'll pass on the beer. Uh, don't take this personally, but just exactly what the hell do you eat, anyway?"

"Most anything that won't eat me, really. Preferably live when I get it, but anything that's reasonably fresh is okay. Strictly carnivore. These small vampire teeth inject a nasty venom into whatever I want that kind of kills it and then softens it up so it goes down. Not much in the taste business, but if the critter's big enough, I don't have to eat or even drink much for days. Don't worry—I'd eaten just the night before we all scrammed out of Hakazit."

Brazil wasn't all that worried, but he decided for now not to ask what, in high-tech Hakazit, the Dahir had eaten.

"Have you ever heard of Dlubine?" Nathan Brazil asked the Dahir, changing the subject.

"No. Sounds like the noise you make when you throw up, sort of. Hell, I'm new here. *You're* supposed to be the expert, right? The god of the Well World, or am I being too limited?"

Brazil chuckled. "No, that's the reputation but hardly the truth. I'm the genuine handpicked successor to the equally genuine handpicked successor of the creatures that helped build this whole thing. We used to call them Markovians in the old days, a term without meaning now, but if I use it, you should know that's who I mean. The highest race in all creation, at least as far as there's any evidence. Got to the point where matter-to-energy and energy-to-matter conversions were old hat. Roamed the whole universe using interdimensional pathways; never needed to take a lot with them because they could have anything they needed by just willing it. They could *become* anything, too—so close, nobody could tell the difference. Just rearrange the atoms. They *knew* they were gods, too. And that's what drove 'em nuts."

"Huh?"

"Well, you ever consider the real problem of being a god? No surprises, nothing more to learn, nothing new to discover, everything you ever wanted or needed there at your whim. Not even time has any real meaning to a god, not in the sense that it does to most folks. After a billion years or so things are absolutely the same, nothing to look forward to, just an endless present. Of course, they built this world as the center—the center of the universe, more or less. All their roads led to here, and from here. A whole damned planet-sized master computer that coordinated all the zillions of lesser ones and was the true source of their power. It's still here, still working, maybe thirty, thirty-five kilometers beneath us now. The whole damned ball except this surface shell is self-repairing, self-maintaining, just going on and on long after there was anybody around who could use its power."

Gus was appalled. "You mean they died of *boredom*?"

"More or less, I guess. I wasn't there, but I've kind of felt an affinity for them over time. But with me it's strictly one-way, from the Well to me, not me to the Well. To get in real communication with it and have access to any of its power, I have to be inside, at the controls, in the form of one of the founding race. No other form I know can handle it. A big lump of a rubbery brain case with six huge but remarkably sensitive tentacles. You don't even need eyes or a nose or a mouth or any of that. You're kind of beyond all that. You don't just see an object in three dimensions, you see it in *all* dimensions, and you see it from all angles at once. Things you couldn't even keep all in your head become so simple and obvious, they don't even require thought. And what you don't know, the Well does, and it's all there and available to you. The powers of God almighty, almost."

"I'm surprised that you change back," the Dahir commented. "Seems to me it'd be kinda hard to give that up, at least until you had your own billion years or so to get bored in."

"No, it's not that simple. Maybe if I *was* one of them it would be, but I'm not. I have strict limitations on what I can and can't do. I've got the form and the power while I'm in there, yeah, but not the independence. I'm not there to tell the Well what to do, I'm there because the Well needs me to do something it can't do itself. And when I do it, it wants me out of there, pronto. Back in the tool chest, as it were, until the next time."

"But it's true you can't be killed?"

"It's true. Something, no matter how ridiculous the odds, always comes along to save my ass. Not that I can't get hurt or have all the other problems that anybody else might have, including all the weaknesses, but no matter what, I'll survive. The Well manipulates probability so I'm available if needed. You know, I once stood in front of a firing squad, and every damned rifle was defective? I've survived massacres, even a crucifixion or so. Even so, I guess I've been shot, stabbed, speared, strangled, drowned, you name it, many a time. No matter what, something happens to save me. I will tell you, though, that it's no fun at all."

"Yeah, I can believe that. Still, I'd think you'd be a mass of stumps and scars by now."

Nathan Brazil shook his head. "Nope. Every part of me constantly regenerates. Cut off an arm and it'll hurt like hell, but eventually I'll grow a new one. Even my brain regenerates, which causes trouble over time. There's not enough room in there to store or copy all the information you get from living so long. Eventually, things you don't need or haven't thought about in a long time just get spooled off, stored by the Well, outside of your head. I don't know how much I've forgotten, but it must be an enormous amount. There were times, I know, when I had no memory of who or what I was at all, until I got manipulated and wound up spending time here. The funny thing is, while I don't remember those periods all that much, I think of them as the happiest of times. After you live as long as I have, you discover that ignorance really is bliss."

"You sound like you'd almost like to join those Ancient Ones," Gus noted.

"Sometimes, maybe a lot of times, I think about that. The last time— the details are hazy, but I know I'd just gotten so damned sick of it, I was ready to at least start the process. See, I'm the safety valve, the one left around just in case there was something those Ancient Ones hadn't thought of. Like my predecessor, I can't quit until somebody else is groomed to take my place and has proved acceptable and competent to the Well."

"This Mavra Chang. She was supposed to be your replacement?"

He nodded. "In a way, anyway. At least it was a start. I took her in, changed her so that she was part of the Well's system, and made her do all the work. I remember that much. Then we had to go through a whole new cycle to see if she could and would be able to handle the burden. I really thought she could, but now I'm not so sure."

"You were—together? For a long time?"

"Yeah, a long time. Oh, we split up on occasion, but we always arranged to meet at some place, some time. Then, one time, she just said she was going down to the bazaar for a few things, walked out of the place where we were staying, and I never saw or heard from her again. We had our fights, but we weren't fighting then. There wasn't anything I ever could put a finger on. She just vanished. I searched for her, of course, not just then but for many long years after. Occasionally I'd hear stories or tales or ninthhand legends that sounded like her, but they never panned out. After a while I just stopped looking. I figured that if she really wanted to find me, my habits and preferences were an open book to her and she'd eventually at least get word to me. She never did."

"Huh! How long ago was it when she split?"

He shrugged. "I've lost count. But the house was just inside the Ishtar Gate in Babylon during the reign of Nebuchadnezzar the Great. What would that be in current Earth terms? A few hundred B.C., I guess."

"Jesus! That's like twenty-five *hundred* years or so!"

Brazil shrugged again. "I said it had been a long time. You ever notice that the older you get, the faster time seems to run?"

"Yeah. It's a cruel joke. I guess it's because each day you live becomes a smaller fraction of your total life, or so I've been told."

"That's about it. Well, you can see how even that kind of time span might not seem so ancient to me. Funny, though. Some of that ancient stuff I can see like it was yesterday, while other stuff, maybe only a few months or years ago, I can't remember at all. I guess we remember the highlights and the lowlights, and the rest gets caught in the cracks."

Gus thought about it, but such a life over so much time made his head spin. "Sure would've liked to have had a camera and tape along back there, though. Man, I bet it was *somethin'*!"

"Yeah, well, it was. But it was also before any real medicine, before mass communication, before a lot of creature comforts. People died young, and they lived lives harder than you can imagine, most of them. Even the rich didn't live all that great by modern standards. Smelled like a garbage dump, too. Folks just tossed it anywhere at all, and almost nobody took baths because the water had so many parasites in it, you could die slowly from a refreshing dip. No, on the whole I prefer things as high-tech as you can get, except, of course, on this particular trip."

Gus wasn't thinking of Brazil's colorful past, though, but of what he'd said before. "This Mavra Chang—this Well computer or whatever it is considers her the same as you?"

"Pretty much, yes. Oh, I see what you're driving at. You're asking if she could do the kinds of things that are supposed to be my job if she got inside."

"Right. Could she?"

"Yes, I'm pretty sure she could."

"She's nuts, Cap. You know that. I mean, livin' as one of those naked savages in the middle of the jungle, all them women—she sure don't have much liking for men. Maybe she did once, but not now. I remember enough of it to say that for sure. Maybe she just couldn't handle it, Cap. Maybe all them years, what you got as memories she's got as hurts. Some guy, or a lot of 'em, put her 'round the bend but good. I hate to point this out, Cap, but you're the only equal she's got, and you're a man. You said she was groomed to take over. If she gets in there first, she could unplug you same as you plugged her in, couldn't she?"

Nathan Brazil felt a numbing chill deep inside him in spite of the tropical warmth as he saw just what Gus was trying to point out. It was the one thought he had not wanted to think or dared consider, yet there it was.

"Yes, Gus," he admitted. "Yes, I suppose she could."

It was something he had long thought about and even occasionally desired, but always before it had been an abstract problem, something safe to think about because it was impossible.

It wasn't impossible. Not this time. Gus was absolutely right.

I might actually die this time . . .

GEKIR

EVEN IN THE NEARLY total darkness it was easy to know when they had crossed the border from Itus into Gekir.

The dense jungle ended abruptly, as if cut off, and in its place was a wide, flat expanse of grasslands punctuated with groves of trees. The nearly omnipresent clouds were gone as well; the sky blazed brightly from the dense stars in the Well World's spectacular sky.

Walking through the hex barrier instantly lowered the humidity to a small percentage of what it had been, and instead of feeling heavy, tired, and dragged down by the earth underfoot, all of them felt a sudden sense of relief as if a very heavy pack had been lifted from each of their backs.

"Now, is this gravity back to normal, or is this place actually *below* normal as the last one was above it?" Julian asked quizzically, as much of herself as of the others.

"Impossible to say," a weary Mavra replied. "It would make sense to have a fairly large disparity, though, simply because it would keep the Ituns from being interested in spreading out over here and probably the other way around, too. To tell you the truth, it hadn't been so dramatic in the places I was last time, at least so I could notice."

"Now what?" one of the centauresses—Tony, from the accent—asked. "Is anybody around here we should worry about?"

"You worry about *everything* on this world," Mavra warned. "Even the friendly places. There's not much chance of diseases—all but a very few don't even travel well between species on Earth, and they're all much closer than the ones here—but meat eaters still eat the meat of carbon-based forms and many plants and animals are potentially poisonous. Even potentially friendly tribes tend sometimes to shoot first and ask questions later. Julian?"

The Erdomese shifted to the infrared spectrum and scanned the relatively flat grasslands. "There are whole herds of creatures out there, most bunched close together and showing little sign of activity. Asleep, probably."

"You think they're natives?" Anne Marie asked, suddenly feeling a little bit refreshed by the lowered gravity and humidity but still feeling sore from the burdens of Itus.

"Who can say? But I tend to doubt it. I've seen the same sort of patterns with cows out on the western ranges and such, and you'd figure that a race would have some kind of night watch and probably fires or the remains of fires that I could easily see. If Earth is any example, and it seems to be to at least *some* extent, then this is a savanna, much like east Africa. That means lots of herd-type animals, which is what the patterns here suggest. Like the antelope. There are probably a lot of other creatures who are also grass eaters here."

Lori had slept for a while and had finally awakened just before the crossing when he'd shifted a bit and his horn had jabbed Tony in the back.

"Where there's a lot of herbivores," he noted, "there are also carnivores. Probably not all intelligent, either. You've got a finite space here, no matter how large a hex is, so something, usually a combination of things, has to keep the population managed. The gravity barrier and maybe incompatible vegetation would keep the animals on this side of the line, but what keeps them in balance?"

Mavra nodded. "We've got to make a camp. Tromping through this meter-high grass for any length of time at night, we're likely to start a stampede, and that's the *last* thing we want. Who knows what this stuff could conceal, too?"

"There is a large stand of trees just about two kilometers in," Julian noted. "It would afford some shelter and protection."

Mavra was dubious. "That's your Erdomese instincts talking. In the desert you head for the trees and the oasis. Think more like the Africa you talked about. I remember a part of it much like this, going on almost forever. It was *huge,* with vast herds of game and great cities and civilizations, until the coastal folks chopped down all the trees and the rains were able to erode and undermine the soft rock and good soil and the whole thing turned into a desert. The last time I was there, it was desert wasteland from almost the Mediterranean shore as far in as I knew. When I saw what had happened and what greatness had been lost, I cried, and I don't do that much."

She paused a moment, remembering the devastation, the eternity of baking hot sand, then regained control.

"Well," she continued, "the point is that when you had thick areas of trees like the ones you describe, it meant a water hole, maybe a spring at the surface, just as in the desert, but it also was where all the nastiest predators went and spent the night. Wouldn't you? They sure don't sleep out here in the grass. Otherwise the herds of prey would be somewhere else. You don't see any signs of some kind of camp, some kind of civilization in that grove, do you?"

Both Julian and Lori looked hard, using magnification as well. "No," Lori answered after a bit. "But you're right; there are some pretty large creatures in those trees."

Julian pointed to their left a bit. "The grass seems to get lower over there. It is possible that there is some surface rock. I do not see anything much right in that area, either. Lori?"

"No, I don't, either. It's a good bet, although it won't give us a lot of cover."

"Better than nothing," Mavra said at last. "We're not exactly inconspicuous anywhere in these parts, you know."

"Or anywhere else, as a group," Lori agreed.

"Well, I for one think we all look just *splendid*!" Anne Marie announced, missing the point.

The area *was* a rocky outcropping that wind and rain had worn clean of soil. It was a large tabular rock, cracked in a few places, that ran about twelve meters by nine. There were some raised sections of what looked like the same material along two sides, although nothing that would really conceal them from an interested onlooker. It was, however, barren of grass and didn't seem to have been staked out by anything else alive, and that was good enough.

"It's basically a form of sandstone," Julian noted, "not unlike on Earth. It's a common pattern. The stuff will eventually erode back to sand—you can see some of that along the back side there—and probably underlies the whole plain. Basically, this isn't much different than Erdom, except that this region gets an adequate rainfall that allows the grass to grow and stabilize the rock."

Mavra nodded. "That's right. You were a geologist, weren't you? Okay, let's get the bedrolls down for us three bipeds. Anne Marie, do you still have the firestarter? I want to check on something."

"Yes, yes. I believe . . . Half a moment!" With that the centauress turned on her forward hips almost all the way around and fumbled in one of the large packs, then said, "Aha!" She pulled out a long, thin metallic rod and handed it to Mavra.

As the supplies were taken off and the three bedrolls were spread out in the middle of the slab, Mavra went over, picked a strand of the grass, and brought it back to the center of the rock, well away from anything else. She pressed a button on the end of the stick, and from the other end came a tiny jet of flame, which she applied to the grass.

It caught fire but went out as soon as she removed the source of the flame. She tried it two or three times, and each time the result was the same. Satisfied, she tossed the remains of the grass stalk away and put the lighter back in the pack.

"If you don't mind, what was *that* about?" Tony asked her.

"Testing fire hazard. Either it's not long after the rainy season or this soil really holds water well. Maybe both," Mavra explained. "It also means that the grass is probably just grass. Plus, it shows that the reason for not seeing any sort of fires or fire remains isn't because it's too dangerous to build one. And *that* probably means there aren't any Gekirs around at the moment, whatever they are."

"Either that or they just don't use fire," Lori noted.

Mavra gave her a look she hoped the Erdomese could see in the darkness. "Don't kill my optimism too quickly! I was *enjoying* this," she said grumpily.

Lori looked around with his night vision from atop the centaur's back. "I wonder what would be the most logical life-form for a place like this?"

"Either carnivores or omnivores," Tony guessed. "Probably carnivores. They would have the most stake in managing such a place, and it would explain the lack of any sort of groves or cultivation in such a desirable spot. I would wager that they eat a lot of meat, anyway."

Lori frowned. "Um, I hate to bring this up, but you Dillians are herbivores, aren't you? And Erdomese are basically herbivores, too." He decided not to mention that another staple of the Erdomese diet was almost any form of insect. He realized that that might well put the others off.

"*That,* I think, was the point," Mavra commented dryly, deciding not to remind them that she was the only true omnivore there. She looked around. "We *could* risk a fire, though, either to ward off our theoretical predators or even to cook something. I'm not going hunting out there, though."

"Get me down first," Lori asked. "I'm feeling a little better. Julian—help support me and I'll see how the ankle is doing."

She came over as Anne Marie lifted Lori off Tony's back and gently to the ground, where Julian braced him.

He tried a few steps, and although he continued to put a hand on her shoulder, it was more as a stabilizer than as a full support. "Not too bad," he said. "It's still sore, but it feels a *lot* better. At least I know now that it's not broken." He took his hand away from Julian and tried an uncertain step, then reached out with his right hand and pushed on Tony's side. "*Ow!* Damn! I think the *leg's* going to be fine, but my wrist feels *terrible!* Shit! And I'm right-handed!"

Julian looked first at his leg, then at his wrist. "There is very slight swelling in the leg, my husband, but as you say, it does not look like much. Perhaps one more day of riding and then you should be able to walk. The wrist, though, looks very bad. It should be in a splint and bandaged."

Mavra came over to them. "Trouble?"

"His wrist," Julian told her. "It is bad, and I do not know how bad."

"Can't you feel along it for a break?"

"No, she can't," Lori told her. "Because our females carry children to term on all fours, they need forelegs, and the way that's done makes their hand basically a hard, fixed surface and a thick separate segment for grasping. But no fingers as such."

It disturbed Mavra that she'd barely noticed. "Let me see. Give me your hand, Julian." She took it and felt it. It was hard and resembled a hoof, but unlike a true hoof, the hand was segmented in two parts, one tapered and rounded and a bit softer inside so that it could be used as a giant thumb against the other, slightly flexible part. When closed, it made a nearly perfect hoof. "That's *awful!*" she exclaimed, then immediately felt terrible because she'd said it.

"Oh, it's not bad once you get used to it," Julian replied sympathetically, remembering how *she* had felt when she'd first awakened and seen those strange hands. "You would be surprised what I can do with them. Not as much as true hands, but about as much as, say, mittens would allow. No, the *real* problem is, since I can use them as forelegs, I have no feeling in them. Having no sense of touch in my hands, I have to be looking at them whenever I am using them. That's all right for many things, but there is no way I can feel Lori's wrists."

"You'd be surprised how much she *can* do with them," Lori assured Mavra. "But not this."

"Well, then, big man, grit those teeth, because *I* sure can," the tiny woman replied. She took his right hand, noting how squared off and hard his hands were, even with three distinct and bendable fingers and a fairly prehensile thumb, then felt back to the wrist.

"*Augh!*" Lori grunted in obvious pain.

Mavra let go and shook her head. "I think you might well have some kind of a fracture there. I didn't feel any protrusions, though, so it's not a clean break we can set. Probably some hairline thing or chip. That swelling *is* pretty bad, though. It's hard to say how it would heal—I don't know enough about Erdomese, obviously, to make a guess—but Julian's right. We're gonna have to bind it in some kind of splint so it's immobile and then bandage it. Bandages we got in the pack, and tape, so if we can find something to use as a splint, we'll be okay. I don't know what I can give you to treat the inflammation, though. The stuff that would help me might kill you or burn a hole through your stomach."

"Believe it or not, aspirin," Lori told her. "It seems aspirin is the number one miracle drug of Erdom. We don't make it, but I ran into a drug trader on the ship to Itus. One of our biggest imports."

Mavra sighed. "Well, I have a small tube of aspirin tablets in the pack for my own use. I wish I'd known—or thought to ask. It sure explains why I was able to buy it in the dockside shops! I doubt if there's more than sixty tablets, though, and you, with your large size and particularly with that break, will need all of it and more. Lie down on the bedroll and I'll get them."

With Julian's help, he managed to get over to the bedroll and sink down on top of it. Mavra came back with the small vial of aspirin and a canteen. "I'd take four of them now if I were you. Damn it! We should have started this as soon as we started out!"

They pried apart the plastic box Mavra had used as a medical kit and were able to form, with the aid of a large knife, a pretty rigid set of splints that were tightly taped to the wrist, lower arm, and hand, then wrapped with a green-colored plastic bandage. When it was done, Lori could not move the wrist at all, and after an initial, intense period of pain, it subsided and he felt some relief. Then it was a matter of waiting for the aspirin to kick in.

Anne Marie came over to them. "I do so hope that does it," she said, concerned. "I know how it feels."

Mavra nodded. "What do you want to do about something to eat?"

"Well, the grass *smelled* all right, so we tried some and it will do. We have to eat an awful *lot*, you know. While I'd much rather have it processed, baked in breads and cakes and pastries, or steamed with veggies and spices, that seems a *teeny* bit impractical here. We'll just graze nearby until we've had our fill. As basic as it is, it is ever so much better than those *horrid* jungle leaves!"

"Okay, but don't stray too far from camp," Mavra warned. "You don't know what's out there."

"We'll be careful. We drank our fill in that stream back in Itus, so water is not a problem. Back as soon as we can. Ta!"

"Are they *safe* out there alone and unarmed?" Julian asked worriedly.

"Dillians are tougher than they seem, or at least they used to be," Mavra assured her. "Those hooves can give a hell of a nasty kick, and while their arm strength isn't close to a male Dillian's, they're pretty damned strong compared to us or most others, and I have a feeling that they can twist and move those bodies in ways we can only imagine. And they're not unarmed, really. They both have the big knives we used on the jungle vines."

"You have other weapons, I assume?" Lori asked.

"Some. The absolute best weapons for the Well World are knives for close in and crossbows for long shots."

"Crossbows?"

"Sure. They're accurate and powerful, and they work anywhere: nontech, semitech, or high-tech. I have some other items, too, but they're for various special circumstances."

"I have a saber and scabbard in my pack," Lori told her. "I was pretty good with it, too, but I'm not sure how well I'd do left-handed."

"Well, you won't have to fight a duel with it—I hope. So long as you can stab something with it, I think it's better than nothing. You sure aren't gonna be winning any fistfights any time soon!" She paused a moment. "What about food for you two? I have a small kerosene-type cooker that'll work here, or there are loaves in the emergency rations that supposedly give any of us what we need. They taste lousy, but they're better than raw grass."

"I could prepare something from the supplies," Julian suggested, but Lori shook his head.

"No, not tonight. Tonight's for resting and taking it easy. If Mavra can stand one of those loaves, so can I. I might like it a lot more than she does."

"Or less. Still, very well, if that is your wish. I could try the grass, but I do not want to leave you alone here."

"No! Eat one of the loaves, too. We're heading for the coast, which shouldn't be that far, right, Mavra?"

"Shouldn't be. Certainly not a day's walk."

"When we are hard up, we will eat grass. Until then we will do what is easiest and most convenient," he pronounced.

"As you say," Julian responded, and went to get the rations.

Mavra was a little irritated. Julian had talked about the confusion over Tony and Anne Marie, but at least there were two of them. She began to wonder if there weren't two Julians as well—the one that led them through a dark jungle safely, reconnoitered the area, and located and approved the campsite and the other one that she now was, subservient, obedient . . . somewhat sickening.

On the other hand, if she had four big tits, hands like claws, arms useless for much lifting and better designed as legs, and if the only hope she had of not being cast adrift as some kind of chattel slave was to keep the one husband who understood her happy enough to keep her around, then maybe she'd be two people, too, no matter how difficult it might be.

She had, after all, been in situations not any better than Julian's. Ancient Earth wasn't kind to most women. The way Tony, Anne Marie, and Julian had talked, that was true even now on much of the planet. Chinese peasant women still toiled in the rice paddies; the women in theocracies like the Islamic fundamentalist cultures were kept without rights, voices, or free movement. It was little better in much of sub-Saharan Africa, India, or even a lot of Latin America. In what they called the Third World, the eighty percent or more of humankind was largely forgotten or ignored by the feminist crusaders in the industrialized west, most of whom also forgot or never knew that revolutions were often followed by reactions that could leave them worse off than ever. She had seen it happen.

She had *lived* it.

Time after time the great civilizations, the great ideas, the progress of whole masses of humanity were stopped dead and thrown back, often for longer than generations. Sometimes the darkness lasted many long centuries. Two steps forward and then one back was the norm, or so it seemed, but the darkness could rise and force one back even farther. If, as she'd been told, the status of women in some parts of Earth, let alone so much of it, was different from that in Erdom only by degrees, then the darkness still loomed, waiting to engulf the rest. And that darkness, the darkness of ignorance and slavery that was the dark side of humanity, would be replayed again and again if Nathan Brazil triumphed, even though he himself would have been appalled at that interpretation.

It didn't have to happen. It certainly didn't have to happen the same way and to the same people again. The Markovians—she still thought of the Ancient Ones by that name although Jared Markov, after whom they were named, had not yet been born this time around—were wrong in believing that there was a level of perfection attainable by races fighting their way up the evolutionary ladder. They were right to try to understand and fight the flaws, but the result was that the flaws were simply perpetuated.

That, at least, she could change. She *might* change. But if, and only if, she got into the Well first.

"I'll take the first watch," Lori said, breaking Mavra's reverie. "I slept most of the way here, and I'm fine now."

Mavra nodded. "All right. Julian and I will try to get some sleep. If the Dillians don't come back in an hour or so, wake me. If they do, then give me at least four hours. I've functioned on that little for days at a time."

She thought a moment. "I don't want to give you a loaded crossbow with that pair still out there if you're not experienced in using one. I'll get your saber so at least you can hit something over the head if it jumps on you, but what I really want is a loud yell. I'll give you my watch. It's a windup type, so it works anywhere, too."

He grinned. "Don't worry so much. I can see in the dark, remember? I've even been keeping track of the centaurs. I'll be okay."

"In fact, I should take the next watch, not you, for the same reason," Julian pointed out. "The nights are long on this world, and it is best that the night guard be those to whom the dark is no barrier."

"I won't argue, but are you sure you're up to it on so little sleep?" Mavra asked her.

"Yes. I do not need a lot of sleep, either. I make it up when I can."

"Okay, it makes sense to me. If all else fails, we can let you sleep and ride as well." Mavra yawned. "Me, I'm gonna take advantage of your kind offer."

"You get to sleep, too," Lori told Julian. "I'll be all right."

"Yes, my husband," she responded, and lay down on the unoccupied bedroll.

Tony and Anne Marie came back a half hour later. By that time Mavra and Julian were both asleep, and the Dillians tried to make as little noise as possible. They didn't need bedrolls or much else; like horses, they lay down only when crippled or very ill. Instead, they simply stood, their legs locked and the humanoid torsos bent back somewhat, and went to sleep.

Except for the occasional heavy breathing of the centauresses, it was soon deathly still.

Lori, too, wondered about Julian's dual nature. He himself felt pretty well adjusted to the Erdomese form and now even to being male. Maybe *too* adjusted, he had to admit, considering some of his behavior of late, but he felt that he was being pragmatic about things. By Erdomese standards, he thought, he would always be a liberal, always remembering that the females had minds and thoughts and feelings and capabilities most of that society rejected and, hopefully, treating them better than most men there did. On the other hand, in *that* society any outspoken advocacy was a sure route to losing everything and to punishments including cutting out his tongue, castration, and beheading. For Julian it would mean instant death. With the church and its omnipresent spies and true believers programmed from childhood to believe in it and with the enforced insularity of most of the population from real knowledge of much of the rest of this world, nothing could or would change in Erdom's society until and unless there was violent mass revolution.

It might well come eventually, but considering how things there were now, it most assuredly would not be in his or Julian's lifetime. It wasn't until experiencing a real totalitarian theocracy that he had realized just how hard a revolution could be, battling not only minds but genuine power. Technology, discovery, enlightenment, the scientific revolution—*that* had started things on Earth, or restarted them. But what kind of science could one develop when a battery would not hold a charge and tended to dissipate in even short transmission? When technology was rigidly and forever limited to water, and wind, and animal and human power? Without mass communication how could anything be organized? When even writing was limited primarily to the church and the hideously complex ideographic language was so complex that even priests were middle-aged before they fully mastered it, how could knowledge be disseminated?

"Some men do in fact run the world—and you're not one of them."

And the price for having a crack at being one of those men who *did* run Erdom was just too damned high.

Still, he had to admit, it *was* different being a man in a male-dominated society. The fact was, he was beginning to *like* this form, even if he didn't like the culture and chafed at the hex's technological restrictions. This form was beginning to—no, it *did* feel natural, normal, comfortable. He never even *thought* about it anymore. Funny. He'd been born and raised an Earth-human female and had spent almost forty years as one; he'd been an Erdomese male for a matter of a few months, no more. Yet Mavra Chang seemed an ugly, colorless, unattractive . . . *alien* to him, while Julian was beautiful, desirable. Lori Ann had never been sexually attracted to women no matter how much she fought the male system. Lori the Erdomese couldn't remember what turned Lori Ann on in a man or see the least attraction there.

Each day it was getting harder and harder to remember what it had been like to be an Earth-human woman. Not the past, not the events of a life, or the people, or the learning and accomplishments, the struggles, losses, and gains, but remembering being the one who had lived it. That person seemed more and more to be someone else, like a character from a movie she'd watched, a movie spanning forty years of a woman's life.

Was that how it worked? First one got the new body, along with sufficient programming on the brain's subconscious level to use it without serious trouble, and a bit of suggestion so that one was not frightened or revolted by what one saw or what one might need to eat, but it was still the original person, superimposed on an alien form.

But that form's brain had to be different from an Earth human's, if only in subtle but important details. Neural pathways would be wired differently; thoughts would need to be rerouted so that action produced the desired results. If there were subtle differences in the wiring of the hemispheres in male and female human brains, how much more dramatic would that wiring difference be in a totally different species? Add hormones and other chemical differences that would eventually influence development as the mind "settled in," and one's old self, one's memories, one's very soul, would be reshaped day by day so slowly and subtly that a person might not even notice. But one day that person would be wholly of the other species, as if born to it.

Lori Ann had been *playing* at being a man, enjoying fooling with the very concept as if it were some kind of masquerade gender-switch game. He wasn't playing anymore, and he wasn't even sure when he had stopped. He *was* a male now. It was one of the basic things that defined him. What flowed from that sense of identity defined his actions and reactions to a host of things both internal and external.

If it had happened to him like this, it almost certainly had happened to Julian. She'd come in months earlier than he had, but her own situation had been so radical a cultural loss that she'd fought like hell against it, while overall, he had to admit to himself that he'd not really fought it in himself at all. Still, by the time he'd met her, she already admitted that she had accepted being female, that it was something that no longer disturbed her. She'd fought not that but the concept that she was property, that she was to be consigned to a base role as if in a medieval harem. It was something Lori Ann would have fought just as hard against.

Maybe those drugs and hypnotic sessions had accelerated the process for both of them; maybe not. But if Julian now felt as normal and natural as an Erdomese female as he did as an Erdomese male, she might also, away from Erdom but still with him, have stopped fighting the rest.

It made sense. He thought of the two Dillians, who seemed so alike outside and so different inside, and knew that they really weren't. Anne Marie really hadn't been required to adjust much, but to Tony it must have been as much of a shock to be a female as it had been for Julian initially—although Julian also had the restrictive Erdomese culture to deal with. They'd been here the longest of any of this party. They'd come through the night the meteors fell.

Tony still thought he hadn't changed inside, partly, Lori suspected, because Anne Marie still saw the old Tony inside the new body because she wanted to see him there. But he *had* changed. He *was* different. They had talked for a bit, being so, well, *close,* during the walk, and since he had the translator Tony could speak Dillian, which was easier. And when she spoke Dillian rather than English, there were only slight differences between her and Anne Marie's speech patterns. In her normal speech, in her manner, her movements, even many of the things she spoke about, Tony was as feminine as Lori Ann Sutton had ever been. Tony admitted that she'd stopped fighting when she had realized that Anne Marie never noticed any difference. In any event, Tony knew she couldn't stave it off forever and would have to let go sooner or later. Now she was just playacting being the old Tony; he was as past tense as the old Lori Ann was.

"I feel real pity for your Julian," Tony had told him. "I would not accept that life. But in Dillia it is different; the practical day-to-day differences in the lives of men and women there are not radical enough to cause alarm, and in the few areas where they are, the benefits of being male are balanced against the benefits of being female. It is not at all like my old culture, nor, perhaps, your old one, either. It would have been nicer, perhaps, and more romantic to have been Anne Marie's husband rather than her twin sister, but we can no more change that now than we could change ourselves before. This is second best, and we will take it."

In truth, the old Tony still existed only when she was required to speak English. Other than that, Tony and Anne Marie had each drawn from the other what they had found most valuable and had become, in Dillian terms, very much alike indeed. It was as if they had been born twin sisters, with the exception that Tony would never be able to grow proper roses or be half the cook Anne Marie could be, and Anne Marie would never be able to pilot a jet aircraft and would never be that good at repairing even simple mechanical things. That difference was enough to allow each of them to retain a sense of individuality and a connection with their pasts, and it really was enough.

Lori had asked Tony why, if things were working out so well for them, they'd agreed to undertake a very long and difficult journey over land and sea to meet a strange and mysterious woman they didn't know.

"Curiosity most of all," Tony had replied. "A way to see more of this strange and mysterious world than we could any other way. Our passage had, after all, been prepaid, and we verified that every hex had a Zone Gate and from Zone we could be instantly back in Dillia no matter how far in the world we roamed, so return tickets were not a worry, either. And, I admit, timing played some part in our motivation."

"Timing?"

"Yes. You see, Dillian women ovulate only twice a year, for about a three-week period each time. It is not that they do not do things recreationally, as it were, but it only *counts* during each of those three-week periods. While we have more control than an animal would, we were told that during that time women of childbearing age get 'turned on,' one might say, and *stay* that way for the duration. I can now tell you that it is indeed true and that it is a whole-body experience, and further that *much* willpower is required to function even close to normally at that time. Dillians grow up with it and learn to cope with their parents' help. In Dillia it is the females who almost always seduce the males. We, neither of us, were quite ready for that as yet, I fear, and if we had done it and even one of us had gotten pregnant—no sure thing, because the Well governs population—we would have wound up *never* traveling."

Lori could well understand. "Um—do you get periods, too?"

"Twice a year as well, and about ten days long. They are *most* unpleasant, but we can function feeling awful a lot better than we can function during the arousal stage, I can tell you."

"I know," Lori sighed. That was the experience that defined growing up female more than any other, and the lack of it now was one of the best things about being male. He looked back at Anne Marie, the twin of the creature he was riding, and commented, "Too bad you and Julian will both miss shopping for shoes, though."

Now, as he sat there in the darkness, he tried putting a little weight on the ankle and was pleased to notice that the pain was very mild now. In an emergency he would have no compunctions about getting up and running on it, even if he might still pay for that later. The hand, though, was another story. If anything, he was more right-handed than Lori Ann had ever been; his left hand was useful mostly for support of whatever the right hand was doing. The aspirin had helped; he never remembered it doing this good a job on a human headache and suspected that there was a different biochemistry at work here, for once in his favor.

Not enough, though. It still hurt, and the fingers felt numb, a lot more than could be explained by the splint and bandages. The automated clinic back on the east coast of Itus was a long way away now. He had no idea how far away the next high-tech hex they might reach was or whether they would know how to repair a broken Erdomese there. What if the hand had to come off? There weren't many prospects for one-handed men in Erdom. He began to feel panic at the thought, and that just made the awareness of the pain worse. He fought it, tried to push it back down, and finally got some self-control back, but he was feeling dizzy and nauseous. Scared, he reached over and shook Julian, who stirred, shook herself awake, then frowned and immediately was up and at his side.

"You have a fever," she told him in a concerned whisper. "A very bad one. You are glowing like a camp fire. How long did you let me sleep?" She reached over and picked up the watch. "Five hours." The remains of the medical kit were on a blanket near them, and she went over and picked up the small vial of aspirin. "Here. *Curse these hands!*" She managed to get the top off but couldn't get the pills out. "Give me your hand and I will try and shake them into it."

Lori nodded, shaking now, and put out his left hand. She shook out a half dozen pills, then scooped up two with the lip of the vial and got him a canteen. He got the pills down, but it would take some time for them to have any effect.

"Lie here beside me, husband," she told him, "and try to sleep if you can. I will be here and keep watch upon both the camp and you."

He moaned and shook and thrashed around for the better part of an hour before finally passing into sleep. Julian wasn't all that certain if he was just sleeping or if the fever had finally put him out, but there was nothing more that could be done.

Julian's thoughts were mixed but all bad. For one thing, she felt almost helpless in the situation. She could comfort him and check on him and see that he got aspirin until that was gone, and she could cover him, but she could do little more. The biggest frustration was that she knew nothing of Erdomese infections or even whether this kind of fever reaction was normal or terminal. She *did* assume that if it didn't break within a day, it was very bad indeed, but *then* what? Should he be kept cool or, as she'd automatically done, warm under a blanket?

She assumed that growing up Erdomese tended to give one at least a rough idea of these things just as Earth people had a rough idea of human reactions and illnesses simply by growing up human. Maybe they shouldn't have bandaged the hand. Maybe that cut off air flow or something, although there was no open wound and the bandages were mostly to keep the splint on.

I'm not even a good First Wife here, she thought miserably. *A first wife should know what to do.*

Of course, if they were back in Erdom, help could have been called. Not here. *All that education, that sophisticated background, and what's it worth?* she asked herself.

Nothing. Nothing at all. The revelation struck to the core of her ego and identity. All that Julian Beard had been, all that he'd learned, every scrap of sophisticated knowledge and the numerous skills he'd mastered, were not merely useless now, they were useless period. Sure, in training he'd learned probably the ultimate in first aid, but how much of that applied to Erdomese biology and what good was most of it without the proper instruments and medications on hand? What could she do if she had a decent kit, anyway? Even if she could put a thermometer in his mouth, for how long should it be in and what would be the correct reading? Useless, all useless. Julian Beard was someone trained for other conditions, another time, another world, another life.

Julian of Erdom was furious at Julian Beard for being worse than useless. *Incompetent, irrelevant, and immaterial.* She had clung to him desperately for so long, even decided at one point to die for him, and he was worthless. She rejected him in her fury. She understood now: this was totally new, a start from scratch, from *less* than scratch. All the feelings, impulses, inclinations that she'd pushed back for the sake of that precious ego had been not a personal victory but a brick wall. Her past was the wall, a useless thing that had kept her unhappily tied to a world and life and viewpoint no longer relevant. But the old Julian Beard wasn't there anymore. He was a ghost, an evil spirit that had led her only to this helpless situation.

It was probably too late, but she hated him now, rejected him, cast him out. She felt him go, like something solid and tangible that had been inside her head and heart and now was removed. It felt good, but—what was left?

Erdomese women served their husbands and families and extended families. She had a husband, but neither he nor she had anyone else, even in Erdom. He was all she had, and she felt that she had failed him. She looked down at him as he slept fitfully, and for the first time she looked at him entirely as an Erdomese female. She looked at his cute horn, the gentle strength of his face, and a flood of emotions and self-realizations swept through her, this time unchecked, unfiltered, without thought or inhibition.

She bent down to his face and whispered in his ear, "I love you, Lori. I love you and I need you."

He didn't come fully awake, but he seemed to hear, and there was a gentle smile on his face all of a sudden, as if he had banished nightmares for a more pleasant dream.

Julian was not really thinking, just letting her Erdomese body and brain act as they willed, performing actions that she neither knew nor cared made any sense or not. She bent over, raised his head gently, and offered him her lower right breast, one of the water carriers in a non-pregnant female's anatomy. He took it and began to drink. At first it was a little, as in foreplay, but after a bit he began really sucking and taking it in, even as she was licking his face with her long, thick tongue.

She had no idea how long she kept it up, but it was probably an hour or two before she noticed a dramatic change in him. The fierce glow was gone; there was only a slight residual shimmer, the natural aftereffect of the dangerous condition he'd had.

Lori's fever had broken.

Julian pulled back, exhausted, dehydrated, but also very, very happy to see and sense the change in him. He was going to be all right!

"We might light a small torch and take at look at that dressing," said a deep woman's voice behind her.

She started, turned, and saw Mavra Chang standing there.

"How—how long . . . ?" Julian managed, her voice raspy and dry.

"Pretty much since you started. *Somebody* had to guard the camp."

Julian felt suddenly ashamed, as if she'd done something *else* wrong. "I—I'm sorry. But—he was burning up with fever. I felt his life burning up inside him. I *had* to do *something*." She paused. "I just wish I knew what I did."

"Don't apologize. I heard him crying out and thrashing around and knew he had to have something nasty—I don't think I've actually slept soundly since I was aboard a ship in space, and you can't *believe* how long ago that was, nor can I. At first I couldn't figure out what you were doing, though," she admitted. In fact, although she didn't say it, what she had first made out in the bright starlight and then watched for a bit seemed pretty damned sick, a kind of prenecrophilia in which one made love to the dying. It took her experience with many alien species and her analytic mind to finally see a method in the apparent madness.

Julian still couldn't. "Uh—what *was* I doing?" she asked hesitantly. She felt really rotten herself at the moment.

Mavra smiled. "A long time ago—it seems like I use that term a lot these days—when I was just pushing puberty, I pondered the Universal Sexual Design Question like most everybody else I knew. If most every mother had one baby at a time and multiple births were rare, why did girls get two tits? The answer, of course, is *redundancy*. Then I saw that Erdomese women had quads, yet Erdomese births are not all that much different in number than Earth-human births. So why *four* breasts? Wasn't that taking redundancy to an extreme? Then I was told that the bottom two were water jugs when the system allowed it, and, probably like you, I accepted it as some sort of desert survival thing. I mean, you only need one guy to knock up a lot of females, but a lot of guys can't produce any more babies with one female than one guy. Made sense. You probably thought the same thing. Probably most Erdomese think that way."

"Yes? So?"

"I don't think so anymore. Oh, maybe that's *one* reason, but it's not the main one. I have nothing but the evidence of my own eyes here and the results, but I'll bet you what you did is done whenever a male is seriously ill. The face licking cools down the head in the only area of the body where your race can perspire to exchange heat. But that water—I don't think that's water at all. It's at body temperature, and the cooling effect is minimal, so what purpose does it serve? Then I remembered the female Uliks from a long time ago. Big, ugly suckers, cross between walruses and giant snakes, with six arms and three pair of breasts. *That* was bad enough, except that they laid eggs and the young were born with developed stomachs and teeth and were fed dead meat. Which of course brought up the question of why they had *any* tits, let alone six, when they didn't nurse their young."

"Yes? And?" Julian was exhausted, but she really wanted to know the point of this.

Mavra handed her a canteen. "Drink all of it. I *know* there's water over there, and we'll get some in a few hours. We have several more canteens, anyway."

Julian took it gratefully and found herself draining the whole canteen in almost a continuous series of gulps. When she was done, Mavra continued.

"See, the only thing you and a Ulik woman have in common is desert. I didn't think about it, but these ancient farts playing God here long ago weren't *all* creative geniuses. They stole a lot from one another. That's why there are so many humanlike life-forms, and why most races here seem to be themes and variations on other races, plants, animals, birds, bugs—you name it. It's obvious to me now that the ones working on desert races would peek at each other's work, steal from each other, even critique one another's work."

"The Ulik . . . ?" Julian prompted.

"The Ulik female takes in enough water to float a ship. Once inside her, the amount she doesn't use, and that's most of it, is stored in a series of sacs that have what look like breasts as outlets. But each 'breast' produces different stuff. There's a salt and mineral solution in a form that can be handled by the body to replenish what's lost. Another takes vitamins from food and creates a vitamin solution of sorts. But the bottom pair have a solution that contains universal antibodies of some kind of supercharged type. Viruses, germs, inflammation, you name it. They attack, destroy, then work to help heal what was damaged. The Ulik males are big; the females are *enormous,* and they don't travel much, but I tell you the males really treat them right and bring them whatever they want. I thought it wasn't a bad system, myself."

Julian gasped. "You mean—my lower set—they're like those super illness fighters?"

Mavra nodded. "I think so now. No way to be sure, of course. I sure wouldn't bet my life on it being fact, but I'd bet a good amount of money it was the answer. I think you shot him up with the equivalent of megavitamins, minerals, body salts, antibiotics, you name it. He can't make that amount on his own, like the male Uliks. In fact, I'll bet the whole harem thing grew out of that. You're basically mammals. When you're pregnant, the body devotes itself entirely to one thing and one thing only, and all this good stuff gets shot into the nursing baby just like Earth-human breast milk transfers antibodies and nutrients well beyond mere food. Tell me—you ever cut yourself? Or had a bad bruise?"

"Yes. When I was being imprisoned, I was chafed and bruised by the chains, and I cut myself once trying to get away."

"Uh huh. And how long did it take you to recover?"

"I—I hadn't thought about it. Once I was freed and out of there, I never noticed."

"Lori injures a lot more easily and heals more slowly. He had some minor cuts and abrasions on him that were scabbed over. You have none, yet you've been here longer than he has and have been treated more roughly. Ever know a sick Erdomese female? Or see one scarred and bruised?"

Julian thought a moment. "No, now that I think of it. Oh, some of the old ones showed the wear and tear of their age, but among the younger ones, no. The men, however, all had some kind of cut or bruise, and a lot of them had dueling scars." The evidence of Mavra's suppositions was sinking in. "Many of the older women were fat and frumpy and didn't take great care of themselves, but I don't remember even one with *stretch marks!*"

Mavra nodded. "So you see, if this secret really got out and was understood, if they weren't kept so ignorant that they didn't even know what caused diseases and infections, the women of Erdom would have a hell of a lot of power over their men. If he tells you he needs you, he means it. I wouldn't push it too far—I doubt if you'll grow back a hand if it's chopped off—but for most basic illnesses and injuries, you women are immune. The men are patsies without your defenses."

"I—I want to believe that it's true. But—*how did I know?*"

Mavra shrugged. "When the Well processes somebody, it has to deal with him as an adult. An adult used to being something else. By definition, you can't have the same lifetime of accumulated experience as somebody who grew up in the new race, so the Well compensates. Biochemically, attitudinally, you name it. The most important parts of what Mama Erdoma teaches her girls, you receive as one-time knowledge, available when needed, like instinct. It was needed. It came out."

Julian shook her head a little from side to side. "I think you may be right—to a point. That, however, was not all that was needed to bring it forward. Somebody I once was and clung to fiercely and needlessly got in the way, too, and he proved useless. Looking at Lori, I knew that. At that moment, feeling so helpless, something snapped inside me. That old self died completely. Died or was killed. It is strange. I know it was there, was the driving force of my life for so long, but I cannot remember much about it. Tomorrow, when my husband awakens, I will ask him to give me a new name. It is all that is left of my past, and I do not want even the reminder."

Mavra had seen this before. Going native was the old term for it, one means by which the mind coped with what to many was an impossible situation.

"If I get into the Well first, you aren't necessarily stuck in that body and role," Mavra pointed out. "You can be anything, any race, any sex you want, here or on a world out there."

"No, no," Julian responded, shaking her head. She knew what Mavra was saying and why, but she did not, *could* not, understand. "I am an Erdomese woman, I am Lori's First Wife, and I wish nothing else. If you can do what you say, and have the opportunity, then his decision will tell me my own. Until then there is no decision. Not until Lori decides."

Mavra shrugged. "Fair enough." She halted suddenly and looked out beyond Julian to the west. "Dawn is coming. At least we'll be able to see what we're dealing with. It may sound crazy, but I've had the damnedest feeling that some pretty big and possibly dangerous creatures are out there. They have moved in the dark here, both on the ground and in the air, although they haven't come near us. That may be caution or fear, or we might just smell awful. I wouldn't take it at all personally if that last is true. In any event, so far there hasn't been anything that kills first and sniffs later. In daylight, who knows?"

They let Lori sleep, and Julian was out pretty quickly, too, but the centauresses were up quickly, bright and alert.

Mavra had some coffee brewing atop a small oil-lit stove. Although she still hadn't reacquired a taste for it after so long, she had decided that caffeine, particularly at the start of a day, was a safety measure.

"Sorry about the lack of tea, but there's only one pot and the amount of rations was limited," she told Anne Marie.

"Oh, no bother, dear. When you live with a Brazilian for several years, you really start getting into the habit. A pity we have no milk, though."

"This is *not* exactly roughing it," Mavra warned her. "Not yet." She looked across at the other centaur. "Where's Tony going?"

"Where I've *been,* dear. I mean, after all, we *did* eat rather a lot last night, bland though it was."

"Oh. Never mind."

With a mug of coffee in hand and some of the pasty loaf inside her, Mavra got out the field glasses and began to take a look around.

"Well, I'll be damned!" she said at last. "Those are the *weirdest* things I've seen in a life of seeing weird things. Whoever dreamed up this place wasn't all that original, but he, she, or it was certainly creative." She handed the binoculars to Tony. "Take a look."

Tony *did* look and had much the same reaction. The fields seemed covered with dense herds of a creature that looked like . . . well, *everything*.

"These Ancient Ones. I think they drank," Tony remarked, and handed the glasses to Anne Marie.

What they all saw was a creature about 120 centimeters tall with a head not unlike a giant beaver or great hare. Its ears, however, were two almost circular extensions that stuck out on both sides of the head like flapping plates. From the forehead, two pronglike horns extended either a mere fifteen or twenty centimeters or, on some of the larger ones, a good forty to fifty centimeters.

"Ten to one the short horns are females and the long horns males," Tony remarked. "Notice how there are far fewer long horns and that they're rather well spaced in the fields. Each oldster watching out for his wives, most likely, with the shorter ones inside probably sons. Oh, my! Look at them *jump*!"

Mavra took the glasses and saw immediately what she meant. They did not run, not exactly; they *leapt*, the larger ones springing free of the tall grass cover. The bodies seemed to be covered in a light, short beige fur, and for a moment they looked like yellowish kangaroos, but in addition to short, tiny arms they had two rather small hoofed front feet and two *enormous* rear feet that powered the leap and seemed all out of proportion to the rest of the creature. They had short, stubby fanlike tails that, unlike a kangaroo or wallaby, could not support them standing on the rear legs alone, so when still, they were on all fours with the long neck craning their heads up.

"Six limbs," Anne Marie noted. "Like us!"

Something panicked a gathering not far from the shimmering border wall—some large reptilian birdlike thing swooping overhead, it looked like. In any event, it almost started a stampede of the creatures, who leapt out of the grass as if one and then came down again, apparently on their front hooves, then launched using their gigantic rear legs once more. The movement of one group startled some of the others, but Tony noted that the larger long-horned ones he'd thought of as males turned and looked up at the threat above them and seemed to act almost in a coordinated fashion to track and if need be fight the predator.

The attacker, an ugly dark-looking thing with an impossibly long snakelike neck and a head that seemed to be all eyes and mouth, swooped down and found itself confronted by a series of male defenders who would leap, horns out, in an attempt to gore or at least scare the creature when it came too close.

It was quite an impressive bit of teamwork and was quite effective; every time the attacker would come down for some wee one in the still-fleeing herd, it would meet one or more of the males. Still, the herd was too large to guard against air attack. Eventually the thing outmaneuvered the defenders, swooped into the madly fleeing and scattering herd, and came up with something small and wiggling. Then the thing flew off toward the nearby grove of trees with its prize.

"Disgusting," Anne Marie snorted.

"Nature, that is all, my dear," Tony responded pragmatically. "One overpopulates; the other manages it. It is the same way on Earth."

"Not in England!" she responded, as if it made sense.

Tony turned to Mavra. "You know, I have been thinking. Do you suppose those herds are the Gekir? They have hands of a sort, or so it appears, and they have some sort of logical defense organization."

"I doubt it," Mavra replied. "Too basic. After all this time they'd be about as sophisticated here as a nontech civilization can get, I'd say. No, you were right. That's instinct and nature. No tools and no weapons that are built with tools. I can't say I'm too thrilled by that thing that attacked them, though. I wish it had gone anywhere but in that grove."

"We can bypass it."

"Yeah, but how many more will we have to bypass if we do? And Julian needs a real long drink or we'll have to let her empty all our canteens." Briefly, and skipping the details, she explained what had taken place in the night.

"Poor dear! But she should *ride* today! I'm certain that either of us could take both of them," Anne Marie responded.

"Yes, particularly if she's the one against my back this time," Tony added, rubbing a bruise where Lori's horn had stuck her. "How far do you think it is to the coast?"

"Not far. Half a day at the most," Mavra told them. "An hour or less if it was just the two of you."

"Perhaps we can repack this differently," Tony suggested. "I think I could take both Julian and you and half the supplies, and Anne Marie could take Lori and the remaining supplies. He's the only one that weighs much of anything among the three of you."

"How sweet," Anne Marie remarked. "You want to ensure that we have matching bruises, too." She sighed. "Very well. Then we can avoid that horrid creature over there altogether."

"I'll go that far with you, about riding, that is," Mavra told them, "but I don't think we can skip water. No, if we run every time there's a predator around, we'll be running all the time. We'll give that pair another hour or two while we re-sort out this stuff. If that thing hasn't decided to leave and find somebody new to play with, we'll see if it cares if we show up or not. It might be too full to care."

DLUBINE

THINGS HAD BEEN GOING well in the sailing department. The oceans had remained generally clear of other ships, although one or two had been sighted either as distant wisps on the horizon or as sets of far-off running lights in the night, but no one had come near, no one had challenged.

They had also managed to steer a northerly course with a good wind at their backs, and thanks to clear skies both day and night, Nathan Brazil now had a relatively decent idea of where they were.

The shortest distance to the north coast would have been straight through Mowry, but the hue and cry for him had to be all over the Well World by now and certainly would have reached a nearby high-tech water hex via Zone long before they got there. He had no desire to face all the locating devices, let alone the speed and weaponry, of a fast, well-armed naval corvette such as the one the colonel had allegedly been waiting to pick up.

They would also probably have come from Mowry to Dlubine with the news, including a halfway decent description of the stolen vessel and her rather distinctive crew, and they would certainly be waiting for him at all the island harbors.

Still, in order to give Mowry a wide berth and make the long crossing to nontech Fahomma—where they'd have a chance of either slipping ashore on the coast of Lilblod or perhaps skirting the coast all the way up to Betared—they would need supplies, and those tiny islands were the best sources. Any searchers would be looking for the ship and for two Glathrielians, male and female, in a hex limited to kinetic forms of energy. They could generate power here, but they could not store it.

Most important to their needs, though, was that those looking for the ship probably did not know about Gus.

Gus had accepted the relative technology levels at face value, as products of the culture. It wasn't until talking with Nathan Brazil that he had realized that the limits were *imposed* by the Well, hex by hex.

"The idea," Brazil explained, "was to approximate as closely as possible what the mother world of the race would provide. Of course, these are only rough limits, approximations, but the general idea holds. The world of the Dahir, for example, is probably mineral-poor, with all the heavy stuff too far down to use and not much surface volcanism—not a lot with which to develop a sophisticated technologically based culture. You're probably more limited here than the Dahir are on their own world, but I wouldn't expect television or trains or a lot of other stuff even after a very long period of development. They'd develop a different way. When resources are there but much harder to get at, and the land and water areas are conducive to some technological development but not on the scale of advanced electronics like computers and satellites, the Well imposes the semitech limit approximation here, too. Planets like Earth, with creatures like the ones we grew up as and with all those resources and conditions, get the high-tech treatment. No limits."

"Yeah? You mean there's an actual Dahir planet someplace? With Dahirs the boss civilization like humans are on Earth? Ain't that a kick in the pants!"

"There definitely is, and don't think that because you're nontech here that they haven't somehow developed a lot more than your people could. It would just be a lot harder than it was for us, and you know how long it took *us*. Who knows how it turned out? Or is still turning out, more likely. Your group here was just the prototype, to see if they could survive and prosper under conditions stricter than they would find out there. There's a huge number of races out there, far more than the 1,560 here. These are just the leftovers. The last batch, as it were. Why they stayed, or were stuck here more likely, I couldn't guess. At any rate, they've been here ever since."

"Huh! Talk about not havin' no future! Jeez . . . Just *here*, huh? Kinda depressing, really."

"Huh? What do you mean?"

"Well, Jeez, I mean, all these people—and all of 'em *are* people, no matter what they look like—bein' born and livin' and dyin' and it just goes on and on. No population explosions, no Tom Edisons or Philo T. Farnsworths or nothin' in most of 'em, at least none that can actually invent things and change everybody's lives, and the high-techs either gettin' fat and lazy or turnin' into ant colonies with traffic jams, seems like. I mean, you talk about havin' nothin' to look forward to! No big changes or revolutions or nothin'. The most you can hope is that your kids grow up to have just what you have. Now, *that's* depressing—to *me*, anyway."

Brazil thought about it. "I guess my viewpoint's different. To me, this is a place where maybe folks can find out what's really important."

"Well, that's 'cause you're the *audience*, not an actor in the play. Even so, I notice you went back and lived through all the shit in Earth history. You didn't stick around here watchin' folks contemplate their navels."

The captain sighed. "I don't know, Gus. Maybe you're right. Your whole life was trying to be where the action was, and I guess mine is, too. Don't exempt yourself, though, from that audience. We're both a couple of ambulance chasers, rushing off to see where the siren's going. Maybe that's the trouble with us. You didn't rush to rescue the child from the burning building or catch the robber or put your life on the line for a cause. You went there to *film* it. I didn't really have any cause, either. I might have tackled the robber or tried to save the kid, but it was just because it was something to do. Now it's *us* who are the story. This time we're the reason for everything that's going on. I doubt if either of us is comfortable in that role."

"Maybe. Maybe I just would rather have been one of them high-tech types here to tape all this for the eleven o'clock news. Maybe that's my problem. Or maybe it's just that this is the only game in town right now, and when it's over, it's gonna be boring as hell."

"Maybe, maybe not. Things *do* happen here, although on a smaller scale. There were some wars here once and might be again sometime, and revolutions *do* happen, cultures *do* get turned. Look at the ancestral home of Earth. Conquered by a nontech hex that forced it to switch places."

Gus looked out over the wheel at Terry, who still relaxed on the deck, seemingly oblivious to everything. "Yeah, and look at what we did with it. What the hell *did* they do to her, anyway? You can't *know* what a difference there is. You can't imagine it."

"I don't know, Gus," Nathan Brazil admitted, shaking his head slowly from side to side. "I don't know what happened at all. They weren't like that the last time I was here, and that was long after the switch. She—they—are the best example that things do change on the Well World. There are other things, too. I don't remember the Dahir being as sleek and streamlined as you are, and I sure don't remember ever hearing about this vanishing trick you do. I've seen some other races, too, races I knew, and they're different as well. A *lot* has changed here, for all the look of it. An awful lot. I haven't figured it out yet, and I doubt if I can get a real handle on any of it until I'm inside the Well, in that incredible form, able to digest all this and figure it out." He sighed. "And that is the only real priority."

And if I fail, I could die here . . .

Brazil was still having trouble with that, still fighting against the idea, but it wouldn't get out of his mind. It scared him, and he hadn't expected that, but there was also a bit more zest to this race because it was there.

For the first time his very existence was at stake. The sense of risk was both uncomfortable and oddly exhilarating. It was something totally new to him, and anything totally new was attractive, even in so perverse a fashion as this.

But then again, the girl was something new and unexpected as well, and for all Nathan Brazil felt for her, he still wasn't at all certain if she represented a true asset or yet another threat.

Why had she joined him in the first place, and stuck with him, considering the vast gulf between them? Why was she so intent on using her powers to help him clear obstacles from his path? Did she want to be put back, become Terry once again? He could do it, inside the Well, but how could she *know* that or anything else about his true nature? Was she perhaps fleeing from whatever had made her the way she was, or had that hidden intellect directed her to join him?

Gus went over to her as she ate some of the hard bread and tried to make her see him. He just couldn't believe that somehow, somewhere, deep inside her, he couldn't make her understand who he was.

She *did* see him when he put his huge reptilian face in front of her and stared into her eyes and began to talk. For a moment she was visibly startled to see this huge creature apparently materialize so close, but then she just frowned a bit and went back to the bread.

He had no way of knowing that at that moment she had looked beyond his surface appearance, looked deep inside him, and sensed only friendliness and a total absence of threat either to her or to Brazil. That had placed him in the category of factors not to worry about, and there seemed little point to anything more until and unless some concerted action was required.

He didn't accept that. "Terry! It's Gus! *Gus!* Do you understand me? It's Gus, at your side like always! You've just *gotta* be in there *somewhere,* damn it! We went through too much together!"

But Gus's words registered only as random sounds, and she could read or infer nothing at all from his features or form. She was aware that it was almost frantically trying to communicate with her, but she saw no possible point to the communication even if there had been a way. It seemed to feel some actual affection for her, which seemed odd, but that, too, wasn't relevant to her, nor was it a problem worth pursuing at this time.

She would, of course, have recognized Gus if he had looked as she had known him; those memories were still there, still accessible when needed. But she had not had the briefing for new entries in Zone. She had gone through the Zone Gate and emerged still human. All her experience told her that the Zone Gate was nothing more than another variation of the gate that had brought her to the Well World; she had no information at all on its transformation and adaptation abilities and functions. There was therefore no way for her to know that her companions of the past now looked remarkably different.

She did consider the problem of why she hadn't been able to see the creature until now. She *had* sensed it, even back on land, and knew it was the same one, but because it radiated only friendship and no sense of danger, it had been ignored.

She heard its heavy steps on the wooden deck going away from her, back toward the Mate, and looked up and was again startled to see nothing. That should not be. She could feel it, sense it, but only in general terms, enough to know it was there.

But where? It was so *big,* so colorful . . . She tried shifting through all the bands, but nothing showed up. *Now,* suddenly, Gus interested her a great deal. It was an unacceptable situation not to be able to see other creatures.

She sat statuelike, virtually all her mental resources suddenly fixed on this one problem, scanning every single energy band, mental and physical, one by one, examining and going through all sorts of tests on each, trying to find one that somehow wasn't right.

Busy with running the ship and with making plans, the two men hardly noticed that she sat there hour after hour, not moving, hardly breathing, all resources concentrated on this one problem.

And eventually she found it. One tiny, thin wave of medium power. She tried to block it off but found that impossible to do without also blocking off needed brain processing power. It was so perfectly located on the mental spectrum that it couldn't be jammed, couldn't be neutralized, without causing more harm than good. The best she could do finally was to narrow it down, localize it, pinpoint its source, then file it away.

She still couldn't see Gus unless he wanted to be seen, but from that point on she knew exactly where he was, which was more than sufficient. It was, however, an interesting capability for all that. The band was a common one, and the broadcast was strictly one-note, designed to do just one specific thing and to do that very well indeed. Given sufficient energy, it might be possible to duplicate the effect from the human brain. Almost casually, without even thinking about, let alone grasping, how she did it, she just *did* it.

Gus immediately popped into full visibility up there next to the Mate. One single narrow frequency; two broadcasts canceled out the effect on sender and receiver. Obvious and simple. Otherwise the creatures could never see one another, either. Once satisfied that she could turn it on or off at will, she filed the information away and finally turned her attention again to the now very old bread.

While all this was going on, late enough in the day to be nearing dusk and only a few minutes later than Brazil had predicted, they reached the hex barrier with Dlubine.

"Looks pretty peaceful," Gus noted. "Big fluffy clouds but not much else. Even the whitecaps don't seem real big."

Brazil nodded. "I'd hoped we'd reach it while we still had some light. I think we're pretty much dead on where I thought we were from the charts, too. I just hope it isn't freezing cold or something over there, although I doubt it. There'd be something of a permanent storm front at the barrier if it was, and while the sky looks a bit different, it's not enough to worry me. Still . . . I gather you're warm-blooded, Gus, or you wouldn't have done so well back in that snowstorm. What's your range of comfort?"

"Can't say for sure," the Dahir responded. "I guess I'm pretty well insulated, since I haven't really felt uncomfortable in any extreme weather. Oh, I knew it was cold back in Hakazit, but it felt like I was wearin' a full set of winter clothes, if you know what I mean. Dahir's kinda high up, sort of a rain forest swamp like you find in northwest Washington, where it rains half the time and can get kinda chilly but not freezin'. I *hope* I don't need no clothes for any of this! I mean, Jeez! Where would I get somethin' to fit *me*?"

"Well, we'll soon know. Here we go."

Pulcinell had been warm and comfortable for Brazil, with both water and air temperatures somewhere in the high twenties Celsius, very much like Rio had been in its spring. He felt the tingle as they passed through the barrier and was suddenly aware that the problem in Dlubine would not be freezing.

It was *hot*. It was a steambath of major proportions, and the sun was almost on the horizon! It had to be close to forty degrees Celsius. Even Gus wasn't unaffected.

"Wow! Feels like somebody just threw a hot blanket over me!"

"Me, too," Brazil responded. "This one's a hotbox, that's for sure. With heat like this near dusk, I'm not sure what midday might bring and

I don't like to think about it. No wonder they had major storm warnings on the chart all over this hex! With this kind of heat and humidity you can get a hurricane between dusk and midnight! Evaporation here has got to be nuts!"

"Yeah, and when it's clear, it'll be Sunstroke City, definitely for you, maybe for me. I dunno. Maybe we oughta figure on riggin' up some kind of roof or sunshade or somethin' for tomorrow, though."

Brazil nodded. "At least it's calm right now, and we're in very deep water here with no shoals or reefs. I can pretty well lock the wheel down and the both of us can look for something to use. Otherwise we'll have to just drift through the day or find some shallows and anchor. Might not be a bad idea to do that, anyway. I can use some decent rest, and I get the bad feeling that there isn't a night in this land that isn't filled with thunder and lightning."

Gus looked out at the darkening horizon. "I'm not too thrilled to look forward to that experience, considerin' the storm we started with, but I'm just as worried at what I see out there." A tiny finger gestured to the northeast, and Brazil's gaze followed it.

"Well," the captain said with a sigh, "we couldn't exactly expect to travel even an ocean without company." He fumbled and came up with the binoculars from his pack and examined the horizon more closely. "Looks like all commercial traffic, anyway, just from the look of the sails. All heading pretty much the same way, too."

He made an estimate of the common heading of the three sets of sails still far off on the northeastern horizon and looked at the charts. "There," he said finally, pointing to a dot on the map with his finger. "Five will get you ten that they're all making for that island." He looked up at the sail. "Not much of a wind, but they should make it in, oh, two hours, I'd say. Maybe less if the wind picks up like I expect once things start to cool—and I say that in a relative sense. They cut it close, but they should be in the harbor there before any big blow comes up."

"What about us?" Gus asked him. "Shouldn't we put in someplace, too?"

"Well, the island, which is called Mahguul on the chart, is the only thing within *our* reach, too. Pretty small—only a few kilometers across by the look of it here, but with some elevation. I'd rather not risk getting bottled up in there if the word's out on us. It would only take somebody from Mowry to come over and post the gory details. A consortium could post a decent reward, but if they just posted that we'd stolen a fellow sailor's ship, it wouldn't take much of a reward." He thought for a moment. "Still, I don't want to battle storms all night even if I'm gonna fry tomorrow. I'm gonna head for it even in the dark. If we can just find some shelter off it, we might be able to get what we need."

"Sounds about as dangerous as takin' on the storms," Gus noted worriedly. "Still, you know the business."

"Yeah." *I hope.*

The night brought a stunning surprise. The ocean was alive with light; greens and blues and reds and yellows and all sorts of in-between shades were all over the place, forming patterns just beneath the surface and giving the whole sea an almost fairy-tale glow.

"Damn! Will you look at *that!*" Gus exclaimed at the unending parade of lights. "What do you suppose causes it? Could it be the lights of the people who live under the water here?"

"Unlikely," Brazil responded, fascinated himself by the beauty of it. "If it was coming from intelligent creatures, we'd see more movement in the patterns, and this is a semitech hex, so there wouldn't be any real power source. The water here is fairly deep, too, so it's not something pasted on or painted on bottom structures. That range of colors means they're not too deep. My guess would be some kind of marine life that forms large colonies that float or swim a few meters below the surface, but around here you can never take anything at face value."

"Terry seems to like it. It's the first really human reaction I've seen her have."

"She's probably analyzing its atomic structure or something equally absurd," Brazil responded grumpily. "Where is she, anyway? I can't see much in the dark, even with the glow lighting things up."

"Right there by the side rail, on the left. Easy to spot her with this light show. You've *got* to be able to see her. Nobody who can grow a new eyeball can have vision *that* bad."

"No, I—oh, wait a minute! Hold on! Damn it! Son of a bitch!"

"What?"

"She's solved your damned trick! Now I can't see *either* of you!"

"You're kiddin'! 'Course, how would *I* be able to tell? So I can see her and she can see me, but you can't see neither of us unless we're talkin' to you or in your face! Ain't *that* a kick in the head!"

"Yeah, for me," Brazil sighed. "And I'm the one that could use it best right about now! More than either of you, since I'm the target."

"Yeah, well, I can't do much about that, but at least you don't exactly fit the wanted poster no more. I mean, they're bound to have the both of you on it, right? They won't expect you alone, particularly when she was clearly aboard when you stole this skiff."

"Yeah, but that won't mean much. She's just an identifier, like me having a beard or black hair. You can lose people all sorts of ways, but my description's pretty well fixed. Still, I wish I could really get through to her, make her understand what we need and persuade her to go get it. You can carry more, but she can climb and get in and out of a lot of places that you can't."

"Tried just about every which way, huh?"

"Just about. The only thing I didn't try, and I'm not sure it would do anything or not, was to try and connect on her level, body to body, mind to mind."

"Jeez! You can *do* that?"

"Of course not. But I have a suspicion that *she* could, if the will to do it was within me and if I could put myself into a trancelike state where I would not resist."

"I don't think *I* could do that."

"Yeah, well, I had some practice with such things while I was in the Orient. In a way, the state she's in and the power she has are very reminiscent of the goals of various schools of eastern mysticism. Thing is, what I've seen ordinary Earth humans do with their minds once they were in a mental state totally removed from the material world awed and scared even me. I think, maybe, deep down it's everybody's inheritance from the folks who built all this. The potential is there, anyway, to some degree."

"Well, why didn't you try that, then?"

He gave a wry smile. "For the same reason I stopped short in the lamasery. Because I'm not so sure if I entered that mental realm that I could get back any more than she can. What if whatever force that has this metaphysical, mental, symbiotic relationship with her were to get that same degree of control inside me? With that kind of power and lack of dependence on most things physical, I could make it to the Well easily. The question is, what sort of mind would I be bringing into it? Could I shake it off when I had to, or would I be bringing a force I don't understand into direct contact and connection with the Well and all its powers?"

"You think this thing is evil, then?"

"Not in the absolute sense, no. It would be evil to some, good to others, I think. But it, itself, is, I think, beyond that sort of definition in the same way that the Markovians, the founding race, were beyond it. I don't know, Gus, but I would have to be in a very desperate situation before I could open myself up to that kind of threat."

"I think I might take the chance at some point if I thought I might be able to become one of them good guys myself. I could stand a billion years before gettin' bored."

"Well, I don't know. I don't know if I would want that or not. God knows I've thought about it enough. And it might not be the kind of godhood anybody would want, anyway." He chuckled. "Besides, I've spent half an eternity as a crook, con man, scoundrel, rogue, and pirate. To be able to do anything you wanted or have anything you wanted by wishing for it would take all the fun out of life. And you've got to ask yourself, What would the Glathrielians want to do? And what would a race of mystics that has sworn off all material desires want, anyway?"

"Um, yeah. I see your point."

They were silent for a while as the wind picked up and they began making some speed again. Off to the west the sky began a dramatic display of lightning, but it was still far enough away that they couldn't hear the thunder.

"Gus?"

"Yeah, Cap? I'm still here, watchin' the fireworks."

"Don't worry about that. It's not heading toward us. I've been looking at the lights, though, and I think maybe I was wrong. I think those *are* some kind of intelligent lighting system. The patterns . . . Well, don't they remind you of something? A bit more color, but don't they kind of look like what a great city might look like when you're passing over it two kilometers high in an aircraft?"

"Yeah! Now that you say it, I do see that. I'll be damned! I *thought* there was somethin' familiar about 'em. But I thought you said this was deep water."

"It is. The first impression, I think, is an optical illusion based partly on the knowledge that this is a semitech hex and they can't have an elaborate electrical grid, even water-insulated somehow."

"Yeah, so?"

"It's the fact that they live so very deep that gives us this overall impression and view. They *do* have some kind of light source, probably organic, arising from chemical means. They've lit their city, their civilization, their little world with it. And to them, we're doing exactly what the vista suggests—we're 'flying,' as it were, on the very top of their atmosphere, looking down. Now *that,* to me, is impressive."

"Yeah." Gus breathed deeply and continued to look at the vast rippling field of lights. He wondered what the people were like down there and whether this was a city asleep or a city alive at night, bustling with traffic and commerce and all the things a great city might offer.

There was lightning all around after a while, and some distant claps of thunder could be heard rolling hollowly over the waves. Slowly, too, the vast undersea city, if that indeed was what it was, began to trail off, the lights becoming fewer, and great dark patches began appearing. Still, a few lines of light continued on almost beneath their ship, as if they were lonely highways stretching out from the metropolis to others far distant.

Suddenly Gus realized that this was exactly what they were or at least what Brazil thought they were, and in fact their ship was following the broadest twin line of lights just as an airline pilot might follow a great road.

"It's going where we're going," Brazil assured him. "It's too bad it's so damned hot here that we get all these night storms. Otherwise this would be a dream stretch of ocean to navigate by eye alone. All you'd need would be a general destination or maybe a road map."

The captain had finally shed the last of his personal dignity in reaction to the steam bath heat. His clothes were designed for a cold climate, and Dlubine was anything but that. He was a little, bony sort of guy, Gus noted, although quite hairy, and it was easy to see why he'd be a hit with the women even though the rest of him was small.

Brazil himself would have preferred at least a pair of briefs, even though he was the only Earth-human male in a vast stretch of the world and the only Earth-human female around had seen him like this many times and indeed seemed to prefer him this way. It was just part of his nature. He had not, however, ever found any nonhuman on the Well World who could get the crotch right.

Yet, it felt better, even if he *was* still sweating like a pig.

"Lights ahead. On—maybe above—the surface," Gus warned suddenly.

Brazil nodded. "I see them. That looks to be a lighthouse to the left, and the lanterns just right of dead ahead— see? Two on the right side, one on the left—they're channel markers. Being northbound, I've got to lay just inside the double lights to remain both in the channel and in the lane."

"Must be coming in to that island, then. Can't see nothin', though."

"You can interpolate it, Gus. Look at the underground highway. The main drag continues right along the markers, but another goes off in a Y to the left, toward the light. It'll probably swing wide before it gets there, though, since the lighthouse is almost certainly marking reefs or shoals."

"You gonna take a chance on the harbor?"

"I don't know. I'm going to follow the markers around to it, that's for sure, and we'll take a look at it. If it's wide and deep enough, we might just slip in, do what we have to do, and slip out before morning. If it's small, active, and threatening, I might just do a go-round and see if we can find some kind of temporary anchorage well away from it. I'm hoping to get in, since the only thing I would like less than climbing over volcanic rocks in pitch darkness is climbing over them when they're hot enough to fry eggs."

The mountain itself, the top of which was the island, could not be seen in the darkness, only inferred, but the channel markers above and the glowing road below made it a simple matter to avoid any nastiness and move slowly around the mass toward the harbor area. Brazil couldn't help thinking, but didn't say, that it would also be simple defense by the Dlubinians to shift that road, extinguish a marker lantern or two, and pile everybody up nicely on the rocks he could hear the water slapping against all around the boat.

Damn it, though, he wished he had a cigar to calm his nerves.

"There it is!" Gus shouted. "Pretty damned small-looking, if you ask me."

"Well, the locals don't breathe air, so they've got little use for the place except as a trading center, and anybody hired to run the place would prefer it nice and compact and manageable, I'd think," the captain replied. "It's probably run by some international outfit. There's bound to be several offering services like this. Hard to say who or what might be running it, let alone what's in there."

"I make seven . . . no, eight ships, all pretty much like ours," Gus noted. "And one medium-sized thing with a smokestack parked off by itself over there."

Brazil nodded. "That's the one to worry about. Those are the cops, Gus. I'm giving the entrance a pass."

"Cops? Here? Whose?"

"Just like the trading companies and maintenance companies. All the hexes that have some concern with the sea or coastal security get together and maintain a multinational force run by a professional, multiracial naval authority. They didn't have anything like that the last time I was here, but I got an earful about them back in Hakazit. They've got a mean reputation. Discipline's about as ugly as a navy gets, but each crew gets a percentage of any seized contraband or reward money. You can get rich at it if you're good, and since it's an all-or-nothing share for the whole crew, if you're not good, you're history, anyway. We can't totally avoid them, but I'd just as soon not tangle with them or answer any nasty questions. You *can* challenge them if they're wrong, but we're a long way from a Zone court here—not that I would particularly want to see what a Zone court was, either, right about now."

Gus nodded, watching as they passed the harbor entrance and continued on past the island. "I see. But you said they only had volunteers from coastal hexes and those doing trade with the water hexes."

"So I was told."

"Then there ain't likely to be no Dahirs among 'em, and in *this* hex there's also not likely to be any automatic surveillance cameras or electric eyes, right?"

"I see what you mean. No, I'd expect you'd be invisible to them, since they wouldn't have much call to counter crooked Dahirs around here. Don't take them or the locals for stupid or ignorant types, though. You can trip a wire or any one of a thousand other traps that don't require any high-tech stuff and be just as caught. I'm also not so sure you're going to do any better over this terrain in the dark than I would."

"I wasn't thinkin' of that. I was thinkin' it wouldn't be much of a problem to swim *this* distance. Even if you anchor on the other side of the island, it's only gonna be a mile or so back, right? I figure I could manage a fair-sized sack and a keg or two for that distance, and I know what you two can eat and drink, havin' had some experience along them lines myself. As for findin' my way, hell, even I can follow these lights."

"You sure you're up to this?" Brazil pressed. "I have to tell you I'd rather not go in there at all if I don't have to, but it could be tricky."

"Jeez! This is a piece of cake! I mean, I got along in Hakazit for *weeks,* and they got all that electronic shit. Of course, I'm pretty fair with that kind of stuff myself, but I never saw cameras like they had or as tiny as they used, and I still never got tripped up. Man, I remember one time we was in the Congo when this riot broke out and turned into a kinda little revolution. They were shootin' anything that moved and had all the exits blocked. Me and Terry, we—"

He stopped a moment, suddenly struck once again by what Terry had become, and Brazil, realizing it, didn't press.

Finally Gus continued, but his tone was more distant, almost sad. "We . . . well, we not only got out of there, we got out with the *pictures.* She told me we had to get the story out and sent me back with it. She insisted on staying to report the end of it. I spent four days in that muddy, crocodile-infested river in a cross between a too-old rowboat and a raft, dodgin' crocs and patrols. But I made it. *She* wasn't so lucky that time."

Brazil was curious now both for the story's own sake and for his own information about the girl and what she'd been like. "What happened, Gus?"

"She never said for sure, but she was a mess. I think they caught her and raped the shit out of her, the bastards. I'm not even sure they knew she wasn't just one of the locals or cared. And yet she *still* managed to get out, somehow, in a few days. Spent ten weeks in and out of hospitals and all. You know what was really weird about what happened?"

"No, Gus."

"When she come back, she still volunteered for the same nasty jobs, and she *meant* it. It didn't even slow her down. It was almost like, well, she'd survived the worst that could happen, and if anything, she seemed to have less fear than she had had before, which wasn't much. That Campos guy I mentioned, the gangster who come to the meteor site with us? *He* tried to get in her, too. I ain't ever been sure, but I think your old girlfriend did him a favor. He'da got away with it then, more or less, but some way or another she'da killed him—*after* we had the story and after the rest of the crew was safe. If Campos turns up somewhere here, no matter if he's a poisonous spider twenty feet tall, if she realizes that it's him and there's any of her old self left inside there, I wouldn't give a plugged nickel for his survival."

Brazil didn't say anything for a moment but finally managed, "Okay, Gus. You've convinced me. You see that set of markers there? That's an inlet, a sheltered cove. It's marked so a ship that might not be able to make it into the harbor can get some protection in bad weather. Ten to one it's surrounded by sheer cliffs, but we don't need to walk if you can get there by sea. I don't see any lights in there, and I didn't expect any with the weather okay—no reason not to make the harbor—so I'm going to lower sail and anchor inside there. *Then* you can go for a swim."

"Suits me."

The craft followed the small oil lanterns into the cove, and they were suddenly aware of high rock walls not just ahead but on both sides of the ship. It was a narrow channel, and it ended in a marked area that was all red-colored little lights.

"Who lights these and turns 'em off?" Gus asked worriedly, pointing to all the small marker lanterns around them.

Brazil was grunting and busily maneuvering several ways at once, hitting levers and turning small deck winches, but when he at last let go of the anchor and felt the ship lurch, then drift a bit to one side and stop, he relaxed.

"To answer your question," he said at last, "if you look closely, you'll see that they aren't oil lamps but gas. Semitech. With the volcano, they probably have some tap on a flammable gas supply, either natural or in a tank. They'll check them in some kind of routine, but only for maintenance. I wouldn't worry about anybody showing up at dawn to put them out, if that's what you mean."

"Yeah, that was what I was thinkin'." Gus sighed, a sound that was more like a soft, hollow roar. "Okay, I guess I'm ready. Anything waterproof that's likely to float that maybe I can use as a stash?"

"Yeah, here in the boat locker. This thing's got a pretty large emergency kit inside it, but if we take it out, it should give you plenty of room for what we need, and it's designed to be both floatable and waterproof at these seals. I won't worry about the beer supply, but we need food. Trust to the grains and veggies. They're pretty well universal among warm-blooded mammals, while meats are, well, questionable at best. Besides, she won't eat meat. She'll starve first."

"Okeydokey. Look, you may as well get some sleep while I'm gone. If anybody else comes in here, you're a sittin' duck before you can weigh anchor, turn around, and get out that narrow passage anyway, and if they take you, they'll probably bring you by the harbor, so I'll have a chance to spring you. Besides, no matter what else she is these days, I get the idea that Terry's one hell of a guard dog."

"You got that right," Brazil agreed. "Good luck!"

"Yeah, I'll do my best, like always," Gus responded, and tossed the emergency case into the water, then slid overboard himself.

Nathan Brazil sighed and sat down on the makeshift bed of spare sailcloth he'd set up for himself. He was too tired, too tense, and too worried to sleep even though he knew he was exhausted.

One of the storms was growing near, and while it didn't bother him in this sheltered area and was still distant in any event, the lightning lit up the sky and played against the rock walls, revealing the shelter in intermittent bursts of reflected light.

It was an eerie landscape, as all volcanic areas tended to be, with no discernible vegetation. The outer rock wall, the eroded remnants of some great eruption, was at least ten meters high, almost sheer on this side but terminating in a series of jagged spires almost like the teeth of some gigantic beast.

He was actually comforted by the wall. It was taller than the mainmast, and thus it meant that he was virtually invisible to any ship passing via the channel outside as well as extremely well protected against any violent blow.

The rest of the area was much like a bowl, perhaps a hundred meters across, ending in sheer dark brown or black rock cliffs that seemed to go up forever. Here and there all along the sheer rock walls, though, were cracks and holes from which spewed steam and other gases, showing that this was still a very active place.

When it was dark between the lightning flashes, only the sky straight overhead showed, revealing the whole upper part of the fog- and mist-shrouded mountain. It helped reflect the lightning better, but it gave the distinct impression that one was in a room with a roof on it.

He felt a little better about the trip now that he had Gus, even if he couldn't see him half the time. At least, finally, there was somebody to *talk* to! Somebody who could speak with a frame of reference comfortable for both of them.

But, too, it was somebody else, somebody extra on the team, and in other ways he felt the Dahir a burden despite all that he was doing tonight. Maybe it was the girl, he thought. From knowing very little about her, he now knew quite a bit, perhaps more than she would have told him had she been able to do so. As much as he'd wanted, *needed* to know all that, he wasn't at all sure he liked knowing it. It was nothing about her; all the information Gus had provided had shown her to be more of a strong, gutsy woman than he'd have thought. It was rather that she was becoming, well, distinct in his mind. Now that he knew about her past, she seemed even more a tragic figure, a real person, not a cipher, and in a crazy way ciphers were often more comfortable to live with.

He wondered if he wasn't also a little jealous of Gus. That was funny in a way—having a two-and-a-half-meter-long snakelike creature as a rival. But Gus had earned her respect and devotion, as she had earned his. Even if they weren't lovers, there was definitely a kind of relationship there that he could not have even now and never could have, or *dared* have, with anyone else. That was what he envied.

And suddenly she was with him, kneeling down, then lying beside him, stroking him gently, as if she knew and understood what he was feeling.

Maybe she did, at least on that empathic level. Maybe more. *That* much he wished he knew.

Gently, he returned her affection and then embraced her and held her to him, as if trying to capture this one brief moment—just the two of them, with no other problems and no other questions, reaching together for the one thing which he wanted most and which had always been denied him because life was so short for everybody else, everybody but him.

The emotions then were real, not induced, not manufactured or manipulated, and not just on his part but on hers as well. The energy field inside her grew bright and enveloped them both, probing deep inside him and through every part of his being. He did not resist.

And when it hit his core, his soul, his true self, a center so strange, so alien that there were no terms of reference for it anywhere, it recoiled, unable to deal with it, powerless to go that last bit and totally absorb him.

Finally Nathan Brazil slept, a deep, intensely pleasurable sleep, the kind of sleep he needed most and rarely if ever could afford.

GEKIR

THE CHANGES IN JULIAN were both subtle and dramatic, but Lori, whose high fever had been the precipitator of those changes, wasn't at all certain he liked it. One thing was clear: while she was as smart and capable as she ever had been, Julian seemed to have lost much of her past life, even though she knew that it had existed. It would probably take about ten seconds for an Earth psychiatrist to come up with a term to cover it, but to Lori it just didn't seem *normal*. Not for Julian, anyway. It was as if something was missing from her, some fire or intellect that wasn't really noticed and certainly not appreciated until it was no longer there.

Lori was feeling a great deal better. The inflammation in the wrist was down, although for a while it meant that the damned thing hurt *more* as it was no longer quite so rigidly bound, but his leg seemed completely normal. He tested it out, even ran on it for a short distance, and aside from a little stiffness it was fine. At least *one* thing was going his way, he decided.

Julian was in far worse shape. She was wan, worn out, and badly dehydrated. They put her, only half-awake, on Tony's back, tied her with the strap that had held Lori, packed up the rest of the camp, and started off toward the thick grove of tall trees about one and a half kilometers away.

There was no sign of the flying monster that had carried off the young "jackalope," as Lori had dubbed them, after a whimsical creature of the American Southwest. But it might well have a nest or den in the grove or be still feeding there, so Mavra broke out the crossbows, handing one to Tony and keeping one for herself. Anne Marie quickly but expertly assembled an obviously handmade, customized bow of great size and exotic design and removed a quiver of professionally manufactured but oversized steel-tipped arrows.

"Archery was one of the few varieties of sport a weak little woman could manage just for fun from a wheelchair," she explained, "and of course the classical favorite of centaurs from time immemorial. It *is*, too, even though the authorities have guns for serious sorts of things. *This* is the hunter's weapon of choice, though, even in Dillia. I'm afraid I'm still not very good at it, though. I have the eye and hold just fine, but I just can't get used to having this much *strength*."

Tony examined the crossbow. "Rather odd design, although I'm no expert on these things."

"You aim it just like a rifle," Mavra told him. "Align the rear notch with the front sight."

"No, no. The use is obvious. I meant this chamber in the rear behind the bolt. I'd almost swear it was for bullets."

Mavra chuckled. "Not bullets. Small compressed-gas canisters. When you pull the trigger, it works in the normal way, but if you have one of these little things in there, it gives a tremendous extra shove to the bolt, and a bit of a twist, at virtually no cost in weight or balance. Use it normally for defense; use the canister if you want to be sure you kill whatever you're firing at. It'll drill a hole through a tree thicker than your middle."

"Not very sporting."

"No, but it's damned effective even against somebody who thinks crossbows are no real threat."

Tony looked down at her. "I see that you are inserting one, but I have none."

"Double insurance. You make the first shot. If need be, I'll make the last one."

"Fair enough," the centauress agreed. "Still, it is almost disappointing somehow that even the crossbow should be turned into something so devastating."

Anne Marie nodded. "Doesn't seem *sporting* somehow," she agreed.

"When it's a sport, you're playing a game," Mavra responded. "On this sort of expedition I don't play games." She turned to Lori. "Can you scan that grove in the infrared?"

He nodded. "I've been doing it. Lots of little stuff, nothing major. It looks normal to me. I smell water, though. Possibly a *big* watering hole. If it is, that means we can expect most anything and everything around it."

Mavra nodded back. "I know. I haven't lost three hundred years of knowledge and experience in wild terrains," she reminded him.

"Yeah." The fact was, however, that the woman beside him was so different in so many ways from even the image of the savage jungle goddess of the Amazon that he had to remind himself that it was the same person. The conversation and the sophistication were large differences, of course, but it was also other factors not so easily nailed down. She had been so dominating, so commanding back on Earth, she'd seemed far larger than her size; now she was such a very tiny creature, he had to crane his neck just to see her. Even her form no longer seemed normal and familiar somehow but rather, well, *alien*. More alien than the Dillians, whose equine parts were more like the Erdomese and whose rears seemed, well, *sexy*.

Sexier than their torsos, in fact.

He began to wonder if what had changed in Julian was changing in him, too. Wouldn't *that* please the priests! But he had no desire to forget his former life and hoped that he could remember some of the lessons from it, as distant as they now seemed to him. Still, it was *Julian* who looked normal and pretty and sexy to him, as did his own reflection. Maybe it was crazy, but he realized that somehow, at some point, his own definition of "human" had flipped. He and Julian were "human"; the twins were, well, not human but kind of distant relatives. Mavra was not human. She was something else.

The grove was large and not at all like an Erdomese oasis, no matter what its geologic and ecological similarities. The foliage was far denser than it had looked from afar and heavy with life. There were hordes of brightly colored and cleverly camouflaged insects and insectlike creatures here, more, it seemed, than in the Itun jungle. Small animals were in the trees as well, some screeching or chattering at them and others just staring, often with huge eyes. There were things like birds, too, in that they had wings and flew, but they were more reptilian than avian, with often brightly colored but leathery skin and beaklike snouts. Even the small, pretty ones looked mean.

The group intersected a wide, well-worn trail that came in from the south, one that was adequate not just for the creatures they'd seen on the plains but for the two Dillians to walk side by side if they wanted to.

"Someone cut this wider," Tony noted, pointing a long finger at a lopped-off tree branch and to other obviously cut limbs and bushes elsewhere.

"Yeah, but why this wide?" Lori wondered. "I've got too many weird scents here to decide what might be odd, but I've sure not seen anything *this* big so far."

"Well, whatever it is, it's *very* large indeed," Anne Marie noted, gesturing toward the ground. "Those are not the droppings of a chipmunk, dog, horse, or anything else so tiny."

"Holy shit!" Mavra exclaimed, not realizing she'd made something of a joke. "I haven't seen turds that size since . . ."

Since where?

Lori stared at the droppings. "Since perhaps some sort of zoo or preserve? Or maybe a circus? Those look like elephant turds to me."

Mavra nodded. "That's it! But not a zoo or preserve or a circus, no. I saw them with soldiers on top of them in both military parades and in fierce battles."

"They're not that fresh—thank goodness," Anne Marie commented.

"And the cuttings aren't recent. Maybe a week or so old, maybe more," Tony added.

Lori looked over and down at Mavra. "Could the locals here be elephantlike? I mean, like Dillians are horselike and so on?"

"There are a couple that I know of who might qualify in that area," Mavra replied, "but none who'd mess up their own trail like that. You have to remember that we're talking intelligent races here. Out in the wild, thinking beings crap off their roads, not all over them. On the other hand, intelligent races ride elephants and use them as work animals as well. And if you ride in on something like that, there's *nothing* in this grove that's gonna argue with you, is there?"

"*We're* not atop elephants," Tony reminded them. "And there is the watering hole. The watering hole and something very much more."

It was indeed. The "hole" was a large pool or basin perhaps fifty meters across. It seemed natural, and the continuous rippling on the surface suggested that it was fed by an underground stream. Someone, however, had taken the natural pool and carved and shaped it until it was an egg-shaped oval with a two-meter-thick lip of mortared stones around it on all but its back side. That ended in a curved wall, with stairs of stone that went up on both sides to a flat stone platform above the pool. In back of it was a cone-shaped structure that seemed twisted, creating a spiral to its point.

The building, stairs, wall, and pool itself were partly overgrown with vines and creepers. A number of creatures from both the jungle grove and the vast plains were moving about the whole area. Still, it didn't seem like a ruin but rather like a place that was only seldom used but was still carefully kept intact.

"Temple?" Tony guessed.

"Maybe. Who knows?" Mavra replied. "Considering that there's something that looks a lot like a boa constrictor covered with peacock feathers and with a mouth showing more teeth than a shark snoozing on that platform, though, I don't think I'm curious enough to find out."

"I thought you were immortal," Lori noted a bit sarcastically.

"I wouldn't die, but I'd hate to waste months growing a new pair of legs."

The current rulers of the pool were two dozen small creatures whose appearance was unsettling. The largest male was only a meter high, and they all looked to be a sort of tailless ape, with thinly spread, soft, down-like hair covering their bodies except the chests, rear ends, and parts of the faces. They walked stooped over but were definitely bipeds, and for all their smallness and crudeness they looked very, very much like humans, even to the long hair on the heads. But there was just enough of the ape in their features to make them seem slightly more of an anthropological speculator's exhibit than small humans.

When the apes spotted the travelers, they didn't immediately run. Instead, the females let out loud, humanlike screams that panicked all the flying things and many of the smaller land creatures as well; the males stared at them, bared their teeth, and growled menacingly.

"Good heavens! They're Lucy's cousins!" Anne Marie exclaimed.

"Lucy?" Mavra asked.

"Doctor Leakey's fossils from Kenya. The spitting image! Claimed they were some sort of ancestor of Earth humans or some such rot."

Lori, in spite of his feelings of alienation from the race of his birth, nonetheless had that primal feeling inside and didn't much like it. "My lord! You don't suppose . . . ?"

"Prototypes or more idea stealing by the makers," Mavra reassured him, although she didn't like how familiar they looked, either. "Odd, though. The mammals we've seen are all six-limbed. They're bipeds. They don't seem to fit in here at all."

"Well, I don't care about mysteries, but some of those creatures best left sleeping are awake now. Whatever these things are, they don't want to move away for us."

"Oh, *pooh!*" Anne Marie said, and with barely a glance, both she and Tony reared up on hind legs, then kicked off and charged right toward the little apelike creatures.

They could see the panic in the creatures' eyes. A couple of the males gave hysterical gasps, then they all ran back into the jungle and vanished as if they'd never been there.

The centaurs pulled up, turned, and looked back at the other three.

"Poor little things!" Anne Marie commented. "I do hope we didn't scare them all *that* badly." There was a trace of a smile on her lips, though, and she added, "That was rather fun, though, I do admit."

They moved in, Lori and Mavra well aware that the feathered snake with the hundreds of teeth was now awake and looking at them from the top of the balcony platform, although it showed no intention of moving from its spot.

Even Julian was awake, looking weak and pale. Tony had forgotten that she was strapped down on her back when they'd reared and charged. Now the centauress's look changed from playful triumph to embarrassment, and Anne Marie quickly rushed over and untied the Erdomese.

"Oh, my dear! We're *so* sorry! Are you all right?" Anne Marie asked in English.

Julian stared back blankly, and Lori ran over to her. "Are you all right? *Julian!* Can you hear me?"

"Yes, my husband," she answered rather weakly and a bit uncertainly. "I—I think so. But I am so thirsty and weak . . ."

She seemed as good as she'd been, anyway. "Come, we'll get you down. When you didn't answer Anne Marie, I got very worried."

"I am gladdened that you were concerned, but I did not answer because I did not understand the speech."

Tony frowned and looked up at Anne Marie. "You *did* ask in English, didn't you? With the translator it's hard to tell."

"Oh, of course. I'd never expect any of you to speak *Dillian*."

Lori steadied Julian and asked. "Do you understand her now?"

Julian looked blank. "I know nothing but Erdoma. Why should I understand the speech of an alien?"

Mavra looked up at Lori. "You better get her a fill-up. I think you bled her dry last night."

The water in the pool seemed remarkably clear and appeared safe. Mavra risked a left little finger and decided that it felt just like lukewarm water. Still, she got out a small test tube device from the pack, added some powder, then stooped and carefully let the tube fill with water. After she brought it up and looked at it, all the powder stayed on the bottom and the water remained clear.

"Unless I miss my guess, it's plain fresh water," she told them. "Actually, it's cleaner than it should be, all things considered. I don't think anybody should get in it, but we'll fill the canteens and Julian can drink all she wants."

"Fair enough," replied Lori, still concerned about Julian's dazed mental state. They began filling canteens and handing them to the Erdomese woman, who drank them down as if she'd been in the desert for months without a drop. The amount of water she finally consumed, particularly considering her size, was nothing short of astonishing. Each canteen held a little over a liter, and she easily and quickly downed a dozen or more canteens full of water before pausing, and she wasn't

through. Even with the Dillians guarding, Mavra kept checking the surroundings for anything dangerous and soon lost count of just how much
water Julian finally took in.

When she was finally, truly done, she looked quite different. The color
was slowly coming back into her, and as the sacs in front of and just
below her rib cage filled, they actually stretched the skin, pushing out
the breasts and making them appear inflated and giving her the appearance of being slightly overweight. She was, too, Mavra thought. At the
very least, she'd taken in fifteen to twenty liters of water, enough to add
quite a bit of weight. Idly, the lone Earth human wondered if the
Erdomese would slosh when she walked.

"I am much better, husband. Now you, too, should drink, for what
you drew from me was not used in ordinary ways and the fever must
have drained you."

Lori had passed a lot of particularly smelly and discolored urine already, but he knew what she meant. While by no means in the kind of
shape Julian had been, he *did* feel a real thirst. On the other hand, he
couldn't down more than five canteens full, and that was about as much
as he'd ever taken in or needed.

While the others took turns, Julian asked him to sit so that she could
clean off some of the muck still on him from falling in the muddy ditch
when jumping from the train days earlier. Using her hands opened as
fully as they could get, she began methodically rubbing and then brushing away the dried mud as if it were something she did all the time.

Since she seemed so much better, Lori asked her, "Julian, can you
understand any of what the Dillians say? Have you remembered English?"

"I cannot understand their speech, my husband, if that is what you
mean. I know only Erdoma. I do not know what the last word you spoke
means, so I cannot answer that."

He lay down so she could work on his side and front, and this allowed
him to see her face. "Have you lost all memory of the past?" *This is crazy,*
he thought. *If anything, it's me who should be having memory problems after a
fever like that.*

She shook her head. "I remember only that I was possessed of an evil
spirit and that now that spirit has fled with your sickness. It would please
me if you would give me another name, one of your choosing."

"But I *like* your name. I'm used to it."

"It is the name of the spirit, not me. It makes me feel bad, and I
cannot even pronounce it as you do. *Please,* I beg you to use the name
chosen at our wedding or any other that pleases you."

He didn't like this change one bit. Not any of it. Even if, damn it, it was the fantasy he'd had since they'd left Aqomb. Now that he had it, he didn't like it at all. She was too much like she'd been when they'd both been under the influence of that hypnotic drug. Too much like, well, all the other young Erdomese women. Still, it wasn't something he could do much about right now.

It was true that the "ju" sound was not in the Erdomese language, or anything else that might in English be pronounced with the "J" sound. Her Erdomese name, Alowi, had been given by the priest at the wedding at least partly for that reason, but they'd never used it except during the post-therapy sessions while under the drug. Ironically, although it wasn't a traditional Erdomese name, "Lori" had been just fine with the priests.

"Very well. For now I will use Alowi," he told her, and she seemed very pleased.

Cleaned and combed, he did feel better and certainly looked better. By this time they were packing up, and he told Julian—*Alowi*—to help but got Mavra aside for a moment.

"You know anything about this change in her?" he asked.

"A little," Mavra replied. "It's not something *I* can understand, and I never thought somebody with her background would succumb, but you can't tell about people sometimes. Basically, Julian Beard's been fighting with the Erdomese body, feelings, customs, and conditioning, and the old personality has been more or less dominant, even when the Erdomese self occasionally peeked through. Last night, in a place alien to both sides, the only person she cared about and really needed in this world was dying, and Julian Beard couldn't save him with all the accumulated knowledge and skill of a lifetime. Beard had to face not only helplessness but repressed feelings and emotions toward you that the Alowi part, the native part supplied by the Well and conditioned by her new body and situation, wanted so much to express. Beard needed you for any chance of survival or reasonable happiness in this life, but only Alowi had both the knowledge and the additional motivation that could save you. Unlike Tony or you, who surrendered on your own terms, Beard could not. It just wasn't in him not to fight. When the crisis came and he wasn't able to deal with it, something gave, and that was Julian Beard."

"But that's *crazy*! They're one and the same! Just as I am. It's true that I'm different; I've changed radically since being here, sometimes in directions I don't like, and I'm still trying for a balance, but it's nothing I can't handle."

"As a woman, did you ever find another woman sexually attractive? Did you ever fantasize about what it would be like to be a man?"

"Well, yeah, sure, but . . ."

"I will bet you that Julian never found another man sexually attractive, at least not consciously, and his fantasies were *about* women, not about being a woman. He could take tremendous stress, great pressure, and still accomplish anything he set out to do. But those same traits created an enormous ego, I think, that had a single and absolutist view of itself. What the Well did to him was, to him, so extreme that finding himself a female, she had to be locked up and drugged just to keep her from suicide. You said as much. When you came along, he tried to compromise with his female self, but all that did was shift her from one extreme to the other. On this trip the male side felt in charge again, but last night the crisis was just too much. To help you, she had to put everything out of her mind that was from her male half, both attitudes and experience, and let Alowi completely take over. When that happened, all that repressed emotion just gushed out, suddenly no longer under restraint. Alowi then saved you by doing something Julian could never do—by *not thinking*. By just letting that Erdomese instinct take control and never doubting if it was right or wrong. She didn't work so fanatically because she needed you, not in the sense Julian had. She did it because she loves you, and being in love with a man wasn't something that Julian Beard could handle. When you push something that can't bend with a lot of force, it breaks."

"You sound like a pop psychologist," Lori noted, but wondered if she wasn't pretty well on the mark.

"I don't know exactly what a 'pop' psychologist is, but I think I understand your meaning. Yes, it's guesswork based on very long experience rather than on being a professional specialist in the mind, and it may not be stated in proper scientific terms, but I've had to read and guess right on all types of people to get anywhere at all. And you will have to trust me that I know what rigid egos can do to people."

"But—what do I do? Is Julian gone for good?"

"You live with it, that's all. All that knowledge and experience is still there someplace; it's just been sealed off in the same way the person she is now was pretty well sealed off. It might not come back at all, it might partly come back if absolutely needed, or it might creep back and merge with the current personality. Only time will tell. In the meantime it's causing some trouble for all of us."

"Huh? How is it a problem for *you*?"

"Since she doesn't remember English, she can't speak to or understand the Dillians. That could be a real pain in a tight situation. Damn! I *knew* I should have sprung for the translator!"

Lori felt a double pang of guilt at the comment but said, "Well, she can still get one somewhere, can't she?"

"I think she'd fight having one now. It doesn't fit with the new personality she's trying to build and lock in."

"I think she'd do it for me," Lori told her.

"She might," Mavra agreed, "but the knowledge of English is still in her mind somewhere, too. These mental things are tricky. A translator is a neat little device that's tuned to a part of the Well and translates speech, then feeds it back to the brain. Since the Well is everywhere, it seems instantaneous to us. But if her mental state won't allow her to accept the translation, won't transfer language except in Erdomese, the gadget is as useless as a computer would be a Stone Age hunter. Data have to be processed, and if the mind refuses, well, it doesn't matter whether you get the data or not."

"Thanks a lot. One more thing to worry about."

Mavra turned sharply toward the wide road leading to the pool and picked up her crossbow. "We have something more pressing to worry about all of a sudden."

They could all hear it and even feel it. Something large—no, *huge*—was coming up that road with enough weight to shake the ground and once again panic all the surrounding wildlife.

"We could retreat into the jungle!" Tony called.

"All right! Move back and take cover if you can!" Mavra shouted, but Lori shook his head and said rather softly, "Too late."

Into the area strode a monstrous creature, in many ways the largest elephant any of them had ever seen, yet not an elephant, either. For one thing, it was covered in thick reddish brown fur from its small tail to its massive head, hanging down like some impossible fur coat. It moved very slowly on six tree-trunk-sized feet; the creature was probably unable to run or move at all quickly, but something that huge was an irresistible force that never needed to move quickly. Even its trunk was hairy, and on either side of the mouth, which was small only in relative terms, grew two very large, cream white, and dangerous-looking ivory tusks.

And riding just behind the massive head was a large orange and black catlike creature with a large, fierce head sporting protruding fangs, and a lower jaw and a mouth that was remarkably expressive, almost humanlike. The cat creature, too, was six-limbed, but the forward pair of arms, while fur-covered like the legs, clearly ended in some sort of hands, one of which held an ornate batonlike object.

It also wore a sash that was equally ornate, from which hung a scabbard with an ornately carved ivory hilt that obviously led to a very large sword.

The cat creature tapped gently on its mount's head, and the beast trumpeted loudly enough to wake the dead. It was clear that the pair was leading at least a small procession, and the sight of the strangers at the pool had signaled a halt.

"Who be ye and why d' ye bear arms against the Gekir in the shadow of Basquah?" the cat challenged, the translation faithfully reproducing the archaic speech pattern. The voice was deep and seemed to have an underlying menacing growl, but it was also unmistakably female.

"Don't do anything!" Mavra cautioned Lori and particularly the Dillians, who were hearing only very threatening animal noises and had their arms at the ready. "She's just asking who the hell we are and why we're here!" It was, after all, a proper question.

They had finally encountered the Gekir.

Mavra lowered her crossbow but kept the bolt ready to go. With the gas propellant loaded, she was certain it would drill even through the mammoth, although whether that would do more than annoy it was impossible to know.

"The bipeds are called Lori of Alkhaz and his wife, Lori-Alowi, of faroff Erdom," she announced. "The other two are from even more distant Dillia and are the sisters called Tony and Anne Marie Guzman. I am Mavra Chang of Glathriel. We mean neither harm nor disrespect and have not entered your building. We are travelers forced by circumstance, not plan, into your nation, and we are here only to replenish our water supplies and move on."

The Gekir, whose feline face was so expressive and rubbery, frowned and cocked her head, looking them all over. "I be Shestah Quom Daahd, elected chief of the Quobok Knights. Put thy weapons away and stand ye all by the far side of yon pool that we may enter."

It wasn't a request; it was an order. Mavra turned and told the others to move where instructed. Right now it was better to try to make friends with these people than to start a fight.

As soon as they were away from the main area, the chief of the Quobok Knights moved her huge mount in and was quickly joined by four others, filling the area rather handily.

The leader's mount carried only the chief and an elaborate chest secured with straps. The next three, however, carried perhaps four or five Gekirs each, riding on top and in two basketlike carriers hanging down on either side of the animals. Another lone occupant sat atop the last beast, along with an enormous hutlike container that clearly carried all their supplies.

"Why does she sound like Long John Silver in drag?" Lori muttered.

Mavra frowned. "Who? Oh, you mean the archaic speech. You can get that and much worse when you're translating a language that's very different from yours. When you meet a race that clearly cannot form our sounds, particularly in a nontech hex, and it still sounds exactly right, watch out. That means the translator isn't translating, it's interpolating."

The Gekir chief was off the high mount almost as the huge creature stopped near the pool and snaked its long, hairy trunk into the water. The Gekir's motion was fluid, very feline, as if she hadn't a bone in her body. The forward pair of big, thick, short-fingered hands were used in this instance as if they were forelegs. But once on the ground, the Gekir chief supported herself on her four rear legs and raised her short torso and long neck in something of a centauroid fashion, although even ripples of skin under the fur gave an impression not of Dillian rigidity but almost of liquidity. The hindquarters, however, were smooth, with no hint of a tail.

The other Gekirs dismounted in similar fashion but made no effort to draw weapons or approach. Instead they simply gathered by the large animals and allowed their chief to handle the business at hand.

Although quite low to the ground, the Gekir projected a sense of bigness and strength. Certainly the creatures were large, and their hands, with the retractable claws, looked both powerful enough and sufficiently dangerous to rip one of the big mammothlike mounts to shreds. The chief came right over to them, showing no fear at all, and first the Erdomese, then the Dillians, and finally Mavra were inspected with large catlike eyes and an enormous twitching black nose. She looked at Mavra the closest, dwarfing the small woman. Mavra was close enough to touch the protruding fangs, and the creature's breath was intense enough almost to cause her to pass out.

Finally the Gekir said to Mavra, "You be like a *zumbaga*. Where do ye say ye was from?"

"Glathriel, Excellency. Type 41."

"Never heard of them."

"Might I ask what a *zumbaga* is?"

"Tiny bipedal apes. Horrid little pests they be. Be a tribe of 'em here somewheres. Can't be touched because they be royal property—protected, y' know."

She nodded. "We've seen them and noted the resemblance. They didn't look like they fit in here."

The Gekir gave a rumbling roar that the translator indicated was amusement. "They don't! They be brought here long ago in ancient times, and the ruler of the time, whose soul should be ever cursed for it, took a likin' to 'em and bred 'em. A royal pain in the arse, they be, but we keeps their numbers managed and limited to religious sites."

"I thought this might be a temple. That is why we did not enter it. We had no wish for anything but water before going to the coast."

"Indeed? And why be ye in Gekir at all, then, when there be all the stuff ye might like or need fifty leagues north in Bug Heaven?"

"We had no intention of coming here. Our business is far to the north and west of this whole area, and Gekir is out of our way." Briefly she explained how their train had gone the wrong way without really giving her suspicions as to why.

The chief was neither stupid nor ignorant. Both Mavra and Lori couldn't help noticing that she took the translator for granted and never once asked how it was they could be understood. "We hates all them things. They robs the soul from ye and make it impossible after a whiles t' tell the people from their machines. But the Bug machines don't go wrong, least not that we hear, and I can see the injury to that one's hand, there."

Mavra nodded, deciding to tell what she could without violating the whole detour's purpose. "Someone has been following us. We don't know who or why, but they have influence and money. They tried to kill me once, but now they seem satisfied to just keep me from going anywhere. We jumped off the train when we realized we were diverted and made for Gekir through the jungle. We spent the night on the rocks out there and hoped today to reach the coast and perhaps pay our way onto a coastal vessel or fishing boat and throw our pursuers off our scent."

The chief nodded. "Aye, we smelled yer camp and tracked you here. Been curious to see what ye might look like. Where ye be headin' to at the end of this business, and why?"

Mavra felt suddenly uncomfortable. "I—I'm sorry, your Excellency, but I cannot tell you that. The knowledge is of no great use to you, but if I told you, even in strict confidence, and you were later ordered by your government to report us or tell what we said and did, it would be your duty to do so. With all due respect, I cannot in good conscience place you in that position."

The big cat froze for a moment and glared fixedly at her, looking for all the world like an enraged lion about to pounce on a crippled antelope. But instead she said, "That big, is it?"

"Upon my honor it is."

Suddenly the chief gave an unmistakable grin, and again there was that growl of amusement. "Well, I think ye be full of shit, but I likes any little one with the gall to tell me to mind me own business and make it sound like they was doin' me some favor! Come on! We'll take ye all to a village on the seashore that might get ye out of me fur!"

The rest of the Gekirs, who'd watched all this not quite sure how their chief was going to react, now showed amusement and relaxed. The ice was broken.

Once the visitors were accepted, the Gekirs proved as pleasant and hospitable as their vague reputation to the north had them. Mavra, in fact, had a tougher time relaxing with the Dillians than she did with the Gekirs. To Tony and Anne Marie, it had been like listening to only one side of a phone call, with the Gekir growling and spitting and making, in Anne Marie's term, "*horrid* little noises." She, for one, liked her cats to be *much* smaller.

The patrol was clearly out on business unrelated to them but also unrelated to the temple and watering hole. There was a certain tit for tat, though, in that Shestah volunteered neither why they *were* out there or particularly why someone whose position equated to provincial governor would be with them. Even so, the old girl was quite talkative about her opinions, and she had one on almost everything.

"It be too damned *civilized*," she told Mavra. "Ain't been a war, so much as a revolution, in so many lifetimes, the young 'uns know about it only from stories. Game's all managed, been peace with the neighbors since forever. Only thing what saves us from slow death by boredom be the no-technology laws. Keeps families together, keeps the good values, makes ye *earn* yer keep. That's why we still got huntin' parties and all the rights and ranks. Afore ye gets rights here, ye got to come out t' *here* or someplace like it, bare of all stuff, make yer own kill, and live the old style. Rest of it's mock battles against the neighbor guv's kids. Just last month a team of me girls got right into old Skisist's office and poured glue on the High Seat." Again the chuckle, but this time with pride. "Took 'em three days to unstick the old witch, and she'll be 'arf a year growin' back the fur it cost 'er!"

She had a lot of stories, and it was clear that she loved telling them to someone, *anyone*, who hadn't heard them so often they were known by heart. Still, it was time to move out if they were to reach the coast in any reasonable time.

Lori looked up at the chief's elephantine mount and then back at Mavra. "You're *really* going to ride up there with her?"

"Sure. It'd insult her if I didn't, and she'll get to tell me dozens more tales before we're there. I know, I know, but it's a small price to pay when you think of it. I'd sure rather have to listen to her than fight her."

Lori nodded. "Amen to that. But—maybe, if you get the chance, you can find out what's really puzzling me."

"Yeah?"

"There are no males. None. They aren't even mentioned."

"Yeah, I *did* notice that," Mavra admitted. "They might well be unisexual. Many races are. Or maybe here the men are home doing the dishes and minding the kids." She shrugged. "We're going to a village, anyway. We'll know soon enough. I just want you to make sure that Alowi and the Dillians behave themselves and aren't scared or panicked by anything they might see. This chief's smart and sophisticated. A full report on us will be on its way to higher-ups as soon as she gets the chance. My only hope is that whoever's screwing us up didn't anticipate this move and enlist the locals here just in case. If not, then that report will be quickly headed southeast to the capital and from there to Zone. By then we should be long gone." *I hope,* she added to herself.

Lori still didn't like Mavra's way of thinking. "What if she *is* in on it?"

Mavra shrugged. "Then we're really no worse off than we were, are we?"

The top of the woolly creature was a *long* way up, and it took Tony's aid from below and the chief grabbing from above to get Mavra up. Once she was there, however, it proved a very wide and relatively secure platform, and the blanket spread out and secured on top was thick enough to kept the beast's backbone from being much of a problem, particularly in the crease between the first and second pairs of the three sets of legs.

The Gekir chief looked down at Lori and grinned. "Ye be all better goin' *aside* us 'stead of in the rear. Not unless ye want t' be steppin' in a huge load of the world's greatest fertilizer!"

It was a good point, one the essentially city-bred and civilized four-some who would walk or run along with the party would not have thought of until it became very obvious.

"We should have one of each of us on both sides of the chief's mount," a still suspicious Tony suggested. "That way we'd have maximum speed and position if anything went wrong."

"Yes, with Chang up there and trapped between us," Lori noted. "No, it's all right. It's still her show, and she is not only unconcerned, she is in her glory right about now. She's having a *lot* of fun. Can't you tell?"

"Yes, the woman's ego is unmatched," Tony agreed, "but you will note that while so far we have been more trouble and expense than aid to her, she wants us along. Why do you think that is? Company? She is an easy one to talk to, but beyond the surface there is someone tough, nasty, and possibly ruthless inside there we aren't permitted to see. If even a tenth of what she claims about herself is close to the truth, then inside her is one of the most dangerous people any of us have ever met. Did you see how confident she was in turning down that chief, for whom being re-fused is obviously a new experience? Could *you* have done it? Or me? And more important, could you have gotten away with it?"

"Well, I—" he stammered. "I hadn't really thought of it that way. So why *do* you think she's taking us along, then?"

"To remove obstacles for her if need be," Tony replied. "Big obstacles she can't talk her way or think her way out of. It might be an idea to remember that she thinks herself immortal, and, true or not, she believes it. We are here to keep her from being captured or badly injured, nothing more, but *we* are not immortal. She said an attempt was made on her life by two assassins before any of us were here. She never said what happened to the two assassins or who she might have been with then. We are . . . what is the term?"

"I believe the word you want is 'expendable,' dear," Anne Marie put in cheerfully. "What Tony is saying is to worry only about yourself and your wife in the end. *That* woman can take care of herself."

Lori looked back up at Mavra Chang thoughtfully. If that was true, and it certainly rang true, why didn't she just hire tough natives rather than transformed Westerners? A Gekir, for example, would make a formidable bodyguard and would probably love the job just for its potential danger.

Anne Marie read his thoughts. "She's short of funds, dear, and we're *much* cheaper."

Alowi was concerned about Lori running. "Are you certain that your leg is not going to go out again? That it is not too soon?"

"The leg is fine," he assured her. "Running on it will actually help me get back into shape. What about you? You were weak as could be this morning."

"I am fine now. I simply needed replenishment. I will not be a burden."

He hugged her. "You are *never* a burden to me! Don't think that!"

"I look up at *her* and I feel a wrongness. I cannot say if the wrongness is me or her, but it is one of us. She rides the monster beast as if she has ridden one her whole life, and she treats the orange and black creatures as if they are old friends, yet she is weak and tiny and could be destroyed by one strike of those hands."

"I know. I knew the first time I met her that she was different from anyone I ever knew, but I did not know how very different she was. Your concern is me. I will deal with Mavra Chang."

"My lone concern is you," she said sincerely, leaving no doubt that Mavra Chang's interests were of absolutely no importance to her at all.

He wished he felt as confident as he sounded. Damn it! What *had* happened to the two assassins?

* * *

The village turned out to be of considerable size, spreading out on all sides of a spectacularly beautiful bay and climbing the sides of low rolling hills to the east and south.

The buildings were basically of stone or brick with thick thatched roofs for the individual one-story houses and red slate for the larger or taller structures. The market and business district was surprisingly well developed, with buildings up to a block square and rising up to six stories high. The port was on the northern side of the bay, set off a bit by itself, including docks, piers, and warehouses. It was about as modern-looking as a nontech civilization was capable of managing. But that wasn't the startling part of the view eastward out toward the ocean; there was something else that commanded attention even more: a shimmering, odd effect, like a thin plastic wall, that seemed to go from north to south and intersected the two far points of land on either side of the bay.

"A sea hex boundary!" Lori exclaimed. "Right up to the town!"

"That be Ogadon," one of the Gekirs called down. "Ogadon takes in part of Muca Bay. The town be Port Saar."

Mavra, too, hadn't expected quite this elaborate a town or this good a port. "Ships *do* stop here, then!"

The chief nodded. "Not like up north in Itus, but that be far away from here, that port. Easier for us to have this and get what services we need direct than to wait weeks to get anything from the big port down at the Point. The wormies, who don't have much of a decent harbor down south, use it sometimes as well. That be why yer train thing be comin' so far south. See, that point of land just outside the border at the edge of the port is really in Ogadon, so they don't need no sail to come in, neither."

"No ships in now, though."

"Don't look it. We'll check the schedules when we gets down there. Don't expect ye'll want no big ships nohow, since they'd be goin' on from here to the wormies most like or south. Ye might be better makin' some deal with some smaller craft for crossin' the Great Bay to Parmiter or Awbri."

She nodded, not knowing if the gesture meant much here. "Do many smaller vessels actually come in here?"

The chief pointed. "Be a few of 'em down there now. The Ogadon, they be proper flesh eaters, so's they don't allow no fishin' as such, but they grows and maybe mines some real strange things down there that some folk of some nations take a real likin' to. Some of it's medicinal to some races, some is used as spices by others, and some's the kind of stuff what some folks like but other folks says is evil, if you take my meanin'. Don't know which races like what, though."

Mavra knew exactly what she meant. Somewhere, deep under the seemingly placid Ogadonian surface, was an entire underwater civilization probably as well developed as this one, and what they ate was some sort of fish or marine animal that was the equivalent of the Gekir's jackalopes or the variety of edible animals on Earth. But deep down somebody had discovered long ago that many of the sea bottom plants and growths produced substances or were themselves substances that affected other races. Southern hemisphere races, after all, had the common bonds of carbon-based life on the whole. As with other Well races, the Ogadon had turned this knowledge to profitable trade, selling the minerals that others might want or need as well as the plant material and chemicals that might be of use elsewhere. Minerals, spices, and medicines, perhaps, but among the variety in such a landscape was bound to be at least one substance that translated to a pleasure drug to one or perhaps many races on the surface. All this would be traded for such things a semitech, undersea race might well find of use but could not make itself.

"Does the government of Ogadon officially approve, disapprove, or ignore the stuff some call evil?" she asked carefully.

"Oh, they *got* to go after it to save their legal trade," the chief responded. "They even got agreements with some of the shippin' hexes to allow surface policin' of the smugglers. It be kinda hard, though, to put a real stop to it. We don't need none of it, so we just keeps out of it all."

I'll bet, Mavra thought, a sour smile on her face. This bay was tailormade for this kind of trade. If the Gekir, and particularly the local authorities, didn't have any use for the products, smugglers would still have a great use for this area. In fact, it explained the apparent prosperity better than anything else. This was a safe haven for such ships and one that served as a convenient place to repack illegal cargo, swap it between vessels, and transfer it ashore so that it could go by Itun train all the way to the Sea of Turigen and from there to other markets. It was a place where trade deals could be consummated with little fear of fancy eavesdropping and where strangers would always stand out.

Such a ship would be absolutely perfect for them—with one hitch. There probably wouldn't be much of a problem talking one of the captains into taking them aboard, but there might well be a problem in convincing captain and crew to maintain their silence and thus getting back off again.

ISLE OF MAHGUUL, DLUBINE

NATHAN BRAZIL AWOKE FROM the deepest sleep he could ever remember in his very long life feeling energized, exceptionally well, and alert. He sat up and opened his eyes and was instantly wide-awake, and he realized that it was daylight.

He sat up, got immediately to his feet, and looked around until it dawned on him how totally stupid that was. "Gus?" he called, then, getting no answer, he yelled *"Gus!"* at the top of his lungs so that the sound went around and around the volcanic bowl the ship was anchored inside.

There was no response.

There was too little sky for him to see the sun unless it was almost directly overhead, and considering that the anchorage was on the north side of the island, that was highly unlikely.

Save for the sound of water within the little inlet lapping gently against the sides of the ship and against the rock walls around and the rush of a small waterfall pouring from a rock fissure high above to the waters of the cove below, there was only silence in return.

He half expected Gus to suddenly pop up at his elbow any second, but when, after a minute or two, that didn't happen, he had to accept the fact that the Dahir had not yet returned. That was bad news; he should have had more than enough time to get around to the harbor, get inside, steal what he could, and get back to the boat.

In other circumstances Brazil thought he'd like this place, particularly this secluded cove, but for now he saw it less as a haven than as a trap.

In daylight the passage in seemed even more narrow than it had coming through it in the darkness, so narrow in fact that it would be nearly impossible for ships of even this size to pass each other once in it and even easier for a smaller ship to block the exit. Nonetheless, he felt as if he had to wait—all day if need be, if he was patient enough to manage it.

But before nightfall he'd have to move out, and he couldn't afford to go looking for the former Earthman. He'd cut him what breaks he could, but his own fate was quite literally more important than Gus's, and if Gus could stay alive, he could do more for the fellow once inside the Well than he could in some naval prison.

It was only after he'd run through all the possible options and decided which ones were valuable that he had time to reflect on himself.

He felt—odd. "Tingly" was the best word he could come up with.

Last night, with the girl, tired and tense as he was, he'd let himself go completely. He remembered it, even felt a shiver of pleasure at the thought, but the bottom line was that all his own defenses had been down.

In a sense he was relieved to be still thinking like himself and able to shout Gus's name. Hell, he'd been wide open last night. He tried to remember, but it was harder to remember emotion and sensation than, say, a conversation or a fight. Still, as he reconstructed it as best he could in his mind, he realized that something *had* happened. Whatever was inside her had taken the opening, had rushed to consume him at the very climax of passion—and for some reason hadn't been able to do the job completely.

In a sense that reassured him, but he was also aware that his body was subject to much of what all mortal flesh was heir to.

He suddenly realized that he hadn't once wondered where *she* was. He hadn't wondered because although she was forward and out of his sight, he *knew* where she was, knew exactly what she was doing, what she was feeling . . .

Knew exactly what she was seeing!

It wasn't telepathy, not exactly. If she thought conventionally, it did not come through. He knew, though, that he could contact her, summon her, send a whole range of basic concepts her way if need be. She knew he was inside her head at the same time he was still himself, and he knew beyond a doubt that she had the same experience with him. He could see, hear, feel, taste what she did, even feel the wind in her hair as if it were his own hair.

Man, this is really weird! he thought.

It was as if he suddenly had two bodies, one his old male self, the other hers, yet most peculiar of all, there was no confusion in his mind over which was which. *I almost feel like I can explain the Trinity to a Christian,* he thought with characteristic humor.

But while he now shared every single real-time experience with her, he had no direct control of that other self. As she lifted some of the little water that remained in one of the water traps to her lips, he felt the water—felt it on her lips, felt it go down—but he could not control any of her actions, only experience them. Taken together with the preexisting empathic link, they were totally, absolutely connected as if parts of the same organism, yet at the same time still their individual selves.

It fascinated him like nothing else he could ever remember, and it troubled him only in one way.

He could not make her body do anything at all, but she had made a sailor of a totally alien race put a pistol to itself and then, when he'd yelled and made his shock clear, made that sailor jump overboard just as if he'd been some kind of puppet.

Could she now, through this linkage, manipulate *his* body?

He very much wanted to know that, but he was afraid at this moment to find out. He *knew,* without having to think any further, that she would never harm him or cause him to come to harm, but that wasn't the point.

He tried not to think of that for now and instead concentrated on other things that were only now becoming apparent to him.

Whatever she had tried to take from him, or alter, involuntarily or not, she had clearly failed to do, but she had certainly given as well.

It was hot here, almost intolerably hot. He could see evaporation even in the secluded cove, and the very air shimmered and twisted. If it had been in the high thirties Celsius well into the night, what must it be now? High forties at the very least, he knew. Certain things were constants. It *looked* that hot, and everything he could check indicated it really *was* that hot, but although stark naked, he felt comfortably warm, quite pleasant, really, as if the air were perhaps just a shade under body temperature.

That enviable protection that she'd had against all extremes of weather had finally been extended to him as well. He had a strong feeling, though, that the ability, and possibly other as yet unknown powers, did not come without some price, and he was well aware that whatever was doing it was coming from her. Something, some power or energy field, now tied them together as absolutely as if it were a great rope tied between them. He realized, *knew,* that the bonds were so tightly knit that there was no chance of one leaving the other any more than his arms could go one place and his legs somewhere else entirely. It gave a whole new meaning to the word "inseparable," he thought.

The question was, Who was binding whom?

Of course *she* had done it, whether by design, nature, or command he didn't know, but the question was one of both motive and control. She was certainly an individual, but an individual who had been repro-grammed to a remarkable degree. The fact that he knew that her total concern for him was not only benign but a matter of genuine affection was meaningless; whatever rules now governed her thinking might have quite a different interpretation of what was in his best interest than he himself might.

He wondered how the insulation worked. It had to be extremely thin and entirely energy-based. Somehow it maintained an internal fixed environment for the two of them almost like an extra layer of skin. Things felt normal to him; the wooden deck was firm and solid and appeared fully capable of giving him a splinter if he wasn't careful. He wondered if something that was boiling hot would feel that way to him or if his tongue would still freeze to a pump handle at forty below. Probably not, considering how well she'd gotten along in the snow, but he wondered what the criteria were and whether a people living in a tropical swamp next to a subtropical region had thought of everything. It would not be wise to take things for granted.

Terry was delighted by the new contact; he felt that as well and also felt that she was somewhat surprised by it. But as joined as they were, they still did not have an effective means of communication. To Brazil's astonishment, it was Terry, not he, who attempted a real start in that direction.

She walked back over to the water collector, almost dry and smelling less than wonderful, and just looked at it. Then she turned and looked back at the entire ship, then over again to the small waterfall on the other side. It wasn't until she repeated the pattern twice more that he realized she was "talking" to him. The message was clear and so obvious that he wondered why he hadn't thought of it himself. If that waterfall resulted from the rain at the top of the volcano coming down through cracks rather than from some internal and probably foul source, just putting the ship under it would allow them to totally refill the containers below with fresh water. But it would be tricky in such tight quarters to weigh anchor and use the little bit of circular current inside the cove to bring the ship around to where that would be practical.

Now, how much of me got transferred as well? he wondered. It was time to find out. He walked forward until he had the anchor winch in sight, then made a turning motion with his hand, then looked back at the wheel, still in view from where he was.

She went over to the winch and stared at it but shook her head. He knew she had understood his suggestion; the problem was that she could not, or would not, compromise her hunter-gatherer principles even to that degree. He was back at the wheel, staring forward, more in her head than in his own but feeling frustrated.

Suddenly she stared down at the deck almost aimlessly and began breathing heavily, and he felt her go into what could only be described as some sort of trance. Her vision blurred; all outside sensations suddenly ceased. Curious, he leaned against the wheel and waited. There seemed to be no hurry.

He felt a sudden tremendous, powerful rush, very much like a gust of wind, only it went into him and through him. He felt sudden vertigo, and then something seemed to be pulling him, pulling him forward, even though he was not physically moving at all. Rather, it was as if his consciousness, his very inner self, were being sucked out of his body and it rushed forward, *through* the top of the cabin, *through* the mainmast, and deposited him forward, where the feelings of the body returned to him, yet the force that had reached for and grabbed him had not dissipated but rather was felt now as tension, as if he were stretched on the end of a taut rubber band. He had felt—*something*—pass him in the opposite direction during the pull and knew that it had been the girl, moving back to his own body even as he moved forward toward hers.

He was Terry.

He was in Terry's body, and it felt strange to him yet natural. When he breathed in and out, the body breathed, the head moved, the arms and legs functioned. Shocked, even dazed, he saw the winch in front of him, turned it, quickly raising the anchor about halfway, and then threw the lock switch. The moment he did it and stood away, the tension broke, and he was pulled out of her body and back into his own body still leaning on the wheel aft. Again he felt himself passing her as she was pulled back into her own body forward.

Sensation and the absence of that force or tension brought him to immediate control in his own body, and he had to make a quick turn and spin the wheel hard as the stern drifted a bit toward the rocks. Old reflexes took hold, and he coaxed the small ship bit by bit out, catching the tiny, subtle spin of the water caused by both the inrush of ocean water and the action of the waterfall, and managed to get it pointed directly for the falls. Now, moving slowly, he locked the wheel and went forward to the winch, the very same winch he'd used before without having left the wheel, unhooked a long grappling hook from its holder on the rail, and waited. As the bow went under the falls, he felt the water wash over him and then lashed out from the rail with the hook, deflecting the bow from going head on into the rock cliff. He almost slipped on the suddenly wet deck as he leaned against the hook, and he let go with perfect timing so that the bow only glanced against the rock and started moving back out, the waterfall now just behind him.

Thank heaven it was just a very small waterfall. A big one would have swamped them for sure. Even this one might.

It was warm water, but it seemed to be good water; he stood under, let it shower him, and he reached out, let his cupped hands fill, and drank it. It went down very well indeed.

Except he wasn't doing that. He was standing there with the hook, ready to try a push-off lest the waterfall flood the deck when the containers below were full and the collectors were backed up to topside. If a lot of water got below, inside the cabin, hold, and other parts of the hull, they could wind up sinking the ship. *He* wasn't enjoying the shower, but *she* was.

He couldn't hear much over the sound of the small falls, but he turned and watched, worried. The girl got the idea and moved out of the immediate stream of the falls, staring at the collector.

There was a sudden gurgle, and the collector filled and began overflowing right onto the deck like a bathtub with no drain. Frantically he pushed off as best he could, but it was the stern that started moving in a semicircle; the bow was getting lower in the water.

Anxiously, he ran back, trying not to slip on the wet deck. He got to the wheel, unlocked it, and tried to steer the ship out of the trap he'd put them in. *Now* he realized why he hadn't considered it. The ship moved a little but not enough.

The girl seemed to sense the problem, too, and now she stepped out of the falls and stared intently at the rock cliff. There was a sudden release of the same sort of energy he'd felt in the switch of bodies, only this time directed straight at the cliff. The ship shuddered and Brazil was knocked off his feet, but the shuddering was the action of the ship moving back slowly out of the stream, away from the cliffside. The falls hit the rail, then actually began supplementing the backward movement.

In a moment they were free of it. He grabbed the wheel, straightened it out, and let momentum take him several meters beyond the splash zone of the falls. He locked the wheel and moved forward to drop the anchor. He would remain in the center of the cove if he could this time.

He did an immediate visual check to see how badly they'd been flooded. The only pumps below were hand pumps, and they weren't the sort one handled one at a time but only in pairs.

It didn't seem all that bad, so he went forward to the cabin and went below. There was maybe 150 millimeters of water below, but it didn't look bad and certainly not enough to use pumps on. It had been a close thing, though; a few minutes more under that stream and there would have been a couple of *meters* in there, and that would have made it very difficult indeed.

Relieved, he went back topside, then aft to the wheel. He sank down on the deck and gasped for air, shaking himself as the tension inside him was released. It was several minutes before he recovered enough to think about all that had just happened.

My God! Did she really draw me out of my body and into hers? How was that possible?

He knew somehow that it indeed had happened, though, and it was another example of power that scared him. She had the power, with no training and no background, to do at least as much as if not more than the greatest of those Oriental mystics he'd told Gus about. If all Glathrielians had this kind of power . . .

Worse, she'd made a decision and split hairs like a theologian. Rather than compromise and operate that winch, she'd worked nothing short of a miracle so that he, not she, could use her body to raise that anchor for him.

And then, having gotten him to go along with her idea before he'd had a chance to think it out, she'd used some of that same power to push a ship that had to weigh more than a stegosaurus back away from the falls and all the way to the center of the channel. The total consequence of what she'd done was that she now felt a little dizzy and lightheaded.

Where did that energy come from? How was it stored? It wasn't from the Well, or anything to do with the Well, that was for sure. Somehow it came from inside her and was stored . . . *as body fat?* It seemed ridiculous, but it was the only explanation that made sense.

It sure beat the hell out of any diet plan he could think of, and it made diets anathema for all that.

She *was* paying a price, perhaps for using two such blasts so close together, possibly because they hadn't eaten very much in several days; she lay down on the wet deck forward and just passed out.

This is really weird, he thought once more. *For the first time I almost think I have a crack at making it before Mavra. I've never had this kind of power on my side before, not until I was inside.*

But *she* controlled the power, he didn't.

Or did she?

He lay down, suddenly struck by an idea. If he was now connected to her so tightly, this energy must be the bond. There had to be some sort of energy field, automatically emanating from her to him, or the bond would be broken at times like this. Surely such abilities, in many ways like what the Gedemondans had been after, at least the last time he'd been there, had to be learned, suffered for, studied, and experimented with for countless years, perhaps countless generations, depriving those who sought such power of almost everything that might provide as the slightest distraction.

At least they hadn't also taken on celibacy, although that would hardly be practical in a grand experiment involving an entire population over thousands of generations.

Maybe that was where the lamas had gone wrong back in the Himalayas. They had brought themselves to the limits of individual higher mental attainments, but the emphasis had still always been on *individual* attainment, and although their belief in reincarnation gave them ample time in their own minds, in reality death had cut them off short. Even without that limitation Brazil had eventually abandoned that life when he'd suddenly realized that the attainment of the absolute, the joining with the That Which Is Behind All That, was oblivion. It was too much like being at the end of the line with the Markovians but not having had any fun getting there. It was, however, a god-awful amount of work, whether it was that traditional system of Earth's or the Glathrielian grand project.

The fact that the Glathrielians had given her the end results of this work, much as one would stick a bunch of programs on a computer mass storage device for easy access, didn't really matter. Everything he'd seen of Glathrielians indicated a total rejection of the physical ways of the world. The most they did was pick some fruit off trees. Even when doing that, he'd observed how their actions were almost hivelike, almost as if they were a collective organism even though on the surface they seemed like individuals. They condescended to the body only in the sense of its need to eat, drink, sleep, and reproduce.

They had given Terry those powers and imposed that overculture as a kind of control program, but she'd not been born into it or brought up with it. It wasn't a natural state to her. Like him or Gus, she had more in common in her background with the Ambrezans than with the Gedemondan mystics, but she had no way of really understanding it. She had been surprised to get any sort of a linkage with him after being together so long. That was the group mind part, the impulse to co-opt those of one's own kind into the greater consciousness. But she was still too much the individual inside, and when she'd absolutely had to, she had compromised the Glathrielian programming in a way that the group mind part of the Gedemondan whole would never have even considered.

Faced with Terry's very appearance, they had done the one thing with her that such a community, insular as it was, wasn't all that used to doing.

They had improvised.

He thought he had them now, although not by any means all their powers and strengths. He doubted that *she* knew what she could do, except it was inside her, like individual programs on disks, waiting to be accessed if demanded by circumstance. A Glathrielian would know. A true Glathrielian *child* would know, would probably have fun switching bodies and moving stones and doing who knew what else. They had the experience of the group mind and were raised and trained to know. But they'd had Terry for only the shortest time. Days or weeks, perhaps.

A television professional would think of things first in visual terms. They must have seized on that as something *simpático* with their own way of thinking. Whole chunks that made a picture, an object rather than a linear assemblage of cross-referenced information. The holographic mind with no intermediate steps, no aids, not even a linear language to slow down the process. Need? *Bang!* Entire solution. Just like that.

He could see them now, considering *him* before they had her. He'd been living very close to them for a while. They sensed his difference, sensed, perhaps, his connection to the Well. They couldn't tap or access that connection, but they understood it on their level, and they understood the potential. But what to do? Problem, even opportunity, but no solution.

Then, suddenly, Terry walks in. She's in shock, she's scared, and she's Earth-human, or close enough to Glathrielian that they recognize her as one of their own. Possibly their communal field was strong enough and she was still shocked enough from her arrival that she sensed and was perhaps even guided by the permeating group mind. They had taken her in, and they had made her one of them, or so it seemed. Compromise was necessary. In them, everything was to a purpose; in her, it had to run on automatic.

Then they sent her back with an absolute command to remain with him at all costs. Sooner or later he might let his guard down. When it happened, she was to copy everything from her mind to his. Make him Glathrielian. Then, when he entered the Well, he would be one of them. The whole of Glathriel could then be connected to the Well itself.

That was how they differed from the Gedemondans. The Gedemondans were seeking a third way, as the founding race had intended, a new way to attain power and an even greater godhood on their own.

The Glathrielians wanted to take over the damned controls!

Well, they couldn't do it, but how would they know that? It was certainly worth a shot. Worth risking one strange girl.

So last night she had made the link, made the attempt, automatically. Not even the whole of Glathriel could do it even with his cooperation, but she'd made the attempt. She'd transferred the programs and linked the two of them so that the energy that was her only tool was shared. His Earth-human body and physical brain and nervous system were still human enough for that. What they could not do, could never do, was get down to the core of his being, his "soul" for want of any better concept, and reprogram at that level. They could control every aspect of his body but not his core ego.

But the programs were still there. Perhaps not in his mind, because of their ultimate failure, but accessible from *hers* over the energy linkage. That linkage had to be physiological to some degree; she'd tapped into something inside him, perhaps inside all Earth-human brains, and activated it. Whether necessary for their plans or not, he would have to accept and accommodate the control program requirements as much as possible, but some of it could be bypassed either by force of will, as when she'd compromised for expediency, or because it was designed to filter *her* input/output, not his. He might not be able to run the whole suite of programs concurrently because of this, but maybe, just maybe, because they'd been designed to be run by someone who didn't have the owner's manual, he might run them one at a time.

He was wide-awake, even a little excited, but he remembered his own long lessons in mental discipline from long ago and relaxed, closing his eyes, clearing his mind, breathing deeply, rhythmically, letting his consciousness roam, but not without a sense of purpose. He felt her, felt everything about her, matched her own deep breathing, thought only of the secondhand but very real existence of her own body, not his own.

This time it was very gentle, very slow. There was no rushing force, no fast-forward pull, not even disorientation. He moved toward her, into her and gently displaced her, sending her, still in a deep, deep sleep, back along the path and inserting himself fully into her body.

He opened his eyes—*her* eyes, knowing that his own body still reclined aft, now sound asleep. Carefully he sat up, then discovered that he was partly sitting on long hair and pulled it free.

He felt the body's fatigue, and there were a few aches and pains where muscles and joints pleaded for more rest, but he wasn't going to do this for very long. He got up on her feet, feeling a bit dizzy, even a little sick, but nothing he couldn't manage. A smile played across her lips.

The old adage holds true again, as always, he thought with some glee. *Never try to con a con man. He'll pick your pockets while letting you believe you're stealing him blind.*

He began to walk forward, keeping one hand on something to steady her body, and considered that it wasn't quite as similar as he'd imagined. The center of gravity was different and took a little getting used to; he was more aware of the large breasts and equally aware of the lack of male genitalia than he'd considered. Still, it was basically the same: two legs, two arms, eyes, and ears. Things *did* look a bit different, and he wondered for a moment if that was something new he was tapping. After all, he was also using her brain, even if his memories and personality were being scrolled off his own sleeping form. Then he realized that it was just that there were subtle shifts in the colors. So it was true—for purely physical reasons no two people probably saw colors exactly the same. But they weren't all *that* different—green still looked green, red looked red. They were just slightly different, often in brightness or degree, although he thought he saw more gradations of each color than he'd been aware of before. There also seemed to be a vastly wider array of smells, both good and bad, indicating that the biochemists had been right in saying that women really *could* smell a greater variety of scents than men. That explained why there were so many varieties of perfume even though most men, himself included, could barely tell the difference.

He tried to speak. "Hello, I am not Terry," he croaked. Her voice was raspy and it was almost painful to awaken those throat muscles so long silent, but it sounded like a decent voice, a nice voice, although he knew it would sound different to her, or to him as her, than it would to him as himself.

This was already more than enough for now, but he couldn't resist making his way slowly and carefully aft, then climbing the stairs and looking down at his own sleeping body.

Good lord! I really am *an ugly SOB*, he thought. As many times as he'd seen himself in a mirror, it was different to look upon his body through another's eyes.

Still, he'd proved his point and gotten something of a charge out of it at that. Hell, he vaguely remembered being an animal once, for some reason, the details of which totally escaped him. But he'd never been a woman.

In the distance he heard the sound of a steam whistle. Something was leaving the harbor, something with power, and that meant the naval corvette unless somebody new had shown up. Instantly he felt a pang of fear at the thought that they might have caught Gus and were now going hunting.

He had to get back in his own body and quickly. Not only would this be embarrassing, her body was too worn out to be of any real use in a fight right now, even if he could get used to it fast enough to do the quick, automatic moves that might be required.

He suddenly panicked at the thought that he might well be stuck in her body; he had not, after all, quite done it her way even if he'd used her inner knowledge and power to do it. And with thoughts suddenly coming to him about the possible implications of that steam whistle, how could he clear his mind enough to do it, anyway?

He had to, he decided. He just had to. There was no other choice.

Carefully, he lay down alongside his body, stretched out, and closed his eyes, resisting the body's impulse to lapse back into deep slumber. *Not yet,* he thought, and tried to re-create the conditions he'd established when he had started the stunt, putting all sounds, all worries, out of the way, concentrating only on doing the one thing.

Although he'd done it more gently, there still was a tiny bit of that tension there, and he was able to use it. He naturally belonged over there, and she naturally belonged here. There was a better fit, for want of a more appropriate term, when each was in the body he or she had been born to. It wasn't like what the Well did, not a bit.

A hand slid over a little and touched his, and he felt himself flow back into his body and her back into her own without any real effort or direction.

He opened his eyes, sat up, and shook his head as if to clear it, then looked down and actually felt around himself just to make sure he was in the form he wanted to be in.

He could hear the sound of engines now, coming closer, coming their way. *Thank God they didn't let go that whistle when I was trying to get back inside,* he thought, quickly running through his options.

There wasn't any real wind; the heat and the high rock walls had created a nearly dead calm inside the cove. His mind raced through all possible combinations of sail, anything that might get him moving if he had to, but he finally realized that it wouldn't matter if he had an atomic engine.

If that cutter came in the passage, its cannon and small arms would be on him no matter what he tried, and it would be like shooting fish in a barrel.

There was only one possible way to escape, and he didn't like it a bit. They'd have to go over the side opposite where the cutter would come in and swim for it to the rock formations beyond. Most of the cliff was sheer, but there was a small break in the outer rocks that might provide a way out through an eroded, irregular crack in the wall. If they could make it through there, they might be able to get up a bit and inland enough so that the cutter wouldn't be able to find them.

They'd be stuck on a speck of volcanic rock with the navy searching for them, but it would be a chance. At least, with the protection he now had from her energy shell, it wouldn't be immediately life-threatening and would give him a chance to figure out something.

The cutter was coming very close now, *very* close. It would be at the mouth of the narrow passage in perhaps a minute or two.

Terry was suddenly up, and he felt her momentary confusion at waking up somewhere far removed from where she'd thought she'd gone to sleep, but she dismissed it immediately. She had slept through all his clever tricks, but she'd come instantly awake when she'd felt his sense of peril.

Using sign language, he pointed in the direction of the passage, then at the water, and made swimming motions, pointing to the far end of the cove where the crack was. He had no idea if that crack was big enough for either of them, having only noted it in passing, but it was better than nothing.

She nodded, and he felt her draw on some reserve of strength and become suddenly energized in the physical sense, tense and ready to jump into the water.

The engine sounds echoed down the passage and into the cove itself; Brazil was certain that the ship would be coming down the passage, was perhaps coming down even now, and that they should wait no longer.

Still, something stopped him. Something subtle, a very slight diminution of the sound, perhaps, that rapidly grew more noticeable. He looked up over the jagged rock wall and saw a plume of white smoke proceed in an orderly fashion down the misshapen spires at the top.

The damned thing wasn't coming in! It had passed them by!

He laughed out loud in relief, grabbed Terry, and kissed her. She was somewhat startled by the action but felt his joy and relief and knew what it meant.

For a moment at least they were safe once again, and, he reflected, it was the perfect end to the business he'd been playing at. Being able to tap all that power, to do all these new things, hadn't changed the fact that he was a fugitive hiding out from the closest thing to a government this world had, stuck inside a bunch of barren and smoky rocks on a fly speck of an island in the middle of an indifferent ocean.

He signed to the girl to go back to sleep. She needed the rest almost as much as they both needed food. At least he was no longer overanxious to get under way; he wanted the navy to be well on its way to wherever it was going and well over the horizon before he ventured out. But more than ever he was determined to leave and to weather whatever the nights in this hotbox hex might bring.

There was no more game playing. While Terry slept, he pored over the charts, seeking some sort of alternative source for food. There were other islands, certainly; this was the start of a crescent-shaped chain of island volcanoes, many quite a bit larger above the surface than this little dot. The question was what, if anything, the Well would allow to take root in the rich soil. Whatever it would be would have to be consistent with the fixed ecology of the hex and not injurious to it or vegetation that would be expected to evolve on the actual planet this place represented.

He examined the topographic information, sparse as it was, on the various charts and guessed by knowing something of volcanic islands and checking elevations that one larger island about forty-five kilometers northwest was the most likely. It was kind of peanut-shaped, two volcanoes that had risen large and whose flows had merged into each other at the center, creating a single unit that appeared to be a lowland plain. He wondered for a moment why the service company hadn't put an anchorage there, but a reference to the island on the chart legend showed that flows were irregular, were not far below the surface all along both sides, and tapered off at an extremely shallow slope for a fair distance. There simply was no decent sheltered harbor available, and the only anchorage spots were marked at four or five hundred meters out even for a ship with this draft. From that distance one would be expected to come ashore in a small boat or raft. It was marked emergency provisions only, and the only indication that there was anything there was the note of the locations along both coasts of the flat region—the sort of place one made for if one was shipwrecked or at least too damaged to get anywhere else. There were no habitation markers, but its position and the stations indicated that it would probably be checked on a regular basis by the company, the navy, or both.

It also would take them even closer to the Mowry border instead of toward the northern coast, but without food it would be touch and go.

Unless Gus came back, and with enough to eat, they had no choice but to try it.

The next problem was how the hell to get out of this cul-de-sac. There was a very slight gravitational tide, but without a clock or a means of recording it he couldn't even use *that*, meager as it was, nor did he know if it would be enough. He looked up at the rock cliff and the forbidding terrain beyond. He had used a slight wind to get in, essentially a land breeze or one created by the nearby storms. It would be enough to get out if it was an every-evening thing. He'd just have to wait and see. He couldn't count on the girl to move the ship again, and they sure as hell couldn't push or pull it.

If there was a breeze, anything at all he could use, he'd have to take it, whether Gus was back or not. He realized that now. Whether it came in two minutes or ten hours, that was the way it was.

For the time being there was nothing to do but lie down, stretch out, and rest. After a while he looked over at the girl and studied her features. For all the extra weight, whose purpose he now knew, she had a good body and a very pretty face. It was hard to imagine her as a hard-driving career newswoman.

That was the problem, of course, and he knew it. He didn't really want her to be any different—he wanted what they had now on the gut level to continue on and on. If he got to the Well before Mavra, or even if Mavra got there first but left his own connection intact, he would have to undo much of what had been done to her. Her future had to be her own choice, not his. He owed her that much.

But if she were restored, even with the memory of all this, what would that *other* woman, Terry, whom he'd never known, think of him? And what sort of reaction might she have seeing him not this way but as something of a monster?

As usual, he was racing to the inevitable ending of a situation that had filled him, for all that, with a sense of participation, care, even . . . love. He was more happy and content with her than he'd been or felt in his long memory, and the only thing he and fate as personified by the authorities and the Well could do was shove him toward ending it.

He wanted the situation, and her, to remain as it was now. The only woman around with no interest in a wardrobe, jewels, makeup, or perfumes and one who never nagged or complained about anything—the perfect mate, he thought sardonically, using his usual defensive humor to mask his inner pain.

Maybe he was just being a sucker again, he thought, unable to dispel his dark mood. He didn't *want* to get to the Well, which represented only a return to that endless existence he so hated. Why not just find one of these tropical islands with abundant food and water to support two people, sink the damned ship, and retire, just the two of them? *Let* Mavra fix whatever was broken and go back through. If she disconnected him, then he'd just grow old with Terry and finally die—and find the peace in that he'd never known.

It was terribly appealing, but he knew he'd never do it. It was this damnable sense of *obligation* he had.

Damn it! There were a million reasons why Mavra might have vanished in that long-ago time and place. But why had she never tried to find him in the two and a half thousand years or so since? If only to let him know, even if not to get together. Even allowing for all that, if only Gus hadn't painted a picture of a man-hating mental case . . . !

Gus had a colored view of her, of course. He might be all wrong, and Mavra might be just fine and fully capable of handling things.

She *might* be, but deep down he wasn't sure he believed it. At least, he wasn't sure enough of her to trust the fate of all those races, all those people out there, scattered, seeded among the stars. He hadn't had to take the obligation or the responsibility for them, and perhaps, knowing what he did now, he would not do so again. But he *had* accepted it, and even if he'd occasionally run from the responsibility, he couldn't really hide. It wasn't just hiding from the Well that was the problem; it was that he could never hide from himself.

Eventually he dozed off in spite of himself.

He awoke in the waning part of the day, feeling very good, very refreshed, but thirsty. But when he got up to go get a drink of water, he discovered that he was in her body, not his own. Her body, yes, but this time it felt natural, neither odd nor different, nor did the sights and sounds and smells seem out of place. Still, he went and got the drink and returned aft, only to see his own body at the wheel and other controls, dropping sail, bringing the little craft about in the wind.

"What are you doing?" he called out in her voice. "You don't know how to sail a ship! I wouldn't even think you'd want to!"

His body's face looked surprised and two dark eyes stared at the figure just below. "You can speak!" he heard his own voice say. "You've got speech back! That's wonderful!"

"What do you mean? It's you who have changed! We've swapped bodies, that's all, probably in our sleep. We'd best swap back so I can take her out. You'll wreck her!"

"Are you mad?" his other self asked. "I'm Nathan Brazil! I was captaining craft bigger and smaller than this before your world was formed! What's this nonsense about body switching? You're Terry, and you've been through a lot of shocks. Let me just get us under way and we'll have some time once we get to open sea! I want out while there's still some light!"

"But—but—you're not Nathan Brazil, I'm Nathan Brazil!"

The other laughed. "This sharing of sensation has restored your speech but given you delusions! Look! What's the name of that sail? Where's the jib? The boom? When should you run with a spinnaker?"

"Uh—I—I—" she stammered, suddenly realizing that she had no answers to those questions. But Nathan Brazil would know, of course, and obviously did know from the way he was operating things up there. She sat down on the hatch cover and tried to think. What did she know? What did she remember? It was all fleeing, rushing out of her head even as she tried to grab on to the memories, the thoughts, the knowledge they represented.

It was all gone in a flash, leaving only the question of whether it had ever really been there. What did she know? She remembered coming into the vast chamber, reaching the place with the giant furry creatures, having met and joined with others like herself in some kind of swampy jungle, then of seeing Brazil and finding him very attractive and going with him . . .

There was no shock, only an intense if incredibly odd feeling of relief, of a massive weight lifted off the shoulders. Why, then, it must be true, she thought. I don't have any responsibilities beyond being with him, helping him, and being happy! I'm not Nathan Brazil, I'm just Terry! I must have gotten enough from him to feel his burden and his pain, and I just wanted to take that away from him. She felt sorry for him, knowing what a burden he carried inside, and she resolved to try to make it as easy on him as she could. She loved him so much, she'd wanted to take that burden off him and carry it herself, but the load was so overwhelming . . .

"Wake up, Cap," said Gus, shaking him.

Nathan Brazil opened his eyes and for a moment still thought he was Terry, but he wasn't. No matter his dreams, he couldn't be let off the hook that easily . . .

"What the hell took you so long, Gus?" he snapped, more irritated to be awakened than glad to see the Dahir.

"Well, they got wanted posters out on you, for one thing. Probably took 'em off a blowup of the recording when you come in. Right now all it says is that you're wanted for theft of a private vessel, and they give a pretty good description of this scow, too. Good thing you decided not to go in the harbor, Cap. You'd never have stood 'em all off."

That was bad. "But what about you?"

"Well, all sorts of stuff. Best-laid plans and all that, I guess. Nobody noticed me, as usual, but when I was through pickin' up information and supplies, I found something for my own belly as well, and after I eat I get groggy and sleepy for a little, and, well, I guess I just dozed off. I still feel like a stuffed turkey, but it was well into daylight when I woke up. I decided to fight off any idea of getting some more snoozin' and get back here. Fact was, I was worried that you'd cut out. Then I heard the boat whistle. All the crew of that cop ship got back aboard pretty fast, and they got up steam and pulled out. I got real nervous that they'd made you and were takin' off after you."

"Yeah, that gave us a turn as well. Went right on by, though."

"Well, I figured that, since word was that one of the small ships that come in sometime today had seen some other ship on their wanted list a ways off to the east. Some kind of big-time smuggler craft—the way they talked, sounded like drugs or somethin' to me. Whoever it is, they want 'em as bad as they want us, and the cop captain pulled everybody out and took off as fast as he could get up steam. Seems these crooks pull the shell game at sea so you can never be sure which boat's got the goods, and they figured this one was steamin' for a pickup."

"Interesting. Well, at least it gets them off our backs for the moment, but don't think there aren't more of them around—and if the posters have hit even a little spot in the middle of nowhere like this, you can bet we're marked. Did you remember to bring the sack with the food?"

"Oh, yeah. Did better'n that, really. Come over here and look over the side. I'll need some help with it gettin' it all aboard."

Brazil was astonished to find not the meter-square aid kit container but a full-blown plastic dinghy filled with cartons. "Good lord! They let you get away with all *this*?"

"Well, they didn't stop me, anyway. Truth is, there was a lot of furry types and all in the cop crew, and this was one of the supply shipments due to go out to their boat. They left it there at the dock in their rush to pull out, so I just kinda slipped into the water and took it instead."

"Great. You're sure it's not ammo and two thousand copies of my wanted poster, though?"

"It's food, Cap. Maybe not all of it's useful, but a lot is. Nothin' looks exactly like it did back home, but fruit and veggies have a habit of lookin' pretty close, and there's flour and some kinda meal like cornmeal and other stuff like that. I checked after I got out of the harbor but before I got too far away to go back. I figured I better let them cops get some distance, I didn't want 'em suddenly rememberin' that they forgot this and comin' back for it. They might not see *me* in the water, but they'd sure as hell see this raft and figure it got loose and floated away."

"Good work, Gus! And quick thinking! This is a real break in a number of ways. If they needed this enough to come back for it, they'd have turned around by now. The company people won't miss it because they'll assume it was taken aboard the cutter, and the cutter might not come back this way for weeks or even remember it if and when it does. Now, if we can only get this aboard and get enough wind to get out of this cove, we're good for the distance."

"How's that? You mean you can't get *out* of this place?"

"Not without some help from nature, or what passes for nature on the Well World. Come on—let's get started getting this aboard so if and when something comes up we don't have to dump it or get stuck until somebody finds us."

"You're ridin' a bit low in the water, ain't you? It looked kinda different."

"Yeah, we, ah, took on a little water, but I don't think it's serious. We might have to get on the pumps later if it proves a real problem, but I'm not worried about it now."

Gus slid back over the side and positioned himself on one side of the raft. "Cap, my arms can't lift their shadows, but I figure I can get under it and get it balanced, I can lift it up on my head. You'll have to grab it and pull it aboard, though. Anything that falls in, I'll try and get after-ward."

"Good enough. I hope *I* can do it. I'm strong for my weight, but I'm only sixty-one kilos or so."

"Huh? What's that in pounds?"

"Old English measure? Jeez, I barely recall. About 135, I think."

"Well, you're not a ninety-eight-pound weakling, so you'll have to do. I'll help if I can. With this flat tail and a head as hard as my mother always said it was, I should be able to give it a little oomph."

The first two tries didn't make it, but they lost only one carton to the water and it floated nearby. On the third try he was aware that Terry was now awake and watching them. When Gus came up again, Nathan grabbed the rope affixed to the raft and pulled up and back with all his might. After almost getting it, he felt it start to slip away again, his arm muscles aching, but suddenly the raft and all its contents came up onto the deck almost as if they were weightless, causing him to fall over back-ward.

He got up, rubbing his bottom and reflecting that there certainly was no energy protection against friction burns, but he knew what had hap-pened. Terry had seen the problem and had added a bit of power to the equation through him. The whole raft was now securely on deck.

Gus retrieved the lost box in his gaping mouth and brought it aboard, then deposited it with the others. There were two very large puncture marks in the carton, and some white stuff was coming out of one of them.

"*Whooo!*" Gus gasped. "That's more heavy work than I've done since I got here! You wanna do inventory on it or what?"

"Might as well, as long as we're still becalmed," Brazil responded. "Besides, if there's anything here ready to eat, I can stand something, and so can she."

This was where the Well's data helped him, although he was barely aware of it. Among the cartons were a number of suspect items, but he instinctively seemed to know which ones to keep and which ones to discard. Gus had been right—most of it was more than useful.

"We're going to have to get this below fairly quickly," Brazil said at last. "Most of it, anyway. We'll leave these three on deck. It's a bit damp below, but I think we can keep these high enough to keep 'em out of the wet. I think I can handle individual boxes. I'd best get to it. Leave this one with the fruit open and this one with the vegetables, too, so Terry can start eating. Watch her, though. She has a tendency to eat absolutely everything, and I need something!"

Individually, the cartons weren't all that heavy, and he quickly transferred the nine remaining ones below to the unused crew sleeping quarters, securing them with netting. The one leaking the powder from the fang marks he could do little about, but the marks were high enough that even if they leaked a fair amount of the sweet-tasting meal, there would still be enough.

The water was still ankle deep, but that reassured rather than bothered him. Nothing more was coming in, and the new load wasn't so heavy that the whole balance of the ship would be adversely affected.

When he came back on deck, Gus commented, "I gotta say, Cap, you were sure right about her appetite. She's just tearin' through that stuff like there's no tomorrow. Better get some while you can."

He nodded, opened the other carton, and found some premade and wrapped loaves of what appeared to be a kind of French bread. Inside, it had a yellowish look and contained small bits of exceptionally sweet cornlike kernels, but it tasted just fine. He was just reaching to rescue a large purplish applelike fruit the size of a small melon from the ravenous Terry when he suddenly noticed something.

"A breeze! I feel a breeze!" he almost shouted. Forgetting his hunger, he ran to the wheel. "Gus! Go forward and raise the anchor. Use the winch! Yeah, there!"

At last! he thought. *Food, water, and even a little daylight left, and along comes a breeze! We're getting* out *of this hole!*

Out, yes, a little corner of him responded. *Out and away, toward harsh reality, outward to smash yet another good dream . . .*

OGADON

THERE WAS NO GOOD place to house the Dillians in the Gekir coastal town of Port Saar, and since Erdomese, too, were basically unsuited for the network of steps and ladders which the catlike natives found no trouble at all, they set up a camp on the edge of town, along the road between the town proper and the port up at the Ogadon border.

The chief, in the tradition of her people, invited them all to the royal guest quarters and to a banquet, but Mavra explained some of the problems the others might have in attending. The governor seemed to understand and instead issued them something of far more value: a provincial conscription note, which was basically an account with local merchants that guaranteed that they would be paid by the local treasury.

As was common in many smaller port towns everywhere, businesses closed promptly at sunset, so they all took advantage of the conscription note in the couple of hours of sunlight remaining.

Port Saar was not the same sort of town as the big seaports they'd seen. Rather, it seemed more like the small rural market towns of much of Central and South America, minus electricity and modern conveniences.

Like their underwater neighbors, the Ogadon, Gekirs were basically carnivores, but nonetheless they spent a good deal of time on small- and medium-sized farms growing fresh fruits and vegetables for export to the railhead just inside Itus or by coastal ships to other nearby hexes. It was, one merchant noted, actually very practical; in the farming business the pickers and other help never ate the profits.

Although adding to and freshening their provisions was the main idea, Lori, with Mavra Chang's permission, used some of the credit on Alowi, as Julian now insisted on being called. In fact, the few times Lori had slipped and said "Julian," she hadn't even responded, convincing him that wherever she was stuffing her past had absorbed even the memory of that name. In fact, it was becoming next to impossible not to think of her as a native-born Erdomese female.

He bought her a necklace she seemed to fancy, some sweet-smelling perfumes, and a set of combs that while clearly not designed for Erdomese, worked rather well on the hair and tail and in cleaning the short fur. There were also some nice-looking and modestly priced clips that were the right size for tail clips; Lori didn't know and didn't really want to know for whom or what they were actually intended.

At Mavra's suggestion, they also looked at heavy coats, since they would be going into unknown climates and might well need them. There weren't too many available for non-Gekir types and none that were really great fits, but a sufficient number of races were to one degree or another humanoid that even the Erdomese found rough fits. The Dillians, it appeared, had brought their own along, and Anne Marie insisted that she could alter the new coats to some degree to make them fit better.

They also finally met a Gekir male.

He was pretty easy to spot; thin, gaunt-looking, and smaller than a female, he was a sort of faded gray color all over except for his outsized lionlike snow white mane. He had a medium-length tail that ended in an explosive puff of white fur, further contrasting him with the tailless females. He also wore matching bracelets and anklets of a golden color with ornate designs in them and a large golden oval nose ring and appeared to be perfumed.

The people had overall been quite friendly, and so Lori couldn't resist trying to strike up a conversation with him in the street.

"Your pardon, sir, but you are the first man we have seen since coming to Gekir, and I was just curious. I mean, it began to look like there were no men at all here."

The Gekir seemed amused. "Oh, yes, there be a lot of us, only not nearly in the same numbers as women. The average be about fifteen women to one man. It be different where you come from, I suppose."

"In some ways, yes, in others, no. In Erdom there are ten females for every male, but as you can see from my wife here, the men are larger, and because of the hand development and upper muscle strength, men run the affairs while the women run the household and bear and raise the children."

"Huh! Think of that! Dunno if I'd like *that* or not! Got enough trouble just doin' me male duties."

It turned out that the males, smaller, far weaker, and fewer in number, ran nothing at all. They also tended to be uneducated and limited in what they could do. What they *could* do was have sex, apparently in nearly unlimited amounts, and they tended to do that essentially as a profession, often doing a "circuit of me regulars" and spending their time at those "regulars'" homes. They also performed services from shopping for busy women to baby-sitting and took little interest in much outside this life. If the male they met was as typical as he said he was, they liked it that way.

"See, all the time they likes us around, and once a month they needs us, so they keeps us pretty happy," the Gekir male told him. The general feeling among the women, he explained in a low voice, was that men were stupid and incompetent except at the one thing they were needed for, and the men had a vested interest in maintaining those attitudes. "They even cook for us," he told Lori. "Think we don't know how."

The male begged off further talk, since he had a "real important appointment just after sunset," but he'd revealed enough.

In Gekir, the women ruled and the men were small and weak, considered inferior, and used entirely as sex objects. It was even more extreme than Erdom by a great deal, and it disturbed Lori almost as much as the reverse would have. It answered one of those nagging questions in a way he hadn't wanted it answered.

The parallel seemed to be with many Earth insects. The black widow was obvious, but many male spiders existed only for one purpose and then died, not to mention male bees and many other examples. A lot of women he'd known back on Earth would have loved this kind of arrangement, but he wasn't so sure. Was his distaste, though, just because he was now a man himself, or was it because the same offenses committed in reverse felt no more moral?

It was a question he pondered as they went back to the camp and set up to cook dinner as the sun went down. After determining that there were quite a number of things both Erdomese and Dillians could eat in common, Lori did not object to Alowi and Anne Marie preparing the meal, with him translating as needed. It did not in fact come out bad at all.

Mavra had remained in town, she said to talk to some people before her official dinner later that night. She told them that they should not wait for her and that they should get some sleep.

Alowi did the cleanup, then insisted on using her new combs and brushes to get the last vestiges of grime from Lori's fur and tail, and he even allowed a little perfume to be used to cover the mild but remaining swamp odor.

The Dillians excused themselves and went off into the shorter, greener grass nearby and eventually seemed to lock themselves for sleep.

With his hand still bandaged and saying by occasional aches and sharp pains that it should remain so for a while longer, there wasn't much for the Erdomese to do but try to sleep themselves. Alowi cuddled up close to him and was soon out cold; after the previous night with so little sleep she had to be exhausted. Still, Lori would have liked to have discussed the oddly different sexual balance of Gekir and perhaps talked about the old days, as they always had, but he couldn't. Those conversations had been with Julian, and Julian, it appeared, no longer existed for all practical purposes.

He felt doubly guilty for that somehow. He'd treated her as less than a partner, all along driving home the division that must have raged within her no matter how much she suppressed it, and it had been his own stupid injuries that had caused the final break.

Nobody else had gotten even a scratch. Not even Jul—Alowi. Mister Macho had to leap before he looked, jump too fast, not notice an embankment. *He* had to be out first, since *he* was going to look out for the others. The poor, defenseless others. *The girls.*

Yeah, right.

Damn it! he thought, furious with himself. *When the hell did I turn into every guy I ever loathed in high school?*

It was not exactly the kind of grand commercial vessel that both the Dillians and the Erdomese had used to reach Itus. It was in fact small, low but with big masts, and had a central funnel so that it could be used under steam where possible. It was built for silence and speed, not for comfort and convenience, and for its ability to run with a minimal crew.

It was also painted a dull black, and even the sails and ropes had been dyed to a very dark gray hue. The bridge was actually exposed as in the ancient sailing ships of Earth, but there was a small secondary cabin between the main wheel and the funnel with a duplicate wheel that could be engaged and that had some very exotic-looking, if now totally turned off, electronic gear.

The captain was from Stulz, far off to the south and west across the great Ocean of Shadows, farther from his own hex than the travelers were from theirs. He was in many ways a fearsome sight, with a dark gray foxlike face filled with sharp little teeth. His beady, reddish brown eyes seemed to dart this way and that without ever settling on any one thing or person, and he had great furry wings that formed almost a cape and a hairy pair of arms terminating in fingers with very long, sharp claws. His bowlegs terminated in prehensile feet that essentially duplicated the hands, while from his back came a long whiplike leathery tail that seemed to be always under total control.

The trouble with Captain Hjlarza, Mavra decided, was that he looked exactly like a drug-running scoundrel in this part of the world should look.

The first mate was from Zhonzhorp and resembled nothing so much as a bipedal crocodile with long, thin arms and rubbery four-fingered hands that terminated in what appeared to be suckers or suction cups. The fact that he wore britches, a sash, a vest, and a tricorner hat with a feather in it did nothing to make him look less fearsome.

The five other crew members did little to reassure by their appearance. Two were giant hairy spiderlike creatures that seemed to be able to use any combination of their eight legs almost as tentacles. Two more were short and squat but looked as if they were humanoid caricatures carved out of very ugly rocks. The fifth was a purple and red creature with a somewhat humanoid face and torso, forelegs resembling a goat's, and a main body that the two legs dragged around, much like a sea lion.

Only the captain and mate had translators, so for most of the passengers it was going to be a pretty nervous trip.

Alowi was horrified at the menacing menagerie, and Tony and Anne Marie hardly looked thrilled, but Lori was concerned only when she sensed that even Mavra Chang was nervous.

The Zhonzhorpian, "Just call me Zitz," was the one who was to get them squared away.

"Could be a rough trip," he warned them.

"Are you expecting trouble?" Mavra asked nervously.

"Oh, no, not *that* kind. The captain knows what he's doing, and we've been at this a long time. Your Dillians, though, will have to sleep up top on the afterdeck, since they just won't fit below, and if we get into a bit of bad weather, it can be pretty nerve-wracking up here, not to mention cold and wet."

"I've briefed them as much as I could about such things," she assured the mate. "I think we'll lash them down if we get into rough seas." She looked aft. "The way you're rigged, we might also be able to set up some kind of tent or at least a shelter if you have some sailcloth to spare. They can rig it themselves if they have the materials and a few tools. If we stretch it between the afterdeck and the main deck, it will have extra support while being out of the way of the mainmast."

Zitz was impressed by her knowledge. "All right. I think we can manage that. You've sailed before, I think, and not as a mere passenger."

She nodded. "A very long time ago, though. If you need an extra hand in weather, let me know. I'm not that good at hauling sails, but I know the basics and I can handle whatever's needed if it doesn't take a lot of strength."

"Very good! I may take you up on that. Weather's been less than great of late, particularly in the northern ocean. We tend to use sail whenever possible regardless of the hex properties and save the steam for weather when we can use it or if the wind's too much against us."

"You're going with cargo full?"

"Not quite, but heavy enough. We'll top it off with a stop at sea. The only nonweather problems we might encounter are in Kzuco, which we can't really bypass. Otherwise we'll be staying on the northern side, which means all nontech and semitech hexes."

She nodded. "That's all right with us. The less attention we get, the better for our own purposes. We have no interest in your cargo or activities so long as this is yet another trip when you have no problems. In fact, I'd prefer not to meet any authorities at all."

The Erdomese and Marva followed Zitz down into the ship. It stank and had that "lived in too long by pigs" look and feel about it. The few cabins were small and narrow, but they would do. Two small cabins that might have been used for storage had been cleared out and were essentially bare; the bedrolls would have to serve both for the Erdomese in one room and for Mavra across the corridor. When Zitz left to go topside, Mavra came over to the Erdomese.

"Not exactly first class," she commented a bit apologetically, "but it will do. It'll have to."

"I wouldn't feel comfortable with this crew if they were carrying Bibles," Lori said nervously. "How long will we be cooped up on this tub?"

"With a decent wind they can make twenty knots, I'd say. Under steam, probably half that. Assuming some foul wind and allowing for the usual lousy conditions for at least some part of the trip, that probably means an average of a day and a half to two days to cross a hex depending if we're going along a single edge or across the center. That's four, maybe five days to Agon, but since they're headed past there to Lilblod or even Clopta, it might well be a week if we don't get off at some place along the way. Call it a week."

"A week! I'll never stand it! And the others . . ."

"We'll do what we have to do. If we can bypass Agon and land in Lilblod near the Clopta border, we'll not only save several days' walking, we might be able to bypass the high-tech hexes and their communications systems almost entirely."

"What about the crew? Can we trust them?"

Mavra grinned. "Not one bit. Not that I'd trust a crew looking like angels, singing like a choir, and carrying that load of Bibles you mentioned, either. In fact, watch out for the Bible carriers more than anybody. Every slave ship that ever sailed back when I knew them carried Bibles on the outbound trip; the crew all had prayer meetings and thought themselves holy and got blessed by the priests, some of whom came along. Give me a good crew of honest crooks any day. You're never surprised, and they're usually honorable if you're not worth the trouble, and the profits these guys turn in one trip make us not worth the trouble."

"Yeah? Then how did you get them to take us at all? We're really in the way."

"Well, if they're stopped, the fact they have multiracial passengers will make them seem legit, since the kind of cops who go after these types know that they wouldn't jeopardize an illegal, high-profit cargo by having innocents aboard. Also, we're not known in the region and so are unlikely to be crooks. That's one reason. The other reason is that they've been highly paid, but in order to keep that payment, they have to deliver us."

"Huh? What are you talking about? And where did you get anything valuable enough to make them consider us as precious as their cargo?"

Mavra chuckled. "It was nice to see how it all came back to me. My original profession and one I always loved. It's paid off quite a bit over the years when I needed it. Of course, I felt bad about doing that to the chief when she was so nice, but not being able to return to Gekir for a few generations is a small price to pay."

"What in the *world* are you talking about?" Lori wanted to know.

"My original profession and first love, learned out of necessity and refined to a fine art before I ever left the planet where I grew up, let alone heard of the Well World. I was the best damned jewel and art thief in the whole galaxy, I'll have you know!"

Lori laughed, finding it hard to believe. "You? A professional thief?"

She nodded, grinning with pride. "That's the third reason. These kind of folks can *sense* when they're dealing with one of their own."

"But—what did you steal?"

"Basically, some of the lesser state jewels kept in the governor's vaults. Not a big deal, but the few I picked were whoppers. They won't discover it for another month or two, though, when their big religious festival comes up and they need to take the things out. By then this business will be done."

"But you said they had to make sure they delivered us! If they've got the jewels . . ."

Mavra nodded. "I know, but they are also aware that I sent a sealed and secured packet with a courier into the Gekir capital and from there to Zone. The package is to be held for my pickup by the Glathrielian delegation, and if I don't pick it up in six months, it'll be opened and *these* boys will be fingered to the Gekir as the thieves. Simple, really."

"Um, yeah, except I thought that the Glathrielians didn't—"

Mavra put her hand up to his mouth, then put a finger to her lips. "*Shhhh!* What they don't know won't hurt us."

Lori decided to let it drop, but he wasn't at all thrilled with the news. If something went wrong and the Gekir somehow discovered the theft before they were out of the country, then nothing could save them.

"I see now why you were a little nervous coming aboard," he said.

She shook her head from side to side. "Uh uh. No problem with that. It's just that I've never had good luck on ships, and even worse on the Well World, so I'm always a little spooked when I'm on them, that's all." She turned to leave. "I'm going topside and help the Dillians. Come on up when you want to."

"Um—Mavra?"

"Yes, Lori?"

"Just out of curiosity—you said you'd been in the Brazilian jungles something like three hundred years or more. How did you get there way back then?"

"I was sold to a Portuguese ship's captain in Macao for a beat-up old musket. The captain took a fancy to me when I was loaned out to him for some hospitality. He wanted something to relieve the tedium of a Pacific crossing. When he grew bored with me, he gave me to the mate. I went down in rank rapidly. I think if he'd been a couple of years older, I would have been with the cabin boy by the time we rounded the Horn and reached Brazil."

"How *horrible!*"

"Yeah, I thought he was going to Africa. Pretty hard to escape when you're in the middle of the Pacific. By the time we reached Brazil, I was so flipped out, I couldn't even think. They painted me up, stripped me naked, claimed I was an Indian, and sold me to a sugar plantation for a couple of bottles of private-stock rum, I think. I wasn't in any shape to pay much attention. For the next several years I cut cane and planted and harvested rice along with hundreds of black and Indian slaves. Slowly I absorbed the local languages, and some of it came back to me. It was okay, but the ownership changed and the new people were pretty vicious; they decided we should be whipped and worked into the ground until we dropped dead. There was a revolt—I don't know the details because the men didn't exactly take us women into their confidence— but somehow I wound up in the middle of it. I got picked up, and they decided to have some fun with me. I flipped out—it was as if the ship's crew had suddenly reappeared. *This* time I fought, but it was hopeless. When they were done with me, they had revenge for my fighting and threats. They cut out my tongue, cut off my hands, and threw me in a swamp to die slowly."

"My God!" he said.

"Instead, of course, I survived, made my way into the jungle, and managed on my own somehow, with no voice and just stumps for hands, until I was discovered by some hunters from a local Indian tribe. They took pity on me and took me in even though I was nothing but a burden on them; by their traditions they should have left me to die. It really wasn't bad, and I was getting to like them, when, of course, I began regenerating, slowly, until it became apparent that I was growing new hands and a new tongue. It frightened the hell out of them. They decided I was some evil spirit and came to kill me, but I escaped back into the jungle, which by that time I knew very well."

She paused for a moment, and Lori said, "You don't have to say any more if you don't want to. I understand."

"No, that's all right. You're one of the few people who has a right to hear this out. Anyway, I lost all track of time, so I can't say how long I lived alone in that jungle, but eventually I came across two Indian girls fleeing from another tribe who'd captured them in an intertribal squabble. We never asked each other questions and just sort of banded together to survive. Those two were the start of my own little tribe. They never asked who I was or *what* I was or anything, even later. Of course, as they continued to age and I did not, and particularly after I lost another limb out of carelessness to a crocodile and *it* grew back, they decided I wasn't human but some kind of goddess. I spent some time long ago in Athens at its peak and in Sparta, and I remembered the legend of the Amazons, and it just seemed fitting. After that we searched out girls who'd been cast out. Centuries later we were still doing it. Frankly, you're the first sentient male I've had any sort of conversation with, let alone friendship, in all that time."

Lori sighed. "I see. You certainly make immortality sound positively repugnant."

"Oh, it has its moments. I think I did some good in that jungle or I wouldn't have stayed, but how long do you think I would have survived there without my special situation? Why did a tribe that threw out its deformed and maimed suddenly take pity on me and take me in? And there were some brief decent periods. Greece was pretty good, and Rome was really even better than its reputation. Sheba was pretty nice, too, and some of the early Hindu Kush tribal groups were okay. It wasn't *all* bad, but I tell you, if you have to live through the history of Earth, make sure that you're a man. It won't guarantee a pleasant trip, but it's a damned sight more fun than being a woman." She paused, then said, "I think I better get up on deck. It feels like they're getting under way, and I want the Dillians settled."

She went off, and Lori looked at Alowi. "You heard and understood all that?"

"Yes, my husband."

"What do you think of it?"

"I heard, but I could not completely understand it. The nearest I could follow was that she has lived a very long time, and many of our lifetimes ago she left her husband and went out on her own in the world. She was thus without status or protection, and bad things happened to her for still more lifetimes. Then she took up with some other wild females, living with them in a wild place, and she blames all men for her misfortune."

He shrugged. "I suppose that summarizes it. But he wasn't her husband. As far as I can tell, she never had one. I'm not sure what the relationship with this man was, but he, too, is here, and they are no longer friends but enemies. Still, you seem to be blaming her for leaving him when we don't know the reason. We don't even know if she left him or some accident separated them and they never again found one another."

"All I can see is that she wants to be a man and cannot accept the idea that she is not. She has the same kind of demon that made my life so horrible, and she will stay miserable, unstable, perhaps dangerous, until she accepts what she is as I did and casts that demon out."

"She doesn't want to be a man," Lori responded. "If she did, she might well have become one, if the powers of that Well are what she claims, and she didn't. She simply wants to be self-sufficient and have the same degree of independence, the same choices and respect, that the man had."

"Perhaps."

He was irritated. "Remember, she came from a civilization we would think of as far advanced, a civilization with ships that sailed between the stars and one that did not have the same attitudes that we have. She was unprepared for the primitive early history of Earth." He paused. Did Alowi even *remember* Earth?

She didn't seem to, but she answered. "I know only that their race is much like ours. There are males and females. They have different bodies and lives and each can do things the other cannot, but they need each other to do those things. I can cure your ills and bear and raise your children. You cannot do these things, but you protect me from the evil that is everywhere and you provide for my own needs. When each does what he or she does best, there is contentment. When each tries to do the

other's role, there is no contentment, and no one can really perform
another's role. You did not make yourself, your role, or this way of life.
Neither did I mine, nor do we truly have the choices we might like. But
to pretend that you are what you cannot be leads to madness. This I
believe."

Lori started to continue the argument, then realized it was useless to
do so. Even Julian might have thought along those lines, although perhaps a bit more sophisticatedly. He'd never been an Earth-human
woman.

Still, Alowi had made a practical point he'd been wrestling with all
along. Here at least, as an Erdomese, on this world, did he really have
that many choices in how to act, how to live, and what he could do? The
priests, the whole culture, wanted stasis. Everyone and everything in its
proper place. Biology was stacked against the Erdomese, too, almost
forcing on them the ancient traditional roles. What was it Tony had told
him? She could adjust to being a woman, but she could never become
what Anne Marie wanted. She couldn't still be Tony, the gentleman pilot
from Brazil; to avoid madness, she had to accept and become what she
now was. Hell, Lori Ann had never wanted to be a man. Never. And yet,
now that she was a he, there were more basic differences than Lori Ann
would have thought, yet few practical differences in day-to-day terms.
When one became a different species of animal, the sexual differences
seemed even more trivial, anyway.

The *practical* differences, the ones that crossed from the old species
Homo sapiens to the new, were in social terms: the ability to walk freely
down strange streets without more than pragmatic caution, for example.
A whole level of *fear* was removed from the simplest social interactions,
as well as the constant uncertainty of whether the strangers one met
were seeing one as another person or as an object. That far outweighed
the physiological differences, and it mattered. He was quickly becoming
accustomed to the physiological change, as was Tony, but it was the so-
ciological change that had made him feel somehow free. There was
much about being a man he didn't like; in its own way it was as confining
and restrictive a role as the female's. Yet he wouldn't want to trade this
absence of a massive layer of tension for anything.

Maybe that was it, he thought. Compromise. Fully accept what one
now was and the role and situation one was now locked into but never
forget the values and achievements of who one once had been. Tony still
had those skills and that knowledge from the past and maybe could
appreciate things more because she'd been on both sides of the coin. She
could retain her kind heart, too, and the love of Anne Marie's spirit and
inner strength that she masked with that little old lady act. Tony wasn't

his old self, and she wasn't Anne Marie, either, no matter how identical they were; she was compromising, no, *synthesizing* into a whole new person. Maybe Lori had to finally do that, too. Accept, become Lori of Alkhaz, an Erdomese male and husband, keeping what was valuable and universal but not letting Lori Ann torture him every time he did something that she might disapprove of. Julian couldn't synthesize, and so she broke instead, retaining only the pragmatic part.

Might that, in the end, be the problem of the two immortals? To go so long, through so many lifetimes and cultures, not only unchanging but unable to change. Somehow he suspected that if somehow ancient folk long dead could be resurrected and taken to either this Brazil or Chang, they would instantly recognize them and find them much the same. Even growing up a person changed, often radically—from helpless infant to dependent child, through rebellious teen years and hopeful twenties and thirties, into middle age, when life's course had been set and for the first time death became a reality as the years passed subjectively at a faster and faster clip, and finally into the combined wisdom and resignation of old age. Just as pictures in the photo album showing the same person at all those stages somehow also showed completely different people, life was a constant series of radical changes.

But not for these immortals. They hadn't changed in so long, they could remember being no other way. Endless, unchanging life—probably passing at breakneck speed to them but never getting them anywhere—had made even the chance of new experiences slim. They could fight against the system as Chang had and suffer, or they could roll with it and drift as this Solomon, or Brazil, apparently did. Eventually, even Mavra Chang had stopped fighting and had withdrawn to the most basic of all human existences. Now she was racing the fellow with an idea to making the next time different.

But would it be?

Just the little he'd seen of the Well World—and his understanding of it as a laboratory for founding new races and seeding the vast numbers of worlds in the universe—had convinced him that those Ancient Ones had probably thought of just about all the themes and variations that could be imagined. In Gekir, women ruled and the men were bimbos. He hadn't yet seen one, but he'd heard that there were asexual and unisexual races here, and other races with more than two sexes. Dillian society sounded as if it was like the better places on Earth, but Tony could never be regarded as "one of the boys" and there would always be a social-sexual separation no matter how equal the opportunities and how safe the roads.

There were 1,560 races here, from the radically different to the fairly similar, and who knew how many had been developed before this final batch was left at the end? And after all this time, had any of them developed the true utopia? If so, he hadn't heard of it.

Mavra might well be able to radically change the race of Earth. But if she did it too much, would it still be human or just another experiment? And if but little, would it make a difference? One might well be able to program all sorts of physiological stuff, but who was smart enough to program social development, attitudes, and cultures over the life span of a race of people? Maybe even this Brazil still believed deep down that there must be a better way but knew he wasn't omnipotent enough to create and maintain it. Greece, Rome, but also the Mongol hordes and the Vandals and Visigoths. Jesus and Buddha and Mohammed, but also Attila the Hun, Napoleon, Stalin, and Hitler.

One might well get something different, but how would one ensure that it was superior when even a race that was close to godhood as evolution could produce couldn't figure that out?

Could it be that the dark side of the human soul was just as essential to the evolutionary development and growth of a race as the beautiful side? Depressing thought, but otherwise why did the Ancient Ones leave it in?

And if *he* could think of this, why hadn't Mavra Chang? Perhaps confusing immortality with wisdom wasn't a smart thing to do. He began to get the eerie feeling that he was better qualified to play god than she was, and *he* had no real desire to take on that awesome and impossible responsibility. He knew he just wasn't smart enough to do it. Nobody was.

Maybe this Brazil knew that, which was why he always remade things the same. The fact that Mavra Chang apparently *didn't* see this trap was unsettling. She wasn't really out to correct humanity; she was out to avenge herself against the forces that had hurt her.

And *that* was the most uncomfortable feeling of all. When push came to shove, as it inevitably would if they got to this Well, on which side of this strange race should his sword fall?

He looked at Alowi. "I think I'd like to go on deck. I can hear all sorts of noises up there, and I'd like to see what's going on. Do you want to go or stay here?"

"I will do as you wish."

"No, this is not one of those kind of decisions. Do *you* want to go up there or remain here?"

"I do not like those creatures above," she admitted, "but if it is my choice, I will go where you go."

"For the record, I don't like them much, either, but come on. We're going to have to live with them for a while, it seems."

*   *   *

Darkness had fallen, and the lights of the city market area were still very close, but they had definitely pulled away from the small private dock and were in the process of turning the ship toward the channel. The two spiderlike beings were up in the twin masts, and the rest of the small crew were tending ropes on the starboard side of the ship.

Lori stayed as far from the action as possible and peered over the side. There, in the darkness, two huge longboats filled with very large Gekirs pulling on oars were guiding the ship like tugs in a big harbor. The captain, barely visible in the darkness, was on top of the wheelhouse getting a view of the entire area. Clearly the creature was basically nocturnal by nature and saw well in just the starlight and the reflected glow from the city. The crocodilelike mate was at the wheel, looking at some basic instruments and taking cryptic cues from the captain and the crew on the lines.

"Away all lines!" the captain shouted. "Clear ship!"

The commands were repeated even louder by the crew on the lines, and the ropes, expertly tied, were loosened and thrown into the water to be reeled in by the longboats.

"Engage rudder! All hands to embarkation stations!"

Now the mate turned and began winding hard and fast on a wooden wheel, which went around and around for a while and then held firm. The mate checked something, pulled up a large lever, then turned back to the main wheel, which had been essentially free but which now seemed to have a mind of its own. The rest of the crew scurried to positions on either side of the sails. Only one small sail was dropped, but the wind caught it and the ship slowly began moving out of the harbor at a crawl, following what appeared to be small oil-fed lamps floating in the water. Just ahead, on spits of land on either side, twin lighthouses gave off amazingly bright beams, easily marking the limits of the entrance to the bay.

The port area was going by on the right-hand side, the buildings suddenly changing in character from dark, closed shops to a small harbor filled with activity just ahead. At the moment where there seemed to be nothing on the shore, between the dark buildings and the lighted dock or warehouse beyond, Lori felt a sudden tingling sensation and started. It felt as if something incredibly thin had brushed against his full body. It was gone in a moment, but suddenly the wind shifted direction and picked up considerably, and the temperature dropped from a tropical twenty-six degrees Celsius to perhaps no more than ten or twelve. Summer had turned to spring in an instant, and the wind did not help the feeling at all.

He looked at Alowi, who was clearly uncomfortable. "Do you wish to go below or perhaps get one of the jackets?" he asked her.

"I am all right," she told him, but she didn't look it.

Mavra came over to them, still dressed only in the thin black clothing and boots she favored and appearing not at all uncomfortable.

"It's pretty impressive when you think about it," the Earth woman commented. "The Well World has no moon and so very little in the way of a tide. That's hell for a sailing ship and cuts off a lot of harbors as too shallow. Magnetic compasses are useless, too, since there's no magnetic pole. The instruments they were using to get out of there are incredibly clever but unique to these conditions. *Now,* however, they've got full instrumentation. That's a computerized compass that always points to true north in the wheelhouse, and they've got something similar to, but much better than, mere radar. It may look like just water, but it's high-tech water now."

"I'll have to take your word for it," Lori responded. "Still, all that fancy navigation equipment only helps in a third of the hexes they sail."

"True, but a good sailor has a hundred means of setting course and position and only needs those instruments in familiar waters to confirm things. You'll note they're going in steps to full sail, even though they could use the main engines. When you have this kind of wind and it's in your favor, you take it." She looked up as the crew made a series of by-the-numbers calls, and there were sudden loud, deep crackling and rippling sounds. "Yep. There come the mainsails."

The ship was clearly at sea now, the water choppy and causing significant spray forward, some of it reaching the deck. There was a pitching motion now as well, often in more directions than one, and Lori found he had to hold on tight to the railing with both hands.

Mavra grinned. "Yeah, I'm having to get used to sea legs as well. It's been a *long* time. You'll find the motion a lot more pronounced aboard this small ship than on that giant you came up to Itus on." She turned and gestured. "See those ropes? They're well secured with steel clips, and they run all around the deck. Use them to keep yourself steady in rough seas." She grinned. "Don't worry. You'll get used to it. Promise."

Lori wasn't so sure. "That's a lot easier to say, built like you are, but hooves designed for sand and rough ground don't do all that well on slick hardwood decks. I think for now we'll be better off below."

Mavra nodded. "Suit yourselves. The Dillians have things fairly well set up back there, but they're also going to have to get used to balance."

"Yeah, well, they've got four feet! I think if I had four, I might at least be able to stay upright." And with that he gestured to a very relieved Alowi, and hand over hand, using the ropes, they made their way below.

For Mavra Chang, however, it was something else, something quite different. Looking aft at the rapidly receding lights, feeling the lurch of the ship, the smell of salt air, the rustling canvas above, and the strong breeze pushing them on, two sets of opposing thoughts and emotions rose within her.

In a positive way she felt *home* somehow, alive once more. The only thing that would have made it better would be if this were *her* ship and *she* was in the wheelhouse charting courses and giving commands. In some ways, perhaps, she would prefer that even to commanding the bridge of a starship, where one was in command of a vast but lonely structure in which the crew was wholly automated and the silence and stillness were ever-present.

But there were darker memories as well, of other ocean voyages where she had been not in charge or even a passenger but *cargo*, and disposable cargo at that, where the days were full of pain and the nights full of horror.

They would never do that to her again. She would see to that.

DLUBINE,
MOVING TOWARD THE FAHOMMA
BORDER

THERE WAS A DRAMATIC scene anywhere one looked after dark in Dlubine. All around, at different very specific locations, one could see lightning illuminate large cloud masses or occasionally but spectacularly snake down to the sea and play along it, often for several seconds, looking like some mad scientist's laboratory experiment. Yet overhead there would be frequent breaks in the clouds, giving windows into the magnificent and colorful night sky of the Well World, while below varicolored lights crisscrossed and weaved intricate patterns, sometimes exploding into huge complex patterns for a while, although nothing on the scale of what they'd seen the first night. And now and then the winds would bring whiffs of sulfur or the rotten-egg smell of hydrogen sulfide. At least once they'd sailed past an island perhaps two or three kilometers distant that, while invisible in the darkness, betrayed itself by showing streams of red running tendrillike down dark self-made mountains to the sea and ending in great plumes of steam. Where hot lava met the sea, the combination created its own very local thunderstorms.

"You could make a million bucks selling cruises through here," Gus noted, just staring out at the amazing sights.

"Well, I suppose the inhabitants would have something to say about that," Brazil responded, taking advantage of the conflicting winds from the surrounding turbulence and making reasonably good time. "Still, what would you do with the money, Gus? What's the top of the real estate market in Dahir?"

Gus laughed. "Not that great. Oh, it's comfortable enough, but, well, this might sound funny, but they're just too much like the small town in northern Minnesota that I got out of."

"Like *what*?" Brazil chuckled. "*This* I got to hear."

"Well, the place is pretty damned dull, frankly, just like home. Nothin' much happens, and what little that does isn't important but it becomes the biggest thing around 'cause it's *something*. Everybody's into everybody else's business 'cause they don't have much else to do, the life's routine, and the pleasure for them is simple. On top of it all it's dominated by a straitlaced church that's gonna make sure you behave and go to heaven, or wherever they think Dahirs go. No imagination, no curiosity. Even the weather's borin'. And I mean, think about this kinda invisibility thing. Even that's a drag there. I mean, so you decide to rough it and hunt your own food down 'cause it's fun, right? Only nothin' can see you comin', so where's the sport? Even back home the deer could see you and make a break for it or hide out, and even the fish had a *little* bit of a chance. Nothing's even really wild in Dahir. It's all carefully managed. I couldn't stand it no longer than I did."

"Um, I see what you mean. You couldn't just find an attractive female and go off and buy your own swamp or something?"

"Not likely. Hell, it's the *women* who run the damn place. They're the bigger ones, they got the muscles, and they're all kinda muddy brown. It's us guys who have all the color and are supposed to attract a female. They lay the eggs, but the guys hatch 'em. I know I'm supposed to have been made comfortable with bein' a Dahir and all that, but that's just the physical part. I mean, the swimmin', the eatin' the way I eat and what I eat, stuff like that, no problem, but in my head I'm still the same guy. I been him too long to be somebody else. And that arrangement just don't seem *natural* to me."

"I know some women who'd like that arrangement just fine." Brazil laughed. "It's not as uncommon among either animals or sentient species as you think, but I can see your point. Some people handle the cultural differences fine, but others find things just too topsy-turvy to adjust in that department. Tell me, what *would* you do if you had your pick? You've seen a bit of this world and its denizens. Would you be something else? Or would you go back if you could?"

Gus thought about it. "I dunno. I guess I ain't seen enough of this place to really decide if there's somethin' neat to be. I sure wouldn't be no Earth-human type, not if it meant havin' done to me what was done to Terry. Go back? Yeah, maybe. I loved the job, no question. That's what I miss most. But I also had started thinkin' that I was gettin' older too fast and slowin' down and the odds were gonna catch up to me sooner or later. You know the worst thing, though? The one thing I dreaded, really hated? And it wasn't bein' shot at or bombed or nothin' like that."

"I couldn't guess."

"Comin' home. Thing was, I didn't really have one. My folks are dead; the rest of my family's as happy not to see me as I am not to see them. Got one sister who married a career navy guy and she's got a couple of neat kids, but I always felt like a stranger when I visited, like I didn't really belong there no matter how much she said she liked me visitin' her. I dunno. You get to a point in life, you don't want to stop what you love doin', but you also want something else, something more . . . permanent, I guess. And I just wouldn't feel right keepin' on doin' what I'm doin' if I had a wife and kids, particularly kids. Be worse than bein' a navy wife. Sort of like bein' a cop's wife, wonderin' if I was gettin' my ass blown off someplace and only coming home between revolutions and massacres. There's some that do it, but I couldn't, and takin' a job runnin' around to the latest drug bust or bank heist or whatever isn't the same thing."

"Permanence but with a lot of action and variety—that's a pretty tall order," Brazil commented.

"Yeah, I know. I guess I'll never find what I'm lookin' for. Kinda like the sign I once saw in a shop. 'Quality! Service! Price!' it read. Then underneath it added, 'Pick any two.' Still, I'd love to go back if I could keep this invisibility or whatever it is. You could still get caught by a random bullet and nobody'd notice you sinkin' in the quicksand, but you could walk right into the rebel camp and film away. Speaking of which, how come you ain't been spooked once since I got back? I really didn't think about it until just now, but you've had no problems seein' me, have you?"

"No," Brazil admitted. He hadn't told Gus about all that had transpired, and he wanted to keep most of it that way. What Gus didn't know he couldn't reveal if he really got captured later on. Besides, who knew how he'd feel about Brazil having that kind of bond with Terry? But a few things had to be addressed.

"I picked up her second sight, sort of," he told the Dahir. "I don't know how, but somehow she gave it to me. At least, when I woke up, I had no more problems seeing you or her just like I'd expect to."

"Yeah? You also got the power to blank out other folks?"

"I haven't the slightest idea," Brazil replied honestly. "Unfortunately, at some point in this trip I'm almost sure to find out. I wouldn't be surprised, though. After all this time I tend not to be surprised at very amazing things happening when I need them."

"You sure got the luck, all right," Gus noted. "I mean, bad as it is for

Terry, she's been a real plus for you this trip, right? Then I'm here as a Dahir with this crazy, built-in disappearin' act, and she figures it out and then gives it to you when they got your picture splattered all over creation. What are the odds of *that?*"

"Very low, Gus, but that's my point. It's not luck. It's the Well—the master computer. I'm just a glorified serviceman, like I said, but I have to be able to be there at the very infrequent times it needs me. So it kind of watches over me, like a guardian angel. It can manipulate probability, make a chain of events happen that serve its interests, although it doesn't do that for much of anything or anybody except me—and Mavra Chang. That doesn't mean that bad things don't happen to me. Sometimes nasty things happen in spades. I got sloppy this time around, didn't remember everything, and wound up spending a year and a half in Auschwitz for my trouble during World War II. It just means that nothing permanent happens. I suffered, I starved, I was treated lower than an animal there, but I survived. Barely, but I survived. That's what it does, Gus. It makes sure I survive."

"Jeez! I keep forgettin' you don't age. But what did you mean by gettin' sloppy 'this time around'? You talk like you lived through the Nazis before."

"I did—but in Ireland last time, I think. That's the scary part of it all, Gus. Inside there, inside the Well, among other routine things, is something I can't really explain but which is, for all intents and purposes, a reset button. It's a last gasp thing, something only I, not the Well, can decide to push. What it does is—complicated. Now *there's* an understatement for you! But anyway, it resets. Not completely, of course. The universe still continues to expand, the *basics* don't change, but all life out there is essentially canceled out. All people, all history, everything pretty much. Time and space become objects of manipulation. In some cases it can use the same planet and solar system again; in other times it has to find material from somewhere else that pretty well matches what existed before and re-create from scratch. Each of the worlds goes through the whole process of development, of evolution, you name it. From the vantage point of the Well World, it happens in the wink of an eye, but it can be a few billion years or more out there. Don't ask me how that's possible. I'm just the guy who has to push the button sometimes, not the ones who built or designed it or the computer capable of such godlike things."

"Jesus! And you've actually *done* this?"

"Twice. The memory of doing *that* is something that's always stored somewhere inside me. I might forget it for a while, but when I get here, I remember. Hitler, Stalin, all the mass murderers of Earth history are pikers compared to me, Gus. I've killed *trillions* with one decision, and worse, I erased all signs of their existence. All their history, culture, everything. Gone. But then I brought them back, in real time. The Well is a master of matching probabilities. Everything repeats as closely as possible. Maybe not an absolute one hundred percent, but it repeats so eerily that you wind up seeing the same people, the same empires, the same dreams, the same wars, the same nations and ideologies."

"Jeez! You mean you killed *me* at some time in the past? Or another me? And another Terry, and all the rest?"

"Well, no. You two were long dead by the time I did it the last time. The time before—I only remember that I did it, that's all. But I was still a captain both times, I'm pretty sure of that. Not of some ship like this, though, or even the big supertanker I was skippering back on Earth. Spaceships, Gus. Mavra, too. She had her own ship. She wasn't even *born* on Earth and might not even have heard of it until she fell in with me here. We moved a lot of cargo and occasional passengers between stars over a third of the Milky Way galaxy. God! How I loved that job! That's my equivalent of your photojournalism, Gus."

"Spaceships. Wow, that's neat!"

"Yeah, only the Well never inserts me at a point where I can do my job. This last time it inserted us, oh, I think maybe 50,000 B.C. or so. Since that time Mavra and I have both been, well, surviving, waiting until Earth once again headed for the stars. This time we didn't make it."

"Holy smoke! You mean you got to reset that thing again? *That's* what this is all about?"

"Maybe. I hope not. I don't know if I can do it again. I can't imagine why I'm here, but I've been here in between for other things. Somebody once was actually smart enough to figure out the mechanics of the Well and some Markovian mathematics. The Well was alarmed, not because he could do anything major but because he had the potential to do some damage right here. Events got manipulated so I fell through a Well Gate shortly after, and it was up to me to solve the problem. No damage done in the end, and I just went back to doing what I'd been doing. The Well doesn't let you stick around to get the universe into real trouble when it doesn't need you anymore. I *can* tell you that something's off kilter and may need adjustment. Something happened, maybe recently, maybe back as far as the last reset, but the tiny differences have accumulated to the point where, over thousands of years, they made a big change or a series of big changes. I noticed that when the Soviet Union collapsed so suddenly. I knew the consequences were terrible for later history that it did, but I kind of hoped it was just the result of a local aberration, just Earth, in other words. There're a lot more worlds and races than that out there."

"Hey! Hold it! That was *great* news, not bad news!"

"Was it? Yeah, I suppose, from your local point of view. From *my* point of view it was awful. Without the tension, the pressure, the competition, discoveries that would eventually spread humanity to the stars were set back by centuries at the very least, maybe even forever unless another such power arose."

"Huh? What? We was sendin' up space shuttles all the time!"

Nathan Brazil sighed. "Gus, you come from the most bizarre nation on Earth. It looks and feels like a European culture or cultures, but its root culture is more alien to the rest of the world than the Chinese or anybody else Westerners think are inscrutable. You invented violent anticolonialist revolution and sponsored it for decades, then you turned around and acted like an imperial power and couldn't figure out why everybody else didn't do the same. A bunch of your people, half of them devoted slaveholders and at least half virulent racists, wrote the world's greatest statement on individual liberty and protecting minority rights. You continue to create and dream up most of the vital inventions and scientific principles of the industrial revolution, and then you let everybody else put them into practice better than you do, so that the only thing you wind up being absolute masters of is varying ways to destroy all life on Earth. One of your people invented the principles of rocketry and couldn't *give* it away, so the Germans copied his patents and used it to bomb London. Then you import the same Germans to make rockets for you, but you don't care even about them until the Russians use *their* captured Germans and create the first satellite. *Then* you decide you got to go to the moon before them to show them up, and you do. But they don't go, and you lose interest, and thirty years later, nobody's close to going back."

"Jeez! You're sure not givin' us credit for much, are you?"

"Well, I credit you with an awful lot, Gus, but you Americans were only masters of one specialty, and that was war. The rest you let go, and when you let the rest go, like space, you become a hollow nation without ideals, a bunch of folks doing research and development for other nations, and you lose that restless creativity that made all those advancements possible. You were rotting, Gus. Drugs, crime, poverty, and an economy mostly based on exporting raw materials and importing finished goods—right back where you started from before the revolution. A service economy isn't an energetic, growing one, it's a nation doing each other's cooking and dry cleaning."

"And the *Russians* stayin' whole would have changed that?"

"Well, it did the last time. Your people need an enemy they think is an equal, Gus. They see the world as a sports contest. Not much fun playing soccer when you're the only team on the field. The Soviets were going to assemble a big, grand space station, Gus. One *hell* of a platform up there, under the control of the Red Army. You know what would happen in your country if that became real. And then they were going to the moon and eventually Mars. Things would turn around. The game would be on again. Instead, their totalitarian regime collapsed, they fragmented, discovered the rest of us weren't so bad and that they really lived at a Third World level, and all the grandiose dreams fell apart as the money and resources got diverted to doing things like producing toilet paper and decent indoor plumbing. Fine for them, but it keeps humanity pretty much stuck on its ball with the only question being whether it'll run out of resources, choke to death on pollution, destroy its atmosphere, or just fall apart in food riots and general anarchy. Don't blame me. It was *your* people who couldn't do a thing without an archenemy. And don't look so downcast. We came from a great era for bang-bang on-the-spot news, didn't we?"

"If you think I'm gonna argue about how shitty the situation on Earth is, you're nuts," Gus responded. "You said it—you remember what I did for a livin'. But you know, I bet you saw worse, experienced worse, during all that time. Kids dyin' of no reason but ignorance or maybe sacrificed to some sun god someplace. You said you was in that concentration camp, saw the worst people can do to each other. Did you ever look up the survivors? Did you ever cry for the ones that went into the ovens? Or did you just sit there, like you was in purgatory, endurin' the hunger and the punishment and the pain and maybe feelin' sorry and disgusted that you got yourself into that fix, but unlike all them other people, them millions, you *knew* you was gonna walk out. You *knew* the Nazis would lose. Hell, you knew that even if they whipped you, even if they pulled out your toenails, cut your fingers off, tore out your tongue, you'd not only pull through, somehow, but all that would grow back. In the end it'd be just one more bad experience and the nightmares would stop and you'd do okay. Not like all them others. You like to pretend that you care, and maybe you do for one person or another right here and now, but you don't really. Not deep down. And the only thing you're *really* pissed off about is the wrong people got a good break and even though it might be better for everybody else, it slowed down what *you* wanted. *Slowed it down!* What the hell's a hundred years to you, anyway? Don't lecture me about my people and my world, good, bad, or whatever. You push a button and we all go away, but while we're here, we're *alive*. You didn't need to see a Dahir's invisible tricks. You ain't noticed the whole course of human civilization except when one comes up and shouts in your face!"

Brazil didn't respond immediately. He felt bad about what he'd said about Gus's native country and history; really, in the long course of things, it was far better than most. But Gus's accusations had hit a bit too close to him at his drifting best to remain totally unchallenged.

"You're right, Gus," he said at last. "About some of it, anyway. The cause, though, is one you should understand as well as anybody. How many people have you seen die? How many corpses have you counted on bloody streets and in killing fields? How many starving kids in some revolution or drought-stricken land have you walked past? A lot, I'd guess, in your short life."

"Yeah? So?"

"What was your reaction the *first* time you saw kids you liked getting blown away or lying in agony? The *first* time you saw a whole village die of starvation, a living death? I think you cried, Gus. If not outside, then inside. I think after you saw a village of kids who looked like walking skeletons and could barely raise their heads, you got so upset, so sick to your stomach, you puked your guts out someplace and maybe cried again. But you had a job to do. Without your pictures, nobody else would know. Nobody who could help would know where to help. A few newsreels of Auschwitz and it would have ceased to exist. The whole rest of the world would have fought like demons. Nobody made it into those camps and back out with those pictures then. That's your job, Gus, and that's part of why you do it. Part of it is a thrill ride, living on the edge, but nobody walks through the starvation in east Africa, say, because they want to see the world."

"I still don't see your point."

"The point's simple. After a while you still believe in the job, but you don't puke anymore. The ten-thousandth kid dying before your eyes of starvation isn't like the first one or even the first ten. The hundredth soldier you capture on film falling in battle isn't like the first one, either. Ask any soldier. Ask any survivor of those camps. You never like it, but you get hardened, you get immunized to a degree, because you have to survive and live with yourself. Pretty soon *you* don't have nightmares about it, either. You just get—detached. Not only to save your sanity but also because you accept that you can't feed those starving people yourself, you can't save the kid looking up at you, you can't call back that bullet to that young soldier's heart. You know it happened to you; otherwise you couldn't still do it. Some people can't. They go nuts or they quit and do something else. You can and you did. I think they call that being 'tough,' or maybe just being a 'professional.' Terry was a tough professional. You admired that a lot in her."

"Well . . ."

"So why condemn me for being the same way? When the ice sheets came down and killed off the crops and moved the people in great migrations southward, I was there. When the first temples were built to long-forgotten gods, I was in the crowd that watched the sacrifice of the children to them. When the Persians and Medes and Babylonians and Greeks marched and leveled whole cities and sowed their enemies' lands with salt, I was there. When Roman emperors threw people to the lions to the cheers of the crowd in the coliseums of the world, I was selling tickets and souvenirs or picking the spectators' purses. When they cruci-fied thousands every few meters of the Appian Way as examples, I ran the dice game for their effects. When the Vandals vandalized and the Goths and Visigoths crushed the Romans, I sold them street maps. Then the Celts, then the Germans, then the Slavs, then the Moslem hordes, as they were called by the Christians. The Children's Crusade—*that* was a good one! All those kids, some not even in their teens, slaughtered as they made their way to the Holy Land singing hymns only to be finished off facing a professional army also convinced that God was on their side. The Inquisition—they actually felt *horrible* after they tortured you to death in the name of God. Wept for your lost soul. Want me to go on?"

"I get your point. But you *knew* better. Couldn't you have done *some-thing* more than be an audience?"

"What? One guy? You can't buck the worst in humanity because some-times you throw out the best, too. See, you have an advantage I don't have. I could at least hide out from the worst of that, I suppose, but I *can't* quit. I can't go home. I can't even go permanently nuts. I can't even *die* with them. After a while you just get too frustrated. After a while you just stop fighting the tide of history and just survive as best you can."

"Yeah, I guess I see, sorta. I still ain't sure how we got on this track. Maybe boredom or tiredness or somethin'. Can you answer me one thing, though?"

"If I can."

"What were you in the last go-round? I mean, maybe this machine god won't let you play really funny stuff, but you got some choice over you, don't you?"

The question actually surprised him. "I—well, yeah, I do. I have a good deal of *local* power over what happens here, on the Well World, while I'm in there, even if I can't mess with the Earth's program. I never really did much with myself, though. Every time I'm in there, I say at least I'm gonna make myself 185 centimeters tall with a face and body to die for, and I never do. It's not a Well prohibition, it's just, well, I'm generally so preoccupied with other folks and other things when I'm there, I never really think of myself. Maybe I'm just so used to being me now, I can't think of myself any other way."

"Jeez! So you're kinda the master of this world of all these races and forms and stuff and you *never* wind up anything or anybody else? You got all them other planets out there and you stick with relivin' Earth history over and over? You're right about not bein' able to go nuts. You *are* nuts!"

This new point struck him even harder than the earlier argument had because there really *was* no defense. He'd always been Nathan Brazil since—well, since this job had begun, anyway. At least he hadn't the slightest, vaguest memory of *not* being just this way. He alone knew why he'd stuck with Earth, or at least Earth humans, but even there he didn't really *have* to. It made no difference in the end to damned near anything.

Sure, he'd been—memory somewhere vaguely said a deer at one time in the past and a Pegasus for a brief time—but those had been *here* and for emergency purposes. He'd become himself again as quickly as he could.

He'd always loved the Dillians, also for good reason, but he'd never considered becoming one of them, living as one of them through *their* history, which was something of a mystery to him. They were fighters, too, and even with far more limited resources they'd managed, as he knew, to attain space consistently ahead of Earth. There were others, too, equally attractive and advanced, yet he'd ignored them all. It seemed stupid on the face of it. No rerun of history and events, new experiences, new people and capabilities . . . Even Mavra, with her own personal traveling version of the Markovian computer, had gone to many other worlds and become many other creatures, he remembered now.

"I've got no answer or explanation, Gus," he told the Dahir. "The only thing I can think of, and I'm not at all sure if it's the real reason or not, is that maybe I needed something that was absolutely fixed, unchanging, always comfortable and familiar, that couldn't be taken away from me."

Gus stared back out at the colorful scenes in the darkness and tried to imagine what it would be like to be Nathan Brazil. Maybe he'd be just as loopy after all this time, he thought, but he wouldn't mind giving it a try.

They were passing another area of active volcanic activity in the distance, and it was a sight he found impossible to tire of. Suddenly his two huge eyes focused on a single spot in the distance, off to the left of the lava flow. At first he thought they were just reflections of some of the lights from under the sea or perhaps lights or markers on the islands, but now, as he stared fixedly at the spot, he saw what had drawn his attention to the spot.

"Cap! Off here, just left of the lava. Those lights *moved!*"

"Could be just an illusion with all the heat and distance," Brazil responded, not terribly concerned. "Or it might well be another ship. There's a lot out here, you know."

"Yeah, well, I been lookin' at it, and those lights are sure not illusions and they're on somethin' pretty big movin' our way."

Brazil looked over at where Gus was already staring, and after a minute or so he saw them, too. "Yeah, Gus. They're running lights for sure. Something pretty big, I'd say. I can't make out much in the dark, though. There's a storm moving almost parallel over there. If it kicks up some lightning, you might be able to tell what it is."

"You want me to douse our running lights?" Gus asked him worriedly. "You never know."

"Maybe. Hold on a minute and try to make sure it's heading for us and not just coming out and going somewhere else. The sea-lanes we're on here run mostly southeast to northwest. If he's legitimate and coming from that direction, he should turn parallel to us in a little bit and head off in the opposite direction. I don't like it, though. What's a ship doing that close to those islands? They're marked as too active and dangerous for landings on the charts."

"He's comin' on toward us! *Whoops!* There was a big flash. Couldn't make out much, though, but it sure looked like a big bunch of smoke. Man! He's comin' on fast and steady! He *can't* be a sailboat and move like *that,* can he? I mean, the wind's against him, right? Yeah! There's another flash. Still can't make out the ship, but that's a steamer all right!"

"Douse the running lights, Gus, quick as you can! I think we're in trouble!"

The sudden rise in Brazil's adrenaline roused Terry, who got up, watched Gus put out the lights so that the ship fell into total darkness, and immediately looked around for the danger she was already directly sensing.

She went through a whole series of spectrum shifts until she spotted the oncoming vessel, and inside of it she sensed danger in numbers beyond theirs by quite a bit. There were a lot of creatures on that ship, and all seemed to be of one mind, to catch and board *this* ship and take them.

A whole range of actions came into her mind, but none of them were useful. She could make it very hard for them to see, or notice, both her mate and herself, but they would still take the ship and sooner or later they would certainly have a means of detecting them. And there were so *many* of them.

There was a sound like thunder off toward the oncoming lights, and suddenly the sea seemed to explode just forward and off to the left of the tiny sailing ship.

Brazil spun the wheel and then began taking down sail, using the levers and pulleys nearby.

"What the hell you doin', Cap! You're headin' right for 'em!" Gus cried.

"We won't be for long, but they had our course and speed damned good there, and I needed to throw them off in the dark. They've got no radar here."

"Yeah, well, they don't *need* radar at this distance! I mean, we must be blockin' off the undersea light show just like they are to us by now!"

Brazil cursed under his breath. He hadn't thought of that! And those guys were surely using just that technique on them. They were used to these waters; he was not.

He took a deep breath, then shouted, "Okay, then, we're gonna have to open range and sail where they can't do that!" as he put out full sail and turned for maximum wind.

"Hey! Them dark places could be *islands,* Cap!" Gus pointed out. "And you're gonna go right into the edge of that storm, too!"

"Just what I want to do!" he yelled back as a second shot landed forward and just to the right. "Damn! Straddled us with two shots at two kilometers! Those boys are *good!*"

They were making very good speed, getting up to fifteen, maybe twenty knots, but they were no match for the steamer still closing on them, particularly considering the angle.

A third shot landed perhaps twenty meters ahead of their bow, and its message was very, very clear. They could hit them any time they felt like it.

They were past the undersea fairyland lights, though, at least, and it was still water at this point. Suddenly, with very loud *splats* like buckshot falling on the deck, the rain swept over them.

The captain of the patrol boat knew exactly what his quarry was doing, and, worse, with the storm and the darkness, he actually risked losing them now that he had them cold. He couldn't wait and take that chance; there were too many reefs and shallows in there for him to follow closely with his craft. "If you can still get it, fire to hit!" he commanded, and the gun crew, also very experienced, made mental calculations, slightly adjusted the forward cannon, waited for a possible last sighting with a lightning flash, and fired a blast.

The shot struck the little sailing ship almost in the stern, and all three aboard were thrown to the deck as their world lurched and shook. One of the smaller masts came loose and dangled, caught in its own rigging.

"Everybody okay?" Brazil shouted in the fury of the wind and rain and thunder.

"Yeah! Terry almost fell on top of me!" Gus called back. "You?"

Brazil got back up, grabbed the madly spinning wheel, and found that it was spinning freely. "Damn! They took out my rudder!" He looked up at the sails and saw the dangling mast hanging precariously, fouling lines, heard the slow rip of canvas, and knew instantly that there was no hope of steering by sail alone.

He made his way to the other two. "I hear breakers not far off, *that* way!" he pointed, a position perhaps half a kilometer away in the darkness from their current position and what looked to be a good three or more kilometers from where the lava flow should be. "We're gonna have to abandon ship and swim for it! The quicker the better, too! We could go down like a shot in this sea if enough water gets in the hole in the stern or we hit a reef!"

"Okay! I'll make it! How about if we split up, we rendezvous this side of the lava near the beach?" Gus suggested. "Hey! You want to throw over the raft?"

At that point the ship seemed to almost stop, and Brazil could feel the bow coming up.

"No time! Just go! *Now!* If she goes down when any of us are close, she could take us with her!"

Gus hesitated, then leapt into the dark waves. Brazil, knowing at least that he and Terry would not be separated but nonetheless concerned for her life, had no choice but to follow. Terry did not hesitate.

Terry had been a fair swimmer in swimming pools and such, but she had never had to swim in seas like this and for a very long moment she was convinced that she was going under for good and was certain to drown.

Then the discipline and control of the Glathrielian mind snapped fully in, and she calmed down, sensed Brazil and what he was doing, and made her way to the surface and toward her mate. Brazil had recovered as best he could but was acting instinctively; later there would be time to think about how much worse he'd been through and reflect on it.

He struggled against the waves to make his way to Terry and finally reached her. Now she would have to pretty well stay with him and trust him absolutely with her life. Her Glathrielian mind understood that sort of logic and did not resist, having no better plan itself.

Using the waves, letting them carry the pair where they willed, Brazil managed to get them both relatively stabilized in the rough sea. At least it was no longer raining, although they could hardly tell, but Brazil was able to get at least a gut-level feeling of where they were headed and even got something of a look in that direction.

They appeared to be heading toward the lava flow and the huge plume of steam offshore.

He doubted if even Terry's bag of tricks could protect her from molten lava, but the Well would protect *him* from it somehow. If he could just stay close to her, linked to her, he might well be able to have her share *his* unique protection for a change. He *felt* her absolute trust in him and felt that she had accepted dependence for this period. She was not doing so well against the waves, though, and that terrified him. In a move as instinctive as his swimming actions, he reached out to her, first grasping her hand, then mind to mind, soul to soul. She did not resist, and now he was part of her and partly still within himself, as was she. They became as one mind, one organism, with Terry surrendering almost total control to him.

They managed for what seemed like a very long time, then, suddenly, there was a large wave that came along and picked them both up and almost threw them against a beach.

It was a granular black sand beach of the sort that new volcanoes built; it *hurt* when they hit it, but it didn't knock them out. Dizzy, disoriented, unable to stand, waves still crashing over them, they crawled as one on hands and knees back beyond the breakers, the black sand sticking to and covering their wet bodies. It took a tremendous force of his will to get them back far enough that there was relative safety. Then, with his inner voice telling him that he was safe at least for the moment, both bodies turned, gasped for air, then passed out cold on the beach.

The sun was high in the sky when Nathan Brazil awoke in a bizarre and yet beautiful landscape.

Terry awoke at the same time, the linkage between them as strong as or stronger than ever, and together the two of them got up on their feet and looked around. Both were battered and bruised and covered in thick black sand that seemed to be stuck everywhere. Brazil, seeing nothing on the horizon, decided that they could risk getting into the much calmer surf and wash it off, and Terry followed. In spite of the energy shell, it was almost like bathing in a Jacuzzi, but it woke them completely and cleaned off the sand.

The bruises were par for the course of what they had gone through, and muscles and joints seemed extraordinarily achy, but both were basically all right considering what they had survived, and that was enough. When you could notice the tangles in your hair and be irritated by them, you weren't in that bad shape.

There was no sign of the ship, not even wreckage, but it was impossible to say how long they'd been in the water or just where they'd gone down compared to where they'd come ashore. There were no other ships to be seen on the horizon, either; if the cutter had searched for survivors, it hadn't found them, but that didn't mean it wasn't still in the area.

Even so, that left the two of them stark naked with no tools, supplies, or anything else, standing on the beach, essentially marooned very much as in his personal fantasy. The trouble was, in a fantasy it was easy to conjure up what you needed, while in reality you had to find it, if anything was available.

The black sand beach stretched in both directions as far as the eye could see. About a hundred meters beyond where they'd come ashore there was a slight rise, and not far beyond that he could see nearly constant plumes of white smoke. While the lava flow itself was invisible to him in the daylight, the lava having hardened a bit on top and flowing downhill in its own thin self-made cocoon, it was clearly still expanding the island from beneath the waves. The muffled sounds of explosions could be heard from the direction of the steam as the molten rock continued to flow into the sea and react with the cooler waters.

Looking inland, it was a long way to anything interesting. The beach extended back for a kilometer or so, then turned into cracked and jagged rock in a fairyland of shapes formed when molten rock had cooled, solidified, and fragmented. It was easily another kilometer or more beyond that to where the older island missed by the most recent flows remained, with thick junglelike vegetation starting abruptly from where the flow stopped.

In back of it all and dominating the entire scene was the massive volcano itself, rising up like a huge lump several kilometers above the water, its top masked by a ring of clouds.

There was no getting around it; they would have to make their way back into the jungle and see whether the island contained enough to sustain them for now. Food and water were the first priorities.

He thought about Gus. He hadn't seen the Dahir since he'd gone overboard, and he wondered how well this kind of place could sustain such a creature. Large animals were unlikely in this isolated environment, fresh water would be more likely inland than anywhere along the coast, and that body wasn't really built for walking or even slithering over this kind of terrain.

Still, Gus had shouted to meet near the lava flow and on this side of it, fortunately, and he owed it to the creature to check before heading inland. He set off across the sands toward the billowing steam, Terry following.

The sight from the top of the rise was spectacular, probably even more so at night, with the lava steaming just below the surface in front of him and then the monstrous, churning, seething, bubbling region creating the steam just beyond.

There was no sign of Gus, nor had he expected any, but he'd done his duty. They could hardly stay there and wait in the expectation that the Dahir would suddenly appear; they'd need the daylight to explore the island. Brazil also didn't have anything he could leave to indicate their survival and presence, nor was there much he could use to create anything. The black sand wasn't even conducive to writing a message in English that only Gus would understand, and even if he could haul some rocks from the lava field inland and build something, a feat hardly possible considering how much he ached, anything small enough to escape the notice of pursuers would be overlooked by Gus and anything conspicuous enough to get noticed might well attract the wrong people.

It was Terry, either by chance or by design, who came up with the somewhat gross but only logical means of leaving Gus any sort of message.

She took a crap in the sand.

Hardly permanent, but a hunter species might well notice such a thing and Gus would recognize the species of origin, possibly the specific scent. Others might do the same, but they would first have to know to come to this specific area of the beach.

That taken care of, it was time to make their way inland to the jungle. If possible, they'd check back at this spot on a regular basis, if only to see if anything had either been disturbed or something else had been left to give them a sign.

I feel like Tarzan playing Robinson Crusoe, he thought. Friday was even the silent type, as always, although he suspected that the old shipwrecked sailor would have preferred *this* kind of Friday to the one he'd gotten.

Walking through the sand wasn't much of a problem, but the sand ended well short of the jungle, and it was a dangerous and slow journey through masses of rock that had flowed, cooled, and frozen, often shattering into huge lumps or collapsing into deep holes. It was a boulder field, but of black rock that was twisted into bizarre forms, some looking like taffy, others looking like frozen rippling rivers. It wouldn't take much of a misstep in that field to twist or even break an ankle, and so it was a slow process of trial and error to get through it, and it took them several precious hours to reach the edge of the jungle.

Volcanic areas were always fascinating for their contrasts. Where they had come ashore had probably been ocean only weeks earlier; now, here, where not much older flows had come, it might have been anything from beach to jungle, but the lava had burned and scoured all in its path, leaving no sign of anything. Yet the wet green jungle had resisted where it could, and just meters from where the flow ended it was as if nothing had happened at all.

There appeared to be no birds or animals, large or small, but somehow insects, or the equivalent of insects, had made their way here on air currents and were the dominant species. Some looked pretty fearsome, huge creatures that flew on multiple wings and were the size of hummingbirds and strange translucent creatures the size of a man's head that made their way up and down trees and vines shooting out long, creamy white tendrils.

To Terry, the jungle gave a sense not of real danger or strangeness but of an odd familiarity. She had spent some time in jungles like this, and while the individual plant and insect life was different, this jungle was no more bizarre than the Amazon had been. She felt almost as if she were in her own element, a cross between the swampy jungle of Glathriel and the dense yet protective Amazon rain forest. Terry the American television producer would have found the region creepy and threatening, but somehow that Terry seemed like another person, someone she barely knew. That Terry would have found the comforts of Hakazit to her liking, while the new Terry had felt only its sense of wrongness and had been relieved when they'd left it.

For all intents and purposes Theresa Perez was dead and had been for quite some time, save for some of the knowledge from her past that might be useful. She hadn't realized it and did not do so now; the Glathrielian way did not allow for reflection and introspection on that level, but that did not change the truth of it. She hadn't even been conscious of when it had happened; it had been quite late, though, when she'd made the decision to be the diversion for the others to get through the Well Gate. Even when she'd told Lori that she would remain in the Amazon until finally she could make her way to civilization, she'd known that she had no intention of doing so. She hadn't known until it was snatched away how much she really had hated her life or how much pressure she'd been under until it had been removed. It had long ago ceased to be anything more than a job, and that job had been the only thing she'd had, the only reason to wake up and exist every morning. She had no personal life, no friends outside the business, and she hadn't even had the glamour of being on camera. It had been over since that horror on the Congo, but she'd had no place else to go and her work was the only thing that she did better than almost anybody else.

She had hid it well, but the rock-hard woman Gus so admired had been terrified to walk alone to her car in an Atlanta parking lot.

Overcoming the initial fear, shock, and terror of the jungle and having been accepted into the Amazon tribe, she'd found a closeness and a sense of herself she'd never been aware of before. She had not thought twice about seducing those guards or felt guilt or recrimination. It had, rather, been the culmination of her transformation before she'd ever seen the Well World; it had been the act of someone who had found an element where life, where action, was a challenge rather than a reaction to fear. Even then, on some subconscious level, she knew she didn't want to be Terry again.

She had followed the others into the Well Gate almost on impulse but partly because she knew that the restrictions on the life of the People were not for her and that her friends, those she had felt closest to of any for a long time, had gone through the Gate. It had been Teysi's impulse, not Terry's. Nor could Terry have walked naked and alone into that alien swamp that was Glathriel, but Teysi could and did. And the Glathrielians, for whatever purpose, had given her the last required links to make the change complete.

They had given her the freedom from all dependency on *things,* leaving the focus only on what really counted—people—and with that the power to survive almost any conditions. They had given her protection against most of the forces of civilization and nature. And in a sense they had given her the ability to accept herself just the way she was, with no pretense or artifice.

So now it was Teysi's persona who was in this strange new jungle with her mate, and Teysi was far better qualified to be there than either Terry Perez or Nathan Brazil.

Brazil was content to let her take the lead, sensing her confidence. Food and water were the first priority, and somehow he was confident she could find them even though he wasn't sure how. On Earth a good although not totally infallible rule of thumb was to watch what the animals ate. Here the only animals were insects of a different evolution.

He watched her examine trees, vines, shrubs, and growths of all sorts and was not even aware that she was comparing them not to anything she knew directly but to elements in the vast Well database she could slightly access through her links to him. Finally, she picked up a thing that looked to him like a purple cabbage, peeled away the outer leaves to reveal a smooth oval inside skin, and bit into it. The deep red pulpy interior was kind of messy, but she kept eating rather than falling down in fits. He shrugged, picked up another—they must be falling from some of the higher trees, he decided—and did the same.

The stuff was disappointingly tasteless, with just a hint of a grapelike flavor, and the inside proved to have the consistency more of mashed potatoes than of oranges or grapefruit, but it went down easy, was filling, and had a high water content to boot.

He hoped they'd find something better and tastier, but unless they both came down with galloping stomachaches later, it was proof that they wouldn't starve here. They could at least survive.

Farther in they found a number of shallow streams that provided welcome fresh water. It tasted strongly of minerals with just a hint of sulfur, but it would do.

They did find a few more palatable things to eat as well, including something that resembled a pink tennis-ball size grape, both in looks and taste, and a thick green vine that tasted a lot like celery with a slight onionlike tang, before the light began to fail. By that time the aches and pains had gotten a bit too much for him, anyway, and she found an area near a huge tree carpeted with a light brown, spongy moss and lay down on it. It would soon be dark as pitch in the volcanic jungle, anyway; not the sort of conditions for exploring.

He lay down next to her on the soft natural matting and found it surprisingly comfortable. Still, as the last light faded and the world was enveloped in total darkness, he couldn't help but feel every ache and pain and consider the absurdity of the situation. There was no way around the fact that they were now shipwrecked on a small island in the middle of nowhere, alone, cut off from continental land by 190 kilometers or more of open sea they had no way to cross, with no means to get off and little hope of rescue by anyone save perhaps their enemies and the final objective, the equatorial barrier and its gateway into the Well of Souls, more unobtainable than ever.

She felt his pain, both physical and mental, and all she wanted to do was help him as he had helped her in the surf. To Terry, the current situation was not bad at all but almost her own concept of how life should be. All that they needed was here, and there seemed little that could threaten them in any way. It seemed as if all the fates had conspired to bring them here, and she could not conceive of it being more ideal. It was his old ways, old life thinking that kept him unhappy, forever searching for what he did not know. He had helped her when she had needed help; now it was her duty to do it for him.

She began by easing his physical pain, both by damping down the pain centers and by applying healing energies to those parts that were badly bruised. She began by massaging him, and as he felt the effects, he did not protest but rather relaxed and enjoyed it. With his pain substantially eased or gone, the massage turned slowly into far more than that, and as passion took control, she offered a unique new experience, a sharing of bodily pleasures that subtly became a sharing of minds and souls as well, in which her own will became dominant. Now, in rhythm with the passion, waves of conceptual objects of her will washed through them, through him, and as they had no words, their significance and purpose could not be divined by him, yet they were unresistingly accepted and understood by his mind as seductive, hypnotic commands in a way quite similar to what the Glathrielians had done to her, but in this case entirely of her own origin and out of her own desires.

Forget the past . . . Wall it off . . . The past does not exist . . . There is no past, there is no future, there is only now . . .

Enter my mind, my body . . . Within is all that you require, all that you will ever need . . . Take from my body, my mind all that you need . . . Leave all else behind . . . See, know, that there is only good inside me, take it as your own, renounce all else . . .

He reached out for what was promised and found within her a shining kernel of something overwhelming, something beyond anything he had ever experienced before. Pure, undiluted, unconditional love; total, absolute, unconditional trust. There, inside her, was what he had never been able to witness or feel, that which he'd been incapable of believing even *existed* anywhere, at any time, on any plane.

Let it in, let it in . . . Let it displace all the darkness . . .

A moment he knew at some deep level would never come again had arrived, and he could not turn it away. His resistance melted; he let it flood into him, not displacing that which could not be displaced but pushing it away, sealing it off from consciousness, not permitting it to interfere . . .

The waves washed through him, overwhelming, sealing off all those things that could intrude or interfere, and once that was done, he returned them until what remained active in his own mind matched the pattern in her mind. The yin and yang merged, the puzzle pieces, shorn of all that was not relevant, fit perfectly and without flaw . . .

They awoke before dawn, the jungle no longer dark to them but seething with the varying colors and patterns of life. They took care of bodily functions, washed in a nearby stream, then started through the jungle, not with any real purpose but because it was so pretty and so alive and was to be enjoyed. Along the way to nowhere in particular they found some of the fruits and vegetables that were good to eat and they ate, feeding themselves and each other and giggling like two young people in the dawn of first love.

After a while they started off again, going deeper, following the trails of some of the larger insects just to see what made them and where they were going. They were hardly aware of the fact that they were also moving uphill, nor did they care, all places and destinations being the same to them. They were Adam and Eve in the Garden before the Fall, and they were more than that. They did not speak because such an act was totally unnecessary. Each felt what the other felt, each knew what the other knew, both thought the same thoughts at the same moment because they were as one. Each existed solely for the other and for the moment.

When they broke clear of the jungle, they were amazed and thrilled at the great sight that was before them. Still relatively far down on the great mountainside, they could still look out from its slope and see the vast colorful seascape beyond, even more beautiful when blended as it was with all the colors of life below.

Then they watched the sun come up and dramatically change the view, not to one of ugliness but to one almost completely different from the night scene. They stayed there for some time, until the sun was well up in the sky, then made their way back down into the jungle for some more to eat and drink.

He found a vine filled with pretty multicolored flowers that had become broken, possibly in the wind or by insects, and picked it up and made a flower garland out of it for her hair. She wanted to see it and so saw it through his eyes, then decided to take the flowers and place them on him, and he looked at himself through her eyes. And when they were done, they put the flowers back where they'd been found and went off in search of more wonders.

And when the thunderstorms came after dark, they did not seek cover but rather stood in the rain and the mud and watched, as if the sound and light show were being put on just for them. Everything was a wonder of a game, and everything was eternally new.

He remembered nothing of his past, his origins, or his unique nature, but he neither wondered about such things nor let them enter his mind. There was only here, and now, and *her,* and that was more than enough. She felt exactly the same, experiencing only the here and now and *him.* Neither remembered or bothered to consider that this had come about only the previous night. There was no concept of time, only the now and the other. So closely linked were they that he was not even certain that he was the *he* and she was the *she*; either could effortlessly become the other, and so such a question was without meaning and thus not even asked.

The food and water were ample for the two of them for an indefinite time. The ship had gone down without a trace, and there was no real sign that they had ever made this or any other island. All their defenses were permanently on; any searchers or landing parties would not even notice their existence, and since they built nothing, created nothing outside of themselves, there were no signs of their existence for anyone to find.

It had not been the intention of the Glathrielian elders, but Nathan Brazil, for all appearances, had been taken out of the game. Terry had allowed for all external factors, it seemed.

All but one, and she could not know about that, even though it was everywhere, not many kilometers beneath their feet.

KZUCO

THREE DAYS OUT FROM Gekir, while still inside Ogadon waters, the small ship its passengers discovered was called the *Star Runner* met up with its transfer ship.

Whatever illegal cargoes were involved in this mysterious underworld, they were both valuable and dangerous, and it was nearly impossible for those paid to find out about such shipments that were in fact taking place. Even deep beneath the ocean waters in Ogadon, where this particular trade originated, there were civilization, law, and effective agencies trying to stay on top of things. The one thing the authorities could not do was fully determine the when and the where across a hex that was, after all, almost four hundred kilometers wide, such activity took place, but it was always a battle of wits.

Even though it would be sheer luck to locate and stop a transfer in progress, once it had been passed off to a surface vessel, the fact became known. The *Star Runner*'s job wasn't to pick up the cargo but rather to meet the pickup boat, which was a relatively local one well known as legitimate to the authorities, and then take aboard the contraband at sea. Ships like the *Runner* were built to all the latest specifications but were particularly intended for speed, speed, speed. As a vessel legally registered to handle charter and consignment jobs, it always had some specific legal mission of its own, although nobody was particularly fooled about its true purpose.

The smugglers' defense was a variation on the shell game; several ships like the *Runner* would take off from various ports on seemingly legitimate missions at roughly the same time. Each would head for a different place, but only one or possibly two would actually pick up transfer loads of contraband. Consistently stopping and boarding the wrong ones could prove embarrassing for the interhex authorities, who were in many ways privateers not much different from the crooks they chased except that they'd chosen a lesser return in exchange for doing things the legal way.

Several large waterproof containers had been taken aboard by the *Runner* from what appeared to be a small and seedy trawler, although it was hard to say just what the other ship really looked like in the nearly total darkness in which it was done. It was now the *Runner*'s job to get those containers to another ordinary and familiar coastal vessel that would take a detour at some secluded part of the coast and transfer them once more to small boats to go into shore and from there to a distribution point.

Mavra Chang was fascinated by the process. Once they were under way under full steam, she went over to Zitz, the friendly mate who'd always liked to chat, and commented, "I don't see how you manage it."

"Eh? What?"

"Linking up with a specific small boat in open ocean, in either direction. I don't see how you can find her unless she sits there like a sitting duck waiting for you, and I'm sure she doesn't."

"You're right," the Zhonzhorpian admitted. "It's actually quite simple. No state secret except for the specifics of every operation. Before we set out, we get a very fine customized grid of the entire hex. Thousands of tiny little squares. The rendezvous ship is a scheduled carrier; we know its route in advance, and we know in which of a range of squares along its route the pickup will be made. She doesn't stop, not even, you'll notice, for the transfer. We just find her and match her course and speed."

"It was impressive—and quick," Mavra admitted.

"Then we proceed to our destination hex, which has another hex map, another customized grid, and another series of scheduled local carriers. We plot them at all times. Once I'm there, I determine where the best one is located, head for it, and reverse the process. Unlike the pickup, I will always have a choice of two or three ships, and even they won't know which one of them will receive the goods from us, so there can't be any leaks ahead of time. Similarly, there were several ships similar to this one, any one of which might have picked up the cargo from the first vessel. They didn't know it would be us, and it might not have been. If anything went wrong, if someone else got there ahead of us, or if they were being shadowed, they would alter their course slightly from the grid and we wouldn't have seen her."

"I see," she commented. "Very slick."

"There are so many spies and agencies out there that it's impossible to keep them from infiltrating one ship or another on the two ends," Zitz told her. "What *is* possible is, since not even the captain knows if he's the one until he passes the pickup point, we control access to the goods. They pick *up*; they transfer to one of a number of similar vessels. What does the spy report when he, she, or it finally makes port? And most of the next ports are nontech hexes, too, by design. *My* crew stays with me, so I know them all. Our rendezvous ship even now does not know it will be the one, so there's no rumors or leaks from its crew. When we do the transfer, same rules applying, they will take it on and proceed immediately to a point offshore in a nontech or semitech hex and transfer it again, being met by crews who pick the position themselves, then proceed into port on schedule. By the time anyone aboard can get the word out, the cargo and pickup people are long gone. As soon as I make the transfer, I destroy the grid maps. My counterparts will eventually intersect the pickup freighter back there, by the way, see that there is no coded sign that anything is to be picked up, and proceed on as if they had picked up something anyway."

"So this is your point of maximum vulnerability," she noted. "You have the cargo and maps aboard."

"True, but for all of that we have ways of dropping the cargo even under pursuit. The captain only needs to remember one grid position and the code number of the grid map no matter where along the route we might be forced to drop it. *We* would not then bring it in, but once he transferred the grid location and grid code upon making port, someone else eventually would."

"Sounds almost foolproof."

"It's very good," he admitted. "I think it might not be improved upon. It is, however, still a risky business, particularly in high-tech water hexes like Kzuco. We try and stay out of them as much as possible, but it's not possible on this run. That makes the money much better, but the risks are far greater. That's why we're running the short side of Kzuco along the Awbri coast. Awbri's nontech, not the best vantage point, and once we're across the border into Dlubine, we're back in semitech and safer. From that point we can remain in non- and semitech water hexes. I *do* worry about Dlubine, but not as much as here."

"Dlubine has local conditions that create problems?"

"Several. For one thing, it's crawling with patrols, sandwiched between a high-tech land and a high-tech water hex and with a lot of islands with small harbors and hidden coves. Also, in Dlubine it's easier to run by day than by night. You'll see what I mean the first night we're there. The water's lit up like a high-tech city, making it easy to spot you. Easier by day, yes, but murder on us."

"Huh?"

"You can almost make soup with the water, it's that warm, and the air temperature in the middle of the day is close to lethal for many life-forms. It averages more than half the point to boiling. Even the islands seem like water kettles. Still, it is a lot of sea to find us in, and we do it all the time. Each hex has its problems, so I don't want to minimize any dangers, but we are used to them. You are not."

She nodded. "We'll stay out of your way. If it comes to a flight, though, you well know I have no stake in being arrested and returned to Gekir."

"Yes. You understand, though, that none of you can be allowed to leave this vessel until after the transfer has taken place and we are well away."

"We understand," she assured him. She did not press him on the nature of the cargo; in truth, she already knew what at least some of it was just from overheard conversations among the crew. It was a drug, an extremely addictive drug, that worked on a large variety of warm-blooded creatures. Called by many names in many hexes, it was apparently some kind of deep underwater fungal growth. Alive, one could actually eat it without harm, although it supposedly had a terrible taste. Out of the water, though, it died in minutes and dried out quickly, causing its natural internal fluids to undergo a chemical change, crystallize, and become a very sweet and addicting drug that could be eaten, injected, or who knew what else? Tolerances varied, but apparently for some races one ingestion could be enough to hook a user.

Lori had come up to get some night air, finding it difficult to sleep below, and had been listening to the conversation. When it was over and Mavra had moved away toward the rail to stare out at the black sea, he went over and stood beside her.

He'd found this business with the *Runner* both disgusting and unpleasantly familiar. "It's the same here as back on Earth," he growled. "It's as if there's no way and nowhere to escape drugs and the predators who sell them."

"The universe is composed of predators and prey," Mavra responded, not sounding cynical but rather as if she were reciting the obvious. "Everyone is one or the other, sometimes both in a lifetime."

Lori's realization that this was a ship in that sort of business and that all the crew were the same sort of creatures as the ones who ran and guarded Don Francisco Campos's jungle operation, which now seemed not merely a million light-years but also a million real years away. He couldn't help but wonder if Juan Campos hadn't already found his niche in this sort of operation here. It was a natural for him.

He often wondered what had become of Campos. How he'd like to meet the little weasel *now*, not rat to woman but rat to man. They said that when a sexual change was done, nine out of ten times it was to a female, to which poor Alowi and Tony, too, attested. He'd often thought how he'd love to discover that Juan Campos had become an Erdomese female. It would be real justice, but while Mavra said that the Well was sometimes perceived to have a sense of humor even though it shouldn't and theoretically couldn't, both Julian and Tony were proof that there wasn't a whole lot of justice as he would think of it built into the system. The bastard was probably nine feet tall with four arms and sharp teeth and more rotten than ever as befitted his personality.

He still wondered about Campos, and not just him. Where was poor Gus, for example? Had he even survived the transfer and transformation? He'd been such a gentle, quiet soul, it was hard to see him outside his element, his cameras and video equipment and other high-tech toys.

He also wondered about Terry quite often. What was she doing now? Still back there with the People in that rain forest? He *knew* when she'd decided to be the diversion that she would get the worst of it. Such a bright, educated career woman, highly competent, courageous . . . There were few superlatives for Terry that he didn't think she deserved. To be shut off for good in the jungle would be *intolerable* to her, he was convinced. But to emerge, tattooed all over, with bone jewelry threaded through her ears and nose . . . She'd be a freak. A news story herself for a while, then just a freak. There was no way she could ever lead a normal life like that, and the amount of removal and the cosmetic surgery on her beautiful brown skin would give her a choice between being a painted freak or looking like a burn victim. What kind of a life could she have like *that*?

In the end, she'd probably stay in the jungle, perhaps leaving the People and joining a true tribe but remaining anonymous otherwise, or she'd find a convent, become a nun, and remain cloistered for life. Damn it, it wasn't fair! Terry would have *loved* this place no matter *what* she wound up as!

He finally talked it out with Mavra. "I know it's a hell of a thing she did for us. I owe her, that's for sure. When we get into the Well, I'll see what, if anything, can be done about her. There's got to be *some* way to influence it, even though the only direct controls available that I know of from last time are on people here. Funny, though. You jogged a memory. When I got information on Brazil and his party from Zone, there was mention of someone coming in alone who appeared from the pictures to be of our race—or so they said; I never saw them. Somebody who came in after us, snuck by them all, and went through the hex gate before they even knew anyone was there. They said the other one resembled us."

Lori was excited at the idea. "You think maybe she—?"

"Don't get your hopes up. She was diverting the guards, and I know just how they planned to do that. The Well Gate would have closed and self-destructed after I—we—came through because Nathan and the other two had arrived long before. I don't think there'd be time. No, what I've wondered is whether one of the other women, one of the perimeter guards, might have watched us go through and decided to follow her goddess. It would be just like Utra or maybe Rhama to do just that. Poor darlings! What if one of *them* wound up in a high-tech hex? It'd be bad enough for them to turn into *anything* else, but a nontech hex they might handle with a lot of work. Still, there was no word of anybody else being reported, so it's hard to say anything for sure. I *do* think that if Teysi had come through, she'd have gotten word to us somehow." She sighed. "No, I'm sure she's still back on Earth, and I'm *pretty* sure she's still in the jungle. Unlike you, she found something in the jungle that she loved. I think she didn't want to come because she'd already found her version of the Well World. I think she really *wanted* to stay just as she was."

"You didn't know her. She'd go nuts living in there like that forever."

Mavra smiled. "Maybe *you* didn't know her. I looked at you over a period of a week or two, and I saw somebody willing to play jungle Amazon and go along because that was better than death, but you were always playing at it. Once you got over your fear and your natural feeling that rescue was at hand, you got into it, but it was always a game with you. You didn't ever belong there. I looked at her, though, and I saw somebody hiding one hell of a lot of inner pain. I don't know what it came from, but it was there. And once she got over the same two hurdles you did, she didn't accept things like you did, she embraced them. I've seen the same thing in countless girls who came to us over the years. Like some kind of horrible burden had been lifted, removed from inside them. You fell into a trap; she escaped one. I wouldn't be surprised if she went totally, completely native."

"We saw totally different people," Lori said, shaking his head. "I wonder which one of us saw the right one."

Mavra sighed. "Well, you've seen it happen with Alowi, and I would have bet you that Julian Beard would never have flipped out like that. We'll probably never know for sure about her. At least I'll try to find out once I'm inside. If I can, and she's still alive, where and what she is back there will kind of settle it and what I do for her—if I can do much. That jungle was already disappearing at a horrendous rate. I wish I knew how long any of those tribes can continue to exist as they want to exist. It's a real shame, but it's the way that whole planet went. Right from ancient times they called it 'progress.' I guess it is—if you're doing the chopping and not being chopped."

That brought Lori back to his original train of thought. "What about this drug trade right here? It makes me feel sleazy. Worse than that, it depresses me. Here, all this time, all this civilization, and they wind up like we were going in *my* old corner of civilization. The whole damned *world* seemed to be falling into the hands of the Camposes and their ilk."

"Well, having used drugs of a sort in the jungle, and earlier in other places, and having done a little smuggling in my time, I can't be too judgmental about these people. In a sense, they're the kind of people I was born and raised with. And I can't really say I'm surprised that this exists here; rather, I'm surprised that it didn't seem to exist when I was here last. At least not in anything that wasn't species-specific and too localized to notice. The biggest problem you have if you're born and raised on the Well World is that you have to face the fact that it's meaningless. I mean, what can you hope to do? These are the descendants of the leftovers, the last races tested out here. They're managed from on high—or, rather, from on low—and on the whole, things don't change very much. That's why they don't keep a lot of the kind of history here that we do, on the whole. Even the Erdomese, on their own planet, *might* discover electricity, *might* discover radio and video and research biology, and *might* even figure out a way to get to the stars. They just have less to work with, and it might take them longer. They might not, but it's possible. Not here."

"Well, yeah, but it's not *that* bad, I don't think."

"No? You were a scientist. I'll bet you know enough to create a small renaissance in scientific knowledge in most hexes here, including Erdom. But it's all useless knowledge, isn't it? Useless because nothing except muscle and some water and wind power works there, and even then, if you generate a current, it'll die before it reaches anything that might use it. That was Julian's problem. Just about every bit of the knowledge she has and the talents she possesses are useless in Erdom. Permanently. She can't even swagger around and be Señor or Señora Macha. Everything in Julian Beard's life was denied him as an Erdomese by itself and by being an Erdomese woman in particular. Build things? Paint? With rock-hard mittens for hands? In a land and culture where anything she *might* do intellectually is considered deviant behavior and women are virtual property—forget it. On top of that he had a ton of guilt over being less than a wonderful human being by his own lights. And his mind-set was so much Mister Macho that he was finally faced with the ultimate problem and it tore him to bits."

"You mean he just couldn't handle being a woman?"

"No, he couldn't handle falling in love with a *man,* you idiot! Even if it was with a man who used to be a woman and still has, I think, a woman's soul."

"Julian? In *love* with me? I mean, *really* in love?"

"Sure. Plain as day. But Julian couldn't be in love with a guy, just couldn't handle it, and Julian wasn't useful in any meaningful way from this point on. So Julian goes, Alowi enters. Call it a split personality if you want, but one of them won. The one who could be in love with you and be of use to you and not go bonkers because of what she could no longer be or do."

Lori sighed. "Well, ain't that a kick in the head. Mavra, I swear to you, even though I never thought it for real until just now, I really *did* fall in love myself! But with Julian, not Alowi. Not that I'm not still, but, well, it's not the same."

Mavra shrugged. "Well, you have a problem maybe unique in romance, don't you? I seem to attract the unique in that department. The thing is, though, you've got the Julian problem kind of the way *he* had it."

"What? Now you've lost me again."

"The Well World changes *bodies* around. That's not unique, you know. It's technology. The same principle as the matter transmitter. I once knew somebody who's a distant ghost to me now who discovered the same principle on his own. An Earth-human type. It's not magic. It's physics and mathematics, and enough of an energy source to do it and enough of a computer to manage all that information. It also does some physiological adjustment so you don't fall over trying to walk on those legs of yours or upchuck when you wake up as a creature that eats live prey or the like. But the process doesn't really change the mind, the personality, the soul, as it were. You can't keep the memories and such and wipe out the rest. You lived too long as Lori Sutton. Somewhere here Juan Campos is still a slimy son of a bitch. Julian completed her own transformation. She became a woman to the soul. Tony—well, that's a different personality. I think he was a tough guy but very gentle underneath. With all he'd gone through and his double suicide plans for himself and Anne Marie, I think he considered himself dead, anyway. He got an easier break in a better culture to be a woman, even though that one, too, has its sexual divisions and problems. Still, in spite of cultural hang-ups, I think he was one of those rare guys who really liked and respected women. At least he doesn't see it as a negative. I think he feels he lived a full and decent life as a man and now he's got a chance to live a second life as a woman. That's the attitude to take. Like the Hindu belief that we're reincarnated alternately male and female. To her it's a whole new life. I'm afraid Anne Marie's more a problem than a continuing love story for him."

"Makes sense." Lori nodded. "But what about me? You said I still had a woman's soul. I sure haven't felt much like it; even my thoughts sometimes would have made the old me *very* mad."

"Oh, you're obvious. You—just like in the jungle—never got to that point. You're having a lot of guilty fun *playing* at being a man. But you're not. Physically, yes, but not deep down. It's always easier for women to adjust to other roles and accept them than it is for men."

He thought about it. "Well, it's true that when you see two guys kissing, you have a whole set of reactions, maybe depending on your own feelings about sexuality, but *everybody* has reactions because it's not done. Women kiss each other all the time, and nobody thinks anything of it. And I *know* women dress more for each other than for men. I can't remember a boyfriend I ever had who ever noticed that I had had my hair redone, and most of them didn't notice new clothes or perfume or whatever until I pointed it out to them."

"But *you* still notice. Even in Erdom."

"Yeah, I guess I do. But a lot of that is how they're brought up, too, isn't it? I mean, competitive sports, competitive grades, competitive businesses, everything's competition. Even in Erdom that's true." He thought of the sword fighting and other such activities. "I wasn't brought up like that. What competition I did was on a different level. All appearances and comparing possessions. Men fight or they get the crap beat out of them. Women try to reach a consensus, and a fight between two girls, when it happens, is real scandal or real news. Yeah, I see what you mean, I guess. I stopped seriously competing real early. I was always the consolation prize, if I ever got invited to the dance in the first place, and the kind of life a business career offered never appealed to me. I just wanted to be a scientist. I wanted to find out how things worked and *why* they worked. I was good at math, and girls weren't supposed to be good at math. I loved computers, and girls were supposed to hate them. I guess I figured that so long as I was already a social geek, I might as well be a total one. I just decided to do what I loved doing. I'd love to do it here, too."

Mavra nodded. "Yeah, I understand that. That's another problem with coming through the Well. The high-tech types already know what you know, and more. The others either don't or can't use it. Coming from the tech level you do and the occupation you do, you not only would have to learn from scratch, you'd have to unlearn half of what you learned as gospel. The very fact that you stand here as an Erdomese man says that better than I could. The same went double for Julian. Pilots of any sort, and particularly jet and space pilots—well, they're useless here, aren't they? So it decided you were useless and dumped you in low-tech. You'd have had a better shot at high-tech if you hadn't been as smart, frankly. Doesn't take brains to learn how to push buttons. Same goes for Tony—airline pilot. I think somewhere there was a theory built into the Well that said that if your skills were useless, you should be put in a spot where they couldn't be used so that you might adjust and use that brain power where it would do some good. Just a hunch—no inside information there. But it kinda holds, doesn't it?"

"Could be. But in Erdom the knowledge that might be useful is held by that damned priesthood and the price is *much* too high, and the guilds leave me out of most of the other trades that might be of any interest. It seemed like the best I could be would be some kind of glorified night watchman or street sweeper or something else menial. I mean, like much of the population there, even though I know seven languages and have a universal translator implanted, I'm still a total illiterate in Erdom, and having looked at that language, I probably will remain so. I think that's why I jumped at your note even though I was under that hypnotic drug's spell at the time. Cut off or not, I knew when I had an opportunity for something better rather than facing my alternatives there."

"Well, I never figured on the hypnotic drugs, but I kind of hoped that either curiosity or ambition or both would bring you. Just a few days more and we'll be ashore in uncharted realms for both of us. I need you. Do the job for me and I'll make sure you have a future you'll like. If we lose this race, you'll have seen something of the world and won't be any worse off. Fair enough?"

"Fair enough. But thinking about those priests' drugs brings me back to what kicked off this talk. I still feel uncomfortable with all this. Did you *really* do this yourself once?"

"Sure. Okay, that shocks you, but as I said, this is a place with 1,560 tiny worldlets with no future and no past, more or less. They're kinda stuck here. They know there's a possibility that their kids might be worse off than they are but won't be better off. Mostly it'll be hard to tell one stagnant age from another. Deep down most know that or at least feel or sense it. It's why life can be cheap here, and it's little wonder some turn to chemical escapes. You mean you *never* tried some drugs out of curiosity or boredom or depression or whatever?"

"Me? Not much. Some marijuana now and then—I did it heavy in college, I admit, but less once I got a job—and some alcohol but nothing hard. I tried cocaine once at a party and darn near choked. Never touched it or anything else again. Why?"

"And these were all legal substances?"

"No. Alcoholic drinks, yes, but not marijuana or cocaine. Not in *my* lifetime, anyway. But it's not the same."

"It *is* the same. Even legal, it's used for the same purposes. Illegal just feeds the whole business. The same ones who got your illegal drugs in also brought in the rest, of which you disapproved. Your money went to help them finance the ships and men like this one. I've not only been with them on this level, I've fought the ugly side of the business, too, against the thoroughly rotten people at the top. You might say that far back in the distant past I saw the future of this as well, and nothing you see here can compare to the depravity of what lies ahead."

"But it's a matter of degree. Some is harmful, some not."

Mavra Chang sighed. "I remember a people once in east Africa. Two tribes, same ancestry, all that, but one of them lived by a great river and tilled the land and mined gold and such from the nearby mountains that served as a barrier separating them from the others. Those others, they lived on the other side, a lot of the same geography and possibilities, but their home was in a virtual cannabis forest. They were a far happier tribe and more content, but for generations they remained no more advanced than the People of the upper Amazon. I don't judge. The tribe that remained in the forest was probably happier than the other one that built a great city, but the happy ones were stagnant, stuck, just like the Well World."

"You're one to talk!"

Mavra shrugged. "We used some drugs from the native forest, you know, and not always as a practical thing. What can I say? After being kicked around for a few thousand years I called a halt. I didn't *like* Earth much, Lori. I didn't like it much at all. It was uglier and more primitive than I could have imagined in ways I never dreamed it could be. I'm sorry, but that is my perspective. I left it. I escaped where it wasn't so ugly, and I remained there rather than come out to face more ugliness. One day things would be different. There would be what *I* considered real progress and advancement, and they would discover interstellar travel. By that time the rain forest would be cut down, and I'd be able to get *off* that miserable planet. I do know that I'm not going back there. Or if the Well somehow forces me back there, I am not going back as Mavra Chang or anything remotely like her. If I can, I'm going to be something else."

"Yes? What, if I may ask?"

"I don't know. If what I believe is true, I won't have to face that problem. If not—I don't know, but I'll think of something."

Since Mavra was in a talkative mood, there being little else to do aboard the ship, Lori was about to go into just what Mavra thought of men—at least, men who hadn't been changed into women and vice versa. It seemed to him as if she hated them in general, on a gut emotional level, even if accepting them intellectually. That Portuguese ship and crew must have been a holy horror, but had it, after so much experience elsewhere and even before, in some former lifetime, driven her over an edge she hadn't been over before? Or had she *never* liked men? Why had she separated from this Brazil guy so long ago, and why did she seem to both hate and fear him now? According to Tony and Anne Marie, this Nathan Brazil sounded like a pretty nice guy. He'd saved two lives out of clear compassion; Mavra had put lives in jeopardy, ruined one or two maybe, and waxed nostalgic for the days when she'd been a drug runner.

He never got the chance. *"Ship! Port, fifty-one degrees, distance nine kilometers and closing at flank speed!"* came a sharp shout from the bridge, where, in this high-tech hex, all the technological gear was active.

The captain was in the wheelhouse in moments, looking at the scope. "I don't like this. It's got the size and speed to be a privateer. How far is it to the Dlubine border?"

"Twenty kilometers, sir!"

"Damn! So close and yet so far! Any attempt at communications?"

"None yet, sir. Instructions?"

Captain Hjlarza thought for a brief moment. "Zitz! Hail them, then. Ask them who they are and why they are bearing down on us. Warn them that we are an armed ship and that we deal mercilessly with pirates."

The Zhonzhorpian was on the radio immediately, barking a challenge and sounding doubly mean. With that crocodilelike throat and mouth, he could make it sound very menacing indeed.

"No reply, sir!"

"They're stalling! Okay, we've given them a legitimate reason for us to turn and run! Kill all lights! Starboard thirty degrees! All ahead full! Zitz! Man the weapons board! Others to arms stations! If they get in range, give 'em all you got! If they call us now, you know the routine!"

"Aye, sir!"

Lori looked alarmed. "I think we better clear out and give them some room," he said nervously.

Mavra returned a wry smile. "Just don't get in their way. These are pros."

The captain kept looking at his scopes. "They're closing a little, but they're only a hair faster than we are. At this heading and speed, we should still have a good two kilometers on them when we cross the border. As soon as we cross it, I'm going to give a sharp turn to starboard and full speed into whatever's there. We'll still be out of visual and off their instruments. When I do, I want everybody at their sailing positions. Engines, I want full until I tell you, then I want a dead stop. We will put on sail the moment after I order an engine stop. Understand?"

There was a chorus of "Ayes," and the crew went to station.

"They're calling us now, sir!" Zitz reported.

The captain gave a low chuckle. "They've just figured out they won't catch us this side of the border. You know what to say."

Zitz, however, was already saying it. "If you were truly legal authorities, you would have responded to our first call with an identification signal," he told the pursuing ship sharply. "We've been suckered by pirate ploys before. No, sir, we would be derelict in our duties if we yielded to you now."

They could hear only one side of the conversation, but it was clear that the gunboat had issued an ultimatum and a threat.

"Well, sir, if you can catch us, then do so. If you are a legitimate naval vessel, we will lodge charges against your captain for failure to respond to a legitimate identification check. If you are not, we will have to fight. If we are fired upon, however, we will take that as confirmation that you are pirates and will respond accordingly and without hesitation."

The captain was just looking at his scopes, throttle wide open. Suddenly he snapped, "Engines, we've just had two guided torpedoes launched against us. I will probably have to turn if they don't both buy the decoy. Be ready." He leaned out the open window. "Torpedoes! Let go aft decoys!"

One of the spider creatures hit some levers, and there were loud splashes behind them in the water. A minute or so later, well in back of their wake, there was a tremendous bright flash and the sound of an explosion.

"One of 'em bought it; the other's still coming," the captain reported. "Launch antitorpedo from aft tube and reload as quick as you can!"

There was the sound like that of a torpedo being fired, and then the spider creature opened a hatch and went halfway down into it, clearly doing something with its forelegs out of sight of the deck. Before it was finished, there was another bright flash and explosion behind them, much, much closer to them than the first one had been.

"Got it!" the captain called with satisfaction. "Zitz, give 'em two rockets! I don't care if you hit them or not, but it'll keep 'em back and make 'em think twice about us!"

Lori's sense of boredom had vanished, but it was replaced with a little bit of fear and concern. Still, all of it seemed somehow unreal, distant. *I feel like I'm in the middle of a cheap thriller,* he thought wonderingly.

The two rockets went away with a twin *thump! thump!* sound, and they saw them quickly rise on small jets of flame and disappear into the darkness behind them.

"I hope the folks who live in the water here aren't the kind to get too pissed off at people blowing up things," Mavra commented dryly.

"One minute!" the captain shouted. "Everybody brace yourselves and be ready to alter course!" He paused, watching the scopes carefully as the stack billowed black smoke and the wind seemed even chillier.

Lori looked forward and thought he could see some lights off in the distance, but everything looked hazy and distorted. Almost as they reached it, he realized that he'd been looking through a hex barrier at night.

They could feel the tingle of the hex barrier as they crossed it, and suddenly all the electronic gear on the bridge failed as if someone had pulled the plug, and the heated air of the new hex hit them like a solid, hot wet carpet, causing some momentary disorientation. The ship, however, continued at full steam.

Without further warning, the captain brought the *Runner* around hard right, so hard that loose things on deck shifted left and Lori felt himself being thrown against the rail, then pitched back, falling to the deck.

It seemed as if the ship would never stop its turn, that it would go on forever, but after a while the vessel, which had itself been leaning to the right, steadied itself and came back to a straight-on course. The captain was counting quietly, estimating the speed of the pursuit and the amount of time it had taken them to make the dramatic turn.

Suddenly he shouted, "Sail crew aloft!"

Expertly, the two great spiders scuttled up the masts virtually to the top, and long tentaclelike legs adjusted the holding straps, while Zitz left his dead command console aft, where the two centauresses were watching the show with a mixture of awe and concern, and moved forward to the sail control position.

There was another long pause, then the captain shouted, "All engines dead stop! Boilers to standby! Disengage engines from drive shaft! Lower center board and deploy mainsails!"

There was a sudden, almost deathly quiet save for the noise of the sails being squeakily lowered and fixed into position.

"Rig full, no jibs," the captain commanded, and first the topsails and then various subordinate sails sprouted, making the transformation to quiet sailing vessel almost complete. The boilers were not out, but since they had been disengaged from the drive shafts, there was a sudden cessation of the steady rhythmic vibration that the engines had sent through the ship.

Mavra went over to Lori and offered a hand. "You okay?"

"Yeah, I think so. Probably gonna have a hell of a bruise on my hip, but it's no big deal. The hardest part is getting back on my feet." He made it with her help but needed to lurch forward and hold on to something. "Great body for running, particularly in sand or gravel, but it's just not good with the casual stuff." He was calming down now and took stock of the surroundings. "Wow! Feels like home, only worse! This is *really* hot!"

"It's at least as hot as Erdom," Mavra agreed, "but with an ocean's humidity. Will you be all right here? I want to check on the girls in the back."

"Yeah, sure, I'll be okay. I'm just trying to get steady enough to go down and check on Alowi." He gave a long, relieved exhale. "At least we made it!"

"Don't feel so confident yet," Mavra warned him. "They're still back there, and they're close. If we don't lose them, we'll have to fight, and we'll be well within their gun range here. This is semitech, remember, not nontech. Cannons do their usual nasty job here."

He stared after Mavra as she went aft to check on the Dillians, then said aloud, under his breath, "Yeah, thanks for telling me that cheery set of facts."

The air felt wet and sticky, and there seemed to be a light rain or mist falling that did nothing to cool things off. He looked to the right of the ship and thought he saw some kind of shimmering, a distortion even of the night fog and mist.

The captain was running directly down the hex barrier, just inside the Dlubine side.

He shook his head and decided he'd better put his trust in the ones who knew what they were doing and tend to his own business, which was going below.

It was a mess there; the turn had spilled more down there than up on deck, but Alowi seemed all right and relieved to see him.

"I—I was afraid something happened to you up there," she told him.

"I fell. Hip's gonna feel like hell later, but I'm all right. What about you?"

"I rolled over, but once things straightened out, I was all right. Everything was flying or rolling around . . . I just did not know what was happening. Come—let me heal your pain."

"I'm all right for now."

"*Please!* Now is the best time. The last time you almost died from a bad bruise. Let me give you what you need to keep it from happening again!"

It suddenly struck him. The key to the entire Erdomese way and why things were more dangerous for him than he'd realized.

The male Erdomese's weakness, its Achilles' heel, was that he and all the rest of them had a kind of hemophilia. The females, in that second set of breasts, carried more than spare water; they carried a clotting factor. The women's nearly total dependence on the men for most things was counterbalanced by the men's absolute need to have that which only the women could make readily available. They hadn't told him or warned him about it. Why would they? Between their customs and their beliefs, and with such a huge proportion of females to males, they took it for granted. No *wonder* the men traveled with as many wives as they could afford to support!

For the first time he realized just how vulnerable he actually was to things that others took for granted. Even without cultural codes or his feelings for her, he would have to protect Alowi with every ounce of his strength and life. If anything happened to her, if they were even separated, out here, so many miles from Erdom, he was dead meat.

"My, that was positively *thrilling*," Anne Marie gushed. "Almost like one of those James Bond thrillers."

"I could do with a little less of that, particularly out here," Tony responded. Although Dillians had a natural ability to swim, it took a lot of muscle power to do so, and they wouldn't have much of a chance out here in the middle of the ocean, any more than a common horse might have. Sufficient to keep them from drowning in a river or enabling them to make a quick swim to shore or a raft, but considering their forward center of gravity, out here they'd be dead ducks.

"Well, I'm glad to see that you two are all right," Mavra told them. "They're slick, these guys. We're outside any capability the gunboat might have to spot us electronically and out of range of any of his fancy weapons, too. Hugging this hex boundary, we're in the natural mist and fog that's usually at such a border, and under sail, there's little noise."

Tony didn't feel as confident. "Wouldn't *they* know that, too? And couldn't they really bear down on us if it were steam against sail in this little wind?"

"They do, and yeah, they could overtake us, but they have 180 degrees of possibility. They'll overshoot coming in and have to turn when they see they lost us, and they'll do it gently. It takes time. Then they have to decide which way to turn. They'll have to cut their engines and run silently to see if they can hear us, and when they don't, they'll know we're under sail. From that point they'll be farther behind and have a fifty-fifty chance of tracking us or missing us entirely. If they don't fire up their boilers, they'll be slower than we are in this slight wind, since they're a heavier boat, and if they do, we'll hear them and have a straight free shot at their bow from the stern gun. I don't think they'll risk that. They'll pick a direction and run slowly along it until dawn, which is still many hours away. By that time the captain will have slipped away."

The captain in fact was waiting until they ran into the edge of one of the local storms, and when the first one was spotted, not too far from the border position, he took a chance and eased out of the cover of the boundary mist and, when nothing was obviously in sight, headed for it.

It made for a rough introduction to Dlubine, but they were alive, the ship was in good shape, and they were free of pursuit by dawn and able to engage the boilers once more and proceed in the heat regardless of the wind.

By midday there was some debate among both passengers and crew as to whether it was worse up top or below. Most chose to be on deck and relaxed under whatever cover they could rig up. Ultimately, it became too hot for anyone to even handle the boilers, and they went to sail and more or less just drifted along, taking four-hour shifts at the wheel.

All five of the passengers remained under the makeshift canvas shelter of the centauresses on the afterdeck. All had removed whatever clothing they'd had on; it was too hot to be wearing *anything* if one didn't have to.

It was a particular shock for the two Erdomese, who were used to extreme heat, but theirs had been basically a desert environment and their bodies were designed to retain and recycle moisture. Both were as miserable as could be.

"I got a reading from the wheelhouse thermometer when I went forward for some water," Lori managed. "Doing a rough conversion, assuming that the top of the mark with the big line is boiling and the black line on the bottom is freezing, I'd say well over 50 degrees Celsius— somewhere over 120 Fahrenheit, Anne Marie."

"Goodness! How do people *survive* here?" she responded. Dillians at least could perspire over most of their huge bodies, but they required a lot of water.

"Because the *people* are a mile or so straight down," Mavra reminded her. "Down there it's probably a nice, comfortable day, although from what I can tell they're nocturnals, like the captain."

"I wish I was," Lori groaned.

There wasn't much more conversation after that. It was too hot to do just about anything.

Still, there *was* a moderate breeze, which helped slightly, taking them almost due west. Again, it was the short leg about twenty kilometers off the Agon coast, a bit too close to avoid the risk of more intercoastal patrols but comfortably far enough out not to be seen or detected from shore. The only hope was to make full speed once night fell and be out of this boiling hotbox by sunup the next day. For all any of them cared at this point, Fahomma would be welcome even if it had icebergs and blowing snows.

Several times in the distance one ship or another would be sighted, but none of them ever closed with them, and such traffic was to be expected in this region. Some were even under steam, demonstrating clearly that whatever was stoking their fires might possibly have Satan as a relative but definitely bore little genetic kinship with anybody on the *Star Runner*.

Who was doing what became moot after a while as all of them drifted into varying degrees of uncomfortable sleep.

Nightfall wasn't exactly cool, but it definitely had a psychological effect on everyone. The captain took the wheel, and the weird creature who usually took care of everything below decided it was cool enough to fire up the engines. The job wasn't physically taxing—whatever fuel they used appeared to be a syrupy liquid stored in large tanks deep in the hull and moved to the engines by some sort of vacuum system—but the boilers got hot, and steam was always dangerous and needed constant monitoring and occasional release and regulation.

Captain Hjlarza wasn't very friendly or communicative, but Mavra had managed to establish at least a working relationship with the vicious-looking Stulz, who reminded her of nothing more than a gigantic fruit bat although she doubted he could ever fly no matter what the leathery wing material might do otherwise.

"How long to the border?" she asked him.

"Dawn. Perhaps a bit longer if nothing happens to delay us. There are always patrols about in these waters, and a full day is long enough for word to have been passed along a pretty good chain, I'd suspect. Still, I expected if we were going to be chased it would have been during the day, when we'd have no chance of running, boilers down, and everyone at their worst. No, I'd say at this point our most probable roadblock would be a series of storms. It *always* rains at night here. All that ocean went up during the day and has to come back down."

"What's this Fahomma like, then?"

"Oh, not too bad. Nontech, which really helps us. Under sail there's nothing that can catch us that might be able to hurt us. Warm, but cooler and more comfortable than this, but it tends to rain steadily for weeks at a time over parts of it. We will transfer our cargo there if all goes well and thus be free of patrol worries."

"Off Agon? They're smuggling into a high-tech hex?"

"Who knows? It goes to another freighter, and it's off here. Where it goes from there is not my concern."

"Well, it can't be soon enough for us, either. I think everybody except me is ready for dry land at this point."

Everyone, from Mavra to Lori, Alowi, and the Dillians, was entranced by the colorful underwater lights that became quickly clear as darkness fell.

"Those can't be electric- or nuclear-powered, can they?" Lori asked, as always as curious about how things worked as about how pretty they looked.

"Not likely," Tony responded. "I rather think they are chemical. Still, the layout, like a vast city-state deep under the water, makes you wonder what kind of creatures they are and what their lives must be like, does it not? I have tended to just regard the ocean as ocean very much like back on Earth. I suspect most of us have. But it takes something like this to remind us that there is an entire alternative set of people, species, and cultures down there. How sad that much of the contact between us up here and those down there involves drugs and crooked elements."

"Well, we know there are centaurs here, don't we, dear? One must wonder if there are also, somewhere, mermaids."

The night was still hot but bearable to a degree, although nobody felt all that energetic. At least there were some very pretty things to look at and a few impressive if less than welcome thunderstorms as well. Still, both captain and crew seemed well satisfied with the progress and also with the fact that the only thing that really was approaching them was dawn.

It was heating up pretty quickly when they reached the Fahomma border, and the captain ordered all steam shut down and shifted entirely to sail. The area ahead, through the hex barrier, looked somewhat forbidding, dark and gray, in sharp contrast to the brightness of Dlubine. As they passed through, the temperature dropped but the humidity got even worse—it was raining steadily, although not the hard driving rain and high winds of a Dlubinian storm.

Late that night, while under full sail, they passed a small trawler that gave the correct recognition sign. Captain Hjlarza was both puzzled and alarmed at this break with procedure and somewhat suspicious of it, but he turned and paralleled the trawler's course. From the deck of the other ship, something big and barely seen in the rain and darkness threw a spear attached to a long rope to the deck of the *Runner*. Zitz ran to it, removed the small attached tube, and then pried the spear from the deck and tossed it overboard so that the other ship could retrieve it. The mate then brought the tube to the captain, who frowned and opened it, pulled out a sheet of paper, read it, then put it with his grids and had Zitz toss the tube, both ends open, into the sea, where it would fill with water and sink.

"Trouble, Captain?" Zitz asked a bit nervously.

"New orders. Don't like 'em. Not at all happy about 'em, but orders are orders. They will owe us all for this, though, Zitz. They will owe us a *lot*. Cost us a damned fortune, this will. Take a look at it when you get the chance and then very quietly pass it on to the crew. I'll need you all tomorrow night, but if anybody spills the beans, they're dead meat."

When Zitz did get the opportunity to look at it, he saw just what the captain meant and liked it even less. It was a new, local grid, a very specific and specialized one, for a new job. Still, there was no question of not doing it. They followed the grids only for a rendezvous, yet the trawler had shown no problems at all finding them in this weather in a nontech hex. Even the authorities had failed to do that except by chance. You didn't mess with the kind of people who could pull off *that* trick if you wanted to keep on living.

The next day, the ocean was relatively smooth, although it continued to rain. The steady, light rain didn't cause any real problems for a sailing ship, and there was always something of a wind but rarely more than you wanted. The air temperature felt almost chilly, although in fact it was twenty-six degrees Celsius or better. The contrast, however, with the neighboring hotbox was dramatic.

Mavra sensed a little difference, perhaps a bit more coldness from the crew, but it wasn't much and could have been put down to a number of things. She knew they'd gotten a message the previous night, and clearly the message had given them some nerves, but they didn't really want to discuss what was in it.

About two hours after nightfall Captain Hjlarza swung in more toward the coast, almost without anyone noticing until they were too close to ignore it. They were still off Agon, a high-tech hex, and there were automated lights and electrically illuminated small settlements within view. Sensing that something wasn't all that right, considering the officers' aversion to getting in close to high-tech coastlines, Tony walked forward and alerted Mavra and the Erdomese, who were below staying dry. Mavra immediately came up on deck and saw that Tony was quite correct. She went to the captain.

"What's this all about? I thought we weren't stopping until Lilblod."

"Change in orders. Special drop just up here," the captain responded. "Stick around. You may find this interesting."

They came in close, perhaps a hundred meters from shore, no more—

close enough to see the hex barrier and the illuminated buoy that was just inside Agon. It was a relatively desolate part of the coast; there were a couple of individual lights atop what might have been high cliffs but nothing approaching a pier or settlement.

Two fairly good-sized black launches came out of the darkness just at the hex barrier, then turned so that the *Star Runner* could come alongside. Zitz and one of the spiders threw down ropes that tied the launches to the larger ship, then lowered rope ladders. Soon four heavily armed creatures climbed slowly up and onto the deck. All four resembled nothing so much as human-sized turtles without shells, wearing black outfits, and they carried what looked like a stylized futuristic automatic rifles over their shoulders and nasty-looking crossbows of equally advanced design in their hands.

Two of them walked over toward the bridge and spotted Mavra. The nasty-looking crossbows lowered and pointed straight at her.

"What *is* this?" she asked the captain, suddenly realizing that *she* was the drop.

"Sorry. Orders. Call the Erdomese man up on deck, very naturally. Try anything funny and I'll kill his wife and the two Dillians. Be nice, no tricks, and I swear that I'll deliver them to safety."

"You swore you'd deliver *me* to safety," she noted acidly.

"Quickly now. Just the man. And I didn't give my word on that to you. I was paid to do it."

"Yeah, and you'll lose that fortune, too."

"I hate the idea like the plague, but I'm ordered to give all the stuff back and report that we disposed of the thieves. A fortune's no use at all to a dead man. Now—call him! Very pleasantly, since there's nowhere he can go down there and all you can do by pulling anything is get your people killed. Don't expect the Dillians to the rescue. Zitz and the other Agonese have them covered."

She sighed. There wasn't anything to do, and she didn't doubt for an instant that he'd kill the others with hardly a thought even if she managed an escape. She'd gotten them into this; she couldn't very well lead them to such an unnecessary doom. But why Lori?

She opened the door. "Lori? Can you come on deck for a minute? Got a problem here I think you can help with."

"Yeah, sure," the Erdomese replied from below. She heard him come out of the cabin and come slowly up the stairs, and it wasn't until he'd squeezed out onto the main deck that he saw the situation and froze. "What the hell is this?" He paused and had that sinking feeling. "They caught us."

"Yeah, but I don't think these guys have anything at all to do with any government on this planet."

"Move out into the open, hands up," one of the Agonite gunmen hissed. "You! Big man! Bend over against the rail! Yes, that's it!"

Mavra started forward, but large, extremely powerful hands seized her from behind and put a foul-smelling mask over her face. *Gas!* She barely had time to struggle and just saw two of them doing the same to Lori before she blacked out.

DLUBINE

EVER SINCE GUS HAD slid into the water, he'd had no contact with anyone for several days. He had looked on some of the islands for Brazil and Terry but hadn't found any sign of them and wondered if, in fact, those were the same islands they'd wrecked on or if he'd been carried along farther in the chain before managing to make shore.

At any rate, he'd been unable to find the one with the lava coming down the side in that pattern, and that suggested that he was in the wrong place or at the very best on the wrong side.

It didn't take him long to discover as well that the islands bore no sign of anything a Dahir could eat. Some of the insects were large enough, but they not only didn't smell right, they smelled very much all wrong, and since being out on his own in this world he'd learned to trust his nose beyond all else. In any event, someone of his size couldn't expect to sustain himself on those things for very long.

That meant getting off, and the nearest mainland was at least fifty, maybe a hundred kilometers away—there was no way of telling for sure, but even if he set off in the right direction, he'd be dead of exhaustion long before he arrived. He was already all in.

He was not, however, the only one who'd lost Brazil and Terry, as he discovered the second day on the island while weighing what few options he had. He heard it first, then saw it—a patrol boat, a big steamer with metal plates on its hull not unlike the one back at the island harbor. Maybe—no, *probably*—the one that had caught and sunk them!

He was angry at them, but clearly they hadn't found anybody, either, or they wouldn't be poking around like that. In any event, with this black volcanic sand not taking much in the way of footprints or other signs, they had the same sort of problem he did and had to send a few of the crew over in small rowboats to look around and check for any signs of anything.

It was a pretty clear way out. If they continued searching and found them, he'd be there to help them out. If they failed, at least they'd head for some place to resupply, and that was the kind of place that might well have decent Dahir eating and he could figure out what to do next.

Besides, the idea of sitting right on the deck of a police launch and having nobody notice him was irresistible.

He worked his way up the island just beyond the beach, then out across some fresh lava rock that extended right down almost to the water, and slid in, swimming to the launch before the men were back. He waited there until the shore party did return so that they'd discount any extra weight or water when he came aboard on the same side.

They went from island to island, beach to beach, looking for any signs of wreckage or of anyone coming ashore, but found nothing. One time they did in fact come right around to a daylight version of what Gus *thought* he'd seen at night, only there wasn't any lava visible. It was only when he realized that the stuff was in fact coming down and dumping into the ocean and that this was what was causing the massive steam eruption over to one side that he understood his mistake. The lava hadn't been out in the open but had formed lava tubes, the rock hitting the air getting solid and forming a kind of roof for the rest. At night it looked like red-hot streams of the stuff, but by day it was a lot less obvious.

And that presented a real problem. If they *had* gotten on the beach and *were* on that island, what help would he be? No food, and instead of two of them being stuck, all three of them would be stuck. If it was the same as the island he'd been on, and he had no reason to think it wasn't, they could eat some of the fruit even if he could not, and there'd been water on the other island, which was much smaller, so there was likely to be water here. The way he'd seen Terry's powers in action, too, he knew they could hold out there a damned long time.

He would do more good to try to find the location somewhere and then come back for them when he could. It wasn't what his heart told him to do, but him dead and them alive and stranded didn't equal all three alive in any reasonable book. He just wished he'd realized his mistake on the volcano, when there had been time to get ashore, look by himself, and still catch the boat.

That night, after the last methodical search, near dusk, the launch gave up and headed out toward open sea. Gus just relaxed and snoozed on the bow and hoped that they were headed some place useful.

Within a few hours they were approaching land, and from the darkness Gus saw that wherever it was was definitely more civilized than he'd like. It looked like the coastline of Oregon or northern California, densely populated and brightly and artificially lit.

After they had slipped into an official naval dock facility and tied up, he waited until all but the watch and maintenance personnel were off and then just walked ashore.

Beyond the buildings, piers, and guards, though, was a kind of lunatic's seaside resort, at least to his mind. All the houses, hell, all the buildings, big and small, seemed like they'd been poured by a five-year-old out of some play-dough set. They looked, well, kind of weird, not at all symmetrical or standard but solid, colorful, and well built out of some synthetic material.

And by bright streetlights he found himself in what he thought of as the Land of the Ninja Turtles.

Well, not exactly, but they *did* sort of remind him of the cartoon characters. No shells, though, and no Ninja gear. And some of them had beards, of all things, and some of them wore what looked like Scotch plaid kilts, but most of them wore ugly, serviceable form-fitting plastic-type clothing.

There were big bipedal turtles and little ones and in-between ones, and except for the occasional oddball in kilts or other nonstandard clothing and the few with little goatees, they all looked just exactly alike to him.

Well, they seemed warm-blooded by their actions, in spite of looking like reptiles, and that made them somewhat akin to him, however different they really were. Maybe, just maybe, what they ate *he* could eat.

For a while he feared they were all herbivores, but then he discovered the refrigerated warehouses and lots and lots of meat. It was all dead, of course, and some of it might take a while to thaw out, although he wondered how long it would take *anything* to thaw in the waters just beyond the breakwater in superhot Dlubine. Rather than be piggy, he picked a half dozen smaller cuts, a mere six or seven pounds of meat of some kind, went down to the shore just beyond the town and waded, then floated out until he was in the warmest water he'd ever known.

The answer was about an hour a pound.

It didn't taste the same, not without the warm blood and all the nice mushy insides and skin and all, but it wasn't the time to be a gourmet or look gift horses in the mouth. He'd eaten a lot worse on this trip, and natural taste and instinct didn't fill an empty gullet. All in all, it was a quite satisfactory beach picnic, even if the company didn't show up.

The next day he tried to find out a little information about where the hell he was and what he might be able to do next.

This, it appeared, was a seaside resort in Agon, so even if the other two had failed to make the northern continent, he had, and he was the only one who didn't give a damn if he ever saw the place or not.

He knew he didn't like the place. It wasn't the locals, or the climate, or even the food so much as it was the fact that it was a high-tech hex. He'd had to bypass several security systems the previous night, and even so, he knew they knew somebody had broken in. In fact, a whole damned busload of uniformed turtle cops had shown up by dawn and were busily going over the place. He decided that they must have found something, because one of the cops lit out for the naval station on a crazy kind of vehicle that seemed to float just off the ground on nothing in particular but had handlebars and a hand accelerator and a hand brake kind of like a motorbike's. He decided to follow, mostly to see if there was any suspicion of a Dahir being involved.

The little fellow on the flying surfboard beat him there by a bit, of course, but he was there with several navy types of various races spouting off a storm. Gus moved closer to overhear.

". . . definitely no race on our local registry. It *has* to be something from one of your crews! You had a patrol come in just last night!"

One of the crew, who looked like a five-foot-tall version of Rocky the Flying Squirrel sans goggles to Gus, who was, after all, a television person, responded, "Now, calm down. What did you say was stolen again?"

"*Zlabruk!* Eight prime filets! Highest quality, too!"

"I assure you we feed our men well," responded another, who looked like a giant frog in full uniform. "And they earn more than enough to not go off after a very hot and difficult mission, break into a place, and steal a bunch of—*steaks*."

"*Zlabruk!* That's imported, you know! Expensive!"

"Well, I don't think—" began the squirrel, then stopped and thought a moment. "Steaks . . . Who in the world would break in and steal slabs of meat? I wonder . . . Wait here a moment. I want you to speak to someone else."

The giant walking squirrel vanished into a nearby building and was gone for two or three minutes while the others fiddled around and the Agonite cop kept muttering about imported filets. Finally the big gray lump of fur emerged, but he was not alone. Following him was a much more amorphous creature, a creature Gus had seen before, and when it spoke through an orifice it formed within itself, it was unmistakably the *same* one as well.

"I am Colonel Lunderman," said the Leeming. "Now, what's this about someone coming in and stealing a bunch of steaks?"

Gus wasn't at all sure whether to be relieved or fearful at the colonel's appearance on this side of the ocean. As much as he needed an ally, he felt he could trust this character about as far as he could throw him.

Just great! he thought to himself. *So* now *what the hell do I do?*

AGON

THEY AWOKE, CHAINED TO a wall by efficient shackles, unable to move any of their limbs more than a very short way.

It was a surprisingly modern room with a glowing ultra-modern ceiling providing more than enough light and vents feeding in air-conditioning at a reasonable level of comfort. Lori hung to the right of the entrance, Mavra to his left. Along the other walls were built-in work tables and fancy computer screens, and in the center were a number of benches with all sorts of science equipment on them, giving the place the look of a college chemistry lab.

Mavra groaned and looked around. "Lori? Are you all right?"

"I—well, if you call this all right, I guess so," Lori groaned, then looked around and tested the chains. "Now what happens?"

"Nothing good," Mavra responded. "You remember that I said you'd never really come face-to-face with what future technology could and would do for criminals? Well, welcome to the future. I'm just *devastated* to see this kind of setup here."

"Yeah, but I thought the equivalent of the UN or something wanted you. This sure isn't them—and why us, too?"

"Well, why don't you just hang around and find out?" Mavra snapped with heavy irony.

Lori sighed. "I guess it doesn't really matter much, for me, anyway. Without Alowi I'm a dead man, anyway."

They did not have long to wait, but the creature who walked through the door was beyond anything they expected.

My god! Lori thought. *It's Daisy Duck with tits!*

In fact, the body appeared more humanoid than duck-like, although it was completely covered by tiny white feathers wherever it was exposed, and the legs, slightly bowed, were of a tough-looking ribbed yellow-orange texture, and while the feet could not be seen, it was not beyond the bounds of imagination to think of two thick webbed feet somehow crammed into a pair of vastly oversized black pumps.

The arms seemed extremely thin, extending a bit out from the shoulders, with a ball-like elbow joint in the middle and ending in two huge mittlike hands, each with three nearly equal-sized webbed fingers and an opposing thumb, without any sign of nails, claws, or whatever. Extending from the underside of the impossibly thin arms was a row of feathers that might have been what remained of vestigial wings but that were now nothing more than decoration. The entire body, which stood perhaps 165 centimeters discounting the heels, was curvaceous and sported two rather ample mammallike breasts that were easily seen thanks to the rather slinky black dress the creature wore.

The head sat atop what appeared to be a very thin, short neck; it was large enough to match the body and began with long, straight black hair parted in the middle and going down to the shoulders on either side; the eyes were huge and oval-shaped, with the longest points vertical rather than horizontal as on Earth-human eyes, and contained large, round jet black pupils. These sat atop a long, curved ducklike orange-colored bill that extended a good twenty centimeters out from the head and was wide enough to be hinged on the sides of the lower face. Two small black slits atop the bill served as the nostrils; no ears were obvious.

Not Daisy Duck, Lori decided. More like Donald's wet dream. Even so, the effect was comical enough that somehow the figure did not seem threatening.

The bill proved amazingly malleable, almost like a human mouth at its front, and helped the creature shape its words. These words, however, came after it stood there for a very long time and just stared at each of them in turn, but particularly at Mavra, to whom the huge black eyes kept coming back.

Finally it said in a deep, throaty feminine voice that seemed to come from somewhere far back in the head, "This is a surprise I hoped for but one that I did not really expect to catch. In fact, I was actually not expecting to catch up with you at all. The net was basically out for Brazil and still is, but you will do nicely. *Very* nicely." That last was said with just enough menace to chill them.

"Who are you?" Mavra asked in as confident a voice as she could muster. "What is this place, and what do you want with us?"

One of the oversized fingers came up and gently stroked under the beak. "Who am I? I am hurt at the question, but I will answer it in due course. *What* I am is a Cloptan. It is not far. Right now you are in an underground laboratory on the border with Lilblod. *It* is in Agon, but above there is something more—ordinary. To get in and out one must go through a tunnel into Lilblod. It solves not only the technical but the *jurisdictional* problems rather nicely. You might have guessed that what is processed and packaged here is not exactly popular among most of the world's governments."

"Drugs," Lori sniffed.

"Yes, drugs. Specifically, two types. One is of little interest to you, but the other is the one you knew was in those containers aboard the ship that brought you to us. It has many names, but in the form we process it here we call it 'rhapsody.' It has different effects on different species. In fact, for a number it is lethal. For others it causes brain and nervous system damage, while to yet others it is simply a tasty spice. When processed into slightly different forms, however, for those races that are similar enough in brain chemistry and share some common enzymes in the cells, it is a drug. A *wonderful* drug, in fact. You take it, and all of your pain goes away. All of your physical pain, if any, and much of your *mental* pain as well. All the bad, negative things, the psychological scars of a lifetime, they all have little effect on you. It's all there, but it can't hurt you. I am told that the initial effects are like nothing else imaginable, but as your body gets used to it, you just sort of settle down into a situation where life is—simpler. The effects last for varying periods, the average being eight to ten hours before it gets down to where you'll need some more—but slowly, very slowly."

"I'm sure you'll spell it out in excruciating detail for us," Mavra commented dryly.

The Cloptan ignored the comment. "First the little aches and pains start returning, then full physical awareness, and looming on the horizon is every single horrible thing in your mind, all your worst fears and nightmares. You can feel them, almost see them coming. Fear turns to desperation, desperation to terror. There is nothing at all you can do. The only way is, of course, to take more rhapsody. Eventually, of course, your system gets used to it, and you level out, becoming more normal on a regular basis and with only one big overriding fear—that the supply will stop and you will face the horrors of your own mind."

"How horrible," Lori muttered. The bitch was enjoying this!

"Even the strongest minds cannot withstand it forever. Some can fight it off for hours, a few for days, but they tell me no one succeeds in breaking it completely. The depression becomes so absolute, you will kill yourself first. It keeps the business—profitable." She walked over and stood right in front of Mavra.

"They say you are possibly immortal, that you cannot be killed. I am not certain I believe that *anyone* can't be killed, but I think it will not

make much difference. It *would* be a nice experiment, though, to see just
how long you could go without it. If you could not even kill yourself,
would your mind crack? What form would the insanity take? I wonder
. . . It *is* tempting, but I think I have other plans in the end. Oh, yes,
the blood tests say that one form of it will work *quite* nicely on you.
Sutton, on the other hand, is sufficiently different from you to require a
different formulation, but the science folks say that it will work on him as
well."

"For God's sake!" Lori cried. "What do you *want*? What are you *doing*
this to us for? We're thousands of miles from home and surely can't be of
any use to you here!"

"I should think it would be obvious to you by now," the Cloptan replied. "Because of *this*," she said, gesturing down her body with her
hands. "*She* made me like this!" she snapped, pointing to Mavra. "And
you—you went along, Doctor Lori Sutton. And *you*—*you* became the man!
The big macho hunter with his little devoted four-titted bitch! I do this
for *revenge*! Venganza! Revenge for daring to drag into hell Juan Alfonso
Campos de la Montoya!"

"Oh, God!" Lori sighed, feeling all hope vanish.

"So that's why they wanted only the two of us," Mavra said.

"The Dillians are nothing to me and too large to have handled in any
case. What are they going to do? It will take them days just to find their
way out of Lilblod. Then what? Report to the authorities? They are
already looking for you and would find you now if they could. As for
Sutton's crazy little bitch, she, too, was nothing to me and just so much
excess baggage. Do not worry, *Doctor* Sutton. The computers here are
excellent. We know of the deficiency in your system, and we have the
means to fix it. If I had wanted you dead, I would have just had them kill
you."

Lori shook his head in wonder, unable to understand this kind of
thinking. "What is it with you? I didn't pick this body any more than you
picked that one. I'd trade you if I could. There are times I would have
killed for a shape like that. But look at you! Is it so *awful* being a woman?
You're young, probably very pretty by the standards of your race, and in
an incredibly short time you've managed to get this far up in the drug
trade. Some new start, but I guess it's what you know. I'm broke and
helpless in a backward medieval desert, for god's sake!"

"Being a woman is bad enough," Campos responded angrily. "It is *hell*
to me! And yes, I am *very* beautiful by Cloptan standards. Do you know
how hard it was to adjust to that? To have every lecherous Cloptan man
pawing you? Do you know what I had to *lower* myself to do to get to this?
I do not own this lab, nor do I control it. Finding the Cloptan under-

world was not difficult, and they were interested in me because I came from the same business but on a different world. No, getting inside was not difficult, but once there I was just another girl, just another piece of *furniture* to them! *Me!* The son of the greatest patriot of modern Peru, the man who could strike and corrupt and bring down the most evil and powerful oppressor of all Latin peoples with a weapon as simple and impossible to fight as common coca! I had to *defile* myself! To swallow all pride and self-respect and put myself in the *gutter*! I am *nothing* in this organization except a powerful man's current favorite toy! But now, now, it is all worthwhile. Here you are. If I can get the others, too, it will be complete. Brazil and that other bitch. Even if fortune does not smile, however, it has smiled enough. For a while yet we will play games so that I may have the satisfaction to repay my humiliation! Then, when the time is right, *you,* 'goddess of the trees,' will willingly and cheerfully *beg* to let me let you put things right. It may take weeks or months yet, I hope not years, but one day you will put things right for me and repay all the suffering that you have caused! Once you are under the drug's spell, you will willingly tell me anything and everything. If you *are* what some say you are, then one day we will take a trip, just us girls, and you will go inside this world and *put me right!*"

So that was it, Mavra thought. One more horror to endure, one more long torment, but the direction that damned Machiavellian Well was taking was now clear. It was sad that Lori yet again had been dragged into this. Mavra had mostly wanted to help them. Well, if he stayed alive, maybe someday she still could. There was certainly nothing to be done now. She just wished she'd listened to them and left Juan Campos back on Earth or finished him off. *Damn* her sense of fair play! One could totally change such as him, but he remained as evil as ever. He had already changed more than he knew or wanted to recognize, judging from what he'd done as a female and even how she now spoke and moved. But the Well did nothing to change that inner self, and Juan Campos had been an insane, evil, power-mad egomaniac in his former life, and the new persona had done nothing to change that but had reinforced it.

Sooner or later, though, no matter what was to come, she'd be taken to the Well. There was no question that such a sophisticated operation could get the truth out of her. It could only be hoped that Campos was so insane she believed that inside the Well, in a Markovian body, she could still dictate to Mavra Chang.

Campos stood back and looked at both of them with satisfaction. "Do the shackles hurt? Well, soon you will be free of them, I promise. And the medical teams here, freed of such stupidities as government oversight and ethical colleagues, can do absolute *wonders*. Even though you are one of the most wanted people on this planet, these people specialize in making wanted fugitives unrecognizable, although in most cases they do not have the level of freedom they have in *your* case. You, Sutton, might be quite useful as a courier once we give you some motivation for making appointments on time. But not *you*, 'goddess.' You are *mine*. From you they will carve a work of art. *Then,* as my *dear* boyfriend Giquazo, who I will definitely kill someday, promised, you will go home with me. You will be my pet, my toy. Oh, we will have a *fun* time, I promise you!"

Mavra's heart sank as one of her bitterest Well World memories surfaced: living all those years with those donkeylike legs, always looking down . . .

But she had survived that and worse, and she would survive this for as long as it took, until opportunity knocked. And if Nathan was having the same kind of luck, she might yet be first to the Well.

"Some technicians will be in shortly to inaugurate you both into our widening family," Campos told them. "I go first to speak with those who will see you next, and then I will see you once more before leaving. But do not worry, my little goddess. I shall be back for you." With that, the Cloptan turned and left the room.

"I think I *would* rather die than go through this," Lori told Mavra.

"Don't! *Never* give up! She's too insane to have them mutilate me so much that I won't be able to speak to her and she to me. To that type, life is all about power. Everything else—drugs, money, you name it—is to gain power. That's what she really hates about being female now. She's lost power, and I'm the only way for her to get it back. There are only two more hexes after Clopta to the equator and an avenue in. So long as Brazil isn't also caught and trapped, he's as much a threat to Campos as to me. If I can just convince her, no matter what I look like, to get me to the Well before Brazil, we win. Stay alive. Even now, hope's not gone."

Lori very much wanted to believe that.

Juan Campos, or Wahna as her name was pronounced by the Cloptan tongue, made her way through the labyrinthine underground complex to the medical section. There she met with Nuoak, a giant creature resembling a huge brown-furred slug with countless long, tiny tendrils that in combination could perform the most delicate operations, and Drinh, an Agonite resembling a human-sized shell-less turtle with long powerful hands and fingers.

"They are yours any time you want them," she told the medics. "Now that you have their scans, have you decided what you will do?"

"Well, the Erdomite is not difficult," Drinh commented.

"He must be castrated!" *Like I was* . . . "But he must not die! I wish him to work for us, becoming what he most fears and helping, even promoting our own interest which he hates so much! And the rest of what I asked as well, so he will always be reminded of me."

"We have not had either of these species before, but they seem to represent no serious challenges. We believe that we can adapt your Erdomite to become a courier for us over possibly difficult terrain. We have noted the lack of proper clotting factor in his blood, but the gland that aids in its production is merely immature, not missing, and so that problem is easily dealt with. Do not worry. He shall be fit to do only what is useful to us, and all that you request be done to him will be a part of it."

"Perfect! Do it! But what about the other? *That* one requires *very* special treatment."

"There's not as much to work with," the master surgeon noted. "Still, the small size and lack of major features and your own requirements make it obvious that the best way to ensure that no one who ever knew her or saw her picture recognizes her is to create from her an animal. It can be a unique animal, since with the countless varieties of the Well World there is nobody who knows them all or will question a convincing appearance. *This* is what we came up with after much study." He pushed a few buttons on a console, and a hologram of a figure appeared.

Campos laughed in delight. "Oh, that is *wonderful!* Perfect! But—can you *do* such a radical thing?"

"It's not as radical as it looks. Mostly a matter of adding a lot of fatty body mass, moving the knees, implanting the natural feathers, that sort of thing. Then reinforcing it with a *pictin*—an artificial virus tailor-made to her and her alone. It will methodically go from cell to cell and manipulate the stock DNA chains that will make the change permanent. Internally there's not much changed, so she'll still have to eat what she normally would and such, you understand."

"That is all right. Appearance is everything. *Delicious!* And her speaking? She must be able to speak to me, and I to her, but with limits."

"Much simpler. We will simply remove her translator and replace it with a synthetic one. As you may or may not know, we've never successfully created a translator crystal, but we do have ones that are very limited. We can tune this one not only to one language but to the specific harmonics of your translator. When she speaks, it will be instantly translated into a preset, encoded binary sequence which can be received and decoded only by your translator. To anyone else it will sound like meaningless squawks and screeches. Similarly, since that code will be fed to your translator alone, she will understand you as if you were speaking normally no matter what language you use, while all other speech will be picked up by her translator, which will overload trying to decode what isn't there and produce meaningless random sounds. No one but you will even think that she is a sentient being. Is that satisfactory, madame?"

"*Perfect.*" Juan Campos sighed. "How long will it be before I can bring her home?"

"Not long. Two, three weeks tops."

"*Do* it, then. Do it as quickly as you can, but do it *right.*"

The Erdomese constitution handled the drug a bit differently but just as effectively from the point of view of the dealers. There was not any massive high but rather a continuous feeling of being just a bit isolated from reality, a "slight buzz" as Lori thought of it. It was when it was withdrawn that its full power and potency revealed itself; the pain, the horrors, the hallucinations were beyond anyone's endurance. He knew he could not exist without the drug but was not so insulated that he did not hate them for doing it to him. That, and the way they treated him, half the time as some sort of interesting lab specimen and the other half as no better than a slave, he thought, the worst possible existence imaginable.

But that was before he met the duo he began thinking of as Mengele Turtle and Frankenstein's Slug. He knew by their detached and clinical discussions that they were going to do something more to him, something awful, but he had no way of knowing what.

Then, shortly afterward, the keepers came for him and gave him an injection, and he remembered no more.

The first realization that he was waking up from a sustained anesthetic-induced sleep was an awareness that he was on all fours. *That* was odd; Erdomese men were *never* on all fours. He opened his eyes, but they refused to focus very well, as if still mostly asleep, but he reached out and tried to stand—and found that he could not.

His first thought was that they'd taken his fingers, and then he managed to put his head down close to his arms and saw hooves.

Not even the kind of hooves Alowi had—real hooves, like on his feet.

But his feet, too, were on the floor. How could that be without him being at an angle or on his knees? It was as if his legs had been shortened and his hips turned so that he was now a four-legged, four-hoofed beast a mere three and a half feet off the ground!

With a sinking feeling he realized that it was exactly what they had done. He still had his tail, but it was down and dragged on the floor, trailing between his—hind legs.

And with less shock than he might have thought, he realized that the tail was the *only* thing between those legs. In far too short a time he had gone from female to male to—nothing. There weren't even any internal muscles there to feel or flex.

You didn't have to go to med school to figure out Campos, did you?

Still, even with blurry vision, he could see that there was *something* in back of his—well, forelegs. He not only could see the shapes in a somewhat blurry way, he could *feel* the dead weight hanging down.

Breasts? Four breasts on a eunuch? What on earth for? Particularly such a large and heavy set, which cleared the floor only by several inches. Sensing something else, a wrongness, he flexed his back a bit so that they did touch the floor, then straightened again. If they had nipples, there was no sensation in them.

He wondered why he hadn't bled to death during their butchery and then realized what the breasts really were. Not just more Campos humor —they had placed in him, or activated by hormones, the internal engine of the female, the healing factors. No nipples, because whatever function they served they did so for his benefit, and he was one of a kind.

The neck was very long and supple. He could look forward or down, although his vision seemed to be limited to about two feet clearly, three before almost everything was lost. Still, he could see very close, and it almost looked to him as if he had some sort of muzzle on, as if he could see part of his nose and jaw.

Then the door opened, and he smelled Mengele Turtle enter. The doctor—if that was what he could be called— began making a lot of very stupid silly noises at him, until finally he heard, "One . . . two . . . three. Ah! I see you can hear me now! Very good! We, of course, removed your translator, among, ah, other things. It has been replaced with an artificial device that interpolates speech both in and out. You can speak, but to be understood you will have to be heard by someone with the same sort of device set to the same frequency. Similarly, you must hear something through the same conditions to understand it. Otherwise, even your native tongue will sound like nothing more than a noise pattern. It is quite useful for couriers such as you will be trained to become. It can't be removed or bypassed without causing permanent damage to the speech centers of the brain, and it can be reset to any frequency we choose or even reprogrammed with a whole new code by remote control. You see how handy that is. You can convey the most sensitive message, but only one who has both the device and your code and frequency can retrieve it. You, on the other hand, sound like an animal making random noises. If anyone attempts to play random sequences and hits it but does not give the code header, it erases, cutting you off completely. Absolutely secure."

"Very clever," he admitted sourly. "But what sort of courier would *this* body make? And what makes you so sure that I'll transfer the right information?"

"Well, you will be trained, of course, both in the uses of the body and in courier technique. You will be used locally, basically between Agon and Clopta through Lilblod. The system itself is simple. There is a specific version of the drug you are on. To survive, you will have to make your assignations, for only they will have it. If any of them find out later that you gave false or incorrect or even incomplete information, they will notify someone and they might well forget your dose. As for finding your way, it will take practice, but you will find that your senses of smell and hearing are incredibly acute. You will learn to follow days-old scents and interpret a vast number of sounds. As most of your route will be through dense forest at night, sight is of little use anyway. The drug will motivate you and ease your pain and exhaustion. Your digestive system can handle most of the ground-level plants of Lilblod. Save for an insignificant amount of the drug you need, you are, shall we say, cost-free and maintenance-free labor."

"Yeah, well these breasts are going to cause no end of trouble in the woods."

"They are tough, and you will get used to them. In addition to supplying your absent clotting factor, they can carry enough food in the form of fat and water to allow you, if need be, to exist for a week or more eating and drinking nothing, so if something happens and you fall behind, you can skip food and water to make up time. You also have a small pouch of which I'm quite proud. It will hold small microencoded materials and even carry the receiving code and frequency for you. It will, however, dissolve such material in gastric juices if you are very late getting your dosage. Withdrawal, in other words, triggers it, so even if you are captured, nothing will be learned."

"You must have studied hard to think up things like this."

The doctor ignored the comment. "Food and drink will be necessities, but they consist of raw leaves and grasses and water—only water will really do—and they'll taste pretty much like what they are. Anything else will make you sick. You won't have much in the way of conversations or companionship, obviously, and you are as asexual as a machine. We were able to locate and neutralize the actual sexual center in your brain. You can't have sex, do not and will not want it, won't even fantasize about it; indeed, if we've done it properly, you won't even be able to figure out why you or anyone else liked it in the first place. It boils down to this: The only thing, the absolute *only* thing that can and will stimulate your pleasure center is our little cube. Over time, as brain and body adjust, it will become your sole reason for existence and our sole expense. Perfect, are you not?"

"Yeah. Perfect." *Drug or not, I'll kill myself at the first opportunity rather than live like that.*

He seemed to anticipate the thought, "If you think of suicide, be sure you do it, because otherwise we'll give you no cube at all for one full cycle . . ."

That was too much. He knew he'd never go through with it, *couldn't* kill himself with *that* kind of threat.

They had won. All this way and the bad guys had won!

For the other captive it was possibly even worse.

At one time or another Mavra Chang had been put on or tried an enormous number of drugs, but nothing like rhapsody. Within minutes it seemed as if every pleasure center in her brain and body exploded in continuous delight while all else, *everything* else, faded into total insignificance. She knew she was still chained to the wall, but it just didn't seem important, nor did it when they released her and she dropped to the floor. Everything, every touch, every move, was a new delight.

She was aware of others, of being asked questions and answering them, but it was of so little consequence, she didn't even remember the specifics of the conversations. Darkness, light, colors, sounds, creatures moving around, all had their wonders and delights. She was being poked and probed and moved here and there, but none of it really *mattered* to her.

It was hard to say how long this lasted, but the coming down was very, very slow. Awareness outside of herself returned in dribs and drabs, shapes and creatures took on more realistic appearances, and things began to seem more logical. Even so, she remained high and knew she was, able to function but still somewhat bathed in a nice, soft, comfortable cocoon. Things being done seemed peculiar or even hilarious but caused no alarm.

By the time real rationality had returned and there was just a glow and slight lack of coordination, they had put her in a small padded cell. Her feet were free, but her hands were cuffed behind her back. Overcome at that point with a seemingly insatiable hunger and thirst, she found a pot of some cold liquid and three very large varicolored loaves of different things, what she couldn't guess. The urge to eat and drink was just irresistible, even if she had to do it on her knees or prone, biting into the loaves as best she could and manipulating the container of liquid with only her mouth and neck. It tasted sweet and heavy with a kind of creamy aftertaste, something like buttermilk, and she managed to drink most of it while spilling only about a quarter, and that she found herself lapping up with her tongue. She had left nothing when she was done.

She now felt sleepy but tried to shake it off and think. That rhapsody was the most dangerous drug she'd seen since sponge. In fact, it might be an ancestor of just that for all she knew. She *did* know that she would be mentally incapable of turning it down if it were offered again, and that brought forth the first and primary fear. They *had* to give more to her! Nothing, absolutely nothing was of more importance to her than that. She'd kill her own friends and betray any trust to get it.

She knew she was hooked, on the line completely, but as much as she hated the thought and those who'd done it to her, she knew they'd accomplished what they had set out to do.

Why keep me locked up and shackled like this? There is no way I can leave this place. Not now.

But she was a new species for them, she realized, and they couldn't be sure of her compliance or even positive that they'd gotten the dosage right. And they were probably scared of her, scared of the rumors about her possible powers. They would make very sure.

Within a few more hours she was in tears, hysterically banging her head against the padded door and begging, pleading, promising anything if they would just give her more and stop the torment. She hated them, hated their cold, callous way of treating her in this, hated Campos for what she'd done to her, hated herself for being so damned vulnerable, but it was horrible, awful . . . Far worse than heroin, which she'd managed to kick more than once. But the withdrawal pains hadn't been nearly at this level. The waking nightmares, the hallucinations of every horror she'd ever lived through, the onrush of all the fear and pain she had ever endured . . .

She was descending into madness with the speed of a spaceliner when they'd finally come and given her some more. Within a minute, maybe two, it was all receding, all going away, things were wonderful once more . . .

After several cycles, as her system became accustomed to having the drug in it, they were ready for the next phase.

She was put under for the bulk of it. She had almost no memories of it or who did it or where or how long it took or how the hell they did it at all. Nor was there any real sense of how much time had passed, only that it had. By the time she was able once again to awaken and move about on her own, it was done.

She felt—odd—beyond the high and knew that Campos had accomplished her total threat. They had done something to her. Something major. It was only a question of what.

She had no feeling at all in her arms. They'd never let her use her arms or hands, not since the beginning, and so it wasn't totally surprising, but it bothered her. She was walking oddly, too, as if she couldn't bend her legs. *Nothing* felt right.

She was in a small but ordinary room furnished only with a thick pillow, but one wall seemed extra polished and she made her way laboriously over to it. Then, seeing the ghostly reflection, she looked down at herself to confirm the worst.

She was almost completely covered in feathers. Tiny little feathers that made a second skin, feathers of bright colors: gold and emerald and crimson and deep, rich blue, making intricate random designs. She couldn't feel her arms because she no longer had arms, or shoulders, for that matter. Somehow they'd managed to transplant some of the muscle tissue, though, because she still had breasts, fattier and larger than before and also feathered right down to the nipples.

But for those she was shaped pretty much like a turnip. She had a large, rotund, feathered stomach and rear end, and they'd widened her hips. That had been done as much for balance as for design, since they'd taken her knee joints and placed them just below those widened hips, as if the upper calves and thighs had been turned upside down, and these terminated in a pair of very wide leathery feet that were more like pads with a flat extension both forward and rear. She did not walk so much as slowly *waddle*. It would take some practice, and she wasn't sure how she'd get up again if she fell over.

She had to get very close to the reflection to see her face. They'd done something to the skin to make it look very dark brown and leathery, extending her nose until it was virtually a hawk-nosed bill of the same consistency as the face. They'd brought in the mouth to almost a pucker and replaced the lips with a short curved birdlike bill. Only the eyes seemed familiar, but even there they'd done something, or maybe it was the drug. She saw quite well but only to maybe one and a half, two meters. After that everything was a blur, even in the small room.

They've made me into a human owl, she thought, more in shock than in disgust. In fact, while the overall effect was somewhat comical in the same way a penguin was comical, the combination of colors and the fluidity of the design were quite attractive. It was also true that she could appear like this in public and no one, not Lori, not the Dillians, not even Brazil, would recognize her.

It was also true that she was now more helpless and more dependent than a captive songbird with clipped wings. She could waddle, first one side forward, then the other, like a penguin, but not very far or very fast. Climbing or getting her own food was out of the question. She might manage a little something with her head and mouth—beak—but not a lot. She was totally defenseless. She couldn't run, fly, or grab or use a weapon or tool, and even her bright colors were a problem, making concealment difficult. That was if the enemy came within two meters so she could see it.

Even her hearing seemed off. True, they'd recessed the ears into the head and covered them with feathers so it appeared she had none, but even so, she thought it odd that all she heard from the corridor outside were what sounded like snorts, clicks, and silly noises.

She suddenly felt foolish. That drug *did* make one stupider, she thought. Of *course* they would have removed the translator. Did they do more? She opened her mouth and called "Hey, out there! Shut up!" but the only thing that came out was a series of awful-sounding squawks. They'd altered her vocal chords or replaced them. And she couldn't even form words with her lips. Not with this rigid beak.

Helpless, dependent, no ability to talk or understand, no way to form words silently or use sign language . . . they'd really cut her off. To literally everyone else, even those she knew and who knew her—save only the ones who had done this with masterful skill and a technology far beyond expectation, and Campos, of course—she'd be seen as—she *was* —the world's first exotic animal junkie.

Well, she'd kept Campos around, a captive, drugged and hauled about through the jungle, and had wound up making him into the world's sexiest duck creature. Now Campos had in her own twisted mind attained the perfect revenge.

What was odd was how she was taking it. She herself noticed this, but only as a curiosity, not because it really bothered her. She just *accepted* it fatalistically as something that was. She knew it was the drug, placing a soft, pleasant haze between herself and reality, but she did not want that haze to disappear. So long as it was there, she could accept almost anything. It was her only friend, her only protector.

Still, there was the practical, pragmatic need to get used to it. She waddled over in the direction of the door, blurry though it was, and the usual food cakes and drink were there. Although a little nervous about it, she discovered that they'd set the balance and center of gravity exactly right. These doctors were geniuses with the souls of monsters. She could bend completely forward on those knee joints, and the bill, serrated a bit, was perfect to break into the loaves and get pieces she could mush and break up inside her mouth proper and swallow without difficulty by raising her head a bit while keeping bent over. Drinking was harder to master and amounted to using the tongue or a back part of her mouth to get some suction through the tiny bill if it was immersed, but it, too, was manageable.

The only real problem was with the breasts, which amounted to dead weight tumbling down when she bent over and which, with no arms and true shoulder muscles to stabilize them, went every which way, pulling on her neck and throwing her slightly off balance. She'd never had large breasts as a human, and they could well have dispensed with them as they did with other parts of her, but instead they'd enlarged them and created a problem. More of Campos's revenge, she understood. She would learn to live with them with practice, she decided.

A technician or guard or whatever who looked like an underdressed turtle gave her the drug regularly, in the form of a solid soft cube. It was far slower to take effect when eaten, but the creature was never late with it. Campos, she worried, might not be so punctual.

And finally the Cloptan came for her. Campos seemed absolutely enthralled by the redesign, and Mavra was again taken aback to discover that thanks to the legs, she was now even shorter, no more than a meter or so tall. She had always been small and mostly looked up to see other faces, but this meant craning her neck.

"Oh, but this is *so* excellent!" Campos gushed. "Revenge is seldom so perfect! Can you understand me?"

To her surprise, Mavra *could.* "Yes, I can."

"*Wonderful!* You see, the little device inside you is tuned *only* to me. It even blocks out other people's translators from your mind. And what it transmits, only *I* have been given the ability to translate and understand. And all I have to do is *think* about it and I can turn it off, or on, at will. So you will communicate, and understand, only to me and when I wish. What you send is a computer code that sounds to all others like the noise of a bird. You will truly be my pet, and you will *act* like it. You will guard me and protect me at all costs if you can, and the rest of the time you will be a nice little trained birdie and do *everything* I say, because *I* and I alone have those nice little red cubes. You will exist to please me and never to displease me, now, won't you?"

"Yes," she replied resignedly.

"Oh, no! We begin right here. It will from now on be "Yes, *master.*' Not even 'mistress,' not 'madame.' *Master.* Understand?"

"Yes—master."

"And you can spend your time thinking of ways to sing my praises. How beautiful I am, how intelligent, how simply *wonderful* I am. You will spend your time thinking of new ways to praise, flatter, *worship* me as your one and only god, and you will do it with *conviction,* with *enthusiasm;* you will *convince* me that you believe it. And in the same breaths you will do the opposite to yourself. Remind me and yourself how low you are, how dependent, how miserable and undeserving a creature you are and how lucky you are to be my property, and you will say *those* things, too, with the same fervor. And any time I find either part unconvincing, I might just forget your little cube for a while. Maybe a very *long* while, until you are totally believable. *Understand?*"

One pang of true abject fear pierced the insulating haze. "*Yes,* my most wonderful master, from whose great kindness all blessings flow. Please forgive this most miserable of helpless wretches who is nothing without you!"

Campos smiled. "It is a start. We shall have many, many long conversations together, and all of them, even the ones that matter, will be partially tests. Practice it in your mind. You will come to believe that what you say is true so that it becomes second nature to use it. Now, come. I have a travel cage for you, and we must catch the return steamer for Buckgrud, the city where I live in Clopta. There, in my flat, I have a nice little place provided for you."

"As you command, most powerful and magnificent master."

The worst part of it was, the words weren't even sticking in her throat.

Still, now would begin the trial, until one day Campos would decide for whatever reason that she'd had enough or wanted more. Then Mavra would be the only means by which Campos could have her revenge on just about everything and everybody she hated, and that was almost the entire universe now. The Cloptan had already thought ahead on this; that was why they could still speak to one another, and she was conditioning her "pet" to think like an obedient slave to ensure complete control. Otherwise, when Juan Campos had the burning desire to get her hands on the Well World controls, how could she make Mavra let her do it?

The worst part was, as she was, Mavra didn't even care.

LILBLOD

"YOU SEPARATED ME FROM my husband! I will *kill* you for that!"

"Now, calm down, I tell you," Zitz soothed. "There was nothing I could do. They'd have killed you anyway if you made a fuss."

"They might as well have killed us both!" Alowi cried. "My husband cannot *survive* without me!"

"Nothing to do with love, I'm afraid," Tony explained. "She produces something inside her that heals his injuries. We've seen it in action."

"Well, it's done, and that's that. I can't even give you a clue as to where they took 'em. I don't know nothin' about the land part of this, and I don't wanna know. I'll tell you, though, that either we did what they said or they'd have took 'em anyways and blown *all* of us out of the water the moment we dropped the load. Blown all three of you away as it was. Think we liked it? We're gonna lose a *fortune* because we gotta give back them stolen jewels! And it'd have been easier for us to just knock all three of you off and dump you in the ocean. We're droppin' you here instead. That over there's Lilblod. It's not a real nice place, but you take care and keep to the trails and keep your nose out of where it don't belong and you'll make it. About fifty kilometers north is Clopta, a high-tech coastal hex where you can get a ride into a Zone Gate and a quick pass back home. South maybe sixty, seventy kilometers is Agon, same deal. Don't think you can go down there and stir up stuff and find them. They probably never made shore there. Got picked up by some other ship and are maybe anywhere or heading anywheres else by now. Go home. It's over."

"Come, come dear!" Anne Marie said sympathetically. "Let's get off this terrible ship first and be on our own. *Then* we can decide what to do next."

With neither the Dillians nor Alowi having a translator, it was up to Zitz to interject.

There was no purpose now to further protests, and Alowi nodded and tried to calm down. "All right." *But I will feed the name of this accursed ship and all of its crew to my people back in Erdom. Such an assault on our honor cannot go unavenged.*

"This *is* going to be a problem, though," Tony commented. "We really can't speak to or understand her, nor she us."

"Sister, if she's nuts enough to go off tramping in that crazy forest by herself, let her," Zitz responded. "You won't find much with a translator in *there,* but it's easy in either Clopta or Agon. Just get everybody out, huh?" He turned to Alowi.

"Okay, lady, here's the way it is. They're gonna head for one or another of these places where you can get home and they'll take you. Maybe you can't talk to each other, but you'll make do. You ain't cut out to be an avenger. You just ain't built for it. Relax. Take it easy. Tell the authorities if you want to once you get there. It's no big deal to us. But one way or another you're gettin' off this ship as soon as we get in a little more. Either you *get* off with all your gear or we shoot you and shove you off and keep it. Your choice."

"We'll go, curse your black heart," Anne Marie responded acidly.

"Oh, yeah, one more thing," the Zhonzhorpian said. "You *can* report this and this ship, but remember that all three of you are wanted in Gekir for jewel theft. And even though they'll still check it out, we'll show that this ship, under an alternative name and registry, was thousands of kilometers away at the time. You're out of your league here. Forget it. You won't find them—hell, the authorities couldn't anyway, could they, or you wouldn'ta been aboard in the first place. All you'll do by stirring up trouble is to make sure you all get sent back to Gekir, where you'll be blinded and sent out for life to work in the salt mines until you die. *Nobody* wins on this one. Sometimes it happens."

It wasn't much of an answer, but it was a collection of hard truths that was impossible to ignore.

The *Star Runner* came close enough to the shore to scrape bottom, and that was as far as it dared. Anne Marie picked up the sobbing Alowi and put her on Tony's back, where she clung as hard as she could, and Anne Marie hefted the saddlebags and packs, and they jumped the short distance from the rails down into the water and quickly struck mud. It was a little tough to get some footing, but finally both of them managed to force their way up and onto the shore, Alowi still clinging to Tony's back, looking wet and disheveled but otherwise none the worse for the wear.

It was very dark and very quiet on the shore; there were no lights to be seen anywhere.

"*Now* what?" Anne Marie asked, trying to see something other than forbidding swampy forest in the thick gloom of the night.

"We camp as soon as we can find a dry place, of course," Tony responded. "We still have some matches in a waterproof container, and we might try a fire, if only to scare away anything unwelcome. When we get some light, we'll see about finding a road."

"Which way?"

"It really doesn't matter, does it? I should think, though, if we have any real chance of tracing them, it should be south. At least they'll have communications, possibly enough to get word to the embassy in Zone. Then we might be able to arrange to get this poor girl home and maybe be out of this and home ourselves. I've had quite enough of discomfort and double crosses. We did our duty as best we could. Now we deserve a chance to live our own lives."

"Duty! *Bah!*" Anne Marie almost spit. "This poor dear won't go home willingly. She'll try to find her husband, even if that's impossible, because it's *her* duty and because she's in love. You heard what they said about that dreadful culture. She'd be married off to some old bum she didn't know and die of a broken heart!"

"Anne Marie, this is not a romance novel."

"Tony Guzman! What in the *world* has gotten into you? It's not like we are innocent bystanders in all this! Nor entirely without some responsibility, too, simply because we weren't all that honest with them, either."

"We didn't *ask* to go along on this adventure!" Tony argued. "We were *drafted!*"

"Nonsense! That nice young man from the Zone embassy came along and *asked* us to do it. To go and link up with this Mavra Chang and find out as much as we could. And we found out a great deal, I think! We were also to get off a report to the ambassador if they lost track of the party. Thank *goodness* we didn't have to do *that*. I would have felt just *dreadful* about it!"

"But it's *over,* Anne Marie! *We're* the party now. The only satisfaction we might have is rubbing it in that smug drug runner's face after he discovers we were not fugitives but shadows."

"Spies, you mean. Spies for our government."

Tony sighed. "Anne Marie, spies are professionals. Espionage is a highly regarded art. We were rank amateurs dropped into a situation where we might have been hurt or killed by a government that wouldn't have really cared, and now we got out with our lives and whole skins. I don't *want* to be blinded or crippled. Not again. Now we have a second chance. I want to go home before something *does* happen. We were very nearly killed back there, you know. Anne Marie, we're sixteen years old again, only this time we're sexy blond bombshells that had the men of Dillia already making fools of themselves around us. I've *been* on that side. I want to find out if it's any more fun on *this* side."

"Well, then, you go home," she told the other centauress. "I suppose I should have seen it coming long before this, but I didn't want to. You've *had* a good life. You were handsome, from a well-to-do and well-connected family, skilled, educated, a pilot and world traveler. I never did *any* of those things. I couldn't. I was homely and plain and stuck mostly in a broken body. I made the best of it, but it wasn't fun, let me tell you! Your coming along, your love, was the one truly wonderful thing that happened to me. I shall always cherish it, and I shall always love that inner part of you, but surely you must have known from the moment we woke up like *this* that it could never be again. In a sense, this is our afterlife, mortal though we remain, goodness knows. I faced it more and more as we went on this trip. I shall always love that memory of you, and I shall continue to love you, but as a sister. This is after the 'death do us part' as surely as if we'd done away with ourselves, and you know it if you'd just face it."

Tony laughed.

"What's so amusing? I'm deadly serious."

"Anne Marie, I've rehearsed almost that identical speech a thousand times in my mind, and up to now I never had the nerve to give it. I was afraid of *hurting* you. And I thought we shared one another's thoughts to a degree!"

Anne Marie laughed in return, then finally said, "I guess not. I suppose it's what we thought we would think if the situations were reversed or some such. Or, since we actually *were* thinking the same, maybe it's true. Maybe we just didn't believe we were." She sighed. "Well, then, I guess this is what we'd call a divorce by mutual consent. Who would have *dreamed* we two would ever say those words?"

"We'll always be closer than any other two women of our race," Tony noted, taking her hand and squeezing it. "But no matter that we see each other in a living mirror, we are two different people who will lead at least slightly different lives."

"Agreed. And if you want to go back and have all those silly fools swoon over you, be my guest. I suppose, if all else comes out in the end, I'll wind up doing it, too, but I'm not so eager to start as you."

"Anne Marie! What can you *do*? It is like the man said—it is *over* for us!"

"For you. Go on, I understand completely. But I know how skin-deep those lusting fools are, and they certainly weren't there when I needed them, going off chasing some—some dumb blond like you. I'm having *fun*, dear! For the first time in my life I'm *living* it instead of watching life go by! I very much *hope* that I'll come through in one piece, but, in the end it really doesn't matter to me. Perhaps it was because I was so devoted, to charities, to the unfortunate, to you. Perhaps it's just divine grace. But God gave me, at the end of my half life, a chance to live a *full* one, at least for a little bit. I shall probably give up in disgust and go home after a few days, but if there is *anything* perhaps I can do, if there's just one little thing I can add, I'll stick it out." She looked around at Alowi. "Oh my! The poor dear's cried herself to sleep!"

"Exhausted, probably. She's been throwing a tantrum for three days now."

"We should stop chattering and build that fire, then."

The next day proved tough going through the thick and ancient trees of Lilblod, but with no sign of who or what was the dominant race there or why they were feared.

Still, before midday they reached a road that, while direct, seemed very well traveled by the depth of the wheel grooves and the marks of all sorts of feet in the clay.

"Runs pretty much straight, northwest to southeast," Tony noted. "I guess this is the main highway to civilization. He said that place—Clopta or some such—was closest, which would mean we might well make it at a trot before dark."

Anne Marie raised an eyebrow. "But Agon is where they took the pair of them. If nothing ate us last night except the bugs—goodness! I itch all over!—then I doubt if anything will eat me if I spend one more night by this road. Give me the poor little darling and we'll head south."

Tony stared at her. "So this is it? Already?"

"I suppose so. It had to come sometime. It might jolly well be now." She gestured with her arms to Alowi to get off Tony and climb up somewhere on her back.

After a few moments' confusion Alowi figured it out enough to act, slid off, and managed, with a little help from Anne Marie, to get up on the other twin.

"Good-bye, Tony," said Anne Marie. "I'll see you in a few weeks, I suppose, unless we have a lot more luck than we have had in this matter so far." And without another word she started off southwest, toward Agon, at a brisk trot.

Tony stood there and watched her go until she was almost out of sight, then muttered, "Oh, hell," and trotted off southwest after them.

JUST OFF THE CRAB NEBULA

THE KRAANG WAS NOT at all pleased. What had looked from the start to be a fairly straightforward affair had now turned into a series of Gordian knots that threatened all its plans.

Nathan Brazil, happily and stupidly diverted making flower garlands for his girlfriend on a desert island well removed from the action, was nicely out of the game, although the Kraang understood the Well sufficiently to know that this would not, could not be allowed to become a permanent condition. Still, thanks to a race playing with powers it was not capable of handling or comprehending, the first job had been accomplished.

The Watcher had been diverted from the Well.

That should have provided more than enough time for the other to reach it first, but instead that mad, sick interloper had captured her and placed her in a situation where she, too, was no longer in control of events but which, instead of representing the Kraang's interests, now threatened to do horrible, irrecoverable harm.

Not that the Kraang didn't have a grudging admiration for Campos. If the vengeful cutthroat succeeded in destroying Mavra Chang's last vestiges of ego and will, she would open the entrance for him but be unable or unwilling to interface with the master control center. That would leave Campos free to roam those vast corridors unhindered, and after realizing that he could not comprehend, much less activate anything inside, he might well do terrible harm in his inevitable rage. Once he was inside its bowels, the Well would be helpless to control events concerning its own welfare.

And because she could still draw on the Well database to the limits of that primitive ape brain, she might even be able to tell him how to do some simple things that even so limited a creature could manage.

Probability was too complex to allow that. As a tiny stone in a pond made great ripples, even a very minute alteration of the basic matrix might, just might, create a series of alternatives that would take the whole universe into uncharted and unpredictable realms. Without one capable of handling and manipulating such power, like the Kraang itself, the results could be disastrous.

Even the Watcher, whom the Well would undoubtedly summon with great urgency if such a thing occurred, might not be able to fully straighten things out.

And yet without Mavra Chang to open the way, the Kraang could not reach those controls itself.

Why hadn't they simply hibernated, as the Kraang had, until they were needed? What could possibly be gained by a Watcher, or even two, living out meaningless lives on some distant dirt ball until rather crudely summoned in time of need?

Perhaps, it reflected, the judgment of eons had been wrong, after all. It had always thought of the Others as wrongheaded and foolish, but until now their competency had not been called into question.

Something would have to be done, and quickly. It was not used to thinking in such terms, but this was clearly not the time to ponder but to act.

But how?

Accessing Chang or even Brazil was out. It had managed a brief access while she was in transition, but once on the Well World, access to either her or Brazil was blocked. As for the rest, so far they were accessible only as viewers, strictly one-way communication. They were neither mentally strong enough to be used nor tied into the Well matrix.

There had to be *some* way, somehow, to break this apart, to create a flood from the logjam. Options had to be weighed, possibilities explored if they existed, and risks taken, even if it used up precious energy it could ill afford to squander if things didn't go just exactly right.

It was a question of divine intervention in a situation where there was no god.

More than ever, though, it was convinced that it was right, that it had been right all along.

This universe required a god and was instead stuck with two incompetent repair technicians.

There *had* to be a way. There had to be *something* that could be done.

But after four billion years of meaningless existence driving to and fro among the stars, finding even vast blocks of time meaningless, it wasn't used to thinking that time, any time, was quickly running out.

Gods of the
Well of Souls

*This one's expressly for
David Whitley Chalker and Steven Lloyd Chalker—
To the future, wherever it leads!*

BETWEEN GALAXIES,
HEADING TOWARD ANDROMEDA

THE KRAANG HAD BEEN wondering much the same thing. The limitations placed on it still prevented it from direct contact with beings on the Well World unless, thanks to the happy accident that allowed it net access, someone was in the transitional stage, totally energy within the net in midtransmission. Otherwise it was strictly read only, and that was proving less amusing now than frustrating.

Monitoring the lives and thoughts of these beings had reawakened in the Kraang a feeling it had thought long dead, a taste of what it was to be *alive* again. It wanted that now more than anything; the lust for it was cracking its heretofore absolute self-control, bringing back longings that it had believed it had long outgrown.

The Well perceived no threat to itself or its master program; it only desired that what it considered an anomaly—the relinking, however tenuous, of the Kraang to the net—be rectified. A simple matter, really, for anyone capable of plugging into the net; not even seconds to find, comprehend, and repair, cutting the Kraang off once more from the system. Brazil was the threat—he'd been there many times, been changed into the master form, and would hardly even think twice about it. He'd do whatever the damned Well said and be done with it, and he would understand the threat sufficiently to be impervious to the Kraang's entreaties and offers. There was nothing Brazil really wanted except, perhaps, oblivion, and the Kraang wasn't so certain that the captain would really take it if it were offered in any event. Brazil was so damned . . . *responsible*. Duty above all.

No, if the Kraang were to effect a return, it would be Mavra Chang. Human, inexperienced, self-involved, and unencumbered by any sense of duty or mission. Mavra Chang would listen before she acted and believe what she wanted to believe. She was certainly tough, no pushover, but she was far too—*human*—to blindly obey the dictates of an ancient race she neither knew nor understood. According to the data, she'd been close to being a goddess before, going from world to world, taking many forms, playing both explorer and missionary to the misbegotten.

The Kraang could deal very comfortably with an activist.

Brazil was at the moment romping in mindless joy with that silly girl on that speck of land in the ocean, but the Well would never leave him there. If Mavra Chang's progress to the Well had been stopped, then Brazil would again get the nomination and be forced to accept. The longer there was no movement or probability of movement by Chang, who was by far closer to the Well gate than Brazil, the more likely the Well would be forced to make the switch. The others would never find her, and it would be all the worse if they somehow did track down Campos but never recognized Chang in her current form.

Campos was the key. Such a *limited* mind! Not stupid, not by the likes of the races there, but sadly warped. Campos was so enjoying her revenge and was comfortable enough in an environment not all that different from the one back on the home planet that had bred and shaped her, that she was in danger of losing sight of the ultimate game. The Kraang had not counted on her adjusting, though, and that was the real problem. Since Campos had been a male from a background that had little value for women, the Kraang had been certain that she would be driven to the Well to reclaim her manhood.

It wasn't happening.

If Campos had gotten hold of Mavra Chang earlier, it would have, but the Well had its own ways of subtly adjusting a subject to a form. The brain chemistry, the hormonal balances, and being completely immersed in a new culture eventually took hold. A transformation that seemed horrible when first discovered began to seem normal; prior life and existence were distanced in the mind as it adjusted, becoming more and more remote. If one were to go mad from the process, it tended to happen rather quickly; otherwise that barrier the mind erected became progressively insubstantial until it either shattered, as in the case of Lori and Julian, or, as in Campos's case, just slowly evaporated to nothingness.

Without even realizing it, or perhaps admitting it to herself, Juan Campos no longer thought it odd, or even wrong, to be female, let alone a Cloptan female. She had managed in a relatively short time to gain a fair amount of power and influence, in part because she was attractive to male Cloptans who already had that power and influence, and she was actually enjoying it. Experience counted. The Well might have played a joke on Campos by making her female, but it also had dropped her into a totally familiar milieu. Being the tough girlfriend of a drug lord wasn't much different from being the son of one, and the knowledge and ruthlessness actually made her a valuable asset to the organization. After that first month she hadn't even experienced much of the fear and insecurity that being a woman in such a society inevitably produced; everybody dangerous knew how suicidal it would be to mess with the boss's girl and how vicious that girl could be if she perceived one as a threat.

Not that Campos didn't want to get at all the power the Well represented; it was just that she was smart enough to know that before she let Mavra Chang near the Well, her control had to be ironclad. And until Juan Campos figured out how to do that or was forced by circumstance to gamble, she'd keep things pretty much the way they were.

It was frustrating to the Kraang. If only Campos would go through a Zone Gate. *Then* some contact, some influence, could be attempted. But Campos wanted no part of those Gates if she could avoid them. She remained where she could ensure protection.

Somehow there just *had* to be a way to kick Campos in the ass. There just *had* to be!

But until and unless it found a way to make contact, the Kraang knew it had to depend on forces beyond its control. The psychotic former Julian Beard—now turned into a complaisant wife for that female astronomer turned male swordsman who was now gelded and trapped as a courier for the Cloptan drug ring—was showing some promise, after all. Aided by the Dillians, who were somewhat in the pay of the Zone Council, she might well disrupt things sufficiently to cause a major move. When one no longer cared if one lived or died unless one attained one's objective, it made for a spicy and dangerous time for all those in one's way. The threat there was the Dillians. If they *did* come upon Mavra Chang by some miracle, helpless though she was, would the Dillians' first loyalty be to their former Earth comrades or to their new leaders and lives? Unknown to any of them, forces were moving in on the region and the situation was getting very, very dicey as the council and the various hexes weighed their own options. If they captured Chang, no matter what her form, while the surprisingly resourceful Gus liberated Brazil, everything could go wrong. Of course, there was always the colonel . . .

Possibilities! Far too many! This was getting much more difficult than the Kraang had originally thought. And there were far too many ways for things to go wrong . . .

BUCKGRUD,
CAPITAL OF CLOPTA

LATELY, IT WAS ALWAYS pretty much the same dream.

A dense, living forest filled with strange, twisting plants shimmered in a nearly constant but gentle breeze. Not familiar in any waking sense, yet familiar somehow to her in her dream. Comforting, safe, secure.

She would awaken into this living darkness in the Nesting Place, along with many others of her kind, and then proceed out from the hollow tree and onto the forest floor. Most of the night would be spent in the hunt, sometimes searching out and sometimes lying in wait as still as one of the bushes that were all around, waiting for prey to venture forth. Tiny animals, large insects, it didn't matter, so long as it was alive and small enough to be swallowed whole. There was always plenty of prey, for they bred all the time, or so it seemed, but much needed to be eaten to satisfy, and it was a task that consumed much of the night. There was no particular fear on her own part, though; there were no natural enemies in this forest for such as they, and the Big Ones who lived among the treetops ate no flesh and seemed appreciative of the service she and her kind did in keeping the crawling things in check so that they could not become so numerous as to threaten survival. She knew each by the scent and by the sounds it made.

The scent from a small mound nearby told her that there were delicacies inside; she moved to it, and her powerful claws dug into it, and she bent down so that her long, sticky tongue could go inside and sift through and find and draw the little insects into her beak . . .

It was near dusk when Mavra Chang awoke. She slept more than she was awake now, it was true, but that was blessed relief in more than one way. It not only meant escape from the sadism and torments of Juan Campos, when, of course, the Cloptan was awake and not busy with other things, it also was relief from the strange and unpleasant sensations that seemed unending.

There were feverish flushes, dizziness, unexpected pains of varying degrees in various places, and, above all else, a nearly universal itch that was driving her crazier than Campos ever could.

At first she thought that the sadistic surgeons employed by the drug cartel had been butchers as well, but over the passing weeks she had come to realize that it wasn't that, either. Something—strange—was happening to her, something even someone with her vast life and long experience in what evil could do had never undergone before. Still, that life allowed her to understand to a degree *what* was happening, if not exactly why.

She had been surgically altered, mutilated, disguised, but that was only the start of it. She had become other creatures before, but always the way the Well did it: quickly, without pain or sensation. She was becoming another creature again for the first time since she had last been on this world, but by a different method, and slowly by the standards of the Well but with astonishing speed by any other means.

She knew that now for several reasons, not the least of which was that what the surgeons had removed, such as her arms, had not even begun to grow back. She recalled that sensation well. Her body was changing. Grafted feathers were being replaced by real ones just as colorful and even more dense. Her center of gravity had moved down, and her midsection had thickened, while her head seemed to be enlarged and set flush on the shoulders, but with a neck that could pivot the head amazingly far. All this had been at the cost of an already shortened height; she was now a bit under a meter tall, but somehow she knew she would grow no shorter.

Her backbone had become increasingly limber, to the point where she could bend backward and almost touch the floor with the top of her head while still standing or lean forward so effortlessly and with such good balance that she could touch the floor with her beak.

From that vantage point she could see that her stubby, mutilated legs were rapidly changing into huge, thick drumsticks; the rather stupid feet they had fashioned for her now were solid, enlarged, and black and were gaining almost the prehensility of long, thick fingers, with sharp needle-like nails developing at the tips. Even the large, curved beak they had fashioned over her mouth was no longer the crude but effective graft; her tongue, now thin and greatly elongated, told her that beyond the beak was the gullet. Bright light blinded her, and even normal daylight was pale, washed out, and difficult to see in, yet the darkness glowed with sharpness and detail. Through the beak, countless strange odors came to her, each somehow separate even when mixed, and it was a bit of a game to try and identify and classify them. It was something to do.

The same went for sounds, although she could understand nothing of speech. She could understand only Campos, and then only when Campos directed something specifically at her; only Campos's translator could accept the eerie clicks and moans, some from deep in Mavra's chest, that passed for her speech. *That* little gift of a dedicated translator remained, but she was glad of it somehow in spite of her hatred of Campos. She knew that the sounds she could make were really bird sounds, animal sounds, not any sort of intelligible language to any race.

The animal urges disturbed her more. She could no longer physically tolerate any vegetable matter. Campos had been feeding her raw, bloody meat strips, it being a bit too civilized in the city to go pick up a carton of worms or grubs, even if Campos would have entertained the idea of live creepy crawlies in her nice apartment. Although Cloptans resembled giant humanoid ducks, they were omnivores and even had tiny rows of teeth inside those remarkably elastic, oversized bills of theirs.

Campos had hardly failed to notice the metamorphosis; it was happening at a rate that could not be seen by the naked eye but fast enough that something new would be evident between the time she left in early evening and the time she returned to sleep.

Now she came in the door and turned on the light, washing out Mavra's vision. The door slammed, and the Cloptan kicked off her shoes and threw a purse on the chair.

Campos looked over at the corner where Mavra stood, held there by a strong chain fastened to an anklet and to a welded-on socket in the wall, allowing perhaps a meter's movement one way or the other.

"Ah, my pet! And how are *you* this evening?"

"Food, master! Please! Food! Birdy begs you!" The worst part was, she no longer even felt humiliated by begging. It said something about Campos's mind-set, though, that she had insisted on being called "master," not "mistress."

"In a minute, my sweet. I need to freshen up and get a drink. It is going to be a long evening, I fear."

"Please, master! Feed Birdy!"

"Shut up! No more, you miserable little shit or I *might* just forget to feed you at all!"

It was not a threat to be taken lightly. The craving for food after sunset was overwhelming, more even than the craving for the exotic Well World drug that Mavra's made-over body no longer needed or even noticed. Mavra had not, however, volunteered that fact.

Campos went into the bathroom, and after an agonizing wait there was the sound of a toilet flush and then water running. Finally the Cloptan emerged, now naked.

Although it was nothing unusual now, the first sight Mavra had had of Campos naked had been something of an odd feeling. The shape was very human to a point, but even the breasts were covered with countless tiny white feathers except at the very tips. The shoulders were unnaturally squared off, it seemed, the arms and thinly webbed hands oversized for the body. The neck was quite long and thin to be supporting that oversized head. Below the waist it became more birdlike, with a definite rounding, almost turnip-shaped, with the turnip top angled back and slightly up, becoming short but large tail feathers. The legs extended straight down, a golden yellow color, and ended in two wide, thickly webbed feet that could still be consciously rolled up and fit into shoes.

She shared the huge apartment with two Cloptan females who were apparently attached to other drug cartel kingpins, but they stayed away from the big bird's area and Campos rarely referred to them or appeared to interact much with them. They ignored their roommate's "pet" and gave it a wide berth and seemed otherwise to be fairly typical of their type.

There had been more than a few naked males in as well. If they were representative of the race, they tended to be larger, chunkier, with almost wrestler builds, bent a bit forward on the hips in a slightly more birdlike fashion but without much in the way of tail feathers at all. Male genitalia weren't visible at all; they were apparently hidden by a thick clump of feathers growing forward between the widely spaced legs, which explained why they all seemed to be bowlegged.

Campos went to the cold storage compartment and took out a box of something, then popped it in a fast defroster that might have been operated by microwaves or some other means.

"Ah! I should tell you that I got word today from those nice doctors who made you so very pretty for me," the Cloptan said as the defroster whirred in the background. "They said you were genetically reprogrammed using the *actual* genetic code of a *real* bird in a hex very, very far away. I forget the name, but what does it matter? They said not to worry, that you would still be able to think and remember but that you'd also have all of the bird's instincts. They even said that by three months or so you would be so physically like this bird that you would even be *fertile!*" She laughed. "Just think! The zoo here doesn't have any of your birdie kind, but you're on their wish list, and the other girls here still seem a bit frightened of you and keep trying to talk me into getting rid of you."

Mavra said nothing. Anything she could say would only cause trouble.

"Just think of it!" Campos went on, enjoying herself. 'The nice zoo people say that if they had you, they could secure at least the loan of a male of the species. That might be quite the answer here. I won't have to worry about your care or suffer your presence here, but you'll be secure and in a happy little nest I can visit any time. That would be *very* amusing, seeing you sitting there hatching eggs, knowing that all your children would be birdbrains. Would you like that?"

"Whatever master wishes Birdy will do," Mavra responded as if by rote, eyes on the defroster.

"You bet your sparkly feathered ass you will!"

It was far from hopeless, but how the hell she would get this stupid asshole to head for the Well was something Mavra Chang was far from figuring out yet. The zoo wasn't a very appetizing new destination, but maybe it would provide some way out. Zoos didn't usually plan on animals being as smart as humans.

Somehow, some way, she had to get to the Well. She was building up too long a list of people to get even with to fail.

SUBAR,
A CITY IN NORTHERN AGON

IT WAS A REGION of thick forests and rolling hills, with mild days and chilly nights; if it hadn't smelled something like an overcooked egg, it might have been very pleasant.

Agon was a high-tech hex with just about everything one could expect of modern life. Private cars were banned; there just wasn't enough room to tolerate them or anywhere to dump the old ones. Still, public transport of just about every kind was available for a very low fee, along with taxis and buses that seemed to glide on air working not only every city and town but every rail and road crossing as well.

The Agonese were a strange lot, looking to Anne Marie like something out of a children's fairy tale. In fact, they resembled nothing so much as squat turtles without shells, but with very tough greenish-gray hides that might have been at home on elephants or rhinos back on Earth. But unlike those animals they were bipeds, walking on two short, thick trunks of legs that terminated in wildly oversized feet out of the age of dinosaurs. The omnipresent if unpleasant odor was nothing less than their collective body odors, to which they of course were oblivious.

"We are strangers very far even from our native Well World homes," Anne Marie noted as they approached a medium-sized city, the first they'd seen since making their way south from Liliblod. "We have no choice. We must contact the authorities and ask for help."

Tony, reluctantly along on this new quest and not liking it a bit, sighed. "You are correct, of course. But it makes me uneasy to do so. Such an operation could not go on in this kind of setting and with this technology without some connivance from high local officials. We are far from the places where the foul stuff is grown and into where it is distributed. This close to the business end, the government official who comes to help us might well be in the pay of those we seek. I would feel more at ease if we could contact our own government. They, after all, sent us on this great expedition in the first place. If we vanish outside their knowledge and contact, then we vanish forever."

Anne Marie nodded. "Agreed. But there *must* be a way of getting a message to our people in—what is that place called?—Zone? Where the embassies are. They have telephones, radios, probably much more, here. I think our best course is not to mention any more than we have to at the outset about why we're here and simply ask as stranded travelers to call our embassy. That would be a reasonable and natural request, wouldn't it?"

Tony nodded. "We have to do it that way, but something makes me uneasy about it. I still do not feel very clean about our role in this so far, even though we had nothing to do with the current problem. And I was born and raised in a very different society than you. I feel, unfortunately, far more at home with the governments here than I ever did with the British government I very much prefer."

There were a great many stares as the two large, blond, twin centauresses came into the city, one with an equally exotic if very different creature on her broad equine back. Alowi, the former Julian Beard, had said virtually nothing and seemed almost disinterested in the city or its inhabitants or anything else. Without a translator, she was merely along for the ride in most of the alien environments. That, both Tony and Marie agreed, would be a top priority. The Erdomese would get a translator or give up any thoughts of tracking down her kidnapped husband. There was no alternative. This was certainly a hex with the technical abilities to install one, although it would take more money than any of them had.

In fact, money was going to be the first problem if they remained here in the north. They hadn't been allowed to take much more than basic packs and provisions when they'd been forced off the ship off the coast of Liliblod, and Mavra had been the dispenser of funds for the group.

They didn't need much to just survive; although all three preferred nicely prepared and cooked dishes, their constitutions were such that they could survive on grasses and leaves if need be. As for clothing, the Dillians in particular could gallop forty or fifty kilometers a day without even sweating hard, and they at least had been allowed to keep their coats for use in colder climates. Still, they were well aware that they were very far away from anything or anyone familiar, and while they could use the Well Gate in any capital city, it would take them only to their home hexes, not to anywhere they wanted to be.

"Not much hope of finding any work around here, either," Tony noted. "Everything that we could do is automated. If the council won't stake us, we're through."

"Yes, I keep worrying that they will thank us for our service and tell us to go home, that they are sending the professionals in," Anne Marie responded. "Still, their professionals haven't been any good up to now, have they?"

Aside from a small Liliblodian consulate, there was nothing in the way of government offices in this fairly remote city, or much need for it, when cheap, fast magnetic trains could take anyone to the centrally located capital in under an hour and a half. While that also implied that the local cops could have somebody who had some authority there in a matter of hours, it didn't prove to be that easy. In fact, it almost seemed as if nobody were interested in doing anything for them except telling them how to get home and suggesting that they do so at the earliest opportunity.

Unable to get any information on anything else, let alone help, they held a conference to decide just what to do.

"You should both go home through the big gate," Alowi told them. "It will take you home, I know, in very quick time, as they say."

"But dear! What will *you* do?" Anne Marie asked, worried.

"I will do what I must. I will *never* return to Erdom. Never. With no husband or family, I have no wants or needs. So far I have been able to eat the grasses, leaves, berries, fruits, and such that grow in these lands. I cannot starve. My body seems most adaptable. I have become accustomed to the chill nights here to the point where the coat is now uncomfortable, so I need no clothing. I will search as I can; if I find him, that is fine, and if I do not, nothing is lost."

"But you cannot even *speak* to people! You have no translator!" Tony pointed out.

"You do, and I do not see that it has helped you much. In truth, I do not expect to find him. I expect to wander this world, or as much of it as can be wandered through, taking little from it and seeing what is seeable. Sooner or later I will find a place for myself or I will die. Either way, it is the most I can expect."

"But you're talking about living like an *animal*!" Anne Marie exclaimed. "You are better than that! Not to mention the fact that by your own admission you are defenseless against the horrid beings that are a part of this world. It is a death sentence either way."

"I will never go back to Erdom," she repeated, "but I will die an Erdomese. Those are facts. I choose my own course. It is more than any Erdomese woman has been able to do before."

Anne Marie sighed. "Then we shall simply have to contact our embassy in Zone and tell them the situation and location. Then we will find some part of this land that has some decent pasture and a few trees and wait them out."

"Or wait until they throw us out," Tony noted.

"Then we will leave, but only far enough to find some hospitality elsewhere," Anne Marie proclaimed. "I positively *refuse* to abandon this poor child to the wolves!"

Tony sighed. "Don't overdramatize, Anne Marie. There are no wolves in a place like this except perhaps the foul creatures who run the place. But we must also be practical. If we remain, we need to find some sort of work, and this is a high-tech hex surrounded by others that are not."

"But the closest ones are water!"

"True, but what of that? If a ship cannot come in to high-tech, then there is at least some point where it must be handled by the old means. Compared to one of our men we are not very strong, but the closest of our men is probably half a world away. In *these* parts we are probably quite strong, and even if we cannot lift what is required, we can certainly *pull* great weights."

"And Alowi?"

Tony shrugged. "She can cook. And supervise if need be. If we must remain in this godforsaken country, let's try and make the best of it."

This time it was Anne Marie who was doubtful. "But for how long?"

Tony shrugged. "Until one or more of us goes crazy or gets fed up or something breaks. It is better than *this*. Who knows? The council might at least extend us some seed money. It was they, after all, who got us into this."

"Oh, Tony! You're such a dear! You're making me feel guilty about dragging you along on this!"

"I have never been dragged," Tony responded. "I followed of my own free will, and I stay for the same reason. And when all hope is gone, *then* I will go home the same way!"

Anne Marie squeezed Tony's hand and then kissed her. "Of *course* you will, dear!"

If there had been no hope, they would have headed home long before this, but the problem was, as Anne Marie put it, they had been placed on hold but no one had hung up on them. Anne Marie noted that in spite of many areas where the Well World seemed futuristic to the point of being magical, the lack of any way to fly or even send signals any great distance between the worldlets led to everything more or less moving at, at best, a nineteenth-century pace. Nobody was ever in a hurry here, it seemed, unless it was to do evil, and so long as they were no threat, even evil seemed willing to leave them alone.

The council, still divided over exactly what course to take and thus taking very little, or so it seemed, asked them in fact to stay on "in the Agon region." They advanced the Dillians some credit and even found the pair a job of sorts, although not quite what they had in mind. Hexes in the region produced a variety of products that were of great interest to Dillia, but it had never been practical to manage much trade with nations so far away without some sort of permanent trade office coordinating things locally. Dillia was half a world distant—almost five thousand kilometers away over a vast stretch of water going west from the Ocean of Shadows and across the entire Overdark. Deals could be made in Zone in the traditional way, but without somebody on site, there was no way to guarantee quality, compare prices and deals, and put everything together. Dillians had never been the sort to relish staying long periods of time in remote and alien lands, and so they'd pretty much had to accept the traditional "take it or leave it" deals from their nearer neighbors. Merely the threat of competition could only help, and here were two who *wanted* to remain, at least for a significant period of time.

Dillia itself was something of a hotbed of semitech innovation, conservation plans and concepts, and agricultural management, particularly forestry, and had much to trade in areas most nations largely ignored. In exchange, it needed steam vessels, particularly for internal lakes and rivers, and other heavy industrial items either impossible or impractical to make at home. Dillians also had a taste for things that could not be grown locally, including many tropical and subtropical products, coffee, tea, cocoa, and tobacco. The Dillian government was more than happy to set Tony and Anne Marie up as a trade office and see what they could do.

Neither of them was under any illusions that this was a permanent job or that the opportunity wasn't created because, for reasons of its own, the Zone Council saw some value in keeping them in the region at that time, but as it served everyone's purposes, there were no objections.

Alowi was not so fortunate. She was nothing to Dillia, of course, and even less to Erdom, who clearly was disinterested even in whether or not one more female came back at all. Nor did the council as a whole see any use for her. So she became basically the Dillians' housekeeper, keeping their new home clean, cooking the meals, and doing other chores, all of which was made much easier by being in a high-tech hex where things not only worked smoothly, they seemed in some ways futuristic compared to Earth.

Because she had no translator, Alowi spent the time studying and learning Agonese, a language that sounded bizarre but that, she soon discovered, followed a pattern not too different from some Earth tongues. It was soon clear that Julian Beard was not dead inside her brain but merely dormant; it was in fact Beard's knowledge of Japanese that gave her the clue to understanding Agonese. Not that they resembled each other in obvious ways, but the structure wasn't all that different.

The trade mission had some initial frustration but then some startling successes. Tony was adept at business, and Anne Marie seemed able to spot a con or a sucker deal almost instantly and knew just when to give in on a negotiation. The initial commissions weren't huge, but they no longer had to worry about going broke.

They used some of the first money to buy Alowi a translator. She made no objections this time, spending much of her time doing a great deal of studying, using the Agonese computer libraries. Their written language was actually pretty basic; for a high-tech society, it appeared that they were surprisingly illiterate and used voice and picture technology for all their information sources. Her greatest frustration lay in her inability to really use her hands; the oversized split hooves proved unable to push even a few small buttons on a console, but she managed by gripping a wooden stick and using that instead.

There was an ancient language of commerce on the Well World that had evolved to cover just about every conceivable situation. It was a written language only—translators filled the gap for spoken tongues—and it had arisen from a pictorgraphic alphabet so ancient, nobody now knew its origins. It was extremely complex—it had to be to cover so many tiny worldlets and so many varying races—but it was used on virtually all interspecies documents and everything from contracts to treaties. If one could learn it, there was nothing really closed to that person. To Tony, its sheer complexity made Mandarin Chinese, with its mere thirty thousand or so characters, seem like child's play, and he barely tried before giving up. Anne Marie didn't try at all, noting that the English had never had to learn other people's languages and she did not intend to start. Alowi, however, managed to read many basic texts at the end of only three months.

It had been learning Agonese that had been the key. With both Agonese and Erdoma to go by, she was able to isolate and assemble key concepts from the two totally different languages and see how the trade language accommodated the concepts of both. It still wasn't easy, but it seemed, well, *obvious* to her, and it had already become merely a matter of memorizing vocabulary.

Tony in particular was impressed. While still back on Earth she'd considered herself something of a linguist, which was useful for an international airline pilot. In addition to her native Portuguese and essential English for aviation, she knew Spanish, French, and German well enough to converse and read a newspaper. *This,* however—*this* was Sanskrit as written by a mad chicken that had gone amok in an ink factory.

"You can really read this?"

Alowi shrugged modestly. "Enough. What I do not know, I can usually interpolate. I think that if I were writing books or treaties, I would need several more years, and about a third that applies to specific races and hexes that I cannot imagine would require some context for me to understand, such as going there and talking with them. But yes, I can make do in it. I will never *write* it, though. With these hands I can stir, chop, pick up, do quite a number of things, but only those things which can be done with broad motion and much toleration for error. To make these fine marks with pen or brush, where slight deviations change whole meanings—no. Even doing block English letters is crude, much like a child just beginning to learn them."

"Then why go through all this?"

"Because the one thing that works as well as before, perhaps better, is my brain. It is odd—I seem to be able to concentrate as I never could before, to grasp and memorize things easily that before would have been much more difficult. I have always been a good learner, but I do not know why it is suddenly much easier. What is not so easy is chemistry."

"What?"

"This body was built for sensation. It *demands* things, and the cravings can become overpowering at times. I have compensated with creativity and with some unconventional use of objects I have picked up in stores here, but it is not the same as the real thing, and the only place I can get what I truly need would also almost certainly give me a lobotomy. Erdomese just are not *built* to be loners. I know that now. I have been kidding myself all along. So I cannot go back, but if I do not go back, I will go mad."

Tony sighed. "So what are you going to do? We're here mainly because of you and because we hope to find out what the hell happened to the others, but time is dragging on and on. The council is only certain that nobody has yet entered the Well. There are certain places at the equatorial barrier, called Avenues, where anyone who knows how—and only two people on this world do—can get in, and those are all carefully monitored. It is almost as if one of those hex gates opened and swallowed the two of them."

Alowi nodded. "I know. I truthfully have expected to hear the worst, but I never expected to go this long and hear *nothing.* That makes it all the harder." She paused a moment. "Do you remember the clinic here that had some doctors of other races as well as Agonese? Where I got the translator?"

"Yes, it mostly serves the ships' crews and passengers and other travelers passing through. There are stories that the doctors are here because they cannot go home, that they are wanted for some sort of criminal activities. Certainly they can't support all this high-tech equipment off what they're paid to fix broken legs and such every once in a while. I did not like the feel of the place when we took you there. Why?"

"The locals tell tall stories about them. About how they do terrible experiments and create horrors, but they are protected because they leave the Agonese alone. It is also said they are of use sometimes to the government and perhaps to criminal gangs. I do not like them one bit, but I have been thinking of going to them. Only faint hope that perhaps my Lori could be found has stopped me."

"Why? Are you sick?"

"As I said, I have—problems. They are the only ones with a data base on all the races, including mine, within who knows how far. Their practice here is certainly honest and above board or they would have been forced to move elsewhere. I have been thinking of going to them and asking if there was something they could do to help me control this or damp it down. When you find yourself not merely sweeping with a broom but making love to it, it is time something was done. I have no money, and they are unlikely to be cheap. I am ashamed that I must ask you if you will cover my bill if I go there."

"Well, yes, of course—if you're sure. But I don't like it, and I know Anne Marie won't, either. If even part of their reputation is true, you could wind up far worse off than you started."

"I'm aware of that, but this will not be some hapless captive coming into their clutches. You will know that I am going there, and it will be all up front. It is not likely that they could stand to create a monster in public, let alone have a distinctive patient vanish, and I will know the options and be able to choose which or whether to do anything at all."

"Very well, then, dear, go to them. I fear as much for your mind and soul as for your body, though. I have already seen you undergo so many personality changes, I am not sure who exactly I am talking to sometimes, if you will pardon my saying so."

Alowi smiled. "I understand. In fact, I understand a lot more about myself than I did. The truth is, I think those all *were* different people, or different parts of me, all mixed up inside. It has taken me a long time, and many shocks, to put any of it together. Julian Beard is essentially dead. I have all of his knowledge, but I have no direct memories or feelings of *being* him. It is more like—well, viewing a very long motion picture of somebody's life. It is very odd. I know every detail, but not as if I had actually *done* it. Rather, it is as if I had been standing there, ghostly, watching it all being done. I can think about how to do things with soft, five-fingered hands, but I cannot really imagine having such a hand. When I look in a mirror, what is reflected there is *me.* And the odd thing is, I like what I see. Nothing else—*computes,* you might say. I hate the Erdomese government, church, and system, and I cannot say that I wish I had been born with the freedom a man has there, but I am who and what I am, and I am comfortable with that. I just wish *they* would be. So, for better or worse, I am Alowi and I am too damned smart to go home."

"I—I *suppose* I understand. At least as much as I could without being you. Certainly I have undergone something much milder myself. I know how to fly a 747, but the knowledge seems academic now, not personal, even though it was what I loved more than anything else. Somewhere, near the end of that last long voyage that left us here, I just suddenly woke up one day and felt absolutely comfortable and normal, not just as a Dillian but as a woman and a woman with a twin sister. And it did not even disturb me—I didn't fight it at all. When I finally admitted this to Anne Marie back in Liliblod, I found that she felt the same. Since then I haven't even *dreamed* of the past, although I have had a few nightmares involving being on a ship at night. Yes, perhaps I *can* understand, to a degree at least."

"You have changed more dramatically than that, starting from when we set out, but it has become a *real* change since we have been here."

"Huh? In what ways?"

"No matter how identical you looked, it was always easy to tell you apart. Anne Marie was more of a motherly type, and she had many affectations that came out in how she spoke and even moved. You moved very differently, with a bolder, prouder manner, a tough, more masculine way of speaking, that sort of thing. If you bumped yourself, you would curse; Anne Marie would say, 'Oh dear!' or something equally quaint. As we went along, I began to notice that the two of you were growing more and more alike. You lost a degree of that masculinity, began to move in more feminine ways, while Anne Marie seemed to pick up that part you lost, becoming tougher and more confident. You have added more feminine words, and she has dropped some of her more obvious old-fashioned quaintness. You now pay attention to jewelry, cosmetics, hair, that sort of thing, even though you are hardly doing it for her or for some man. You are doing it for yourself, and it is exactly why *she* does it. And then there are the half conversations."

Tony was fascinated by this. "The what?"

"I am sure that neither of you is aware of it, but when you talk to each other, what must seem like whole complicated dialogues are really often sets of unconnected half sentences, words, and such, and often you will finish one another's sentences."

"I—I never *realized*—"

"I did not think you did. Physically you are absolutely identical, I think more so than any natural identical twins could be. Together, over time, while I have sorted myself out, you two have been doing the same, only less dramatically, more slowly and subtly. You are not really Tony anymore, nor is she Anne Marie. You are someone different, an average of the two. Only the difference in your *knowledge* bases keeps you from being almost one individual in two bodies. That alone will keep you slightly different, which is, I suspect, all to the good. Everyone should have a *little* something to make them different. But that *is* the extent of it."

Tony thought about it, not sure if she was pleased with the idea but seeing the ultimate point, which was the same one Alowi had made about herself: they were who and what they were. One either accepted that and learned to live with it or one killed oneself. Period.

The Well World worked some of the magic; the rest had to be supplied from inside, from the mind and soul.

"Make your appointment," Tony told the Erdomese. "But make no rash or irreversible decisions."

Doctor Drinh was an Agonese, and after all this time in the province, learning the language and the culture, Alowi *still* couldn't tell one from another without a uniform or badge of rank. He specialized in treating aliens but was a diagnostician and planner. Others, some so alien that they made Erdomese and Agonese look like relatives, did the actual work.

Drinh put the Erdomese profile on the computer, then took samples of blood from Alowi for comparison, then ran them through a myriad of automated tests and looked over the results.

"Well, I *can* say that your feelings will not get much worse than they are, but they won't get any better, either. It must make for early marriages and active honeymoons, at least." He paused. "Sorry if the attempt at humor was offensive."

"No, no," she assured him. "It is absolutely correct. Child marriage is the norm in Erdom."

"Yes, but you see, in this sort of thing the tension builds up, releasing an overdose of all sorts of brain chemicals, and it stays pretty well 'on,' as it were. You seem extremely intelligent and self-controlled, but I would be remiss if I didn't tell you that if a male of your race, *any* male, came within your eyesight, you would become, pardon, a whimpering, begging fool. It is inevitable with these sorts of readings."

"I know that. It is why I am here. The odds of me meeting a man of my race while I am over here are pretty slim, but as you say, I am smart enough to know that I cannot go home and remain so."

"Just so, just so," Drinh muttered. "We don't have much on culture here except those sort of taboo listings so that we don't do anything to someone that would cause social or mental damage or the like, but I *did* note that the society is labeled 'patriarchal.' So what would you like me to do, assuming it is doable?"

Alowi sighed. "I—I need it to be damped down. Some way to put it under control so I can live with it."

"Well, the most obvious way if you never intend to have children or have any sexual relations with another of your kind would be to remove the sexual organs. It is a radical and permanent solution, but it would cause the hormones and psychochemicals to shut off eventually, and with it all sexual desire."

It was a more radical solution than she wanted, but she couldn't quite dismiss it out of hand. "It is something to think about if all else fails, but I would rather not. It would change me in other ways, too, would it not?"

"Well, I couldn't know, although I can put in for research notes via Zone and find out. Logic and experience with other races suggest that there would be complications, yes. With someone of your type, basically mammalian, the breasts would sag and be encumbrances, you'd probably get extremely fat, there might be some long-term problems with bone integrity and the like, and your energy levels would tend to be down, at the very least."

"I like myself as I am. I think I would rather try going for the one problem rather than something that radical."

He shrugged. "Well, there are drugs that might work, but they would have to be specially formulated for your species—we wouldn't exactly be expected to stock Erdomese materials—or brought from Erdom via Zone, and either would be expensive and require that they be taken regularly over *decades,* judging from your apparent physical age. If you are wealthy, well connected, and will be in one spot, like this city, it would work. Otherwise. . . . And if you came off them, particularly suddenly and dramatically, your system might go wild. There would be a danger of losing all control, of becoming little more than an animal in heat, and how long this would go on until you came back to present levels is impossible to say."

Alowi was feeling less and less like she had any way out.

"There is a third way," the doctor went on, thinking. "Radical and somewhat costly up front, although possibly not, depending on how much work is actually involved."

"Yes?"

"Before going further, I must tell you that it is not approved medicine. Strictly experimental, although we have had tremendous successes with it and few failures. I am quite certain that it would work in your case. It has come out of our own research work here."

"Go on."

"The process is complex, but basically it is rewriting your genetic code, rather rapidly. Do you understand what that means?"

She was shocked at the idea that they had such abilities, but she nodded. "Yes, I do, at least in its implications. Can you really do it?"

Drinh sat back. "We can do more than you ever dreamed with it. We take only a few cells, and we alter the code. Then the mathematics of the coding is fed into tiny semiorganic devices, machines if you will, but on a scale so small, they could be seen with only the finest microscopes. They replicate themselves with astonishing speed, enter every cell in your body, and rewrite the code. Then they die and are passed out in the normal way or allow themselves to be consumed by the body's defenses. The process is quite rapid. The cells quite literally become other cells. Major changes can cause a great deal of temporary discomfort and disorientation, but relatively minor ones such as we are talking about might well not be noticed, or no more than catching a minor virus at the worst."

"You can really *do* this?"

"We do it regularly. Of course, there are limits. I could not, for example, turn you from being an Erdomese into one of my own race. At some point you would be neither one nor the other, and the stress would kill you. But if you merely wanted to *look* like an Agonite, *that* I could do. Of course, we are talking far less than that here."

She couldn't believe what she was hearing. "Look like an Agonite? The process is *that* comprehensive?"

"Oh, yes." He seemed somewhat uncomfortable all of a sudden, though, as if he'd already said more than he had intended.

She had a sudden thought. "You could not turn me into a man, could you? An Erdomese man?"

"Alas, no," the doctor sighed, and seemed to relax a bit. "The reverse, yes, because in your race and many others the male contains only half the genetic makeup; the other half is female, coming from the mother. But you have two sets of female genes, so there is nothing there to edit. If you were male, I could remove the male chromosomes, duplicate the female ones, alter them somewhat, and recombine them so you would turn into a perfect, fully functioning female. But the other way—well, one must have *something* to work with, and your race is even more peculiar than most bisexual races in that you have no male hormones or male psychochemicals at all. Disappointed?"

"No, not really," she answered, realizing that what she was saying was true. "But what *could* you do to me?"

"Oh, a lot of things. The possibilities are vast. To address the immediate problem, it would be a matter of finding the triggers and dampening them down. The work is complex because it is subtle, exacting, and challenging. It must be done just right. If we got it wrong, we might not catch the problem; or it could throw you off and create violent mood swings, intermittent pain, or even psychotic episodes. If we had an Erdomese clientele, it might be rather simple, but as we do not, it would be a matter of trial and possibly error. In fact, let me put the data into the computer and see what the risks might be."

He turned in his chair to a console, and although it had full audio input capabilities in Agonese, he used a complex keyboard instead.

All the better to keep trade secrets and control the conversation, she realized.

In less than a minute a string of Agonese text came up on the screen, much of it punctuated with graphic images of things that were beyond her comprehension. Also, the screen was angled sufficiently to keep her from reading more than bits and pieces without being obvious.

Finally he turned back to her. "There are two possibilities that seem just about equal. Now, understand, I do not mean two different things we might attempt. Rather, there are two equally possible outcomes to the attempt as postulated. There is absolutely no way to be positive short of, well, experimentation. We have no case histories to tell which way it will go."

She couldn't imagine where he was heading. "Yes?"

"Well, there is about a three percent chance of serious complications. I tell you that up front, but that is actually a very small percentage in this kind of process. There is no risk-free solution. Beyond those unknowables, there is a better than forty-nine percent chance that it will decouple your mind from your desires."

"I beg your pardon. What does that *mean,* exactly?"

"Basically, you would be fully capable of performing as a woman, but you would lack all desire to do so, even in the face of stimulus-response. You would simply be incapable of arousal. There is a medical term for this, but I do not know how it would translate. It is physiological frigidity."

She nodded. "I understand the idea. I would be turned off of sex, as it were." She thought about it. "Is it—reversible?"

"I would not recommend attempting a reversal. Changing the changed is always a hundred times more dangerous, because we would have even less to go on and the risk of things going terribly wrong would be major. Of course, you could always take injections or oral hormones to artificially restore it to some degree or another, but it would be temporary and administered by a clinic like this one, which could determine and synthesize what was needed."

"I see." It was in many ways an attractive possibility. "But Doctor, I can add. You have left almost forty-eight percent unaccounted for."

"Um, yes, I was coming to that. The problem is, the same regions of the brain and the same chemical balances serve more than one function, and without prior research we can be only so delicate. The nearly equal chance would be to achieve not a neutral balance but opposition. You would have no arousal or desire to copulate with males, but you would find yourself attracted to and potentially aroused by other females. You would not suffer the borderline psychochemically induced nymphomania that is at the heart of your problem, but you would be vulnerable, as with most sexual creatures, to stimulus-response."

"You mean I would react like a man."

"No, not precisely. In the sense of stimulus-response to females, yes, but you would not think of yourself as male or have male responses and desires. In some races a small percentage of people are born this way. It *would* solve your problem, because you would be unlikely in any event to encounter females outside of Erdom, but not as completely as neutralization, and of course drug and hormone therapy to restore normalcy would be *very* unlikely."

She considered it. Bizarre—that the worst-case scenario would be to wind up viewing women close to the way Julian Beard was brought up seeing them. But Beard had always been fully capable of giving up almost anything, even sex, for very long periods, and certainly, if it couldn't be Lori, she would rather not ever be tempted, even accidentally, by one of those native men.

"How—how soon would I see a difference?" she asked him.

He shrugged. "Impossible to say for sure. Still, only automatic and stimulus-response chemical actions in your brain would be affected, so the change would be quite rapid. The practical effect might be noticed in days, perhaps hours, although total and permanent change might take a few weeks. We are dealing here only with a very small reprogramming of an even smaller area. But the permanence of the process is important to remember; if you wish to have anything else done, it is best to have it done all at once."

"Anything else?" She could see his gaze. "Oh, the hands. I thought about that after what you said, but . . . Well, you said it would take away my desire. Would it do more? Would it make me antichild, for example, or incapable of loving someone or having other normal emotions?"

"Again, you'd need an Erdomese physician to fully answer that. It is not like this has been done before, let alone repeatedly, with someone of your race. There are bound to be some ancillary changes we can't foresee, but not drastic ones. I doubt if you will become some sort of emotionless, cold individual or anything like that. It might even work the other way. You might find that your emotions in other areas are stronger. There is often that sort of compensation. But would you love your child if you had one? Of course you would."

"Then I cannot have the hands done. If you check your data base, you will see that these are essential for one of my kind to have a normal childbirth. I want as few options closed as possible. I just want relief."

"Then you shall have it," Doctor Drinh assured her. "We have your residence here. I will get our computers to work on this and see what is what, then call with price and such. I really do think this might well be the best thing for you, considering your circumstances."

Alowi left, and the doctor immediately went into the back of the clinic and walked briskly into the laboratory portion of the building, where a huge, sluglike creature was working at a machine using countless wormlike tendrils.

"You heard and followed, Nuoak?" Drinh asked the other.

"I did. The problem she seeks relief for is real."

"I know, I know, but I haven't felt fully comfortable since they moved here. I almost told her there was no help, but I think that would have been worse than the truth in arousing suspicion."

"Your professional pride and bragging got the best of you, and you know it. She is *exceptionally* bright and knowledgeable and as an offworlder has the education and possibly the cultural background to eventually put two and two together, particularly with the added detail you gave her. I don't like it."

"But what can we do? We can hardly dispose of her. The Dillians are her comrades and titular employees of their state. They have council contacts that make them too dangerous to involve. But if we play normal, she will almost certainly put the facts together and start snooping in earnest. *Then* what?" He thought a moment. "I suppose we could slow down her data processing speed and limit her retention. Do it slowly, and she wouldn't even be aware of it or even care if she did notice. If the Dillians noticed and wouldn't accept it as some natural mental problem, we could always claim it as an unfortunate side effect."

"Too obvious," Nuoak responded. "The data that we got from the security police suggest she learned Agonian in only a few months and is well on her way to reading Standard. No, looking over the data, a more interesting suggestion comes to mind."

"Yes? You have an idea?"

"I do not believe that she is a direct threat to us. The chemistry here is fascinating. She is almost totally nonaggressive, quite literally incapable of defending herself against any significant threat. It must have taken every bit of her willpower to just come here on her own. She might well suspect the truth to a very great degree, but she would be incapable of acting upon it."

"She had the guts to come in here and be pretty cool about it."

"That is less a function of biology than force of will over biology, resulting from the fact that before Well processing she was male and, to some degree, by her mind battling against her body. The urges inside her must be excruciating. But no, we must accept that she will suspect, or already does, and perhaps even tell her friends about her suspicions. The fact is, though, that they can do nothing at all about it. They remain here only as her friends and protectors and possibly out of a bit of fear of actually returning to Dillia and taking up normal lives there. It must be quite a difficult thing to actually bring yourself to do. Still, they must be unhappy here, and bored and frustrated. They would leave if they saw a way, I feel certain. They are held by the one pressure this Erdomese girl can bring to bear; a version of passive aggression. 'If you leave, I'll stay here and die.' Remove *that* and you remove the problems, all of them."

"I am listening."

"The odds you quoted were correct, but surely you noticed that we can tip the scales on one of them. We have the orientation model from the male Erdomese in the computer now. If we use that as our model, it would also be possible to introduce a tapeworm of sorts. It would search through her catalog of memories while she slept looking for the specific pattern of her memories of her husband and their time together, and allow her mind to restructure those events."

"A tapeworm is the most dangerous thing you can do in a sentient creature," Drinh noted nervously. "We might as well change *all* her memories for the mess it would be likely to cause! Best to just kidnap her and be done with it if *that* is your solution!"

"You misunderstand. The limited nature of this program is so subtle, she probably will not even be aware of it. At worst, she will either blame it on the results of the reorientation and accept it as a minor side effect or take it as an inner revelation of something that's been there all along. It won't matter. It will not change her relationship with the Dillians one bit, and it will produce a logical result. She will not only have little motivation other than friendship to want to find this husband of hers, she will have an even greater motivation for fearing finding him as she remembers him. As this plays out, we can find someone, perhaps connected to the Great University at Czill or some lesser institution, with the potential to offer her some sort of position. She would be among many species and would not stand out as particularly alien, and her knowledge of Standard would allow her to do academic research. I believe her offworld profession was some sort of geologist, at least judging from those secret police reports. A passive, productive, rewarding job in a protected setting. You see?"

"I see. It is a good plan."

"Only you do not agree?"

"I agree because I have no choice," Drinh replied, "and nothing better to offer. But you are a logical scientist from a race that does not have the sexual context both her race and mine share. People do not always react logically in this sort of situation. Nor do I think the Dillians stayed for her alone. Not this long. There is something to be said for comradeship and for the sense of personal violation, of insult, when it is broken up the way their group's was. I don't even think the two lost people are at the heart of it, not anymore. Some people simply have a strong urge to see justice, and I think that may be in play here."

"There is no such thing as justice if you have a good enough attorney," Nuoak commented.

"There you go being *logical* again!"

The call came in only a day later. The clinic could perform the procedure at any time, given a few hours' warning to actually synthesize and program the tiny microgadgets. They were confident, it was a simple procedure, and the price they quoted was considerably less than the translator had cost. *Considerably* less.

"Well, I don't like it," Anne Marie said flatly. "It isn't *natural*. And what's to keep them from fouling your brain chemistry all over to hell and gone? Why, suppose they *can* do all they say! Why, after that stuff's inside you, you won't be able to *stop* it! You could wind up being turned into a cow or something worse!"

Alowi shook her head. "I do not think he would do that. He might if I were some captured guinea pig, but not to paying patients who come in the front door. I got the impression that they were a *lot* more experienced with this than they want to admit. And they have probably won friends by doing big favors—fixing congenital defects, perhaps regrowing limbs, maybe even the reverse of what I am thinking of."

"But what if, somehow, sometime, we or somebody finds and liberates Lori? How's *he* going to feel with a permanently frigid wife?"

"I—I thought about that, but I can no longer let that enter into my plans. If I am to be the first totally free Erdomese woman in history, then I have to go all the way with it. If he is found, then I will still be me, and if he wants more, well, Erdomese are polygamists. Actually, I have had more dark thoughts about Lori since consulting with Drinh."

"Huh? What do you mean?" Tony asked her.

"Well, everybody says that the clinic works with criminal gangs, and we know who is most likely to have that kind of clout and protection. Suppose there is a really good reason why nobody has seen a trace of Lori or Mavra. Suppose they were two of the clinic's guinea pigs for its ambitious experiments. He said he could actually make me look Agonese. What could he make either of *them* into?"

"Oh, *my!*" Tony exclaimed, sounding *exactly* like Anne Marie.

"But that makes putting yourself in their hands even *worse!*" Anne Marie protested. "If they *did* do something to Lori, something monstrous, then they almost certainly know who you are. Suppose they think you're *really* there to spy on them! That you're on to them! They could do something to you and then, when it was noticed, say, 'Oops! Sorry! We made a big mistake! But it *was* experimental and we didn't know *everything* about Erdomese women and you were warned of the dangers.' What could we do? Nothing!"

"I thought of that, but I do not think they are the kind to panic, and I really believe they will be extra careful *not* to do anything wrong simply to keep us at a dead end. Besides, if I do not do *something,* I am going to go crazy. If they are the ones who stole the life I was content to lead, then they owe me a life of independence at least."

"I have a bad feeling about this," both centauresses said in unison, another thing they did more and more often. "But if you are determined, we will not stand in your way."

"Thank you."

"If they do anything other than what they promised . . ." said one.

". . . Then we will be on them like a ton of lead," the other finished.

They set up an appointment with Doctor Drinh.

Alowi sat there on the stool as before, in the outer office, feeling nervous but determined.

Drinh was the competent physician now, taking final samples, giving her a thorough checkout, and running the resulting data through his medical computers. Finally he said, "All seems in good order. All that remains is to ask once again if you really wish to go through with this, because once done, it is done."

She nodded. *Sorry, Lori, but I just can't stand this otherwise.* "I would not have returned if I had not already decided. Let me get it over with."

Doctor Drinh walked to the back of the office and opened a compartment, removing a clear rectangular container in which there was some equally clear liquid. He took out an Agonian syringe, which resembled a small flashlight with two nubs, put it against the container, and pushed a button on the syringe. Almost instantly the fluid was gone, drawn into the syringe. He then walked over to where Alowi sat and stood by her. "This is it," he told her. "Say no now or it is done."

She swallowed hard. "Do it."

She felt the two nubs of the syringe against her right rump, then a sudden tingling sensation much like a minor electric shock, and then nothing.

The doctor put away the syringe and replaced the container. She sat there a moment, wondering what was next.

"You may go now," he told her, sounding satisfied.

She felt surprise. "That is it? That is all there is?"

"That's it. Period. You might feel some dizziness or disorientation off and on, and you might run a slight fever, so take it very easy for a few days. There might also be some confusing or bizarre dreams and thoughts for a bit, but that should last only a day or two. You should certainly notice a lessening in your tension by tomorrow at the latest. Also, I would walk back rather than ride if you feel up to it. It will help distribute the serum in your system."

She got up. "I hope it works," she told him.

"I hope it works, too," he responded with a sincere smile.

LILIBLOD

LORI, TOO, COULD NOT help but notice that Juan Campos's well-planned and fiendish revenge was not as complete as it had been intended to be. Overloaded with the mind-numbing drug, sent through a training course over and over and over again until all action was automatic, he had been beyond even caring what had happened. Weeks of Pavlovian training and then the real thing, trips back and forth by night without the slightest deviation along back trails laced with an overpowering scent unique to him, all seemed to be one continuous blur, without a sense of time, place, or event.

How long this had gone on, he could not know, but slowly, ever so slowly, he began to come out of the stupor. Rational thought returned with the same slowness, in fits and starts. He was unable to distinguish what was real from what was dream, but eventually he came to understand that for some reason that drug no longer affected him, that its power was fading with increasing quickness.

There was some sense of denial about that fact. He didn't *want* to come out of it, didn't *want* to think and perhaps face the pain and monotony of this life, but his own inner strength denied him the oblivion he needed.

What did it matter that he was no longer addicted except to add to the torture? If they found out, they might not trust him anymore, and that would mean his finish.

But that, too, was an odd thought. Wouldn't death be preferable to a life of *this*?

The answer, though, was no.

That left escape, even though he was a four-footed freak far from any home or help, forever cut off from rational communication with the outside world. Even if that weird new translator didn't encode everything in and out, it would probably be useless. His mouth felt funny; it wasn't malleable as it always had been. Even the limited communication he'd had with the handlers who had special translators to make themselves understood was now one-way. The only sound he seemed capable of anymore was from very deep inside and sounded more like a bray and meant nothing. His handlers, usually none too bright underlings, had found that amusing.

Still, it had been a shock to find out that indeed he had changed so radically and that after all this time of staring down at the ground, his neck was somehow now long enough and flexible enough to allow him to look straight ahead. In fact, it became increasingly flexible as time wore on.

They had fused his hands to form hoofs and, after castration, had filled him with female hormones that had produced grotesque travesties of Erdomese breasts. Yet now the breasts seemed to have shrunk away while the legs and hooves seemed to have solidified and changed. Through the fragmented and confused mental haze he was in, he realized at some point that he was very, very different from what Campos had intended or how he'd started out under the hands of those maniacal butchers.

His vision was weak, distorted, and without color, but it had tremendous contrast abilities. It was hard to imagine that there were this many scales of gray. Vision was short-range but sharp straight on, but there was little if any peripheral vision to speak of. To see something to the side, he had to move his head rather than his eyes. It took some getting used to once he started to try to use his vision again for more than spotting things to step over. Anything outside a two- to seven-meter range was a gray blur. This was true day or night, although night was more comfortable. Bright light, even reflected, blinded him for a minute or more after he turned to avoid it. Hearing and smell were much more trustworthy than sight.

I've become some kind of a horse, he realized after a while. Not any horse he knew, but close enough. The forelegs were true forelegs, the front hooves true hooves, and the joints angled like a horse's joints. Everything was proportional, comfortable, balanced. His nose and mouth had elongated and combined into an equine head, and somehow he'd grown a long bushy tail. His ears felt funny, too, but he couldn't tell why. The one thing he still had as before was the horn.

A unicorn, he thought at last, the old vision coming from deep in the past. But a unicorn with no interest in virgins; most definitely a gelding.

How did it happen, and how long had it taken? No way to know, but it was likely that those butcher bastards had access to technology far in

advance of mere mutilation, perhaps some kind of rapid genetic manipulation.

Still, how rapid was "rapid"? Not only were the days under the drug's
influence a blur, but even when his mind had returned, his sense of time
had not. When he was hungry, which seemed to be most of the time, he
ate large quantities of grass and bushes and whatever else looked green
and tempting. He wondered how much he weighed. He didn't seem all
that much bigger, certainly not true horse size. Probably the size of a
Shetland pony, but perfectly proportioned.

The thought of the virgins made him aware of just what had been
removed. He remembered Alowi fondly but could not even recall what
kind of sexual attraction she'd had. It was more than the loss of ability or
desire; he seemed to have totally lost even the memories of the feelings
that sexuality had brought, human or Erdomese, male or female. He
knew the lack of it should have bothered him, but it didn't; instead, it
only bothered him that there was now a hole somewhere inside him
where something once valued and prized had been, something now ut-
terly excised. It was in many ways the same as the loss of any sense of
time and, oddly, no more disturbing or important to him.

There was a certain satisfaction in that. To deny him sexuality had
been the heart of Campos's revenge. That he neither missed it nor gave
it any more thought after this was another slap in the bastard's face.

He had become a unique animal but a consistent one. It was stupid
and meaningless to dwell on anything he lacked, particularly something
that was now no more than a set of definitions for how a species repro-
duced itself. If he could get a better handle on what it had once meant or
felt like, perhaps he would think it a tragedy, but for now it seemed
somehow—*liberating*. When one was without sex, one had no stereotyp-
ing, no fears or expectations based on a factor that did not apply to one,
and when one was one of a kind, as lonely as that might become, there
were neither expectations nor fears from peers. It was gone, every last
bit of it, and being gone, it took with it all sense of deprivation or loss. It
was irrelevant. "Relevant" was learning everything there was to learn
about what he now was and how he interacted with everything else.

The scent he followed, whose slightest trace he could pick out of hundreds of others, he soon realized was the scent of his own excrement. It
interested rather than revolted him to discover that he had virtually no
bladder or bowel control. It came out when it was ready and had to, but
only when he was in motion, never when he was still or asleep. Once
discovered, that fact, too, was simply discarded and not thought of again
because it didn't matter. That was how he was, period.

Each trip through the dim forests of Liliblod found him growing more and more comfortable with this new form and thinking about things that were important rather than dwelling on his twin pasts, both of which seemed to have decreasing relevance or even interest to him. Instead, he concentrated on developing his superior sense of hearing, which could pick out the song of a distant bird or a chorus of sonorous insects with ease, and in determining and cataloging what each sound meant. Similarly, classifying every scent, every odor, analyzing not only the ground and trees but the very breezes, provided vital information once he'd matched scent to source. Since there was a mind behind that classification system and nothing else to do but walk, smell and sound proved to be more precise than sight had ever been.

He knew he'd have to become an expert at this, since the same line of thought told him that he would have no choice but to escape as soon as he felt it was safe to do so. Not that he had any illusions about the rest of his life even if he *did* get away. He would neither understand nor be understood by anyone else, he had no hands or tentacles with which to write, and he didn't know how to read any native languages. He'd be an animal, period, able to perhaps study and explore for the sake of knowledge but not to interact. It wasn't what he would really want, but it was absolutely preferable to staying where he was. *Death* was better than that and more moral, but somehow he didn't want to die. Not now. Not yet.

The fact remained, though, that he was carrying a drug that allowed evil people to poison other people, to steal their very minds and souls, and he simply could not continue to be a part of that. He felt bad about what he'd already carried for them, but to continue to serve them once he felt confident enough to get away was unthinkable. And, too, his careful studies of Liliblod had revealed something of the nature and nastiness of its inhabitants, and he knew that when someone got a whim or when he was older or perhaps got sick or hurt, those who now worked him would not hesitate to feed him to those damned tree-dwelling monstrosities.

He'd seen them clearly only once, although he knew their sounds and scents and knew that they were always there, high up above, a thought that also made escape seem attractive. Accompanied by one of his handlers, he had carried in a huge load of what smelled like monstrous chocolate bars. Part of the payoff, he understood, for the creatures keeping the back trails used by the couriers open to the drug runners and no one else. And down they'd come, from the very tops of the trees, where their vast ropelike webs created almost a roof over the hex. Huge spiderlike creatures the size of a ten-year-old child, with eight hairy legs that ended in small but malleable pincers and bright, shiny brown bodies topped by demonic heads with gaping mouths and hateful, bright red eyes. He and the handler left as quickly as possible, since chocolate had been known to send the Liliblodians into a frenzy of uncontrollable and often violent behavior. All female, the handler had told him. The tiny, mindless, wormlike males crawled literally into the wombs and were sealed inside, their outer skins dissolved by special juices releasing the sperm, and the remainder provided the food for the brood until they were ready to be hatched.

It was not a nice thought that so many of them, perhaps tens of thousands, were clustered up there and could drop down at any moment if the bargain suddenly seemed not to their liking. That was why they used "mules" like Lori for most of the work.

No, there would have to be an escape, and if this trail went only from Agon to Clopta, then his escape would have to happen at one of the ends of the route. He was pretty sure that there was no real escape in Liliblod.

He wished he knew what had become of the others. Although he felt no physical attraction, poor Alowi, or Julian, was still as close a friend as he had here, and without him she was in a real mess. She would never go home, but she might well kill herself, and that was the most worrisome thing of all. The Dillians were probably well out of it—he'd never really understood why they were *in* it in the first place, except that they'd once been human and were at least still a bit human, as were the others. Still, they had potential lives back in their home hex and no stake in this affair.

And then there was Mavra Chang. If they had done *this* to *him*, what had they done to her? Or was that a long-term concern? Didn't Mavra claim that she could not be killed, that anything injured or lost would regrow, that no damage was permanent to her? Sooner or later, no matter what monster they'd made of her, they'd have to take her to that Well, whatever it was. They'd have to risk it, whoever "they" might be, because the other fellow might get there ahead of her if they didn't. *Then* she would be in real trouble, but then, whoever had Chang and hadn't at least made the attempt would probably be in worse shape.

Well, there was little chance he'd ever find out how any of them had made out. It was enough to try to figure out how and where to escape.

Agon would be better geographically; it hadn't seemed overly developed for a high-technology hex, and there was a lot of rough country in the north, and it was connected, if he remembered correctly, to other hexes for vast distances. The trouble was, he wasn't ever technically in Agon; the cleverly concealed entrance to the headquarters was in Liliblod even though the whole underground complex was under Agon's soil. It wouldn't be much of a run to bypass it, but there were so many guards and so much in the way of defenses that it was a sure route to capture and disaster.

That left Clopta, which seemed almost paved over from the moment one reached the border, as overdeveloped as Agon seemed just right. But the warehouse there where the trail ended was well within the border and was in the middle of what appeared to be an industrial district. Most of the time a handler was right there, waiting, but every once in a while they missed him, and he would have to make his way several blocks along dark back alleys between warehouses and factories to the rendezvous. If they did it again, he would go. He felt as ready as he would ever be, and the alternatives seemed increasingly bleak. They wouldn't expect it; they thought he still needed that drug.

He was always surprised when he reached the border, even though he could smell a bit of Clopta as he grew near. With no time sense and no more drug craving, he never seemed to know how long he'd been on the trail or just how far along it he might be. It was daylight by the time he reached it this time, and that meant he would have to stop and wait. There were clear instructions that under no circumstances was he to enter Clopta in daylight or while there was any traffic in the immediate area.

The hex boundary remained the most dramatic feature of the Well World, even now. It appeared to his altered eyes as a thin but infinite piece of semitransparent gauze at which the endless Liliblodian forest stopped with amazing suddenness, replaced by a brightly lit but sterile-looking mass of metallic buildings. It was hard to look at them too long; sunlight would catch some window or piece of polished metal, and he would be suddenly blinded. Muffled sounds of much activity came through the barrier: sounds of machinery operating, men yelling, vehicles going this way and that, huge doors sliding open or closed—all the sounds of a manufacturing district, although what they made there he did not know.

They had built right up to the boundary, too. Space was at a premium in lands with rigidly fixed borders, and they used it well. Most likely this had always been an industrial district; it was possible that the whole border with Liliblod was this way and that all heavy industry was concentrated in a strip. If *he* had these kind of neighbors, that was what *he* would do. He certainly *hoped* that it was so. It might mean that the rest of the hex was a lot more livable and perhaps had trees and forests into which he could disappear. If no one met him, it would make sense to go right, then left, keeping to the alleyways but off the trail. That would take him into the hex and away from any sort of activity.

The trail had only ten or so meters in the open before it went into a thin alley between two tall, smelly structures. It *did* have to cross a few broader streets, some with loading docks on either side and a set of rails going down the center—he had to watch his step in order not to get a hoof caught in the gap. But the trail mainly kept to the back alleys and side streets until it reached the one warehouse where things went on after dark that were probably unknown to those who worked in the area during the day.

He hadn't seen Campos, there or anywhere else, since the first couple of runs right at the beginning. Apparently she was satisfied enough by her first visits and didn't need to see much more. It didn't matter, anyway. *Some* things of an emotional nature had not been excised, and one of those, now that the drug had no more hold, might well cause him to impale a certain person on his horn no matter what the cost to himself and any future he might have, no matter how bleak. *That* might well be worth it.

I'll bet Mavra spends at least a little bit each day regretting she didn't listen to us and kill the little turd or at least leave him to the mercies of the People.

He ate and slept most of the day, waking up occasionally but not for long and mostly to eat some more. It seemed like no time before the shadows fell and night came upon the Well World.

He went close to the boundary but didn't yet cross. He wanted all the sounds to vanish into the distance first.

Maybe this is it, he thought anxiously. *Maybe nobody will show this time.*

But somebody did. No Cloptan except someone expecting him would *ever* go through that barrier in this direction, not unless it was on one of the main roads. The spider bitches would just love a little duck.

He recognized the little man by his scent. The Cloptan was a decent sort as handlers went, not too bright and very loyal but not cruel to the mules, either. He looked like some bastard relative of Gladstone Gander, except that he wore pants.

"Ah, it's you, is it?" the man, whose name was Banam, commented, although it sounded like nothing but deep melodic rumblings to Lori. "Well, you can come along now. It's a holiday here tomorrow and everybody's taken off early, anyway. I'll just get my pushcart and follow you in as usual."

Lori was used to people speaking to him when he couldn't understand a word. In a way, he was even more cut off than a *real* horse, since even real horses could pick up a few common sounds or terms. It was the worst part of it all, an utter loneliness that came from having no way to truly communicate with anyone except, of course, the absent Campos.

There was a pronounced difference in air pressure when he penetrated the boundary and also a marked rise in humidity. He couldn't tell much about the temperature, though, except that Banam wore only a light jacket, so it probably wasn't very cold. That was another thing Lori seemed to have lost; he wasn't very aware of, or very sensitive to, temperatures of any sort. Early on, Clopta had been cold enough for him to see people's breaths, but he'd barely felt a thing.

His hooves clattered against the paved street, echoing off the close-in walls. He'd been a bit annoyed that they hadn't shoed him, since there was always the danger of a split hoof, but now he was glad of it. There wouldn't be any blacksmiths able to provide the service if he cut out.

"Your design's been a big hit with the bosses, I hear," Banam commented chattily, never knowing if he could be understood or not and really not caring all that much either way. "I watched you change over the past coupla months from a real mess into a pretty slick-lookin' animal. Heard 'em say they're gonna do it to anybody who can stand the operation or whatever it is. Ain't for everybody, of course. They'd need black magic to make *me* into somethin' like *you*, I think." He chuckled at the thought. "Only thing different'll be that horn. No horns on the others. Makes some of 'em kinda nervous, y' know. Dunno why."

The old fellow just kept chattering as they came up to the warehouse and the end of the trail. Then Banam walked to the front and pushed a series of numbers on the security lock. There was a sudden rumble, and the door slid up, allowing them to enter.

It was pitch dark inside, as always, but when the door came back down and settled with a crash, the lights came back on automatically. No sense in shining a beacon to the world that something was going on here.

They had a sort of stall for him in the back, reached through a maze of shelves, boxes, and palettes and well hidden from view even when the day shift was in. There were a couple of bales of hay there, a tub with water in it, and some thick straw on the floor. That was pretty much all he required.

Banam unhooked the cinch and let the packs drop before he went into the stall area. He fumbled inside, removed a greasy-looking cube, and put it over on top of the hay. "There's your big reward, fella. Enjoy. I gotta get help and get this up to the boss."

It was the drug, of course, and now it smelled and tasted as bad as it looked and did nothing for or to him, but he had to keep eating it just to make sure that they didn't suspect.

The one thing that seemed certain was that it would be another round trip before he could escape. Or was it? Had he been thinking the wrong way, perhaps? They almost always accompanied him back to the border but no farther. If he hugged the border and walked down quite a ways, he might well be able to escape on the way *back.* It made more sense than the other way, and the thought excited him.

If he escaped just after leaving *here,* then they wouldn't expect him at the other end for quite a while. They might even write him off as having been injured and thus made a banquet of by the Liliblodian locals. Now, *that* seemed to make real sense!

He tried hard to remember the maps. Clopta, Liliblod, and Agon were all on the coast. That meant Liliblod would be the border along this segment of the hex, going—what?—probably northeast. Southwest would mean the ocean, and that was no good, and north would most likely take him through the heart of Clopta, not a good option. In a high-tech hex it would be impossible to remain hidden forever. If he only knew how far along the border they were! It might well be *shorter* going north if they were near the point where three borders came together. Best not to take that much of a chance, though. Stick close to the border, check every once in a while, and go when it no longer smelled of spiders.

After that it would be time to stop running and start exploring until he came up against something with an appetite as bad as a Liliblodian that he couldn't outrun or impale.

No. Wait a moment. There *was* a potential destination, wasn't there? The same one they'd had since the start. That place, that break between the hexes at the equator where those who knew how might be able to enter the inside of this strange planet. If anyone got there and could get inside, he wanted to be there. It was the longest shot in the universe, but it was all he had.

If he could just survive, get up there, get to that entranceway, and wait, no matter how long it took . . .

It wasn't much, but it was better than nothing. It was somewhere to go and something to do, and it was at least a sliver, no matter how microscopic, of hope.

If not this trip, then the next. The first time they gave him an opening, he had to have the guts to take it. To get away, to get free, that was the first objective. Then, once safe, use the sun as a guide and head north all the way to the barrier, which he assumed was much like the barrier that formed the southern boundary of Erdom. Then west, toward where the sun rose on this backward-turning world. West until there was a door.

If not this trip, then the next. Or the next. Whenever it was possible. As hopeless as it all was, it was the only thing he had.

AGON

ALOWI HAD WALKED HOME from the clinic feeling nervous and uncertain about what she had done. Nearing the place where she and the Dillians were staying, essentially a huge tent struck on some deserted landfill north of the city, she began to feel light-headed, and by the time she was inside, she had the start of a serious headache. Dizzy and sick, with a throbbing head, she lay down on the pillows in the rear area of the tent and pretty much passed out.

More concerned and suspicious of everything were the Dillians, who found her out cold and decided that there was no purpose to rousing her. Some of this was to be expected from a radical injection, but as Doctor Drinh had feared, they were also quite suspicious at what Alowi had told them about the capabilities of the process. While Tony took care of some business at the port, Anne Marie put in a call to the capital.

While embassy operations on the Well World were best handled within Zone, most hexes had small offices whose function was to pass messages to and from Zone via Well Gate couriers. Reciprocity gave any race the right to use the service of any hex at all, and under diplomatic seal. It wasn't beyond being compromised, but it was effective, and any hex found compromising the system would of course lose its own rights and privacy.

Anne Marie had no intention of giving an oral report but used a recording cube of the type standardized by Zone and put it under a password that was known on the other end only to the Dillian ambassador. She dispatched the cube via messenger service on the next train to the capital, where someone alerted by her call would pick it up and stick it in the next courier pouch. She had no idea who would ultimately hear the report and no real hope that those bureaucrats could decide on whether they had to go to the bathroom, let alone anything important, but it was worth trying.

In the message she had simply summarized Alowi's experience to date and related the claims of Drinh and his reputation and voiced her suspicions with hope that all this would be relayed to the inner council committee that was in charge of the "immortals problem," as they so euphemistically put it.

At least the committee had proved honest and reliable. While it had been next to impossible to sit on the rumor that the ancient and legendary Nathan Brazil might be back, the fact that Mavra Chang might be an immortal equal to Brazil had been suppressed to a remarkable degree. The most that seemed to have leaked was that Chang was wanted because she had known Brazil and *might* prove useful in motivating the mysterious man to make a deal. Brazil, however, remained the real target for all the factions out there nervous about either his possible powers or his potential; Chang's cover story had been increasingly reinforced to the point where no one outside the council took her as more than a minor player, of no great advantage unless one had Brazil and perhaps not even then.

Now, with the readily recognizable Brazil missing for so long and the Avenues well covered, even the mild hue and cry of earlier times had faded. Most believed him a fable and the missing man simply a man, no more or less, a man who had caused stupid panic and rumors and who was now probably dead. The council was doing a nice job of covering up, but it had neither of its own objects in sight, let alone in hand. Brazil had vanished and was possibly at least neutralized as far as could be surmised from current information, and Chang had been abducted by the drug cartel and was undoubtedly a prisoner or worse by now. The fact that the drug lords had done nothing with her, though, indicated that they didn't know who and what they had, and it was feared that any attempt to find her might just tip them off to a key to potentially vast powers.

It was for this reason that they had allowed nothing to be done, since that was what they preferred as a normal course of action, anyway. Now, though, the report from Anne Marie caused a great deal of concern. If the drug lords had worked their usual tricks on Mavra Chang, she could literally look like just about *anything;* if she really was Brazil's equal, then she could not be killed and thus eventually had the potential to get free —or, worse, break under the strain and try to make her own deal with the drug lords out of desperation. If Mavra Chang no longer bore any resemblance to Mavra Chang, then the guards at the Avenues had nothing at all to go on, and they could hardly be obtrusive about barring all and sundry from those equatorial entrances without tipping the game to everyone.

If there was a chance of locating Mavra Chang, the committee knew, then it had to be taken. But patiently and with sufficient safeguards, no matter how ruthless, to keep the true value and nature of the quarry from those who might use her.

Once they decided that they *had* to move, they wanted to move yesterday, but it had to be done *right*. Still, it seemed to them that their long lag time had finally run out.

"The Dillians in Agon will almost certainly move on this if we do not," one councillor argued. "This cannot be left to amateurs. If they move, they will certainly fall into the hands of the cartel, who will be merciless in finding out why they were willing to make such a risky move. If the cartel even suspects Chang's true value, all could be lost."

"True," another agreed, "but neither can we leave them out, unless we want them disposed of."

The Dillian ambassador objected. "That is out of the question! Only if the future of the Well World and our authority were clearly at risk would we permit that! Besides, if Chang now looks nothing like she did, they may well be the only ones who could establish that a suspected being *is* Mavra Chang. Remember, *two* were taken, and we have no way of telling if we capture one just which one we have. We agree, however, that this is no job for amateurs alone. Who do we have in the region?"

"The Agonese authorities are compromised," another pointed out. "That leaves only that immigrant Leeming and the renegade Dahir in the area, both trying to find Brazil. The Leeming has proved reliable and has some feel for this sort of work—"

"But he lost Brazil!" the first councillor pointed out. "He enjoys the work but clearly isn't all that competent at it!"

"And we are, I suppose?" the Dillian retorted. "We've managed to lose *both* of the immortals while we engaged in endless debate and delay. Still, I agree that a native, one of us who is beyond reproach, must be in charge. Preferably someone who knows the area and has familiarity with the drug cartel. Any candidates?"

The problem was fed to the Zone computers, and after a process of elimination, one name, and only one, stood out.

"Now the only trick is to prepare a cover story for going after Chang," the Dillian ambassador said, nodding. "That and convincing the Agonese government to give him full authority in this matter without their corrupt elements tipping off the cartel."

"That," said another, "will be far easier than what we are asking *this* fellow to do!"

Anne Marie, however, had finally galvanized the council into action. The long wait was about to end.

For their part, the Dillians, knowing nothing of this, waited to see what the disreputable clinic might have done to poor Alowi.

The answer, at least from their point of view, seemed to be nothing more than what had been claimed. Alowi seemed more content with herself and more confident and no longer seemed troubled by runaway inner drives.

No one, of course, was more nervous about this than Alowi herself. Becoming a guinea pig possibly at the hands of one's enemy was an act of desperation but reasoned action nonetheless.

At first she simply felt, well, *normal,* and for a while that was enough. Those inner urges, those bouts of losing control, of nearly sick cravings, seemed to vanish while leaving little in their place. This was not, of course, normal to an Erdomese, but it seemed normal in almost any other context. She felt, well, much like Tony and Anne Marie seemed to feel, or Mavra. She was simply herself, but in complete control, not *needing* anything just to remain sane. Free.

Free to study, free to learn, free of any thought of returning to Erdom. Yet when she looked at herself in the mirror, she liked what she saw. If anything, she liked it more than she had, felt more comfortable about the person who stared back at her. Although those urges and emotions had at times been overwhelming and omnipresent for what had seemed forever, it now was difficult, even impossible, to remember what that had felt like. She felt every bit a female, no less than before; certainly she didn't feel sexless or frigid or an "it." And yet, well, those things she'd gathered around or made or picked up in the markets that were so obviously *phallic* now seemed pretty silly. She wasn't quite sure just what sort of change other than allowing her independence the doctors had wrought, but if this was the extent of it, well, it was something she could surely live with and might have died without.

Tony came back from the city with what she hoped was an answer to Anne Marie's report of only a few days before. Anne Marie, at least, was excited. "This is the first time they *ever* sent a reply to one of our reports! And so *quickly,* too! Perhaps they've found something out! Play it!"

Tony removed the cube and pressed her thumb firmly on the one side that had an inlaid red surface. The cube took a few cells of skin, compared them with the genetic code it carried, seemed satisfied, then said in a voice that came through as a soft and pleasant woman's voice, "Please do not play the rest of this inside your home. Take it to an open area well away from any others, particularly natives, and repeat the process. The cube contains a small zonal scrambling device that will cover an area about three meters square, so be close to it. The message will play only once, erasing itself as it plays, so pay close attention. When done, burn the cube in any open fire. The message will now pause until you take these precautions, and you will not hear this preamble again."

"My goodness!" Anne Marie exclaimed. "Sounds rather *serious,* doesn't it?"

"It certainly sounds as if *something,* at least, is going to happen," Tony agreed. "Let's take the precautions and go down to the jetty and see what they have to say." She paused a moment and had a puzzled look. "I wonder why that many precautions. Surely they do not think that even this tent is bugged—could they? I mean, who would bug *us?*"

"Someone who is certainly near death from boredom," Anne Marie responded. "Still, let's do this cloak and dagger business by the rules, dear."

They all left the tent and went down perhaps two hundred meters to the jetty, where the gentle ocean water, softened by far-off undersea reefs, lapped against the sides. It was a nice, bright day, warmer than usual and with a gentle wind. There was nobody else around close enough to observe them. The three gathered close, and Tony took out the cube and pressed again on the red area.

"This is Ambassador Aliva speaking for the Special Committee," said the female voice in Dillian, which the two centauresses understood directly and made an extra authenticity check possible as well. "We have evaluated our report on this clinic and its specialists, which coincides with intelligence from other sources, and we believe that you have stumbled on the key to the disappearances and also to why action is now mandated. As a result, we have arranged for an Agonite whose character is beyond question and who has both knowledge and authority in combating this criminal syndicate to assume command of a special unit that will follow up this lead.

"His name is Janwah Kurdon, and he is an officer in the Agonese Secret Police. Please do not be put off by this; Kurdon has been in something like an exile since mounting a campaign against the syndicate and being blocked by corrupt higher-ups. We have arranged for his restoration of rank and position, and it is understood that any Agonite official who gets in the way of the special unit will be placed under suspicion by the Zone Council of aiding and abetting interhex criminal activities. It is very likely that they will do their best to stay out of your way to avoid even the slightest hint of corruption, but it is inevitable that they will use their own people to try to anticipate your actions and report them to the criminal gang. Agon itself has become too industrialized to be self-sufficient in food; it is also clearly understood that anything less than government cooperation could mean a blockade and embargo. We have already notified the government of this and have heard the protests, but we have the votes here on our side."

"Goodness!" Anne Marie said. "They can certainly knock heads if they decide they want to!"

"You may, if you wish, become part of this special unit, but understand that the personal danger is very great, that this cartel is totally ruthless, and that while we can act against officials and the nation if need be, we cannot protect you individually. Also, you must accept Agent Kurdon's complete authority and act only under his orders. Otherwise, you will have to leave the country and return home or go elsewhere. You may also not travel to Liliblod or Clopta without being under the unit's authority; the former does not consider what the gang does a criminal act and operates under a different and not altogether scrutable logic, while the latter is at least as corrupt as the government of Agon and far less competent. As we cannot protect you and as you must suspect Kurdon is less than excited about being saddled with those he considers both aliens and amateurs, nothing will reflect on you if you choose not to continue, and you will be informed of any results. However, if you *do* accept the terms, complete what business you might have yet to do and meet the special unit in Subar, the northern city where you first made contact with us, in precisely four days. Go to the Central Prefecture there and simply ask for Agent Kurdon. He will then brief you on what will be happening next.

"One more thing," the message concluded. "Do not return to that clinic or contact the staff there again even if something is scheduled or they call and ask to see any of you. Make any excuse, but do not go. Operations are already under way as regards them that you might only jeopardize or, worse, alert the staff about. For the record, the cover story is that we believe genetic reengineering is being employed to possibly replace or enslave existing officials or whole populations and we are going after the proof of that. Under *no* circumstances is anyone, least of all the gang, to suspect that we are after more than that. We have also planted information that your two missing comrades have vital information for the council and that if they are located, in *any* form, and the reengineering stopped, we will not act further against the organization. We can only hope that this will buy them their lives, or at least enough time to locate them.

"May the blessings of all the gods be with you in this endeavor. This message is at an end. Please burn this cube and do not attempt a replay.

The message in it is already gone, but another attempt will produce nasty consequences. Farewell."

"I'm not sure I liked the last of that," Tony commented. "It really sounded like a rather formal kiss-off. Like she never really expected to hear from us again."

"Well, we will just have to surprise her, won't we, dear?" Anne Marie responded, then looked over at Alowi. "Well! Why so glum? This is what you wanted, isn't it?"

Alowi nodded, but slowly and hesitantly. This *was* what she'd wanted all along, of course. So why did she feel so little like following up on it?

Lori, after all, had saved her life at the start of all this and for a very long time had been her only friend.

"I am glad something is happening, of course," she answered lamely, "but, well, I am just concerned. Concerned about what we might find, where this is all leading. I will be all right."

But it was more than that. After the Dillians began their preparations to shut down their trade operation, leaving her to begin the packing-up process, she tried to put her finger on it. She really did know at least a part of her problem, and it was tough trying to get around that. Lori wasn't just a friend, he was her *husband,* and the last thing she wanted right now was a husband, now or ever again. Memories of long conversations, the sharing of intimacy down to her very soul with him, now seemed distant and colored with an unpleasant veneer that seemed somehow impossible to remove.

She certainly wanted Lori liberated, but their relationship couldn't be like it had been even if by some miracle he was unchanged or could be restored to his previous form. *Particularly* not in that case . . . A whole litany of things that had attracted her and turned her on to him in the past now seemed in retrospect to be the opposite. Even his personality, mannerisms, the way he interacted with her and with others seemed distant, alien at best, and in some ways downright repugnant to her.

Finding him a malformed invalid seemed at least less threatening to her, and she felt awful for thinking that thought. Even so, she felt no duty toward him, no real attraction at all.

She had been happiest right here, with Tony and Anne Marie, free to explore her own potential without any feelings of repression or any demands she didn't like. Tony and Anne Marie had remained for her sake, and she loved them for it, and while she knew deep down that this arrangement could never be permanent, she didn't want it to end.

One had to have been on both sides of the sexual boundary to know just how defining the roles were, how they shaped and misshaped people. Seen from Alowi's perspective, she hated, despised Julian Beard.

He'd been swaggering, loutish, and self-centered to a fault, committed to his own goals but seeing no commitment toward others—it was no wonder he couldn't stay married to anybody. Yet she saw the essence of all that was wrong in him in just about every male she'd met or could think of, regardless of race. It was almost as if every quality she valued seemed lacking in every male yet present in the vast majority of females. Lori—Lori by the end had been no more a former woman than Alowi had been a former man. Instead he'd become more and more like . . . Julian Beard.

Here, during this period, she'd also discovered something else. She liked herself now. First she had struggled to expunge all that was Julian from inside her, then she'd become someone else, a creature with no ego or sense of self-worth unless it was defined by what she could do for Lori. That creature, too, was gone, and for the first time she was an individual again with the qualities and capabilities she desired. She didn't want to be anyone else. Here the heavy weights placed upon her by her past and by the Well World and Erdomese culture and biology had been lifted, revealing a real person. Now it seemed as if some of that weight was being forced back upon her, and there was nobody else who could understand her problem.

It had to be done, of course, but it seemed as if freeing Lori was the worst thing that could happen to her.

If everyone elsewhere noted that the Dillians were genetic twins, it was harder for them to tell one Agonite from another. That meant that the creature who showed up at the police station in Subar where they'd been instructed to check in looked very much like all the other natives, except that he wore a yellow sleeveless shirt and a pair of baggy denimlike trousers. It was clear from the reaction of the police in the station, though, that he was far more important than he looked.

"My name is Chief Inspector Janwah Kurdon," the newcomer told them, "of internal security."

"We are—" Anne Marie started, but the newcomer waved her off.

"I know who you are. I know who all three of you are and how you came to be here. What I *don't* know is why you are here in Agon or still anywhere in this region. After all this time, I'd think that you would have grown weary and be on your way home by now."

Anne Marie gestured toward a sullen Alowi. "She has lost her husband. In her culture that is about as close to being killed as you can get. Her honor demands that she find him or, for her, life would not be worth living. Since she's alone and friendless and because we don't like being pushed around and, yes, betrayed ourselves, we've remained with her."

Alowi said nothing. She didn't want to disillusion the Dillians or make them feel as if they'd wasted their time for nothing, and frankly, she'd taken an instant dislike to this chunky little reptile.

The secret policeman sighed. "So what did you think you could do?"

"Us? Probably not much. Not without a great deal of help, anyway. On the other hand, we must do *something*. Even if we fail, we *can't* simply let this go. Surely you understand that."

"I understand that you were stuck in a strange country with no resources and you actually thought you could find and take on one of the most powerful criminal organizations in the history of the Well World," Kurdon replied. "Amateurs," he sighed. "You realize, I hope, that these people will kill at the drop of a leaf and that they can do things far worse than death."

"We more or less assumed that, yes," Tony put in. "We are not unfamiliar with such groups. They exist on our original native world as well."

Kurdon glanced around. "Come. We will walk a bit together. It is a nice afternoon for the highlands."

They walked from the police station, one of the few buildings that was large enough for the Dillians to comfortably enter, and out into the street, following the inspector. For a while he said little except to comment on the nice weather and give a little inconsequential local history, but eventually they reached a large public park. Some locals were there playing various games or sitting around, but much of the area was empty in the predinner hour and the inspector was able to find a large area without trees or nearby people.

"I prefer to discuss other things in settings like this," he told them. "Of course, we can still be spied upon, but it is much more difficult to do so without being obvious. Subar is a nice peaceful city, but it is also one of our most corrupt." He reached into his pocket and brought out a small conical device that seemed to have no features except a red tip, which he pushed. "This will keep anyone from overhearing us by electronic means. Not totally foolproof but more than adequate here, as I know from experience."

"I take it that we are in the midst of our enemies," Tony said nervously.

"You are in their hometown, as it were, at least the homegrown sort. They live here, work here, do many good and charitable works, and launder their cut of the illegal money through the banks here, which are among the richest and most successful in the nation. They used to be very good at what they do, but in recent months they have become even more efficient and creative. We believe that it is because another of your origin species has affiliated with them. Do you know the name of Campos?"

Both Dillians nodded in unison. "Mavra Chang spoke of him. A vicious man, she said. Is *that* what this is about?"

"Man? Interesting . . ." The security man thought for a moment. "As to the other—yes, I believe that it is exactly what all this is about. In fact, it explains much that was puzzling, particularly why *both* of your friends were kidnapped. Chang we could understand—there are reasons I believe you might be aware of why such an organization might like to get hold of her, although it seems they don't know just who or what they've got or they'd have done something with her by now. It was the Erdomese that puzzled us. Now it becomes much clearer. Not politics, not power in the sense that we'd originally thought. Revenge. Pure revenge. How typical of that type. Reassuring in a way, too."

"How's that?"

"We have no particular drug problem here. Can you guess why that might be?"

Tony saw his point at once. "Because they are protected here. The government and the cartel have an agreement."

Kurdon nodded. "Exactly. It is not official and is never mentioned, but it exists. Not everyone is involved, of course, but they have clever ways of getting around just about anything. Once, a year or so ago, I came very close to breaking some of the big shots involved in it. Their laboratories and most of their operation are run out of a vast headquarters complex not very far from here, along the border with Liliblod. I had everything ready to go and spread out for my superiors to approve. We would have gone in with an army team and cleaned them out. Instead, I found my plans and papers confiscated, my informants met quick and untimely deaths or simply vanished, and I was made division chief of the coastal watch unit in the southeastern city of Magoor. Nobody said I'd done a poor job or that I wasn't right; technically the new job was a promotion in pay and authority—but a shift away from all my previous investigations and contacts. I wasn't stupid, and I knew the choice was to accept or follow my informants. I am still a young man."

"Our message indicated as much," Anne Marie told him. "But I must say it doesn't sound very encouraging."

"On the contrary. A few days ago I was called to the capital and told to stand by. Much of my original paperwork mysteriously reappeared. Then, yesterday, I was promoted to chief inspector, given a great deal of power and authority, briefed on your situation, and told to form a special unit and proceed here. Some very important government ministers whose honor has not been for sale have been involved in the watch for these two alleged immortals that the council at Zone has been most concerned about. They lost not one but both of them. Then word comes that two creatures were taken off a courier boat by agents of the cartel just off the northwest coast, and the remainder of the party fits the description of three members traveling with the Chang woman. The three of you are rather difficult to mistake in this region. Everyone from the ministers to the council was initially panicked that Chang had fallen into the hands of the best organized criminal organization on the Well World. Then, for months—nothing. The only logical conclusion was that the ones who had Chang had no idea who or what they had and for some reason hadn't even bothered to interrogate them in the manner that they have of extracting your closest secrets. Why? The bottom line was that they felt any search or heavy pressure would simply alert the still-ignorant criminals of the value of their captive. Now we know why. A revenge kidnapping probably arranged directly by Campos without any of the higher-ups even being aware of it."

"But surely someone would know!" Tony exclaimed. "Or at least notice!"

"Not necessarily. You have no idea of the range and scope of their operations. It probably seemed quite routine for the people at the headquarters, and it is not healthy to ask questions. Now, I ask you: If you were Campos, bent on revenge and now having the means, and you had seen or heard of what services these so-called physicians could and probably routinely perform for the gang, what would *you* do? Campos was once of the same race as your birth race. You tell me."

"Turn them into monsters. Unrecognizable, tortured, probably addicted," Tony said flatly.

"Why not just torture them to death? Wouldn't that satisfy?"

"I do not know this Campos, but I know his type," Tony told the agent. "He would not want to just kill them, even painfully. If he had the means, he'd want to see them in a continual torture, to spread his sadistic revenge out over a very long time. They could be killed any time, but until then . . . no. He would want to *enjoy* it."

"I thought as much," Kurdon said, nodding. "It is not common here, thank heavens, but it does occur. That is another reason why Campos got away with it so far. It is *not* a common attitude in Agon or Clopta; both races are far more pragmatic. They torture for information, kill when someone is in the way or no longer useful, but this sort of prolonged torture for personal gratification isn't something they would think of doing. Risky and wasteful. We have found that your doctor friends were mostly using such creatures for experimentation and eventually doing away with them but that they did some pragmatic work as well, primarily in converting creatures into couriers. I wondered why *two* women were targeted, since clearly only one was of interest to them if they suspected her true nature, and now you have told me that what I suspected is true. It is something I did *not* bother to suggest to those who are suddenly my friends."

"Couriers?" Tony repeated. "Why turn people into couriers? Couldn't anybody do that?"

"Not this type. They are designed—reengineered as couriers, dedicated to that specific task, while being physically limited from doing much else. Essentially pack animals smart enough to be autonomous yet limited enough that they had nowhere else to go and nothing else they could do."

"You know what they've been doing, then!" Anne Marie said excitedly.

"We do now. Thanks to you, we were able to wage a clandestine operation in their clinic and tap into their computer banks. Very difficult to break their codes, but Zone has capabilities beyond anything else on the Well World. We found the entire genetic codes of many individuals from a number of races in there, but we found only one male Erdomese and one female Glathrielian in the memory banks. It would take a very long time, however, to match up precisely the original and the changed structure and get a true picture of just what they became. The work is extremely advanced and, I must say, extremely frightening. Frightening enough that this alone has outweighed any loyalty to, and even much of the fear of, the organization in Agon by high officials. This explains my free hand."

"What do you propose to do?" Anne Marie asked him.

"I have a clear directive. This Chang is to be found, arrested, and brought to Zone no matter what her shape or form or condition. I may use whatever resources I require to get this done, step on any toes, go through any barriers. When I suggested that this might require going straight through the cartel's headquarters, they did not even flinch. To not do it ourselves would at this point almost certainly mean it being done in spite of us, with Agon the object of an invading army of other races. There is already a council military man in the south setting up this possibility. I find myself, therefore, with a very strong hand. Our objectives are not quite the same. If we can recover both, well and good, but it should be understood that Chang is my objective."

"Our first objective is to recover Lori for this poor dear's sake. We've been through a lot together already," Anne Marie told him. "As for Mavra, well, I don't see any other choice for us or for her. She is quite a capable individual, and if she must deal with the council, so be it."

"Agreed. Most pragmatic and satisfactory, actually. You should be aware, though, that they are both unlikely to be anything like you remember them, and it is entirely unclear whether anything can be done for them."

Anne Marie sighed and looked at Alowi, who seemed still curiously ambivalent about all this, then turned back to Kurdon.

"Somehow I do not think that will stop Mavra Chang," she told the agent. "Not if half her own stories are true. But . . ." She decided not to finish now. There was no sense in panicking Alowi, at least not yet.

"When do you move?" Tony asked Kurdon.

"In a few days. I want more information from the local agents here before I begin. I do not underestimate this bunch."

"What about going directly for Campos?" Tony asked him. "I cannot imagine such a type not having the objects of revenge close by so he could lord it over them."

"Campos is a Cloptan. Out of my jurisdiction. If we turn in a report linking Campos and the kidnapping, it will be out of our hands immediately. Besides, there are dangers to the direct approach. The quarry could go underground in its own home territory or even be killed in such an attempt, in which case we might never find those we really seek. Or our objectives could be destroyed in a final act of vengeance before we can reach them. Remember, too, that they could be literally *anywhere,* just as long as Campos can get to them. No, when I move on Cloptans on Cloptan soil, I want it to be *my* party, fast and unexpected, but with the full authority of the council. At the moment I have no idea where Campos even *is,* except somewhere in the port city of Buckgrud, a high-tech metropolis with a population of more than a million. Think of this as well: Can you *honestly* tell one Agonese from another aside from size, weight, and clothing? Honestly, now."

"Uh, um, not without great difficulty, I admit," Anne Marie managed.

"So how do you expect to directly penetrate a criminal organization and pick out the one correct Cloptan from the masses? You see? In the end we will require Cloptan help, but that will have to be very carefully done. I don't believe that they are even as honest as we are, and that is not going very far. I would prefer we deal with the Cloptans *after* we strike here. Trust me on this. This is my territory and my profession. It will be difficult enough having to somewhat involve Liliblod. Nobody can really deal with them, and they will not like this at all."

"It seemed a nice, quiet, peaceful place when we went through," Anne Marie noted. "Yet we keep getting horrid warnings about it."

"Yes. By the terms of their agreements, the roads are kept absolutely safe for travel. They are not without their own odd vices, and so some commerce is permitted as a concession to their own needs. But they are not— *rational*—in the sense that we are here. They have a rather egocentric view of the universe and are quite unpredictable beyond certain bounds. The organization pays them well for protection in a sort of currency that they could not legally acquire, and they will not like to see that cut off."

"Another corrupt government?" Tony sighed.

"You misunderstand. The Liliblodians believe that all other races were put here as their prey. By—consuming—others or, more accurately, the fluids of others, they believe they gather in inferior souls and all the strengths of the prey. The cartel pays them in two ways. It provides live prey for them of the type they love—alien flesh, as it were—and the one other substance which is their own drug weakness."

"Disgusting," Anne Marie commented. "Eating live beings for *pleasure* . . ."

"Yes, it is almost as bad as their own drug of choice. You cannot imagine anything more bizarre than seeing a mass of Liliblodians literally rolling in a chocolate stupor . . ."

DLUBINE

THE MASTER COMPUTER THAT was the heart of the entire planet called the Well World was just a machine; its powers were far too vast to have ever trusted making it self-aware in the sense that it could act outside its makers' predetermined instructions. And while it was true that machines had infinite patience, they could also have very little if something required was not getting done. Now, as the Kraang continued its assaults and made tiny slivers of inroads into the system, it calculated that the time to solve this problem was no longer inconsequential. In that sense the Well could be said to have become impatient with the progress of events, and when the Well wanted something, it tended to be less than subtle about it.

To summon the two Watchers to see to repairs, it had sent huge meteors crashing into the planet where the Watchers were living. Extricating Mavra Chang so that she had any reasonable chance of success appeared to be very difficult and would require a great deal of subtlety and patience. Going after Nathan Brazil, on the other hand, would not. The fact that Brazil had willingly taken himself out of worldly care was to the Well entirely irrelevant.

Nathan Brazil had been on the Well World for over eleven months, having come in with Tony and Anne Marie. It had been almost seven months since Theresa "Terry" Perez had come through on her own, following Mavra, Lori, Gus, and Juan Campos by a mere hour or so and quickly coming under the influence of the bizarre Glathrielian Way that the race that shared common ancestry with Terry's had followed. Prepared by the Glathrielians, she had attached herself to Brazil within only a week, and they had been inseparable since. For four months they had been deliberately held up, stalled, far from the goal of the Well Avenue, and then for two weeks they had broken free and escaped across the sea, been reunited with Gus, and then lost him again as they crashed on an undersea reef in a storm.

But on their tiny tropical volcanic island in the middle of a fairy-tale sea, Nathan Brazil and Terry had no concept of the passage of time or any cares or thoughts beyond sheer childish fun. The tropical rain forest on the windward side of the island provided enough wild fruits and vegetables to feed them, and the frequent but brief storms always provided a supply of fresh water. Brazil had opened himself to the Glathrielian Way but not to the elders' master plan of co-opting him as he entered the Well. There he had remained, happy and carefree, unaware of that nonhuman part of him, that deep alien nature that had thwarted the elders' control.

The tropical sun had browned him almost as dark as Terry's natural color, and his hair and beard were long and unkempt, giving him almost a wild man's appearance. His bare feet were hard and callused, toughened from months of volcanic rock and soil; the day-to-day life of climbing for treetop delicacies and over the craggy rocks had bulked out his muscles.

Terry had not been as active of late, for she'd developed a large, hard belly and some considerable fat and felt unbalanced and odd, but she accepted it as the way things were. Part of the Glathrielian Way was acceptance of whatever was and dealing with it as best one could.

This proved difficult suddenly, though, when they were awakened one morning just at dawn by a series of severe tremors. The ground shook, and trees swayed, and rocks fell from the high mountain. This went on for a day or more, and suddenly a huge piece of the mountain about halfway up the side seemed to collapse, opening a gaping wound from which belched forth steam and black ash. Then beginning what seemed a wondrous light show, a volcanic fountain played against the sky. But the earthquakes continued in increasing frequency and intensity, and from the masses of grainy rock laid down by the fountain there came puffs and plumes of smoke and ash that set part of the forest on fire.

They made their way around to the beach on the opposite side of the mountain from the eruption, having to stop or risk falling down with each tremor. Something inside them knew that they had to leave this place, and quickly.

But leave for where? And how? There was nothing on all sides but the water.

There were other islands, of course, some of which could be seen across the expanse of sea, but they were not as close as they appeared. None would be a problem to reach with a boat or a raft, but they had nothing but themselves. An inner sense of urgency told them that there was little time to consider any alternatives. Reluctantly, they entered the water and made their way out past the reefs, Brazil using his strength to support Terry and keep her afloat.

They made it to perhaps a kilometer from the beach and found themselves suddenly carried along on a warm current, able to pretty much just float and let the water do the work, which was more than welcome. The current carried them at a steady pace away from the erupting island and toward the calmer ones beyond.

Then a sudden, tremendous explosion hit them like something solid, deafening them both, and they could see the onrushing wall of water from where the island, now a vast and dark mushroom-shaped cloud, had been, a huge tidal wave coming straight for them. It was taller than the tallest trees and with a roar that sounded like thousands of caged beasts roaring at once, and they stopped swimming and watched it come, knowing it was death.

When it struck, their world became all water and whirling forces and then oblivion.

The Well had issued its wake-up call to Nathan Brazil.

The island exploding, the rushing wall of water, then . . . What?

She awoke as if from some strange dream, much of which had been very nice yet only dimly remembered, like some great childhood treat now far in the past and unrecoverable.

But watch that last step, she thought. *It's a dilly.*

She sat up painfully, groaning and stretching. She felt as if she'd been beaten to a pulp by some gigantic fist, but just as everything seemed bruised, nothing seemed broken.

The beach was warm and wet. It was made of yellow sand, the kind built up from the discards of coral reefs over thousands upon thousands of years, but it was soft and somewhat comfortable.

She shook her head, trying to clear it, trying to think. She remembered a tremendous bang and a big wave but nothing afterward.

And nothing before.

It was as if she'd just suddenly come into existence here on this beach. A big bang and here she was.

It was quite dark, but out in the water she could see a million lights underneath the gentle waves, burning with a multitude of colors and shapes and patterns that she knew couldn't be anything from nature, although she didn't know how she knew. And on the water, too, in the distance, things seemed to float, lights up upon the water rather than deep below it.

Boats, she understood at once, although again she had no idea where this information was coming from.

I've lost my memory, she realized. *Something, some accident or shipwreck or something like that caused me to lose my memory.* She had no idea who, or where, or even what she was.

She ran her hands over her body in the dark. It was a woman's body. It wasn't that this was wrong so much as basic information about herself that she had had no sense of before. Somehow, she hadn't seen herself as a woman, and there was a sense of wrongness about it somewhere deep inside her.

She knew so many things! There were all sorts of facts and behaviors and other pieces of information swirling around in her head, yet about herself she had no information at all. No past, no memories of actually being anywhere, doing anything, interacting with anything or anybody at all. *I am a woman* became the first, and so far only, definition of herself as an individual.

It seemed to her that there had been Another somewhere, somebody very important. A girl . . . Another girl? That didn't seem right. But who and what?

She cast about with her mind, never even considering speech, but there was no response from the immediate area. She was alone on the beach, without memory, without anything at all, in a place she couldn't remember for reasons that were a total mystery.

Perhaps . . . Perhaps out there, among the floating lights? She cast a mental net and caught far more than she expected. Thoughts . . . *Lots* of thoughts from what seemed to be lots of different creatures. Their words, their very sounds would mean nothing to her—she knew that—but thoughts were assembled from stored information into holographic concepts before they were translated as sounds, and *those* she could pick up if she concentrated.

The power came naturally to her, although something inside said that it was a new thing, something she hadn't done before, yet something she *had* done before. That didn't make sense. Nothing really did.

It seemed somehow indecent to peek into their thoughts, to see who was tired, who was bored, and who was thinking of killing the captain. Indecent but kind of fun, too. Some thoughts, though, were a lot harder to figure out than others; some of those creatures out there weren't even close to her form, and their thinking wasn't much closer, either.

She cast about for others of her own kind but found none. Wherever she was, she was more than merely unique in her own psyche; she was one of a kind.

No, that wasn't true. There were others. Something told her that. Men, women, children . . . But not here.

In the general casting about, though, she found spots where in fact not only words but complete sentences came through to her as if spoken in her native tongue—whatever that was. But it took some mental fine-tuning until she could fully understand those thoughts, kind of like tuning a radio.

Tuning a radio? Where had *that* come from? God! She sure knew a lot for somebody who couldn't remember anything except what was discovered by direct examination.

Maybe *they* knew. Maybe they were looking for her. If so, she'd better find out if it was in her best interest to want to be found.

". . . *Still getting reports from the Dlubinians that there is a great deal of damage and loss of life below. . .*"

Those underwater lights. There were *people* of some kind who lived down there! If that explosion that seemed to start her existence wasn't just some metaphysical memory, then . . . Oh, God!

". . . *No previous indication of volcanic activity in the area in any recent period, and it's monitored as closely as you can in a semitech hex . . .*"

Some of that made sense, some of it didn't. A volcano—*that* would account for the explosion and the big rush of water that had followed. If she were anywhere in that area, she would have been hit with tremendous shock. That had to be it. But it didn't explain anything else.

She listened for quite some time, gathering details of what had happened but clearing up her own personal mystery not one bit. Had she been on a boat, or on an island, or what? Not alone, surely. Not out here in this strange and alien place. But if not alone, then with who? How? And why?

The aches and pains made it impossible to just sit there. She began massaging the stiffness and found herself somehow mentally surveying her physical condition. Bruises, twists, all that, but nothing serious. As each region was surveyed, she dampened down the pain there and went on. Only one area stymied her, the area around her abdomen. It seemed odd, at once detached and yet not detached, but certainly *different*. Well, it wasn't anything she could figure out now. She was aware that she was using, almost matter-of-factly, powers that were extremely unusual, powers that even she hadn't realized were there. But she thought nothing about using them.

She felt a strong urge to pee and then find something to eat and drink, if she didn't have to wander too far in the darkness. She certainly hoped that there was some sort of food and water on the island; otherwise a lot of choices would be made for her right off.

Her body felt clumsy, unfamiliar, and it took some getting used to before she felt confident enough to really try much. She wished it were light; there was nothing but darkness beyond the beach and no way of telling what might be waiting for her there.

Almost at once, unbidden by any conscious thought, the darkness was replaced by endless colors, all soft pastels with occasional flashes of brightness, and without a lot of difficulty she began to make out which were trees, which bushes or flowers. She intuitively understood that other colors represented living things great and small. It seemed magical, a counterpoint to the great lights beneath the waves in back of her, but after a while she realized it didn't help. This new form of vision didn't show rocks or fallen dead timber or other hazards. Best to stay out of the jungle until she knew it better and was more comfortable with the way her body moved.

Instead of going inland, she walked along the beach, not quite sure what, if anything, she was looking for, but the terrain was at least manageable by the light of the spectacularly bright starry sky. Here and there were great rocks—perhaps spewed by volcanoes, perhaps eaten away by the sea—and all sorts of wood and shells and coral washed up and deposited on the sandy shore. Walking closer, she thought she heard something, a gurgling sound, almost drowned out by the sound of nearby breakers. In a couple of minutes she found it—a tiny spring coming out of the rocks and jungle, cutting its way through the sand, and flowing into the great sea beyond. She got down on her knees, cupped her hands, and brought some to her lips. It was fresh! At least she would not die of thirst! It was lukewarm, but she splashed some on her face to wash away the last of the cobwebs that seemed to be lurking in her mind.

She drank her fill and got up unsteadily and went on down the beach, feeling a little better. After a few minutes more the beach ended, tapering to a stop around a fair-sized cove. There was a large rectangular box where the last of the sand vanished, clearly there to be accessible by land or sea, and she went to it. It was the first artificial thing she could remember ever seeing. For a moment she hesitated to get close to it, let alone touch it. When everything was an unknown, then everything was a potential threat, if not directly then because of her own ignorance of the world around her. It was such an odd feeling to have a lot of facts in her head but not be able to relate them to anything until she had some logical reason to do so.

She realized on at least one level that this was the next step in defining herself. She'd exercised caution and stayed out of the forest not out of fear but for very practical reasons. She *was* afraid of this box, though, just as she was afraid of the boats out there and the creatures on them. Now she had to decide if she was going to let that fear rule her and hide out from everything or if she had the guts to explore and discover new things. That really wasn't a choice; she did not like being alone and without any memories in a place she had no knowledge of.

Cautiously, she approached the box until she stood right next to it, examining it as much as she could in the starlight. It seemed featureless, colored some kind of bright yellow except for a bunch of marks in a dark shade etched into the front of it. Those marks made sense to somebody —what was it? Writing. Yes, writing. But they might as well have been just marks to her.

She reached out hesitantly and touched it, then immediately pulled away as if it were some burning hot fire. Nothing happened. Emboldened, she ran her hands over it and around it and found in the top a series of indentations with small marks inside each one. Touching one didn't seem to do anything, so she ran her finger along each in turn.

There was a sudden, terrifying *woosh!* from the box that so startled her, she fell over backward, then scrambled away on hands and knees, staring.

The box lid rose up as if being opened by a giant hand until it was a bit more than straight up; pulses of light began emanating from it, aimed toward the sea. As suddenly as it started, the flashing stopped and the light burned steadily. After perhaps a quarter of an hour of staring, waiting for some horror to climb out, she finally felt bold enough to go back carefully and see what she'd done. Curiosity was outweighing fear; if that light or whatever it was kept going, somebody would see it and come anyway, so she might as well check it out before they did.

The box was a bit more than a meter high and deep and perhaps two meters long. Conscious for the first time that she wasn't very tall, she stood on tiptoe and peered in.

It was full of more boxes.

Big boxes, little boxes, square boxes, long thin boxes—boxes and boxes. She wondered if she could pull herself up and stand inside and whether it was a good idea to do so. That lid might well come back down . . .

The inside of the lid itself was a long, very shiny surface with a bar of bright glittering lights along the top and both sides. The light was irritating, but that shiny surface inside was very, very tempting. Angled just enough that it showed no reflection of her head at ground level, it would certainly do so if she were at or near its height.

She looked back out at where the beacon was shining and scanned the area. Lots of thoughts out there, as before, but no signs that anybody had yet seen, let alone was coming toward, this new beacon. Not yet.

She *had* to risk it. She just *had* to. She tried various ways of pulling herself up and into the box, but while she'd get close, she just couldn't seem to manage it. After a few minutes of frustration she remembered the driftwood nearby and went and carried some thick loglike pieces over to the box and stacked them one at a time. She was winded after a while, but she managed to build herself enough of an unsteady pile to get high enough to pull herself the rest of the way into the box.

Standing on the smaller boxes in the center of the big one, she could see herself from the thighs up in the smooth mirror of the lid's interior surface.

Staring back at her was the unfamiliar face of a very young woman, perhaps no more than midteens, with big brown eyes and finely wrought, attractive features, the hair thick and black and curly, making a frame around her face. The face did show definite chubbiness, although it did not detract from her overall pleasing looks. The weight also showed in large fatty breasts and in a fat ass and thighs, and there was a fair bulge of a tummy centered on the navel that didn't seem as natural-looking as the rest of her and was clearly the cause for her feeling ungainly when she walked. She stared and stared at the image in total fascination as it was illuminated by the beacon lights around the lid.

It was the face and body of a complete stranger.

And yet it was *her* face, *her* body without a doubt.

Who are you, girl? she wondered. *And how long will it be before I am no longer surprised to see you staring back at me?*

Reluctantly she tore herself away from the image and concentrated on the boxes. Most used the same system—one put a finger in some indentations one at a time in a line, and it hissed and opened. Clearly the seals weren't designed as locks but rather to keep them from being opened and unsealed by accident, waiting until somebody needed them.

Some of the stuff inside the boxes was weird, some of it was bizarre, and some of it was downright disgusting. However, one box contained what smelled like cake, and in fact, it *tasted* like plain yellow cake; another held hard biscuits, and yet another had something that looked like a miniature loaf of baked bread but turned out to have the taste and consistency of soda crackers. There was also, in one larger container over in the corner, a deep box that contained a liquid—one of the terms flying around in the back of her head leapt out at her: "beer." After the cakes and biscuits and crackers, she drank a fair amount of it.

When she finished, she was feeling a little light-headed and had to pee again, and she realized she had to get out. Piling up boxes got her to the top, but turning around and getting down to the logs and from there to the sand proved challenging.

She slipped and fell back, landing on her rear in the sand, but she wasn't hurt and the whole thing seemed somehow very funny. She tried to get up, but her body responded even more awkwardly than usual, and she finally was forced to crawl on hands and knees. She finally made it perhaps twenty or thirty meters away, back onto the beach but up near the rocks and the start of the jungle. It was all she could manage, and she picked a spot that seemed comfortable. She sank onto the sand and lay there, awake for quite a while but not thinking of anything at all except a vision reflected in a mirror by a glittering of light, of a face and body that said, *You don't know me, but I'm you.*

And, for a little while, until sleep took her, it didn't make any difference.

It had been a typical Dlubine night; clear one minute, fast-moving thunderstorms the next. In between the brief bursts of rain, fog and mist lay in patches all over the open sea, some natural, some the result of activity below the waves, lay where the people of the hex lived. For most of the evening visibility to the west had been obscured by fog, but now it was lifting, dissipating as the first signs of false dawn came upon the ocean. A lookout on the patrol corvette *Swiftwind Thunderer* spotted a flashing light through the thin mist and called it out to the watch. It was soon verified by other lookouts, and the watch officer located it on the chart. Then it was time to notify the captain.

"Sir! Emergency beacon activated on Atoll J6433!"

Captain Haash, a Macphee, stirred from his sleep and opened his blowpipe, cursing semitech hexes and their limitations. "Probably nothing—those things malfunction all the time on their own, and when there are earthquakes and eruptions . . . Still, might be survivors from a ship that got swamped. What's the weather like?"

"Squall moving in, sir. Looks to be one of those short but nasty types."

"Hmph! How soon?"

"Ten, fifteen minutes, no more."

"Too short to make a run in and send in a shore party safely. How long to sunrise?"

"About forty minutes, sir."

"Well, we'll wait until full light and, when the storm clears, take her over and investigate. No use in getting banged up or beached. I'll be on the bridge by then. Make to other ships that we'll handle the beacon so they don't have to bother."

"Very well."

The storm hit within minutes with the usual ferocity of small storms in the hex, but it was no volcanic eruption or tidal wave, and the crew was used to this kind of weather by now.

While riding it out was routine, sleeping through it wasn't much of an option, and it wasn't long before the captain was pulling himself up through the bridge hatch. It wasn't easy to catch his mood at this moment, but then, it never was—unless one was another Macphee. His huge eyes always looked as if they were about to rip somebody apart, and beaked creatures always tended to have less physical expression, even those which didn't also look like a large squid covered from enormous head to halfway down his tentacles with thick brown hair.

"What's that banging I hear?" the captain demanded.

"Not sure, sir," the mate responded. "We think it might be debris and such from the explosion in the water striking the hull. We can put somebody over to check if you like." All the cutters had several air-breathing water species aboard for any such eventuality.

"Absolutely not! I'll not have anybody brained by a tree checking to see if we're being struck by a tree! That hull is tough; it'll take a few dings."

It was one of the reasons his crew would go almost anywhere with and for the old man. He was as tough as they came in a fight, but he cared about every member of his crew. He'd willingly risk all their lives for good reason, but never for nothing. It was a bargain he had with them, he liked to tell other captains. The Macphee might have resembled squids, but they were not aquatic creatures and the thick hair was not particularly coated. If he fell overboard and could find nothing to hold on to, that waterlogged fur would cause him to sink like a stone. That meant that he had to always sail with a crew that would be anxious to throw him a line just in case . . .

In a little over a half hour the storm was over, and the captain immediately ordered the crew to check the condition of the ship and see what, if anything, was still in the water near them. Two Effiks, large green and yellow banded insectoids whose legs could stick to just about anything, went over the side and down it, walking around the hull as easily as if they were walking on the deck. The one on the port side suddenly gave a yell. "Here it is! *Big* sucker of a tree; looks almost like it got launched straight up, it's in such good shape! Hey! Wait a minute! There's something stuck in it! An animal, perhaps. Hey! Everybody here!"

There was a general rush to the port side, and two otterlike Akkokeks slid off into the still-choppy seas and approached the big tree cautiously from both sides. Seeing what might have been a leg or some other appendage sticking out of the still-green fronds near the former treetop, they turned upright in the water, bouncing like corks, and hands carefully peeled away the greenery to get a look at the whole creature.

"Never saw anything like *that* before!" one exclaimed. "What the heck *is* that, anyway?"

"Looks like a sentient race," the other remarked. "Bipedal, hands with opposing thumbs . . . Definitely a male. My! That's so *exposed!* Let's see . . ." It carefully began poking and probing and was suddenly startled to see the jaw open, then close. "*Woof!* Reflex action, or . . . Hey! This thing might still be alive!"

"Lower a stretcher on floats and send it out with Doc!" the captain ordered. "Don't touch it until Doc gets there! If it's been stuck in a damned tree since the explosion, it's probably beat up all to hell. Don't want to do anything that'll kill it now, not after it came through all *that*!"

It took some time to get the float to the far end of the tree and for the bewildered medic, who had a lot of practice on dozens of races but knew nothing about this one, to supervise extricating the body from the tree and moving it as gently as possible onto the flotation device.

"Take it easy!" Doc cautioned. The doctor, a birdlike Mosicranz, had little strength in the long, spindly arms beneath her white wings and had to supervise without directly manipulating the body. Once on board and in the clinic, she might be able to do a bit more, since those same fragile limbs possessed an incredible delicacy in control, although she would have preferred to be in a high-tech hex where all the medical equipment that would easily answer her questions would work.

"How should we lay it out, Doc?" one of the Akkokeks asked her.

"How should *I* know? I'm going by deduction here. Flat on the back, I should think, face up. Keep the legs together and the arms against the body. Damn! Whatever he is, he sure looks like he's been through the dominion of evil! Yes, that's good. Fine. Make sure the arms don't drop off or out and let's get him aboard as quickly as possible. I can see some respiration, although I look at the rest of him and I can't understand why. I don't have to know anything at all about his species to know that there's no rational reason in the world why he isn't deader than a stone!"

It took about ten minutes to get the new find aboard and below and another ten or fifteen minutes before the doctor came back up to the bridge.

"There's very little I can do except lay him out and hope for the best," she told the captain. "Anything I do may finish him—if he doesn't die beforehand anyway. There's been some loss of blood from all those gashes and tears, impossible to tell how much, and probably some broken bones, although I can't say without a full scan, which I can't do here. The gash in his head is particularly deep and nasty, and there's some swelling in the skull. If we're going to try and save him, we have to get him into a high-tech facility, and fast. There is no such thing as fast enough."

The captain thought a moment. "We could make Mowry in less than an hour and a half. That would activate your onboard equipment."

"Yes, but it might not be nearly enough. I need *data*. What good is a full scan and examination if I don't know how much blood and fluid he needs or its composition? In order to fix him, I have to know his definition of 'normal.' That means a land hospital."

The captain thought a moment. "All right. The fact that we have a survivor who is of no race known in the region is worth a risk. If we get up full steam, I can get us into Deslak in . . ." The mean-looking eyes went to the mate.

"About three hours, sir," the mate responded.

"That be good enough?"

The doctor sighed. "It will have to do. He's likely to die before we get there, but the gods only know how he managed to live this long. Maybe his will to live is so strong, he'll make it."

"Very well. Notify the company we are rushing an injured survivor to Agon and will be off station for eight hours," the captain said to the bridge staff. "Order the engine room to get up full steam and proceed to Deslak at flank speed as soon as practical."

"Aye, sir. Um—sir? What about the distress signal?"

The captain froze for a second. "Oh, yes. Totally forgot about that. Let me think . . . All right, head for them now. Do as quick a shore recon and pickup as you can. If nobody's there, don't hunt for them, but if there *is* another survivor there, they might even know who or what this fellow below is and what he was doing out here. At the very least, they'd have to be taken in somewhere, anyway."

"Captain, I really think we ought to head for Deslak straight away," the doctor protested.

The captain gave a clicking sound that was more or less the equivalent of a sigh. "Doctor, I appreciate your concern, but he probably won't survive to get there anyway, and if he does, he does. He's held out this long. Another half hour to perhaps save somebody else probably isn't going to make a whole lot of difference."

On the beach, the girl had woken with the coming of dawn. With the morning light, she had lost some of her fear and was beginning to wonder what to do next.

It was strange how clearly she could think and see things yet know so little about herself or much else. There were a lot of terms that meant nothing, a lot of concepts that seemed more confusing than clear, and absolutely nothing at all to anchor her own self upon. She did know that as far as she could tell from the thoughts she could intercept, she seemed to be the only one of her kind.

The storm itself took her by surprise; she didn't run from it but rather was fascinated by it. All that energy, all that sound and fury and noise and light, and all that rain.

The rain in particular fascinated her. Not that it fell in such great quantities but that it seemed unable to quite touch her. It was like she had some kind of second invisible skin that was keeping her and even her hair dry. She could feel it as a series of constant pulses against her skin, but it didn't penetrate. With a little effort she could see it, a thin and transparent layer of energy that gave off a vague lavender glow. She reached out her hands and cupped them, and the glow receded to the wrists, allowing the torrent to strike and quickly overfill her hands. The force of the rain and its weight startled her, and the glow quickly shot back around the hands once more.

They couldn't do that, those creatures out there. None of them could. She didn't know that as much as sense it through the mind's eyes of the unlucky sailors who had to be on deck awash in wind and rain and crashing waves. It wasn't merely that they didn't want to have it; they simply didn't. That was clear.

So whoever and whatever she was, she had powers they did not. She was not, however, so naive as to think that those powers would give her more than a slight advantage over the rest in some situations. They could hurt her, even kill her, if they wanted to do so.

That knowledge brought things right back to the start once again. What was she to do? Run into the forest here, hope that there was enough to eat and live on, and remain here alone, one of a kind? That didn't seem very appealing. But what would those creatures out there do if they found her? Would they take her to more of her own kind, or would they put her in a cage or, perhaps, eat her? It was impossible to get a handle on that because they really didn't know she was here and didn't seem to have any concept of her kind in their heads.

It was lack of knowledge of the world out there that was so disturbing. Surely she must have a past. Those terms which kept popping up in her mind now and then had to come from someplace. And yet, hard as she tried, there just was nothing there. The only thing she knew for sure was that she was here and that somewhere out there there was another, one of her kind yet not like her. She knew this not from memory, though, but because there was some kind of link between them, something she felt. She tried reaching out through that link, but what she got back was unintelligible, confusing, like a thick fog.

Yet, reaching out, there *were* a few such sensations she could decipher. Water . . . wetness, and something sharp and misshapen. Then something—some *things*— grabbing, moving the other out of the water, up onto one of the boats . . .

There was suddenly no choice on the course of action she had to take. One way or the other she had to get on that boat. The other was the only link to any existence beyond what she now knew, the only other one of her own kind. For her own safety she could rely only on instinct and on the strange powers that came unbidden. Basic logic just wouldn't work here; she didn't know the rules. Best to go with feelings until she knew enough to make decisions on her own.

They were coming for her now; the very boat on which the other had been taken was approaching, apparently drawn by the lights she'd triggered. She left her hiding place and went down toward the big box to meet them.

AGON,
SOUTH COAST

THE COLONEL OOZED INTO his temporary headquarters on the patrol dock and formed an eyestalk to better focus on his surroundings. It looked quite empty.

"Come! Come! Gus! I know you are here!" he said rather casually. When there was no immediate response, his irritation was clear in his tone. "What would you like me to do? Send off a report to Dahir that they should come and pick you up?"

"If you were gonna do that, you'da done it by now," responded a deep growl of a voice behind the Leeming.

"Ah! What a talent! If I only had such as you back home in São Paulo! There would have been no secret closed to us!"

"I was in the news business," Gus reminded him. "Maybe it's *you* who wouldn't have had no secrets. All the stuff you did in them cells and damp basement rooms woulda been on the evening news. Now the only joy I have left in life is making you as paranoid as you probably made half of São Paulo."

"Ah, my friend! How many times do I have to remind you that my country was a democracy?"

"Not in your version of the good old days," Gus responded. He didn't like the colonel very much, and he knew the colonel didn't much care for him, either, but at the moment they needed each other. "Any news? We've been wallowin' here for too long now."

"There was a major volcanic eruption on one of the islands a couple of days ago."

"So? I understand that's pretty old stuff."

"Maybe. But it was in the very area we searched so long and so hard, my friend. On the very island where you were convinced they had to have been."

Gus was suddenly concerned. "*That* one? You think maybe they . . . ?"

"Who knows? If they are, it is the end of this part of the problem since this Brazil person would obviously not be an immortal and would certainly not be the man with the keys to the Well, now, would he? But if he is, and many people do believe he is, then, my friend, either he was not there or he would escape, no?"

"But Terry—the girl! *She's* no immortal!"

"That is true, and I understand your concern. She was a friend. Perhaps she lives, perhaps not. What would you do if you found her? Found her separated from the captain, I mean? I have heard of some odd couples in my time, but *this* is a bit much, I think."

"It's not like that! It wasn't sexual. It was different than that."

"Indeed? And which planet are you from? I know where *I* was born and where I am now. Or perhaps you are a throwback to the days of romance and chivalry, to Platonic love and honor and duty and all that? Or were you honorably married and religiously faithful? Or perhaps it was *she* who was married?"

"No, she wasn't married, and neither was I."

"I can see why not! You might as well be a monk. Or did you perhaps not find women sexually attractive?"

"I wasn't gay, if that's what you mean, and I wasn't no monk, neither. If you want to know, I didn't want to make it with her because I thought it would spoil things. She was the closest thing I had to a best friend. We had what they call mutual respect, and she sure as hell had guts. Maybe I'm wrong. Maybe we were *both* married. Not to other people but to the job, to the life-style. There wasn't nothin' neither of us wanted to do with our lives than what we was doin'. Both of us. If either of us had been willin' to stop, I guess it mighta worked, but we was two of a kind, you might say. I guess you could say we shared the same lover, if you want to make it like that. No use beatin' this horse anymore. If you don't get it now, I could never make you understand it."

"To each his own," the colonel responded. "I think perhaps that things are not so different here as they seem. Only back on Earth we all looked pretty much the same, so we thought of ourselves as one when really, our cultures and natures were as alien as, well, a Dahir and a Leeming. And perhaps, too, we change less here than we think we do, eh?" The colonel sighed. "Well, that is neither here nor there. The question is, What do we do next? Do we go back out and see if we can find anything in the aftermath of this, or do we wait and see what gets picked up?"

"I'm for going back out," Gus replied without hesitation. "If either or both survived, then things got really stirred up, didn't they? It might have spooked 'em—and remember, they got the knack like me. If they don't want to be seen, you can't see 'em. *You* can't, but *I* can." And that was precisely why the colonel needed Gus. For his part, though, Gus did not underestimate the colonel, who had managed to accumulate a whole hell of a lot of authority and rank, which implied trust, in a very short time on the Well World. That kind of man was dangerous in and of himself, but even more so when it was not at all clear to whom the man gave his loyalty.

The colonel considered Gus's response, then said, "I think perhaps you are right, my friend. If I'd had a boat at my disposal, we would have left at the first reports, but they have a veritable armada out there, from patrol boats to scientific teams, and that left them thin in other areas. There's one due in for refueling and reprovisioning this afternoon, though. I think when it sails, you and I should be on it."

The colonel's question had bothered Gus more than he let on. What *was* he going to do if he found Terry? What sort of future did he have in mind, particularly considering the state she'd been in when he'd found her? Her only hope was the captain, and while he seemed like a decent enough guy, he didn't seem to be all there in a number of ways. In a sense, *his* only real hope was the captain, too, since he sure couldn't go back to Dahir and didn't see much of a future anywhere else. In point of fact, until things had stalled, this business had been the most fun he'd had since he had arrived in this strange place.

They'd probably let Terry go. She wasn't much good to anybody, but she wasn't very good company as it was, either. But Brazil—that was a different story. At best, they'd lock him up and try to get enough guts to trust him on any deal he might make, or they'd march him into that whatever it was up north with guns pointing at his head. Not a good condition for granting favors, although Brazil always seemed confident that if he got in there, he could handle anything.

Still, old Gus wasn't one of the folks likely to be invited to the party, and Brazil would have a lot more on his mind than his brief acquaintance and shipmate.

Damn! he thought. *Kinda like* The Wizard of Oz, *only you got to steal the wizard and carry him off, too.* Yeah, and when they'd gotten to the wizard, he'd proved to be a fake, anyway. Wouldn't *that* take the cake! All this crap and you get Brazil inside and he's just another con man. Hell, the captain had even described *himself* as a con artist! Seemed damned proud of it, although where had it gotten him up to now?

As always, he'd have to just wing it. At least those two somehow had learned the same knack for not being noticed that was built into the Dahir; they might be pretty damned hard to keep locked up. *That* was something of an advantage, although, as the colonel said, it wouldn't take forever to get somebody else here, somebody native, who could see through the trick.

"Ship off the port bow!" the lookout cried. "Coming landward and at full speed! Looks like one of ours!"

"Make to approaching craft by signal lantern as soon as she's in range," the ship's captain instructed. "Ask them for identification and the reason for coming in. They might have some problems. Nobody was due in for another thirty hours."

The semaphore lantern was soon clicking away, and after an interval during which time the approaching craft had covered a good deal of distance toward them, the signalman read out the reply.

"Corvette *Swiftwind Thunderer,* carries two survivors, unknown species, one in critical condition."

The colonel snapped to. "It's *them*! I *know* it is them! Captain, tell them to approach and lay to next to us. My companion and I are going to board that ship and ride it back in."

"Might not be who you're looking for," the officer pointed out.

"It is. I will chance it anyway. Just give the order before they get so close that they pass us." He paused a moment, then called, "Gus? You hear?"

"I heard. Might as well see what they caught."

The two corvettes were nearly identical, and when alongside they secured to one another with grappling hooks and lines, close enough that a metallic plank could be laid between them.

Watching the colonel move fast when he wanted to was an education. While he normally seemed to just ooze across the floor or deck, his great translucent blob now seemed to shrink, and then an object the size of a basketball extruded and fairly shot across the gangway. The rest of the body followed as if the whole were a rubber band that had been stretched and now was released. It was a bit harder for Gus, but his feet gave him a good grip on all but the smoothest surfaces, and he was able to leap the last meter or two.

"I'm here," he told the colonel, who signaled for the two ships to disconnect.

Captain Haash oozed down from the wheelhouse himself as soon as they were again under way. "What the blazes is all this about? And who are you?" he demanded to know.

"I am Colonel Lunderman of the Royal Leeming Forces, currently assigned to South Zone Council duty. My orders and authority are at the patrol base at Deslak, if you have any doubts."

Haash thought a moment. "Well, I doubt if you'd be on old Shibahld's ship unless you were who you said. Still, can't say as I can figure out if you're comin' or goin'."

"Neither, Captain. I was headed out for another search for certain creatures wanted by the council. I am looking for two Glathrielians, and you have two unknowns from the right region. Am I correct?"

"Glathrielians? Never heard of 'em. So *that's* what they are!"

"Perhaps. If we can just see them? That is the only way to make sure."

"Sure. No problem. 'We,' you say? More'n one of you in that blob?"

"He is referring to me, Captain," Gus put in.

Haash proved that a Macphee could move even faster than a Leeming —and up a bulkhead, too. Then the huge head peered back over, and two enormous but very human-looking eyes peered down. "Don't *do* that to somebody like me! Don't *ever* do that again! I'm likely to take your head off!"

Gus decided that it was the better part of discretion not to point out that the captain's reaction had been not to fight but to flee. After all, it *was* his ship. "Sorry. Can't help it. A defense mechanism that's just built in. I couldn't turn if off if I tried. You haven't noticed this sort of thing with either of your survivors?" Gus was beginning to worry that they'd just blown it on a wild-goose chase.

"No! And from the looks of things it's gonna be touch and go if one of 'em don't disappear into the grave."

The colonel felt impatient. "May we just see them, Captain?"

"Infirmary below. At least the one that's wracked up is there. The other one roams all over the place but generally stays out of the way. Anybody can point you the way."

As they went below, led by a crewman, Gus wasn't at all sure that he wanted it to be they. If it was Terry who was down there, near death . . .

It was pretty clear, though, in the small infirmary that they hadn't wasted any time at all and that Gus's fears had not been realized, either.

Hooked up to a forced breathing apparatus and submerged in a fluid tank that at least insulated the injured man from the effects of the sea was clearly a battered, bruised, and cut Nathan Brazil.

"Jeez! He looks *awful*!" Gus noted, examining the man through the plastic casing. "What the hell did they *do* to him?"

The colonel, too, stared at the man floating in the tank. "He's survived many weeks, probably with very little, on a tropical atoll," he noted. "I doubt if he had a comb, razor, or medical kit. However, note the scars."

"I'm trying not to," Gus responded.

"Be observant! The scar tissue is brown but of roughly the same uniform age, shade, and thickness. The bruises and black and blue areas also look to be rather similar. This says that most of what we see happened in a relatively short period of time. I think that Captain Brazil might very well have been on that island when it exploded and was somehow blown away with the debris. Strange . . . He seems, well, so much *smaller,* more frail-looking than I remembered him. I suppose, like many small men, his personality and energy are in inverse proportion to his real size and strength."

A Mosicranz, looking something like an anemic and sickly angel to Gus, although with a more birdlike head, came into the room. "I am the doctor," she told them. "I understand you know who and what this is."

"He is a Glathrielian," the colonel told her. "Not likely to be an extensive entry in your medical books, I fear. They are generally a very closed and primitive society and do not travel. This man was an exception to the rule."

"I can believe the primitive part," the doctor responded. "The female seems to be totally ignorant of the simplest things, almost like a little child."

"She is not so badly hurt?" Gus asked anxiously. Predictably, the doctor started but recovered quickly. Clearly she'd seen that trick before.

"She's not hurt at all. She apparently made it to a nearby island with a lifesaving chest and beacon and apparently triggered it by accident. That's the only reason we knew she was there and picked her up. She seems very concerned about the male—they were mated, perhaps?"

"In a way," Lunderman acknowledged. "Although I don't think it was necessarily mutual. This man is quite sophisticated about things, while the girl seems about as primitive as you can get."

"You knew them before, then?"

"Yes, indeed. We both did," the colonel told her. "My companion goes back even further with the girl."

"Is that so? Well, I'm afraid that might not count for much anymore," the doctor told them.

"Why? Something happen?" Gus asked. "You said she wasn't hurt!"

"Not *physically,* no. But we Mosicranz are very good healers, sir, with our own set of inborn attributes. I am mildly telepathic. Only surface thoughts, no deep probes, but sufficient to read and respond. She, too, has this ability—to what depth I can't say, although it appears to be very similar to mine. When I say she is like a child, I mean that literally. She has no memories at all before waking up on that island. None. She doesn't know who she is, where she is, what she is, or how she got there. She is here only because she has a permanent connection of some sort to the male and sensed that even on the island. It is impossible to say where they were when the eruption took place, but I would think it was quite close. They became separated in the water. She made it to the island; he did not, struggling in the channel until he found a large tree floating there and managed to wrap himself in it. That is all deduction but is probably correct. He was so badly injured that it's incredible he managed as much as he did. As for the female, there is no clear evidence of head trauma, so I can only suspect that the memory loss was due to either shock or internal concussion when the thing blew—literally a shaking of the brain inside the skull. I should like to examine her more thoroughly when we get to a high-tech port to see if there is any brain damage or internal hemorrhaging that I can't now detect."

"Huh? You mean she might really be hurt, after all?" Gus asked her.

"Perhaps. I would have kept her here, but I had no knowledge of what she was, so sedation was out of the question. What dosage? Which drug? You see? And she's not one to be kept lying down without forcible restraint."

"Where is she now?" Gus asked her.

"Somewhere aft and almost certainly topside. She doesn't like to be inside for long. But don't expect too much from her. If she is capable of vocalized speech, I haven't been able to get anything out of her."

"She is, but she may have forgotten how," the Dahir replied. "Still, I'll see what I can do. Maybe later you can act as a bridge for us and I'll see if I can stir up anything in her memories."

"That might be a very big help," the doctor agreed.

Gus went out to find Terry, leaving the colonel with the doctor.

"So, Doctor, what is your best guess, and I realize that it is only that, on *this* one?" he asked her.

"Frankly, I can't understand how he's still alive. Just looking at the external injuries, I can well imagine what is inside. If he lasts long enough, I hope to be able to do as much for him as possible, but frankly, unless he can somehow heal himself of mortal wounds, I would be shocked if he lasts more than a matter of days."

The colonel thought for a moment, then said, "Perhaps he may surprise you, Doctor. In any event, if you wish to stick with him, I certainly have no objections, but even in the terrible shape he is in, I will insist that from this moment there be a guard posted here or just outside and that he not be moved or treated anywhere without a guard being present."

"That man is not going anywhere!" the doctor pronounced confidently. "Period!"

"If he were on fire and we were watching him burn, I would not trust 'that man,'" the colonel told her. "You and your ship are going to be a little bit famous, I think, Doctor. You see, that man is Captain Nathan Brazil."

There was a long pause, and then the doctor asked, "Who?"

"Nathan Brazil. There's been an all wants and warrants out on him since he stole a sailing ship and vanished many weeks ago."

"I don't pay attention to that. I have enough trouble keeping up with the medical biology of the nine different races represented on this crew alone, let alone others I might have to patch up, regardless of tech level. It keeps me busy."

The colonel was still a bit incredulous. "You have *never* heard the name before?"

The doctor gave a mild shrug. "Well, seems to me that there's a name that sounds something like that in ancient mythology, but I'm afraid I didn't pay much attention to myths and legends."

A pseudopod oozed out and gestured toward the man in the tank. "Well, there lies a genuine mythological legend, Doctor. Nathan Brazil, the immortal who alone remains to work the great Well World machine."

"You're joking, of course."

"Perhaps. Perhaps not. Let's just say that there is ample evidence that such a person exists. Enough to satisfy the Zone Council that he exists, anyway. And this man, who came through the Well Gate from another world far from here, not from ancestral Glathriel, knew an awful lot about the Well World for one from a civilization still not really even into space."

The doctor stared at the man in the tank. "An ancient god? *That* one? *Here?*"

"Wiser heads than we believe it. Certainly it will be a moot point if he dies, won't it? But if he doesn't . . . If he in fact makes a full and complete recovery . . . What then?"

"You kind of expect your ancient mythological deities to be, well, a bit larger, more imposing, to say the least."

The colonel chuckled. "Only if they *want* to be noticed, Doctor. Not when you want to sneak in."

She hadn't entirely lost her fear, but she was much more relaxed now, convinced at least that she'd done the right thing by coming to the other, hurt though he clearly was. Everything on the boat was so interesting, so new. She understood that the crew members got a lot of amusement at her ignorance. Of course they were sometimes not so amused, like when she'd just taken a piss on the deck, but she didn't mind. A lot of it was too confusing to worry about, anyway. What did it matter if some had clothes and some didn't? What did it matter how one ate, or slept, or whatever?

And they kept going around and working all these things on the boat that didn't make a lot of sense. Some of them even did things that seemed silly on the face of it, like washing the deck when they were on an ocean—when it got rough, the waves washed it anyway. That was why she didn't understand why they got upset when she peed on it. Either they or the waves washed it anyway, and it seemed like she had to pee a lot.

They also had a lot of gadgets and gizmos that made no sense to her. They'd sometimes try to show her the simplest things, at least to them, and she'd try, too, really try, but she just couldn't figure out how to work them. She *had* finally managed to figure out how to open doors, but then they got mad when she kept practicing on every door on the boat. Doors seemed stupid, anyway. All they did was block her way from one place to another. If they didn't have doors, they wouldn't have to bother opening them all the time, she reasoned.

She couldn't figure out why the boat didn't sink, either. One threw something in the water, it sank. Why didn't this big, heavy, ugly thing sink? It didn't make any sense. Well, she didn't worry much about things she couldn't figure out.

From observing and listening to the surface thoughts of the crew, she'd gotten the idea that there were smart people who understood or could figure out most anything, there were others who understood some things, and finally there were dumb people who just couldn't figure out things. Some of the crew members whom others in the crew considered stupid didn't seem so stupid to her, but they also didn't seem to be sad or upset that they might be stupid. All of them thought she was pretty stupid, even the ones the others thought were stupid, too, so maybe she was. She'd asked the nice doctor about that, and the doctor, who everybody said was the smartest one on the boat, had told her that people who tried their best and didn't worry about what they knew or didn't know were happiest, and that seemed like good advice. She'd just try her best and learn what she could and not worry about the rest.

And then there was the other downstairs. It didn't look at all like her, but it looked more like her than anybody else on board. The doctor said he was badly hurt, something that she hadn't needed to be told. The doctor also said that while he might wake up and get better, he probably wouldn't. It was funny, but that news hadn't really affected her. There was just something inside that said that he'd be sick a long, long time but wouldn't die. That just meant that it would be a real long time before he woke up and could tell her about herself, if in fact he could and didn't have the same problem remembering things. She might stick around until he got well, but she knew it would be very long, and what could somebody like her do just staying around? Of course, she didn't have anything else to do or anywhere else to go.

She'd watched unobtrusively when the two boats had pulled up next to one another. It was kind of neat how they could do that. They probably had to be really smart to do something like that without crashing. The two new people who'd come aboard had gone below, and she hadn't found out much about them yet, but maybe she would. She didn't really like the big blob thing; she couldn't say why. The other one almost seemed like, well, like somebody like her, but that was silly.

Gus found her on the afterdeck, just sitting there and seemingly oblivious to the world. Her hair was a tangled mess, but otherwise she seemed unmarked and remarkably the same.

"Terry?" he said gently to her. "You understand me? If you do, nod your head up and down."

Terry. He acted as if he knew her, but the name was unfamiliar. Well, she didn't have one, so maybe that was as good as any. She nodded and felt his glow of joy at actually communicating with her.

"Do you know who I am?"

She looked blankly at the colorful dragonlike creature. Know him? Should she?

"It's Gus, Terry. Gus. Do you remember me? Remember me at all? Even like this? Shake your head up and down for yes, back and forth for no, like this." He demonstrated as best he could.

She thought it looked funny but shook her head no.

"Well, I remember you," he told her, and in his head she could see a lot of images, memories, right at the surface, where she could look at them. Memories of her wearing stupid clothes and working all sorts of strange stuff and in a whole lot of places she'd never seen before. It was like being a character in a story. It was fascinating but bore no relationship to reality at all. The only thing it said to her was, *I was smart once.* That was good to know. Maybe she could get smart again someday. The doctor had almost said as much, although without a lot of conviction that it would happen.

The visions of her doing incomprehensible things in settings totally unfamiliar soon bored her, but something else was interesting, too. It was the creature's vision of himself at these places; he seemed to be of the same kind as she and the other down below. A tall, thin man with a very pale skin and yellowish hair. It confused her. For some reason this person thought of himself as that other one as well as what he was now. He couldn't be both, could he? It was all too mixed up. Like the rest, it was just something she wasn't smart enough to figure out, she guessed.

Still, she had an unmistakable feeling that the creature was important. He wasn't trying to fool her or anything like that; in fact, he seemed to be totally open to her. He *had* known her before she had lost her memory, and he definitely had genuine affection for her from that period. The trouble was, she wasn't that person anymore, even if she wanted to be. It was as if that person were gone, dead, and somebody new had set up shop in the old body, somebody not nearly as smart. She certainly would trust this Gus, but could Gus ever see her as who she was now and not as who she might have been in some past life?

There was little more that either of them could say to one another beyond what had been done. For Gus's part, he began to understand that Terry had changed again, from the mysterious girl of great power to this very childlike creature who didn't even remember the *second* incarnation. This wasn't going to be easy, but at least now he had a little bit of purpose to his life. She sure needed *somebody* right now, and he was the only one she had.

Glathrielians were in the medical references at all only because of the work of some Ambrezan physicians and anthropologists, but the information was about as complete on the physiological side as it was for most other races and certainly more than adequate. In high-tech Agon, with a diagnostic computer set up and armed with all those data, it was relatively easy to do a thorough checkup on both patients.

"By all rights Brazil should be dead," the doctor told them. "In fact, after going through these data, I'm almost inclined to believe your stories about the mythological god. Virtually every rib is either cracked or broken. One punctured the right lung and caused massive internal bleeding. Several of his organs are in horrible shape, too, and he has lesions in the brain in areas that might well control motor development. As far as I can see, he's been going on sheer will to live. The aggregate of these injuries is enough to kill just about anything carbon-based, but in all cases there is something like a one in a million chance that it might not be fatal. I swear that instant death versus horrible injury was a matter of microns one way or another in a few instances. A surgical team has been on the case since he was brought in, and they're now working on him."

"What you are saying is that he will survive," the colonel noted.

"What I am saying is that he should not have survived and that there are very poor odds that he will survive this massive level of surgery. Synthesizing that quantity of blood alone was a monstrous job, and I have no doubt they will use all of it. If he *does* survive, well, there is no way to know what areas of the brain are affected, but there will almost certainly be some serious problems. In addition, there is major damage to the spinal cord which is *perhaps* reparable over a very long time, when he can stand the additional work, and assuming that it is similar to other spinal cord injuries in the races that have similar torsos. Then again, that is never an exact science. The odds are great that he's going to remain in a coma, which will make him your ward and no longer our problem. If he *does* come out, then he will probably be unable to move much of anything below the neck. They tell me that they can do nothing on the spinal cord injury at this time. They have to do the other repairs first, and it is best if he cannot move anything down there, even involuntarily. The problem is, the longer the spinal cord is left untreated, the less likely it is to respond to treatment. I believe that at best, you will have a being who is totally bedridden and will never be able to move anything beyond his head again. That's the best estimate."

The colonel thought it over. "Oddly enough, if that were true, it might be a very convenient result. He could be questioned but would hardly be a threat. On the other hand, we have information that leads us to believe that he is capable of regeneration, perhaps total, over a long period of time. If he is the man of the legends, then that is what will happen, but it is still a result that my superiors will not find too terrible. It buys time, a lot of it, and no matter what, leaves him in our official custody."

The doctor shrugged. "Suit yourself. Sounds grotesque to me, but considering that he *is* still alive after all that, I begin to think that I can believe anything about him. What I *cannot* believe is that he is going to get up and walk out of here, or even crawl out of here, in the next year or two, if ever."

"A year might be most satisfactory if one remaining complication can be resolved," the Leeming told her. "Unfortunate that he might remain comatose, though. If we cannot resolve our problem, we might have to deal with him much quicker."

"You never can tell for sure, but I wouldn't bet on any conversations," the doctor told him. "Whatever your complication is, you better resolve it."

"What about the girl?" Gus asked her. "Did you run all the tests on her, too?"

"We did. She's in remarkably good physical shape, all things considered. *Mentally* I'm not so sure. From what we were able to get from the Ambrezans through Zone, we have a theory but only a theory. That is one strange race there in Glathriel."

"Yes?"

"We think she probably woke up in Ambreza near the border and, after seeing what she could only perceive as monsters, made a run into Glathriel. There they've developed some kind of deliberately primitive society that shuns all artifacts, machines, tools, whatever. That doesn't mean they are savages, though. Like some other races here, they went in the other direction, developing powers of the mind, realizing what might be just a slight potential in most of them, developing and honing it."

"Back on Earth I've seen men walk barefoot over red hot coals and suspend themselves on sharp nails," Gus told her. "And I've seen a lot of other strange stuff, too. Is that what you mean? They went strictly that way?"

"Well, I think it's a lot deeper than those types of things, but you get the idea. Ambrezan anthropologists believe that the Glathrielians have developed something of a group mind, a sort of insectlike social and mental organization without any hierarchy in which all of them are connected to one another. They convert their body fat into energy that can be used for things far beyond mere physical work. I think you've seen examples of that in her."

Gus nodded.

The colonel gave a mock clearing of his nonexistent throat. "I believe I shall go file my report. We have no interest in the girl, so I will leave her fate entirely in friend Gus's hands." And with that, the Leeming oozed out of the hospital lounge.

"You were saying they used fat to do things with their mind?" Gus prompted the doctor.

"Yes. Fascinating, really. Still, it's only the background here. What is really the point is that she walked straight into a place where the people were *organically* the same as she was but mentally and socially were far more alien to her than physically different races. She had no foreknowledge and no defenses. They co-opted her into their mental net. She would have seen it as an offer of friendship, security in her most vulnerable moment. She didn't resist, almost certainly expecting communication. She got far more. We think they literally rewired her brain. Not organically but electrically. The memories were still there, but they were no longer relevant or needed because the whole frame of reference was different. We can't say why, when she saw Brazil, she latched on to him with such tenacity, but we can guess that she knew he was someone from her old world and she wanted out. The problem was, she'd been re-wired. She could leave, but she couldn't rewire herself. That would take the collective knowledge and power of a pretty large Glathrielian group. That meant she was suspended, neither here nor there. In our world she thought like and acted like one of them. But in their world she couldn't completely wipe away a lifetime of experience, memory, personality, and ambition to assimilate."

Gus nodded sadly. "Poor Terry. She deserved better."

"Then we get to the situation where you were present. She reached out somehow, using what must have been instinctive Glathrielian mental methods, and hooked into Captain Brazil's brain. Again, this is on an energy level, not physically. It was probably out of fear he might aban-don her, but the link, once established, worked both ways. He gained access to some of her powers, and she gained a connection that might as well have been steel chains. With only the two of them, stuck for weeks on that island, more in her element than his, it's difficult to say what happened or if anything did, but it might have. Then came the eruption, probably a terrified leap into the sea and an attempt to get away, the big explosion, and, in the course of it, Brazil was seriously, horribly injured. The link between them, something like a telepathic bond, would have carried through to her as well. The shocks and his own physical and mental trauma, combined with what must have been sheer terror for her, overloaded her system. Linked to his more 'normal' wiring, going through all that with her Glathrielian wiring, the shock loosened and perhaps destroyed the careful patterns they'd built inside her. We think —and this is mere theory and probably can never be any more than that —the patterns were wiped out, as if the whole brain were flooded with a massive electrical charge. The Glathrielian powers, which are there now not because of wiring but because they'd been used so much, probably saved her life."

"I'm followin' about a tenth of this," Gus told her. "What is the bottom line?"

"Sorry. It's just such a fascinating study that I tend to run away with myself. The bottom line is that we haven't any 'normal' Glathrielian or Earth-type patterns for comparison—Brazil is hardly a good sample right now—but there are a dozen or more races here that share similar brain and nervous system structures with the Glathrielian physiology. More important, they share a lot of commonalities, so we can compare and at least build a *theoretical* model of what a Glathrielian brain pattern should look like and how it works. Your bottom line is that whatever was there was erased by the shock, and her brain then rebuilt what it could based on what it had left—the link with Brazil. We've tried all sorts of tests, always reliable on those others. Her memory isn't blocked by shock or brain damage—it's gone. The Glathrielian protective powers she had were constructed to be autonomic—automatic like a heartbeat. Those remained. So did the other basic autonomic systems. The rest? A simple vocabulary based on what little snippets of information were stored in areas closest to where memories are combined into thoughts—possibly her thoughts, possibly his. This has built up to more complex thinking by what she's able to get from the surface-level thoughts of others so long as those thoughts create holographic images in the thinker's mind. If you were to think of an image called 'boat,' for example, she knows what a boat is. I do not, however, see any real evidence of abstract thinking or much chance for it."

"Huh?"

"It's linear thinking, like we do, which means the pattern probably came from him," the doctor went on. "But it is very limited thinking, very limited processing of information. She has no patience and little interest in learning most things. If she decides she wants to learn something but doesn't get it quickly, she loses interest. She's entirely in the present; she has no concept of the future or any interest in it. She can be thrown a ball and is just as amused if she catches it or watches it drop and bounce. She learned to push down on latches aboard ship to open hatches but never could get the idea of closing them behind her, and she's been frustrated here because she's been trying to push down on doorknobs to open doors and it doesn't work. The woman you knew is gone. Accept that. What you have is a young child in her body. And there is no way of knowing at this stage if she will progress beyond where she is in more than very small degrees."

Gus felt the hurt of losing someone very close, but it wasn't quite like that. "Tell me straight, Doc. Can you say for absolute certain, beyond the shadow of any doubts, that Terry will never regain any of her memory? That it's a dead-on medical certainty that she'll be like this until she dies?"

The doctor considered her words carefully. "No, I can't. Not with absolute certainty. It is not like we've ever had a case like hers before or know exactly what we are dealing with. Not even the consulting Ambrezans really understand what's inside the Glathrielian mind. All I can say is, absent any evidence of physical trauma, it is a *very* remote possibility that much of anything would come back. And if anything were still there, it would come back in pieces, over a very long period of time."

"But it's possible? As possible, say, as Captain Brazil surviving all those wounds?"

"Well, yes, but—"

"She's tied to him, Doc. You said so. Maybe some of that immunity rubbed off as well. If I just send her back now, it's over, period. She can never come back. The door's closed forever. See, I just can't write her off yet, send her back to what is a certain life as part of a group mind living in the mud. She was so much more than that."

"But what else can you do?"

"Well, what are my options here?"

"Not many. She can't stay here. The law says that anyone likely to be a ward of the state must be returned to its native hex. Of course, she is free to go anywhere she likes as well, but I still feel that this is the best course to take. The Glathrielians could probably restore her to their state, but unencumbered by the baggage she brought in the first time. She'd live what for them would be a normal life."

"Not yet, Doc. When I'm convinced, but not yet. There's still some options open, no matter how wild the odds. If nothin' else, I want to see what happens if Brazil wakes up."

The doctor sighed. "Well, as I said, I will get religion and go study the ancient gods if *he* recovers, let alone walks. But there's another reason for possibly sending her back. Perhaps a compelling one. It explains the other major mystery—why the Well preserved her pretty much as she was instead of translating her into another race as it did with you."

"Yeah?"

"She's pregnant, Gus. According to the Ambrezan material, about six weeks from normal full gestation. Counting back, that means she was pregnant when she came onto the Well World and almost certainly not much before that point."

"Oh, my God!"

"It's in the records, although extremely rare even in ancient times, it seems. The Well has no trouble taking one race and making of it another, but when you complicate it, give it what it perceived in its analysis as two in one, it didn't have an answer for that. So it pretty much optimized her for survival here but otherwise left her just as she was. She is going to have a baby, Gus, and she doesn't even know what a baby is or how it's made."

Gus sighed. "Jeez! *Now* what do I do?" If he sent her back, she'd probably be okay, but he'd be dooming forever any chance she might have to recover normalcy. But if he didn't, then what of the baby?

"Well, you heard the colonel. I'm afraid that since she isn't capable of deciding for herself, it's entirely up to you."

* * *

"We have exciting news," the colonel told Gus. "We have a real lead on the other one, this Mavra Chang. She is in the hands of an international drug ring whose headquarters are on the northern border of this very hex. A fair amount of money and death have gone into protecting them until now, but this changes just about everything, as you might suppose. The more things are different, the more they seem like home. Is it not so?"

"You should know," Gus muttered.

The colonel ignored the sarcasm. "Well, they are going to attack their headquarters in utmost secrecy, led by one of the few really honest policemen in Agon. With Brazil safely incapacitated, I am going north this very day to be in on this other operation. After all, if we have Brazil but not Chang and Chang can also access the well, then we have gained nothing. Still, I feel we are closing in and that this matter is about to come to a head. There are others from Earth in this raiding party as well, so it will be pleasant to have yet more of a connection with the old home. What do *you* wish to do, my friend?"

"Others? Anybody I know?"

"I don't think so. Someone *I* knew, at least for a little while, and two associates of Captain Brazil's who came in on his initiative, I believe, from Rio de Janeiro. One is a fellow countryman of mine—in the old life, that is. Two Dillians—they are much like the centaurs of our ancient Earth mythology, I am told—and one Erdomite."

Gus sighed and shook his head. "I don't know. Much as I'd like to, the only person I *really* know well is right here, aside from you and the captain, anyway, and I'm just not too sure what to do with her yet."

"Someone I believe you may know *is* involved, after all," Lunderman commented, looking over reports. "Do you know a Juan Campos?"

Gus's reptilian head shot up, and the eyes blazed with a menace not seen before. "Yeah, I know the bastard! If it wasn't for him, none of us would be *in* this damned fix! He's in this group, too? Don't sound like his style."

"You misunderstand me, my friend. Campos is with the drug cartel. In fact, it might well be Campos who had Mavra Chang abducted."

That menace in the eyes didn't fade. "Same old Campos, then. He was dirty back home, and he's *still* dirty. Guess he just don't know any other trade. Figures. What'd *he* wind up as?"

"A Cloptan. They look something like cartoon ducks, but there is nothing funny about them or cartoonish, either." He paused a moment. "A Cloptan *female*! Most interesting!"

"He's a *girl*?" Gus found it impossible not to laugh, although a Dahir chuckle sounded far more threatening than amusing. "Well, at least he got *some* justice, the bastard. He won't be raping any more helpless women."

"Perhaps not, but Cloptan society isn't as traditional as most. Women have some real power there, in the government and in the rackets, too, it seems. I would say that whatever was done to him was compensated for by the society in which he found himself. He's come a rather long way to be influential in such an operation so quickly. Campos is the sort to have a deadly grudge against this Mavra Chang?"

"Yeah, he would, at least in his own mind. I was sick or drugged for most of it, but I remember enough, so I'm pretty sure he does, too. I want in on this one, Colonel. I want to see Campos squashed like the bug he is."

"I had hoped that you would say that. I should like to bring the girl along as well. Protected, of course, and well out of the action, but even if she can be of little help, the detective in charge says that he would like her up there."

"Huh? I hadn't really considered it much. Of course, I guess if I'm not gonna just send her back to that Glathriel forever, at least not yet, she has to stick with me. She trusts me pretty good, but—I dunno. I guess she could be sent back by *any* Zone Gate, so there's no real rush in that regard, but I'm not sure I want to get her exposed and active too much right now. Why would this drug agent want Terry?"

"He does not say. The only way to know is to go up there and ask him. But why do you have such concern over the girl now? She has certainly managed to take care of herself with minimal help so far, and even if she has lost her memory, she still has her unique abilities."

"Damn it, Colonel, she's gonna have a baby in like a month and a half. That's why. What if she goes into labor? What if she gets stressed or even accidentally hurt and the kid gets killed? *She's* no immortal."

The colonel thought a moment. "That *does* complicate things, I do agree. And yet Agon, and Clopta if we have to go there, are both high-tech hexes, and I believe she would probably be as safe as or safer in one of them than she would be back in that primitive no-tech homeland. You've seen the medicine available here already."

The colonel knew that Gus was only easing his conscience, that he very much wanted both to go and to keep the girl with him, pregnant or not. Gus would *have* to face the birth sooner or later anyway; it seemed pretty obvious he wasn't going to send her back to what was tantamount to oblivion forever. Somehow, deep down, it was obvious that Gus still clung to the belief that Terry, his old Terry, might well be down there someplace, buried deep inside that girl's head. Until he was absolutely convinced that this person was forever but a memory, if he ever was, he would cling to her out of honor, out of friendship, and because it was the only thing that kept the Dahir himself going.

There was, of course, no purpose in telling Gus at that point that what the Agonite cop wanted her for was bait.

SUBAR,
NEAR THE LILIBLOD BORDER

SHE KNEW GUS WAS troubled by something, something concerning her, but she couldn't, or wouldn't, dig down to find out why. It just wouldn't be *right* somehow, and besides, she might not understand it, anyway.

She liked Gus a lot. She trusted him absolutely, maybe the only one she'd met so far that she could say that about. Oh, she trusted that nice doctor, too, but the doctor was way, way too smart for her to really feel comfortable with. It was nice being able to actually talk to somebody, but most of the time she couldn't follow what the doc was saying, so it wasn't that big a deal. Deep down she was just an interesting patient to the doctor, but Gus really *cared* about her, although why he did was still a mystery to her.

She had come to terms with the fact that most of the world was and would remain a mystery to her; most everybody seemed a lot smarter than she was, and after a while she realized that would be the way things were and accepted it. It wasn't as if she had anywhere she wanted to go or anything she wanted to do.

It would have been easier on Gus if she could speak, but the doctor thought that the Glathrielian business had done something to the area of the brain that controlled vocalization. She could make some sounds, but they were just sounds, not words. This was something else that might or might not reconnect, depending on how she developed from this point. Because she *could* understand others, or *most* others—there were some creatures that seemed a total blank to her but not many—Gus had worked out what was still a simple sign language for her. It was okay for the obvious basics, but it would hardly serve as an alternative language.

Gus finally decided he had to tell her the situation, no matter how much she might or might not understand. The concept of pregnancy proved less difficult than he imagined; some mental pictures, along with a simple child's version of how it worked, seemed to get the message across.

She was fascinated by that. A little person growing inside her that would someday pop out and then grow up to be a *big* person. It made sense and answered a few questions she'd had about how all these people got there and why some were small and some were large, but she never wondered about how one got that way.

"Now that you know," Gus told her as gently and simply as he could, "you will have to be careful. Things could hurt you, or the baby, or both. You could go back to the people who are like you and be safe, or you can stay here. But if you stay here, there is a chance you or the baby could be hurt. You understand that?"

She nodded. She had picked up graphic images of what her people were like from Gus, the doctor, and others, and she didn't think she would like that life. Gus couldn't come, and she knew from his mind that if she went back, she couldn't talk to or hear anybody else but her own kind. She didn't like that idea at all. Not only did she want to stay with Gus, Gus's own thoughts about the way her people lived came through as something scary. She let him know that she understood he was worried about her and the baby and that he didn't want her to go.

It didn't ease his conscience, but it helped him go with the flow of events and accept that, risks or not, she was staying. He had the distinct idea that no matter what the colonel had said, they wanted her for something and wouldn't let her go in any event. He didn't want to be conned by these types; he knew them all too well. If she was going to be put in harm's way, then he was going to be there for her.

That afternoon they met the colonel at a sleek, silvery transport station and boarded a magnatrain for the north. She found the station itself to be a place of wonder, and the train was really neat.

"I spoke to Inspector Kurdon before we left," the colonel told Gus. "He seems quite happy to have us, and he's particularly interested in you. He thinks your little talent might well be very useful to him."

"Maybe, maybe not," Gus responded. "It's handy, yeah, but it's not as much as it seems to other people. If they have the equivalent of a television scanner, I'd show up on it, and I'll trip any alarms. This place has got to be guarded like Fort Knox. It's not like I can just walk in there and do what I want."

"Agreed. But I'm sure he has something in mind and knows all that. Well, we'll see this evening, won't we?"

They pulled into the northern terminus station at Subar about an hour after dark. The welcoming committee wasn't that hard to spot. Two Dillians and an Erdomese female stood out from the Agonite crowd as much as or more than they did.

"Oh, my! There's only that gruesome blob and that poor girl!" Anne Marie exclaimed. "I thought there was another!"

Julian looked at the Leeming oozing off the train and frowned. "I see that Colonel Lunderman hasn't changed a bit. It's just that you can see him so much more clearly now," she commented dryly.

"Greetings, my fellow expatriates, greetings!" the colonel said with his usual oily tones. Gus had wondered if Lunderman could say "Good morning" without sounding insincere. "I am Colonel Lunderman, and we might as well get the usual shock over with right off the bat. Say hello, Gus."

All three of the others were somewhat startled when the Dahir did just that. To have a huge dragonlike multicolored creature suddenly appear where one hadn't really noticed it before was always startling.

"Strictly defense," Gus assured them. "We're too big and bright to hide, so we have this ability. You'll get used to it. I can't turn it off."

Julian recovered first. "Whew! That's *some* trick! Could have saved us a lot of trouble if *we'd* had something like that!" She looked over at the colonel. "You've come a long way since we last met, Lunderman."

"And changed a good deal. I would not have known you at all, Captain Beard." While forewarned, the colonel in fact was amazed at the transformation in the person he'd known. In voice, tone, movements, manner—in virtually every category there wasn't a trace of the Julian Beard he remembered in the Erdomese female he addressed.

"Julian, Colonel. Just Julian," she responded, grim-faced. "Captain Beard is dead, or as good as dead. Think of me entirely as you see me. I have buried him forever." *Too bad the same didn't happen to you,* she added to herself. If she'd despised the human colonel, she positively loathed what she was seeing now. Gus, too, made her feel very uncomfortable. He was *creepy.* She turned to the third, silent member of the party and softened immediately. "And this must be Terry."

Terry smiled at her, capturing the sudden warmth inside the Erdomese. She was *very* pretty and seemed smart and strong, too. Terry couldn't figure out why Gus wouldn't produce the same friendly feeling, but it wasn't anything she could do much about right now.

The four-legged blond twins were also beautiful but not easy to catch thoughts from. Their thinking seemed to go back and forth between one and the other so that it was almost as if they were the same person in two bodies. Trying to follow it made her head hurt, and she turned back to Julian.

"Come," Julian told them all, even though her attention seemed to be drawn more and more to Terry. "This is not the place to speak of things. You never know who or what's around. Let's get to the people running the show, and then we can all fill each other in on everything."

Gus looked around the station with the experienced eye of a professional cameraman. It wasn't very crowded, and all the Agonese looked the same anyway except for size and dress, but he could spot the shadows and the tails. They had a way of not looking at a person and not being even curious about that person that made them stand out to a professional's eye in the same way they did in a crowd back on Earth. He wondered which were from the cops and which were from the bad guys, but there was no way to tell that. The breed was made in the same factory.

Inspector Kurdon proved to be another of the same type, but very dry and very professional. He greeted them almost perfunctorily, and Terry couldn't help but feel that he, too, had more of an interest in her than in the others for some reason, although there was no sense from him of the friendly, warm interest radiated by Julian.

"I know you all want to compare notes, so I won't keep you long," he told them. "My people will be able to provide appropriate if not very exciting meals for all of you. I'm not going to tell you to get an early rest because the later you go to sleep and the later you wake up tomorrow, the better. We are going in tomorrow night, but not until nearly midnight. Surprise will be very important to this operation."

"Surprise? With all these people and all this security you think you really fooled 'em, Inspector?" Gus asked him.

Kurdon looked at Gus with a bit more respect. "You are absolutely right in that sense. We can hardly hide the fact that something is up here, but our intelligence assures me that they still can't figure out what it is. My advantage is that they really believe the headquarters to be both politically and physically secure. Even if they *think* that we're moving against them, it doesn't mean as much as you might believe. First of all, we are not after drugs or even criminals of any sort. We're after their computer records, which are not easily transportable."

"Won't they just erase them the moment your people break in?" the colonel asked.

"Maybe, but they have no equivalent to this headquarters anywhere else. I'm sure they have backups, but they aren't linked because such a link can't be run through other hexes and they can't be stored here and be totally secure from us. Putting this headquarters out of operation will severely cripple their entire operation worldwide. It might be months, more likely years, before they get things running with any degree of efficiency again, and not without great cost in the interim. A lot of other hexes, not to mention the Patrol, have been wanting to move on this, but they couldn't so long as Agon and Liliblod allowed this center to continue. If it's destroyed, they will move, and the politicians in their pockets will scramble to be on our side all of a sudden. For that reason, I believe they will try *not* to erase the active records but rather depend on their own security to keep us from getting to the information. Then, when it blows over, they could have their own people mixed in with our crews and download and recover what they need. That is not going to happen. I believe we *can* crack their codes, but whether we can or not, the computers there and all their data will be either in our hands or completely destroyed."

"You sound pretty confident you can get it," Julian noted with skepticism dripping from her tongue. "What if you can't?"

"The drug business is the inspector's problem," the colonel told her. "*Our* interest is quite different. Some suitable prisoners, people who work there routinely day in and day out, should be what *we* need, although getting access to the records would make it simpler and surer. If our quarry is in there, we will have her. If not, we need to know where she might have been taken."

"If they don't just kill her when you break in," Gus put in.

"If they can kill her, she's not who we are interested in," the colonel responded coolly. "However, I have already seen enough evidence on my own to suspect that this is not a problem."

"Yes, but *Lori* isn't some superman!" Tony pointed out. "We could be killing *him*!"

Kurdon looked up impatiently at the Dillian. "We have been through this already. Everything we know suggests that if we cannot free him, he's probably better off dead. He is certainly addicted to a particular mutation of this drug in any event, which will cause enough of a problem. I am open to any suggestions on making it safe, but so far I've heard none. Until I do, this matter is closed. Now, if you will excuse me, I still have a lot of preparation to do. If there are no further questions, you should go and get acquainted and eat and finally sleep."

"Just one question," Gus said. "How you gonna get *in* there?"

The impassive turtlelike head looked straight at him. "Come tomorrow night and you'll see."

As Kurdon expected, the rest of the evening was much more relaxed, with a great deal of talking and comparing stories and experiences. For the first time Gus heard the account of the kidnapping of Lori and Mavra Chang and got a picture of the latter totally at odds with any memories he had of her back in the jungles. In fact, the Mavra Chang who emerged from the descriptions and tales of the twins and from Julian sounded to Gus an awful lot like a female version of Nathan Brazil. This at first glance seemed to make even more mysterious their estrangement from one another, but, Gus thought, often the pairs that seemed to work best together were ones one would never put together on one's own. A ship with two equally strong-willed captains was a ship that sailed forever in circles.

The colonel was something of the odd man out in the circle. There was something about him that made everybody who met him feel slightly uncomfortable, and aside from some reminiscences with Tony of their shared homeland in their original native Portuguese, the colonel did not participate all that much. He excused himself early, but the rest of them went on talking well into the night.

Terry liked almost everybody except the colonel. Somehow this group of very strange-looking creatures seemed very comfortable, very natural. It was something in the way they thought and interacted; no matter how alien they now were physically from one another, they were more alike in the way they thought than any of the other creatures she'd met, including the doctor. It was a familiar, relaxed feeling that was hard to describe, but it was comfortable to her. Somehow, in a way she didn't quite get, she knew that all these people were *her* people, the same way she'd felt about Gus from the start. She didn't really try to follow much of their conversation; it was kind of dull, and a lot of it made no sense to her. They seemed to be able to talk and talk and talk on the same topic over and over without getting bored, but it didn't matter. The underlying din felt like a warm, safe blanket, a haven from the unknown and truly alien world out there.

Finally, when it was quite late, they couldn't keep it up any longer. Gus told them that he would find a place suitable for himself and not to worry; Terry was physically best suited for Julian's tent, which had that floor of soft pillows.

Gus couldn't make Julian out at first. She'd been a guy, Mister Military Recruiting Poster, then was turned into a woman in a society that did not value females, had been rescued from it by Lori, and now, with Lori gone, seemed like a strong but dedicated man hater. It was almost as if she'd literally hated, disowned, and, as she'd told the colonel at the station, killed off every trace of who and what she'd been back on Earth. After hearing the colonel's description of the old Captain Beard on the train coming north, he hadn't expected this at all. In a very different way, Julian had reinvented herself as thoroughly as Terry had.

Terry, stay with Julian. I'll be nearby, he thought in the girl's direction. *She doesn't like men much, so if you see me inside and she can't, just pretend I'm not there. Okay?*

Terry seemed a bit confused but nodded.

The inside of Julian's tent was a veritable Art Deco wonderland of colors and exotic perfume scents, and it even had a full-length mirror tall enough for the Erdomite to see her whole self in. Terry found the whole thing a little dizzying and the scents a bit overpowering, but she got used to them after a while. It was the mirror that fascinated her the most, though.

She'd seen her reflection before, but never her whole body at once, and it fascinated her. She was still not used to that face staring back at her. The thing was, she had no comparison with what she was *supposed* to look like except Gus's mental images of the old Terry, and while she could see her in the reflection, it wasn't anywhere near the same. Chubby, bigger thighs, bigger ass, bigger breasts, and there, the tummy that kind of stuck out and didn't look like the rest. *That's where the baby is growing,* she thought, more in wonder than anything else. She felt it, much like a hard lump inside her, and every once in a while, when lying around or sitting, she felt it move.

Julian watched her for a little while, then came over. "I was told you're going to have a baby. You shouldn't be anywhere near here, let alone on this kind of trip. These men don't care about you or it. I was one of them once, and I know how they think. My husband was a woman once, but the Well World made her a man, and before long he started acting and thinking just like the rest of them." She sighed. "You're a fish out of water, just like me. You can't go home, and neither can I, even to our homes here. When this is over, I'm going hunting for a place for fish out of water. Maybe an island like the one you were stuck on, uninhabited. Maybe a little multiracial place where we could live our lives and just be ourselves without having to be what we're expected to be." She paused. "You just stick with me. I'll see they don't let you come to any harm."

Terry didn't think anybody meant her harm, but a place to just live and see the baby grow without all this other stuff sounded pretty nice.

Kurdon had his Agonite commanders there as well as the foreigners about three hours after sundown.

"All right, I've briefed the advance teams already, and some of this operation is already under way," he told them. "We've taken out every shadow and spy we can't control, so they're pretty well blind, and we're set up with the explosives, drills, and weapons in the forest above the headquarters complex. The raid is set for exactly midnight. At eleven fifty-eight the gang in the market will be out cold from gas being introduced there now, and a team will enter and cut all communications from the subbasement there to the headquarters. That will set off alarms, but at exactly midnight, only two minutes later, the charges and borers will start, and we will blow the main entrance, which is in Liliblod. This may cause a diplomatic problem later, and absolutely *no one,* and I mean that, is to cross the border. The charge should be enough to bring sufficient materials down on the entrance that it will be blocked. If by any chance it is not, we have sharpshooters just this side of the border to make certain nobody gets out from that end. The only emergency exits they have are into Agon, which will be easy to control since they're in line with the air exchangers. I want every unit in place behind the borers. Get in there as fast as possible. Stun or freeze anything that moves; kill anything you see that doesn't immediately surrender. Clear?"

The Agonese, mostly in black armored outfits with helmets and clear faceplates, nodded gravely.

Kurdon turned to the visitors. "There is no sense in risking the girl at this point. One of you should remain back here with her, and there will be a guard here in case there are any nasty surprises."

"I'll stay," Gus told him.

"No, not if you're willing to come at all," the inspector responded. "I need that cloaking of yours. The design is such that once we reach the main corridor of each level, we have to use it. Once the obvious resistance is taken out, you would be very useful in scouting ahead and spotting ambushes. Your background says you've been under fire before, which makes you even more valuable, since most of my men really haven't. That true?"

"Yeah, I guess so. If you really need me, I guess so." *Though if I'm gonna stick my neck out a mile, I wish to hell I had a camera and a network to send it to.*

"Julian, you can ignore a lot, but you have a personal objective in there, and if any of your old memories and reflexes remain at all, you've had real military training and experience. Am I wrong?"

"No," she admitted. "You're right. This is a little out of my line, though. I was an air officer." Julian was startled by the offer. She'd never even considered that Kurdon would want her anywhere but back in the rear. Now she found herself nicely trapped by her principles; if he was willing to trust a woman, she could hardly say no.

"You know when to duck and can anticipate how these men will move and how they'll operate, I think, and that's enough. For you it's all volunteer, though. Go or stay."

"I'll go," she told him. She didn't really relish this any more than did Gus, but it was do it or shut up about what she could or couldn't handle.

"Good. I can't armor somebody of your type, so you'll be in the rear of the formation, but I need your eyes, ears, any extra senses you have, and your experience. I'll outfit you with a small transmitter. Use the troops as a shield and move forward as they do." He turned to the Leeming.

"Colonel, as the other military man here, I'd like you up with the main corridor force as well," Kurdon said. "Remember, though, that you're vulnerable to energy weapons and there's no way I can armor *you,* either."

"We will do as we discussed," Lunderman replied. "I assure you I will be in no more danger than anyone else."

"I was in the same air force as the colonel," Tony pointed out. *Flying fat asses like him around with his cronies and equipment to make war on his own people,* he added to himself. "Dillians are also excellent shots."

"Well, maybe, but Dillians are also exceptionally huge targets," Kurdon responded. "If you want to come, okay, but you'll be in the rear. I'm not going to let you down there until things are secure enough that you have a chance to survive. Otherwise, you'll just be in the way. I may need you for interrogation or ID, though."

"Oh, dear! That doesn't leave very much for me, does it?" Anne Marie noted. "All right, then, I suppose I'm elected to remain back here with this poor child."

"You can monitor what's going on from the command post right here," Kurdon told her.

Anne Marie looked at Tony. "*Must* you go? I'm afraid I've gotten terribly used to you."

Tony smiled and kissed her. "Don't worry. As the inspector says, I'm going to be well out of range. But I *have* to go. You understand that, don't you?"

"No, but I accept it. Take care."

Gus turned to Terry, who clearly hadn't the faintest inkling of what the hell was going on. "You stay here. They want me and some of the others to go catch some very bad people and maybe save some very good friends. You can't come because you can't help and we might get hurt protecting you. Do you understand that?"

She frowned, then hesitantly nodded. She didn't like this at all, but if Gus said to stay, then she couldn't exactly argue. She suddenly realized that some of her new friends, maybe even Gus, could get hurt, though, and it scared her. He saw the somewhat sad, somewhat panicked look on her face.

"Don't worry. You'll be here with Anne Marie, and I won't let them hurt me. You have to believe that."

It would have been easier for her to believe it if she saw that Gus believed it, too.

"Where's the Dahir?" somebody asked, and Gus responded, "Here."

"Oh, that *is* kind of nerve-racking, isn't it?" one of the Agonese soldiers commented. "Wish I could do it, though, particularly now. Okay, any way to get this headpiece on you? It's pretty small and flexible. If you can, you'll be able to hear what we say and speak to us, even in a low tone. It will also be monitored here, so if anything goes wrong, a message can be relayed. Think you can handle it?"

"It's uncomfortable, but yes. Over the head and then below the snout on my neck. That will put the output mike right against the translator."

"Fair enough. You *have* done this before?"

"Yeah, but in another life and with a lot more equipment."

"Okay, people! Let's take a little walk in the woods!" Kurdon called to them all. "And keep it quiet, huh?"

Someone tried to hand Julian a rifle, but she refused, holding out a hand. "I'll make do with these," she told him. *I have to.*

It was a cloudy night, which helped conceal their movements but gave Tony some vision problems. Someone handed her an Agonese helmet, which was extremely loose on her and pinched her hair something awful in the back but which proved a little high-tech marvel. It probably would have been even more of one if it had been connected to the rest of the armor-plated suit, but the faceplate proved to have pretty good night vision abilities.

Basically nocturnal, Gus managed to keep position, and Julian needed no special gear, simply relying on infrared.

They walked for what seemed like a great distance through increasingly thick woods and rolling terrain until at last they came upon a large unit already in place and surrounding what looked like a giant pencil the size of a small house on some kind of treads.

Kurdon went to the device, nodded to the technicians standing by it, and looked at his watch, then signaled for two of the technicians to move. They got up on the treads, pressed something, and a small room in the very rear of the thing was revealed. They got in, sat down, strapped in, threw some switches, and then the entry closed behind them. There was a dull whining sound from the device now, and Julian's eyes could see a sudden glow from not just the "point" of the pencil shape but from the tapered area as well.

"What *is* that thing?" she asked a soldier near her.

"Construction machine. It's used for tunnels on the railway, for reshaping rock formations, that kind of thing. There are only three of them in existence, and somehow he's got all three here tonight."

"You mean he's going to bore holes right into their roof? Can we follow? I mean, it's bound to be molten."

"It cools pretty quick. You have any feeling in those hooves?"

"No, not really."

"Then if we can go in with these boots, you can, too. Don't worry about it. We'll see that you make it."

The comment irritated her, but she stilled her tongue. No use pissing off somebody who was supposed to give her cover.

"Market is secure," Kurdon told them, the news coming through everybody's communicator at once. "Demolition team in place. Air exchange patrols check in by number."

They couldn't hear the responses, but apparently Kurdon was satisfied.

Nervous and scared, as he should be, Julian thought, *but he's having the time of his macho life. I bet he's dreamed of this moment.*

"Borer to full. Demolition team ready at my count. Ten . . . nine . . . eight . . . seven . . . six . . . five . . . four . . . three . . . two . . . one . . . *Now!*"

Just to the northeast of them a massive explosion sounded, shaking the very ground. Liliblod was a nontech hex; Julian had to wonder what the hell they'd found that would make that big a bang.

At the same moment the entire tapered part of the borer glowed red and then suddenly shot a blindingly hot white energy beam so powerful that Julian's eyes reflexively switched to day vision. It didn't matter. The whole forest was lit up, and nobody could watch that beam. Not far away, there were similar illuminations in the no longer dark wood.

Kurdon's plan was simple given the technology he had to work with. The first borer, almost on the border itself, would open up the main entrance to forces that could drop in and secure the hopefully trapped but panicked and confused denizens inside in one stroke. That done, they would move to secure all the security controls, taking command of them, then move a force back along the first level. The colonel would go in with this team.

The second borer, with Julian, would move in and secure the middle area, followed by a ground force larger than the other two. These would proceed in both directions, linking up with the first group on that end and the third group, with Gus, coming in the back and pressing forward. Once the first level was secure, they would use internal access if they could to go down; otherwise, portable borers would come in through the ceilings. The rear part of the second level was said to hold the cells; the forward part was the labs. Then the procedure would be repeated on the third and final level, where the computers, living quarters, and more cells were. *That* was the main objective and might possibly be the toughest—or the easiest. Few crooks bottled in so thoroughly liked to go out shooting; their chances were far better if they were taken prisoner. Or so it was theorized.

The borers cut off, and it was suddenly *too* dark once more, except for a dully glowing, perfectly symmetrical tunnel going down at an angle just where the borer had been pointed. The technicians moved the borer back on its treads; its job was done.

A small rectangular vehicle now moved up to the hole and, parked right in front of it, was opened by two soldiers. Water or something like it gushed out and down the tunnel, creating a cloud of steam that quickly cleared.

"Tunnels safe and coated," Kurdon reported to them. "Prepare to move in. Take it slow and easy. Don't slip. The angle's a good twenty degrees."

That worried Julian, with her hooves, but while the tunnel appeared perfectly round from a distance, up close it proved quite jagged and irregular inside. The first group had also strung a rope along each side and secured it, so there was a handhold to use if need be. She found it tough going but not impossible, and she was well in before it suddenly occurred to her that at the end of this thing there was bound to be one heck of a drop and there was no way she was going to be able to get down on a rope or temporary ladder.

It was eerie at the end, a dark hole filled with lots of lights—like dozens of flashlights waving around in a black cave—lots of echoing shouts, and the sound of both conventional gunfire and energy beams not too far off.

She brought herself as close to a sitting position as she could and was relieved when she saw an Agonese soldier on a ladder reaching up to grab her. They were remarkably strong for their size, she noted, accepting the offered hand and feeling not at all good that she had to do so.

There was the sound of muffled explosions both forward and in back of her. "Concussion grenades," a sergeant told her. "We're lobbing them in every doorway and opening we find. They'll knock most anything inside cold but don't do much damage."

She switched again to infrared and saw a well-organized operation going on. It was also *some* headquarters for a criminal operation. The corridor seemed to be four or five meters high and carpeted, and the conventional lights from the soldiers' helmets revealed a place that looked less like a drug hideout and more like a luxury hotel.

"Entrance area secure. Lights coming on on level one only," Kurdon's voice came to them, and soon the whole ceiling flashed on, bathing them all in a soft but ample indirect light.

For the second time Julian had an ego-killing thought. *My God! What am I doing here? These people are more professional than I am!* If Kurdon had invited her along to prove a point, he was doing a damned good job.

She could still hear firing in back of them.

"We're moving out toward the back end with this squad, ma'am," the sergeant told her. "You can come, but watch it. As you can hear, this place is a lot bigger and more complicated than we thought."

She could only nod. "Shows you what you can do with unlimited money, doesn't it? Go on, I'll watch your back." *At least that's something I can do here,* she thought ruefully.

It wasn't until they had the lights back on that the officer in charge of the rear complex team called for Gus.

"These rooms go into rooms that go into rooms," the officer said in a mixture of wonder and disgust. "We can't be sure what's still in there. Just go ahead on your own and scout it. We can tell where you are by the transponder, so you won't get stunned or shot. Here's a pistol. You look like you can handle one. We need to find the location of a downward stairway as quickly as possible, so that's your objective."

Gus stared at the pistol but felt very uncertain about it. *I don't kill people; I take pictures of people killing people,* he thought, with a sense of unreality about it all. He didn't know if he *could* kill anybody.

But he still took the gun. It felt heavy and all wrong in his tiny, four-fingered hand, but he knew he could hold it and fire it. It was one of those Buck Rogers ray guns; no problems with recoil or ammo, at least so long as the battery held out.

He was appalled at the size and scope of the place. *Jeez! Don Francisco Campos was a two-bit piker, wasn't he? This place is the fuckin' Maui Hilton! Wonder where the swimming pool and saunas are.* He wondered how Juan Campos managed to fit into this kind of setup. For crime, this was strictly first-class, and classy to boot.

He was careful not to enter any of the rooms until after they'd tossed in the stun bombs. It was quickly clear, though, that the complex went off in both directions for some distance, and just tossing those things in the first room in a series of rooms didn't get too many people. Oh, there were a couple lying about in the first room he entered, but the others either stayed back out of that exposed area or came in after the blast, when the soldiers would feel safe.

Damn if some of 'em *didn't* look like real live Donald Ducks. Not too funny-looking, though; some of 'em looked real tough. Even so, there was a veritable United Nations of the Well World represented here. Gooey things and mean-looking suckers and women with goat heads and humongous breasts and a walking toadstool or two, not to mention a couple of two-legged alligators wearing pants and the biggest damned frogs he had ever seen.

He went from room to room to room, cataloging what he saw in low tones and warning the squad if any of the critters emerged with weapons in hand or lay in wait. He reckoned he was saving a number of lives, and that made him feel good, if not any less scared to death. With *this* big a zoo, there was no telling if he'd run into one or another creature that might not have a problem seeing Dahirs.

Finally, in one rear room that looked like a luxury suite at the Waldorf except for the fact that it was clearly built for some large humanoids with bull heads and horns and some of their cowlike girlfriends, whose unconscious forms he'd passed two rooms earlier, he found the jackpot. This was clearly a visitor's suite, and visitors could easily get lost in a place like this.

He couldn't read it, but it sure as hell looked like a map of the whole place.

Welcome to the Drug Lord Ritz, he thought with some amazement. *Man!* Had they ever been cocky and arrogant!

He made his way carefully back out to the main corridor and hunted for the officer. "Got something that will make life a lot easier if you can read it," he told the startled Agonite.

The officer looked at the maps, and his reptilian jaw opened in amazement. "I should say you did!" He looked at the first level map, then the second, then looked up and pointed. "Nine more doors up. Emergency stairs."

"I'm surprised they don't have elevators," Gus commented, still amazed at the place.

"They do, but they don't have power now. Besides, do *you* want to be in the first car when the door opens?"

"You got a point there."

"As soon as we do a linkup and get a first level secured, we go down. I'll radio command and control where the other access stairs are."

"How are we doin' so far?"

"Well, we knocked out about a third of 'em. The rest so far have been equally divided between giving up and fighting it out. We hope it'll be easier below, since they know they don't have a way out if we get down there, but you never know. A lot of their security people will be down there, and the bosses probably kept their loyalty with drugs. When an addict is faced with losing his drugs or is charged up on them, who knows?"

"Yeah. Thanks for the optimism," Gus commented dryly.

As expected, they had captured a huge number of the staff trying to flee out of the main entrance into Liliblod. The explosion hadn't completely sealed things off—there were more entrances and exits than they had thought—but it had trapped enough.

The colonel had come in with the first wave but didn't stay for the wrap-up. Instead, he pressed himself against the wall and slowly and carefully oozed up it to the ceiling, then began a slow but steady flow back toward the middle group well ahead of the commandos. A Zhonzhorpian with an energy beam rifle emerged from a doorway beneath the suspended Leeming, huge crocodilelike jaws open and dripping saliva, eyes blazing mad.

A pseudopod shot out and struck the gunman on his head. He dropped the rifle and roared in pain, clutching at his head, but his hands went into thick goo and seemed to be stuck there. With slow deliberation, Lunderman flowed down and around the man and engulfed him. He remained like that for a short while. There was a sort of hissing sound as if something were being dissolved in acid, and then a larger Lunderman reached up and flowed back onto the ceiling area. There was no trace of the very large gunman who had been there except his rifle, still lying where he'd dropped it. A few moments later various metallic and plastic pieces fell from the ceiling to join it as the Leeming rejected what could not be digested.

Far from being satiated, Lunderman was instead irritated. There was a limit to how many of this size he could absorb without going dormant and dividing, and this bubble-brained idiot had known nothing of importance.

Worse, Lunderman had no idea what his limit was. He hadn't ever eaten more than one a week until now, and that had been sufficient. Even dissolved, the additional mass of one was significant if not any sort of handicap. Judging from the added mass of this one, the upper limit might well be no more than five or six. If he doubled his size, he could not stop the process.

It was unlikely that there would be many of the cartel on this level who had any information except by sheer chance, anyway. He began to search for a way down. Best to find it quickly, anyway, lest some nervous soldiers spot him and not recognize him as a friend.

As he heard the concussion grenades going off not far in front of him and just as the lights came on, he found it. Some sort of service elevator, he decided, linking the upper rooms with perhaps the kitchen or even the labs. It didn't matter. The door was easy enough to dissolve with the extra energy he'd absorbed, and to his great relief the car was down at the bottom. He flowed along the tiny, meter-square shaft until he reached the second level. The automatic trip on the door was obvious from this side; he didn't have to burn through it to open it.

On the other side was a small room that possibly served as a crew lunch room or break station. Nothing special, and expected. It was deserted, and he moved to the door, listened carefully, but saw no crack or opening where he might extend a pseudopod to scout what was beyond. He flowed back up to the ceiling, reached down, and used the manual grip to push the door open slowly.

The room beyond was lit by recessed emergency lighting, giving it a dull orange glow. It was a big place and looked very much like a state-of-the-art, high-tech lab, which it was. There didn't seem to be anybody there, although some things were still cooking and bubbling away.

It *still* wasn't what he needed, but it was one step closer. Below this, if he could find another easy way down, would be the master computer room.

There was no way Tony could get down one of those tunnels, something Kurdon surely had known when he had agreed to allow the centaur to come along. Now she stood just inside the border, staring out into dark Liliblod.

"Damn! They say there's like *three* entrances out!" one of the soldiers commented. "We got the main one, but the other two are beyond our reach by this point. They say the complex is bigger than an office building! Crime sure pays sometimes."

"Until now," Tony commented. "What about those other entrances? Anybody covering them now?"

"We sent a few people up there, but any of the big fish who wanted to get away are well into Liliblod right now, and our people are heading to shut them down from inside by now. One's just kind of a side door, I guess, for private comings and goings, but the other one's like a stable. They say they got some very strange animals in there."

Tony was suddenly alert. "Any of them with a body like mine? Animal head, perhaps with a horn, but a body like mine?"

"I dunno. I'll check. Hold on a moment." The soldier said something into his communicator and waited for the reply. "A few with bodies kinda like yours, but nothing with a horn."

"See if you can have somebody from the middle group contact Julian.

That's the name. Report this to whoever you can get and ask them to get word to her. If he's anywhere around there, she'll recognize him."

"Who?"

"Just do it."

The soldier complied. "Message received and relayed, they say. That's all. I can't guarantee it'll be passed on. They'll be linking and going down to level two shortly."

Tony thought furiously, frustrated at not being able to get down there to see what was going on for herself. "How far is this stable? And how far in from the border is it?"

"About four leegs that way, and maybe just a harg inside, but that's far enough. Why?"

Four leegs was maybe half a kilometer, and a harg was no more than ten meters. "I was thinking maybe I could enter from there."

"Lady, you don't wanna do that. You got colonies of them Liliblodians right up there in the trees; I don't think they're real happy with us at the moment, and they don't give a shit about diplomacy and protests and all that other crap. They'd be on us like a plague if any of us went across that border, high-tech weapons be damned. They got sense enough to know they'd be wiped out, but they'd take a ton of us with 'em before they went and might figure it's worth it. They're probably so mad at us for blowing up the main entrance in their territory, they're just *waiting* for one of us to stray ever so slightly in."

"I came through there once before, and they didn't even show themselves. And I'm not of Agon. They *might* hesitate."

"Yeah, and if they don't, you'll be dead in ten seconds. Don't think your size will save you. Dozens of 'em will drop down on top and cover you, and you'll get enough poison in the first few seconds to kill half the world. Besides, even if you managed to get in, how would you ever get the heck *out*?"

It was a good point. Still, she was determined to do *something*. "Tell your men up there I'm coming and not to shoot. Don't worry. I accept your argument; I am not going to try it. But if I can be very close, perhaps I can be of some help."

With that, she trotted off toward the north.

Julian was frankly relieved to get the call. Frustrated and feeling useless, she was in no mood to follow them down to farther levels.

Assured that at least level one was now secure, she made her way forward toward the main entrance, from which someone would guide her to Tony. She was most of the way there when, just behind her, something came out of a doorway roaring with fury and charged right at her back.

She didn't even think, she just acted, shifting forward on her forelegs, rearing up the powerful hind ones, and kicking with all the strength she could muster.

The hooves struck the creature in the face and snapped it back. The thing gave a startled cry and then was flung backward against the far wall with the force of the blow.

Julian came down slightly unbalanced and with her hind legs splayed. She was a moment realizing what the trouble was and easing herself back up. Turning, still on all fours, she could feel her heart pounding in her throat and whatever the Erdomese used for adrenaline coursing through her. She feared a second attack, but the creature was not moving at all, just lying limply like a rag doll thrown to the floor by a bored child.

With some shock, she realized that the thing was dead. Looking around lest there be any more ugly surprises, she carefully approached the body as a couple of Agonite commandos ran toward her.

The thing looked like somebody's nightmare of a teddy bear, perhaps a meter and a half tall when standing. Those teeth and that fierce expression, now frozen in death, were never on any teddy bear *she'd* have around, though.

Two commandos approached the creature cautiously, then checked it out. "Dead," one said, and the other nodded.

"Lady, that's some *mean* kick you got," the first one commented to her. "I think you broke its neck and maybe its back."

"Yeah," the other agreed with grudging respect. "That guy must've weighed three times what you do, and he *flew.*"

She was beginning to calm down a little and realize what she'd done. Now, where had *that* come from? It had been so natural, so automatic, she hadn't even had time to think before it was over, but she sure hadn't known she could *do* that.

Maybe *she'd* been the one to underestimate the Erdomese female.

The only thing was, she couldn't stand back up. She was locked in the four-footed position. She didn't mind that much; it was both comfortable and natural, and she used it often by choice, but now she guessed that it was part of the defense built into her. About the only problem was, it made her slightly shorter than the Agonese, even with her head up and forward on her long neck. Oh, well.

She felt suddenly *terrific*—euphoric, even. She'd actually done something! She wasn't as defenseless or helpless as she'd thought!

Not wanting to admit that at the moment she *couldn't* get back up, she said confidently, "I think I'll go the rest of the way on all fours, boys. I don't think my arms could take too many more bounces like that."

They watched her go on with obvious respect in their eyes.

"I hope my wife doesn't have any hidden tricks like that," one of them said.

The other felt his own throat. "Yeah."

Gus carefully scouted the stairway down to the second level. It was quite dark, and even his night-adjusted eyes had a problem with it, but there were small bumps of yellow lights running down both sides, powered by some internal source, that made footing not a problem. *Seeing* was something else again, but the sterile, flat walls carried sound well, and he could hear nothing close by.

If they were waiting for company, those on the second level certainly weren't doing it on the stairs or landing. Gus figured that they would expect a grenade to be tossed down the chute here, and with the echo, nobody would last very long. Most likely they would be waiting beyond the doors to this level.

While they might not be able to see Gus, they could certainly expect the door to open and probably wouldn't wait to find out who or what had opened it. He pressed up against the door and could hear voices which made him pretty sure that a nasty welcome awaited.

"Armed party probably barricaded just beyond the second level doorway," he reported into the mike. "No way I can open it without exposing myself. Stairs clear to level two."

"All right. Why not move down and check the bottom level, then," came a tinny-sounding voice near his ear. "If the stairs are clear, we won't give them a warning by blowing anything there. I'm sending down an advance party now to take out whatever's behind the door. If you can get into the bottom level safely, use your own judgment. Otherwise proceed back to two after the opening is secured."

"Okay. Heading down."

The bottom looked like the second level, but unlike there, he couldn't hear any signs of life on the other side. *Okay, Gus, how lucky do you feel?* he asked himself. *Are you Clint Eastwood or Mickey Mouse?*

Mickey Mouse, he answered himself, but he was still tempted to try the door. Once inside, he'd be virtually invisible to whoever and whatever was there.

He heard the commando team come down to the second door above him. There would surely be some explosions and shooting before too long. Maybe, just maybe, if he could open the door and get through quickly at the same time they opened up above, it would panic and confuse anybody with a bead on the door.

Hell, it was either that or get his eardrums broken sitting there.

He took hold of the door, then waited. *Come on, come on, let's get it over with!* he thought to the commandos above.

Suddenly there was the quick sound of an open door and a big explosion and then the nearly deafening din of weapons fire just above. He pushed back the door, standing to one side, and when it seemed as if nothing was coming out and nobody was nearby, he slipped quickly inside it, leaving it open.

There was emergency lighting here as well, only better than up top. It made the area glow a very dull red, but it was sufficient for him to see and get around.

If he remembered the layout, he was now in the area where they kept prisoners. Ahead would be the living quarters, the master kitchen, and then the computer complex.

It definitely had the look of a prison or, more accurately, a dungeon. He found why there hadn't been a welcoming party for him there immediately. The whole entrance foyer was little more than a giant cage of thick mesh with an electronically operated door at the end. There was no lock, latch, or knob on this side; it clearly was intended to be opened only from the inside.

That meant a guard or guards with some kind of surveillance system. He looked around the ceiling and upper wall area in the dim red glow and finally spotted where the camera just had to be. That left him with a problem.

If everything sealed when the main power went off and there was always a guard or two inside there, then the guard must be in a sort of in-between cage between prison doors. He might well be trapped in there. In fact, he was pretty sure he could hear somebody moving just beyond. How the hell could he deal with that guy?

He had a thought that was so nutty, it just might work. It was, after all, very thick mesh.

"Hey!" he called out. "You okay in there?"

The guard stirred and hesitated, unsure of who this was or whether to respond.

"Cm'on! I'm one step ahead of them bastards upstairs. They're gonna blow through here like butter with all the artillery they got, and right now I'm gonna be right in between 'em like the filling in a sandwich!"

The guard was more scared than suspicious. "You're with *us*?"

Gus gave a loud, impatient sigh. "If I was with *them,* this door would be blowing up about now. Cm'on, man! It ain't much, but it's the only chance I got!"

The guard still hesitated. "I got my orders. If the power goes, nobody in, period. Not without an okay from the boss or security."

"What the world you think this *is*, you dumb ass? It's the cops. It's a whole damn army. They already got the top level, and they're working on the lab level now. We're finished. All you can do is either make a break with me if we can or stay and die."

"Ain't gonna break out from *this* level!" the idiot said, almost with pride.

"No? Well, then we can fight or give up. If you gotta give up, you don't want to be the guy who's handy when they start checkin' the cells. Huh? Now, stop clowning and let me in!"

"I—I—I dunno. I don't know what to do."

"Anybody come up and reinforce you?"

"N—no. They all lit out for the front."

"Leaving you here to either buy 'em more time or take the fall. You're a sucker. I don't have any more time for this. I'm gonna open up on this door, and either it's gonna give for me or I'll run out of ammo. Maybe if I cut through this cage with this needler, I'll accidently hit the dumbest asshole in this whole complex."

"I—no. I, er—don't do that! Here!"

There was a fumbling sound and the turning of a manual key and a wheel, and the door swung open. Gus entered and found a sorry-looking little guy in a black outfit sitting there on a stool with a big energy rifle cradled in his lap. He was a little twerp, like an anemic otter in full dress, and he actually had a tiny pair of glasses sitting on his snout.

"W—well? Why don't you come in?" the guard asked, the rifle coming up.

"Right here, you dumb shit!" Gus shouted in his face, grabbing the rifle and bringing the stock down hard on his head. The guard collapsed in a heap, and Gus, rather than worrying if the little guy was dead or alive, felt a little thrill of satisfaction.

"Sucker," he said, checking the rifle and seeing that it was still in good shape. He decided it was handier than the little pistol if he could manage to hold on to it.

The inner door was easy to open, although the wheel was hard to turn with his small and relatively weak arm muscles. Finally the lock clicked and he was able to pull it open.

Inside was a long and ugly chamber of horrors.

LILIBLOD

HE HADN'T DONE IT, and it made him feel worse than ever. He'd actually had the chance back there in Clopta, and he hadn't done it. He'd meekly gone back over the border and started following the same old trail, just as before.

What bothered him most was that he was well inside Liliblod before he realized that he hadn't done it or even remembered what he'd intended to do. It was almost as if he could have his opinions and dream his dreams, but he could only act on what he was told to do.

Maybe it's still going on, Lori worried. *Maybe just changing me physically into a packhorse isn't the end of it. What if even my brain is becoming more horse than human?*

The more he thought about it, the more certain he was that this was the case. He could think frantically and hard, even plan, but for how long at a time? Was he thinking slower, or were there very long stretches of time when he just didn't think at all? He'd made this trip countless times, over and over, but how many times and for how long? He didn't know. How long did it actually take him to walk the trail from Clopta to Agon? Again, he didn't know, not even how many days it might be. How long had it been since he'd meekly walked back in? Was it today? Or yesterday? Or was it further back than that?

He had no idea.

There were times when he was totally lucid, remembering a lot of specifics about everything, and there were other times when he couldn't remember much at all. Why, just back there, when he had thought of escaping, he had remembered most of a map and how to get around. He *knew* he had. But try as he might, he couldn't get that information back now.

He had been losing it little by little, piece by piece, and he hadn't even realized it until now. Maybe the process was speeding up. Maybe it was nearly done. How many facts could a horse's brain hold? Not too many, because it didn't need to hold all that many. He ate, he slept, and he walked the same trail. Could it be that deep down that was all he really wanted to do?

Or was it that he no longer had the *will* to do anything different and was making excuses? That his old self said "Fight!" but his current self wanted only peace and contentment? How much of him was gone, and how much had he himself pushed away so he couldn't make use of it?

He didn't even know how long he had mused on these depressing topics, but it was quite a while.

One thing he suddenly *did* know was that he wasn't far from the end now. Close enough from the scent that he could smell and taste the hay and oats and other good stuff they had at the headquarters, far better than just grass.

He usually stopped after dark and slept till morning, but he was close and he didn't really *need* to see all that much to make it. Not far, not far . . .

Suddenly, ahead, there was a massive explosion! The noise startled him so much, he reared back and shook his head in disbelief. And then came the sounds of guns firing and loud shouting by lots of people.

Suddenly terrified of what lay beyond, he stopped right on the trail and just stood there, unsure of what to do.

The tumult ahead died down after a while, but not the one *overhead*. The tops of the trees were alive with hissings and buzzings and sheer rage, and he heard those *things* begin to move along the treetops, move toward the border and the noise.

Suddenly two figures, a Cloptan man and a Zhonzhorpian, came running toward him on the trail. He tried to back up and back off a bit to let them by, but suddenly a flashlight beam caught him square in the face.

The two men were out of breath, were half-dressed, and looked to be in a terrible way. Soon they began arguing and then shouting at one another, and after a moment the Cloptan took something from a case he was carrying and a bright white beam caught the Zhonzhorpian full and enveloped him; suddenly the tall crocodilelike creature was no more.

The Cloptan then approached Lori, and he was even more terrified after seeing what had happened to the other, surely a companion rather than an enemy.

The Cloptan patted him on the side, trying to reassure him with the gesture and meaningless talk, and oddly, it *did* have a calming influence on him.

Then the Cloptan climbed up on his back and latched the case to the saddlebags while keeping the gun in one hand. Firmly, the rider turned Lori around, away from the end of his journey and back toward where he'd come from. Cloptans weren't horribly heavy, but this was going to be one heck of a walk.

He wished he knew what had happened back there, but whatever it was, it sure wasn't good.

AGON-LILIBLOD BORDER

"LIEUTENANT, I THINK YOU better get some men down to the third level as quick as you can," Gus said into the mike. "I left the door open. I think I killed the lone guard, but if he isn't dead, he's too dumb to do anything but give up."

"What's the matter? What did you find?"

"Monsters. Monsters in the basement. You might want the inspector down here as well. If Agon doesn't have capital punishment, I think it will by tomorrow."

There was silence for a moment, then the officer said, "All right. I'll send a squad down and relay your message. Will you wait for them?"

Gus looked around and shivered slightly. "I don't think so. The guard station at the other end is empty, but the door's locked. I think I can blast through it, though, now that I've seen how the doors are made. I'll report when I can."

"Resistance on the second level was light after that initial barricade. It's mostly labs, and it looks like they ran when things started happening. Watch yourself, though. Any of them that didn't come up to level one are pretty likely to be down there—and desperate."

The cells were of the highest quality for dungeon cells. High-tech, Gus thought. State of the art. Thick, shockproof, probably bullet- and rayproof doors made of some material that nonetheless was totally transparent save for the electronic locks and a small slit for feeding prisoners not otherwise restrained inside.

There were 1,560 races, it was said, on the Well World, and he'd seen only a tiny fraction of them. And even though many were bizarre in the extreme, none of them could be as bizarre as some of the *creatures* in the cells. Hybrids, genetic mutations, people whose own bodies were in the process of re-forming themselves into the visions of insane designers.

Some screamed, some cried out, others sobbed, but he could not help them or look at them.

Now, what the hell does any of this have to do with a drug ring? he wondered.

Designer creatures. For what? Designer jobs? Animals with the smarts of humans to avoid detection, follow complex orders? Traitors, people who'd failed in their work for the gang, now forced to become monsters at the beck and call of their masters? Why kill them when they could be turned into something useful? Recycling taken to its ultimate degree.

There were a few that weren't like that, but they weren't much better off. Chained to walls, scarred, ripped open but still alive in agony . . . They must have had information somebody wanted. At least it was more familiar. He'd seen this sort of stuff back on Earth in central Africa, in the Middle East, and in a few of the less pleasant Far Eastern beauty spots. In some ways the mentality was the same no matter where you went, even here. The others, the monsters—that was just a high-tech extension of the same idea. New toys for the depraved.

The idea of a Campos with this kind of power was disturbing. The original incarnation was bad enough. Gus remembered what a big-time syndicate boss had told him once. It wasn't about money. Money was rarely a concern after a short while. It was all about power.

"Hey, Lieutenant, you got a news crew here in Agon?" he asked through the mike.

A moment later, after a request to repeat the question, the answer came. "Yes. Several."

"Well, get 'em down here when you can. Let 'em see this, photograph it, broadcast it. Even though it'll make every viewer sick to their stomach, it'll legitimize this raid and your government more than anything else. Some of those corrupt bastards who protected this place all these years should watch it, too. And if they don't know how to cover it right, call me. I'm an expert."

He reached the jail door at the other end. Knowing where the locking mechanism was, he fired the rifle on full blast, holding it steady until the lock turned first black, then red, and finally white. He released the trigger, then reared back on his tail and kicked with both powerful feet. The door resisted the first time, but the second kick saw it move back. He had been so angry, he saw he'd actually bent the material.

The secondary door had been left open, since it was never designed to be more than a security lock for people wanting in. As he went through it, shots rang out all around and tracerlike needler rays rained down on him. For a moment he thought they could see him, but then he realized that they were just firing blindly at the sound.

"Hold your fire, you idiots!" somebody called. "Don't waste energy! Wait until they actually come through!"

Good advice, Gus thought with nervous release. They wouldn't have had to do much more of that before they'd have winged or even killed him. Blind shots were his worst enemy.

They'd overturned tables, beds, sofas, everything they had, and made a pretty fair barricade. This was *not* going to be easy, and he was suddenly acutely aware that he was between them and the commandos he'd just urged to come down behind him.

There didn't seem to be much of a choice. He picked a weaker and less sturdy part of the barricade, went over to it, took a deep breath, then simply charged in with a roar, making furniture and appliances fly all over the place.

The gunmen were so startled that the ones closest to him pulled back in total fear, while the ones on the other side again opened fire on the now-deserted corridor.

He didn't wait for them to figure out what was going on. He was, after all, a very large target even if invisible. He opened up on the fleeing men with the rifle, forgetting he still had it on maximum. The whole corridor was bathed in white energy, and those caught directly in the beam were disintegrated, while those farther away found their clothing and skin in flames.

He turned to the others who were just turning to bear on him and charged into them with a hideous roar that echoed terrifyingly down the corridor, so close in and so violent that they had no chance to use their weapons. There was no rifle this time; Gus's huge reptilian jaws opened and closed with savage fury as his targets futilely struggled and fought to break free. One down . . . Two . . . Three . . . Where the hell was four?

Running down the hall right into the cells, where he would undoubtedly find a welcoming party by now.

His mouth was dripping with blood in three colors, and there were pieces of people from three races all over the place, but nothing alive.

And the funny thing was, he felt *great*!

He looked around on the floor and didn't see his own rifle but saw a furry dismembered hand still clutching a nearly identical one and pried it away.

Staff living quarters and kitchens. He could just walk right through them to where he really wanted to go, but he didn't think he would.

He wondered what the current record was for the Agon commandos for killing these turds and also whether it was possible for him to break it. The ghost of his old Lutheran pastor shattered in his mind. Hell, he was really starting to *enjoy* this!

Julian's walk back to what they had called the "stable" entrance had calmed her somewhat, and she was finally able to relax enough to stand on two legs again.

She wasn't sure just what they were bringing her this far away to look at, and when she saw, she *still* wasn't quite sure.

"What *are* they?" she asked an Agonese sergeant.

"Beats us, ma'am. We were told maybe *you* could tell *us*. We ran 'em through our own system by shooting video up to the command center, but they can't place them, either, at least not by species or hex."

They looked mostly like horses and mules, but not *quite*. No two were nearly alike beyond the basic form, but no two rang exactly true, either. She could see what the Agonese meant and why they hadn't really been able to explain it.

There were tall ones and short ones, big ones and little ones. They divided first into two classes which she thought of as equine and elephantine. The equine had thin legs of varying lengths, balanced torsos, and heads on long necks. They tended to have camouflagelike colors, dull and mixed, with lots of browns and olives. Hair was short or long; tails were optional and of varying lengths and designs. The heads, though, were what caught her attention. They all looked different, and many of them looked unsettlingly like caricatures of the faces of some Well World races.

The elephantine were more bizarre, with very thick legs; wide, round padded hooves; and large, squat bodies that tended to be hairless and dull-colored, with pink or gray or mottled variations, as if they'd once had hair but it had fallen out. They, too, had faces, but the faces—again all different and with some hint of familiarity—were virtually looking out from the top front of the torsos without distinct heads or necks. She couldn't imagine how they fed.

The worst thing was, they all looked at her and the others with eyes that seemed very intelligent indeed and expressions, when they were capable of them, of extreme sadness.

"Did you capture anybody alive from this area?" she asked them.

"Yeah, but they haven't been too talkative yet. We asked them what these things were and why they were here, and all they said was that it wasn't their area but they thought they were couriers."

"Couriers!"

"Yeah. Apparently this is a fairly new batch still being trained. They have some that run through Liliblod to Clopta, but most of them go to other areas where they can run stuff by night through backcountry areas without being seen."

"Do they make sounds?"

"Uh huh, but they're just crazy screeches or bellows. Nothing intelligible, even on translator, if that's what you're thinking."

She was thinking worse than that. She was thinking of those two doctors she'd gone to see with their miracle experiments and records that had included information on Glathrielians and Erdomese.

I actually let them put something into me, *too! My God! Am I going to turn into one of these things?*

She told herself to calm down, that they wouldn't have been crazy enough to try anything like that and risk exposure, but she couldn't quite convince herself. *I'm going to be a paranoid hypochondriac for months,* she admitted ruefully to herself.

She tried to pull herself together. "Are they—natural? I mean, do they seem, well, normal in the sense of being put together right?"

"Well, as far as we can tell, they're all sexless," the sergeant told her. "Of course, with *those,* who could tell what's really missing?"

Julian thought of Lori and Mavra Chang. Couriers? Like *these* monsters?

"I want to talk topside if I can," she told the sergeant. "They told me that my Dillian companion couldn't get down here. I'd like to contact her if I could. I need to compare some notes. Is that possible?"

"Could be. I'll call the command center and see if they have a channel open."

Inside of five minutes she was talking to Tony. "Where are you?" she asked the centaur.

"If you're where they said you were, I'm probably about five meters on top of you," Tony told her. "What's the situation?"

As quickly and as adequately as she could, she described what she'd seen and her thoughts on the missing pair.

"I agree, but we must remember that these poor wretches were probably their own people being punished for failures, while Lori and Mavra were objects of revenge. I can see them perhaps making Lori one of these poor creatures, but I cannot see Campos doing that to Mavra Chang. If I remember Lori's account of his adventure in the jungle, I can see why Campos would want some revenge, but not the kind of long-term suffering that would be due to Mavra. I know something of the code and the way people like Campos think. It was that sort of person that caused me to stay away from my native country until democracy was restored there. Lori was a point of honor, a detail, even though an important one. But Mavra Chang by direct action impacted personally on

Campos. She stopped his attempted rape, she kidnapped and drugged him in the jungles, and then she caused him to wind up here. No, Mavra Chang would be special, someone who would have to be in permanent hurt and humiliation, available for frequent lifelong scorn. Considering what you have told me, who knows *what* these people were capable of?"

Tony thought for a moment. "A pet, perhaps. A dog or cat or whatever would be appropriate but not too obvious. Something that could be walked on a leash through a public park. You see what I am getting at?"

"Yes, I'm afraid I do," Julian replied.

"Someone should be able to remember Lori and what they turned him into," Tony said confidently. "They are still in a state of shock, but interrogations should bring results. That is a big place, but it is not *that* big, and I would suspect that the permanent staff knows pretty much what is going on throughout the place. But Mavra—I fear that unless we can get into that computer and find out precisely what they did or unless we can crack those two butchers open, we will have to reach Mavra by going through Juan Campos."

"I've never met this person," Julian told her, "but I am beginning to think that I *want* to meet her. Preferably in a nice dark alley . . ."

In a hex with the kind of technology that could put a very powerful computer into something the size of a claw, the computer center was incredibly huge. How much information did they have here? What could these rooms of memory cubes, each capable of holding trillions of facts, possibly contain? More than merely all the data on the drug business, that was for sure. Blackmail on thousands of leaders in every hex they went to? Biological information on every single race, with details on how to make something for each that would addict them? Probably, Gus thought. At least that.

He was as surprised by the size of the place as he was by its emptiness. He'd expected at least a few people here, just to make certain that this stuff didn't fall into anybody's hands, but the place was completely deserted.

Or was it?

Over there—a terminal of some sort and something, something large but indistinct, sitting at it . . .

Colonel, what the hell are you up to?

Jeez! The Leeming was *huge*, a blob fit for the horror movies almost. At least twice the size he'd been a few hours earlier, anyway.

The large projection-type screen above the terminal booth was alive with flashing data. Gus couldn't read any of it and was surprised that the colonel seemed to be able to do so. Come to think of it, even if the old

boy *had* somehow mastered the writing, how the hell had he gotten past
the security system and inside to the data?

And suddenly, with the cynicism born of covering countless wars and
tragedies, it all fell into place.

"I always wondered how you got so much authority and power so fast,
Colonel," Gus said loudly, his deep voice echoing slightly off the walls.

The colonel was startled. "Gus? How did you get *here* so quickly?"

"This is Education Day, Colonel, at least for me. Today I found out
things about myself I never knew before, and I also found out why the
Dahir have such a strict and pacifistic religion and don't want their people wandering all over this world. We're killers, Colonel. Natural killers.
It's in the blood, in the genes, the hormones. We *enjoy* it. *I* enjoy it. It's a
tough thing to keep down once you've started doing it. That's why the
Dahir faith is so strict and life there so god-awful boring. It's the only
way to keep us civilized. Nothing worse than a natural killer you can't see
wandering around, is there?"

"You are a rational man, Gus. You only have killed your enemies."

"That's true, but I have a strange feeling that it's going to be very easy
to be defined as an enemy of mine from now on. But I haven't told you
the whole story yet, Colonel. Education Day is still ongoing. I learned the
best part just by stepping in here and watching you."

"What do you mean?"

"Nothing this big, no operation this slick and this huge, could possibly
get to be this way on its own, and I don't care what drugs they sell or
how much money they spread. We ain't talkin' just a gang here. We're
talking governments, or parts of governments, at the highest levels. Pres-
idents and kings and dictators and probably South Zone councillors as
well. Not that they were in on the details, of course. I doubt if they were
ever here or even imagined how some of their money was spent, but in
on the top levels of control. Not all of 'em, sure. Not even a majority,
'cause what sense would *that* make? They didn't care about the details.
They were busy using that power to weaken and take over governments
of hexes they didn't even know how to pronounce. Control economies,
trade, you name it. Pretty soon the whole Well World's workin' for them
and it don't even know it. It must've drove 'em crazy when they figured
out they had to sacrifice this place, but their little underlings did something, and they can't afford to even let their own people know what it
was. Uneasy lies the head, huh, Colonel?"

"Go on, Gus. You are quite entertaining."

"So it's going along really good, and then, suddenly, *wham!* Here's the
legendary Nathan Brazil unmasked, and he's headed for the internal
works sooner or later. They can't kill him, so they try and slow him

down, make him feel comfortable, that kind of thing, while they consult and figure out what the hell to do. I mean, they can't let him get *inside*, can they? If they do, he'll see their racket right away and queer it. I can just imagine the nightmares. And then it's not just one of 'em but *two*. Either one's the worst thing anybody could imagine. Both together might be unbeatable. *Two* unkillables. But they're pretty clever. The two clearly haven't seen each other since the last ice age on Earth, so it's easy to make each of 'em think the other's out to get them. They won't get together then even if they could. But how to keep them from getting up to the equator? *That's* the other problem."

"It is quite an amazing fantasy you weave, Gus. You should have quit news and gone into the cinema."

"It gets better. You, for one, are there as a member of a race that was one of the insiders. The Leeming. Somehow, right off, they see you as just the kind of guy who's perfect for them, but you can create a friendly, human face. All the power, all the authority—and one job. Just keep Brazil happy and anywhere but heading north and always where you can find him. I don't know why you didn't just have him arrested and jailed right off, but I can think of a number of reasons."

"For one thing, Nathan Brazil is a legend, a part of mythology, like Odin and Jupiter back home. Bringing a sufficient number of leaders to the conviction that he was more than that and that he was a possible threat to the Well World's very survival takes time. The last is next to impossible, really. No one fears the repairman; they welcome him. They fear the demolition man, and they fear their gods. Ironically, Brazil himself tipped the scales on the required religious conversions merely by surviving what no creature of his makeup should possibly survive. And the more he recovers, the more nervous they will get. They will endlessly debate how to enforce any deal or bargain they can make with him, but who can truly make such demands of a god once that god is on his throne? So they will keep him locked up. There is your story. One day he may escape, but by that time they will be long dead."

"Uh huh. And who had your job with Mavra Chang?"

"You would not believe me."

"Try me."

"The Dillian twins."

"I don't believe it!"

"They didn't know anything about the rest, unlike myself. They were just given an all-expenses paid chance to see the Well World if they would simply make a few reports on the location and whereabouts of one Mavra Chang as things went along. They didn't know Chang, and they were made just aware enough that she was more than she seemed and something of a threat to peace, stability, and order. Armed with that, it was rather easy to make her miss connections, foul up her bank accounts, that sort of thing. And unlike the captain, who truly gave me the slip, she actually contracted with those very forces which wanted her out of the way to carry her here. It was Brazil we were worried about. We didn't give a thought to Chang. Now, though, we find that Chang is not here. Somehow she slipped through our net and into the hands of a minor player about which we know very little overall but whose mental profile in the records indicates that she would do almost anything to keep Chang out of anyone's hands but her own."

"That still bothers me, Colonel. You know where Campos lives. You could have gone there at any time and forced her to show you Chang, but you didn't. You went through all this, which must cost them plenty."

"It did. It is painful and a real setback," the colonel admitted. "But you still fail to appreciate both Campos and the man she ingratiated herself with. If one inkling, one *thought* that Chang might be another Brazil entered *his* mind or the minds of his associates, they would vanish, and Chang with them. The hold they would have over the entire international organization would be nearly absolute. Surely you must see that. Chang must never be the object of all this except to such as we. And when we bust them, headed by fearless and incorruptible policemen like Inspector Kurdon, even they will have no suspicion until Chang is in our hands and locked away in Zone next to the captain with the so-pleasant name."

"And now you're here finding out exactly what they did to her, what monster they turned her into, and precisely where she is. And after that, making certain that nothing in that computer will *ever* be read by the inspector or anyone else. Tell me, Colonel—how'd you learn to read that stuff so quickly? And how'd you learn how to use their computer system? You ain't been here much longer than me."

"Long enough, my friend. Besides, we Leeming have more than one way to learn things. In fact, with certain kinds of races, which make up close to ten percent of the south's racial makeup, we don't have to do anything more than feed. You can see by my size that I've been a very gluttonous soldier."

"You mean you can learn stuff by *eating* somebody?" Gus was incredulous.

The colonel chuckled. "Friend Gus, you are on an impossible world full of impossible creatures such as the two of us, turned into a big colorful lizard who can not be seen unless he wants to be, discussing a worldwide takeover conspiracy for which there remains no proof at all and which you only learned about because of a hunt for two demigods. And you find my alternative learning method unbelievable?"

He had a point there, Gus had to admit. He kept his rifle on the colonel, but he expected a trick any time now. The colonel hadn't moved, but did he seem suddenly more like his old self in size? Or was that imagination?

"You're a rotten son of a bitch, Colonel," Gus told him. "You had a second chance here, a real chance of a new life and a fresh start, and you decided to remain what you were back on Earth. Don Francisco must have paid you pretty good, too, I suspect."

"Not nearly enough, but after the return to democracy there were problems for many of us, and we had to find alternative sources of income to maintain ourselves and our families in the style to which we had become accustomed. This is not the same thing. This is the equivalent of military rule, which we imposed to prevent the communists from dominating our beloved land. In that I followed orders and remained true to my country. I am doing so again, and I feel that it *is* a new start for me. Again I have honor. Again I serve my country and my people."

That shimmery SOB *was* shrinking! Gus shut up and moved back toward the entrance. It was barely in time; a thin layer of goo rose up and grabbed for him as he moved.

Nice try, Colonel. You are better than I gave you credit for, Gus thought, nervously eyeing his narrow escape. If the colonel had kept him talking just another thirty seconds, he'd have been history!

"Gus? Where are you?"

Ready to take aim on your slimy guts the moment you pull yourself together, you fat pig, Gus thought, but he remained silent but vigilant.

"I'm sorry, Gus. I won't make another stab at you," Lunderman assured him. "Look, no one will believe your story, not even Kurdon. You have no place to go and no way to act on what you know. You can't win, not against this kind of power. But you don't have to lose, either. You are a very resourceful man, Gus. *Very* resourceful. Just as they found a place for me, they can find one for you. Anything you want. What have you to look forward to, anyway? You can't go home—particularly now. You know that yourself. The Dahir church would probably have you sacrificed to keep from corrupting the rest of the flock. You are both a man and a creature without a country, Gus. But with your unique talents and awakening appetites you needn't be an unhappy one."

I wouldn't be tempted if you were giving me a straight offer, Gus thought, *but I can see your puddly self flowing all around the floor and in between the consoles, feeling for me even now.*

The colonel had grown large, but not *that* large. It was relatively simple to keep out of his way if Gus just paid attention.

Gus could see a fair amount of him now, but too flattened and too spread out to make a real target. Still, Kurdon had warned the Leeming that he was vulnerable to energy weapons, and that happened to be just what Gus had in his cute little hands. Time for a continuation of Education Day.

Gus set the rifle on wide, aimed at the largest concentration of Leeming he could see, and pulled the trigger fast and briefly.

The colonel screamed an unholy scream as part of him fried and vanished. It suddenly occurred to Gus that this might have been the first real pain Lunderman had felt since becoming a Leeming. Reflexively, the rest of the amorphous creature withdrew inward toward the central mass. But where *was* the central mass now? Gus wondered. Not at the console.

Cat and mouse, Colonel? Gus thought. *Suits me fine, but I frankly didn't think you had the guts.*

Lunderman didn't. Suddenly, across the room in one corner, a great mass rushed upward with tremendous force and speed. It was so fast and so blended against the dark that Gus was slow to react, and by the time he got off a shot, the thing had vanished into the ducting above.

Gus didn't like the fact that the Leeming was around up there somewhere and nursing both a wound and a grudge, but he could hardly follow *that* exit. At least the colonel couldn't see him or anticipate his actions. Even so, the faster he was out of here, the better, he thought.

Still, he had to risk some communication.

"The colonel was working with the gang," Gus reported. "I am in the computer room. He was in here erasing records. I shot at him but only winged him. You can't capture him, but he's the only one of his kind here, and he can be fried. I recommend a shoot on sight, particularly since he eats people by absorbing them." Suddenly the magnitude of what he'd done hit him. "And get some people in here really quick," he added. "Lunderman's left the computer turned *on* with the damned security already deactivated!"

The sun had been up for hours when they struggled back to Subar, but all of them felt it had been worth it. Terry almost cried for joy when Gus came back and ran to hug him.

There was no sign of the colonel, but all the entrances and exits were heavily guarded and it was felt that he was still in there somewhere.

Inspector Kurdon looked exhausted but generally satisfied. "Sixty-eight of ours killed or wounded, but at least two hundred of theirs dead and almost a hundred in custody, and we broke that cancer that has been eating into the soul as well as the soil of my nation for far too long. It has been a worthy night indeed."

"What about the computer? Have your people learned anything?" Gus asked him.

"Not as much as we might have had the colonel not gotten in there first but far more than I think any of them would have wished. What you caught him doing was unleashing what my computer people call a tapeworm." The term wasn't exact, but that was the way it got translated to Gus. "A program that goes in and finds and destroys specific information. A second was ready to load, and a third was found nearby, but thanks to you only the first was run."

"Any idea of the nature of the information destroyed? Or is that a ridiculous question?" Anne Marie asked him.

"No, it is not altogether ridiculous. We can deduce a little of it, although we have barely scratched the surface of the thing. It will be *months* before we get everything we can out of that data base, and we need to make certain that no one who does not have the most impeccable honesty gets in there in the meantime. I do not like it that the colonel is still at large in there, but we do not believe he could actually operate the computer. Rather, he knew how to run the tapeworms and where they were stored. In a sense, merely losing what we did is a fair trade for having the security system opened up. We might have learned far less over a much longer period had we had to attempt to crack it."

"And the erasures?"

"Oh, sorry. As I say, by deduction. Political names, big regional names, that sort of thing. We won't get a payoff or politician's listing from that, I'm afraid."

"It's bigger than you know," Gus told him. "You wouldn't believe how big. I got it straight from the colonel."

Kurdon gave a weary nod. "I believe I know how far this had to have gone just by looking at its scale and by the sheer number of hexes where deletions were made. Do not worry, Gus. It wouldn't matter if the entire council was corrupt, as they probably are in one way or another. This complex and the computer are in *Agon*. Agon alone has authority here. *And I know who is who in Agon.*"

"What about Lori and Mavra? Any word on them?" Tony asked, concerned over Julian's report.

"It is the first minute of the new information age," the inspector said. "Give us a little time. This is of the highest priority. Get some sleep, all of you! Even *I* am going to attempt it. By the time we awaken, they will have news, perhaps very exact news. *Then,* I believe, we will be on our way on a journey to the northwest."

"*Clopta!*" Gus breathed. "And Campos."

Kurdon nodded. "Also by that time I expect that I will have so many high Cloptan officials terrified of me that I will be carried to this Campos person on a litter with politicians as bearers." He smiled, the first time any of them could remember seeing such an expression on an Agonite. "It was a *very* good night."

By late afternoon, when they struggled back to the command center, most still half-asleep but unable to go any further toward resolving the problem, the trusted technicians inside the computer room had some answers.

"A bird and a unicorn," Inspector Kurdon told them. "Neither are monsters in the sense of the ones we discovered down in the cells. They are in their own ways works of art—if, of course, the results proved equal to the computer estimation. Your friend Lori was something of a compromise, it appears. The original order was for a grotesque, like what we saw. But when they saw the genetic potential and also discovered that Campos was just going to make him a courier like the rest, they had second thoughts. They made the monster part come out early, then later fade as the *real* program kicked in. Campos was apparently furious at the start but later decided she liked it after all. At least, there's no sign of any attempts to do worse again."

"You got this from the computer?" Julian asked him.

"Not entirely. Our doctor friends seemed to have pulled a very slick vanishing act in the middle of a cordon I'd have sworn was unbreakable, but their assistants weren't so fortunate. And the assistants know the medical computer quite well and helped with all the detail work. With what we got from the clinic, we were able to go to specific points in the big machine and get virtually a replay of the entire discussion and debate, almost a step-by-step explanation and tutorial. They were sick of making monsters. They wanted to make pretty, living works of art." He reached into a pouch and pulled out a picture. "Here is what your Lori looks like now."

The pretty beige pastel colors had been retained, and the hair, and much of the elements of the original Erdomese, Julian noted. Only the body had thickened, becoming less wiry and more equine overall, and the forearms and hands had become traditional horselike legs with fixed hooves much like the Dillians'. The head had been thickened, and the head and face reshaped into a rather cute horse's head, but retaining the curved horn in the forehead that was the mark of an Erdomese male. Compact, sturdy, cute.

"Kind of like a cartoon Shetland pony," Gus commented.

Kurdon cleared his throat. "The worst news, I fear, Madame Julian, is that the specifications set down by Campos included that he be a gelding. It was actually designed that way. There are no genitalia at all."

Julian knew she should have felt shock and grief for Lori, but somehow she felt relief. Still, she noted, "I wouldn't exactly be the proper mate for a pony, anyway, would I, Inspector?"

"Um, no. I hadn't thought of that. We also discovered why all the poor wretches we found made only unintelligible sounds. It seems the practice was to install within them a type of artificial translator that intercepts both incoming and outgoing language. Only someone with an identical translator tuned to each individual's code will be understood by the— pardon—creature, and vice versa. That way, if something happened, if one of them escaped or fell into the hands of the law, they could never reveal anything they knew. And the total sexlessness made them docile, passive, easily trained, and nearly incapable of rebellion. No aggression, no initiative. They may hate it, but they'll do exactly what they're told to do."

Poor Lori, Julian thought, and somehow that very sentiment, spontaneous as it was, made her feel a little better about herself. "Where is he now? Do you know?"

"He was on the Liliblod route, and he was due in Agon either the day we hit the place or today. So far no sign of him, and we can hardly go hunting in Liliblod for him, not for *quite* a while."

"They won't *eat* him, will they?" Tony asked worriedly. She'd already decided to make a run in to see that stable area for herself when a soldier had given her a pair of night vision glasses and shown her the denizens of Liliblod. That had talked her out of any such foolishness. Giant furry spiders with glowing white death's-heads dripping with venom . . .

"Tony!" Anne Marie scolded.

"No, it's a fair question," Kurdon said. "My feeling is that they will not break their own end of the bargain. They are a strange lot, but they have an odd sense of honor and consistency. In all these years they never once touched anyone who stuck to the agreed-upon routes, although frankly, I'd not like to test them *too* much right now. There's some evidence that a number of higher-ups had emergency escapes down to the stable area just in case, and since we didn't nab them, we must assume they got away into Liliblod as well. Best case I suspect is that he'll eventually turn up, possibly after getting over confusion over all the new people there. Worst case is that he met up with some of these fleeing bigwigs and was turned around and pointed back toward Clopta. If that is the case, he should be snared when we move on the gang there. They can hardly send him back again. To what purpose?"

"They might kill him!" Julian said worriedly.

Tony shook her head. "Not Campos. She's not the type. She's more likely to put him in a horse stable, if they have such things in Clopta, and ride him around the park on nice mornings."

Kurdon nodded. "That is our assessment as well."

"But what about Mavra Chang?" Tony asked him. "You said a *bird*?"

"Yes." Again a hand went into the case and brought out a picture. "Probably something like this. It's an even greater work of art than this Lori, in a way. You see, that's a real creature, albeit a rare one from a hex far away from here. A real bird. The only thing that's different is the size of the braincase, which was accomplished with some clever bioengineering. Campos wanted her mentally intact, to *know*."

"Odd-looking thing," Gus noted. "Kinda like an owl, but with a long bill and pretty colored feathers."

"It's flightless," Kurdon told them. "The wings have completely vanished. It is also quite large—about a meter high, and it can weigh upward of thirty-five kilos. It spends basically all its time rooting with that long, curved bill and sticky tongue, eating mostly insects. It needs to eat a great many of them, but it can also eat raw meat and even a little grain if need be. It is nocturnal, practically blind in daylight, which, aside from its size, is its only defense. The legs are too short and stumpy for speed. I doubt if it can run at all. Sort of like walking on your knees. They made certain she wasn't going to go anywhere."

"The poor dear!" Anne Marie exclaimed.

"Will you be able to do anything for them, all things considered?" Julian asked him. "I mean, you said this was genetic data here, and I went to those—those *doctors* myself. They said doing it more than once could lead to instability, deformity, death."

"Hard to say, with our two most knowledgeable experts among the missing," Kurdon noted. "Probably we can do very little. What we *can* do is outfit them with translators that restore their communication with the outside world. At least that will give them some voice again in how they want to cope and some help in doing it."

Julian thought about the pair. *Another couple of one-of-a-kinds,* she thought. The population of her mythical dream island was growing.

"Well, we should be able to get them when we get Campos," Kurdon assured them.

"Shouldn't you send ahead and have them arrested now?" Julian asked him.

"Too risky. Clopta is not Agon, and without a bit more authority from that nice big computer, it's not dependable. Remember, even the two maniacs who created this managed to escape us, and that was *here,* in our own backyard."

"Shouldn't we be off, then?" Tony asked him. "I mean, it's likely some of those escapees are even now heading toward Clopta with the news of the raid. They may go underground before we can get to them."

"Liliblod is the same size as Agon, and they are on foot," Kurdon reminded them. "We, on the other hand, will bypass Liliblod and sail directly into Buckgrud, the Cloptan main port city, which is where our quarry happen to live. Besides, even with what happened here, I am pretty sure they'll still feel safe in Buckgrud, which the cartel more or less owns and operates, and under the protection of their own bought politicians."

"I hope you're right," Julian said, looking at the photo of the new Lori. "It must still be awful for them now. I'd hate to get this close and lose them."

"Don't worry about it," Gus said confidently. "I mean, hell, the hexes aren't really huge, and outside of their native hex they'll be easy to spot. Hell, I bet Juan Campos looks like Daisy Duck."

Julian nodded. "A very dangerous Daisy Duck."

BUCKGRUD
CLOPTA

JUANA CAMPOS WAS MADE up and dressed to kill—if one was a Cloptan male. In fact, it was the large eyes and pliant oversized bills that gave Cloptans a ducklike appearance, but they were not related to ducks, nor were they exactly birds in spite of the featherlike covering—rather, they were egg-laying mammals that incubated the eggs in the marsupial-like pouches which both males and females had. Aside from the oversized heads, the body shape was quite humanoid, the female's particularly so, although the males tended to be more pear-shaped and actually rather dull-looking. The females even had thick, lush hair growing from their heads, while the males were universally feather-topped and rather bald. The females even tended to be taller than the males, but while short, squat, and fairly ugly as a rule, the males were built like tanks and abnormally strong for their size. Much of their bodies was protected by invisible but quite effective thick, bony plates right down to the genitalia.

In Clopta, women were literally soft and men were literally hard.

Gen Taluud was built like a bank vault and had a face to match. Ugly, raw, with a curl on one side of his bill that revealed the otherwise seldom visible sharp teeth lining the inside. He looked like the kind of Cloptan who might walk right through a wall, and he radiated that kind of toughness even when saying nothing. He had spent twenty years doing all it took to become the top man in Buckgrud, the man who owned the mayor and the provincial governor and whose very word was law. But it hadn't been merely by strong-arm tactics, bribes, double crosses, and murders that he'd risen to the top; he was anything but the stupid muscle he appeared to be.

He'd initially gotten interested in Campos simply out of curiosity, someone who had once been something entirely different. That made her exotic and interesting, and the fact that she also had a hell of a figure didn't hurt. Campos had initially been appalled at the circumstances the Well had forced upon her but also realized that this was a golden opportunity, maybe a chance to rise high and fast in spite of the changed circumstances and in a way overcome the sexual change and get both power and protection. She'd learned, observed, and played the part Gen Taluud expected of his mistresses. Campos recognized the Taluud type immediately as the same sort of boss his father and other cartel members had been back on Earth, and she also understood the business. The only one who'd stood in her way once she'd accepted the situation and her own self as permanent had been Taluud's longtime existing mistress, who wanted no rivals. But when she'd tried a hit on Campos and failed, thanks to Campos's own experience, she had become easy to handle. Campos had pulled the trigger on the woman herself and disposed of the body in a time-honored way so that it would never be found.

If Taluud suspected or knew, he never said, but instead of being upset, even forlorn about the loss of a longtime companion under mysterious circumstances, he'd given Campos a free ticket to the top and treated her with a fair amount of respect, in some cases giving her the authority usually reserved for his lieutenants. Campos understood the bargain. So long as she was at his beck and call, jumped when he snapped his fingers, and served him loyally, she otherwise had nearly free rein within the organization. Still, service to him could be unpleasant sometimes, as the big man was fond of rewarding certain underlings and bigwigs with his girl's services for an evening or two. But with no assets other than the body and a shared ruthlessness, she'd learned to use that, too, to build a ring of powerful friends in the organization that might well outlast even Taluud.

But no matter what else she had planned or what she felt like or wanted to do, when the big man called, which he could at any hour of any day, she was expected to drop everything and show up, always looking her very best. This was just such a time. The fact that it was three in the morning on a weekend did not mean anything particular to her.

Taluud was in his penthouse, clothed in a fancy dressing gown, sitting in his big, overstuffed chair and puffing on an imported cigar. The cigar was as much a badge as a habit; he went through a dozen a day, and a box of them was close to the average annual wage of a Cloptan. Around him were a half dozen fully dressed lieutenants, all of whom she'd known intimately in the past, and one fellow in the chair opposite who was anything but properly dressed and looked like he'd just crawled out of a sewer after battling angry crocodiles. Other than Taluud, he was the only

one seated, which was unusual only in that usually nobody sat in
Taluud's inner sanctum but he. She stood there, taking in the scene and
wondering what it was all about.

Taluud in turn looked straight at her and took his cigar from his
mouth to use as a pointer. "Glad you could get here so fast, doll. This
guy here is Sluthor. Up until a few days ago he was transport chief at the
complex. He tells me a goddamned *army* just blew it to shit."

Campos's lower bill dropped a bit. "But Genny, that's *impossible!*"

A clenched hand came down so hard on the coffee table that the table
almost broke. "You *bet* it's impossible! Not only was that place a fortress,
but we *owned* the Agon military!" he shouted. "But it *did* happen! And
only a few of our people got away. They're straggling in now from
Liliblod in ones and twos, all looking at least as bad as Sluthor here. I
been on the communicator the last two hours to the capital, and you
know what, nobody's in who knows *nothin'*! You hear me, doll? *Nobody's
in!* To *me!*"

"I—I don't understand." Campos had a very bad feeling about this
that had little to do with the mere loss of even such a wonder as the
complex.

"Well, neither do I. I got one of our people in the capital to go into
Zone and get some face-to-face answers, but he ain't back yet. Too soon
to get many details, but we got some basic stuff from Sluthor and the
others straggling in. It ain't just the loss of the complex—we can always
build more—and nobody there was so important we couldn't afford to
lose 'em, but *how* in the name of the six hells of Dashli did they have the
fuckin' *guts* to do this?"

Slowly, through the big man's tirades, what little was known came out.

They'd suspected for some time that something was up, something not
at all good, but they'd never expected anything on this scale. This kind
of scale would take approval by and the active support of the council, yet
nobody on it had warned them or tipped a hand. Instead, they'd given
full authority and support to the raiders under an overzealous cop
who'd been neutralized, or so it had seemed.

Campos thought it over. "Sounds like somebody very big and very
powerful but not on our side got the idea that some of the council was
bent," she suggested. "And the ones that were had to save their own tails
by letting this go through. If they'd tipped anybody, it would have been
a sure sign they were bent, so they had to let it go. It's the only thing that
makes sense."

Taluud nodded approvingly. "That's what I figure, too. The question
is, just how much and how many are they willin' to sell out to cover
themselves? They had their own man, one of them jelly blobs from the

south, in on it. Probably to get in there and protect their asses by deleting the records. That we know because we knew about him before, and he suddenly shows up there just before the raid. The question is, what are the others doin' there?"

She blinked. "Others? I don't understand."

"Them two horse-assed girls, the goat girl with the four tits, and, with the jelly blob, some unknown type ape girl who don't say a word and somebody else we never got a handle on. Thing is, our people reported to the complex that all these critters had one thing in common: They all knew each other. Even the jelly blob. Word was that every single one of 'em had come in from offworld and gone through the Well. Just like you."

Now she understood why she was here and what this was about. "You mean they're *all* there? Together?"

"Pretty much. Who knows if there are any missing. We already had run a check on 'em. The two horse asses and Four Tits got there on one of our courier boats. They been snoopin' around for months but weren't much of a threat. Seems they were there lookin' for somebody—God knows why else you'd stay in that lizard heaven. Somebody snatched off the same courier boat. Another of their own, most likely. Sluthor did a check on the ones that stayed in Agon. None of 'em seems to have come in with you, and none of 'em seem to have any connection with you other than comin' from the same planet once. That goes for the jelly blob, too. That's in your favor. But I know you went down there and did a lot of checking a while back. Where's the ones who came here with *you?*"

She thought a moment, realizing that there was great danger here. The whole truth might cause nasty problems, but a lie could be deadly—or worse. She needed time, and Gen wasn't giving her any. Maybe a half-truth was best . . . for now.

"I was a prisoner when I was dragged here. You know that," she reminded him. "Right at that time I hadn't realized how good I had it, and I was boiling for revenge. Two of the sorry bitches who got me into that fix were on one of *our* boats and heading right here. I couldn't resist. I'm sorry, Genny, I just couldn't resist, particularly after I visited the cells and saw what they were doing down there. It seemed like heaven had delivered my enemies into my hands. I . . . persuaded Arn Gemalk, who was head of security then, to divert the boat, have them taken off at the pickup point, and delivered to the docs at the complex. I wanted revenge, and just killing them seemed not nearly enough at the time."

Taluud nodded, interested but not apparently upset at this. "And what did they do to them?"

"Turned them into couriers, I suppose. The idea was to make them live out the rest of their miserable lives as cut-off monsters serving what they hated."

"And you don't know what they became or where they are now? The odds are they were the trigger for this—now, don't worry your pretty self about that! You didn't do nothing to them I wouldn'ta done myself. Thing was, though, the horse asses were doin' a favor, trackin' one of 'em for the council, so when they were lifted, it went straight to the top. There was too much heat, and after a while they couldn't stall it anymore. Yeah. This all fits together now. Shit, I wonder if we can find that pair and give 'em to them. Might take the heat off. Otherwise they're givin' the cops and patrol and all the excuse to take us out base by base, station by station."

"Beg pardon, sir, but even if we *could* track them down, they will hardly be in a condition to be recognized. Would it make any difference?" one of the lieutenants asked worriedly.

"Yeah, yeah, it would. They wouldn't like gettin' back two freaks, but they'd have what they was after, anyway. Provin' who they were is just a matter of a new translator. Even if somehow they could talk or they got one of them mind-reader races to get through, what could they tell? We're still in the clear, right? And they get what's left of who they're after."

"Wouldn't they soon be in agony from lack of their variety of the weed?" Campos asked him. "It might not be much of a victory to hand them over."

"Even dead, they'd be found," Taluud noted. "But the weed's no problem. We found that the ones who go through that monster stuff get immune to it over time. Don't matter. We got much better control by that point, anyway."

So they don't need the drug anymore. Interesting. "But how would you tell who and what they were, let alone where?" Campos asked him. "I mean, once they're processed, I thought they were just assigned and all traces of them erased."

"Yeah, well, they don't exist, true, but people got memories. Maybe they can't be found, maybe not," the boss responded. "How many we done of these? A hundred, give or take. Not too many, and there was always a contingency plan just in case for a lot of things, including them doctors. Sluthor says they were in their clinic on the coast and not at the complex when it was raided. If they managed to give their tails the slip before the cops moved in, they'll be on a courier boat right now headin' for a safe hideout west of here. They may have to dodge some patrols, but they should be there before any muscle gets in these parts, and maybe they remember these two. Neither of them was from races we see anywhere in these parts, if I remember. You remember what they were, doll?"

"One was a male from somewhere far off; I think it was Erdom or something like that. The other was still the same as when she left our old world. I understand they're called something here, but nobody seems to know much about them."

"Glathrielian," Sluthor said tiredly. "I've been trying to think of it myself. That's what they called the apelike female who came in with the Leeming."

Campos was suddenly *very* interested, enough to dampen her fear although not enough to make her disregard the sense of danger. "This was a female of the same type? Dark skin, perhaps, no body hair to speak of except on the head and crotch?"

"Yes, that is pretty much a good description of the pictures I saw. Do you know her, then?"

"Yes, I know her. She is the one I *truly* hoped to get my hands on, but she was not with the others."

"Well, you lay off her now, period!" Taluud told her firmly. "She's untouchable. History. They may even have an idea that she'll draw you out. You don't go near her, you hear me? We may all have to disappear for a while until this blows over. Keep your bags packed and be ready for a call. They lure you with her and nail you, the next stop's right here!"

"I doubt if I'd get the chance at her unless it *was* a trap," Campos sighed. "Still, it's too bad. I could have had such *fun* with her."

"What's the point? Sluthor here says she don't talk and is like some brain damage case. Besides, it's gonna be a while before we can use those docs again no matter what."

Campos nodded. "I know. But she's unchanged, and I know from the other that the weed will work particularly well with that kind. Make her an addict, put her on a leash, walk her around like a pet . . . It would be *very* satisfying."

"Yeah, well, get that out of your head now. No personal vendettas while we got bigger trouble. Besides, you already got a pet. That big ugly bird, right?"

"No, I gave her to the zoo," Campos told him, suddenly nervous that two and two would be assembled in the room. "They are quite rare, and the zoo is going to breed her."

Fortunately, it never occurred to the gang leader to consider that the process didn't always create monsters or sterile mules, either. "Yeah, well, no more of that. We got enough trouble from this missing pair if we're guessin' right. All we need is a third to vanish and we may have to bury ourselves, and I do mean bury."

"I wouldn't *dream* of doing anything without your permission, Genny. You know that."

"And you better hadn't, not anymore. Still, bad as it is, we got a few days to play with here; let's not panic. Ain't no raiding army in Clopta yet—they couldn't keep *that* from me. Figure if they didn't find their friends in the complex, then this is where they'll head, though. Take 'em a few days to sweat the details, a few more to get here by boat, a few more than that to set up things so's they can move here. We got at least a week. If they got away, them docs should be in before that, so we may get a jump on the law in finding that missing pair. Also send out the word. Anybody who remembers them when they was in the complex or being seasoned, they tell us just what they are and where they might have gone. Get on it!"

There was a chorus of "Yes, sirs!" and it was clear that the meeting was over.

Campos remained for a bit, wondering if Taluud had anything else for her and hoping to get more information, but the boss dismissed her. "Get lost, doll. Go home, pack, and stay close to the phone. I got calls to make."

She turned and walked out.

By the time she emerged at street level from the private elevator, she'd already started to think about things on her own. What if somebody remembered that she had been there for the whole process? What if the doctors had backup records or clear memories of just what they had done? Taluud was no dummy; he would figure out that she'd been holding out on him and already knew the information he wanted. *Then* life would get *really* unpleasant. But she didn't want to turn them over, particularly not Mavra Chang. Campos wasn't fooled by the drooling servile act, not now that she knew that the bird bitch wasn't even addicted anymore and had never let on. Chang in the zoo or under her control was one thing; Chang with a voice and a mind was something else, even if she stayed a bird. There was something too familiar, deep down, about that bitch. Given the chance, Mavra Chang would spare nothing to arrange a similar fate for Juana Campos.

But why was the council, the kind of United Nations of this world, so worked up about Chang and the Erdomite? The Erdomite was just somebody with that news crew; he *couldn't* be important in the long run to anybody. But Chang—that "goddess" stuff, playing jungle Indian high priestess . . .

She had been pretty damned sophisticated when she had gotten here. Those Indian bitches had thought that she was immortal, that she'd been there like forever. Stupid superstition from the dumb-ass Stone Agers? It had seemed so. But what if . . .

What if those rumors of her being some kind of creature who could work the whole damned Well World had been true? They'd recalled the wanted bulletins, said she was just a minor player for the guy they were really looking for, but maybe that was a blind.

First they said she was some kind of real god if she got inside, then they said she wasn't really. What if the first story had been true? What if Mavra Chang could somehow get inside whatever ran this world and do pretty much whatever she liked to everybody and everything? And they got afraid that somebody else, somebody like Genny, would snatch her and somehow make her do what Genny wanted when she was there . . .

That would explain everything that had happened, wouldn't it?

If they find out my birdie is Mavra but don't figure out the rest, they'll give her back. Sooner or later she'll get away, get in there, one way or another, but they won't care what she orders for a Juana Campos.

In the hands of Genny and the cartel things might be even worse. Even if she could somehow talk her way around the deception, which was highly questionable, *they* would be playing for all the power, not her. A world remade by Genny wouldn't be a fit place for anybody. Not with that kind of power. He'd go nuts. If he made a deal and they ran things together, it would be even worse. Two nuts. And no place at all for Juana Campos.

But what to do? What to do? In a couple of days, a week at best, it would be out of her hands if she just let events take their course.

Wait a minute! Maybe there is *a way out of this!* She walked down the darkened, rain-slicked street, deserted at this hour, the only sound the sound of her heels clicking on the hard pavement.

What if she did her own vanishing act? By the time Genny figured it out, the shit would be hitting the fan here. And if she had her two treasures with her, there'd be nothing to stop the cops. They'd come after the organization here like that army'd gone through the complex she'd thought impenetrable. Looking for her, most likely. If she'd checked up on them, they *had* to know that she was here. They had probably already figured it out; they just needed the clout to come after her.

But what if neither she nor they were here? The cartel would be underground for quite a while, particularly in this region. But to where? And how?

Liliblod would be out of the question. She'd never felt comfortable in that creepy place, anyway, and right now it'd be even worse. Likewise, nowhere in Clopta would be safe. By ship? Too risky, and if they tracked her, she'd be trapped with the goods. Due north was Quilst. She didn't know much about it, but it was nontech, so it would be damned hard to trace her, and she was pretty familiar with roughing it in primitive conditions far worse than she'd seen here. Lori ate mostly grass and shrubs now, and Mavra ate bugs and carrion. Not a real supply problem. Lori could haul stuff, and if it got so Mavra couldn't find anything to eat, then Lori might be a good feed if need be.

But what if the Quilst was as nasty as or nastier than Liliblod? She needed to know. There were semitech hexes to the east and west, which *might* do. She needed information, and the first thing to find out was if Lori was an option at all. She didn't have much time—maybe a day or two. First thing to do was to check on Lori. If he wasn't in when she was ready to leave, the hell with him. She'd get a real horse or something like it. A few weeks, or maybe months, away, just marking time, would be worth it. After they'd scoured Clopta and Genny and his gang were history, she could come back. Maybe not to Buckgrud but to one of the other big cities where she could lose herself or, better yet, to the northwest, where there were farms and ranches. She had a number of IDs in the system. Cut and dye her hair, do a few other things, and she might just get away with it.

If she had Terry in her clutches, it would be just *perfect*, but one couldn't have everything. Not yet, anyway.

The clicking of her heels sounded for all the world like the ticking of a clock. A clock counting down the window of opportunity . . .

She had a lot of calls to make.

Lori had tried to keep track of how long the nightmare journey had taken, but either exhaustion or the creeping dullness in his mind had made it impossible. It certainly *seemed* like forever, particularly with that very heavy bastard on his back urging him on and making him miss needed water and food stops.

Still, the guy had to sleep and drink, too, so there'd been just enough of a break to survive. How much did these ducklike things *weigh*, anyway?

Still, once in the warehouse, he'd slept the sleep of the dead, and when he woke up, still feeling pain in every joint, he was at least able to eat and drink.

Still totally confused by what had happened and why he was back *here* instead of *there*, he nonetheless started to get the idea that things weren't normal on this end, either. There were lots of Cloptans around, including many he'd never seen before. They were all frantically loading stuff into huge vans that pulled up one after the other, and he realized that they were emptying the place.

Maybe the good guys finally won one, he thought hopefully. Not that it would do him much good. They were clearly just shifting operations for a while, and where did that leave him? Either they'd shoot him or they'd take him with them to put on some other courier run. It wouldn't even matter if somebody found him. What would they see? A nice little horse with a horn, that was all. Too small for real horse work and, as a gelding, not handy for any other reason. How could he even contact somebody else to tell them he was more than he seemed?

More important, would it make any difference? It was getting harder and harder to remember things. Not just little things, big things. Before he was a horse he'd been a man, but a man who did what? He had memories of a desert and some tent towns and a city by a big wall, and he remembered a woman of the same race, but even she was kind of blurry. And before that there had been someone, something else, but that was so distant and so confusing, he wasn't sure about it. He tried frantically to think, to remember. *I'm not a horse! I'm a . . .*

But he *was* a horse. He couldn't get around that. No matter who or what he'd been, he was now a horse. He was always going to *be* a horse. What was the use of fighting it, of dredging up those old memories, of worrying about things that he could not do anything about?

Someone . . . somebody else . . . had struggled with a big change, and it had driven them nuts. The woman. And when they'd stopped fighting and accepted who and what they were, they were finally able to find some happiness, to stop torturing themselves.

Maybe that was it. Maybe he should just stop trying to be anything else and accept it. Stop the thinking, the remembering, the deep thoughts. Just . . . live. If he *was* going to just be a horse, what would his wants be? Food, water, sleep, and maybe a little care and grooming by somebody nice. What else could he ever want or need? Nothing *these* men had. Nothing *anybody* had that he could imagine.

Then why did he feel such a sense of loss? That was why he'd been searching around in those memories, but while he could come up with all sorts of memories, episodes, and mental pictures, he couldn't come up with anything any of those past lives had offered that seemed at all important or interesting to him now. All it seemed like was an endless search to find things he hadn't had. But he'd never really found them, he knew that, because he had never been sure what he wanted.

And now, here he was, and he knew exactly what he needed and wanted, and the simple things on the list didn't go beyond the basics.

Maybe what he'd lost were all those problems and worries. His big problem now was that he hadn't been thinking like a horse.

With that idea in mind, he drifted back to sleep, but it was a lot easier to decide on this course than to stop the dreams.

The Quilst were a kind of cross between animals and plants, it seemed. The pictures made them look like walking, talking turnips who ate dirt. They weren't said to be particularly hostile, but they didn't really build roads and seemed to spend most of their time training hordes of insects to do stuff. Maybe the data was true, but the fact that the Quilst hadn't even put a Zone ambassador down south in recent memory meant that if the information was out of date, she was up the creek there.

The Betared were those horrid little bear things. They were well involved with the cartel at the highest levels, but they all had the temperaments of Genny on a bad day. The Mixtim looked like giant multicolored grasshoppers, but they supposedly had taken steam energy to its highest levels. They were so totally omnivorous that they could, and did, eat almost anything, but aside from often disturbing visitors with their culinary tastes, they weren't threatening and were very civilized, if specialized, like lots of insect cultures. She'd never seen or heard of one with the cartel, though, and they certainly looked like the best of a bad lot. Even if it proved less than inviting even for a getaway, Mixtim was well located with a variety of other hexes available.

They'd also take international credits there, which they used for trade, so at least it would provide options. Mixtim it was, then.

Now a haircut, and a dye job, some practical working clothes, and a bit of an identity switch, and she'd be ready to reclaim her little living treasures. She hoped the zoo wouldn't be too sticky about it, but if they were, then there were other ways.

First, though, she went down to the warehouse, which was getting pretty well cleaned out. "Moving the stuff offshore mostly, to islands and to boats, until this blows over," one of the supervisors told her.

"I called earlier. They said you had a courier come in, looks like a pony?"

"Yeah, he's in the back there. We have no instructions on what to do with him."

"I'll take him," she told them. "Mister Taluud is looking for specific couriers for some reason and doesn't want any harmed or lost until he finds what he's looking for. I'll take full responsibility."

The supervisor shrugged. "Fine with me. One more worry off my shoulders. But what are you gonna do with him, lady? You can't put a horse up in downtown Buckgrud, and you sure can't take him into an apartment."

She laughed. "Let that be my problem. Just show me to him."

Lori was only half-asleep when Campos walked into the rear stall area, and when his vision cleared and he saw who it was, he felt sudden fear and loathing. This was *not* the kind and gentle groom of his needs!

"Hello, Lori," Campos said, almost as if she were greeting an old friend. "Time for us to go."

It was so strange to hear words, whole sentences, that he could comprehend that it shocked him out of his stupor for a bit. "Go where?"

"Oh, you can still *speak*! Well, that will make things even easier."

But he couldn't, not like before. He no longer had the physical equipment to make the variety of sounds necessary for the translator to pick up. Still, the device worked by direct implant into the brain, so as long as *something* came out, however much it was like a whinny or a gurgle, the whole thought came through.

"We have to leave this place soon. Tonight, I hope. I have much to do myself, but I have a place for you to stay until I am ready. I'm taking you to a nice park where you'll be tied up but able to eat and drink and relax in the open air. There's a nice old fellow there who'll see that you're all right until I can come back for you. It's a very nice day to be outside, anyway. Later on we're going to take a train ride, at least part of the way. Right now, just you, me, and our old mutual friend."

"Friend?"

"Yes, indeed. I wouldn't *dream* of leaving without the pride of my little collection!"

Mavra Chang was not having a very pleasant existence, but she was in far more command of herself than Lori had been.

Then again, Lori had never been this low before. Mavra, as she was remembering, had been so low sometimes that this seemed downright optimistic. And of course, Lori might not have much of a future. Mavra knew she'd have that, or at least she hoped so, depending on where the hell Nathan was.

That was her greatest fear. If Nathan had made it inside the Well, maybe she *was* stuck like this and doomed to die. Somehow, though, she didn't believe it. She was still getting information, memories from the Well data base as she thought of them, and going over bits and pieces of her past long forgotten. Nathan sure as hell would have cut that if he'd already been there.

Maybe he was having as much trouble as *she* was, she thought hopefully.

Still, this was not a promising beginning. The Buckgrud Zoo was state of the art, but that meant that she'd been placed in a large area with few places to hide. A large, fake, hollowed-out tree was the only real place of escape, but it had little in the way of maneuvering room inside it. Around it was an area about ten meters square with a heavy glass or glasslike window on one side and very dark walls on the other three. The lighting let people see inside but to her looked like a cloudy night.

The glass was coated with some sort of nonreflective substance, and she could not see herself in it or see much beyond, although if she went up very close, she could barely make out a variety of overdressed giant ducks gawking at her. She couldn't help wondering how many times, if any, Campos had been by just to gloat. There was water in a simulated spring and small pool, and there was food.

That was the worst part, the food. Live insects, mostly worms and crawlers, were introduced several times a day, along with an occasional carcass of something that might have been an unfortunate zoo accident or roadkill for all she knew. The problem wasn't that she was going around gulping down the squirming critters or picking at the festering dead meat. She'd long since passed the point of being revolted at that aspect.

The problem was, she really liked them.

What she didn't like was how even the apartment and its window had offered more attractions than this dump, which was so boring, it risked driving her into the madness she'd been fighting all this time. The only entrance or exit was at the top of the cage, a good four meters beyond her head. The occasional cage attendant would come in now and then on a rope ladder, which was impossible for her to manage, without arms to hold on to it with. The ladder was taken up when they left, anyway. The glass was as thick and unbreakable as she'd ever seen, and there wasn't a chance of getting through it.

She was even more worried that they were going to breed her with a male, as Campos had threatened. It was what zoos did, after all, but what would it do to her? She still had her mind, she could think as a human even if the thoughts were dulled by who knew how long in this incredible boredom, but if she just let her mind wander into fantasy, the bird genes just took over. What if they brought in a male whatever it was and she got knocked up? Would she start building a nest and sitting on eggs and thinking about little squawkers?

The Well was notorious for not making it easy, but damn it, it shouldn't make it *impossible*. But try as she might, she hadn't been able to see a single way out of this mess.

What was even more depressing, was that if there *was* a way for her to get free, flat out she could make maybe a hundred meters an hour, and not for very long. She would also need to spend a lot of time keeping the metabolism going with food. No wonder this bird was rare. Figuring at maybe a kilometer a day if she was lucky, she could make the Avenue and the equator in, oh, maybe three or four years under absolutely perfect conditions.

Yeah.

And so she was quite startled when, in the early evening after the zoo had closed for the day, she heard the cage door open and saw not the usual attendant or the vet but the new model Campos climb down the ladder.

"Hello, my pretty birdie," she said with mock concern. "You needn't play with me. I know you don't need the drug anymore, and I'm not someone to trifle with right now."

"Are you here to taunt me?" Mavra asked her, despondent as ever.

"Oh, my, *no!* In fact, I am here as your liberator, believe it or not. It seems that you have become too popular for your own good and are far too valuable to be left in a musty old zoo. We are going on a little trip, you and I, along with my other pretty little treasure, and we will not be back for quite a while."

"You're taking me *out* of here?" Mavra's heart soared, even though she didn't expect to be going to a nicer place.

"Yes, indeed. In fact, Algon, he's a nice attendant here, will help you up out of the cage. He is a sucker for a pretty face and a few credits. Here. Get into this netting, and then I will tell him to pull you up."

Mavra suddenly felt a little contrary. "You can't lift me. What if I refuse?"

"Refuse? You mean you *like* it in here?"

"Not particularly, but they feed me regularly. You wouldn't go to all this trouble if you just needed to skip town. Somebody's got a line on what you did to me, haven't they?"

"You are quite sophisticated for a jungle primitive, aren't you? Yes, my precious, they *are* looking for you, but it will do you no good to hope. Even if they found you, you would just be kept here in a cage much like this. They might even keep you right here, although with a *much* better lock. I suspect, however, they would take you south, perhaps *very* far south. *I*, on the other hand, am going north, at least for now. Better the devil you know than the devil you do not." Her tone grew suddenly lower, more menacing. "Besides, you little shit, if you don't do it right now I will take one of these rocks, beat you into unconsciousness, and *roll* you into it. Now, *get in!*"

Mavra didn't have any doubts about Campos doing exactly that, so she complied. *Out and going north* . . . There was some hope again. Maybe she was too hard on the Well. One had to have patience with the gods before they answered one's prayers.

Algon took her, still in the netting, and placed her in a box with air holes that sat on a rolling cart. Soon they were out into the night air and, with Algon's passkey, out of the zoo and onto the street. The air felt good, although she was frustrated at being so completely and literally boxed in.

For somebody sneaking out of town, Campos certainly had a lot of help that could reveal her plans no matter what bribes she'd paid. First she was put in the back of a small truck that was certainly driven by somebody else, since Campos remained with her. There were also a number of cases and a steamer trunk.

They stopped after a while and shortly loaded on what certainly sounded and, from the tiny bit visible through the air holes, *looked* for all the world like a small horse.

"You're sure you're not too conspicuous?" Mavra commented, but it was ignored.

More hands unloaded them, and then the box was opened, but only to cut away the netting and transfer Mavra to an even larger box, one apparently designed to transport live animals. Inside was a fair quantity of raw meat and a gadget that would give her water in small amounts.

"Just relax," Campos told her. "You will be in there for a long time, but we shall meet up again before you run out of food and water, I promise you."

"Meet up again? Where are *you* going?"

"The same place you are, only by a different route. I have no time for questions or need to give answers to such as *you*." And with that, the box was sealed and began moving again.

Mavra could hear Campos speaking with others, but since the conversation wasn't directed to her, it wasn't picked up by the translators.

She was puzzled, no, totally confused. What in the *hell* was this maniac doing?

If Mavra was confused, Lori was even more so. For one thing, two female Cloptans had shown up in the park later that day and had set up for what looked like a horse bath and rubdown. It turned out to be a dye job; his pretty beige and all the rest were now jet black, and his mane and tail were snow white. Even the horn had been painted black, and it still smelled awful.

Then Campos had come with the van, loaded with a number of cases and baggage, and eventually had unloaded it at a freight stop on the Cloptan high-speed train line. He was collared there, and a whole bunch of routing tags were attached to it, then he was led onto a livestock flatcar which also contained a large number of animals that looked like a cross between a cow and a camel but with a kind of rounded, platypus-like bill. In a very short time the train began to pull out into the darkness.

The first time they unloaded Mavra Chang's box and reloaded it onto another train, she had a glimmer of what was going on.

She was being transshipped over half the damned hex, on one freight, then on another, in a pattern that probably looked like a baby with a crayon had created it. All of the other stuff was being shipped the same way, but on different trains, and it all seemed to be designed to eventually wind up somewhere together. Shipping agents, working from wired instructions, would reroute the packages so that no one would know the final destination or be able to easily trace them.

It was amazing what money and a computer could do, she thought.

The fact remained, though, that if she was attempting a getaway with everything, including Mavra, then she was traveling very heavy, and if she stayed in a high-tech hex, they would eventually track her down. That meant lowering the technology standard, but to do so with this much stuff would be pretty rough for a Cloptan female on her own. That one horse certainly wouldn't do the job.

Mavra's train reached the end point first, and she sat there, now inside a warehouse, the only sounds occasional trains whirring past outside. She wondered what was coming next and how Juana Campos figured on pulling this off. She didn't mind the wait; that was all she'd been doing for a long time, anyway, but that had been waiting for nothing. Now something was happening. Things were *moving* again, and so was she.

That was worth waiting for.

Just before dawn some automated equipment unloaded several cartons, and they were placed very near Mavra's box. She guessed they were the rest of the stuff from the van. Now all that was lacking was the horse.

It wasn't lacking for long. Just as the sun was starting to come up, Mavra heard the sound of hooves clicking on the hard floor of the warehouse and picked up the unmistakable scent of live horseflesh.

Lori, now tied up to a metal stake near the boxes, was totally confused. All night it was on one train, then onto another, going back and forth, and sometimes, he was sure, on the same train over and over. Unlike Mavra, he didn't like it or understand it one bit.

None of them had long to wait after Lori at last arrived. Whether on a schedule or because the loadmaster didn't like having a horse fouling up his nice warehouse floor, a crew entered and began transferring everything once more.

In the daylight, even with his poor vision, Lori could see that they were at some kind of border stop. On the other side of the sleek magnetic strip that served as Cloptan train tracks there was a very different looking building and beyond it a very different looking terminal. It was a little hard to see as well, as if he were looking through a discolored gauze curtain.

A hex boundary! And not the one to Liliblod, either!

The Cloptan crew and its robotic equipment moved everything across right to the border. The boxes were then put down flush with it and pushed across slowly by small rams that came out from the equipment. Lori alone was led through, feeling the familiar tingle as he passed into a new hex, and then he could see more clearly what was beyond.

It was suddenly chilly. Not cold, but there was a definite chill in the air, and signs of light frost were still around, slow to melt in the rising run. Lori didn't really feel the cold, but it was still something of a shock.

More of a shock was the crew that awaited them on the other side.

They were bugs. *Huge* bugs. And not just huge bugs but bugs of just about all shapes and sizes, the smallest still the size of an alley cat.

They were quite colorful creatures, and the two that were enormous, at least two meters long and standing taller than Lori, looked like nothing he'd ever seen even in a nightmare or in the Amazonian jungles. They seemed closest to praying mantises.

He was scared, nervous, and yet somewhat excited and didn't even realize all the old memory connections he was suddenly making again.

A big beetlelike thing crawled up to the pallets on which the boxes rested and with two whiplike hind limbs took the lead pallet and started pulling it effortlessly toward the station beyond. Other, similar creatures did the same with the rest. Finally another, who looked more like a bipedal grasshopper, approached Lori, who shied but couldn't pull away, being tied to a post. But the thing didn't eat him; instead, it wordlessly untied him and began to lead him after the boxes.

The railroad warehouse was a wonder of cogs, levers, belts, pulleys, and other such automation, all of which was apparently driven by external steam plants and which rumbled and hissed and gave off occasional steam through vents. Steam also seemed to heat the place, at least somewhat; it was certainly warmer here.

Overcoming his fear and revulsion at the sight of the giant insects, Lori began to watch them work with fascination. They all looked so very different, yet he began to wonder if in fact they really were. Each seemed to be physically designed almost as a tool would be designed, to do one or two specific tasks well. The big low ones were the strong-arm types, the longshoremen who could move and lift loads much larger and heavier than they. Sleek, small, fast bugs went up and down the conveyors and pipes, oblivious to whether they were right side up or upside down, apparently checking to make sure that everything was operating properly.

The big praying mantis types were primarily lifters, almost like living dockyard cranes using huge mandibles that form-fitted into specially designed containers.

Suppose an insect society, many of which had different specialized varieties anyway, could really breed and design to order or need? Each individual hatched, shaped, and endowed with the capabilities to do specific jobs and serve the whole? That obviously was what was here.

It was an ideal thing for a nontech hex, but the steam power and degree of automation said this was semitech. The bugs of the industrial age, adapted to fit the new requirements.

If they were as durable and as prolific breeders as most bugs, this was a race that might well be able to survive and even thrive anywhere, under almost any conditions.

Outside, both Lori and Mavra could hear the shrill sounds of steam whistles large and small going off and the rhythmic *chug chug chug* unique to one kind of mechanical marvel moving about.

Steam locomotives.

Neither was aware of the other's identity or proximity, although there was little they could have done about it had they known, yet both suddenly shared the same thought.

The crazy dance of the trains might not yet be over.

ANOTHER PART
OF THE FIELD

GEN TALUUD WAS VERY uncomfortable in the presence of the colonel, but he needed information and needed it bad. He might have some business to do with this jelly blob if the answers were right.

"It was a complete disaster," the colonel told him. "They even managed to prevent me from destroying a great deal of the computer files. Fortunately, I *did* manage to eliminate information on certain major figures and also some details of the divisions within the hexes such as yours."

"You think that'll help *me*?" Taluud thundered. "Hell, everybody there knows me, and so does everybody here. I ain't in the quiet part of the business, you know. If they'd flush something as big as the complex down the toilet, they wouldn't think twice of flushin' me along with it." He bit off the end of a cigar and spat it out with such force, it traveled halfway across the room. "So what's the price, Colonel? What in hell will get 'em off my back?"

"As you surmised, the pair kidnapped by Campos, and particularly one, Mavra Chang. Find them, turn them over, and you are likely to find the pressure turned well down, so much so that you might well be back in business within six months to a year at best."

"Then we'll find 'em!"

"Um, yes. *That* is a priority. The question is, Do we really wish to turn them over to the council when we do?"

"Huh? What in hell does that mean? Of *course* we do. You think I want to be ruined?"

The colonel had considered his course on the journey here, accomplished mostly by sea and not without its own danger. Leemings had great power on land, but in the water they were helpless, and in salt water they could not help but absorb great quantities and sink like stones. Even these amorphous creatures needed to breathe oxygen, and they were not equipped to fashion working gills.

"Mister Taluud, have you thought beyond what's happening to consider *why* it's happening? Why our mutual bosses would allow such a catastrophe?"

"Savin' their own asses, that's all, just like everybody else."

"In more ways than one. They are scared. They are frightened of something so much that they are willing to pull down an important part of what they had built with such care and patience. This Mavra Chang isn't merely someone with a lot of friends. They would *never* have sacrificed the complex for as simple a reason as that."

Gen Taluud really hadn't thought about it, but what the creature had said made a lot of sense. "Go on."

"Let me tell you what they firmly believe about Mavra Chang," the colonel said calmly. "And I'll also tell you about my experiences with a man of the same race. A man named Nathan Brazil."

Taluud listened, fascinated, not knowing whether to believe this stuff. Still, it was clear that the big shots, the rulers and politicians behind all this, were totally convinced, and they had greater resources than he did. Still, it was hard to swallow.

"You really believe all that crap about her, Colonel? Honestly? And this guy who they think is some kind of ancient god, too?"

"Does it matter, sir?"

"Huh? Whatddya mean?"

"Let's assume it's all true. Every word of it. You could never make a bargain with that sort of creature. Even if you thought you had a deal, once inside, at the all-powerful controls, what would bargains with mere mortals count for? How would you enforce the bargain? You see what I mean. There is no way we can allow her to actually get in, so it doesn't matter if I believe it or even if it is true. It doesn't matter if *you* believe it, either. *They* believe it. The raid and the massive actions still to come here prove that."

"Yeah, so what? What's that get us?"

"Perhaps a lot. If *they* got her, they'd just lock her away under guard with Brazil and try to keep them there until all that we know passed away. But what if *we* had her? You and I, together. What if we had her and she was salted away safely in a place only we knew? Think of the possibilities. What do you want to be? Emperor of Clopta? Governor general of the district? Permanent chief councillor? No running, no fear of the law at any time because you *are* the law, secure in the position because if they don't give you everything you want, if they even *dare* to act against you, you can give one order and Chang will get into the Well. You see the potential? You are a powerful man, but only in this city and to a lesser extent in Clopta. Like me, you still take orders from those higher up. The kind of people who are now selling you down the river, as it were. Isn't it tempting to turn the tables and have *them* deferring to *you?*"

It was a masterful scheme, absolutely brilliant. Taluud's estimation of the colonel went up a great deal in just that one moment. Only one thing made him hesitate.

"All very well, Colonel, but what do *you* get out of this? What's to stop *you* from just eating me and becoming ruler of the world yourself?"

The colonel was ready for that one. "For one thing, I don't want to be ruler of the world. I think it would be far too much work to be fun. Much better to be an adviser to that ruler and have his ear when needed. No, sir, I don't want that. But you see, all my life I have taken orders. All my life I have served governments and cartels and bowed to Don Francisco this and General Hernando that. It's been no different here. I do their dirty work, I cover up their mistakes, and still I am dependent on others. I am a man of modest and humble beginnings. The army of my native land on my native world saved me from poverty and starvation. I worked my way up, doing whatever was necessary, whatever could advance me. I did not have the relatives, the connections, or the old military school ties that counted. Finally, with the air corps, I managed to attain basically the level I am at again here—but I was *still* subject to miserable pay and the whims of my superiors, always with the sword at my neck. One of those—those high-and-mighty generals could in an instant declare me dangerous or push me aside. When I got here, I had certain unique qualities and experience and managed to achieve this level rather quickly, but I am still the servant, the outsider. I am not a native. I can never be at the top."

"What do you want, then, Colonel?" Taluud asked him with growing interest, wondering if he could trust any of this.

"I want to be the grand leader of Leeming, the most supreme general and president for life. A modest position of power compared to what *you* might attain but more than enough for me. There are certain—characteristics, if you will—of a Leeming that have the potential for me to live a very long time and for a part of me to live on almost forever. Within my own land I would be absolute ruler. You would have all the rest."

Taluud thought it over. Maybe the slime was telling the truth, maybe he wasn't, but Gen Taluud hadn't lived this long without being able to judge when a fellow as unencumbered with morals as he himself told stories like that. Besides, he could always get the bastard fried if it looked wrong.

"Very tempting, Colonel. Very tempting, indeed. But we're missing one thing to make such a deal, and that's this what's her name. We don't even know where she is or, at the moment, *what* she is."

"I know. Both from the computers and from the medical records of those curious doctors. She is an *anuk,* a very large wingless bird. They were quite proud of her; the genetic remake was so complete, she is said to be capable of reproducing—as an *anuk,* of course."

Taluud's cigar almost dropped from his fingers. "A what? A bird? How big a bird do you mean?"

"Oh, a meter, give or take a bit. About this high, I would say." A pseudopod shot out and hovered in the air.

"Why, that lyin', double-crossin' bitch! I'll fry her ass for this! *Nobody* does this to Gen Taluud!" He picked up the communicator. "Get me Campos. *Now!* No—wait a minute! Go over there and pick her up— *personally.* I want her here in ten minutes, you hear?" The communicator slammed down.

"I gather you already know the location of our quarry," the colonel commented. "How convenient."

"Yeah, maybe. Seems to me she said she'd given it away to someplace, but I can't remember. Don't matter. She'll tell me anything I want to know soon enough."

The communicator rang, and Taluud picked it up. "Yeah? *What!* Well, what about the other two broads? Them, too? *Shit!*" He looked back at the colonel. "They flew the coop! All three of 'em flew the coop! Like they can hide from *me!*"

"I would not underestimate this Campos. I have information that on the old world Juan Campos was in some ways an equivalent to you here."

"Yeah, yeah, I know, but he ain't got no control. I never trusted guys who got to be big because their father was big. You work yourself up, you don't have to prove nothing."

"My point exactly with my own case," the colonel noted. 'We agree on a great deal, sir. I believe this could be an excellent partnership."

"The zoo!"

"I beg your pardon?"

"She gave the bird to the zoo!"

A few calls brought the news that the zoo, too, had someone missing. He was back on the communicator again.

"Look, how tough can it be? Three broads and a bird the size of a teenage kid. You put the word out. Naw, they probably are outta here by now, maybe on a ship—check all the docks and passenger and cargo manifests. Also check the trains, border controls, you name it. *They got to be somewhere, and I want the 'where' and fast, hear?"*

"I admire the way you move on things," the colonel said approvingly.

The communicator signaled, and Taluud grabbed it. "Yeah? Well, you get movin' on this other thing. As soon as you find 'em, you get a dozen of your best men and meet me. We'll go after 'em personal. *Then* we pull the plug. Hear? First we want them girls. Period."

"What was that about, if I might ask?"

"Your buddies from Agon are here. They're in the capital right now, armed with lots of information on certain political types, and they're gonna have a pretty free ride by tomorrow. The rats are deserting the ship up there and fallin' all over themselves to be helpful."

"My—'buddies,' as you call them. I assume this is the centaurs, the Erdomite, the Dahir, and the Glathrielian girl?"

"Yeah, yeah. Them and that holier than thou Kurdon, too. I *knew* we shoulda made him have an accident years ago! Well, that's what I get for bein' a softy! No more!"

"This—bird. It was well known?"

"Yeah, around here, anyways. It was so weird-lookin', anybody who saw it remembered it. *Shit!* Right under my nose! Right under my fuckin' *nose!"*

"If even the more common elements in your own organization will remember it even slightly, it is serious. And she was last in the zoo, too . . . Probably on display. That means even more will remember. Honest, upright folks. We will not be too far ahead of them, I fear."

"Maybe not. But if it's always ahead, I'll settle for a few steps. The only one's gonna laugh at the end of this is the one who winds up with the bird, right?"

"I would say that was a fair statement."

"Then *we* get there first."

"What of these other two females? Might they be with Campos? How much of a problem might *they* be?"

"They're all looks, no brains. Campos was the one with the looks, brains, and guts. I don't know how she even got the other two to go along, but they're dumb enough to fall for a lot of stuff. Well, I'll fix all three of 'em when I get a hold of 'em!"

The communicator signaled. "Yeah? What? *Oamlatt?* That's on the border with Mixtim! You *sure* she crossed over there? Absolutely positive? Yeah, well, it's a lead. Let's get on it. We got anybody in Mixtim that's handy? Shit. Well, it shouldn't be brain surgery to find information. See what you can find out, if you can find anybody there who remembers a *second* woman, or a big bird, or whatever. Call me back." The boss turned to the colonel. "Mixtim."

"Problems?"

"One of the girls—not Campos, one of the others—arrived this morning. I said the other two weren't all that bright. She made a call back here just so's her sister wouldn't worry about her. They're sure she went over into Mixtim at the Oamlatt border crossing. It's a rail intersection and trade center. Makes sense."

The communicator buzzed.

"Yeah? A black pony? That don't sound like no bird!"

"Wait a minute!" the colonel said in an urgent tone. "Ask them if the pony had a horn on its head."

"Hold it. Did the horse have a horn on its head? How do I know? Stickin' up, I guess." There was a pause. "It did!" Taluud looked over at the colonel. "Okay, it did. So?"

"The other one. She's taking *both* of them with her!"

"You get to work on the Mixtim side. See if you can get any information on trains and such. I want to know where they bought tickets to, hear?"

He pressed a button on the communicator, then redialed another number. "All right, we're on 'em. Have your team meet me at Central Station. Call ahead to Oamlatt and make sure we have supplies for a long trip and the firepower we'll need that'll work there. Yeah, Oamlatt. They went into Mixtim, and we're gonna have to go get 'em. You meet me at the station after gettin' that set, you hear? I'm pullin' the plug."

He looked at the colonel. "You like bugs?" he asked.

"Depends. Raw, boiled, or fried?" Colonel Lunderman responded.

"Everybody's flown the coop," Kurdon told them. "It was to be expected, but I am still disappointed. At any rate, we've broken the main connection for this entire region for quite some time, and we have enough on the local boys both here and in Agon that it's unlikely to be restored on a scale like this in the near future."

"You mean you've actually destroyed the cartel?" Julian asked, somewhat awed at the concept. "Because of *us*?"

"Because of you we have hurt them, yes," the inspector agreed. "And we have given two hexes and perhaps many more in the area a breath of fresh air and cleanliness, which is more than I dared to hope when this began. As to the cartel, though, no. It is damaged but far too large and too spread out to be killed. To truly kill it we would need a means to get at the ministers of many governments, to clean house at the very top. What we have gained is a bit of local joy and some pride; we have finally hurt them. But destroyed them? Hardly. You cut off a few heads from this kind of monster, it still has far more heads than it needs. You cut off *all* its heads and somehow it grows new ones. Just winning a battle of this magnitude is incredible, but the war? No. Take it from a career policeman. So long as there are greedy and power-hungry people at the top and corruption festers, you cannot win. You play to tie, that is all."

It was pretty depressing looked at that way.

"What about Mavra and Lori?" Gus asked him. "I mean, that was part of the reason for all this."

"Yes, it is, and the council is still very anxious to have them. But there is a limit to what I can do myself, and I am already overburdened here. My main concern is my own country, as you must understand. If I cannot cure the worldwide cancer, I can at least try my best to ensure that Agon becomes fully cancer-free. You will have whatever funds and authority you require and the aid of any official that you contact. It would be better to work through the locals on this, anyway. They know their own territory."

"That certainly helps," Tony told him, "but I gather you mean that we're on our own from this point."

"Hardly. As I say, this remains a top priority with the council. You will find cooperation along the line in most civilized areas, and we now have descriptions and bulletins going out from Zone to governments throughout the Well World. Make no mistake—we will find them."

"I want Campos," Gus said with a low growl. "I want Campos *bad.*"

"Then your next stop is Mixtim," Kurdon told them. "Take the train to Oamlatt. I'll arrange for Cloptan authorities there to brief you on what we know so far. After that, you will have to pursue. Please do so. If they are chased, then they cannot stop, and if they do not stop, they are bound to be seen and reported. If they *do* stop, you will be on them. I have seen you all work now, and I have every confidence in your abilities to do the job."

Gus sighed and looked at Terry. Damn it, he *knew* he should stop, but they were so very close. And for Terry's sake as well as his own, he *wanted* Campos.

He wanted to eat her alive.

MIXTIM

IN THE ANCIENT TIMES when the Well World was operated as a biological and social laboratory rather than simply existing, there was the problem of simulating the limitations of real planets that would logically evolve such races and ecosystems. In many cases that meant placing limitations within the hexes on everything from the losses in electrical signals over a distance or whether certain levels of technology would work at all. The semitech hexes had the most variations, but in all such places the great emphasis had been on steam. Mixtim had a generally flat landscape and a somewhat dry continental climate where the rains were seasonal and the rivers broad, fairly shallow, and winding. It was a land best suited for growing hardy crops, mostly grains, but without the practical use of rivers to move large quantities of harvest from where it was grown to where it was needed.

The answer had been a vast network of steam-powered locomotives pulling long trains of produce to and from major population centers and also to ports of entry with neighboring hexes, where it could be traded for goods either impossible to manufacture or not worth the trouble to make within the hex. They were sleek, fast trains like nothing ever seen on Earth, but they had the unmistakable sound and fury of the classic steam engine. The network was particularly remarkable because of the inability to use a telegraph or maintain the integrity of an electrical signal through the tracks. Nonetheless, they had a fine safety record, and the trains of Mixtim ran on time.

In fact, it almost seemed as if the whole population were involved in running or servicing the trains. While the trains occasionally passed clusters of high twisted mounds filled with teeming denizens of the insect world, after more than two hours there wasn't a sign of a major city and the villages they passed were more likely trade centers and farming communities. On the other hand, there appeared to be one every time two different rail lines crossed, and there were an *awful* lot of rail lines in Mixtim. Juana Campos was counting on that and the fact that they had little in the way of computers or even written records for nonroutine shipments. Everything like that was more or less off the book.

The natives crammed into cars and resembled festering colonies, but there was little provision for visiting travelers. On the other hand, the Mixtimites had plenty of surplus boxcars along every siding, and it was no problem at all to hook one on for special purposes.

The society was, as expected, totally communal, so there was no money or other favors exchanged for services, but outsiders were in fact valued and expected to pay, the fees going to whatever local jurisdiction for the purpose of buying imports. Some of these were specialized or customized farm tools and implements or finely machined parts for irrigation systems, and some were as simple as candy and other delicacies.

The largest import, however, was chemical fertilizer, and *that* made Mixtim and its railroad less than ideal for visitors. The Mixtimites, it seemed, either had no sense of smell or liked the smell of it. The stench of fertilizer was everywhere.

"This is totally gross," said Audlay, one of the two former roommates with Campos back in Buckgrud, as they sat on a layer of wheat or some kind of grass on the floor of a boxcar heading into the hex.

"Look at it this way. At least we won't have to worry about gaining weight here," Kuzi, the other roommate, responded in a tone just short of I-think-I-have-to-throw-up.

"Quit complaining!" Campos snapped at them. "I don't like the smell any more than you do, but what do you want me to do about it? You knew it would be rough when you decided to come along. You also knew when you came that there was no going back. Not for a long while. Now, make the best of it!"

"Yes, Juana," Audlay responded, sounding almost like a small child.

Campos had dominated the other two since she'd moved in six months earlier. They were of an all too familiar type, very much the kind of people the old Juan Campos thought most women were. They seemed to live in fear of almost everything, and in spite of their protests, they *liked* being dominated. What power and confidence they had they drew from another, and that other was the one whose power they feared. They were both afraid of Campos, but it wasn't just out of fear that they'd agreed to come along. They both felt that this was the only way out of an existence they didn't like and one which had no real future.

Audlay almost defined the word "bimbo." If there were two thoughts in that head of hers, they were jumbled from being blown around by the air passing between her ears, Campos thought. Still, she had just enough pride and sense to realize when she was being humiliated, even if she didn't understand the joke. The men had her do silly, ridiculous things and played all sorts of pranks on her when they weren't insulting her or slapping her around. She had found herself oddly attracted to Campos from the first, though. There was something inside the strange woman that radiated the power, the authority, and occasionally the attitude of the men she'd known, yet Campos wasn't a man. The newcomer had often defended Audlay against some of the more oafish lieutenants. A woman capable of standing up to the men and protecting others had been an unbelievably attractive individual, and Campos had shown her all sorts of new and different positions and turn-ons she had never dreamed of before. She would do just about anything Juana said, but not without whining and complaining about it all the time.

Kuzi was different. Older and tougher, she was very much the product of a rough and morally ambivalent life and had taken everything she could get. She, in fact, had only one fear, and it wasn't Campos; she was getting older, and while she was still attractive, every time she had looked at herself in the mirror for the past year or two, she'd seen more and more bloom coming off the rose. Her man was coming by less and less, and fewer others were interested in coming around when they had other, younger women to fool around with. She'd seen the handwriting on the wall and hadn't liked it one bit. The guys also weren't exactly young chicks anymore, either, and where did they get off dumping her? She didn't like Campos all that much, but she saw a lot more there than the men had. The strange newcomer had hated the life almost from the start, and it was clear that she'd been biding her time until she could do something about it. Well, now that the time had come, it was time for old Kuzi to fish or cut bait.

Campos regarded Kuzi not much more than she did Audlay, but she did recognize the armor plate that was there. A gun might be as dangerous to them as to anybody else in Audlay's hands, but there was no question in Campos's mind that Kuzi could and would blow away anybody she had to.

Still, Campos wished that she had a couple of better and stronger allies than this pair. There just hadn't been enough time to build the kind of alliances she really knew were necessary before it had fallen apart, and these two were the only ones she could depend on upon such short notice. Still, sitting in a boxcar that smelled like warmed-over shit going through a landscape that was kind of like the Argentine pampas overrun with human-sized grasshoppers and cockroaches, she was under no illusion that she was biding time until something came up that would give her more of a plan.

"What are they all so scared of that damned birdie for, anyway?" Kuzi asked after a while. "And why load ourselves down with that pair?"

"The horse will be handy. He carries things, remember," Campos responded. "Besides, there is no other animal of that type who can understand a complicated order. As for the birdie, that's the prize, and I did not really realize it. They are all afraid that my precious little birdie can walk inside this world and play God. Would you believe that?"

"*That* thing?" Audlay commented, her upper beak rippling in disbelief.

"She was not always 'that *thing*,' as you say it. Inside is still the brain, the mind, of the person it used to be."

"So you gonna take her up north, let her go inside, and fix things for us?" Kuzi asked her.

Mavra, still in the box but well within earshot, could not help but note that she was being talked about. "Don't believe it? Take me up there and I'll show you how it's done," she offered, knowing the response.

"She says she can do it," Campos told the other two, to whom Mavra's words were just unpleasant squawking. "The trouble is, what would she do to *us* if we let her, eh? *That* is the problem. That is *everybody's* problem with her."

"So where are we goin' and what're we gonna do?" Audlay asked her.

"We are going to change trains a few times just for insurance's sake, and then we are heading for another border. This is a nice place for a getaway, but it is hardly the kind of place where I think any of us want to spend more time than we have to. Have either of you ever been this way before?"

"I went down to the place in Agon a few times and once or twice to the islands, but that's about it," Kuzi told her. "I don't think Audlay's been out of Buckgrud since she ran away from the farm. Right?"

Audlay nodded.

"That makes us all strangers, but I have more experience being a stranger in a new land than either of you," Campos told them. "Still, I admit I have never been in *this* strange a place before. We need some information. We need to know what is in the hexes that are around this place."

In a way, Clopta hadn't been nearly as alien as she would have expected if she'd just heard of it. The buildings were odd, some of the customs were very strange, the people looked different and had in some cases different needs and comforts, but overall, it really *hadn't* been that different from Earth. That was what had made it easy for her to fit into it. Deep down, they were the same *sorts* as those she'd known back home. Agon hadn't been all that different, either, no matter how different the look of the people or what they ate or what their houses looked like, and some of the other races she'd met at the complex hadn't been alien enough where it counted to really worry her. *This*, though, was unexpected. There *were* places, nearby places, on this world where things were so alien, she could not fit in. It had added a layer of difficulty almost from the beginning that she hadn't counted on at all.

"Find one with power, a real bathroom, and running water," Kuzi said, half in jest.

"It will get harder than this, I think!" Campos warned them. "We cannot use the modern hexes. Modern hexes have computers and electronic identity checks and efficient policemen and probably corrupt officials with ties to those we left behind. No matter where we go, we stick out. We are a different breed. Best for the time being to stick to places where it is difficult to find people who do not want to be found, where news travels very slowly, and where the government is a three-day ride. We need food, and shelter, and privacy. We must move until we find it."

"What then?" Kuzi asked her. "We just sit and hope they bust Taluud and his whole rotten lousy crew?"

"For a start," Campos told her. "Still, I feel that there is something else, something valuable that I am missing here that will be the answer to all our problems."

"Yeah, well, so long as you have something they want, they'll keep looking for us," Kuzi noted.

Campos's head snapped up, and her long lashes almost hit her forehead. "What was that? What did you say?"

"I just said that so long as we have the birdie and they want it, they'll keep coming."

"Yes! That's *it*!"

"Huh?" the other two both said at once.

"I wonder what price, what guarantees we might get at the highest levels for her. I have been an idiot! We have a treasure this whole world wants, no matter what the reason! It is simply a matter of making sure we can safely cash it in!"

"Yeah? How are you gonna do that?" Kuzi asked her. "You know Gen and his mob. Would you trust them on any deal once they had what they wanted and didn't need us no more?"

"Not a bit," Campos admitted. "But if it were from the government, in writing, and public, then perhaps it would be honored, no? A full amnesty, a full pardon for anything we might be charged with first and foremost. Some money—reward money—for returning what was lost.

Quite a lot of money. Enough to buy all the finer things. A villa, perhaps, or a ranch, and some strong-necked, simpleminded men to carry out our orders and see to our needs. It has possibilities, does it not?"

"You think you can get 'em to buy that?"

"Over time. It will have to be well thought out and carefully done, but yes, I think we can get at least that. But first we must have that place I spoke of."

"You mean the ranch with the cute dumb guys?" Audlay asked.

Campos ignored her. "We need to hide out for a bit. Make them uncomfortable, even desperate for a solution. *Then* we can make any sort of deal with confidence."

She needed more than ever to find out about the hexes farther on. Somewhere on this crazy world, where every country seemed no larger than Ecuador, there was the kind of place she sought.

"Yes, three Cloptans, a horse, and a lot of baggage," the colonel said. "We know they came at least this far."

"Oh, yes," the stationmaster responded, standing on her hind legs and looking very much like a parody of a human. "I remember 'em. They *did* change here. Kind of odd, two groups of foreigners coming through. We don't get much of that here, you know."

The colonel and Taluud were counting on that. It had been frustrating to stop at every transfer point and make the queries, particularly with the train crews so insistent on keeping the schedule so perfectly, but it had paid off.

"They took another train from here?" the colonel pressed impatiently.

"Oh, yes."

"Which train? Going where and in which direction?"

"You know, we've been hoping to replace the roof on the main silo over there before the rains come," the stationmaster commented.

"Just let me have a few minutes with the little bug, boss," one of the gunmen whispered to Taluud. "I'll find out what we need."

Taluud slapped the man hard in the face with the back of his hand. "Idiot!" he commented. He could estimate the number of bugs within shouting distance, and he didn't like the mental image of what would happen to them if they roughed up the key official in town.

"So you need a new silo roof?" the colonel responded. "And how much will it take to get one made for you, say, in Clopta?"

"Oh, not a lot, but more'n we got," the stationmaster responded. "Maybe six hundred units."

Lunderman could hear Taluud choking slightly in back of him, but he knew how much cash the man had in those suitcases. "You'll have your new roof, sir. Now, as to the others?"

"Train 1544," the stationmaster responded. "Eastbound."

"When is the next train due in that direction, if I may ask?"

"Oh, there'll be one by in an hour and forty-one minutes," the stationmaster responded, looking at the enigmatic station clock.

"Then we'd also like passage on it when it arrives. How much will that be?"

"Can't say," the Mixtimite told him. "I don't know how far you want to go."

"How far did *they* buy passage to?"

"End of the line. That'd be the Hawyr border."

Gen Taluud saw a long string of such transactions ahead and groaned.

"Don't worry so much," the colonel told him. "After all, they don't have nearly the cash with them that you do. They can't keep this up for long."

"Long enough," Gen Taluud growled, turning to one of the gunmen. "Pay the man. And add six hundred for his damned roof."

For a society without money, they all sure seemed to have a good knowledge of the finer points of the system, he thought ruefully.

"These documents from your own government railway commission tell you to give us full cooperation as well as free passage," Julian argued.

"I see it," the stationmaster told her. "Trouble is, we haven't been on the friendliest of terms here with the Mother Nest. Been hard to get materials."

"He's sayin' that the government's all well and good, but his three hundred babies all need shoes," Gus commented. He turned to the stationmaster, who had reacted as everybody always did to Gus's sudden and fierce appearance.

"Tryin' to scare me poppin' in and out like that?" the stationmaster asked nervously.

"It's a habit. We understand what you are getting at, but they didn't give us a great deal of cash, just enough to get by, and we may have a long way to go. We've spoken with other stationmasters here, and they have understood the problem. What makes you think we can give you more?"

"Got a new silo roof out of the last bunch."

"The *last* bunch? You mean there's more than the Cloptan women?" Tony asked.

"Sure. *Was* they women? Can't tell the difference myself. But first the one bunch comes in, and they buy tickets for themselves and freight for their stuff. Then this second bunch comes in, also Cloptans, but with a real strange character like nothin' I ever saw before—as strange as all of you. And *they* seemed right interested in payin' whatever it took to find out where the first group went. Guess I shoulda held out for more than a roof, huh?"

Julian thought a moment. "What did this other one, with the second group, look like?"

"Didn't look like anything at all. No, I mean it. Just a giant ball of goo. Nice manners, though."

"The colonel! The colonel's after 'em!" Gus hissed. "Okay, look, we could give you a paper that would authorize you to go to Clopta and place a prepaid order for something if you want, but we can't give you cash."

"I dunno. We don't work like that here."

"Yeah, well, I'll tell you how *we* work. We try and be reasonable and hope for cooperation," Gus told him, some menace creeping into his already intimidating voice. "If we don't get any cooperation, we note who didn't give it to us. Then we have to send a message to our people and to your government that we could not do our jobs *because we couldn't pay his bribe*! Might not get us what we need, but it sure brings us satisfaction."

"Oh, goodness, yes!" Anne Marie put in, getting the drift of things. "I wonder what happened to that last one who did this to us. We never did find out because when we had to backtrack to check, they were marching out the whole population of his town somewhere. It was *most* distressing!"

The stationmaster's limbs twitched a bit, and the antennae atop her head seemed to cross.

"Give me a sheet of the official notepaper with the seal," Gus told Tony. "I'll put it on the next train to the Mother Nest. Then all we'll need from you, sir, is your name and title and the name of this lovely little town here."

The twitching continued, and finally the stationmaster said, "First batch took 1544 eastbound. The second group followed 'em."

"And when is the next train?"

"Sixty-four minutes."

"We thank you for your cooperation," Tony told her. "We will report our satisfaction with the line to the authorities."

"No, just leave me out," the stationmaster responded. "They'd just come and take away the money I already got . . ."

"Amateurs," Gus hissed contemptuously.

* * *

"Hawyr is out," Juana Campos muttered, looking at a map which she couldn't read but which she'd marked up in Spanish. "High-tech and reported not very friendly anyway. Karlbarx is nontech, but they're said to be some sort of giant rat thing and they eat meat. I don't think they sound too great, and there's not much trade there or a line going all the way to the border, anyway. Quilst I'd already ruled out, so that leaves Leba. I don't like it, but that seems to be the best choice."

"Are they all full of flesh-eating monsters or what?" Audlay asked plaintively. "I mean, gee, it sounds like a horror show."

"Well, the Lebans are plants, and they supposedly don't need much except dirt and water, so that's something," Campose commented. "They're also semitech, but the only use they seem to make of it is that they've allowed the Mixtimites to extend a few railroad lines through."

"*Phew!* More smelly boxcars?" Kuzi said rather than asked.

"Maybe. We'll have to see what it looks like. The trains are basically through to the other borders and don't seem to have many stops in Leba. I doubt if a plant that gets all its nourishment from the sun, rain, and soil needs much from anywhere else. Trouble is, we go up there, we can get boxed in fairly easily. There's only one more hex to the equator, which, I am told, cannot be crossed. The Leban trains don't go there; they head for Bahaoid or something that sounds like that, which is a high-tech hex to the west that they *do* trade with. So we got this plant hex, and then a nontech hex up against a wall, and a high-tech on both sides. Not great."

"We could turn around and go back," Audlay suggested. "Maybe they wouldn't figure that."

"The *last* thing we want to do is go back toward Clopta, believe me. We'd be in jail or worse, and most of them in there with us would be part of the old organization and maybe not too keen on seeing us, either. No, I don't think so. Not now." She sighed. "Leba it is, then."

"You say they're *plants*?" Kuzi asked her. "I just can't imagine that. A flower garden that talks back."

"Somehow I don't think it's going to be like that," Campos responded. "We can only go and see. And I hope we can arrange for some fresh food for our little troublemaking prize here. As an insect eater, she's probably been going nuts being unable to eat this whole population."

LEBA

LOW HILLS BEGAN AS they traveled north toward the border in Mixtim, and soon the countryside began to be broken and interesting once more. Along the rivers there was lush green vegetation, but beyond the hills were covered with grassland, too arid to really farm effectively, considering that the water had to come uphill, but sufficient to provide sustenance for a few small villages that seemed to exist primarily for the railroad.

There were no border controls as such there, but the station and small yard right against the hex barrier were used to rewater the engines and give them a checkout as well as to change engines and crews for the haul through Leba. The steam engines used had a different look to them; they were much larger, with long boilers, and had huge coal tenders just in back of the engine in place of the wood carriers of Mixtim. While the engines were prepared and checked out, there was a two-hour layover.

"Figures," Gus commented. "You wouldn't want to burn wood in a land where the people were the plants. They might take it personal."

"They must mine the coal elsewhere," Tony noted. "There didn't seem to be any signs of such mining or of coal, period, anywhere we passed." She sighed. "Well, time to at least find out some information. Excuse me."

Anne Marie stood looking at the ghostly border and what was beyond. "Looks rather ominous," she commented. "And certainly wet."

The skies within Mixtim were bright, with just a few clouds, while the skies on the other side of the border were a low uniform gray. The place was certainly green, though; it seemed like an endless forest, perhaps a rain forest from the looks of the fog and mist curling through the tops of the trees beyond.

Tony returned a few minutes later. "News good, not so good, and in between," she told them. "First, no more switches. They went into Leba, all right, and so did the colonel's bunch following them. The ladies went through many hours ago, the second group only on the train before this one. We are certainly catching up, but I fear to the wrong group. I am *most* worried about the colonel, Gus."

"He's a slick meanie, all right," Gus agreed, "but I handled him."

"Yes, once. I remember thinking when we spoke to one another of Brazil and Carnivale and old times that I was glad he was on our side. Now that it seems he is not, my fears are realized."

"I still say he can be handled."

"In a high-tech hex, yes. He is as vulnerable to the energy weapons as we are. But the energy weapons do not work here, Gus, or in Leba, either. Regular guns, crossbows, that sort of thing, *they* will work, but what would be the effect on a creature like him of shooting him full of bullets and arrows? Not much. He can drown, yes, but we are far from the ocean, and I doubt if we will be able to entice him to jump into a deep lake. We need a way to counter him or we might rue catching up to him."

Gus considered it and nodded. "I think I see what you mean. In this kind of hex you gotta think like you're in a western, and they didn't have Colt .45 disintegrators back then. There's gotta be *something*, though, that'll get him. If those things weren't mortal, they'd have eaten this whole damned world by now!"

"That is a point," Tony admitted. "But what?" Her eyes looked around the rail yard, not really knowing what she was looking for but hoping for some kind of hint, something that would give them an edge.

"What is that little beetle doing with the small tank up in front of the engine there, dear?" Anne Marie asked.

"Putting oil in the headlamps for the dark, I would say," Tony responded.

All three of them suddenly said at exactly the same time, "Say! Why not?"

"I wonder how much they can spare and how much we can safely carry?" Anne Marie mused at last.

"Yeah, and don't forget the matches," Gus added.

Tony sighed. "That is still a worry. It looks *awfully* damp in there."

"Look on the bright side," Anne Marie said with a smile. "If they are all intelligent plants over there, at least we won't be executed for starting any forest fires."

* * *

There is a sort of train service area and such right here, in the middle of the hex, just before the line branches off to the east," Juana Campos noted. "That is where we must get off."

"What're we gonna do about all our bags and stuff?" Audlay asked. "I mean, we can't carry all *that,* and not even your cute little pony can take all that much."

"Yeah, we're gonna be in the middle of nowhere," Kuzi agreed.

"I had hoped we could take more by hiring natives or animals when we needed them," Campos told them both. "It seems like we can't count on anything being what we think of as normal up here, though. We're just going to have to go through the stuff, see what we *have* to take and what we *can* take. Anything else will have to be left."

"You can leave that bird for all I care," Audlay commented. "That thing's gonna be what takes up a lot of room."

"We can use some of the clothing to make a kind of brace, and she is light enough to be able to be carried by our pack mule here. If she is truly charmed, she won't starve. With all these plants there must be insects by the millions, so if we just tie her to a stake at night with a very long rope, she can go find her own food. The Mixtim say that the natives here are not hostile but demand respect and that fruit and such are available if you do. We will have to depend on that."

When the train stopped for the servicing in a wooded glade near a rushing waterfall, it was already very late in the day. They had spent a full day and night going back and forth on the trains of Mixtim and now, at the end of a second day, were in the middle of nowhere in Leba. The two companions were not at all thrilled with this adventure anymore, and Campos was beginning to wonder if she hadn't made a mistake herself.

It was gray and depressing, there was a light rain falling—there *always* seemed to be a light rain falling—and they were in a wilderness setting surrounded by mountain-sized rolling hills. Where there wasn't grass or puddles there was mud.

"You sure this is a good idea?" Kuzi asked her. "I mean, we're gonna go off in this *muck* toward who knows what. And we don't even know if anybody's really following us! If they just got an all-points out, hell, we oughta go on to that high-tech place at the end of the railroad and be comfortable for a night or two until we can figure out what to do next."

"Sounds good to me," Audlay chimed in, looking at the mud as if it were acid about to swallow her up.

Campos shook her head. "No, I have been hunted before. You get a feeling for it. Still, we cannot do much, starting this late in the day. Perhaps before we *do* figure out anything, we ought to see just who we are up against. I propose that we stop here and camp out, no matter how miserable that sounds, but not close to here. Up there, overlooking these yards, might be far enough if we can fool these Mixtim staff into thinking we went some other direction. Then we wait for more trains and we see who gets off. There is one late-night train and then not another until morning. There is also no question that we can hear them when they come. If we look and no one gets off of either train, or no one gets off who does not then climb back on, we can decide what to do, perhaps even take something of a risk and catch the *next* train after that toward civilization."

"But what if a bunch *does* get off?" Kuzi asked her.

"Then *we* will be in back of them rather than ahead. Then, if they do not discover that we remain near here, they will go off into this wilderness in search of us. If they do figure out our plan, then we will have to deal with them. Come. We are in for some very heavy lugging that will take all of us and Lori to do and then a more miserable climb and a miserable dark, wet night. But by tomorrow we may well be able at last to act."

Kuzi looked around nervously. "I wish we'd seen some of these Lebans. I'd like to know what we're dealin' with here."

"Oh, *yuck!*" Audlay said with obvious disgust as she sank ankle-deep into thick brown mud. "I don't think I'm gonna be able to take this!"

"Just pretend you're back on the farm you ran away from," Campos told her. "You weren't city born and bred."

"Yeah, but that was *comfortable!* I just didn't realize it till now."

Campos grew alarmed. *"Don't you cry on me, you silly wimp!* Give me a hand with this—*now!*"

It was said in the Campos tone of voice that few ignored; those who did lived to regret it.

They had managed, with Lori doing some pulling, to get what gear they'd saved a hundred feet up the mountainside, although it was exhausting work. Mavra was finally out of the box and on a rope tied to her ankle, but she was expected to walk, and she managed, her feet actually able to dig into the mud and turf, although she moved slowly.

Although near exhaustion, Campos made sure that they had a tent up and that the gear was either repacked or sufficiently hidden from view. The station crew had paid them no real attention, but they were certainly bound to be remembered, so after all was said and done, leaving everything on the bluff overlooking the yard, the three of them and Lori managed to make a show of going down, through the whole yard, across into the darkness beyond, and off toward the northwest. They then circled around, came up below the yard, crossed the tracks, and at last made it back up to the camp.

If anybody in the yard was asked, he would swear that the trio had gone off in that direction.

It was enough, but it had been done only with Campos threatening and cursing. In the latter stages she was pretty physical with them, particularly Audlay, but it was accomplished.

Now there was nothing to do but huddle in the tent, in the sleeping bags, and wait for the sound of a steam locomotive.

The late-night train had brought nobody familiar, nobody suspicious, and nobody who didn't look like a large insect. Campos didn't know whether to be relieved or worried, but she decided that finally she might be able to get some sleep.

It seemed like only an instant, but somebody was shaking her, and hard. She resisted, then started, reflexes taking over, and grabbed the nearest strange arm.

"Take it easy!" Kuzi snapped. "You was out like a light! I heard the train and went down and took a look, and you'll never believe who got off."

Campos shook herself awake. "Who?"

"Your jilted lover, the great himself!"

"Gen Taluud? *Here?* But he never goes *anywhere*! And he *never, never* does his own dirty work! This isn't his style!"

"Well, it's him, all right. Think I could mistake that son of a bitch, fat cigar and all? And he's got five guys with him; looks like Pern and the whole bodyguard."

This was an even more unexpected curve. Campos hadn't expected to be chased by Taluud at all. "Anybody with them?"

"Maybe. I dunno. There was this—this *thing* with 'em, and they all seemed to be talkin' to it, but I couldn't tell you what it looked like even now. I *will* tell you they got *horses* with 'em, but the horses sure don't like whatever it was."

Campos pulled herself out of the sleeping bag, every single muscle aching, including some she had never known she had. "Are they still there?"

"Last I saw, yeah. I figured I better get back here and wake you up fast."

"You did exactly right. Stay here and keep Audlay quiet if she wakes up and don't tell her about this yet. If she hears it's Genny in person, she'll panic. I'm going for a look myself."

Kuzi was right; it *was* Taluud in the flesh, and she really couldn't make out what the hell that thing with the boys was, either. One thing was for sure: he'd come in style. Not only horses for all the boys but pack animals, too. He must've spent a fortune on that outfit. This wasn't personal anymore, that was clear. She knew him too well. He'd have ducked underground under most circumstances and just sent out feelers to everywhere to report to him if the girls were found. No, for Genny to do it himself, there had to be more to it.

There was only one possible explanation: Genny had found out or figured out who the bird was and had come to the same conclusion she had. He'd have stayed in character if he just wanted to give them back as he'd said. No, clearly he knew of Mavra's value and was determined to use her to work his own deal.

Back on Earth her brothers and father had always teased her about thinking too small. Maybe they were right. What would amnesty mean to Genny? He was so crooked, he'd have new charges in a week. And as for riches, he probably had enough stashed away to buy his own hex. She'd had a certain admiration for him from the start for what he'd built and how much he'd accumulated and how comfortable he was with all of it—very much like her own father. Now that admiration was justified. That fat old SOB was rolling the dice for all the marbles, winner take all.

What *was* that thing with him, though? It kind of flowed or oozed, but sometimes it looked almost like a very large man—an Earth-type man. What could one do to stop it if it found one? she wondered. It would be like shooting into a giant wad of gum. It would be best not to find out. Genny alone would be bad enough.

She watched, worried and impatient, until they finally mounted and rode off slowly in the direction they'd faked the crew out on the night before, leaving one of the bodyguards at the station just in case. The *thing* with them had gone, too; although the animals hadn't liked it, it had assumed its manlike shape and managed to mount a saddle.

They'd be back because they lost the trail, because there wasn't one, or because they would finally figure out the deception. Still, where could they go? What could they do at this point? Where they were was as safe as anywhere else around here, and it would be pretty tough to surprise them.

At least it wasn't raining. It was still as humid as the jungles but much cooler, and there was still a lot of fog and mist around. Without the rain there seemed to be something saying that not everything was hopeless.

Audlay was up by the time she returned, and Kuzi had made a small fire with the camper oven, really just a metal device with a chemical fuel that could be used to heat one thing at a time. It didn't give off a lot of smoke; Campos decided to let them eat something.

Both Lori and Mavra looked wet, muddy, and miserable, but they were still there and still secure.

"You are very popular," she told them. "We will see who gets who, though, in the end. Do not get your hopes up. No matter *who* winds up with you, you will still be what you are and they will still lock you away. In a way, you are both very fortunate to be with me and not them. *I* need you. I need both of you. They only want my little Mavra."

Lori's head jerked up. *Mavra!* So *that* was what all this was about! If only there was some way to communicate directly with her and not just through Campos!

"Yeah, I'm real popular," Mavra responded. "And hungry. There were some pickings around here, but not enough."

"You will have to eat what you can. I have nothing to spare right now," Campos told her. "Would you prefer I shot my pretty pony here and let you feast on *him*? He's another like you, you know."

Mavra turned and looked up at the pony and for the first time noticed the horn, painted black though it was. *No. Couldn't be,* she thought. *But then again, maybe it could . . .* Like Lori, she tried to think of some way of communicating.

An hour later there was the sound of another train pulling in, but it turned out to be going in the opposite direction. For a moment she was tempted; that certainly was one option, considering their fix. But if Genny had left one man here, had he also left others elsewhere? There was that long layover at the border coming up; there was probably a similar one going back and nowhere at all to hide.

After another hour there was no sign of Taluud's party returning, but another train was coming up from the south and it stopped at the station. More people did indeed get off, and they stuck out worse than Cloptans.

Two centaurs—blond and beautiful, Campos thought approvingly. And an unmistakable Erdomite female. Probably the little bitch they said was with Lori on the boat.

And then, suddenly, her bill opened in complete amazement. It couldn't be! It just *couldn't* be! But it *was!*

Theresa Perez, naked as the day she was born and fatter than a stuck pig but otherwise looking much the same.

Campos couldn't take her eyes off the girl or fight the near lust for complete revenge that was rising within her. *I could have them all! Even now! I could have them all to play with . . .*

But how?

She saw the Cloptan left behind start to walk out toward the train, spot the other foreigners getting off, and quickly duck back behind a shed, pulling his pistol.

Shoot them all, you idiot! Just leave me the girl . . .

He looked as if he might well be going to try to do just that, perhaps to all of them, but just as he steadied his arm and aimed, *something* had him. Something that somehow hadn't been visible before but now was a huge, monstrous lizard, wide jaws chomping down on the man, who struggled once and was still. The pistol fired once, a totally wild shot that seemed to go nowhere, and that was it.

Campos was upset less at the scene than at the sudden appearance of their savior. Where had that creature come from? And for that matter, where was it now?

This was going to take a great deal of thought.

"Sorry to mess up your station. It was not intentional," Anne Marie told one of the Mixtimite workers. "I'm afraid he was going to shoot us."

"We have an absolute dictum neither to judge nor to interfere in the strange customs of other races," the creature responded philosophically. "Please just clean up any messes you make before you leave and take only your memories and what you brought in with you."

Gus stared at the large insect as he walked off, apparently unconcerned about what had happened. Finally he said, "Why do I feel like I'm about to be arrested by Smokey the Bear?"

"Forget it," Julian told him. "Good job. How did you spot him?"

"Just luck. Even Dahirs have to take a leak now and then."

"Well, we ought to be more careful from now on," she warned them. "Tony, see if you can find out what this was all about from some of these workers. I want to know what Cloptans are doing here trying to take us out."

"You aren't the only one," Tony agreed, and trotted over to some of the workers who were tending the water tank.

Julian looked around at the high mountains and dense forest with its puffs of fog and frowned. "I don't like this. I feel very exposed here."

"You went through that whole nasty business at that underground nest of cutthroats, and *this* beautiful spot makes you more nervous?" Anne Marie responded, a bit amused by the contrast.

"We were attacking there, and *they* had to contend with *us*," Julian reminded her. "Now *we're* the sitting targets." She looked around and above them and then seemed to see something. Her Erdomese eyes adjusted for the long view, bringing the bluff into clearer view as if through mild binoculars.

"Something?" Anne Marie asked, a bit nervous again.

"I thought I saw something on that bluff, but I can't be sure. Whoever it was is gone now, though." She kept watching the area just to make sure.

Anne Marie twisted around and rummaged through her saddle packs, bringing out a medium-bore rifle with a scope and a clip of ammunition, which she inserted into the stock. She checked it, then raised it to her shoulder and panned the area, looking through the scope.

"Can you really shoot that thing straight?" Gus asked her worriedly.

"My great uncle Reggie used to sit around and tell the family stories about his war in Burma. I'm not sure we believed them, but he was a member of the Aldstone Downs Shooting Club, and he took me with him once when I was still rather young. Took pity on me, I suppose—young girl in a wheelchair and all that. I watched them shoot some clay pigeons, but it looked rather silly. They had a rifle range there, though, and Reggie wanted to show off how good a shot he was to his unbelieving niece. He was *quite* good, I might say, and just for a lark he let me try it from the chair. It proved quite a good platform for small-bore. He'd take me back now and then because I liked it so much. Finally stopped, though, when I began outshooting him." She sighed. "He's long dead now, but these are stronger arms, better eyes, and a *much* better platform."

"I wish I could hold something that would shoot," Julian commented, still looking. "My own abilities seem to be purely defensive and useful only close in." She finally looked away, and after a moment Anne Marie lowered the rifle.

"You are *sure* you saw someone up there?" Anne Marie asked her.

"I'm sure. But who knows? It might be one of the elusive natives for all I can tell about them."

"Stay here, all of you," Gus said. "I'm going to go look for myself."

Terry started to follow, but he cut her short. "No! They can't see me, but they can see *you* now."

Tony came back over, noticing the rifle. "What happened?"

"Julian thinks someone is up there. Gus has gone to check," Anne Marie told her. "In the meantime, I thought we'd be ready just in case."

"Interesting," Tony said, thinking and looking at the bluff. "The Cloptans—almost certainly Campos with what might well be Mavra and possibly Lori as well— arrived just before dark last night. They went off in that direction, toward the northwest, leaving much of their baggage behind one of the train sheds, and weren't seen or heard of again. The colonel and five Cloptans came in this morning, fully armed and with horses and pack mules, left that one back here, and set off after the first group. They, too, haven't returned."

Julian shook her head slowly from side to side and said, "I wish Gus was back from his scouting. I seem to remember him saying Campos was from a pretty wild area, maybe the jungle, back on Earth."

"So?"

"Nobody with *any* survival experience would go into an unknown wilderness at nightfall. No roads, no trails to speak of. It doesn't make any sense. And why northwest? Why back yourself up against the equator, which I am told is a solid wall like the Zone wall in Erdom? I kept trying to think what *I* would do in their place." She clicked her two hoofed hands together. "That's *it!*" They never went *anywhere!* I'll bet you they're right up there in a solid defensive position!"

"We should know when Gus comes back," Tony said optimistically. "Until then I suggest we move a bit more toward some protection from that bluff just in case there's a rifle as capable as the one Anne Marie has up there."

"I agree, but I wouldn't worry *too* much. After all, they can't see Gus, you know," Anne Marie reminded her.

"I wouldn't get overconfident," Julian warned. "That is Gus's one big weakness. I do not think that this Campos is any pushover. If she saw Gus in action . . ."

Mavra had been trying to figure out a way to communicate with Lori. She walked over to the black unicorn pony and looked at the ground. There was a fair amount of mud there, and slowly she began to smooth it over with her broad bird's feet. Lori, on a short rope tied to a stake, was nonetheless able to come over to the area and watch.

Language . . . What language? Greek had worked before. Try it.

The feet weren't adequate for writing, so she leaned over and began writing in the mud with her sharp, slightly curved bill. MAVRA.

Lori understood what she was trying to do but couldn't make out what it was. Once he had known these things, once he'd read many languages, but it was so hard, so hard to remember . . . He shook his head no.

Mavra was elated that she'd gotten any reaction at all but disturbed at his inability to read what she thought looked fairly clear. She wished she had been able to learn this English tongue the others knew or at least the alphabet it used. English . . . England . . . England was a part of Britannia, right? The Portuguese had hated the English and spoke as if they were not distant in their native lands. So England, Britannia . . . Conquered by Rome, as had been most of Europe and north Africa. Latin? If something was wrong with learning Greek, he might not remember Latin, either. But what if the alphabets were the same thanks to the Roman conquest? It was worth a try.

M - A - V - R - A.

Lori twisted, took a look at the letters, and tried to remember, tried to bring *something* back. A, B, C, D, E, F, G . . . The old rhyme came from somewhere, and out of the depths of his brain he saw MAVRA there.

A nod of the horse's head.

Mavra felt better. Something was better than nothing. But how was Lori spelled? Did it matter?

LOWREY?

Lori thought he was losing it but got hold of himself and read it again. Lowrey? *Lori!* Enthusiastic nod. He'd grade for spelling later.

This next one would be harder. Mavra looked over, but if the two women with Campos saw anything odd there, they surely gave no sign that they noticed.

ESCAPADUM, she managed, with a *lot* of effort. It looked awful, but maybe it would come through.

Again Lori puzzled over the word. What the hell did *that* mean? Escapa . . . *Escape!* A very enthusiastic nod.

He moved his head and managed to almost grab the rope around his neck in his mouth. Mavra watched, got the idea, and went over to the post. It wasn't much of a knot, more a casual loop, but since she had only a bill designed for digging out insects, untying it would not be that easy. Still, looking over at the two Cloptan women, she started to work on it.

It didn't matter where they were or what they were. As Campos had pointed out, they were self-sufficient in most surroundings and had no real needs beyond food and water. They had been coming north, so they were still headed for the equator. If they could make it, what difference did it make if they were on their own as animals and would have to take some time to get there?

She almost had it when Lori gave a deep neigh and shook the rope. Mavra turned to see Campos coming back and knew she had to back off.

Lori didn't feel too disappointed. If they were going to have to walk in this place, then Mavra would probably be stuck up on top of her somehow, because otherwise they'd move at a crawl. The first chance they got, he'd make a break for it no matter what. If they could make it into the woods at any kind of speed at all, those three Cloptans would never catch them. They would be forced to give up any real chase after they realized that their supplies were also gone atop Lori's back.

Maybe what Mavra had claimed was all true. Coming from such depths of despair and hopelessness to a point where they not only were brought back together but might actually make a break for it in a region better suited to them than to any pursuers had been too much to hope for. It had taken Mavra to make him realize it, though.

For now they had to wait. He looked over at Campos. What in the *world* was she doing with that machete?

"Just some vines and those metal cups," Campos was instructing the other two. "That will do, yes. Kuzi, get the pistols and put clips in them, then bring me one, and *fast!*"

Quickly Campos sliced through a small tree so that only a small stub remained above the ground. She twisted some thread from Audlay's sewing kit around it, secured it in a notch, and tied the two metal cups to it so that they touched just off the ground. She then unreeled the thread over to another stump so that it crossed the most obvious path. She then tied it off to another cut trunk on the other side.

Kuzi brought the pistol to her, looking nervous. "What is this?"

"Just get back behind the tent and keep Audlay out of the way," Campos whispered. "There's something down there you can't see until it is too late. If those two cups hit each other, stand and just fire as fast as you can anywhere between the threads. Straight out. It's taller than we are."

"What is it?" Kuzi whispered back, suddenly scared. "That thing I saw?"

"No. Something else. Like a big lizard from hell, only for some reason you cannot see it until it is eating you, so just *shoot!* I will be over by the rock and doing the same. If we fire quickly enough, we may get it or at least knock it back."

"Gee . . . she really does know this stuff," Audlay whispered, terrified but still confident in Campos—more now than ever.

"I hope so," Kuzi responded. Giant blob creatures, invisible killer lizards . . . This wasn't exactly the picture she'd had in mind of the trip.

In spite of his confidence at not being visible, Gus still proceeded cautiously. The mud was slippery, and if he lost his balance and fell, he'd be seen, all right, by just about everybody, maybe before he broke his fool neck.

He reached the bluff where Julian thought she'd seen something, and sure enough, it looked as if somebody had been there, maybe for quite some time. What was that—some kind of root there? He'd seen Cloptans chewing on that stuff, but only the menial types. Somebody said it was some kind of mild drug, he remembered, more a habit than an addiction. He picked one up and sniffed it. It smelled like, well *root beer,* sort of. He dropped it and looked around. Well, if a Cloptan had the habit and was stuck here watching things as a lookout, that would be about what one would expect.

They couldn't have gone much farther up, not in the dark. There were certainly signs of some kind of boots or shoes, and was that a hoof-print or two? Maybe.

He moved on up, being extra careful, and as his head cleared a flat area just above, he saw the tent and campsite and, over to one side—holy smoke! Could that be *Lori*? The horn was right and it was kinda like the picture Kurdon had shown them, but the colors were certainly all wrong.

They could dye the hair, but they hadn't cut off the horn.

And over there near the pony—a meter-high ball of feathers that kind of gave off a whole riot of colors. Looked like a damned big owl, though, except for that long pointed beak. Could that be Mavra?

His heart started pounding with excitement. This close! Here they were!

With nobody else in sight, he moved swiftly to get up to the top and try to introduce himself when he suddenly felt something catch on his foot. There was a dull chatter.

Suddenly, the whole place seemed to explode. He felt something slam into him like a hammer, and he fell backward and then began to slide down the slope, bits of grass coming off as he slid farther and farther down the mountainside toward the freight yard below.

"Did we get it?" Kuzi yelled.

"We're still here!" Campos pointed out. This was the most excitement she'd had since waking up in that burg. The sense of danger coursed through her and invigorated her in a way she'd felt only briefly since becoming Cloptan, that having been when she'd disintegrated that bitch on the docks months earlier.

"*Now* what?" Audlay squealed, uncharacteristically excited more than scared. She was actually *enjoying* this!

"I don't think that thing will be climbing up here anytime soon again," Campos told the others, "but there are three more down there, and now they'll know we're here. Get together what you can! Never mind how it's stuffed in! Roll it all up, tie it off, and get it somehow on the horse! We are going to have to move fast! Keep the ammo out. Get me another clip and take one for yourself!"

Kuzi threw Campos a clip, and she ejected the old one and inserted the fresh clip in the pistol. But even as she moved with Audlay to strike the tent and get everything together, she called, "Move? *Where?*"

"Into the forest and then down!" Campos told her. "Get down toward the tracks if we can, I hope. I'll keep us covered while you get packed! *Move!*"

Terry had followed Gus mentally all the way up, and when he'd been hit, she'd cried out and started toward the trail. Julian moved to try and stop her, but Tony called, "No! Let her go! It may be the only way we'll find him! Stay here! I'll get him if he's still worth getting! Anne Marie, keep me covered. If they start shooting again, shoot in their general direction. Keep them back!"

But Juana Campos had no intention of exposing herself again, only of blocking anyone else from coming to the camp level.

It was also pretty easy to find Gus; he was totally visible, sprawled out, covered with mud about halfway to the bluff, and from his side a pool of yellowish liquid gathered.

Terry reached him first. He groaned and tried to get up, but it was too much for him. Tony was there only seconds later.

"Gus! Are you all right?"

The Dahir's eyes opened, and he took in several deep breaths. "You've got to be kidding."

Tony examined the wound. "It looks like you've taken a bullet in the side. Small caliber, but a mean-looking wound. Can you stand? I will try and help you down the rest of the way."

"I—I dunno. It ain't really hurtin' yet. Here . . . pull me up—*Jesus!*" He stiffened and sank back down. "Man! It hurts like hell *now!*"

"Well, we are going to have to get you down somehow. If I help you, do you think you could get on my back and just cling there?"

"I—*augh!* I'll do it! Gimme a moment . . . Okay—*now!*"

The female centaur's arms, so weak in Dillian terms compared to the male's, were more powerful than anybody else's they'd met along the way. Pivoting around at the nearly universal hip joint the Dillians had, she pulled Gus to a standing position, then grabbed him and pulled him up onto her back. He was barely on, and sideways, but by force of will he managed to turn himself around. Tony immediately started down, Terry following worriedly.

Once back on level ground, Anne Marie helped Gus back down, and they turned him on his side. "Looks like it passed clean through," Julian noted. "That's actually a good sign. Trouble is, we can't tell if it hit anything vital internally because we don't know what 'vital' *is* to a Dahir, and the only doctors I know of in this whole region aren't ones I'd recommend to friends."

"We should wash off both the entry and exit wounds," Anne Marie told them. "We can get buckets or something from the Mixtim, and there's plenty of water around here, goodness knows. Stopping the bleeding, though, is going to be a real problem, and there's still shock and infection to worry about. The best we can do is use some of the big bandages in the kit and tape him up and then wait."

"No! Stop! You *can't* wait!" Gus gasped. "Too close! Too close!"

"Just take it easy," Tony soothed.

"No, you don't understand! *They're up there!* Mavra and Lori both! I saw 'em! *Ow!* God! This hurts!"

"Mavra and Lori both?" Julian responded, looking up again toward the bluff and beyond.

"And a lot of guns and a willingness to use them," Tony reminded her. "One thing at a time! Where can they go? They are on foot now, as it were, and Cloptans would have a lot more trouble in this landscape than *we* would. If they can get off there at all without coming back through here, they will be off trail and going down into a wilderness. Our biggest danger is that they will come down, guns blazing. You and Anne Marie see to Gus. I will ensure that if they *do* come down, they will not get far. Do not worry about them. At the moment I would rather be in our position than theirs, actually."

"I don't know about that," Julian commented. "This Campos seems to be a devil, almost supernatural in the harm she can cause. What if they *do* get down? What if they flag down a train?"

"These trains do not stop for flags, I don't think," Tony assured her. "The Mixtim will allow nothing to interfere with their punctuality."

Gus was no ideal patient while the wounds were washed and dressed, but after a while he passed out, and that helped a lot. They rigged up a kind of litter from wood and a freight station tarp and got him under a shed which held maintenance tools. It was all they could do.

Julian sighed. "Look, I'm going to go down the tracks and see if I can pick them up. Oh, don't look so alarmed! I'll be careful, and I won't *do* anything, only locate them and get back here. They won't be expecting anybody to do it, anyway."

"I don't like it. We've already got one wounded member, and he was in many ways the handiest of us all," Anne Marie said, shaking her head.

"You said it yourself about Campos," Tony reminded her.

"I know, I know, but don't you see? It's something I can *do*. Something that makes sense that I can do better than either of you. And of all of us I'm the most expendable, anyway. You two have futures when you finally get back home, and even Gus has the girl here in a kind of sweet, Platonic way. I can't go home, and you know what they did to Lori. Mavra Chang might be my only way out of this. Don't worry." She paused, then added, "But even if for some reason I don't come back, don't give up. I'm going to do what seems best at the moment. I don't intend getting caught or shot, but no matter what, you find them. You find them and get them to that Well."

They knew that nothing they could say and nothing they could do short of tying her up would change her mind, so they let her go.

Once outside, Julian looked around until she found what had to be the messiest, gooeyest mass of dark brown mud anywhere and then got down and rolled in it until she was literally covered with the stuff. There was a heavy mist starting up; it wouldn't dry out very easily.

Then, on all fours for maximum traction, she started off up the tracks in the direction of the end of the line somewhere far off, searching less for individuals than for hope.

Juana Campos was thinking as they made their way slowly and laboriously down the mountainside, almost tree by tree. The girls had acquitted themselves well in their first real trial; for the first time, she was beginning to have actual respect for their potential.

All along I have been thinking like a woman, she told herself. *I have been thinking like the mistress of the local don. I am more than that. That I am a woman I cannot change, but I am also Juan Carlo Rodriges Campos de la Montoya, son of Don Francisco Campos, the greatest man of modern Peru. If I am a woman, so be it, but I will not think like one. Taluud, you will not be the one to rebuild in Clopta, this I swear! Before I am through, they will bow and scrape to me as they did to you. Here begins the future of power in Clopta!*

No more thinking small, of amnesties and rewards. Those who truly had the power in this world would have to acknowledge her, or a certain little birdie would go visiting the Well. Take it or leave it.

Those amateurs hunting for their friends would not climb up the mountain again, and the only real threat from them had been taken out. Gen Taluud would not be so timid. He would send his *men* up there and find them gone. Then they would see the signs and figure out what she'd done, and they'd come hunting. Hunting on their big, fat horses. If they could shoot an invisible thing, then how much easier to shoot them off their mounts! Hell, just potting Genny would probably do it.

Once down the hill, she'd find the perfect place, and there they'd camp and lay their ambush. They would wait until the others came. *Then* whoever was left would have to deal with *her!*

And part of that price would be completing the set. *Then* it would all be right. *Then* this world would also dance to a Campos melody!

It was easy to find the railroad; a train came by every hour by day and every two or three by night. Whatever they traded, the Maxtim sure traded a lot. Finding the spot in a light rain before darkness fell would be more difficult but not impossible. The trees and rocks around there were almost made to be natural fortresses, and she knew how Genny and his men thought.

The other two listened in amazement to the plan, but with growing excitement. Not just Kuzi, the new supreme lieutenant, but even Audlay was saying, "Can I have a gun this time, Juana? *Please?* I been wanting to shoot some guys for the *longest* time!"

"Pretty one, if I thought you could even hit a *mountain* with a gun, I would gladly let you," Campos told her. "But you can be just as important and cover the one area that neither Kuzi nor I can. Just be patient. We must find our spot and prepare it well tonight. I think they will come tomorrow."

Julian had worked her way slowly along the tracks until well after dark before she decided that she had to have gone too far and started back.

At that, she almost missed them. They were quite well dug in and nearly invisible from the road. It was only the fact that they expected their trouble to come from the southeast that betrayed them at all. Once or twice the one on guard looked out from this direction toward the freight yard, and when that happened, Julian's infrared vision abilities caught a glimpse of a head.

Now that she *had* found them, though, she didn't know quite what she was going to do. Something inside her told her that no matter what situation she was in, she simply could not take offensive action. It was something inside her that was part of what made her a very different person from the one she'd once been. She could instinctively defend herself—that she'd discovered in the complex—but to go in there and harm someone not trying to do immediate harm to her—it just wasn't in her.

She had no weapons, anyway. In fact, she had come with nothing at all, her earrings and nose ring being the only artificial things she had. That and her brain, which was at least working efficiently—or was it? She'd had this idea to come here and find them, but that efficient thinking machine hadn't a clue as to what to do with what she'd discovered.

She wondered if she could get around them and spot where Lori and Mavra were and what their situation was. It might give her an opportunity. She moved into the forest and up and around the Cloptans' camp.

They had picked their spot very well. No matter what the angle, Julian couldn't quite get in back of them or above them with any kind of clear view. She knew better than to try to get in really close. They'd trapped Gus somehow, so what chance would *she* have?

She realized she was making excuses for herself, but it didn't matter. She was still too much the Erdomese female to be capable of aggression or even of doing most things on her own. It was like knowing everything there was to know about flying a plane and then discovering that she had acrophobia. In fact, although she knew that the only rational course was to go back and warn the Dillians, she found herself unable to bring herself to risk detection by the ambushers. For all the false bravado at the complex, she still had nightmares about it, in particular about being jumped from behind. She'd done it once, because that had been the group and she'd gone with the group, but she doubted she could do it again—especially on her own.

I'm as much of a freak as Mavra, Lori, and those poor things back in the complex, she thought miserably. *I'm still the same scared, wimpy little Erdomese cow I was before, only they made it impossible for me to like guys who can defend me.*

She tried to figure out some way to actually act, to make something happen, and came up with a hundred different things, but she just couldn't do any of them.

She wondered what she would do if the Dillians came walking up the tracks into the ambush. Would she have the nerve to warn them, or would she be forced to watch them be cut down?

Shortly after dawn there was a change in the camp. Voices and the sound and scents of things being prepared for a breakfast.

Women's voices, unmistakable even with that Cloptan rasp.

Julian envied them even as she hated them. It wasn't *fair,* she thought, finding tears of self-pity rising within her that she was also powerless to stop. *A bastard like Campos gets to act decisively, and I can't even work to save my friends!*

About two hours after dawn came the unmistakable sound of horses, and Julian feared she was about to witness what she'd worried about all night. However, it wasn't the Dillians who were coming up the tracks but somebody else. Those voices were definitely all coming from men.

"Only three Cloptans!" Campos hissed. "Three and that blob thing." She looked over at Kuzi, who had her rifle out and poised, and then back at Audlay. "You ready?"

They both nodded.

"Hold it! I hear a train coming—from the south, I think!" Campos whispered. "Wait until the train is almost to them. Then take out the two on this side first. The noise might keep the other two from even noticing the shots. They won't have a clue where we are or even that we're here until the train passes, and then we've got them cold."

Gen Taluud heard the train as well. He and the colonel were on the far side of the tracks, and the other two were on the near side. As the train approached, he said, "Let's all get over there and let the train pass! There's not much maneuvering room for horses over here!"

Campos could hardly believe her good fortune. "Back two first! Same idea!" she hissed, and Kuzi nodded again.

Suddenly the train was upon them, belching steam and smoke, the Mixtimite engineer sounding the whistle as a warning.

Campos and Kuzi fired their rifles from braced positions dead on, and the two gunmen in back fell off their horses. One of the horses bolted forward, startling Taluud and unbalancing him, and Campos's squeezed-off shot caught him in the shoulder instead of the head. He whirled in the saddle and screamed at the colonel.

Kuzi's shot struck the colonel dead in the "chest" area of his manlike riding form, but it passed right through and didn't seem to do much more than knock him a little off balance.

Campos had expected that, but now she actually stood up, fully exposed, as the train rumbled off into the distance, and shouted, "Hey! Genny! Over here, *baby!*"

The big boss of Clopta looked up from nursing his wound, saw her aiming directly at him, and shouted, *"No! Doll! Wait!"*

She fired, and his head nearly exploded, with brains flying as he toppled off the horse in a heap.

"That is very impressive," the colonel shouted to them. "But you may shoot me as much as you like. It is very difficult to find my vital spots, you know, and I am coming up there to embrace you all!"

The shape got off the horse, and Kuzi pumped five heavy-caliber shells into him before his manlike shape dissolved and he began flowing toward them up the side of the sheltering rock.

Suddenly it was not the two shooters but Audlay, teeth showing, who stood atop the rock holding a pot filled with something. "Hey! Blobbo! Want a little bath?" she asked, and emptied the contents of the pot on top of the colonel.

The colonel froze, then asked, "What is this? Do you think this will stop me?"

Campos and Kuzi emerged from either side of the rock outcrop. Both of them were holding torches.

"No, sir, it is more like a relative of kerosene," Campos said. "Would you like a light?"

The colonel didn't have a ceiling or corner to run to, and he had no knowledge that Audlay wasn't at the top with a torch of her own.

"No! Wait! You need me!" he cried out.

"How do we need you?" Campos came back, hesitating and wondering if she was a fool to do so.

"I had a deal with Taluud! He was going to run everything! The whole show! I was to get my own home hex as absolute ruler!"

So *that* was it. "So why do I need you now?"

"You don't know who to talk to! I do! I know who pulls the strings up to the councillor level! You can only deal with the government up front!"

"Oh, yes? And perhaps we put out these torches and you eat us, huh? I think perhaps we do not have enough guarantees. We will do this ourselves!"

"My word was always good to a Campos!" he retorted. "I am Colonel Jorge Lunderman!"

"Lunderman? The one who worked for my *father*?"

"*Sí! Sí! Yo siempre encontré su padre para ser un hombre más honorado! Y él, a la vez, tuvo no razón para me dudar. No una ves!*" the colonel said urgently.

Campos was impressed. "*¿Yo tengo su palabra ahora, como estuvo con mi padre, tan estará entre nosotros también?*"

"*Sobre el honor de mis ascendientes y antes de el Dios y el Virgen Santo, sí!*"

"Colonel, this may be the one fatal mistake I make, but I believe you," Juana Campos told him. "Kuzi, it is all right. Put out your torch. The colonel and I have just come to an agreement."

Kuzi looked hesitant. "You're sure? What was that you were saying in that funny language?"

"Nothing is certain, but I think so, yes. I asked the colonel if he was willing to pledge his service to me here as he did for my father back where we both come from. He agreed and took a most solemn oath to that effect. Now, go see if you can get the horse back. We can use them. It is all right."

The colonel oozed nervously back down the rock and re-formed facing Campos. "I am honored that you would trust me still," he told the Cloptan. "I am, however, a bit amazed. At this very moment I could reach out in a second and swallow you, and what could you do about it? No, no! Do not worry! I am a man of honor. I ask of you no more than I asked of Taluud, and I might tell you that I feel that things will be much better in your hands than in his. I am just curious as to why you trusted me at this point."

Campos gave a Cloptan smile and looked up atop the rock. "It is all right, Audlay. You can put your torch out now, too!" she called.

The colonel started quivering like gelatin in an earthquake, and soon peals of laughter issued forth from the mass. Finally he said, "I do believe, madame, that this is the beginning of a most wondrous partnership."

The Cloptan nodded. "Where are the other two men who were with your party?"

"Back at the freight yard. The Dahir's in pretty poor shape from your shot, and the others remained with him. They are now, I should hope, disarmed and well under control. I don't think either the men, who were only bodyguards, or the Dillians will give us any trouble from now on."

"And the girl? She is there, too?"

"Oh, yes. She is of no consequence, however. She had some strange powers at one time, but she appears to have lost her memory and control of those powers. She appears able to read surface thoughts but cannot speak. And she is very much pregnant."

"Pregnant! By one of our old kind from that place here? Or from before?"

"They think before. They think it is the reason that she was not changed physically into a different race by the Well. Is it important?"

"It *could* be. Before they brought us to this place, they had us more or less service many of that cursed tribe. I was drugged; I do not know for sure which ones. It might well be someone else's, but it might, just *might,* be my own child!"

"It might be obvious in at least general terms once it is born. The features . . ."

"Yes, it might at that! Well, well, this puts an entirely new complexion on things. We will want to ensure that she has that baby before we think of other uses for her."

"And where are the other two in this little drama?" the colonel asked her, still reeking of flammable oils and nervous about the fact.

Kuzi was bringing up the horses, which had not gone far, when they all heard Audlay give a shriek. All of them headed for the camp behind the rocks.

"They're *gone!*" Audlay cried. "Them no-good animals lit out on us durin' the fight!"

OTHER PARTS
OF THE FIELD

LONG BEFORE THE GUNFIGHT Mavra had started to work once more on Lori's rope. Being a nocturnal creature had certain advantages, one of which was seeing quite well in the dark, even if not quite in the same way she used to think of as clear vision.

It was clear that the women were setting up an ambush; the odds of all three of them being required to pull it off were equally good. She and Lori were virtually ignored once they had been staked out.

Campos was very smart, a lot smarter than Mavra had given her credit for in the past, but the Cloptan was not without some basic human failings, one of which was that she'd clearly begun to regard both Mavra and Lori as the animals they appeared to be, forgetting the minds buried within. This was often a fatal mistake on the Well World, and while it couldn't, unfortunately, be fatal here, it meant that Campos never thought that Mavra would be able to untie the slipknot holding Lori or that Lori, with a patience and dedication no horse could maintain, would simultaneously be chewing through the rope tied to Mavra's leg.

By morning it was merely a matter of pretending to still be restrained and hoping that the women would be too concerned with the coming showdown to check on the pair, who were in any event within clear eyeshot of them.

When the sound of oncoming riders was heard and the three Cloptans scrambled for their positions, Mavra looked at Lori and Lori just nodded. When the first shots rang out, Lori went down on his forelegs and Mavra scrambled aboard as best she could, then grabbed the rope still around Lori's neck with the claws on her feet and held on for dear life as Lori took off.

Watching nervously, Julian was startled to see the break and immediately moved away from the ambush and followed them.

Mavra could stay on only for so long in that precarious position, particularly with a trailing rope, and fell off two or three hundred meters into the woods. Lori felt her slip, stopped as soon as he could, and turned back to help her. Suddenly a ghostly, filthy mud-caked shape moved from the trees toward Mavra, who was struggling to get up. At first Lori thought it had to be one of the mysterious creatures who were the dominant race in Leba, but he soon realized that it was someone far more familiar, someone he knew . . .

Julian put up a hand to Lori to reassure him, then examined Mavra, who'd stopped trying to struggle to her feet when she realized somebody else was there.

It was easy for Julian, even with her hard mittenlike hands, to get the rope off Mavra's leg and then set her on her feet. She then gestured to Lori to approach, put Mavra on his back, then used the rope she'd just freed to secure the large bird to the pony's torso.

"Can either of you understand me?" she whispered, as only a few voices could be heard in the distance, the train and shots now long past. Getting no immediate response and not wanting to waste any more time, she pointed to Mavra's bill and then to the other rope around Lori's neck. Holding on with the bill and relying on the wrapped-around torso rope to keep her body on, it looked like she might actually be able to ride.

Julian pointed farther into the forest, away from the sounds in back of them, and they proceeded onward. Mavra was uncomfortable but fairly secure upon Lori's back, and Julian reverted to all fours to set a steady but not exhausting pace that covered ground without risking more spills.

They did not stop for hours, not until Julian's thirst was too much to ignore. As soon as she passed a pool of water off to their right, she slowed and headed for it, Lori following, and together they drank. Then Julian untied Mavra and set her down so she, too, could drink and perhaps exercise or feed.

In the darkness of the thick forest Mavra had some reasonable vision, although nothing like what true night would bring. Everything was there but washed out, as in a faded photograph. She was exhausted and felt like she was starving, and her back was killing her from riding like that. And yet . . .

She hadn't felt this good since she'd reentered the Well World.

She was free again! It didn't matter what she was or where she was; it only mattered that she was again delivered from her enemies.

Different insects were out in the day from in the night, but she had enough practice now to figure out where they were and find them. She wanted to make sure that she didn't get out of sight of the other two, but she also wanted to eat as much as possible. She hoped that Julian would discover by herself or somehow be made to understand that they should travel long and hard but only at night, when they would have the advantage of better vision.

After Julian ate some fruit that she found on the forest floor, she went into the pool and tried to wash out as much of the mud as possible. It usually wasn't a good idea for an Erdomese to take a bath of this scale, but once in a while didn't hurt and this was certainly necessary. It was also damned cold water, which meant she had no urge to linger.

Still, she did feel better when she got out and was more her old self again, although there did seem to be places where the mud would *never* wash out. What she really needed, she thought, was dryness, the heat and near absence of humidity for which her body was designed. Thoughts of the desert and its feel and its beauty had crept into her mind off and on of late, particularly while she was just sitting there in Agon. As much as it would kill her, she could not banish Erdom's call to its own. She very much wanted to go back there, but not like this and not while that foul system endured.

She wondered if Lori felt it, too, or whether he felt much of *anything*.

Clearly the two of them had hatched this escape plot, but did that mean that they could understand each other? Somehow she doubted it, at least on a verbal level. They hadn't exactly been making bizarre sounds at one another, anyway.

Think, Julian, think! You may not be much good at anything else, but you are very good at thinking!

That had been her trouble in the beginning, she realized now. Unable to face her position and limitations, she'd stopped thinking and started to let others do all her thinking for her. That was exactly the wrong way. Thinking things through, learning all that could be learned, solving problems and delivering solutions—these were things not everybody was very good at. If she couldn't physically, psychologically, or culturally carry them out, there was always someone who could.

What about writing? Translators did nothing about writing ability any more than they covered up one's previous language skills. They were an enhancement to vocal communication, that was all. She looked around for a stick, found one, and went back over to Lori. She might not be much at writing with those hands, but she sure as hell could block print.

In the mud near the pool she scratched, in English, CAN U READ THIS?

Lori watched, then came over and looked down at it. It was so *hard* to dredge up those old skills, but he managed. It was a little easier than it had been with Mavra; at least this was English. He nodded his head.

Julian was excited. At least there would be *some* way to get through.

R U OK?

Yes. It was an absolute answer to a relative question, but there wasn't any way to add qualifiers.

WHAT DO U WANT TO DO?

That was a deliberate attempt to provoke him into finding some way to get a more complex answer back. He understood its purpose but wondered how the hell he could do it. He tried writing with the stick in his mouth, but it wasn't any use. Then he tried scratching in the mud with his hoof, but that didn't really produce anything intelligible, either. Finally, he gave a big sigh and shook his head negatively.

Maybe Mavra would be better for this, Julian thought. But what language did they have in common?

In an instant she realized that would be a good test of whether they actually had a chance or were just adrift until caught or killed. If Mavra knew the commercial standard language that Julian had spent so much time in Agon studying . . .

It was some time before Mavra had her fill and wandered back. She couldn't help but wonder at how those two were reacting to one another. Julian needed the old Lori, and the old Lori was gone. She approached where they were resting and saw the regular scratches in the mud. She hadn't thought Julian capable of it; maybe she'd changed personalities yet again since the last time they'd been together.

Julian had been dozing but awoke when she sensed someone nearby. Spotting Mavra, she reached for the stick and then went over and smoothed out the mud. The basically ideographic Well World standard commercial language was versatile but not easy, and she had only a limited command of it. Still, Mavra could have no better command of it than she if Mavra were just another person from Earth. But if she was who she claimed to be . . .

CAN YOU READ THIS? Julian scratched, then carefully placed the stick in Mavra's bill. Mavra went over and looked at the writing and was so surprised at what she saw that she almost dropped it. How the *hell* did Julian learn *that*?

Don't ask stupid questions you can't get answered, Mavra, just answer if you can.

I CAN READ IT, Mavra scratched back. It looked awful compared with Julian's, but it was sufficient.

WHAT DO WE DO NOW?

Mavra wrote back, RUN LIKE HELL.

Julian laughed. If somebody could give an answer like that after being like *this* for so long, she was something special indeed.

THEN?

Mavra took the stick. HEAD NORTH THEN WEST TO AVENUE.

Avenue? What was an avenue here? It was a formal and distinct ideograph all its own; that indicated an important noun, a real place.

WHY?

GET IN WELL. MAKE THINGS RIGHT, Mavra wrote.

Make things right . . . Right for whom? Julian wondered. Still, it was the answer she had both hoped for and expected.

GO BY NIGHT, SLEEP DAYS, Julian suggested.

THEY WILL BE WAITING FOR US.

They? Campos? The colonel? The Dillians? WHO IS THEY?

EVERYBODY. ARMIES. WHOLE WORLD.

That was alarming. NO OTHER WAY IN?

MANY. LONG WAY. TOO LONG.

HOW FAR?

ONE HEX LENGTH N, HALF WEST.

That meant maybe 250 miles north, give or take, and half that west. A *really* long way to go on foot, and with nothing but themselves and their wits. She had thought, or at least *hoped,* that they had traveled farther by train, but she hadn't really paid attention to the map, and Mavra probably was guessing, too. It could be less.

Or more.

YOU WILL GET IN, she scratched to Mavra. *Somehow or another we have to.*

They'd be coming for them, that was for sure, but even Julian knew that the odds of catching anybody in this environment were as slim as the odds of their actually pulling this off. On the other hand, at least there wouldn't be a lot of talkative natives.

Or would there? All this way and she still hadn't the slightest idea what the natives of this hex really *were.*

She got up and started looking around. They hadn't come very far, that was for sure, but they'd come *some* way inland. Did the natives leave the forest as wilderness and cluster in places off the beaten track?

The trees were huge, creating a vast canopy of green above. There were scads of insects, both crawling and flying, and while they looked suitably bizarre and like nothing on Earth, they were clearly recognizable as insects. There *might* be birds, but if so, they remained pretty high up and weren't apparent.

About the only really odd thing was a kind of vine that seemed to grow in thick clumps down the trees, giving them almost the appearance of wearing skirts. She wondered how strong the vines were. The rope solution for keeping Mavra on Lori's back wasn't a good one, but the vines might give her more flexibility. Julian went over to a low-hanging mass of them and examined them.

The vines looked back.

She was so startled, she backed away. There were *eyes* of a sort on the ends of those things! Or at least they sure *looked* like eyes, one per vine ending.

And now the vines moved in a cluster. Quite slowly and lazily, yet as deliberately as snakes, which they reminded Julian of.

She walked a bit to the right, and the clump of eyes slowly followed her. Back to the left, the same. She *wasn't* imagining it!

Were they all part of a single organism, part of the tree, or parasites on it? Some sort of plantlike worms, perhaps? She'd better find out, she decided, because now that this bunch had blown their cover, as it were, all the vines on all the other trees were looking at her, too.

This may be the dumbest thing I've ever done in a lifetime of dumb things, she thought furiously, *but it's worth a try.*

"Hello," she said. "We are strangers here, brought here by others. Bad people we are now trying to escape from. We don't want to harm anything, but we do not know the rules here. Are you the Lebans?"

Did translators work even on plants? Or was she talking to a common variety of parasitic worm with no more intelligence than any other worm?

The vines got very agitated and seemed to speed up their motion, curling in and out, back and forth among one another until it looked like they were caught in some sort of windstorm. The other clusters on other trees were doing much the same.

It's almost like they're talking with each other, discussing me, she thought, still not sure if she wasn't just imagining this. She looked nervously upward into the trees for perhaps a giant open mouth at the end of the tendrils, but while they did vanish into the upper reaches of the tree, there was no clear body to them.

But *how* were they talking, if that was what it was? While the translator might be able to get through to them if, presumably, whatever they were attached to had some way to hear or feel vibrations, what if they communicated by a totally different means? That was *still* assuming that she was talking to Lebans. *Now is the kind of time when I wish I could confer with the others,* she thought.

There was suddenly the sound of a wind, although she could feel no air moving against her skin.

Then there came a deep, melodic bass tone that seemed to come from within the tree itself. Incredibly, it seemed to be forming words, although they were a bizarre-sounding monotone, like trying to listen to conversation from the world's largest one-note tuba.

"You may pass in safety," the voice seemed to say. "Do not touch the vines. Do not harm the trees. Eat what you will of the forest floor but pick nothing."

She *wasn't* crazy! These *were* the Lebans! "We will obey all of your rules. I promise," she told the clusters of eyes. "We go north by night to the equator beyond your lands."

"We have heard what the others have done," the monotonous horn responded. "They will not find you in Leba if you give Leba respect."

"It is a very pretty place," she said, trying to butter them up a bit, still wondering if they were the vines, the trees, or something inside the trees and out of sight. "But it is not our place. We would not harm it, and we need to leave it. Um . . . You wouldn't happen to know which way is north?"

The vines swirled, curled, and then pointed off in one direction. "Thank you," she told them. "I must get some sleep now. We have a long way to go."

"You will not be disturbed," the voice promised.

The vines slowly subsided in their rhythm, then hung limp and still once more.

It was very odd, but she felt like she *could* sleep here now. She wasn't exactly sure why and she probably could never explain it to the others, even if they'd believe it, but she felt suddenly more secure, no longer watched but rather watched over.

If you are polite to the Lebans and show respect, they are very friendly . . .

Somehow she'd just have to make do with the ropes.

She wondered what would happen to somebody who *wasn't* polite and respectful. The ones who would be after them might be such people. One could certainly outrun a Leban, but one couldn't run out of them. She wondered just how strong those tendril-like vines could be . . .

Somehow Anne Marie was not surprised to see three Cloptan men and the colonel ride out and three Cloptan women and the colonel ride back in.

"Ever the Talleyrand type, aren't you, Colonel?" she said with acidic sweetness.

"What's she talking about?" Juana Campos asked him suspiciously.

"Talleyrand," the colonel explained, "was a pragmatist in royalist France. A minor functionary, he saw the French Revolution coming and, when it happened, helped the revolution find royalists and arrest them. He survived the reign of terror, survived the excesses, and in the end supported a young officer named Napoleon who became emperor himself and made Talleyrand a count. When Napoleon faced defeat, he negotiated with the old royalists and brought them back to power. He died a wealthy and respected statesman, in bed, of old age, but he never betrayed those he served or lost his honor, which is why they all trusted him. I do not consider her comment an insult but rather a compliment."

The two gunmen were more shocked and not as understanding. *That* had to be put right immediately.

"Listen, you two, you are very fortunate to have been here!" Juana Campos told them. "You are still alive and you have futures, if you wish to take the colonel's example. Taluud is dead. His empire in Clopta is even now being crushed. You have a choice to make. Serve me in the same way you served Taluud and you will prosper and be high in the *new* organization I will build when this is over. Choose wrongly and I will allow you to enjoy the colonel's embrace. I do not *need* you for controlling this lot, but I can certainly *use* you."

The two men didn't like it; their own world was being turned upside down in the same way their captives' had been. Still, the alternative was certainly worse. "All right, ma'am. We'll stay with you," one said.

She nodded. "You will take orders from me and from Kuzi here as if she were speaking my own words. You will keep your manners intact as regards all three of us and will keep your hands off. Be faithful, and your rewards will be great. Hesitate, foul up, or betray us, and you will be dead. Remember that if you are testing any of us with your *manly* strength, you are also testing that strength against all of us, including the colonel. You understand that? *Do you understand that?*"

"Yes, ma'am," they both said.

"You call *them* 'ma'am.' You call *me* 'boss.' "

"Yes, boss."

Campos looked around and saw Terry. For her part, the girl was totally confused as to what had gone on, but she understood that Gus had been hurt and that those who had hurt him were now in control. Of them all, though, it was Campos who terrified her. There was something there, inside her, something *awful*, particularly when she looked at Terry. It was not something that could be explained but rather something that was intrinsic, something ancient, something rarely glimpsed. The colonel had elements of it, and so had the duckmen, but in Campos it was not hidden, it was not partial, it was the essence of her, and it was frightening.

It was pure, uncompromised, unequivocated evil.

And yet somehow, while she felt Campos's particular evil whenever she looked at her, she also sensed that at least for now, that evil was not a direct threat. Not yet. For some reason Campos did not want to harm the baby.

Campos felt such satisfaction at finally having Terry in her clutches that it was a moment before she realized that something was wrong. The two Dillians, the girl, the big monster in the shed . . .

"Where is the other? The Erdomite?"

"These were the only ones here. We checked the whole place out thoroughly," one of the gunmen said.

Campos turned to Tony and Anne Marie. "All right—where is she? And no games!"

"We don't know, and that's the truth," Tony told her. "She left us yesterday evening to go to scout for where you might be. She thought you'd head for the tracks and perhaps lay an ambush. We haven't seen or heard from her since. When she didn't come back with you, we thought perhaps she was a casualty."

Campos shook her head. "So that was how it was done. While we fought with Taluud, your friend came in and liberated the others."

"Likely," the colonel agreed. "We had no knowledge of it. I wouldn't think she'd be much of a threat otherwise, though. Their women don't have the proper hands and are not otherwise built for fighting. You are certain that the other two cannot understand each other or anyone but you?"

"I am certain of that, yes. They cannot talk, which means they cannot plot with each other. I see your point. But they are going to be very difficult to track and to catch in this terrain."

"Perhaps. Perhaps not. They will *feel* us at their backs no matter where they run and whether we are there or not. They will zig, and zag, and perhaps get lost a few times, but eventually they will get their bearings. In the end, we know the direction in which they *must* go. They *must* go to Verion, then west, to the northwest corner of that place. They have no other choice."

Campos looked at the Leeming and frowned. "You believe it, then? That if she can get inside, she can become like a god?"

"Until I got to know Captain Brazil, I thought it was nonsense," Lunderman admitted. "And then, after, when I saw him survive what would have, *should* have killed anything alive, I was nearly convinced. But it was when talking with Tony here, back before the raid, that I became certain that this is not nonsense."

"Why?"

"*You* were dragged here. So was Gus. Lori and even the girl here were more or less brought here by Mavra Chang. I and our missing Erdomese fell through by accident. But there is no getting around it. Nathan Brazil walked here, knowingly, of his own free will. He invited these two to come along. He promised them what they achieved. And Mavra Chang, too, took great risks to voluntarily come through. Of all of us, only Brazil and Chang came freely, knowingly. Why? Because they *knew* what they would find here. And of all of us, only they and the girl here, whose pregnancy prevented a change, remained Earth-human. All the rest of us were dramatically transformed. No, it is beyond chance. And where does that pair try and head once they set out separately, independently? To the equator. To the door inside the world. No, it more defies logic to deny their true nature than to believe in it, however fanciful. They are not human. They have merely chosen to appear that way. Brazil may heal, but he is out of this. Safely away. That leaves Mavra Chang, and I do not believe that she will let any obstacle stand in her way."

"She could just wait. Bide her time and wait for Brazil to save her. After all, she cannot know he is a prisoner."

"No, I believe we took care of that possibility. They are rivals. Each is convinced that the other means to assume total and sole control. As far as Chang is concerned, this race is still on. She cannot afford to wait."

"She'll know that we know this, too. Is Verion the only door?"

"No, there are many, but she will be forced to go for Verion because it is closest. Any other choice means more travel, more hexes, more chances of discovery, and, most of all, much more time."

"Will it be guarded?"

"There is a token force there. There is one at all of them. Nothing that cannot be handled, though. I have authority with some of the council even now, and those two have authority with others. A nontech hex, a boring and routine guard assignment—it should not be much of a problem."

"What makes you think we'll help *you?*" Tony asked him.

"Several things. First, it is your only hope of returning to Dillia alive. Second, there is still one of your number that you might well be able to help, and that is all you were ever promised. And third and finally, your friends here will need you. We can transport our party and supplies, but Gus either travels with you or he must be disposed of here and now. I would like to keep him around because it will keep the girl in line and certain to stick close to us as well. By the same token, concern for her safety will keep *him* in line, even if he fully recovers. But you must understand that you are the most expendable of us all."

Campos looked at the centaurs. "Think about this, Dillians. It would take very little to spoil those pretty looks for good. You will do *nothing* except what you are ordered to do. You will take no hostile action against us. You will say nothing to others except what we tell you to say or both of your tongues will be cut out. Do anything, *anything* that displeases me and I will blind you. You are packhorses to me, nothing more. Raise a hand or a weapon against me and you will lose both weapon and hand. Try and escape and I will kill you. If you make it, the ones who remain will suffer your punishment. The girl, for example, does not need eyes or ears or hands to do what I am interested in. She will not leave her strange paramour, and she will be kept close to me and the colonel at all times. Do we have an understanding here?"

"I believe we do, yes," Tony said gravely. *But if I could kill you, even at the cost of my own life, I think I would do it.*

"Well, get the big lizard ready to move, then," Campos instructed. "Even as he is, I want him tied down to the litter at all times, and one of you must always be watching him. With these horses and supplies, where they can go, we can go; where we cannot, I doubt if they could, either. We will track them if we can. If we lose them, we go for Verion immediately. Now, *move!*"

VERION

JULIAN HAD NO WAY to mark time in Leba, but it had seemed an interminable journey, made all the more so by her inability to really *talk* with anybody.

Sure, she did some questions and answers with Lori, who seemed to need some mental contact anyway, and some more bits-and-pieces discussions with Mavra by the stick method, but those were almost always to ask specific things or just to keep from going nuts. The Lebans remained friendly and true to their word, but they weren't exactly conversationalists, either.

The journey had been an extremely rough one, and it wasn't over yet. The whole place was mountainous and wet, much like the Olympic range of Washington state but without the trails. The Lebans could be counted on to recommend a route or keep them pointed in the right direction but not for much else. They were certainly friendly, though, in their own way; as they'd gone on, the Lebans would often shake fruit right off limbs when nothing obvious was available to eat.

Still, there had been no distinctive landmarks or anything to mark the progress of their journey. After a while one stream valley looked like another, and all the mountains looked pretty much alike as well. It was impossible for someone with her build and hooves to walk bipedally and not lose her balance over and over; still, she'd been walking on all fours so long by this point, she wasn't sure she remembered how to use just two. Once she'd threatened, even prepared, to go off and live in the wild alone. How stupid that seemed now!

Thus, when sunrise neared to mark the probable end of yet another day, Julian, like her companions, was just silently trudging along, coming over yet one more rise. Suddenly she saw something she hadn't seen in so long, she'd almost forgotten what it looked like.

Sunlight. Sunlight just creeping over the landscape, a little bright on this side, much duller beyond what seemed like a vast semitransparent curtain.

The border! It had to be! And if the Lebans hadn't been playing an enormous practical joke on them, beyond lay Verion.

She shrieked with such delight that Lori stopped, and both he and Mavra looked over, concerned that Julian might be in some trouble. Julian turned to them, put out her forearm, and pointed.

She felt like rushing to it, and the hell with the daylight, but she knew that would be the worst thing to do. If there was sunlight in Verion, then perhaps there were Verionites who were not as friendly as the Lebans.

Best to remain on the same regimen, she knew, although it was hard, really hard, not to push on. That boundary didn't just mean that they were passing into a new climate, a new land, but the *final* land, the destination point. And even though it would still take them a great deal of time to reach that destination, they had been safe, almost protected in a way, in Leba, with the natives watching out for them and with plenty of food and water and at least reliable help with the directions. That, out there, was more than just another unknown land and people.

Somewhere beyond that final curtain was the enemy.

They had no illusions about that, Mavra the least of all. It didn't take a genius to figure out that the Verion Avenue was the only practical choice they could make, and so they'd be waiting there, right near the end, waiting for them to walk into a trap.

That was another reason Mavra had insisted they not go elsewhere, though. Verion was a nontech hex; nothing but muscle, water, and wind worked there, as in Erdom. That also meant no radios, no instant communications, no tracking scopes and sophisticated monitoring systems. The enemy knew *where* they would wind up but not when. *They* could pick the time and the opportunity.

A lot, then, would depend on the Verionites, whatever they were. Would they be searching for them with a reward for their capture? Would they be hostile to everybody? There was no way to know in advance.

In fact, Mavra had been almost insistent on finding out something about them. If the Verionites were nocturnals, for example, they might do better moving by day and remaining just this side of the border until they were close to the Avenue.

The Lebans knew, but it was no use asking them directly. Simile wasn't always effective in a translator conversation, particularly when one party didn't have one.

Still, she tried. "Are the Verionites animals?"

"Yes."

"Do they eat meat or grain?"

"Anything."

"Are they larger or smaller than we are?"

"About the same."

"Are they friendly to visitors or unfriendly?"

"Unknown. They seem all right to us."

Not exactly a great deal of help.

"Will we be able to find food over there?"

"Probably."

"Are they day creatures like you or night creatures like us?"

"Day mostly."

"Is there anything else we should know?"

"Yes. Remember to look up."

She was startled. "They fly?"

"Some do."

She hadn't figured on that. Flying in a nontech hex meant some kind of bird or other winged creature. That wasn't good at all. *Definitely* a night crossing, and with extra attention given to concealing them from the air.

Still, she couldn't help but feel excited. Although there were many long, dangerous days or weeks to come, it was the first measure of real progress since she'd taken up with Mavra and Lori.

"One last question. Do you know the way this world usually measures time?"

"Yes. The railroad is quite punctual."

"Do you know how long it has taken us to reach this border?"

"Yes. Fifteen days."

Fifteen days. "Sorry—one more and then I thank you for all your assistance. At this rate, how long would it take us to reach the Avenue?"

"Another twelve days to reach the equator, then ten. If you can go exactly northwest, ten to twelve days for the whole journey."

"I thank you. I will always hold the Lebans in my heart as true and trusted friends. I have had very few since I came here."

"We are pleased to know this."

It was time to make some plans.

Mavra was all for heading straight for the destination by the shortest route. Lori wanted to take it slower and more cautiously, not feeling the same sense of urgency.

In the end it was up to Julian, of course. Their opponents might *expect* them to take the shortest route, but then again, how would they know when she and the other two would emerge from Leba and where? In a sense, straight to the goal was the safest course; it meant the least distance to move, and that lessened their chances of being spotted and reported. Mavra didn't like the idea of fliers, though, any more than Julian did. Fliers could cover pretty good distances in short periods of time, vital for reconnaissance in a no-tech hex. But if the Lebans were right, and Julian interpreted their answer to mean that the Verionites probably saw about as well at night as Earth-humans, then they had a chance if they could conceal their day camps.

It was an all or nothing roll of the dice at this point, but it seemed like the only way to play it.

Near sunset they moved out, down and through the final valley and to the Verion border. Just looking across it, even though the hex boundary made it dark and hazy, they could see a dramatic change. Many rivers and streams crossed boundaries, as did landforms, but clearly Verion was a much drier place. The hills continued, but the trees almost completely stopped, replaced with grasslands and occasional bushes and other small shrubs.

Not a lot of cover, Julian thought worriedly. Still, there was no other way to get it done. She stepped through the border, feeling that now-familiar tingling sensation, and into Verion.

It was suddenly very hot and surprisingly humid for a place that far from an ocean. There wasn't much transfer between hexes beyond the immediate area of the border, where some convection was inevitable, so this was probably how it was going to feel.

They proceeded in, although intending only to find a reasonable place to camp out of sight and wait until the next night to begin their real journey.

The sky was clear, although there were some lazy-looking birds off in the distance which Julian hoped weren't the local equivalent of vultures circling over a kill.

They traveled down the first hill, into a ravine, and then back up the gentle slope of the next, slightly higher one, which revealed a whole new vista.

Beyond, the land flattened out considerably, although there were various isolated landforms standing like bizarre sentinels as far as the eye could see. The lowlands clearly had eroded away over great periods of time, leaving pockets of harder rock, possibly volcanic.

In the middle of this strange landscape of bizarre shapes and flat plains were clearly developed areas. There *were* trees here, but they were far different from the ones in Leba: tall, thick, but without branches and with leafy growth only at the very tops. Julian thought they looked like palm trees that had fallen off their diets.

More important, they were clearly planted, both for ornamentation and in groves. Nearby were large fields that showed definite signs of cultivation. A fair-sized river cut through the middle of it, leaving a jagged canyon that looked pretty formidable. There were, however, two clear suspension-type bridges over it, showing a great deal of nontech sophistication.

Well, none of us are tree climbers, Julian thought, *and those trees aren't going to conceal us too much, but the fronds will give us air cover.*

The real problem was going to be the canyon. The only practical way across was over one of those bridges, and during that time they would be exposed with absolutely nowhere to run or hide.

She wished she knew more about the people here. She wished she knew a lot more about everything having to do with this place.

By the time they reached the first of the trees, it was clearly too close to dawn to consider risking either of the bridges that night. Best to camp, get some rest, and watch and see if any of the natives showed themselves. She wanted to see them, but not all that closely.

It wasn't long after dawn, just as they settled in under the trees, when she got her wish.

The sound of what seemed to be a wagon drew her, and she crept over to the edge of the grove, making certain to keep as well hidden behind a tree as possible, and looked out. What she saw was one of the strangest sights yet on this bizarre world.

It was a wagon, all right, and it was huge, with two big solid wheels that had to be two meters high holding it up. What got her was that it appeared to be pulled by two oversized, very fat Earthwomen, and on top, on a tiny seat trying to keep his balance, the one who held the reins looked for all the world like an Earth-human-size pig in a very wide brimmed straw hat and wearing a pair of overalls.

A closer look with her ability to magnify things showed that her first impression of the creatures pulling the wagon was wrong but that her notion of the driver was pretty well dead on, although Porky Pig it wasn't. That was one *ugly* hog up there.

The creatures pulling the wagon did have a humanlike shape, were bipedal, had enormous rear ends and thighs, and seemed to have breasts as well, but the faces were very apelike. Their backs and sides were covered with brown fur, while their fronts appeared a hairless purplish skin color. For such large creatures, though, they had remarkably scrawny arms, and if those were hands, they weren't much more useful than Julian's, if that. They looked to be at least seven or eight feet tall and proportioned to that height save for the arms and huge hairy feet. They weren't pulling the cart by walking or ambling but by a kind of slow jogging canter that seemed almost horselike.

The draft animals had been the startling things, but the driver was more interesting because he didn't match what she expected at all. He certainly had no wings, and if pigs could fly in this hex, it surely was by some means not obvious to her.

Were the Lebans wrong, or was there more here than she could see right now?

She knew she should go back and stand a better guard as the first watch—Mavra and Lori couldn't speak, but they could surely wake the others up in a hurry if need be, and their judgment was the important factor in a watch—but she wanted to see how that thing got across that bridge.

The answer was that it didn't. Instead, several more pig creatures—*hogs*—emerged from a lemon-drop-shaped hut near the bridge and began operating an oddball system of pulleys and gears that revealed strong cables strung parallel to the bridge. When the cart reached them, Verionites climbed up and began stringing cable through slots along both sides while the driver unhitched his odd "team." Another set of cables was then attached to another series of poles with gears and pulleys, and the "team" was hitched to a circular master gear on these and started going around and around slowly.

Julian watched in amazement as the entire cart body was lifted off its carriage and huge wheels and into the air, suspended by the cables. An operator at the far end and another at the assembly right at the rim of the canyon threw a series of giant wooden levers, changing the gearing, and the cart began actually to move along the cables down to the second set of gears and poles and then out over it, powered by the team on the far end.

It's a cable car system! she realized. A very clever and elaborate cable car system using the sheer muscle power of those beasts. More interestingly, it was also a kind of basic container system; they didn't move the carriage and wheels, only the container and its cargo.

Once the container was across, the team was unhitched from the system and led across by the driver, the bridge swaying a bit under the weight of the two behemoths but hardly stressed. On the other side the process was reversed with a new carriage. It was slow but efficient.

The other, parallel bridge did not have such an assembly and was probably built later for routine foot traffic, which would not have to be held up waiting for teams to pass. With those draft animals and the rather imposing girth of the Verionites, traffic was pretty well limited to one way at a time, anyway.

The natives were clever, quite modern, and industrious; that much was sure. She had the opportunity to take a magnified view of a couple of them while they were setting up the cables, and while the faces were ugly and their figures matched the sort bipedal hogs might be expected to have, their arms and hands seemed quite muscular and flexible, and their feet, supporting that form and weight, more resembled those of a hippo or an elephant than a hog's. Large, wide, and flat, almost like tree trunks, they provided pretty good balance and flexibility.

But if those suckers could fly, she wanted to see it!

She wondered if perhaps such clever folk might have hot air balloons or something like that which the Lebans would consider flying. That was a thought, although it wasn't at all something she would have thought common in a hex like Verion. Like Erdom, Verion was against an impenetrable barrier, in this case the equator, and so wasn't hex-shaped at all. Balloons might well be practical in a compact hex-shape, but unless they were pretty well staked down and used only for lookout purposes, they were unlikely to be practical for travel here.

Still, after seeing those bridges, the cable car, and the container apparatus in action, she wouldn't put anything past these people. In a sense, she admired them from what little she'd seen. Most of the nontech hexes seemed to have accepted their lot and mummified their culture and society. Erdom was a perfect example of this—static, with change considered a threat. The Verionites, though, had refused to accept their limits and become at least in part a culture of engineers. It was almost as if they'd said, "Okay, here are the limits, and here's what we want to do. Now figure out how we do it!"

That made them dangerous as well. They couldn't afford to treat this society as a standard, lazy nontech culture.

Remaining in the groves all day, Julian also noticed one other characteristic of the hex that seemed quite odd. Everything animal appeared to be bipedal for some reason; even the insects ran around on two legs, looking almost like miniature varieties of Mixtimese. Yet another very odd place, but not nearly as strange as Leba or even Mixtim.

That night they had to face the problem of the bridges.

There was no way around them; who knew how long this canyon was or how far it stretched? And even if it didn't go on forever, what of the river at the bottom, which certainly seemed large and wild running? There was a sort of tollbooth, but both it and the cable crew and shack seemed to shut down shortly after dusk; they had watched the creatures lock up and leave. Lights indicated a town not too far on the other side, probably a farming center and way stop for bridge travelers, and everybody on this side seemed to cross the bridge and go off in that direction. Whatever justified the whole system was either to the east or to the west of them; they certainly did no traffic with Leba.

There was no way to be completely safe crossing the bridge, but nothing in the infrared showed that they had left any kind of guards around, although Julian had half expected to be barked and growled at by bipedal dogs or something. The big problem would be that they had no idea what was on the other side. The guards might be there, where the bulk of the people were, since a barrier on either side would do to block passage, or they might ring alarm bells over there by merely shaking the bridge up and down as they walked. Although Julian had heard nothing specific, an alarm system might be hooked up when they closed, or it might be something she wouldn't recognize as an alarm but they would.

What they found was a solid wooden gate, a sign, and a large bell. The sign was in Verionese, not commercial, so it was impossible to read it, but they could all guess what it said: "To use bridge, ring bell for attendant."

There *was* an opening on either side of the gate, but it was much too small for either Lori or Julian. Mavra went to it, looked in and up, and saw that the gate was secured from the other side with a large wooden bar. This was one time when her lack of arms might be an asset, although not for actually moving the thing. She was, however, able to wiggle through the opening at ground level with minimal loss of feathers and get on the other side. That left the bar, which was a bit above her eye level. It looked to be a simple enough system, but how to move that bar when she didn't have any arms?

Ultimately, she pressed her back against the gate, got her head under the bar, and tried to straighten up as much as possible. The bar moved, but not enough to come out of its latch.

After several frustrating attempts, after which she realized that she needed to be about her old height, small as that was, to get it high enough, she decided to step out and look at the thing.

It was just a board, nothing spectacular but effective enough. She finally decided that the only chance was to lift the thing as high as she could and then, when the weight of it, which was not inconsiderable, was on her head, to move sideways and hope she could slide it enough so that it would fall outside the latch on one side.

Several attempts failed, but finally she managed it, her head hurting like hell, and the end of the board fell to the floor of the bridge with a *clunk!* The other end remained precariously balanced on the other latch.

Dizzy and with a whale of a headache, she nonetheless stepped back and gave off a single low squawk. Julian heard it and slowly and carefully pushed against the gate. The board jammed a couple of times, but Mavra was able to help free it, and finally they had it open enough for Lori, then Julian to squeeze through.

The trouble was, if word had reached here about them and the Verionites were on the lookout for signs of strangers, the open gate would be a signal. Julian pushed the gate closed and strained to lift the board back up into place, but she just didn't have the strength. Lori, seeing the problem, didn't stop to wonder why she was doing it but came over and put his head and neck under Julian's arms and lifted slowly, giving her the added strength she needed. It wasn't neat, but the gate was again locked and bolted.

Julian helped Mavra onto Lori's back but didn't bother to tie her. At the speed at which any of them could cross the swinging span, it was unnecessary and would take time they couldn't spare.

The roar of rapids came from far below, masking out much of the sound once they were out over the chasm, and the bridge rippled and swung back and forth as they crossed. But it was a sturdy and well-built structure that had seen much traffic. At least the idea of alarms rigged to the bridge seemed remote; there was a distinct night breeze that caused it to sway slightly entirely on its own, making it more difficult to keep one's own balance on it but possibly explaining why the crossing was usually restricted to daylight.

There was a small house at the other end with a light inside, apparently the toll keeper's house. Before they even reached it, the pungent smells of Verion's masters hit them, and it wasn't much more pleasant than the odors of Mixtim, although it was more varied—the scent of massive sweat, garbage, and pungent spices all rolled into one unappetizing and somewhat sickening perfume.

Just before they reached the other side, somebody came out of the house and started fooling with something unseen on the side of the building. They froze, and for a brief nightmare moment they had the swaying, the winds, and the odors all at once.

Then whoever it was went back inside, and they finished the walk slowly and quietly, trying to keep hoof sounds to a minimum. They were relieved to see only a small wooden crossbar on a pivot where the bridge again reached land. As quietly as possible, Julian raised it enough for Lori to get through, then ducked under it herself.

The wind really started up on the other side; while unpleasant, it had the effect of masking their own sounds as they moved between bridge and town, across the road, and around the main settlement.

Well over a hundred more miles of this, Julian thought nervously. Too long in such a civilized country. They had gotten lucky this time, but there was no way of knowing what other obstacles this land had in store for them before they reached the final and largest obstacle of them all.

Beyond the town the bizarre mixture of twisted landforms—spires, pinnacles, tiny table rocks—grew even more dense, and the Verionites had planted virtually every available space in between. Here and there were virtual herds of the huge, lumbering bipedal draft animals just wandering about or lying around sound asleep and snoring loudly. The wind rippled the grains and grasses as if they were a gigantic sea and made its own series of groans and moans as it twisted in and out and all around the natural statuary.

As morning approached and false dawn was illuminating the western sky, Julian searched for a good camp. She was beginning to wonder if perhaps she had misunderstood the "up" warning of the Lebans or if there were Verionite sentinels, like shepherds, atop some of the broader rock forms as watchmen. It was still hard to see, though, how they'd get up or down without wings.

They would have to camp at the base of one of them, though—a particularly large tower of twisted black rock that had shallow cavelike indentations at the base that would provide at least some cover. There was no choice; it would have to do.

Julian, as usual, took the first watch. Mavra's own sense of time from watching the shadows seldom failed her here; her second watch was as reliable as Julian's. Only Lori seemed to have little sense of time, so he took the last watch, since it was fairly difficult to miss the sun going down if the others weren't already awake by then.

For Mavra, so long out of the chase, every step took her closer to her goal. Somehow, some way, she would get inside. Nothing and no one was going to stop her this time. Lori, on the other hand, was going through the motions with little hope; everything that could go wrong up to now had, and he fully expected, after such an epic walk, to wind up caught and back in the hands of the enemy when they reached wherever it was they were going.

It hardly mattered to him anymore if they even got there. Seeing Julian and being so dependent on her all this time could only remind him of what he had lost. Considering how she'd handled herself so far, she needed him or anything he might do other than carry Mavra about as much as he needed a sewing kit. He didn't even have desire, only a sense of guilt and loss.

For Julian, although taking it one day at a time, there was a sense of the endgame in this. She hadn't the slightest idea if they could get Mavra into this Well place or not or what would really happen if they could, but either they would or they would not. If they did, then at least victory would be denied the evil people both from Earth and from this world. If they couldn't, she was pretty sure they'd not be given a second chance at it.

Anything you desire. That had been Mavra's promise to them. *Anything you desire.* A nice phrase, that, but what did it mean? Was it like the ancient genie, granting wishes? That was always an easy one in fairy stories. They wished for wealth and romance and happily-ever-after endings. It wasn't that simple in real life. It particularly wasn't simple for her. She'd had a series of shocks and psychological changes that almost outdid her physical ones, and they'd even messed with her mind with her own consent.

What did Julian now, today, really desire? Not to go back, to become Julian Beard again. For all his glamour, she hated his stinking guts. Still, why had that earliest incarnation wanted to become an astronaut? Because of a need of adventure, of challenge, the excitement of the new frontier. That much remained of him, she thought. She didn't want a happily-ever-after ending; she wanted new challenges, new chances to do something different, worthwhile.

Erdom was hardly the place for that, permanently and happily stuck as it was in a kind of bizarre variation of the permanent twelfth-century Earth.

And yet she'd come to like who she was and what she was and dreamed of the desert lands that she'd hated when she'd been there.

It seemed as if there had always been something tearing at her since she'd been here. Male, female, master, slave, rebel, wife, loner, lover of the herd.

The way they'd rearranged her head, she could never go back; the society would burn her at the stake as a witch. But if it could somehow be countered or removed, she'd become that servile little wimp again, and *that* she didn't want, either. What if she could go back as an Erdomese man? It solved most of the conundrums, but the trouble was that she didn't want to *be* a man, not anymore. She'd been one once, and while he'd loved it fine, she didn't think very much of him now, and that was just what she would become. Look at what it had done to Lori, whose own contrasting Earth background was the opposite of hers. She didn't exactly want *that* guy back, either, let alone want to become another one.

There was a real catch in that three-wishes business that the fairy-tale writers hadn't ever faced. In order to make decent use of them, one first had to know what to wish for.

On the third day they passed near another small town and then another. The roads, which they stayed off but which they watched carefully, seemed to grow more frequent, wider, and better maintained, not to mention more crowded.

And on the third day they also saw that pigs could fly.

The last thing anybody would have expected to come across in even the most sophisticated high-tech hex was an airport, but that was exactly what it was. There was even an unmistakable wind sock on a large reflective pole. Making camp in some trees not far from it because the timing was right more than because they wanted to be this close in, they actually could watch it in operation.

There were two types of fliers: the aircraft and the kites.

Watching a kiter take off was something of an amazing sight. Strapped underneath a massive width of a canvaslike material, the hoglike Verionite was then placed on a wheeled dolly. Then a team of the big, lumbering creatures that Julian had dubbed bigfoots were brought out, hitched as if they were pulling a cart. When the omnipresent wind was right, someone gave a signal, and the four-bigfoot team would start lumbering down a cleared path, gaining speed until they were running flat out. This plus the wind would catch the leading edge of the kite, and it would rise into the air, the dolly dropping away, and up it would go, breaking free of the ropes or whatever they were that the bigfoots used to pull.

In fact, once aloft, the kite fliers seemed to have some sort of rudder control and perhaps ways of seeing the wind currents aloft, which must have been pretty tricky from what Julian could see. She had been a pilot once, too, and had done some hang gliding off Maui, so she knew that this would have been nearly impossible, no matter what the design of the kite, under Earth-type conditions.

But this wasn't Earth, nor was it supposed to simulate the Earth. It was simulating some other world somewhere else.

At any rate, once aloft, the pilot had lift, could get up farther, and could clearly steer. The amazing thing was how the device kept climbing until he was just a speck in the distant sky. Watching the aerodynamics of the thing, though, Julian had to wonder if under these conditions a skilled and highly trained pilot might not be able to stay up there for hours and possibly cover a fair distance.

Even Mavra, who piloted spaceships and other craft far more sophisticated than anything Julian had ever more than dreamed of, was impressed. Even with the level of automation in her day, there were minimal atmospheric flying skills that had to be learned before one was allowed to pilot a massive spacecraft.

There was another kind of flier as well. This was an oblong gondola supported by a matching hot air balloon suspended over the top of it. One Verionite was in the gondola, controlling the flame, although it was unclear just what the source of that heat might be or how they managed to get a sufficient amount of it in a controllable and obviously compressed form to allow for the level of controlled blasts he could give it.

And then there was the bigfoot pedaling the bicycle.

It was an absurd sight, but its logic was pretty clear. Once the gondola lifted off—with the bigfoot, obviously trained to do this without panicking, sitting strapped in the seat at the front—the man at the flame gave a command and the creature began pedaling. This in turn started a large propeller at the rear, sheltered in a frame with a vertical rudder that the man at the flames appeared to be able to control using a long pole.

Once aloft, with these winds, the balloon would have been at the mercy of the currents and would have picked up speed; the bigfoot, however, was able to overcome this, and its energy and the prop in the back provided a forward momentum that looked as if it might reach, oh, three or four kilometers per hour in the face of the wind. Altitude was controlled by the fire and the master gave the craft direction by manipulating the rudder poles. The thing could actually travel. Julian suspected that the winds blew at different speeds and levels at low altitudes and that, again, an expert pilot could find the right one for wherever he wanted to go, attaining maximum speed. At that rate, he could make the equator in just a couple of long days or almost anywhere in this land in four. Not fast, no, but that thing could carry a limited cargo, such as mail, packages, and news, at a speed that a nontech civilization could hardly match on the ground. Such a system would be vital for emergencies and would make communication practical. It bound the hex together, she guessed.

It also meant that if there *was* a wanted poster out on them, as there almost certainly was on Lori and Mavra, the odds were that there weren't many in Verion who didn't know about them.

It also made travel by night a good decision, virtually essential, as they were clearly moving toward a denser population center.

On day five they were on the outskirts of a major city, where the skies were filled with flying pigs in variations of the two devices they'd seen at the airport but with such a variety of color and design that it was clear that the Verionites had a far different aesthetic sense than Julian.

More dramatic, off well beyond the city on the farthest horizon, was a solid dark line, easily seen through the more prairielike and less obstructed land that the hex was becoming. It wasn't much, but it was too regular and too consistent to be either natural or an optical illusion. Still forty or fifty miles from them, it was nonetheless visible.

The equator!

The position of the sun told them that they had been heading more or less true northwest, which meant that as of now, they were less than a week away from the Avenue.

Mavra had given up trying to explain or describe the Avenue to Julian in scratch writing. Apparently she would just have to go there and see it for herself. The only thing Julian got was that it was sunken, like a very broad culvert, flat on the bottom, smooth on all sides, and that it led to one of the doors into the Well.

That meant no cover and low ground at a point when forces could be all along both sides shooting down at them. All kinds of technology would work there, but it wouldn't matter. When they were exposed on the floor of the thing, Julian knew that rocks could get them, never mind bullets. Nor, Mavra informed her, could one just enter the Well even if one made it to the doorway.

"Automated. Opens only at old shift change," she told Julian. "Midnight."

"Can *anybody* enter it at midnight?"

"No. Only authorized. You come in with me. I am authorized."

"How long does the door stay open?"

"About fifteen minutes unless I close it first."

Julian sighed. "So we have fifteen minutes to get down there, run a gauntlet, and somehow get inside without them killing or capturing us. It's *impossible!*"

"See layout, defenders first. Then we'll see. I think I may have a way."

"You want to give me an idea of how you're going to do it?"

"Wait. When I know it is possible, then I tell you."

Julian shook her head, wondering if any of this was worth what she'd gone through the past couple of weeks. If it was anything like it was described, it was absolutely insane to even attempt to enter. Even if Mavra Chang were who and what she claimed, it made no difference. Until she was inside, she was just a big, heavy helpless bird who couldn't outrun a child. This whole business *had* to have driven her insane; that was the only explanation for why she even could think that she might get in there.

Mavra understood Julian's attitude, but she could *feel* the Well, feel the contact with its power and even some of its knowledge at this point. The Well *knew* where she was, *knew* that she was close.

And the Well had gone to a great deal of trouble to get her here. With Nathan out of it in some southern hospital and Mavra this close, it wasn't going to let her get away now, of that she was certain.

THE AVENUE

CAMPOS AND THE COLONEL had tried every means that they could think of to find some sign of the missing trio in Leba, even bringing in expert trackers from other hexes that the colonel knew about, but to no avail.

The Lebans themselves had seemed singularly unimpressed by their problem and had declared themselves neutral and uninterested in the affairs of other creatures. Not even Campos or the colonel could think of anything to offer them that might tempt them into cooperation.

There were times when some of the animals brought in seemed to pick up a scent, but it always led to a dead end, with the creatures going around in confused circles. At one point the colonel swore that if he didn't know better, he'd swear that someone was pulling a drag over the "foxes'" trail, confusing the scent and leading them away, but he couldn't imagine why anyone would do that or how he could without betraying himself. He finally decided that the land was just not conducive to finding the fugitives' trail.

Score one for the prey, they both were forced to admit. On the other hand, the endgame was what counted.

The colonel had hoped, though, to avoid the endgame simply because he was none too secure about showing up in his old role. Kurdon had certainly put out the word on his betrayal at the complex; it was unlikely that he'd have real authority even if his friends in Zone were able to keep the law off him with some cover story.

More than that, they would have to deal with armed soldiers whose loyalty was to their own hex and then to the Zone Council and not to any third parties. And there always the chance that in spite of threats with real teeth in them, their captives might be able to betray their real status as prisoners to the army personnel at the Avenue.

Campos, too, wasn't pleased with that prospect. "I think perhaps we should get rid of them now, before they can cause trouble later," she suggested. "All except the girl, of course. If we cannot control the likes of *her*, no matter *what* her wishes, we do not deserve to be in this game in any case."

The colonel, however, didn't like the idea of finishing them off. "We can't do it *here*," he explained. "The executions would be witnessed by Lebans no matter where we did it, and the Mixtim are under their protection as well. I don't know what all those tentacles could do, but I *do* know that if we got out alive at all, a message would somehow be sent to Zone, and we would be as wanted as the ones we chase. This isn't Clopta, after all. There are times when diplomacy and a light touch might yield better results than the heavy boot. Bring them along. If they cause trouble, we can dispose of them when we get to Verion. But consider this: The Dillians and the Dahir still have the official weight of the Zone Council on their side. *They* can legitimize *us* with the army. So long as one or more of their companions are within easy range of either of us, I think they will go along."

Campos frowned. "You are not playing both sides again, are you, Colonel?" she asked suspiciously.

"I took an oath and I meant it! This is not some sordid drug business here; it is for the highest of stakes! This will be very, very tricky no matter what we do!"

Campos thought it over. "All right, Colonel, I will play it your way for now. Please just make certain that I do not see you changing sides once again."

"I *swear* to you . . . !"

"Never mind. We have wasted far too much time here. Let us get the party together and head out for this Avenue, whatever it is. But remember, Colonel, if they betray us at the last moment, they have nothing on me at all of a criminal nature. What have we done? Fled a drug baron and defended ourselves against a monster and the baron and his henchmen? Gone where I have a right to go? Taken these people where they wished to go, anyway? You see?"

"You are forgetting that the condition those two are in was your doing," the colonel pointed out. He did *not* point out that the only witness to his treason was Gus, who could hardly afford public charges and testimony in Zone because it would mean leaving Zone and exiting in Dahir, a place that very much wanted him back to ensure that he would not leave again.

"So? Even if they can prove that, which is not a certain thing, how could the poor mistress of a gangster have such authority in the gang in so short a time here on this world? It is hardly an international crime like the running of drugs. Even kidnapping is a local crime here, did you know that? Had I kidnapped or held prisoner a fellow Cloptan, *that* would be a different story, but *these*? No, I think not. And as I am certain that you, as usual, always have a way out of a tight situation, the fact is, the way this world is set up, neither of us has committed crimes for which anyone is looking for us other than those we directly committed crimes against." She considered that and found it highly amusing.

"Come, come! My friend and son of my patron!" the colonel said. "What are we *doing,* passing blame back and forth to one another? I believe there were 160-odd nations back on the Earth we left, perhaps a few more. There are *780* sovereign and independent nations here, each with its own unique race and needs. Consider how little could get done back on Earth and you have only a shadow of how little can truly get done of an international nature here. Without this unpleasantness with Brazil and Chang, they could not have even *touched* the cartel! What have such as we to fear from such as them?"

"Yes, you are right," Campos said after a moment. "Well, we will let them live, at least for now. As you say, what can they do?" She paused a moment. "Of course, if those army people get our birdie, then we *might* just have to commit one of those crimes, you know."

"True," the colonel agreed, "but if that happens, we'll have Mavra Chang, so what difference does it make? If the king—or queen—is the state, can that person commit a crime against themselves?"

It was a *most* amusing idea, and both of them laughed.

For the first time on the journey Terry felt really frightened. The images in that Juana's mind about her were bizarre and nightmarish. She couldn't imagine what she might have done to deserve such complete and utter hatred, but Juana Campos was scarier than anything she could imagine, even in her surface thoughts. They were also so inconsistent as to be totally crazy. How could Campos on the one hand imagine blinding and maiming Terry and treating her like an animal and at the same time look upon her with genuine concern?

It took a couple of days before she realized that Campos's gentler nature, what there was of it, was directed not at her but at her coming baby.

Gus was improving but still in no condition to do very much, and the travel didn't help his healing at all. There were times when the pain was such that he was very much afraid that he was going to die and other times when it was even worse and he was afraid he wouldn't die. Still, Terry's presence kept him from giving up and provided the determination to heal no matter what.

He had never expected to still be here this close to the birth and headed away from the kind of medical help that she might well need. He knew of women who still *died* in childbirth, particularly in Third World countries, and he'd seen too much infant mortality for one lifetime already. He cursed himself for ever agreeing to leave Agon with her as well as for being stupid enough to get shot.

Now it was clear that Kurdon had wanted her handy as bait in case Campos had to be lured out of some underground hiding place in Clopta. Well, Kurdon joined a lengthening list of people, including Gen Taluud and himself, who had underestimated Campos. Trouble was, it was no skin off Kurdon's ass what happened; Gus had paid with a painful, debilitating wound and capture, and Taluud had paid with his life. But it was Terry who might well pay the biggest price unless somehow he could get well enough to save her.

The Dillians, too, felt less than noble about the help they'd been in all this and were pretty well defeated and resigned. A few times one or possibly both might have escaped, but they could hardly have taken Gus and Terry with them, and they had no doubt that either Campos or the colonel would make them pay for any transgression by Tony or Anne Marie.

In point of fact, Tony for one was surprised to be alive at all. It didn't make a lot of sense not to have killed them, but since they hadn't, there was at least the possibility of getting out of this with a whole skin. Whether the same could be said for Terry, Mavra, or Lori remained to be seen, but as Anne Marie had commented, "We started this as grownups. It would be maddening not to be there at the finish."

On Taluud's sturdy horses and with well-provisioned pack mules, they made the Verion border in just three days.

"It would be tempting to run our trackers all the way down this border and see if there is a scent now," Campos commented, "but whether or not they have gotten here yet is something we cannot say. We wasted so much time back there trying to find them that it is not worth it at this point. Let us push on to this Avenue; I want to see what the devil this setup is."

"Shall we cross over to Ellerbanta? They are high-tech over there, you know. It would be much easier to travel. We might well be able to ride up on something that has real power and eat decent food again."

"It *is* tempting," the colonel agreed, "particularly considering what these Verion hogs think of as high cuisine, but I think not. Our odds of making headway with any guards are far better on this nontech side than on the other, and they will *have* to come this way."

In another three days they reached the point where the Avenue intersected the equator. None of them had ever actually seen a Well World wall before; its scope and sheer sense of permanence awed them all. It rose from the ground as if placed there by the hand of some enormous giant, rising up, up, as far as the eye could see. There *was* a top limit, of course, but it was impossibly high up, and beyond that there rose an energy barrier that still stopped any sort of passage across it.

The southern hemisphere of the Well World was dedicated almost entirely to carbon-based life; the few exceptions were primarily silicon variants that still required much of the same ranges of environment for life and sustenance. The northern hemisphere, on the other hand, was entirely non-carbon-based and in fact had so many varieties that they had their own separate lexicon up there. Most of the northern races, it was said, were so alien that they made little sense to those in the south. Ammonia breathers gazed out on methane oceans, and sulfur oxide breathers found it chilly at a mere ninety degrees Celsius. There were whole regions up there where even crossing from one hex to the next would be lethal to the native of the first, and not a single condition there would support any of the life in the south without an artificial environment.

The only way back or forth was by a special gate in the two Zones, north and south. The equatorial barrier kept everybody else, and everything inside the hemispheres, from mixing.

If it wasn't for the Avenue, there would be no way to tell that this was any sort of unusual place along the otherwise totally smooth, impenetrable wall. The Avenue simply went up to it and essentially merged with it, with no apparent sign of a seam. It was almost as if it continued on through, although there was nothing to show that it did or didn't.

When they reached it, it was certainly impressive. The border ran right to the edge of the Avenue entrance, and there were cuts every few kilometers where sloping ramps switchbacked down. Campos went a little down one ramp, through the border, and found that the other border, for Ellerbanta, was along the opposite side. The Avenue was a place all its own, broad, smooth, and finely machined, which showed the otherwise invisible artificial nature of this world.

Campos took out one of the energy pistols she had, which hadn't been anything more than a weight since leaving Clopta, and fired it at an angle to the opposite wall, which was impressively far away. The shot hit and seemed to be absorbed by the material. There was no ricochet, not even of the light from the energy beam.

Impressed, Campos tried it on a section of wall right next to the ramp. The same thing occurred, and she then gingerly touched the spot, which showed not even a scorch mark at a beam level that would have atomized the horse. It wasn't even warm to the touch.

There was no question that even by the standards of the Well World, the Avenue was beyond any of the technologies here and stood like an artifact, perfectly preserved, running straight as an arrow due north as far as the eye could see. Campos had had the same sort of feeling when seeing the great Incan cities and those of the Aztecs and Mayas as well, somehow out of place in their junglelike settings, suggesting another world, another time, and a civilization that could barely be imagined.

At night the Avenue glowed with an eerie light, this one a golden yellow, revealing a pattern in the Avenue floor and walls not so obvious in daylight. By night, by this internal glow, the "street" level seemed to be made up of hexagonal blocks of absolutely uniform size.

"Gives you the creeps, does it not?" Campos said to the colonel, looking down in the darkness.

"I find it astonishing. What incredible creatures they must have been! So far beyond us that we could probably not even imagine their civilization and way of life. This whole *world* nothing but a laboratory for them. It must have been like Mount Olympus or the angels around the throne of heaven."

"But still they died out, just as the Incas, but not by conquest," Campos noted. "Maybe things were not so heavenly, after all, I think. They are dead. Gone. All we are doing is looking at their toys."

The colonel wasn't so sure. "Perhaps. But if they left at least one gatekeeper, as I believe they did, then they didn't think they were going to die out, and they certainly didn't die out due to external or accidental forces. To reach *that* height, they had to have destroyed themselves somehow. What was it that they did, I wonder, and why? *They* certainly didn't think of it as an end, else why leave a gatekeeper? I wonder if we can even *conceive* of what they did. I doubt if we could understand it even if one of them explained it to us. Why build a laboratory, set it up this way, and then leave? And where did they go? And why?"

"Such power they had," Campos breathed. "They would never have given it up willingly. Still, we will never know, eh? Not unless your Captain Brazil wakes up and decides to talk about it."

"Oh, he has. Gus told me all about it. He claims he's nothing more than a man who accepted a bargain with the previous keeper, who was so sick of immortality that he simply wanted to die. And that our captain finally had reached that same point himself and had chosen Mavra Chang as a candidate replacement. Apparently she flunked the initiation."

Campos thought about it. "You know, if that is true, I almost wonder if we could *still* make some sort of deal with her. What does she owe *him* or the builders? Think of getting inside, in the control room of this whole thing. It must be like nothing we can imagine, yes?"

"Indeed. But I hardly think she'd be in any sort of mood to keep a deal struck with you, not after what you did to her," the colonel pointed out. "Even if she kept her word, it would be, I think, like making a deal with the devil. She might make you a queen, all right, but a queen who looked like she does now and with the same limitations. No, I don't think I'd like to trust her on that. Our original plan is far more practical. In that case, we *know* the sort of minds we are dealing with and the limits on their power and authority."

"I think you are right," Campos agreed. "Still, I have to admit that if your captain is telling the truth, then perhaps he did not pick so badly, after all. Consider how far she has come and under what circumstances she has managed to do it. I keep wondering if, considering all that, she will not somehow manage to slip inside."

"Not if we get there first," the colonel responded firmly.

The soldiers stationed here were Verionites; there had been a larger and more mixed force earlier, but it had been discontinued because of its expense, because of the complaints from other races about the tedium and lack of amenities to no apparent purpose, and because the Verionite government wasn't exactly thrilled with the idea of any foreign troops on its soil for any length of time.

They were almost laughable, these troops, except that they had a certain imposing look about them up close. Those pig snouts and big, ugly hog faces and tiny, nasty-looking eyes were atop large mouths from which lower canines often protruded, giving them a very fierce look indeed. Their arms were thick, powerful, and muscular, and their hands had very long fingers that ended in sharp black nails.

They were, Juana Campos decided, really *mean*-looking.

They wore metal helmets that came to points and uniforms of a filigreed wool-like material that included crimson jackets, gold buttons, and black trousers with gold stripes. There were perhaps fifty of them at any given time, under a single officer and two NCOs, and they were rotated frequently.

And they considered their orders to be a very big joke.

"We're to stop anybody from going in *there*," Major Hjazz, the current officer in charge, told the newcomers. "As if they could!"

"There is nothing really there at the end of the Avenue, then?" the colonel asked him.

The major chuckled. "Well, yes. Every night at midnight you'll see it. It'll click on, a kind of glow—the usual hexagon, you know. But you can go up to it, bang on it, butt your head against it, anything you want at all. It won't make a damn bit of difference. It's still just wall."

"Indeed. But tell me, when this light is on—can you see anything? Anything inside?"

"You can see for yourself any midnight. There's tourists come up to see it all the time, both from our own people and from Ellerbanta. Most of the nonlocal races, they come in on tours through Ellerbanta, though, where they got that stuff that makes you soft and lazy. When it's turned on, you can *sort* of see something in there, but you can never really make out what it is. They been tryin' since a lot longer than I been alive, I tell you! Hey, it's just a light on one of them timers like they use in Ellerbanta. It turns on, stays on maybe fifteen minutes, it turns off again. No big deal. Most folks don't come back. It's not much of a show."

"Well, with your permission, we'll camp near here for a little while. We were supposed to meet some others here, and it is pretty clear they haven't shown up yet. They were coming in via your country and on foot, so it might well be a few days, even a week or so, until they get here. It's vital that we speak to them, so would we be in the way if we stayed around a bit?"

"Naw. Feel free. It's the off season, anyway. Still, if your friends are recognizable, I could see if they've been spotted anywhere along the way and how far they might be from here."

Hardly, I think, the colonel said to himself, but aloud he said, "Indeed? Any runners or riders you might send might not cross their path, and we don't know their route in any event. We might ask if things drag on, but it's not necessary at the moment."

"Oh, we wouldn't send runners or riders," the major replied. "We send and receive mail every day by air."

"By *what*?"

And thus it was that the party learned of the aerial accomplishments of the Verionites.

It was the source of endless fascination to the party to watch them take off and fly like that, and the bored soldiers were more than overjoyed to show off, explain things, and particularly emphasize the problems and dangers of doing it so near the barrier and the border, where wind and such could cause serious problems or even disasters. "We've scraped up more than one from the bottom of the Avenue," one private told them. "Messy."

"I'd think you'd just sail right over to Ellerbanta," Tony commented.

"Oh, sure, that's what you *try* to do, but it's not that easy 'cause you don't have a lot of height from this point. That area right in there between the borders ain't all that wide when you're flying, it's true, but it's dead air. You start to sink like a stone, and you don't have much tolerance between those walls for landing. You hit one, or the barrier, and it's all over."

Tony and Anne Marie had been given a good deal of freedom, and they made some use of it. Even Campos seemed to have tired of them as prisoners; she and the colonel more than once tried to talk them, rather nicely and almost as equals, into simply heading over to Ellerbanta, taking a train to the capital, and using the Zone Gate there to go home. There was nothing more here they could do and very little that they could do to Campos or the colonel, in spite of all.

"And Terry and Gus?" Anne Marie asked them.

"Gus knows that as soon as he's recovered enough, he's out of here," Campos told her. "As for Terry, she remains here with me. We are old acquaintances, she and I, and I feel sorry for her."

"She of all people should be sent home now!" Tony argued. "She's going to have that baby any day now!"

"She is a strong, healthy girl. She will do all right," Campos told them both. "Back home in Peru I have been at many home births. It is the way of my people in the backcountry. More than once I assisted doctors of Shining Path with such things. What few things are needed I have had brought here thanks to the ingenuity of our host countrymen."

"Well, I'm not about to leave until she's through it!" Anne Marie told her adamantly.

Campos shrugged. "Suit yourself."

Terry had ridden with them and watched all this in growing confusion and uncertainty. At least Gus seemed better, although still in great pain, and it almost seemed as if the two centaurs were completely out of danger. She knew *she* was still in danger, but she could do little about it. Running away wouldn't do anything but maybe make them hurt Gus. Besides, she couldn't run or even ride right, not anymore.

She had trouble sleeping; every time she changed position, it woke her up. She couldn't walk far or easily; it was more like a waddle, and it was very tiring with this big, hard, increasingly heavy lump in her belly. Her nipples hurt, her breasts seemed swollen, and she had to pee every ten minutes. It didn't take anybody smart to see that she wasn't going *anywhere*.

She, too, was getting pains and the weirdest feelings down there, where they said the baby would come out. She couldn't imagine a baby coming out of *that* little place, but if they said it did, then maybe somehow it did.

After a day or two the pains got worse and more frequent, and those strange feelings got even stronger. It was a kind of pain like no other she could remember, and she got very worried about it. Anne Marie tried to reassure her, telling her that it was all normal and that all women who had babies went through this. But Anne Marie had never had a baby. She'd been too sick. Even she couldn't know how *awful* an experience this was turning into and how it seemed to keep dragging on and on.

Early one morning, when she was walking from the pit toilet back to the tent for the umpteenth time, she felt something different, and all of a sudden all sorts of smelly, gushy, yucky watery stuff was flowing out and down her legs. She knew that she hadn't peed again and that it hadn't come out of *there,* and it confused and frightened her enough that she went to Gus, who was just lying there as usual, and pointed.

Gus hadn't much experience in this himself, but he knew something had happened, and he called for Anne Marie and Tony.

"Why, I believe her water's broken!" Anne Marie said happily. She turned and looked straight into the concerned Terry's eyes. "That means the baby will come very soon now. Not much longer. Hold on, girl! Hold on!"

That was going to be really hard, because the pains were coming back now full force, a *lot* stronger and a *lot* more often.

"Shouldn't she be lyin' down?" a concerned Gus asked Anne Marie.

"If she wants to," the centauress replied. "Otherwise, let her stand or sit or whatever. In one sense she's better off than in some hospitals where those stupid male doctors don't let women stand up or sit and treat this like it's some kind of illness. It's not an illness, it's the miracle of birth, quite natural, and about as amazing as anything that has happened to us."

Over the next few hours the pains got even worse, and they just kept coming and coming. She was getting to the point where she no longer cared about anything, not even the baby. She just wanted it *over* with.

"Get Campos in here," Anne Marie instructed.

Tony looked at her oddly. *"Campos?"*

"She claimed she could deliver a baby and had before. I haven't. *You* certainly haven't. And I don't want that nasty colonel within a mile of this."

"But—the way Campos thinks of her! She could *kill* the child!"

"She won't. I've talked to her. She thinks the child is hers. Don't argue! *Get her! Now!"*

It was the most miserable, painful time of Terry's brief memory, worse than anything, worse than dying. The pain, the exhaustion, the people yelling at her—she began to hate them all. And it went on, and on, and on . . .

"Push! Now push!" someone was telling her, and she felt as if she didn't have enough energy to do anything else at all, but she pushed . . .

And then the girl who never said a word, never uttered much in the way of sounds at all, screamed. Screamed with a length and depth that were almost unbelievable and sent panicky nearby Verionite soldiers running for their weapons.

It felt as if she had passed a stone the size of a watermelon, but now, suddenly, it was over. Somewhere off in the distance she heard the incongruous sound of a baby crying, but then she simply passed out.

"Santa Maria! It's a boy! A *big* one, too!" Campos shouted with unrestrained glee. She carefully clipped the umbilical cord with a small clamp she'd gotten from the Verionites, then washed off and wrapped the baby, a rough and tumble type who clearly didn't want to be out in this weird, cold new environment at all. Anne Marie took care of the placenta and otherwise cleaned up the mess.

"Poor dear! She's passed out, totally exhausted."

"Shouldn't wonder," Campos commented. "Twelve hours. *Ai!* But here is the result, and not a blond hair or blue eye to be seen. These are Latin features on the child! You see? No Mister Gus with his lily-white north in *him!*" She laughed. "Even here, in this place and in this muddled mess, a new Campos is born!"

"Well, don't kill him by taking him all over and showing him off!" Anne Marie scolded. "Give him to me. He should be here when she comes to, and she will have to nurse him, considering the conditions here. You can go brag all you want. I'll take care of things at this end."

Actually it was Tony, who had remained nearby through it all, who had the worst reaction. She wasn't at all sure now that she wanted to have children, not one bit.

Gus was not one to be put off by the fact that it wasn't his child. In fact, it had never once occurred to him that it might be. He'd almost injured himself all over again when he'd heard that scream, but when he heard the baby's cry, he'd sat back down again.

He wasn't at all sure if it was or wasn't Campos's kid, either, but he was glad that Campos thought so. It would keep Terry safe for quite a while longer.

The fact that mother and baby were doing fine was enough for him.

It took another three days for Mavra, Lori, and Julian to reach the camp at the end of the Avenue, but they'd managed an epic cross-country trek without, they felt, once being detected, and that was something of a victory in and of itself.

By that time Julian had a very good idea of what Mavra had in mind, and she wasn't at all sure that it was any crazier than simply rushing the place.

In the wee hours of the morning Julian crept in and examined the soldiers' little airport. It was dead quiet, the bigfoots asleep out in the field and everything quite still. There wasn't even a guard on the place, because what purpose would *that* serve here?

There were several of the kites in a storage shed, and all of them looked like they'd seen a lot of work. Still, they looked about as reasonable as one could expect, and the belts and such would probably hold Mavra if, of course, she could steer it by head movements.

She brought Mavra in to examine them, and the bird woman looked at them long and hard. Finally she nodded.

They would not do it tonight, but they would certainly do it quickly. It was *much* too dangerous around here to stay long.

The other question was how to launch and how to get Lori and Julian in with her. In that regard, there was nothing much she could do except use them to get her aloft, and then, if she managed to gain altitude in the darkness and make the proper turn, they would just have to rush full speed through the camp and down the ramp as soon as Mavra vanished inside the Avenue walls. If Mavra was through, they'd get through. If she wasn't, what difference would it make?

The next morning they tried as best they could with the writing system they'd developed to make whatever plans they could.

"You are sure you can fly it?" Julian wrote.

"I am sure I can. I understand the principle. If I can maneuver the front struts with my head and beak, I can do it."

"This is crazy," Julian told her. "We could do as well by just rushing them with you on Lori. They are sloppy, not on guard."

"No," Mavra scratched. "Too risky. Bad guys will try anything to stop me, even killing you. If I am not with you, they won't. They will be trying for me."

"When do you want to do it? We do not even have a watch. How do we know when it is time?"

"Guard changes," Mavra told her. "Last night they had two after dark. Second was at time the door opened. We go on second guard change."

"The odds are very poor."

"The Well will not let me fail. Watch out for yourselves, not me."

She was so confident that this insane, harebrained scheme would work that Julian almost believed it.

Even so, it was hard as hell to get to sleep just thinking about it. All this way, all this accomplishment, and for what? How much training and experience did it take for those Verionites to fly those flimsy things? What did they know or what might they see in the wind currents that was unknown to Mavra? Could she and Lori even provide enough speed to get lift at all?

And most important, what was she most afraid of? That she'd fail? That Mavra would fail? Or that Mavra would succeed?

What then?

Would the wonderful wizard have a heart, a brain, and courage to give away? Or would it just be a small woman behind the curtain pulling levers?

At least Dorothy had had an idea of what she wanted, as had her companions. And she'd never had to fly an unfamiliar aircraft just to get there. She'd even missed the balloon, hadn't she? And all she'd had to do was click her heels together three times . . .

This was gonna be a hell of a lot more complicated, and who knew what all the assembled wicked witches would have ready to stop them?

They'd seen the centaurs, of course, Campos and her bunch, and the colonel, as well as the brutal-looking if rather sloppy soldiers. At least nobody seemed to want to camp out down there at the bottom of the Avenue. It was just too lonely, too spooky, and too bereft of water and other necessities.

There had been no sign of Terry or Gus; they could only hope that nothing bad had happened to either of them.

Maybe that was enough reason for this crazy business, Julian thought. It's too crazy to work, and it's too risky as well, but if it does . . .

At least they might be able to get even.

For all the agony, Terry had delivered quite cleanly. Campos had been ready with a borrowed and boiled scalpel, but it hadn't been needed. When the baby had decided to come, it had come, with Terry sitting mostly in an oversized Verionese chair, gravity doing much of the final work. There was also no real sign of tearing, although there almost had to be some inside.

The girl, they decided, was a hell of a quick healer.

She awoke about an hour after the birth, feeling as if she'd just delivered boulders. Then she was handed the baby and the baby was placed gently to a breast, started to suck, and really gorged himself.

By the next afternoon she'd slept off a lot of it and was feeling remarkably better and a *lot* thinner and lighter to boot. She kept the baby with her at almost all times, except when Campos wanted to see it or show it off, and, wrapped in a soft blanket, the baby seemed quite content.

The second day, as she grew more ambitious, walking with the baby along the barrier, always accompanied by someone, she seemed to grow more and more interested in the Avenue. That evening, after dinner and feeding the baby, she went out accompanied by no less than Campos and Tony, the latter just because she didn't trust anybody around the girl. Terry surprised both the guardians by going through the barrier and partway down the ramp, holding the baby gently.

Campos stared at her, wondering. "Sometimes I think she can see inside there, see what we cannot," she remarked as much to herself as to Tony. "I wonder what draws her to it. Does she see or hear something, perhaps?"

"Hard to say," Tony responded, but she, too, had noticed it. The girl hadn't shown the slightest interest in the wall or the Avenue in all the time they'd been there, but now, after the baby had been born, it was, next to the child, the *only* thing that really fascinated her.

Later on Campos discussed this with the colonel. "You would almost swear that she saw inside," she told the Leeming. "That she thought that she could just walk right through."

"She is such a strange one," the colonel responded.

Campos was not ready to let it go at that. She'd watched her face staring into that blank wall too often now.

"I wonder what would happen if we *did* take her there when the door opens," she mused. "What if that 'rewiring' or whatever they did to her back in that so-called human hex tuned her to the signals in there? What if it is some sort of mental signal, some frequency that is denied those of us created by its machinery?"

"You are actually suggesting that she might be able to walk through?" The colonel thought about it. "I find that highly dubious, but even if she *could*, what good would that do us? She is such a simple sort now. She wouldn't know what to do once she was in there, I shouldn't think. I often wonder if *we* would or if even the controls would be so alien or so beyond our ability to understand."

"I grow very tired and very bored here," Campos told him. "I began to think that our quarry is never going to appear or certainly that they are not going to appear here. Perhaps they have more patience than we thought. Or perhaps they weren't as good as we thought they were. There have been no signs, no signals, no reports. It is as if this world swallowed them up."

"I share your frustration, but what can we do? If we give up now, it has all been for nothing."

"Perhaps. Perhaps I am just playing mental games with myself to keep from going insane with boredom. I just wonder, though, What would it hurt to take her down there when the door opens up tonight? If she walks in, she walks in *with us*. With *all* of us, perhaps. As you say, it is probably incomprehensible to us, but what of that? If she could just walk through, and we with her, in front of the amazed stares of the guards! Think of *that*! We would not need Mavra Chang at all to work our will! Inside, then out. We two and the girl. That alone would be enough to cause terror in the highest places, yes? And only *we* would know that we did not do a thing!"

"It is foolishness. You are simply letting a poor unfortunate girl throw you."

"Still, think of it. If she could, and we did, I would be right, would I not?"

"Well, yes, but . . ."

"But what? She is almost certainly not going to be able to do it. I admit that. But where is the harm in trying it? Just once?"

"And who would be down there with her?"

"Just us. She, we two, and the baby, of course, which she, as a good mother, keeps with her. If we can get in, I would like that baby to go in as well. Think of the possibilities. Think of what powers we could claim for that child! Why, there would be *cults* built around the child! More power to those who control the growing child than from any drugs, because there is no product to move except belief. Campos the god-child! And Madame Campos, the only creature known in the history of the universe to be both a father *and* fully female! And you, the high priest of it all. Makes you think, does it not?"

"Well, I will only say that if you want to be humored, I will go along. But do not be too crushed if nothing at all happens at midnight. I still believe Mavra Chang will eventually show up here and that she, not this foolishness, is the key to it all."

"Worth a try, though, no?"

"Whatever you say. On the other hand, on the off chance that this impossible idea actually works, have you considered that we might not be able to get back *out* of there?"

"You do not need to come."

"Oh, no, I did not say anything about that. I will be there with you, I assure you. If there is the chance of *anything* happening, even a change in the texture of the wall or the transparency of its opening, I should like to be there to see it."

Tony watched the evil pair talking and went over to Anne Marie. "I don't like it. Those two are up to something, and whenever they are up to something, it is always bad for everyone else."

Anne Marie looked over at the two, perhaps ten meters away, and nodded. "I agree. And anything they might be up to might well not be good for Terry and that sweet little baby, either. I think we'll keep a good watch on her tonight."

The Well had sent meteors to summon them and bring them through; it had slowly, subtly manipulated probabilities to ensure that at least one Watcher would come to it. It had used all its tricks, major and minor, to accomplish the simple goal that its ancient, automated instructions required of it, and because it was a machine, it had used a circuitous route that would be inexplicable to the linear thinkers who had been the targets of its convoluted, bizarre program. Now all the sequences were run; now all the mechanisms were in place. Even Nathan Brazil, who knew it best of those alive, had tried to fight it in the past and failed, but while patient, the Well would never be denied. Now all the means and methods were in place, the players assembled, each well suited to do what was required to accomplish the Well's own ends, although they themselves were unaware of it. And only Mavra Chang had confidence in it even though she could not feel its hand.

It was time.

The wind was up, blowing directly in their faces across the flattened field. Mavra Chang had examined and even played with the large kite under which she was now strapped but had refused a test flight. Much too risky, too much chance of a crash, and no chance then to make another attempt. One shot for everything. Fifteen minutes of window, fifteen minutes to win the game, set, and match in spite of all the forces arrayed against her. The only thing she was certain of, though whether the knowledge came from her own ancient experience or had been fed to her by the Well, was that a hang glider was guided not with hands and feet but with subtle shifts of the pilot's weight. She was lighter than any of the natives of the hex, but she was sure she weighed enough to maneuver the craft, perhaps higher and faster than even the creatures for which it had been designed. It was more than a hope; it was a necessity that it was true.

Julian watched, only half-concealed in the brush, and frowned as she saw Terry come out, carrying something indistinct in her arms, flanked by both the colonel and Juana Campos. The latter was even smoking one of Taluud's cigars, the puffs of smoke rising and dissipating in the wind.

She was happy to see Terry; it allayed one of her worst fears. Still, what *were* those villains doing with her? And—*what?* They were walking through the border, down the ramp to the Avenue! *What the hell?*

She checked the guards who stood overlooking the vast alien entryway below, bathed in the night glow of the Avenue's strange luminescence, and saw them getting nervous but not yet moving.

Now the *Dillians* were moving toward the Avenue rampway! One of them halted, then the other, and they conferred for a moment. Then one trotted over to a large tent nearby and entered, the other waiting at the start of the ramp, dividing her attention between the tent and what was going on below.

The one in the tent emerged with something large and strange-looking on her back. Could that be *Gus?* Why take *him* down there? And why was he so visible?

Something was definitely wrong. There were four Cloptans as well, two males and two females, and they began heatedly conferring with each other, then they checked their guns, and they, too, were heading down!

My God! Julian thought. *Who's next? The whole damned Verionese army?*

Her eyes went back to the guards, who were visibly nervous at the sight of so many people going down into the Avenue. One of them shouted something, but if there was a reply, Julian couldn't hear it.

Over to one side there *was* activity in the Verionese army camp.

She thought of calling the whole thing off for the night, but Mavra was already strapped in, Lori was hitched up, and it was all ready to go. Mavra would never understand or forgive her if she didn't launch now, but maybe this was all just as well. If Mavra saw the assemblage down there, she might abort the thing herself. At least, Julian hoped so. This was getting ridiculous, and there was no way to warn *anybody!*

She frantically considered trying to write something that Mavra could read, but now the activity from the army camp revealed itself as the changing of the guard; two privates and an officer or sergeant were marching over to relieve the two agitated guards.

She had no choice and no time! There was absolutely nothing she could do about this!

Oh, my God! Here we go!

MIDNIGHT
AT THE WELL OF SOULS

JULIAN RACED FOR THE field, saw where Lori was set up, and barely checked to see if Mavra was okay. It didn't matter anymore. Either it went right or it was over.

She pulled up next to Lori, fumbling with the stupid makeshift pull strap. She finally got it, took a deep breath, and tried to get hold of herself, then clamped it around her neck and shoulders. She turned, lined up with Lori on all fours, then said, "*NOW!*"

Lori might not have understood the word, but the intent and emotion were clear. He kicked into action, and the two of them suddenly felt the straps tighten and then something dragging along behind them. There was no chance, no way, to look and see if it was working; they just had to keep running at full gallop and hope for the best.

Mavra wasn't as prepared for the yank and the move forward as she had thought, and the pull tab that would release the straps fell from her beak. She strained forward, tied into a kite never built for somebody like her, trying to get the last little fingernail-width distance to grab the ring again while rolling forward on her stomach, bouncing on the makeshift carriage.

She felt the kite's leading edge bite into the wind, start to lift, and then come down again. Then it caught once more, and she felt herself rising free of the carriage and of pressure below. With a last desperate attempt that felt like she was tearing her neck from her shoulders, she got the ring, pulled it, and then, with her head, forced the kite up, up as the straps dropped away.

It was a *lot* trickier, bouncier, and rougher then Mavra had thought it would be. No time to look down, no time for bearings; she had to keep it into the wind and with sheer head and neck motion force it up, up, like climbing stairs in the air. Once or twice she almost lost it and had to use the controls rigged to her feet to roll and stabilize while losing altitude, and it took every single ounce of strength and will to fight the thing and get another updraft and climb, climb, climb all over again . . .

Suddenly she was well over the whole field and banked south, trying to gain more and more altitude so that she could get some feel for the craft and sight her objective. The nearly absolute blackness had been the equatorial wall; now she was up, maybe several hundred meters, and angled so that she could see much of the landscape beyond.

For a moment the view, the tiny lights, torches, lamps, and glow on the horizon of the capital were hypnotizing. She had forgotten what it was like after all this time . . .

From somewhere, something was giving her more and more the feel of the thing with each moment aloft, how it steered, how it angled, climbed, and dove, and she didn't fight it. The glider was controlled with very subtle shifts of body weight, and the greatest problem was resisting the urge to overcompensate. As her skill at maneuvering increased so did her confidence. This wingless, flightless bird was soaring now!

She banked back across the field and turned toward the camp and the Avenue. Below her, she could see Julian and Lori going much too slowly, trotting toward the camp. *Hurry up! Hurry up, you idiots!*

It would be tricky, but she decided to make a single trial pass and see what she was dealing with inside the Avenue if she could. The border kept vision a bit dimmer and less clear than she would have liked, but she thought she could see *people* down there. That was bad, but she couldn't afford to risk a second pass. There was some commotion in the Verion army camp, and a lot of soldiers seemed to be rushing to the edge of the abyss, even though some of them were half-dressed.

She couldn't worry about any of this. Something inside her, or perhaps beyond her, from beyond that equatorial wall was saying, *"Now, now! You must come to me now!"*

She took a wide swath around the camp, the airfield, and beyond, proceeded a bit south again, and steeled herself to make the attempt at the door. It would be dead reckoning, and she would have to guess the distance and descent right the first time. The only sure and reasonable way in was to cross the border, straighten up, and fly directly at the door, hoping she sustained enough lift to reach it and did not crash against the wall or drop like a stone.

Below her, Julian had taken her time to get her breath and to disconnect Lori and herself from the other end of those straps. Then she'd started off toward the Avenue, but slowly, at not even a brisk trot. Lori matched her but wondered what was wrong. The messages he'd read said that they had to move quickly at this point and that time was of the essence once Mavra was away. What was holding Julian back? Why was she almost slowing to a dead stop?

Suddenly he sensed that she was afraid. After all this, she was afraid to take the last gamble herself!

Lori had neither much hope nor ambition for all this, but he damned well wasn't not going to see it through. He dropped back, reached over, and nipped her on the ass right near her tail. She started and involuntarily speeded up, and now he raced forward, taking the lead, charging as fast as he could go right into the middle of the Verion army camp.

For some reason Julian found herself unable to take her eyes off him. She just ran after him, and ran, and ran, right into that camp herself.

The major, the sergeant, and several troopers were all arguing and grunting over jurisdiction and procedure and what the hell they were supposed to do. Nobody had ever *really* gone down there without permission before, and nobody wanted to take the responsibility for doing anything at all. Everybody kept making excuses and passing the buck, with the result that nothing was decided at all.

Suddenly somebody yelled, "Watch it! Animals coming!"

And the brave helmeted troops of Verion scrambled to get out of the way as first a pony and then another—*pony?*—ran right through them and to the Avenue ramp.

Lori found it hard to put the brakes on, but there were four turns and no guardrails in the ramp going down. He only hoped that Julian was behind him and that she wouldn't push him over.

She *did* almost fall over the first turn and down into the hard culvert below, but while one leg slipped off the edge, she managed somehow to keep a grip with the other three and scramble back up. She wasn't thinking at all; she had this irresistible impulse to follow the horse ahead of her, and she was going to do it come hell or high water.

Ellerbantan monitors on the other side were far more comfortable but no less bored than the Verionites opposite. Two of them sat watching control screens more or less, dreaming about anything but being there, when one of them suddenly jerked up and punched the other with a tentacle.

"Look at that! It's a whole *mob* going down there from Verion for the midnight show!"

The other one devoted all three eyes to the scene, then relaxed. "Don't worry about it. See how many races are there? It's just one of those damned tour groups."

"Yeah, I suppose you're right," the other agreed. "Still, it's funny they didn't follow the usual routine and come over and warn us."

"Aw, you know those Verionites. Walk all the way down, across, and back up here just for that?"

"Yeah," the other sighed in disgust. "If there was something wrong, they'd be here in a flash, shoot off one of those flares or something. Heck, if those were anything more than tourists, they could take 'em out with arrows."

"My point exactly. So relax," said the first one, and went back to its daydreaming.

On the Avenue floor the colonel and Tony flanked Terry and the baby and watched with curious apprehension as the great yellowish hex switched on just in front of them.

Terry seemed to think it was funny. She gave a kind of delighted giggle and went right up to it, cradling the sleeping baby as she did so. She approached so closely that she could see her reflection in it, as well as the ghostly reflections of the pair behind her.

"She's going to *do* it! She's actually going to *do* it!" Campos breathed.

"I think she may *try*," the colonel agreed.

At that very moment Mavra Chang, hoping that ancient instincts and the Well's own aid hadn't failed her, crossed over into the Avenue's space and tried to center herself as she felt the lift give out. She was going forward still and reasonably straight, but there was no way in hell she could climb or in any way pull out of a shallow but definite forward dive.

Ahead, she saw it. *The door to the Well! Open! Waiting for her!* If she could only stay airborne long enough to make it!

It was going to be very close, and ahead now she could see figures standing there. A Cloptan? Could that be *Campos*? But who, or what, were the others? Jeez, that almost looked like a human woman just at the door itself. She hoped she wouldn't crash behind them; that would be the worst result of all, to fail so very close to the goal. But if she didn't, she risked knocking down the woman.

Well, the hell with it! Precious little she could do about it now!

What the hell? Suddenly the two *Dillians* were there, and one of them had a big lizard on her back. *Get out of my way! Get out of my way!*

She gave a horrendous, panicked screech that echoed through the whole of the Avenue. All of the ones inside heard it and turned, as much in curiosity as in fear. Eyes widened as they saw the huge kite coming, and only Campos had the presence of mind to realize what it must be.

"It's Chang! *Shoot her! Shoot her down!*"

Mavra Chang came over the Dillian's head, so close that Anne Marie's hair was blown by her passing. The four Cloptans who'd just reached the floor themselves drew their weapons when they heard Campos cry, but the thing was too low. Not only did the Dillians block any decent shot or view, if they shot through them, it would be too late.

The colonel sent out a pseudopod that actually touched the kite, wrenching it a bit, but even though he had hold of it, he was too close to the door and the thing still had too much momentum for such an unthinking chance grab.

The girl, having seen what was coming, moved to one side and crouched low so that first the kite went through the door with Mavra Chang still tied under it, perhaps a meter off the Avenue floor, then the colonel was dragged in, too, still clutching it.

Campos had hit the floor when she'd seen that the kite couldn't be slowed. As she got up, she watched in amazement as the girl looked at the baby, smiled, and then stepped into the hex opening and vanished.

"*No!*" Campos cried, and lunged forward, and was herself swallowed up.

Tony and Anne Marie looked at each other quizzically.

"I don't care if you have to throw me, get me the hell in there!" Gus growled at them.

Anne Marie shrugged, and Tony shrugged, and the two galloped right at the opening and went through.

The four Cloptans were totally confused by all this, and finally it was Kuzi who screamed, "I don't give a damn 'bout *nothin'* no more! I say we follow the boss!"

The others nodded, guns still drawn, but as they ran for the door, they were almost knocked down by two horses, or something very like them, running at full gallop toward the Well access. First Lori, then Julian ran right into the thing and disappeared amid some wild but inaccurate firing by the Cloptan guns.

Finally Kuzi started for the door, and the others followed, all angry, confused, but determined to go through and find out what the hell was on the other side and why everybody else had disappeared and to where. Kuzi marched right up to the still-outlined door and right into a solid wall that knocked her down and sent the others sprawling in back of her.

The door remained visible for about another minute and a half, and the Cloptans tried just about everything from firing energy weapons and conventional pistols at it to pounding on it, but it did no good. Then it winked out, and they were left alone in the suddenly silent and very deserted Avenue.

"It ain't *fair!*" Audlay cried. "Everybody got to go but *us!*"

THE WELL
AT ENTRANCE HALL 9

THE COLONEL WAS TOTALLY disoriented, and it took him a few moments to disengage from the kite which lay, crashed, nearby and re-form himself into a practical shape.

He was most conscious of the silence, sudden and absolute, but he was too experienced to dwell on it at the moment. Instead, he went over to the kite, put out two strong armlike pseudopods, and turned it over.

Its struts were splintered, and it was virtually broken into two pieces; whatever had ridden in on it must have taken a terrible jolt.

But there was nothing in the harness. It looked in fact as if the straps had been *burst*, as if by something suddenly enlarging to a point where the straps could no longer contain it.

If so, where was it?

He looked around and saw the door behind him, as transparent as glass. He saw the girl check the baby, smile, and walk through into the chamber where he now was, the invisible surface parting as if it were a thin curtain of water.

The girl stopped, then looked around in wonder at the whole of the enormous chamber. Then the baby moved and made a sound, and all her attention came back to it.

Now Campos, looking very comical, picked herself up and almost *stormed* through. She spotted the colonel immediately, paying little mind to the girl. "So? Where is she?" Campos asked, eyeing the broken kite. Her voice echoed in the vastness of the hall.

"She's not here," the colonel responded, gesturing toward the under-side. "I can't explain it. It couldn't have been more than a matter of seconds, a half minute at most, until I was able to regain my composure and check it. I still had hold of it!"

Campos reached into a pocket, took out another in the dwindling supplies of Taluud's cigars, and lit it. "I don't like this. I say we go with the original plan and all get the hell out of here before it closes on us!"

The colonel looked around at the eerie, empty hallway with its incredibly high, nearly endless ceiling and vast expanse, and said, "I tend to agree. I—"

Suddenly, the Dillians burst through the door, Tony with Gus on her back.

"Who the hell said you all could come?" Campos snapped at them. "And why bring *him*?" It was clear she meant Gus.

"Because he asked us to," Anne Marie answered matter-of-factly. She looked around the great hall, as did Tony, and both gasped at the scale. It made all of them seem like a speck of dirt on a nice, clean floor.

"Well, everybody can turn around and get out right now!" Campos thundered. "All of us!"

"Lost your nerve? So soon?" Gus taunted, then frowned. "Hey! I don't hurt no more! In fact—"

He rolled off Tony's back and onto the smooth floor, then looked down at his side. Almost on impulse, he tore off the bandages. Underneath there was nothing but smooth, undisturbed skin. Not even a scar was visible.

"Well, I'll be damned! I'm beginnin' to *like* this place!" he said wonderingly.

Campos was growing increasingly nervous. "Well, *I*, for one, do not! We go! *Now!*" She looked at the other Cloptans coming toward the door. "If we don't, it's going to be an even *bigger* mess! About the only ones missing are—"

At that moment Lori and Julian came into view behind the Cloptans; they could see but not hear the Cloptan group scatter as they passed and saw the Cloptans firing wildly, but then first Lori and then Julian were inside the hall, their hooves abruptly clattering against the smooth floor.

"I had to open my big mouth," Campos said grumpily. "All right! *Out!*"

"Who's gonna make us?" Gus asked him. "*You?*"

"Colonel, I am suddenly very weary of that one. He has been a burden for too long," Campos said to the Leeming. "Will you please see to him?"

The colonel moved close to Gus, who had no armor and no defense and was still all too visible to everyone there. The Leeming hesitated just a moment, and Gus asked him, some obvious nervousness in his voice, "Well, Colonel, you and I gonna finally finish it here, huh?"

"Gus, I don't really want to kill you," Lunderman said with apparent sincerity. "Just take the girl by the hand and let us leave."

"No, Colonel. I don't think so. For some reason, I got this funny feelin' that the rules are different here." He didn't sound very confident, but he wasn't going to move, that was clear.

"Finish him, Colonel, and get out!" Campos screamed.

"Sorry, Gus. You chose it yourself," the Leeming said, shooting out a pseudopod and flowing a part of himself up and around Gus's midsection.

Gus's tooth-filled mouth opened in amusement and obvious relief. "That tickles, Colonel. If I'da known that was all there was to it, I wouldn'ta bothered to waste a shot on you back in Agon."

The colonel withdrew rapidly.

"What is wrong?" Campos asked, sounding nervous herself now.

"It didn't work, that's all. It was as if there was something, some very thin barrier surrounding the whole of his skin. I could not get through it."

"Leave him, then! Get the baby and the girl and let's go!"

"I wouldn't be all too certain that leaving is an option, Campos," Tony commented, gesturing at the door, where even now the other Cloptans were trying as hard as they could to penetrate without success.

Campos broke for the door, ran to it, and reached out as if to show that it was just a thin piece of nothing.

It was hard as a rock.

"Sorry, Campos. I want you right where I can see you," came a voice unfamiliar to most of them but very recognizable to others. It was a deep, melodic woman's voice, and it came to each of them in his or her native language.

"Mavra! Is that you?" Tony called, her voice echoing like all the rest in the vast chamber.

She gave a low, gusty laugh. "Yeah, it's me. I made it! Against all the odds, I made it! Me! First in and in control. Hey, *I* didn't call the Well to get here; *it* called *me*! When I got this close, I knew that whatever the odds, it would provide whatever I needed to get inside. I got to admit I was doubting it myself there, particularly at the last minute, but I'm here now. I'm not sure why all of *you* are here, but it seems appropriate somehow."

"Where are you?" Campos yelled at her, defiance still in her voice. "Why do you hide yourself from us?"

"Well, you know, when I get in here, I'm really not myself," Mavra responded. "I guess I wanted a little time for you to settle down. But if you want to see what's become of your little birdie, then so be it!"

All the lights inside the chamber came on, illuminating them as if in daylight. "Oh, my *God!*" Julian gasped. They all turned toward where she was looking and had a similar reaction.

The creature that was approaching them was over two meters tall and reminded most of them of nothing so much as a huge beating heart, skin a sickly blue and red, pulsing rhythmically, moving forward on six powerful-looking, sucker-laden, squidlike tentacles.

"I *told* you I wasn't myself in here," Mavra's voice came from somewhere within it. "You see what I mean about the shock value. It's a pretty practical form, really, for this sort of thing, although it's not exactly current fashion. This is what they looked like, the people who built this place, at least at the end. By then they'd advanced far enough that they didn't need all the handy stuff evolution had provided earlier. I can't describe it to you. I'm doing a thousand different exchanges with the Well right now, each perfectly clear, while I'm using just the tiniest part of myself to hold this conversation with you. I'm running and checking out math and diagnostics on a scale even I can't believe. I'm also seeing everything the Well is sending me, and I have 360-degree sight and absolute hearing through all the frequency ranges. And even with all that, I couldn't *begin* to build something like this. Imagine a whole race with this kind of capability. It's staggering."

"You—you really *were* one of *them,* then?" Julian managed, amazed.

Mavra laughed. "Oh, no. I couldn't *imagine* being one of them, or how they lived and thought. The Well just re-creates me in the image of its makers, so to speak, because otherwise I couldn't work the controls here. I guess by *their* terms I'd probably be a low-grade moron, but the capacity and speed of the brain are such that I can handle the routine stuff."

"Everything—the whole Well World—is maintained and controlled from here?" Gus asked, losing his abhorrence of her form and becoming more the old reporter again.

Again Mavra laughed. "No, that's just one tiny little area here. A kind of microcomputer, compared to the whole thing, that does relatively simple jobs. The *main* job of this thing, if you must know, is keeping the universe running."

It was so staggering a concept and so impossible to believe that nobody had a follow-up on it for a while. Finally Gus said, "So God is a computer?"

"You *might* say that. I get the idea that this isn't all of it, but there are limits on what I can understand or do here. They didn't want their repair personnel playing too fast and loose with the universe. We're just dumb lunkheads. We make decisions that are basically moral ones, ones the Well isn't programmed to make for itself. If the fabric of space and time itself is damaged, the way it was the last and only other time I was in here, *we* have to choose to push the button and reset the universe. It's a mean responsibility if you think about it. I wiped out whole worlds of civilizations last time, probably killed multiple trillions of beings from all sorts of races, not just the ones on the Well World. They didn't think a machine should ever have to make decisions like that, so they assigned somebody to do it. The closest translation to the job would be 'Monitors,' but it often comes out as 'Watchers,' 'cause that's really the job, too. We just exist, and watch things, and make sure they don't fall apart, while waiting for the phone to ring."

Campos was appalled. "You mean *that* is what all this is about? A stinking *computer* calling its *repairman*? And for *that* all of *us* were wrenched from our lives and twisted and reshaped and dropped into this nightmare of a world?"

"Something like that," Mavra admitted. "It *does* have a way of making its summons a bit dramatic if we can't get to one of its doorways in space, and I'm afraid a lot of people *often* get dragged in. It wasn't designed that way. I doubt if it ever occurred to the builders that people like you even existed, Campos, let alone that they'd be hauled over here to cause even more misery. I doubt if it ever occurred to them just what trouble it might be for the Watcher to get in here, either; otherwise they would have made it easier. But I'm here now in spite of the best efforts of quite a number of people to prevent it, including some of you here. The only ones I *expected* and *invited* were Lori and Julian. Ummm . . . Yes, minor detail to set right."

Lori's body was suddenly misty, then distorted, and when it was again clear and distinct, Lori of Erdom, fully restored, stood in their midst. He shook his head as if clearing something out of it, something rattling around inside. Finally he sighed and said, "I feel like I'm waking up from some awful nightmare. I have all these crazy memories, impressions, but most of them don't make any sense."

"Well, you were a horse," Mavra pointed out. "I'm afraid all that information in your head couldn't always fit in that horse brain, but your spirit, your drive, remained, and in the end you still did what you had to do."

"Julian, I—" he began, and stopped, seeing something in her eyes and manner. It was readily apparent that Julian was less than fully thrilled to see her husband back to normal.

"Lori, Julian's going to be a little bit complicated, so just hang on for a little bit," Mavra told him.

The colonel spoke, although they all were awed at the display of power

Mavra had just performed. "You—you can do *that*? With your mind alone?"

"I just order it. I don't bother with how it's done any more than you bother with how the electricity gets to the lamp when you turn it on. It's easy in specific cases, but it gets more complicated if you have to do something on the scale of a hex. When you get beyond that, to whole civilizations and worlds, I'm not so sure I'm up to it. Still, we may see."

Gus, too, was awed and fascinated, but not to the point where he didn't want to press things a bit to satisfy his curiosity. "So what's wrong?" he asked her.

"Huh? What do you mean?"

"Well, we all got stuck here for *some* reason, right? I mean, it called you and the captain, and that was to fix stuff. What's broke?"

Mavra seemed disturbed by the question. "I—I've been trying to find out. All of the diagnostics so far are turning up just fine. The universe isn't in peril, no world is about ready to die, nothing appears wrong. Still, we were called here for *something*. The Well went to a great deal of trouble to get us here. I guess I haven't hit it yet, although that *is* rather odd. If something's broken enough to summon us, then something in the Well's diagnostics routine should have told me straight away. So far —nothing. It's very strange."

As if in response, she began to receive a data stream from somewhere deep within the Well. Something about a "Kraang Matrix Formula," but it didn't make any sense. It didn't correlate with anything in the Well's operational system, in the symmetry of its physics and mathematics. What the hell was a Kraang Matrix Formula?

Before she could even request research information on it, another signal broke in, one she'd heard only once before but one that had provided a major motivator for her to reach the Well.

"Mavra! Mavra! You've done it! Now free me! Free me!"

"Obie? Is that really you? Can you really live again?"

Once, in the past cycle of existence, before the last reset, she had roamed the universe with Obie, a moon-sized computer built by some of the most brilliant minds of her own time, a self-aware computer that could in a limited way do some of the things on a vastly smaller scale that the Well could do. She could never explain Obie, but having to see him —Obie had always been a "him"—wiped out with the rest of that universe had been the most horrible thing she had ever had to face because of its permanence.

"How can I do it, Obie? I don't know a lot about working this thing."

"I'll send you the instructions. I already knew a lot, so I could follow what was being done here. Just pass the instructions along exactly as I give them to you, no

changes, no hesitations, and I'll once again be formed in orbit around this world. Think of it, Mavra! The two of us together again!"

No more horrors of existence on that grubby Earth, no more crawling before the likes of Campos, no more pettiness and Earthbound strife . . . Together again, with that power, no matter how limited, roaming the universe, exploring, learning, helping out . . .

"Brazil never told you because he wanted me to die," Obie sent to her. *"He thought that my power was too great a potential disruption to the Well. He couldn't help it, but he did it, Mavra! He killed me, Mavra! And now you can bring me back! Now you are in charge! Take the data stream and command the instructions! Free me! Free me!"*

"Go ahead. Send. I'll try, Obie. I'll try!"

All the exchange, her internal debate, and the final decision, had, to the others, taken place within the blink of an eye. They barely knew that something was going on.

"So what will you do with us now?" the colonel asked her. "Revenge? That seems a rather petty thing for one in your current circumstances."

"You are right," she answered him. "Revenge is something beyond a superior creature such as this one. When I am human, I am very vengeful, but not like this. Not now."

She could see Campos seem to relax, and the colonel, more suspicious, also seem a bit more comfortable. "What will you do, then?" Lunderman asked her.

"Justice," she answered, sending new fear into them. "Justice is the highest calling of a higher intellect."

"Sequence completed and program running. Done. Input accepted. Result nominal," the Well reported to Mavra.

But what did that mean? Was Obie reconstituted, alive again in orbit? All the Well's local sensors showed no change. Nothing but the usual random debris up there. What had she just done?

"Obie? Where are you, Obie?"

"Obie couldn't come," said a strange, commanding, powerful voice that seemed to fill the whole of the great hall. "So I came instead."

"Holy shit! It's *another* one!" Gus exclaimed. "And this one sounds like Darth Vader!"

And from the center of the hall another shape appeared, very much like Mavra, but not *quite* like Mavra. It was bigger, more than three meters tall and half again as thick, and it seemed to be bathed in a radiant glow.

"How *wondrous* it is to be free once again!" the Kraang exclaimed. "I did not believe that it would ever happen in spite of my best efforts!"

Mavra had no conception of who this newcomer was, but she knew pretty damned well that it had been the result of her commands to the Well, which was now reporting a return to "nominal" status, meaning no more repairs were necessary.

Mavra Chang tried to retrieve information on this newcomer, this bizarre new creature who seemed to have come from nowhere, but she couldn't. Suddenly she felt the Well closing off from her as if a series of switches were being thrown one by one, shutting her out, diminishing her . . .

She tried to fight, but the Kraang was out of her league. Suddenly, for the first time, she realized that it *had* all been for nothing, that she'd been played for one of the biggest fools in the history of the cosmos.

She stood there, suddenly just Mavra Chang again, a tiny Oriental-looking woman, slightly built, naked, and looking very, very small indeed.

"Don't feel so bad," the booming voice of the Kraang said to her. "I have been most impressed with you. *Most* impressed. You couldn't know about me because I was outside of the entire system, outside of the entire Master Program. It was designed that way so that I would drift forever in space, neither fully alive nor dead, never intersecting or interacting with anything. Designed that way over five billion years ago."

"*You!* It was *you* sending me those messages!" she said, openmouthed, never feeling more like a sucker in her whole life than right now. "And *you* were what was wrong! You were what I was called to fix!"

"Clever. Yes, it is true. You know the principle of the fifty million monkeys. That sooner or later fifty million monkeys at fifty million typewriters will write the works of Shakespeare if given an infinite amount of time. Well, *my* condition was like that. Eventually, in a coincident situation during the last reset, the Well was supposed to give a course correction that would have continued my endless lonely isolation. At that moment, however, the reset was executed, and that command was not completely given. Eventually, an intersection was made in spite of it all. I was able to tap into the data stream, although only in limited ways. I've been watching you—all of you—since you were processed through the Well and became part of the minor data stream. I've seen it all through your eyes, heard your thoughts, monitored your dreams. But it was all for naught. All for nothing if someone came here who understood the problem and corrected it. Fortunately, you made it in first, my dear. That will stand you forever in my favor."

"Nathan," she said guiltily. "If Nathan would've gotten here first, he would have been able to deal with you."

"Yes, that's true, I suspect, although I am still not terribly clear on who or what he actually is beyond being a pathological liar. Severing him from the data stream will take considerably more work, but there is no hurry now, is there?"

"You are one of the founders? An original of this race?" Lori asked.

"I am."

"Then why did they imprison you so? And where did the rest of them go? Will you tell us that?"

"As a race they went collectively mad," the Kraang responded. "This insane project, this march to oblivion, began with nobler motives, but eventually the infection was complete. Only I stood against them. Even those who agreed with me were eventually won over, co-opted. Those who thought as I but did not have the courage to speak or act against it were carried along in its momentum. They did not exile me. They came to kill me. They came to put me through the Well, to make of me what the Well did to you. *I* was the one with the courage, and I was too smart for them. Deep below here, in the workrooms and stations of the Well, I arranged my own exile. *I exiled myself* rather than be forced into their madness! And I did it in a prison of my own devising, one that was controlled by an endless loop that the Well itself could neither monitor nor touch. I suppose they might have been able to break it in time, but they apparently decided to let it go, seeing how perfect my exile was. To them, I had committed a racial sin, and I had devised my own punishment, my own hell, as it were, and sent myself forever to it. They did not know that I was in a suspended state, shut down, all but the most minute part of myself in semioblivion so that the passage of such a great amount of time would be as nothing to me."

"But then, you must have known that somehow, sometime it would break down," Lori noted, fascinated as they all were, even if still terrified of this strange specter from out of ancient epochs.

"I was a mathematician," the Kraang explained. "I knew of randomness, of chaos, of the infinite amounts of time before this universe. *Would* it happen before the universe began to contract in upon itself once more and finally die as quietly as it had been born so noisily? *That* I could not say. It was nonetheless a vast amount of time in which, even with the Well, almost anything could happen. I must say that it never occurred to me that it would be this soon. Now, though, I am here and they are gone. Now the Well serves me and me alone. Overall, this universe is a patchwork remade by amateurs. *I* shall proceed to perfect it. Not right away, not so frighteningly dramatic, but slowly, with subtlety, with conscious interaction. I will provide the way, and the universe will choose to follow me and perfect itself. That portion which does not will be destroyed. My vision is a challenge to me, to the Well, to all the peoples and worlds of the universe! Those who see and accept me and my vision and follow shall inherit it under me!"

"It sounds like you're thinking of becoming God Almighty," Anne Marie said somewhat scornfully.

"I AM GOD ALMIGHTY, MASTER OF THIS UNIVERSE AND ALL THAT IS WITHIN IT!" the Kraang thundered.

Then, in still thunderous but more moderate tones, he added, "That happened the moment my program was canceled. How can I explain it to your puny, primitive intellects? The moment I returned to the point where I had left was the moment that the Well came under my total and complete domination and will, an instrument of myself. You are honored to be present at the coronation of the one and only true God of the universe. Now and forever."

"Amen," Gus said a bit sourly.

Mavra just sat there, head down, thinking over and over, *What have I done? What* have *I done?*

The Kraang, however, was going on. It was, Gus supposed, the first time he'd had a captive audience in billions of years.

"What is God?" mused the Kraang. "The *ultimate* leader. Immortal, all-powerful, able to call up any fact, any bit of information, no matter how large or how small, as he chooses. One able to reward those who worship him and follow his instructions and to punish those who transgress his will, his whims, no matter how petty. You all had gods—at least, virtually all of you—and one, Mavra Chang, played goddess for centuries to a bunch of people even more ignorant and primitive than she. The god of the Jews slew whole populations because one person transgressed. He punished individuals who did nothing more than slip once in an otherwise pious life with death and damnation. He set down a list of rules so arcane, so complex, that no one could truly follow them all. And yet he could take someone who murdered, who committed adultery, who violated almost every one of his commandments and make him a beloved king in spite of all that. Now where is the logic in that? Yet on your world that god became god of the Christians, god of the Moslems, the most influential and important god on the planet. The Hindus—we won't even talk about the destroyer of universes; it is self-explanatory. They perhaps had the clearest idea of the system as it truly was, but to what end? So that a rigid class structure could always be maintained on the people by the ruling elite in which even social climbing would be a mortal sin. The Buddhists—they saw through everything. Existence proceeded stage upon stage, until you reached the That Which Is Beyond. Oblivion. And that's just *your* world. You cannot *imagine* what some of the others came up with! Am I so much worse than the gods you *did* worship? The gods you tried to follow? Or am I merely a threat because I am real, I exist, you cannot deny me or my power or doubt it? You—none of you can rationalize *me* away!"

Mavra's head came up. "This is an unlikely group of prophets to begin your reign," she noted.

"Not at all," the Kraang responded. "Why, right now I can see that you are contemplating either suicide or some futile and fatal heroic gesture to ease your conscience. The colonel is trying to figure out the best way to ingratiate himself with me, as always the pragmatist. Campos is a bit torn between her Catholic upbringing and her lust for power which she finds potentially vast in my service. The Dillians are aghast but fatalistic. Lori and Gus are curiously similar in their desires to just be out of all this, although Gus is far more offended by me than Lori. And Julian —my pretty Julian has been on the verge of suicide since she got here and is still confused about her purpose, her role, and how she could possibly fit in anywhere at all. Let me demonstrate how easy it is."

Julian was suddenly bathed in an unearthly glow, a radiance that gave her a nearly supernatural look. Subtly, she was changing, not from being an Erdomese but into the absolutely ideal image of the Erdomese female, a change so perfect, so precise, and so beautiful that even those who weren't Erdomese could see it and even feel it. And upon her face was a look like no other, an expression of total and abject worship, of complete and utter innocence and joy. She fell down and prostrated her new self before the Kraang.

"And you shall henceforth be called *Sowacha,* which in Erdomese means 'Daughter of Heaven,' and all who see you and speak with you will know that your name is of me and my power and that you wield it in my name and with my authority," the Kraang intoned. "You will seek counsel only of me and return to your land as my servant and agent. I shall bless and protect you, and you shall be unsullied, without blemish or sin, and the church, and the land, shall know you as one who is my own. You shall lead the people in my name, and in my name you shall remake the land and people as I command."

"Yes, my lord and master," she responded, never getting up or looking up.

"You see?" the Kraang said to the others. "It really *is* that easy. I do not *need* or *require* your loyalty or your consent. It is merely a matter of reprogramming your rather simple minds."

The others were frightened to death by the demonstration, but Mavra Chang was just consumed by anger. She moved to rise but found she was frozen, stuck where she was. She couldn't outthink the Kraang; he had the whole damned Well at his beck and call thanks to her.

Damn it! The bastard had won! When he finished his ego trip, they'd all march out of here like Julian, slaves to the Kraang, devoting all their lives and thoughts and energies to whatever he wanted. And there wasn't a single damned thing they could do about it!

Suddenly, out of the darkness, the baby cried. They had all forgotten about Terry and the child. Even the Kraang for some reason hadn't included her in his survey of the group. Now, though, all the attention was diverted to the small, dark girl with the infant.

She walked steadily out of the shadows, looking expressionlessly at the Kraang. When she got to Anne Marie, she stopped, looked up at the Dillian, and said, "Anne Marie, take the baby. I think I've had just about enough of this egomaniac's bullshit."

If anything could shock them more than the Kraang and his demonstration of pure power, it was Terry speaking and speaking so determinedly.

"Terry?" Gus managed, but even though it was Terry's body and Terry's old voice, it just didn't *sound* like Terry. It sounded like . . . like . . .

The girl went up to a stunned and frightened Juana Campos, reached in her pocket, and pulled out the last of Gen Taluud's cigars, biting off the end and sticking it in her mouth. She didn't strike a match; she just pointed at the end, and it burst into flame.

If anybody was more shocked than all the people present, it was the Kraang.

"Ahhh . . . That's *so* much better," said the girl after a few puffs on the cigar. "You can't believe how I missed these. Pure Ambrezan. That Taluud was a scumbag but he definitely had good taste."

The Kraang stood there on its tentacles, saying nothing, moving not at all, but the heartlike pulsations of its body were reaching a fever pitch.

"Keep trying, Kraang. If you try hard enough to control me, then you might just bust something. You're still flesh and blood, you know, renewable or not."

The Kraang was suddenly aghast, his enormous triumphal return spoiled by an anomaly his great brain could not understand, comprehend, or get data on. Massive quantities of data were going by at the speed of light itself, but the Kraang was coming up totally empty, as empty as Mavra had been in trying to find out about the Kraang.

"You weren't the only one, you know," Terry said, letting some ash fall to the floor. "*I* took a different route. I always was a better programmer than you."

"*YOU! It's—impossible!*"

"Not impossible, just damned hard. I just gave birth to a goddamned *baby,* for Christ's sake! Not even Mavra's had to undergo *that* wonderful experience! It was hard as hell switching in and out to keep me out of the data stream you were monitoring. Fortunately, the Well measured the probabilities of Mavra getting here first and factored in a few extra wrinkles. Those damned Glathrielians thought they were going to control me with their powers, but all they did was hand them to me to use. Handed them to me just as the Well figured when I rotted lazily back there in Ambreza instead of coming immediately to answer its call, in the person of one very fascinating and exceptional young woman named Theresa Perez. And it still had to explode a damned *volcano* under me to get me to do what I should've done right off! I'm as crazy as you are, Kraang, and just as much a shirker of responsibility, but *I'm here now!*"

Mavra's head came up, and she stared at the girl. "*Nathan?* Is that really *you?*"

In an absolute instant, without any sense of any time passing between, the girl was suddenly gone and in her place stood another being, a being slightly smaller than but otherwise identical to what Mavra had been and what the Kraang was now.

And in one tentacle it still held the burning cigar.

The tentacle shot over to a frozen Juana Campos and stuck the cigar in her mouth. "Here," Brazil said. "I don't like to see cigars that good go to waste."

The Kraang was appalled at the vision. "It really *is* you! How—how is it possible? I had everything, *everything* factored in! There was no mistake!"

"Sure there was. As soon as you bought my line on the life history I gave to Gus the same way Mavra bought your disinformation about Obie and Brazil," Brazil responded. "I was just another *amateur,* just like her, only more experienced. Isn't that what you said not long ago? A universe re-created by amateurs? Did you really think I'd leave the Well so unprotected? I never did figure out what happened to you, but I always figured that if *I* beat the system, then others must have, too. In a way I'm glad it was you this time. Mathematicians are so damned *logical.*"

Only Gus among them had the nerve to inject himself into a discussion between two gods. "So what were *you?*" he asked.

Brazil chuckled. "Me? I was an *artist!*"

"This is more an inconvenience than a defeat," the Kraang told him. "I have full access to the Well. If I cannot touch or harm *you,* neither can *you* do anything to *me!* At the moment we are at a standoff. But I know from your own histories stored here that you cannot exit the Well on your own as you are. *I can!* You must remain here, imprisoned in the Well alone, forever, just to retain your access and retard my project.

Every god must have a devil, I suppose. We will play a game. I will go everywhere, and you will try to stop me from doing anything you do not like. But *you* must do it *from here! Yourself!* I, on the other hand, will be free to ride the whole of the trans-spacial nets and roam the stars! I can be anywhere, anything, any time I wish to be. And eternity is a *very* long time."

"Tell me about it," Brazil said sourly. "Still, as much as I *hate* to spoil your godhead and coronation or even your lofty dreams, I'm afraid you're going to be in for a very, very big shock. Still, you want to leave, leave. Go ahead. I won't even try to stop you. You know where the exit is and how to use it. Go on, go ahead. *Try* to be a god. You'll quickly see how boring and silly it gets."

The Kraang thought that Brazil was being too smug and overconfident, and he knew enough not to trust anything the other said or claimed, particularly now. But try as he might, cross-indexed and fully researched, the Kraang could find absolutely nothing that Brazil had left as any sort of trap.

"Lost your nerve, have you, Kraang? Pretty poor performance for a god to lose his nerve. Of course, you can stick around here. Plenty to do, I suppose. Been five billion years and then some since we matched wits with some of those games that are still in the core system. Or do you remember that you used to beat me all the time when we were setting up but after a while you couldn't beat me ever again? That's because you never were willing to take risks. You had a grasp of math that's truly godlike, but you never, ever went against the probabilities. Even your clever exile trick was done with a keen eye to probabilities, given the limits placed on you. I cost you this round at the last minute by taking some risks, but maybe you'll win the next time. It'll relieve the boredom, anyway."

The Kraang seethed with anger and frustration, but he had been trying any number of combinations and at no time could he supersede Brazil's command of the Well. While they had been talking in normal time, a massive battle of intellects throughout the computer that took up the entire inner surface of the Well World had been going on, a battle of such speed and complexity that those who watched could never have comprehended or described it.

Mental thrust . . . parry . . . access denied *. . . backdoor . . .* access denied *. . . wall off . . .* sector not available *. . .*

Even in his enhanced form, the battle wasn't easy for Brazil nor was the outcome certain. In a sense, both he and the Kraang were equals here, equals before the Well computer, equals in knowledge, skill, and the ability to use the vast power and ultra-complex engineering of the master world, at speeds and on dimensional planes that were far beyond mortal comprehension. It wasn't one parry, one thrust, one end-around attempt, but thousands . . . millions . . . *quadrillions* all at once, like some vast chess game at superlight speeds with unlimited pieces.

Whole lifetimes of mental battle had taken place in the space of one second in real time. Brazil realized that he'd been far too cocky, far too confident in his power here. He'd forgotten what it was like to come up against an opponent of his native race, one fueled by eons of hatred and a lust for power. *I've become too much a man,* Brazil thought worriedly. He could not sustain a defense against the level of sheer emotion that had been stored up in the Kraang for so very, very long.

Equal! Equal, damn it! Dead even! Brazil began to see this as an eternal struggle in which strength of will was paramount and patience everything. There was no way he could keep this up forever and he knew it; more, there was no purpose to doing so. There *had* to be an answer! As it stood, neither he nor the Kraang could make use of this vast power beyond the automatics that served them both. Equals. . . .

There just *had* to be an answer! Some way in which they were not equals. Some way, no matter how minor, in which Brazil had some kind of edge.

And in the countless moves and countermoves between two more ticks of the clock, he had it. It was too obvious; it had been handed him on a platter right at the start. That was why he'd had to endure so much before he suddenly realized that it was there. The one thing that separated the two of them. The one thing that made the Kraang vulnerable. The one thing anyone not so desperate or so close to the problem would have seen immediately.

The Kraang eased back to where he'd appeared, which they now saw was a hexagonal plate embedded in the floor. He moved onto the plate, shimmered, and was gone.

Brazil waited there a minute, saying and doing nothing, then relaxed. "Well, I'm glad *he's* gone! Yessir, ridin' those hyperspacial nets . . ." He seemed in great spirits, as if enjoying some little private joke. Then he saw Julian, still the radiant daughter of heaven, although at the moment a wee bit disoriented. She suddenly lost her radiant glow, although he let her keep that perfect Erdomese form. It wasn't bad, he thought appreciatively. Maybe the Kraang *did* have a little artist in him, after all.

"Go on back over with the others, Julian. You've just been unconverted," he said lightly.

Mavra could not see why he was in such a wonderful mood. "You—you can just let that *monster* roam at will out there? After seeing what he can *do?*"

"Oh, come on, Mavra!" Nathan Brazil scolded her. "You know when a con's working as well as *I* do. Or at least you used to. I begin to wonder after the one you fell for yourself. Talk about *amateurs!* You fell for the worst, most basic, most obvious con I could think of—and it almost cost us everything. You've got to know deep down that this was one *hell* of a lot closer than I let him think it was."

"I understood that much," she responded. "And I'm aware that an awful lot more probably went on between the two of you than we'll ever know. Did you *really* set up the Well so that you'd have to be here if any other Markovian managed to survive?"

"Well, not exactly, but I think I'll add that capability now before we leave. You see, the time when we were in here together so long ago, I added a condition that so long as I was around, alive and kicking, you couldn't enter the Well except in my presence. Until we got here, I had no idea that the Kraang was still around, let alone that he was potentially loose, until you did."

"You *what!*"

"What are *you* so sore about? If I *hadn't* done that, look at what would have happened!"

"You didn't *trust* me!"

Nathan Brazil chuckled. "Hey, kid, you only had your learner's card. Still do, in fact, considering how *this* turned out."

"But—but—what *about* the Kraang? He's still *out* there! And he's still connected to the Well!"

"Yeah, he is, I guess," Brazil sighed. "Only even *he* knew a con when he heard one, and he *still* fell for it once I realized what his weak spot was. And he'd *told* me—told us *all*—just what that one weakness was. He really *was* a god. He'd almost always *been* a god, or at least a god, junior grade. Man! Anything you wanted—the energy-to-matter transformers made it for you just like you imagined it! Anything you wanted to *be*, to *experience*, to use, to own, to look at. There it was. That's how I conned 'em during the Great Transmigration. I became Nathan Brazil, or a reasonable facsimile thereof anyway, in Glathriel, which was a kind of pet project of mine, anyway. I conned 'em into thinking I'd gone the whole way, that I'd *become* a Glathrielian. The way I worked it, I showed up as just another guy, even to the Well. The only thing was, the Well had special instructions and links to me. I conned 'em. Designed it right into the program."

"But the Kraang—"

"Is *not* designed into the program that way," Brazil told her.

"Wait a minute," Lori put in, feeling an immense weight slowly lifting from him. "If he's not designed in like you or Mavra, then . . ."

"You got it!" Nathan Brazil responded lightly. "There's hope for you yet, Lori."

"Well, *I* don't get it!" Gus said, "and I don't see nobody else gettin' it, neither."

But Mavra Chang suddenly did, and she started laughing, and the laughter grew so loud and long that it echoed through the great hall and woke up the baby again.

"Mind letting us in on this, since you woke up the kid?" Gus called to her.

She got control of herself. "Let me see if I got this right. When he left, he rode the hyperspace nets as he said, whatever the hell *they* are, and he came out someplace, just as he always did when he was back in ancient times. But all those worlds are dead now. They've been dead for billions of years. So he's going to come out on a lonely, barren, incredibly ancient world of the Markovians, and he's going to see only artifacts and death. He's probably doing that right now. And then . . ." She started to laugh again and tried to fight it. "And *then* he'll have no choice but to move on! He'll probably have big, big plans, but to do them he'll have to use the gate that's there! And when he *does* . . ."

Lori suddenly saw it. "He'll wind up back here!" he finished, open-mouthed. "But in Zone. North or south, just like *we* did. And the only way he can get *out* is to use the Zone Gate, and *that* will process him just as it was designed to do so many years ago!"

"Wait a minute!" Gus put in. "Are you tellin' me that the only place that egomaniacal bastard can go is right back here? And that when he comes through, his only choice will be to be transformed into one of the races here, just like *us*? So he'll be as mortal, as ordinary as *we* are?"

"Unless he figures it out, sitting there on that world," Brazil replied. "He might. Probably will, in fact. He was never a dummy, even back then. But then, so what? What's his choice? To live like he did before, with everything at his beck and call, but alone, on a deserted world, not comatose but fully awake, looking at the skies all the time and not being able to do a damned thing about it. Totally, completely, thoroughly alone."

"Until somebody comes along in a spaceship," Mavra said worriedly.

"He's waited this long. He can wait."

"It's a pretty big universe," Nathan Brazil pointed out. "But we can check and see just where he wound up. And maybe, before we leave, we'll kind of nudge the probabilities of his ever being found a little more toward the infinite. Besides, even if he got off that world by conventional means, he'd be off the net, out of the loop. He wouldn't dare ever go through a Well Gate. His data links will only be as good as his proximity to one of the ancient worlds, so what will he be? Not a god. At best a very smart freak. I think we can deal with the Kraang. The one absolute guarantee we now have is that at worst he can never be more than a local menace. He can't get back in here, and he can't get back on the net. He's back to reality, just the way he was before he took himself out of the loop. All the old rules apply again."

"Maybe you're right. I hope so," Mavra said.

"And now we can go on to lighter fare," Brazil told her.

"You mean taking care of this bunch?"

"No, no, something far more of a puzzle than *that*."

"Huh? What?"

"Why'd you walk out on me in Babylon?" he asked.

CONTROL ROOM 27, WELL OF SOULS

"I WANT YOU ALL to come down with me to my control room," Nathan Brazil told them. "Just follow me. It's not a long journey, not after the one you all have taken."

Nobody objected. Nobody was in a position to object much to anything, having seen what one creature like Brazil could do.

"Do you really want to know?" Mavra asked him as they crossed the great hall.

"Huh?"

"Do you really want to know why I left you in Babylon, or were you just being your usual self?"

"Yes. Of *course* I want to know."

"You can read it from the data stream."

"Not really. And that's only the facts, not what's inside you."

She thought about how to explain it. "Nathan, you really were comfortable there. And in all the other civilizations and cultures we passed through and lived in."

"Well, a few were new to me, but mostly, I'd been there before," he admitted.

"No, that's not what I mean. You were in your element there. I'm not just talking about it being primitive, I'm talking about the fact that in spite of it all, you succeeded. You talked to tons of people, you ate and drank and sang songs with them, you had no trouble worming your way into their societies and getting what jobs you wanted. You'd already been captain of two trading vessels, one in the Red Sea and the other in the Mediterranean, before we ever *reached* Babylon."

"Well, it takes some practice to—"

"No. You're not connecting in spite of that super brain of yours at the moment. Don't you see? While you were off with the boys drinking and carousing and telling tall tales, which is where *I* wanted to be and what *I* wanted to be doing, I was stuck back in wherever we were living. Or I was stuck with the other women—most of whom were ignorant, dull, and had never been out of the confines of their native cities or towns— doing the only stuff women were allowed to do. I didn't fit with them; it's not my style at all. The roles were so stratified that there was just no way to break out, really *do* something, interact with the *interesting* people, who were almost always men because the men got to do the interesting things. After a while I just couldn't take it. There was a lot to see and do even in that ancient world, but I wasn't allowed to do it, and your secondhand recountings only made it worse. Women were *property* in those societies; even at our levels they were expected to stay home and be protected and do womanly things. Break the rules, try something outside of those roles, and you got stoned, burned at the stake, or raped. You've never *been* a woman in those times. You can't *imagine* what it's like."

"I've been a woman for part of *this* trip, even pregnant, and while it's *different,* I can't say as I can see the problem."

"You experienced some of the physical aspects but not the social. Nathan, the only man of Terry's race that you interacted with was, well, *you.* In fact, it's *much* more liberating to be a woman here, particularly if you're *not* in your own home hex. To all the other races you're just another funny foreign creature. They may have hang-ups about their own men or women, but they don't apply that to other races. You never *once* had to face the simplest challenge for a woman back on Earth, walking down a dark street at night in a strange city alone. I can't describe it. I can do the same thing here, just like this, and it's totally different. Both Julian and Lori understand what I mean, even if Lori kind of forgot it in a power trip that I find totally understandable. Even Campos had a taste of it, for all she learned from it. In my own era I lived with elements of it, but I had more freedom, more opportunity; I could become a spaceship pilot, go where I wanted, and be one of the group singing the songs and telling the stories. On Earth I felt shut out —and there was no relief in sight! It wasn't any one thing, it was a lot of things. I walked into hell when I walked out on you, but it was no worse than the hell I was stuck in. That's why, when I finally did get away, I didn't come back. I couldn't take that role again. *I couldn't live my life through your experiences.*"

Brazil was silent for a bit, thinking over what she'd said and sifting it in his mind. "In primitive societies I don't see a way around it, really. With their lives so very short, they built their societies to ensure propagation. 'Women and children first' was the old rule, and women were noncombatants because each woman could bear a child only once every nine months while one man could impregnate one woman a day. It's ironic, really, that much of this evolved more than anything else out of the basic social realization that men were expendable. Even conquering armies would slay all the men but carry the women off. There were exceptions, of course—there always are. But we can't be the exceptions in any of those societies; sooner or later somebody will notice that everybody else is aging, growing old, and we aren't. The exceptions—Hypatia, Cleopatra, Joan of Arc—*they* get written up in history books."

"Yeah, and most of them die violent deaths at young ages, anyway," she noted. "I looked for the Amazons in Greece but never really linked up with them. I think I'd have been a little small for their lot, anyway. The only place I *did* find any peace and equality was on a little island off the coast of southern Greece that was an all-woman society, but it turned out to be a lot more boring and more a matriarchy than I figured. Besides, I didn't 'look' right to them. I was accepted as a guest, but I couldn't stay, not with *these* features. I began to wonder, though, whether you had to have an all-female army or an all-female society to just get some sense of freedom."

"And when you found it, however basic, in the Amazon rain forests, you just stayed. Yeah, I can understand the situation, but it's not quite the good and easy life being a man, either. Still, you should have come out and taken a look once in a while. Things changed, dramatically. Not all the way, but a *lot* better, even in my namesake Brazil and more to the north in America and in Europe."

"I found *that* out with Lori and Julian. A woman astronomer and professor, a guy who flew in spaceships . . . It was so damned *slow,* and then everything seemed to happen in a hurry. But by that time I was so isolated, so set, and had been doing it for so long, I barely remembered any other life. And all I saw there was women's pain, and heard stories of more of it, and I had no desire to move."

"Um, excuse me," the colonel interrupted. "I hate to intrude, but just where are we going? And why?"

"Just come down the moving ramp here and follow," Brazil said in an irritated tone. "We're going down to the control room so we can decide just what the hell to do with all of you."

Campos crossed herself.

The moving walkway went down into the bowels of the planet. Every once in a while it would take them right through a hexagonal portal of deepest black, as if going into a tunnel, only there was no tunnel there.

They quickly became aware that every time they did that, they moved a tremendous distance in a very short time.

Finally they reached Brazil's destination, going through a bizarre workshop whose size was on a scale that dwarfed their imaginations. Everything was massive, was apparently working, and looked as if it had been built two days earlier and cleaned just before they arrived.

There were openings all around in a massive hexagonal shaft, not just on their level but going up and down as far as they dared look. The openings were marked because they were not hexagons but great semicircles, and inside each was darkness—darkness but not inactivity, as countless small bits of energy flew and routed and shot around almost as if they were tiny galaxies in accelerated motion.

They went in between two such openings and down a short corridor and found themselves in a room that bore no resemblance to any they'd seen before. The wall was filled with tiny triangular shapes, each with a unique code on it in some kind of luminescent dots. In the center were two very strange looking pedestals, and as Brazil glided to one and crawled into it, it was suddenly obvious that these were in fact chairs for the race that had worked here.

Mavra, still human, pulled herself up on the other one and sat cross-legged on it, looking at the others. They in turn all stood looking back at them, both fearful and nervous.

"You'll pardon me if I have to remain in this form," Nathan Brazil said to them. "I need to do that to interact with and control the machinery with any precision. I think we ought to conclude our business as quickly as possible now, and we'll start with the easy ones. Tony? Anne Marie? You got what I promised you back in the hills west of Rio that night. You got yourselves involved early with the wrong folks, but you also stuck with Julian and saw the consequences through. I can only ask you what you want to do now."

Tony and Anne Marie both frowned. "Just what exactly do you mean, Captain?" Tony asked.

"Just what I said. Would you like to return to Dillia? Would you rather go to where the Dillian project wound up? A world still a bit primitive but civilizing fast, much like our old one in that regard, in which your present kind are the dominant species? Or would you rather be someone, something else? Tony a man again, perhaps?"

"Oh, dear. This is for real and forever, isn't it?" Anne Marie responded. "I—I'm afraid I don't know what to say. I'm quite satisfied the way I am. I'm young, healthy, and attractive, and other than being young before, the other two are still very new to me. I hardly feel like second-guessing your computer."

"I have but one regret," Tony told them. "I regret that in this form I cannot fly again. I *did* love it, you know. But this is not a bad form, and it has a great deal to recommend it. I never did put much stock in what people looked like on the outside, anyway. Anne Marie is my dearest friend, but I would never even have met her had not misfortune sat so heavily on us both. As opposites, we would of course marry, and our course would be fixed, and that perhaps would be a shame. We would never know our potential or be able to become *individuals*. I think this machine is perhaps wiser than we. I would never have dreamed of this solution, but it is the one that is right for both of us. As for the Dillian world, it would be fascinating but not, I think, as fascinating as the endless variety right here." She took Anne Marie's hand and squeezed it, and the other smiled knowingly.

"Let's go home, dear," Anne Marie said softly, and she meant to Dillia. She took the baby and gave it to Gus, who looked *most* uncomfortable with it, and after he did what he could to support the child, he looked back to complain to Anne Marie that maybe he wasn't the right one for this job.

But the two centaurs suddenly weren't there anymore.

"And now we have you, Colonel," Nathan Brazil said with a stern tone creeping into his voice. "You have a *very* warped view of honor and duty, I think. Anne Marie compared you to Talleyrand. I *met* Talleyrand once, and I checked to make sure I still had my purse when I left. Still, everything he did, beyond ensuring his own survival, was because he believed that he was doing his best to serve his country and its people. In a sense he was a pragmatic anarchist. He knew that his nation was going to have a government, and he firmly believed that no matter what that government was, it wasn't the one France truly needed. He was trying to save what he could through it all, and he did a reasonable job, considering the obstacles. But you're no Talleyrand, Colonel. You never cared about your country or your people. You climbed up from virtually the bottom, and then you forgot what it was like to be there. You didn't just sell your service to get out, you sold your soul. You never even *thought* of the people you hauled in during the dictatorship as real people. And you sold your services and honor on the side to some petty drug lords of a neighboring nation whose product infected your own people as badly as those to the north. Then you got here, and what did you do? The Leeming accorded you rank beyond anything a newcomer deserved, and you sold it again—*to the same damned types of people*! And then you rationalized every single bit of it. You're amazing, Colonel. You're the only man I know who sold his soul twice to the same bidders."

"You are unfair! I *never* betrayed my country! *Never!*"

Brazil gave a big sigh. "That's the tragedy, Colonel. You can't even understand what you did. 'I didn't gas the Jews! I just followed Himmler's orders!' My, I heard *that* one enough! No, Colonel, you didn't betray anybody. And all those homicidal fanatics in Peru got a lot of their money because you arranged transit to Venezuela for their goods. And then those goods went all over the planet and poisoned thousands, tens of thousands. But *you* didn't do it. Like those death squads you allowed to go through Rio and São Paulo and the other cities of Brazil, killing off all those poor children—*children,* Colonel!—because they were bad for business. Just tidying up. Doing your duty for God and country, going to confession once a week to be absolved of all your sins. Take the Eucharist on Sunday with a clear conscience."

"Do not lecture me! You! The mighty immortal! How can *you* know what it is like to have to fight and starve and claw your way to anything before you die? You *know* you will survive, ageless, through the generations!"

"Oh, I've seen death, Colonel," Brazil told him. "Death is a very old friend. I admit he's never come for me, although I had a little glimpse of him when I thought I might not make it here. I've seen death clearer than almost anyone. It's all around me. *Always!* I see it take everyone, the rich and poor, young and old, innocent and guilty alike. Sometimes I have to run from it. I have to make myself hard in order to stand the view. But I hate it. I hate it more than I hate anything else. Maybe I can't understand what made you this way, not really, but I *can* understand that for everyone in your position when you began, most did not make the choices you did. No, Colonel, I reject your thesis."

The colonel drew himself up and became the semblance of the man he'd been, impressive and ramrod straight. "Then we can never resolve this. I am your prisoner. I die with *dignity,* like a *soldier!* I will not crawl or beg!"

"I'm not going to kill you, Colonel," Nathan Brazil told him. "I'm not going to kill anybody here, not even Campos, who deserves it more than anybody. I'm going to give you an opportunity you never gave *any* of your victims. I'm going to give you one last chance to get your soul back."

The colonel vanished.

Campos was increasingly nervous. "Where did he go?" she demanded to know. "What did you do with him?"

"I sent him back."

"Back! Back *where?*"

"Home. To Brazil. In a little while he'll wake up and discover where he is. He'll find that a few things have left him. The knowledge that comes from education, reading, writing, a wide vocabulary, other languages, that sort of thing, but he will *know*. He will know even though where he will wake up is in a corrugated box in a garbage dump on the outskirts of São Paulo. He'll be a child again, but this time an orphan dressed in rags, along with all the other such people who try to survive day to day on the garbage of the well-to-do whose homes they can see way off in the hills and in the downtown high-rises. The original child died of exposure and malnutrition the instant he went into the body. *He* won't die, though. Not right off. Not if he moves fast enough and hides well enough. It's lower than he's ever been. It's about as low as you can be. And I've given him an added little factor, an added degree of difficulty, so he can have a real appreciation of those he never saw in life except as victims. The child I chose from far too many available to me is a nine-year-old girl."

"You bastard!" Campos cried. "And what will you do to me? The same sort of miserable thing? Well, go ahead! No matter what you do to me, I shall always be a Campos! Not even being a female *duck* could stop me! You better kill me or I will rise from *whatever* depths you plunge me into! And unless you wish to bathe your own hands, or whatever they are, in innocent blood, remember that there is *still* a Campos here!"

"No there's not," Brazil responded. "The baby's father is Carlos Antonio Quall, a sergeant in the Brazilian Air Force, and the union wasn't even forced." Before Campos's expression had even fallen at this, Brazil added, "And I just *love* challenges!" And with that, Juana Campos vanished as well.

Mavra looked at him. "Well?"

"Well what?"

"What did you *do* to the SOB? I think he was right, by the way. *I* didn't kill him when I had the chance, and look at the horrors he caused here. I was never really positive before, but now I know that there really are some people so totally evil that you just can't teach them."

"Who said anything about teaching? Maybe I'm wrong, but he gave me a challenge and I accepted. I sure wouldn't put *her* in a box in São Paulo. In ten years she'd probably have the most vicious girl gang in that city. Still, let's see."

"You're not going to tell me?"

"Later. We have other business before we can get to *our* business."

"At least—the kid *really* isn't his?"

"No. That's how Terry diverted attention from the meteor while you and the others got through. It was your own plan, remember."

"Um, yeah. I'm not feeling so great about that now. Still, I'm glad to know it hasn't got any trace of the Campos bloodline."

"Yeah, what're you gonna do with this kid?" Gus asked them. "I'm getting real nervous just trying to hold him right, and he's pissed all over me once already!"

"Patience, Gus, we'll get to you," Brazil said lightly to the Dahir, and then turned his attention more to Mavra. "Well? *You're* the one who made the promises to Lori and Julian."

She shrugged and looked at the Erdomese, who both felt that they were present at the Last Judgment. "I promised you two anything you wanted if I got here. Well, I'm here."

"Yeah, but I don't know what to ask for," Lori responded. "I'll tell you what I would *want,* or at least I *think* I do, but I can't say how. I put a lot of time and effort into my field because I loved it. Maybe I was trying to prove something to myself, maybe I was trying to excel as a woman in a man's field, all that, but the bottom line was that there were a *lot* of places I could have done that. When I got here, I *enjoyed* being a man in a man's society for once, but it was a society I didn't want to live in. I could *look* at the stars, more than I'd ever known, through Erdom's bright, clear skies, but I couldn't *study* them. I couldn't work in physics at all. The most I could be, under optimum conditions, was muscle. A strong arm with a sword. I wanted more than that. I had more than that back home. I *like* this form, its strength, its power, the absence of the kind of fear Mavra told you about, but what good is it if it's all you are or can ever be? The only thing of *real* value I got out of Erdom was Julian."

Julian gave him a humorless smile. "And that's what I am, even to you. A 'thing' of value," she noted. "I can't blame you any, really. When we came through that hex, that matriarchy, where the women ruled supreme and the men were no more than objects, there was no real difference. I'm *still* not even sure if I think like a woman, really, or like a guy who was forced to take what he dished out. I know that most women can't see the serious problems that men have in society—their lack of freedom—and part of that is that they don't want to. When you're down, you resent the ones that are higher up. When you're a higher-up, you forget what it was like to be down. And neither side can ever really come together. Me, I've got the impossible problem. I finally came to terms with this shape and form and sex. I *like* it. I like the way I look, the way I feel, and I've found I can do things many of the men couldn't. But I don't want to go back to being a piece of property, a 'thing of value,' without a voice, without rights, without even the freedom to think serious thoughts. *I* was a scientist, too, you know. I kept faith because I needed Lori, and he needed me, but, let's face it, I don't need Lori anymore."

Lori seemed shocked at the statement Julian made and shook his head sadly. He didn't understand this at all.

Mavra shook her head sadly at Julian. "You're wrong. You're *still* wrong. You've been through all this, more experiences and more damned personalities than most folks could ever imagine, and you haven't really learned a thing. A person alone who needs nobody else isn't a whole person at all. Even the plant creatures here interact. And I don't know anybody, except maybe Nathan and myself, who needs somebody more than you do. In a sense, the Kraang was right about you. What don't you like about Julian Beard? That he was self-centered, egotistical, that he saw everybody else as kind of props in his life? I got that much from you the moment you stepped in here, but he wasn't a bad man, just vain and selfish to the core. The Well took that away from you, and in a vain and selfish fit you decided death was better than not being the center of the universe. Lori rescued you from that, but *he* didn't make you the center of the universe, either. Within the limits of that atrocious society he tried to make you a partner, but you couldn't stand it in the end. You couldn't survive that way, or at least you didn't *want* to, and you couldn't survive any other way. You were so desperate to break free that you let those butchers mess with your mind even though you had a pretty good idea that they'd mutilated Lori and me. You were *relieved* when you found Lori as a horse. That put *you* in the center again, the one controlling *him*. Even then you needed his guts to get here."

Mavra sighed and looked over and up at Nathan's pulsating bulk. "Well? You got the big brain right now. What do you think?"

"I think that while we're going to have to correct Erdom a bit, these two just don't belong in a nontech environment," Brazil commented. "On the other hand, a kind of compromise that *you* sort of suggested with your comments and a few things said elsewhere here present a possibility."

"That *I* suggested?" Mavra came back, puzzled.

"Yeah. It's going to take some really *major* work here, though. Let me see. Gus? You've been the most solid one through this whole mess. If there's anyone I'd want with me in a nasty situation, it would be you. You've also got more moral sense than the rest of the bunch put together."

"Nice to hear," Gus told him. "But it don't count for much, does it? I'm a big, fat lizard holdin' Terry's baby, but all that time I thought I was stickin' by her, it turned out to be *you*."

"No, you're wrong, Gus," Brazil told him almost tenderly. "She was there. I had to hide myself so thoroughly that not a trace of my true self emerged. Occasionally I had to switch back and forth between that damned rehab tank in Agon and her body. She *knew*, Gus. She was there all along."

"Until your comin'-out party. Where is she *now*?" he asked.

"In that body, my old body, which has healed with astonishing speed, at least from the point of view of the medical people there. *They're* the ones keeping her sedated for the moment. In fact, they've taken it out of the tank, restrained, still sedated, and have transported it to the Agonese capital for shipment through the Zone Gate there. I'm afraid they're in for a nasty shock this time. That body's linked to *me*. Everything they've done to it I've known, felt, just as if I were still in it. I've deliberately kept it alive and healing. When it comes through the Gate, oh, almost any minute now if my timing's right . . ."

One of the hexes in the floor of the control room turned black, and a figure was suddenly there, as if faded in. It was Nathan Brazil's own body, with long, wildy flowing hair and beard, lying stark naked on the floor.

The body stirred, sat up, and looked around, a very confused look on its face. "What? Who . . . ?" it asked in his voice, then saw Brazil in his native form and scrambled backward.

"Come on, Terry! We didn't go through all *that* together to be put off by looks, now, did we?"

The figure frowned, then got unsteadily to its feet, eyes on the pulsating creature. "You—you're—*him*? You *are* him!" Then, suddenly aware of the beard and other odd feelings, it said, "Or am *I* him? This is *crazy*!"

"You played around inside me before," Brazil reminded her. "Now we'll have to keep you there for a little bit. Don't worry, it'll all work out."

"Terry?" Gus said hesitantly. "Is that *you* in there? I mean, if it is, you can *talk*!"

"Yeah, I—what happened to me, anyway? I followed those signs into that swamp, and then there were these people, and then everything seemed to be all different all of a sudden. I—I remember *all* of it, I think, but half of it doesn't make any sense! Neither does *this*, for that matter!"

"I had a tough time figuring out the Glathrielian system," Brazil admitted. "If we hadn't spent all that time together on the island, I might never have gotten it to the level where I could manage what I did. When that volcano blew and I got conked by the tree keeping you from drowning, there was a moment when my human part and all of you merged inside that head. The only part of me that was left in your body was this, the part you could never reach. It took a couple of weeks of healing in that hospital in Agon before my—*our*—brain began functioning well enough that I reestablished contact and was able to sort us out. Now that *my* old brain, which repairs itself like the rest of the body, is functioning normally, all that was you can use it. You're back, even if not quite as you were."

"I, uh—" Terry reached down and shook his head. "I'll be damned. I always *wondered* what it felt like to have one of *those.*"

Gus cleared his throat, which was a somewhat menacing sound although not intended that way. "Um, Terry. You remember *this?*"

He went over and looked down at the baby and smiled. "Yeah, I do. Whose is it, anyway? I'm not my own kid's father *and* mother, am I? That would be too much!"

"No, I'm sterile. I have to be," Brazil assured her. "Remember your diversion at the meteor back in the Amazon?"

"Oh, *him!* Damn! Still, he *is* cute. Let me hold him!"

"Gladly," Gus responded, handing over the child. "Um—do you remember me, Terry?"

"Yeah. You could flip in and out, like, so folks couldn't see you. For a while you were my only real friend."

"Terry, that's Gus," Mavra told her. "I'm Alama, and that tall furry creature with the horn on his head is Lori."

Terry gasped. "Oh, my God! *Gus? Lori?*" He laughed, and it wasn't at all like Brazil's laugh. If one knew both Terry and Nathan, one could see Terry in every move and hear her in every spoken word. Finally, still gently cradling the baby, he said, "So we're all kind of scrambled up here, and we're all standing here before a talking turnip with tentacles and the queen of the Amazons. If I ever got this story on the air, they'd lock me up in an asylum."

"Well, that brings up our situation," Brazil said, finding even himself a bit disconcerted talking to, well, himself. "We have four—actually, now *five*—people left here, all of whom have problems. The child was born on the Well World to a creature who'd been processed. Because of the laws and limits of probability, the only way I could send you, Terry, and the baby back without making a real mess of things would be to Earth at a point in time *after* the gate closed. Nine months plus a few days, to be exact. As far as reality was concerned, you'd have spent the whole time as you'd originally planned, in the Amazon jungle with the People. That's the way the math runs here. Terry alone I could deal with in any way I pleased, but the baby complicates it beyond belief. From your standpoint, you wouldn't have made that last jump. Instead, you would have stopped short. You wouldn't remember anything that's happened here, and you would have spent nine months with the People and had the baby with them."

"The baby's a boy, so you'd have to give it up to one of the regular tribes or leave the People," Mavra pointed out.

"I'd leave," Terry said flatly.

"I know," Brazil told her. "But you would never go back to civilization. You'd join one of the tribes there, and both you and the boy would remain with them. You know that if you ever went back to civilization, you'd be a freak, a ten-minute story for two or three days on your own old network, and then that would be that. You'd stay, you'd have many more children, and you'd grow old watching them grow up as members of the Amazonian tribe."

"That's not much of a future," Terry noted.

"It's a choice. If you stay here, you'll be racially Glathrielian, but you won't be rewired again. What limited powers you can use without that, you will retain. Your baby will be safe, too. I'll see to that. I'm going to keep tinkering with that bunch until I get them right! But they've got a long way to go even to get beyond the Amazonian stage themselves."

"You're saying it's jungle or swamp? My choice? *Some* choice!"

"Not necessarily. I'm going to attempt something that is very, very difficult here. I've never done it before, but there's no reason it can't be done. In fact, in theory it should be easier than most other things around here because it's built into the old mechanism. When we started off here, the hex attributes were symmetrical. High-tech to semitech to nontech in repeating radial patterns. Over time, as races proved out, we moved them out the worlds and built new races that often required different limitations than the previous tenants. Over time it became a jumbled mess like today. But the mechanism for switching them around is still there, still accessible. The effect will be so unnoticed in most places that it'll take some time to discover it's been done. Only one of them will know right off, and it'll most likely destroy their current civilization. As far as I'm concerned, it's worth bringing them down a notch. Anyway, they're clever people. They'll survive."

Mavra stared at him. "Nathan? *What are you going to do?*"

"After we make a few adjustments in the Glathrielian Way, ones that will start them on a new track. I'm going to upgrade it from nontech to semitech. Since doing this would cause the Ambrezans to contemplate genocide, I'm going to downgrade the Ambrezan hex to semitech as well. By the time the Glathrielians rise, the Ambrezans will have re-worked their own system to adjust. They're agriculturally based, anyway; they won't suffer in the long run from this." He paused a moment. "And I'm going to upgrade Erdom to high-tech."

"*What!*" both Lori and Julian cried at once.

"The same lovable climate and people—changing *that* is a lot more complicated—but with a major difference. And, oh, yes, it seems that there's going to be an epidemic there soon. It won't bother most people more than a bad cold. But it won't be curable by partaking of the women's curative milk supply. It's going to infest the males mostly, with their lack of natural immunities, but it's going to find itself allergic to testosterone and related substances the males have naturally. All, of course, except the castrated ones. I'm afraid it's going to be *very* fatal to them very quickly."

"You—you're wiping out the *priesthood*!" Lori said, mouth agape.

"I'm afraid so. They've kept that place in the dark too long. Now, if a couple of people, one male, one female, maybe married so that they're socially acceptable, *knew* this and also knew that high-tech works there now, well, who would be the only two there who really understand the new technology that will be brought in? And what is needed? Who will have to be the founders of the first university of the new electronic age? If you're sharp enough, and clever enough, and work together on this, you might just pull it off. You might not, and things aren't going to change overnight, but they *will* change. You two want a challenge?"

"It—it's more than we could hope for," Lori told him. From minor associate professor to founder of a new technological civilization. Not bad.

"That's what I always went for," Julian told them. "Challenges. It sounds like a big one. I hope it's not *too* big."

"Well, these things seldom work out the way you plan, but sometimes they work. Give me a week and then check it out. I'll send you a little gizmo when I throw the switch so you can know it's started."

Julian winked out, but Lori stayed. "What—where'd she go?"

"Suspended in transit. I wanted a word with you alone. When she emerges, she's still going to be that bombshell Kraang made her, but I've removed that stuff that idiotic pair of butchers did to her head. You saw how he made that attitude adjustment, too. I don't think Julian can ever completely conquer her own egocentrism, not on her own. I decided the hell with it and did it for her. It's nice to be able to shortcut these things. She's going to be just as smart as she ever was—smarter, I think, than before—but she's going to forget that she ever was a man. She's going to find us males as inscrutable as every other female. And the next time she sees you, she's going to realize that she's maddeningly, passionately, completely in love with you. She won't question it or reflect on it as any sort of change; she'll realize it's been there all along. *You*, on the other hand, I *want* to remember your life as a woman, what it meant. You won't ever forget it again. You forgot it once, and it didn't help Julian's mental health or your own. That race is the most sexually interdependent on this planet. Use it when you go about re-forming the system."

Lori stared at him. "Thank you," he said, and vanished.

Mavra nodded approvingly. "Well, you did *that* pretty well. I hate to put building a new society in the hands of two *physics* majors, but what the hell. I guess you work with what you got."

"What about us?" Terry asked. "What happens to *us?*"

"You have the biggest job of all. Both of you," Brazil told them. "Gus, you remember what you told Kurdon? Bring in the press? Take all the pictures? Let everybody see what this filth is all about?"

"Yeah, I remember."

"Well, that's your job. Yours and Terry's, and others, from many races, if you do a decent recruiting job. I'm sending you both—all three of you, actually—to a place you haven't been. It's called Czill, and the creatures there are walking, talking plants. No kidding. But they have one great purpose—they've assembled the most massive, highest-tech library and information resource on this planet. They're going to know you're coming—their computers will tell them. And they're going to know just what your job is going to be. The idea will be so fresh, so new to them that they'll love it. They'll fall all over each other helping you get it going."

"Yeah? What . . . ?" Gus asked, not really following.

"An independent news source. Printed where it has to be, broadcast where it can be. Carried all over with the same speed and efficiency with which the cartel dealt its poison. You've already got a few stories, including the hex changes and the cartel. You'll have more right off. A number of very high-ranking councillors are going to have serious health problems very soon, and some of their associates back home are going to suddenly find that there's a lot of evidence in the open on just how corrupt they were. But that won't stop the evil. It'll flare up again in a different form. It's endemic. If everybody here is a reflection of his or her creators, well, you've met the Kraang."

"You mean a syndicate? A worldwide *news* organization?" Terry gasped. "And *we'd* be *running* it?"

"That's right. And training others and sending the scholars from all the races who come to Czill to study back with the knowledge of what a free press can do. You two think you're ready for that kind of job?"

"Are you kidding?" Terry responded. "Jeez! From naked little twerp who couldn't even talk to Ted Turner!" She turned to her old friend. "And with you right there, just like old times!"

"As much as the Dahir's talent for hiding is handy, I don't think being a Dahir is right for this job, though," Brazil continued. "If you can't go back to Glathriel, at least for a while, maybe it's better if you were a pair."

"You mean I get to be *me* again?" Gus exclaimed. "Yeah!"

"Well, not quite. But if you don't like it, go through the Zone Gate in Czill any time in the next seven days and you'll be pretty much as you were born. If you don't, then my revisions stick. Okay?"

"Yeah, well, I guess that's fair enough."

"Good luck, then. I'm counting on both of you. *All* of you! Oh—by the way, Dillia's not that far from Czill. You might check in with our friends there from time to time."

"Okay, we will. Hey! Wait!" Terry called. "I'm not gonna be a *guy,* am I?"

"No, you'll be who you want to be. I promise. Farewell."

They winked out, and Nathan and Mavra were alone.

"What did you do with them?" she asked him.

He adjusted the program and put her back into the matrix. Almost immediately she became a smaller version of him.

"At least the stool fits now," she said. She looked into the Well and traced Gus and Terry and the as yet unnamed child to Czill. "Wow! Gus is nothin' to complain about, is he? I may go to Czill myself!"

"You can't. The only way out for us is back out into the universe."

"Oh, yeah. But where'd you get *that* stud's picture from?"

"Terry's mind. It's her idealized fantasy male."

"I see you didn't make *her* any different."

"No need. He loves her. She already *is* what he wants. Besides, she has absolutely no competition."

"You got that right." She sighed. "So here we are again, sitting here just like before, doling out happy endings like some fairy tale and solving all the problems of the universe except our own."

"Seems like," he agreed.

"Nathan—you're remaking all sorts of parts of *this* world, but you keep putting *our* universe back the same old way again."

"I can't help it. *This* world's easy. It was designed as a lab. All the controls and instructions are available. But Mavra, I wouldn't have the first idea in the *cosmos* of how to rework something as complex as an entire planetary civilization and ecosystem, let alone all of them. It took the whole damned *race* working *together* with this thing to do *that.* I'm a button pusher. If I can push a button and do something or throw a switch or issue a command, that's fine. Even the Kraang knew better than that. He was going to be god, but he needed disciples to do his dirty work."

She sighed. "I see. So it's back to that crummy old Earth again, is it? After we fix up a few more things here?"

"Pretty much. Now, we *could* go other places, of course, but there's no guarantee they'd be any better. I tried it once, and it was worse, if you can believe it. Don't think about all that past, either. Where we'll be going they'll have electricity and aircraft and video and all sorts of stuff you haven't seen in ages. It's still violent, and it's hardly close to perfect, but it'll do if you watch your back. The same evil strain that shows up here sometimes shows up there as well. Besides, it *will* be different this time in the long haul. The Kraang's interference seems to have caused some rifts in the usual probability program, at least for Earth, and I'm sure as hell not going to push the reset over *that!*"

"You mean—you don't know where things are going, either, this time?"

"Not really. I was shocked at the changes in the Well World from last time. You saw those streamlined Dillians, for example, and many of the others were equally refined."

"Yeah, so?"

"They're evolving, Mavra. Changing. Becoming something newer, maybe better, maybe worse, but different. Even here change is coming. Back on Earth—well, I no longer know the specifics, but in general things will work out. There'll be wars, and violence, and hatred, and drugs, and things we haven't even thought of yet, but science is already on the fast track, technology is already running wild. Eventually they'll pick up the pieces, put themselves together, and head out for the planets and then the stars. They have to. It may take a while, but we'll be a little more comfortable getting there. They already have women captains of aircraft, so you've got some potential right off. It's no more or less dangerous or risky than it was, but it's a damn sight more *comfortable* at this stage."

She sighed. "Well, okay, maybe. At least we can play for another tie, huh? Accelerated change, everything, everywhere, even here. Everything and everybody but us and this big old machine."

"Well, somebody's got to be around to appreciate it. That's what's so damned wrong with all this, all this time, I think. The worst possible sin happened to me long ago, and I just couldn't deal with it."

"The loneliness?"

"No, even worse. This endless, unchanging perspective turned me from an artist into a damned art critic!"

She laughed. "You never told me what you did with Campos. I'm going to see."

THE JUNGLES
OF EASTERN PERU

JUANA CAMPOS WOKE UP as if from a dream and shook her head as if to clear it. She suddenly remembered what had happened and started, then sat up and checked herself.

She was still female, but she was *human* again! And, well, if she had to be a woman, *what* a body! This figure was a killer; she knew that without having to examine it further.

She felt her face, and it seemed normal, too, not horrible or disfigured. Her skin was smooth but copper-colored, and it looked rather nice.

She got up, still puzzled that Brazil would have made her like *this* and looking for the snake. There *could* be one here, that was for sure. It was jungle, dense and deep, much like back home.

She walked on a little way and then stopped and gasped. It *was* home! There was the airstrip over there! And there the house where, as Juan Campos, she'd been born!

A truck full of her father's men roared toward the back end of the airstrip, when somebody looked over in her direction and shouted. The truck stopped at once, and suddenly they were all piling out, staring at her.

"*Ai!* Would you look at *that!*"

"That is the most stacked Indian bitch I ever seen!"

"I think I'm in *love!*"

She didn't turn. She knew them all. Pablo, and Carlo, and Juan Pedro, and Pipito Alvarez . . .

She started to shout to them, to tell them she was not what she seemed, but when she opened her mouth, nothing came out! She tried again to shout, to talk, to make any sort of sound, and she couldn't do it! She was *mute*!

They started coming toward her, leering.

Writing. Maybe something, *anything*! But how? And what to write? How did it go, anyway? She couldn't remember!

They were still coming, and now Carlo started into a running trot and the others followed. *No! No! I'm Juan Campos, you fools!* she wanted to shout, but nothing came, nothing at all.

Suddenly she was filled with panic. She turned and started to run back into the forest, back to where she could hide.

But she'd waited too long. They were too close, and she knew it.

They already had their pants off by the time they caught her, and they took an awfully long time, before they picked her up and took her back toward the compound, exhausted, bleeding, and nearly unconscious.

Hell, *this* bitch was good for the whole damned bunch of *campañeros*! With a little more seasoning and discipline, why, she might last for *months*! Don Francisco wouldn't mind. The only danger was that the old boy might take her for himself!

THE BEACH
NEAR CANNES

MAVRA CHANG CAME OUT of the water, happy but exhausted, and looked around for Brazil. It wasn't great yet, but *this* was definitely more like it! And with the film festival only three weeks away, she could look forward to some real glamour around.

She spotted Brazil and still had to chuckle. Nathan Brazil, infallible god, provider of happy-ever-after endings, always the same old stick-in-the-mud himself. Wise as Solomon, ancient as history itself, always confident.

For the first time in his five-plus billion-year life the great man had goofed. A *minor* goof to be sure, but from her standpoint an absolutely *perfect* one.

They'd spent the week redoing the hexes, adjusting, tinkering, fine-tuning, trying to think of every little detail that they actually *could* do something about. They'd taken several days to check it out and run simulations to ensure that they'd gotten it right.

Nathan had even remembered to send Lori the sleek, motorized camera and reflecting telescope.

Everything was just right. The Glathrielians were set on a new course with a fine subtlety, the Ambrezans were going absolutely bananas but they'd ensured that nobody would starve or die when all their high-tech stuff just stopped, and Gus, who had *not* chosen to revert to form during his week's trial—and little wonder—was settling in with Terry and little Nathan, a touch Brazil had loved.

And finally, they'd gone down to the exit gate and set the positions and the probability adjustments so that they would have real identities when they materialized back on Earth in their base forms. Brazil had already stayed too long as the Egyptian David Solomon, so he'd specified that a new identity be created consistent with his base form and relative to Mavra, who, not wanting to become a jungle goddess again, was getting an extensive identity makeover. It was so automatic, he just did it without thinking, issuing the bare minimum commands needed to accomplish the goal.

"Well," said Nathan Brazil, "that's about it. We're actually in pretty fair shape, although it's interesting that the Kraang's interference has put us on a whole new historical track. Endless possibilities this time. Should be kind of fun. No resets necessary, I guess. Not this time. Just go back, pick up living, see how it all comes out. You ready?"

Mavra Chang sighed. "I still haven't seen much to like on that little dirt ball, but I'm open to persuasion. All right, Nathan. I think I like you better as a human, anyway; you're a lot less like some pontificating god. I almost wish sometime you'd make a mistake. Not a *big* mistake, mind, but *some* mistake. Just enough to take a little of the wind out of those sails."

Nathan Brazil chuckled. "Let's go home, Mavra."

"Computer: open Well transfer type forty-one to native mode. Reset Watchers to prior human form but create new identities this timeline and insert subjects . . . now!"

Just one little detail . . .

While Nathan had remade his old, now mortal body into the image of Terry, he'd forgotten that he was still inside the *real* Terry's body. The Well had simply taken this rather than the old form as the default, since all shapes, forms, races, and creatures were all the same to it, and Brazil's own instructions for insertion had been to revert them to their "prior human form."

And so Nathan Brazil had rematerialized back on Earth not as his eternal old self but rather as a dead ringer for Terry Sanchez, stretch marks and all. And he'd be stuck as a she, and looking *precisely* that way, until they had to travel back to the Well World once more and could get inside.

Although startled, Mavra was more than pleased to see her wish granted so quickly. It wasn't necessarily permanent, of course; all Brazil had to do was go back into the Well and change things. That, however, was easier said than done; once in Watcher mode, travel to the Well World was at the convenience not of the Watchers but of the Well. It had taken thousands of years for it to need either of them the last time. Who could know how long it might take again?

In the meantime, although she was sorry Nathan couldn't experience the more negative side of being female in ancient times as she had, Brazil would sure as hell have a *very* different life for *quite* a while, and into a future that was not as certain as before.

It almost made Brazil bearable this time. Mavra thought they might stay together for a while, maybe a *very* long while, this time, now that Nathan would have a taste of *her* side of life. In the meantime, Brazil was already struggling to adapt, but given enough time, *she* would get used to it. She'd already played the role to perfection, after all. And, she'd noted, there was a bright side. When they came through again at last, nobody would be looking for a big-breasted brown woman whose documents said she was Danielle Brazza of West Palm Beach, Florida, USA, just as Mavra Chang was now from a city called San Francisco that she'd never really heard of in a country she'd yet to visit. Next time should be a piece of cake.

And she had a *very, very* long time to practice . . .

A DEAD WORLD
IN THE CONSTELLATION ANDROMEDA

THE KRAANG HAD REALIZED the trap the moment he'd stepped into it, but by then it was too late.

He went out regularly and just stared at the Well Gate, which opened and closed with monotonous regularity whenever he approached, as if inviting him to come on in.

It wasn't awful here; the internal planetary computer was rusty, but it still worked, at least on the limited basis that the Kraang needed for his requirements.

But it was a dead, silent world, offering only regrets and memories.

Somehow I'll do it! the Kraang swore. *I will survive here as long as I must! As long as the universe survives, I will be here, building my hatred, plotting my revenge! One day, one day, I will find the way out! One day, someone will come, or something will occur, to liberate me again! Then, my old nemesis,* then *we will see who is the better!*

But only the darkness, and the memories, and the aching loneliness heard his cries or felt his rage.

He was God! Absolute ruler!

God of loneliness!

God of the dark.

ABOUT THE AUTHOR

JACK L. CHALKER was born in Baltimore, Maryland, on December 17, 1944. He began reading at an early age and naturally gravitated to what are still his twin loves: science fiction and history. While still in high school, Chalker began writing for the amateur science-fiction press and in 1960 launched the Hugo-nominated amateur magazine *Mirage*. A year later he founded The Mirage Press, which grew into a major specialty publishing company for nonfiction and reference books about science fiction and fantasy. During this time, he developed correspondence and friendships with many leading SF and fantasy authors and editors, many of whom wrote for this magazine and his press. He is an internationally recognized expert on H.P. Lovecraft and on the specialty press in SF and fantasy.

After graduating with twin majors in history and English from Towson State College in 1966, Chalker taught high school history and geography in the Baltimore city public schools with time out to serve with the 135th Air Commando Group, Maryland Air National Guard, during the Vietnam era and, as a sideline, sound engineered some of the period's outdoor rock concerts. He received a graduate degree in the esoteric field of the History of Ideas from Johns Hopkins University in 1969.

His first novel, *A Jungle of Stars,* was published in 1976, and two years later, with the major popular success of his novel *Midnight at the Well of Souls,* he quit teaching to become a full-time professional novelist. That same year, he married Eva C. Whitley on a ferryboat in the middle of the Susquehanna River and moved to rural western Maryland. Their first son, David, was born in 1981.

Chalker is an active conversationalist, a traveler who has been through all fifty states and in dozens of foreign countries, and a member of numerous local and national organizations ranging from the Sierra Club to

The American Film Institute, the Maryland Academy of Sciences, and the Washington Science Fiction Association, to name a few. He retains his interest in consumer electronics, has his own satellite dish, and frequently reviews computer hardware and software for national magazines. For five years, until the magazine's demise, he had a regular column on science fantasy publishing in *Fantasy Review* and continues to write a column on computers for *S-100 Journal*. He is a three-term past treasurer of the Science Fiction and Fantasy Writers of America, a noted speaker on science fiction at numerous colleges and universities as well as a past lecturer at the Smithsonian and the National Institutes of Health, and a well-known auctioneer of science fiction and fantasy art, having sold over five million dollars' worth to date.

Chalker has received many writing awards, including the Hamilton-Brackett Memorial Award for his "Well World" books, the Gold Medal of the prestigious *West Coast Review of Books for Spirits of Flux and Anchor*, the Dedalus Award, and the E.E. Smith Skylark Award for his career writings. He is also a passionate lover of steamboats and particularly ferryboats and has ridden over three hundred ferries in the U.S. and elsewhere.

He lives with his wife, Eva, sons David and Steven, a Pekingese named Mavra Chang, and Stonewall J. Pussycat, the world's dumbest cat, in the Catoctin Mountain region of western Maryland, near Camp David. A short story collection with autobiographical commentary, *Dance Band on the Titanic,* was published by Del Rey Books in 1988.